Fulfilment

AND ATTAINMENT

Fulfilment

AND ATTAINMENT

K.M. GOLLAND

Book 3 and Book 3.5 in
The Temptation Series

HARLEQUIN®MIRA®

FULFILMENT first published 2013
ATTAINMENT first published 2013
First Australian paperback edition 2014

ISBN 978 1 74356 863 7

FULFILMENT
© 2013 by K.M. Golland
Australian Copyright 2013
New Zealand Copyright 2013

ATTAINMENT
© 2013 by K.M. Golland
Australian Copyright 2013
New Zealand Copyright 2013

Published by Harlequin Mira
An imprint of Harlequin Enterprises (Australia) Pty Ltd.
Level 13 201 Elizabeth Street
SYDNEY NSW 2000
AUSTRALIA

°and TM are trademarks of Harlequin Enterprises Limited or its corporate affiliates. Trademarks indicated with ° are registered in Australia, New Zealand and in other countries.

Printed and bound in Australia by McPherson's Printing Group

ABOUT THE AUTHOR

'I am an author. I am married. I am a mother of two adorable little people. I'm a bookworm, craftworm, movieworm, and sportsworm. I'm also a self-confessed shop-aholic, tea-aholic, car-aholic, and choc-aholic.'

Born and raised in Melbourne, Australia, K.M. Golland studied law and worked as a conveyancer before putting her career on hold to raise her children. She then traded her legal work for her love of writing and found her dream career.

Our eyes are not only the windows to our soul;
they guide us through a life that should not be travelled blindly.
Open them.

PROLOGUE

Bryce

I've always had goals to strive toward in life. Goals, that with hard work and initiative, were still achievable regardless of how remarkably high they were set. But damn, it was amazing how quickly your lifelong goals, aspirations and priorities could change when faced with new information — information that had the capacity to blow existing plans right out of the water. In my case, all it took was the news I was about to become someone's father.

The night before, when Alexis had confirmed she was carrying our baby, everything I had previously been working for my entire life seemed meaningless in comparison to what my life held next. Leading up to that moment, I had been hellbent on expanding and building my family's legacy, as a kind of tribute to my father.

Now, I didn't only see it as a tribute to him, but also something I could pass on to my family, and this new revelation excited the fuck out of me.

* * *

As always, when I stare at Alexis' naked back lying before me she fucking takes my breath away, and even more so now that she is carrying our baby.

I gently trace my finger down her back, careful not to wake her, as she needs her sleep. She got up three times during the night to piss. Three times! I can't figure out how a person can possibly piss so much. Although, I did have to chuckle to myself last night when the bed dipped for the second time, waking me, and I heard her curse to herself, and I quote, 'pathetic bladder, you need to harden the fuck up.'

She makes me laugh. My heart literally hurts at how much I love and adore her, to the point where I think she somehow has some form of supernatural hold on it, controlling whether it beats or not.

* * *

The moment Alexis confirmed that she had feelings for me, I knew that I would do absolutely anything for her, and ever since I have made it so that my world revolves around the very spot on which she stands — and I wouldn't have it any other way.

She is just everything I have ever wanted: beautiful, kind, smart, funny, nurturing and feisty, my favourite part of the day being when she challenges me. Of course, I know that I will always win, because that is just something I cannot and will not change. She doesn't know that though.

God, just thinking about her — let alone being in her presence — makes me so bloody happy that my cheeks ache. I'm even sitting here right now, staring at her and grinning like the fucking Cheshire Cat. I should be ashamed of myself. Sometimes I think I need a good reminder, tell myself to man up and stop acting like a fucking love-sick teenager. After all, I am thirty-six years of age and have a fucking decent set of balls between my legs.

* * *

When Alexis confirmed that she was pregnant, I couldn't say that I was shocked. In fact, to be brutally honest, I had hoped she wasn't on birth control in the first place. It wasn't something I had ever discussed with her for a reason. Why? Because I hadn't really given a shit. She was the woman of my dreams and I had fallen in love with her from the word go, so the idea of her possibly falling pregnant with my child was ... well ... fucking great!

Now I know that sounds completely fucked up and bordering on evil, because on paper she was still married and she already had two wonderful children of her own. But I make no excuse for getting the things I want in life, and I certainly make no excuse for how I go about getting them.

I made myself a promise the day my parents and brother died, the very day my life was ripped out from beneath me. I decided I would take care of the ones I loved, and instead of wallowing in self-pity asking 'Why me?', I would make it my lifelong ambition to get what I wanted. After all, I fucking deserved it.

I've never been one to say that life will hand you what you want on a silver platter or that fate will bring you what you deserve. No, I've always said life is what you make of it. That you rule how your existence in this world plays out; that no one else controls the decisions you choose to make. When you think about it, it's quite simple really. The direction in which you head is determined by your own conscious decision to go there and no one can take that away from you.

I wanted Alexis. I'd never wanted anyone or anything more in my life. So I knew I would do whatever it took to have her, regardless of what or who I had to overcome. Yes, it was selfish and callous, but I didn't care. I knew only too well that life was too fucking short to spend it wasting time accepting the second-rate dividends that are handed out.

Essentially, life is what you make it, and I have one more thing I need to accomplish in order to make mine the best it could possibly be. I want to marry Alexis, make her my wife, and make her the happiest woman on earth. I want to wake up next to her every day because, fuck, she makes me the happiest man alive. So as soon as I get the green light to do so, Alexis will become my wife.

CHAPTER

1

Your body, while incubating a baby, is capable of many amazing, miraculous and, well ... let's just say, interesting things. Not only does it transform into a protective cocoon, shielding your unborn progeny from the outside world, it also experiences some batshit crazy adjustments in the process — both physically and mentally.

My body had been experiencing these things in the two weeks since Janette — the City Towers precinct nurse — visited the apartment to check me over after being sick.

I remember the moment when she pulled the test strip out of the cup which held my hormone-affected urine, and said — in what I heard as a low, deep slow-motion voice — 'You're pregnant, Alexis.'

At first I hadn't known what to think, apart from feeling incredibly shocked. However, as the disbelief wore away, I found myself angry at my own stupidity for forgetting to take my contraceptive pill in the first place. Yes, I had been a little preoccupied and distracted by the crazy turn of events my life had taken during that time — my husband having confessed to having an affair being one of them. But I had taken my birth control pill on and off for half my life and to so easily forget it like I had was completely careless.

* * *

I was having another baby, which was not something I had planned, nor had it even been in my foreseeable future because, let's face it, my life had recently been turned upside-down. I had just left a marriage of twelve years after finding out my husband had cheated on me. Then he hadn't. Then he had.

And on top of his infidelity, I also found out that the cheating bitch had spawned his offspring.

If that wasn't reason enough to feel that carrying a baby in my 'retired' womb was not such a great idea, then surely the fact that I had recently fallen deeply in love with my new employer was.

Bryce Edward Clark had pursued me tirelessly while I thought I was happily married. He had also taken it upon himself to go behind my back with an indecent proposal to my husband of an obscene amount of money to — in my words, not his — 'pimp me out'.

So was gestating, birthing and mothering another little human being at the age of thirty-five something I had planned? Hell, no! Remarkably, though, pregnancy hormones had a sneaky way of altering your thought patterns and it was definitely these hormones, together with constantly seeing the joy and elation Bryce displayed every time he looked at me, which had somewhat changed my mind.

If I had thought my Mr Love-Smitten Clark had been absolutely and undoubtedly in love with me before carrying his child, then I was wrong. Because the way in which he looked at me now, and the way he had been acting around me for the past two weeks, was nothing shy of full-blown adoration and worship.

He kissed and touched my belly every chance that he got. He rubbed my back during the morning — and sometimes noon and night — sickness sessions. And he delighted in cooking fresh, organic meals for me. He was just amazing and attentive and I was so lucky to have him.

The thing is, all the beautiful, loving and sentimental gestures came with many annoying and aggravating ones too. Like demanding I let him give me a foot rub nightly, which I was still dead against. He practically carried me everywhere within the apartment, which was getting beyond a joke. And, he had been sparse with 'I need to be inside of you' — because, apparently, 'Having sex may be dangerous'.

Dangerous! Ha, I will be the one who is classified as dangerous if my Mr Over-protective Clark does not have sex with me within the hour.

Lucky for me, this was a foregone conclusion due to the fact that we were sitting together in the waiting room of my obstetrician's office. You see, I had every intention of asking her to kindly inform Bryce that hot, loving, penetrative sex during pregnancy was not only safe, but essential in keeping the mother stress-free and happy.

* * *

'Do you need some water?' Bryce asked while draping his arm over my shoulder and placing the other on my lap.

'No, I'm fine.' I squeezed his hand with my own as I read an article slandering Princess Kate for being too brazen in her choice of sunbathing attire. *I mean, really, give the poor woman a break. Stupid paparazzi. Get out of the bush you're hiding in and get a life. Grrr, they annoy me.*

Certain things had really upset and annoyed me lately, and I mean *REALLY* upset and annoyed me. Things I wouldn't normally blink at, like privacy-invading paparazzi for one. But there were other things like roadkill, and Stephanie dying on *The Bold and The Beautiful*, which had me turned into a blubbering mess.

'Do you need anything at all?' he asked again. *Apart from your long, glorious love-wand to enter my abandoned yet eagerly-awaiting pleasure tunnel? No ... no, I don't.*

My frustration turned to a smug inner smile as I thought of something I did need. 'On second thoughts ... yes,' I replied.

With an eager expression on his face, he appeared ready to be put to task and perform his fatherly duties and requirements. 'What, honey?'

I lowered my voice. 'I want to fuck you in that bathroom over there.'

Without taking my eyes from the magazine, I pointed to the door with a picture of a little man and woman on it. I had spotted the toilet the moment I walked in, my toilet radar currently being on high alert.

'Alexis, we've spoken about this. I'm not making love to you until the doctor has performed the ultrasound and given us the all clear.' He clenched his fist and released it as it sat upon my shoulder.

'Bryce ...' I said, keeping my voice calm but sarcastically sweet. 'I know we've spoken about this and, again, I will tell you it's perfectly safe to make love to me.' I didn't look at him as I spoke and kept scanning the magazine I had rested on my lap. 'Don't get me wrong, I love your tongue and all the mind-blowing things you do with it, but I need to feel your cock inside me and I need to feel it *now*.' I dramatically flipped the page in my magazine. *Seriously, what the fuck?* There was a full page advertisement for a KY lubrication gel with a picture of a naked man and woman gloriously tangled around one another. I was beyond jealous.

Dropping my hand to Bryce's lap, I slowly moved it up his leg without raising my eyes from the pornographic picture in front of me.

He groaned and stopped its wandering with his own.

'You're fucking killing me,' I whispered as I snatched my hand back. 'I need sex and I need it now!'

He smirked. 'It's your hormones, my love.'

'Hormones shmormones. I don't care what it is.' I casually placed the magazine back on top of the coffee table and leaned over him so that my fuller than usual breasts brushed his arm. Then, pressing my mouth to his ear, I whispered, 'Listen here. Your long, hard, delicious cock will be in between my legs within the hour. I guarantee it!' I discreetly bit down on his ear lobe, then pulled back and eyed him intently.

'Ms Summers,' Dr Rainer called from the doorway of her office.

I removed my hungry stare from Bryce, stood up and smiled sweetly at my doctor.

Bryce sat there for the smallest of moments, then eventually rose from his seat and relaxed his fist again.

We sat down in front of a large, hardwood desk in Dr Rainer's office. She had been my obstetrician during my pregnancies with Nate and Charlotte and, when I booked my appointment to see her, I had to explain my current 'situation': Rick and I were no longer together and my new partner, Bryce, was the father of my baby.

'Hello, Alexis. It's been a long time.' She flicked through my file. 'Six years, in fact,' she finished.

'Yes, it has been a while,' I replied.

Dr Rainer held out her hand for Bryce to shake. 'And you must be Bryce, the father.'

He obliged and gave her an enormous grin. 'Yes, that would be me,' he answered confidently, but shifting in his seat just a little.

He had been fidgety all morning and even more attentive than usual. Don't get me wrong. I love his devotion and thoughtfulness, but he had a tendency to go a tad overboard.

Dr Rainer motioned toward the examination table. 'Okay, Alexis, hop up on the bed, and we'll have a look at your baby.'

Bryce shot up out of his seat and helped me as if I were his elderly grandmother. *Grrr, he is so adorably aggravating at times.* I desperately wanted to roll my eyes at him and refuse his over-the-top assistance, but allowing him to fuss over me seemed to calm his nerves. So I let him, swallowing the need to chastise him about it.

Bryce walked me to the black vinyl-covered bed where I laid myself down, while Dr Rainer washed her hands at the basin. She dried them with a paper towel then sat down on a swivel chair and made herself comfortable.

Moving around to the other side of the stretcher, Bryce took hold of my hand.

'You all right there?' I asked with a slight smile.

'Couldn't be better, my love,' he smiled back.

I was abruptly pulled out of my loving gaze into Bryce's eyes when Dr Rainer grabbed the bottle of gel and squirted it on my lower abdomen. *Jesus! That shit is always freakin' cold. Can't they at least microwave it for a few seconds. Surely that's not too much to ask?*

No matter how many times I experienced the application of that bloody gel, I never once remembered to mentally prepare myself for its cold shock. Therefore, I grudgingly adjusted to the sudden temperature change on the surface of my skin.

Dr Rainer switched on the monitor and moved the ultrasound wand over my tummy, prompting Bryce and I both to simultaneously move our heads a little closer to the screen while squinting.

Okay, to be honest, I've never really been able to distinguish what was what during an ultrasound. All I could ever make out was grey, black and white swirling patches, and trying to distinguish what was supposed to look like a jelly bean with a large head was pretty much impossible for me. So when the image appeared on the screen, I made more of an effort to watch Bryce's reaction rather than try and figure out my baby's head from its bottom. As long as I heard that wonderful, amazing, ticking sound of Baby Clark's heartbeat, I was going to be more than happy.

Almost instantly, Dr Rainer started calculating our baby's measurements on the monitor. I squeezed Bryce's hand as he stared intently at the screen. He looked down at my hand, then up to my face, so I gave him a knowing wink which prompted him to raise my hand to his mouth to place a soft kiss on it.

'Okay. Your baby measures one point seven centimetres, which would put baby at eight point one weeks gestation.'

'One point seven centimetres?' Bryce asked in confusion as he spread his thumb and index finger apart.

'Yes. At this stage in the pregnancy, your baby also has two arms, two legs and eyelids,' Dr Rainer replied.

'One point seven centimetres?' Bryce repeated a little louder, still looking confused.

'Yes,' I giggled. 'One point seven centimetres.'

'How is that even fucking possible?' he asked, astonished. 'Shit, I'm sorry. Please excuse my mouth. I'm just slightly blown away here.'

'You're excused, Bryce,' she offered with a smile, then continued recording the measurements. 'Okay, let's see if we can take baby's heart rate.'

Dr Rainer moved the ultrasound wand, this time pushing it further into the base of my abdomen and increasing my already strong urge to urinate. *Don't need to pee. Don't need to pee. Who am I kidding? I need to fucking pee!* I was willing myself to clench my pelvic floor muscles tighter, when a ticking noise sounded through the monitor and distracted me from my desperate need for the toilet. Instantly, I gripped Bryce's hand as that wonderful repetitive popping — which made any doubt or worry disappear into thin air — sounded throughout the room like music to my ears.

I lifted my head to look at the monitor's swirling shades of grey, which was again annoyingly useless because I couldn't make out shit.

'Baby's heart has 165 beats per minute, that's excellent,' Dr Rainer informed us.

I smiled. More than smiled. I gleamed. I was pregnant again at age thirty-five, my baby had a heartbeat of 165 beats per minute, he or she measured one point seven centimetres and had limbs, and the father of my little precious jelly bean was standing next to me teary-eyed. *Hang on, back the fuck up. He is teary-eyed. Oh my god, he is teary. Shit, now I'm teary.*

He leaned down and pressed his lips to mine and a lone tear fell from his eyelid onto my cheek. I placed my hands on either side of his face and kissed him back.

Bryce broke free from my lips and rested his forehead against mine. 'I love you,' he whispered.

'I love you, too,' I replied softly.

He stood up while Dr Rainer turned off the monitor and wiped my belly with a towel. We were staring at each other, both of us still highly emotional and amazed by the little miracle growing inside of me. It was just such a wonderful feeling.

'Okay. Now, Alexis, seeing as your blood is type A negative, I would like to give you an anti-D injection at the twenty-eight week mark of your pregnancy. I'd also like to schedule another appointment for an ultrasound and standard screening tests, in, say, three weeks?'

'Yes, of course,' I answered.

'Now sit up on the bed nice and slowly for me, please.' Bryce stood behind me and helped me into a sitting position. 'What's an anti-D injection?' he asked with scepticism.

'Alexis' blood Rhesus factor is negative, Bryce. Therefore her blood does not contain D antigen. Both Nate and Charlotte had positive Rhesus factors; if their blood had mixed with Alexis' at any stage, antibodies would have formed. Now, if those antibodies cross the placenta and mix with your baby's blood, it would cause serious complications. The anti-D in the injection destroys any trace of Rhesus positive blood in Alexis' circulation. That is why we give it to mothers with negative Rhesus factors during and after pregnancy. It's precautionary.'

'Right ... and it's perfectly safe?' he asked, his voice laced with worry.

'Bryce, I've had it before. I had to have it during both my pregnancies with Nate and Charli. It's fine,' I reassured him.

'While we are "just checking" things, Dr Rainer,' I said, giving Bryce a smirk — *yes, Alexis now has a smirk of her own* — 'can you please inform Mr Clark that it is perfectly fine to have sexual intercourse during pregnancy?'

She laughed. 'Yes, it's perfectly safe. Alexis has a mucus plug that seals her cervix and helps guard the baby from infection. The amniotic sac and her strong uterine muscles will also keep baby safe. So go ahead, have as much sexual intercourse as you like.' She smiled at Bryce and he seemed satisfied, so I smiled at her. *I love you, Dr Rainer.* I then shot Bryce an I-told-you-so look as he helped me climb off the bed.

'Here is your blood test referral, Alexis. If you have any other questions please don't hesitate to give me a call. I will see you in three weeks, okay?'

Both of us thanked Dr Rainer and made our way out of the clinic.

* * *

I watched Bryce very closely as we drove home from my obstetrician's office, having the incredible urge to launch myself on top of him. The problem with that was the driving ... placing myself on his lap would prove not only dangerous but also slightly crazy. I had to sit there, as horny as hell, and wait. *Maybe I could just lean in and lick his one-day-old stubble, or nibble on his juicy ear lobe.*

Salivating, and pulsating from what I knew was not far away, I decided to utilise the aggravating delay by carefully taking in everything about him.

While scrutinising the sexy beast beside me, I spied what I normally spied: the sexy blond hair that fell to his ears, the defined cheekbones and jawline, the soft, full lips, and that short delicious stubble. However, this time I also spied something new: a smile that was unlike his normal, fun-loving and heart-stoppingly cheeky smile. No, this smile was an excited one, an incredulous one, and an unreservedly proud one. My sexy, Mr I'm-Going-To-Be-Daddy Clark was simply over the moon happy and he had the perfect smile to prove it.

I was already incredibly turned on and horny as hell, but having to sit there and look at him, with that particular expression on his face, had my sexual desire going through the roof. *For the love of all fucks.*

I bit down on my lip — because I couldn't bite his — and then swallowed heavily. 'When we get home, I want a screaming orgasm. And seeing as I am not allowed to drink alcohol, I'm talking about the non-liquid version.'

I licked my lips and waited for his reaction. He didn't say anything, but I noticed his eye twitch.

'When we get home, I am going to have my screaming orgasm by riding the fuck out of you in this Lexus,' I continued.

This time he looked over slightly as I bit down on my fingernail. He returned his gaze back to the road, only to grip the steering wheel tighter.

'You have deprived your pregnant lover of the sex she has so desperately needed and she is not happy, Mr Clark. Nor is she going to wait a second longer once in your basement car park —'

'Honey,' he interrupted. 'I did it for a reason.'

'Bryce, you didn't listen to me.'

'Honey, I wanted to be sure.'

'Bryce, you didn't listen to me.'

'Honey, I fucking love you and my baby so much. There was no way in hell I was going to put my dick and its needs ahead of you both.'

'Bryce ...' I waited for him to look at me.

'What?'

'I fucking love you and our baby so much too, so I forgive you. But ... you are going to have to make it up to me for the next twenty-four hours. Do you understand?'

'Yes.' A small smile appeared across his face as he pressed his foot on the accelerator just a tiny bit harder.

CHAPTER

2

I was already unbuttoning my shirt as we pulled into his garage.

Bryce didn't bother parking the Lexus in its normal place, instead driving it to a spot just short of the elevator doors.

Wrenching off my seat belt, I watched him with hungry eyes while he slid his seat back, an indication he was completely aware that I was about to climb on top of his lap, which I did. To say that I was desperate for the feel of him inside me, caressing me, stretching me, was an understatement. It had been almost two weeks since I had felt that. *Two freakin' weeks!*

Obviously, we had indulged in other forms of sexual release, and I had enjoyed them immensely. But the experience of his rock-hard cock sliding in and out of my pussy could never be outdone. It was not just the physical pleasure and sensation that I felt when I completely surrounded him. No, it was far more in-depth. Bryce and I shared an unbreakable and undeniable connection that started at the very spot we both became one and it travelled deep within me until it reached my heart and controlled it entirely.

Placing my hands on either side of his face, I kissed him with passionate force as he unclipped my not-so-sexy wire-free maternity bra, releasing my swollen and fuller-than-usual breasts into his waiting hands. He groaned at their plumper feel.

They had been tender of late, but what they were experiencing right at that moment when he tongued my nipples was pure relief. I swear to God, when you're pregnant every single sense in your body is heightened and my sense of touch and feel were no exception.

Feeling the wet, warm glide of the tip of his tongue as it traced small circles around my nipple, I shuddered in delight, only to cry out with a mixture of pleasure and pain when he gently tugged at it with his teeth. *Holy fuck!*

As his tongue continued its delicious assault, his hand firmly squeezed and massaged my other breast, pleasing me with his superb simultaneous actions. I loved it and, in response, began to rock my pelvis on top of his cock, which in its position underneath me had become more prominent. He groaned at my movements while continuing to worship my chest with his mouth, forcing me to drop my head back and let out the moan I know he liked.

'Mm, I fucking love you,' he mumbled into my now exposed neck.

'Good. You should,' I arrogantly replied, while bringing my head back down and shooting him a cheeky smile.

He growled, then grabbed hold of the back of my neck, pulling me forward to meet his mouth while I lifted my hips just enough for him to pull down his jeans and free his mouthwatering erection.

I wrapped my fingers around his warm, hard length and murmured. 'Mm.'

'Fuck, Alexis,' he slurred in response as he pushed my skirt up around my stomach, revealing my underwear.

Before I could say anything, Bryce tightly gripped the waistband and swiftly ripped them apart with ease. The purely erotic look on his face as he released me from them nearly tipped me over the edge. *I will never get tired of watching him do that.* I moaned again and lifted higher, waiting for his touch — which didn't take long.

Slowly and with intricate precision, he trailed his finger over my clitoris, sending a jolt of pure pleasure right through my body, inevitably making my head drop forward to rest upon his. The feeling his finger afforded me as he dragged it back and forth was nothing short of sensational and before I knew it I was panting and breathing heavily, causing the windows in the car to fog over from my fierce exhalations.

'Put your cock inside me now!' I demanded, almost at a loss to voice the words coherently and having come to my absolute threshold after two weeks without it. 'I'm not waiting a second longer, Bryce.'

He smirked salaciously and took hold of his erection, positioning the tip so that I could lower myself onto it. I placed both my hands on his shoulders and didn't hesitate, dropping down and instantly forcing a groan to escape us both. My hips sprang to life immediately, moving up and down his incredible length, the motion divinely plaguing my body with a sensation so heavenly and delightful ... in that moment, I reaffirmed that, yes, my heightened sense of touch was definitely my favourite perk of pregnancy.

Gripping the back of his seat for balance, I placed one hand against the roof, allowing me more control over my movements.

'You have no fucking idea how much I have missed the feel of you, Alexis. I belong inside of you.'

'Oh, trust me, I know,' I moaned.

Bryce's head fell back against the seat revealing the sexy veins in his neck and, unable to resist the urge, I leaned forward and dragged my tongue from his collarbone, moving over the veins and up to his mouth where I savoured the taste of him. He grabbed the back of my head and he pressed me into him, prolonging our hungry kiss.

I broke away, gasping, my eyes now widened with the need to bring us both undone, so I replaced my hand against the roof and quickened my pace, pumping as hard and as quickly as I could — facilitating my rising orgasm.

I felt his fingers tightly grip my hips, indicating he was right there with me. 'Are you ready?' I asked breathlessly. 'I can't hold off any longer.'

'Yes, come apart on me, honey!'

Without hesitation, I moved my hand from the roof and grabbed his head, pressing him to my mouth as he stiffened and released while I clenched and contracted. *Fuck, I have missed that.*

After screaming out the relief of finally having a fuck-induced orgasm, I massaged his tongue with my own and slowed down my movements.

Bryce released his grip on my hips and placed his hands on my arse. 'Mm, I love your arse,' he mumbled, while gripping it tightly.

'You won't for long,' I mumbled back as our tongues continued to caress one another's.

He pulled away with a confused expression on his face. 'Why?' he chuckled. 'What are you talking about?'

'You won't love it much longer, because it is more than likely going to double in size.'

My heart started to pound within my chest at the realisation of what I had just described, knowing from past experience that my body was soon going to balloon. *Oh, shit. I am going to resemble a beached whale. He is going to find me hideous.*

Look, I know it is said that we possess a radiant glow when we are pregnant and that we are the essence of beauty when carrying a child. Well, excuse me for bursting that incredibly bogus bubble, because when I was last pregnant I felt nothing but frumpy, moody, sore and highly undesirable. And I am not the type of person to degrade myself or put myself down. However, if history was anything to go by, during pregnancy my self-esteem went out the window.

Bryce noticed my sudden dread and pulled my head in closer, kissing my neck as he spoke. 'You are the most beautiful and exquisite creature I have ever laid eyes on. That is *not* going to change. Yes, you are going to grow in size, but that just means there will be more of you to worship and enjoy. And trust me, my love, I am going to worship and enjoy every single bit of you.'

* * *

Bryce made good on my request that he make up for refusing to have sex with me for the past two weeks. Let's just say the man has stamina and he was eager to exploit that trait many times throughout the day and night. My sexual deprivation was temporarily fulfilled. And I reiterate, *temporarily*.

* * *

Both of us had made the decision not to inform anyone of my pregnancy, and had no plan to do so for at least another month. With so much happening in our lives in recent times, announcing another addition to our family at that point would probably be just a bit too much for my children to have to comprehend. Deep down, I knew they would be excited, especially Charli. I just didn't want to over-whelm them any further for the time being; both of them had already had to dissect and cope with more than enough change in a short space of time.

My baby-bump was not yet visible, and the vomit-express only vis-ited me once a day. So there were no obvious signs that I was harbour-ing a teeny-tiny human inside of me, therefore spilling the beans that I was expecting was not yet a necessity.

Keeping our pregnancy quiet was terribly difficult though, because Bryce wanted the whole world to know our exciting news. He literally wanted to shout it from the rooftop and, in fact, had done just that the night after he found out I was pregnant. He had stood on the balcony and shouted to the city skyline, 'I'm going to be a fucking dad.' He was over the moon, ecstatic, making me laugh as he repeated it over and over. But as excited as he was, he also knew that keeping it a secret for the time being was the right thing to do.

Initially, that had not been an easy task to accomplish. We would get comfortable mentioning it to each other when the kids were not around and then when they were in our company, minor slips of the tongue were inevitable.

Nate and Charli had been spending Saturday afternoon till Tuesday morning with Rick — their father — and Tuesday after school till Saturday afternoon with me and Bryce. I had found this arrangement terribly difficult at first, because I was not used to being away from my children for such a considerable amount of time. However, this agreement wasn't a strict schedule and we could change it whenever we wanted, which suited me just fine as the nights I couldn't tuck them into bed were absolutely dreadful and I hated it.

Being away from my children for consecutive days on a regular basis had been challenging, possibly the most challenging thing I have ever had to endure. But I continued to face life's challenges, jumping over the hurdles that arose before me and, because of that, my hur-dling skills were becoming world-class ranked. I also had to allow Rick to have his quality time with the kids.

As hard as it had been for me — after discovering his sordid, secret past — I had made the executive decision to bury my feelings of anger toward him for the sake of our children. The kids were innocent in this entire life-changing situation, and keeping the peace so they could adapt a little easier was what I, as their mother, had to do, whether I wanted to or not. At the end of the day, Rick adored his children and they adored him in return.

Nate, however, still refused to meet his half-brother, RJ — Rick's five-year-old love child. He had been so hurt and upset after finding out his father had another son that he chose not to speak to Rick for days, having refused outright to have anything to do with either of them. During the past week though, Nate had relented a little and some of his anger toward his dad dissipated, but he was still adamant he wanted nothing to do with RJ. Charli, on the other hand, had met her half-brother very briefly during a trip to a cafe for a milkshake. She had mentioned to me afterwards that 'He sort of looks like Daddy,' except RJ was not as tall and 'He doesn't have little bits of hair on his face like Daddy does.' She had also said 'he's quiet' and 'he likes caramel'. I stopped asking questions after that.

* * *

The kids no longer had to go to before- and after-school care when they were staying with us. Bryce had arranged for Danny to drive them to school and pick them up whenever I couldn't. At first this bothered me a little, because Danny had not signed up to chauffeur my children to and from school. But he never complained and both he and the kids seemed to get along really well, high fives being a regular thing between them all now.

Nate, the typical nine-year-old boy that he was, had requested they be driven to school in the limousine, my response having been, 'In your dreams, bucko.'

Yes, having a limousine at our disposal was convenient and, well ... to be honest, really cool. However, I didn't want that particular privilege adding any more unwanted attention to my children's lives. Rumours of my relationship with the illustrious Mr Bryce Clark were already circulating around our small community thanks to the bitchiness of the 'mummy mafia' at school. And because of this, Nate and Charli had been the target of some negative and truly horrid taunting from kids in the playground.

I hated to admit it, but apparently the troll-gene that some parents seemed to possess was passed down a generation to their children.

When Nate had requested being chauffeured to school, I'd noticed Bryce give him a wink shortly after I had said 'no', which made me think that he and my son were in cahoots about the whole thing behind my back. Being undermined where my children were concerned was definitely a big no-no in my books, but as Nate and Bryce had been getting along really well I was willing to let some things slide. It was just such a relief seeing my son interact in a positive way with Bryce, as I could have sworn Nate would have hated the idea of another man being in my life — being the massive Mummy's boy that he was.

Surprisingly, Nate had acted quite the opposite and had really taken a liking to him. Maybe it was because he could see how much Bryce loved me, but at the same time, I was not forgetting about that thing Bryce had plenty of — money. I'd really like to think it had nothing to do with the money but, in saying that, kids would be kids and I honestly couldn't rule it out.

Charli-Bear had adapted to our entire situation a lot slower than Nate, but overall she was accepting it really well and had even asked me if one day she would refer to Bryce as her second dad. My answer to that was, 'One day, if you would like to, but for now just call him Bryce.' Second dads, stepchildren, new babies, long-lost half-brothers — it was all happening just a bit too fast.

* * *

I had woken early this particular morning and made my way out of bed before Bryce, which never usually happened. It must've had something to do with my body preparing to be awake for feeding, and the times I would then be recouping those lost hours of sleep. It was either that, or I was simply excited that in a few hours I would be seeing Nate and Charli again.

I decided that as I was awake before Bryce — and that it was, in fact, a rarity — I would make him breakfast for once. The problem with that idea was that I prayed to God I'd be able to keep the contents of my stomach exactly where they should be — in my stomach. Having a heightened sense of smell was definitely not one of my favourite perks of pregnancy. Touch ... yes. Smell ... no.

I swear I had developed superhuman smelling abilities and, unfortunately, most of the scents I picked up on would send my tummy into a state of nausea. Just the other day, a client had entered the foyer, bringing along with him the smell of onions. I must have resembled a Customs sniffer-dog, sticking my nose in the air as he walked in, practically giving the poor man an interrogation as to where the onion smell was coming from. Mr Onions had quickly revealed that he'd eaten a salad roll containing them for lunch, and I'm guessing he'd hoped that his confession was enough for me to drop the questioning. It was. But as soon as he entered Bryce's office I'd had no choice but to run to the bathroom, only to be greeted with my half-digested morning tea. *Oh, hello, banana and hot white chocolate, nice to see you again. Urgh!*

So, as I contemplated my plans for our breakfast, I knew onions were not going to be on the menu. Instead, I opted for some bacon and eggs with a fruit salad as a side. However, cooking this particular meal could also be a risky move as eggs were definitely a vomit-express trigger as well, but I knew Bryce loved his eggs for breakfast, so I was willing to take that gamble.

I decided I would have a little work-out on the gym set before breakfast. I hadn't exercised in a long time and, quite frankly, I felt very blah, tight and sore. Working out during pregnancy is perfectly safe and I knew from past experience that moderate exercise early on in pregnancy could be extremely beneficial, not only for weight control but also for mobility and the prevention of aches and pain.

Stepping on the treadmill, I started with a five minute warm up walk. *Ah, this isn't so bad.* I felt good, so I eagerly moved across to the exercise bike for a twenty minute fat-burning cycle on a low setting. Again, easing myself back into it.

After my subtle fat-burning cycle, I figured I would try some light weight training, being pretty sure my muscle mass had packed its bags and pissed off elsewhere due to neglecting to use my muscles for anything of late, including sex thanks to Bryce. So the loss of my flexed biceps saddened me.

I gave them a little jiggle. *I'm pretty sure they are not supposed to just wobble and flap like that.* I gave them another jiggle. *I'm pretty sure I look like an idiot.*

Self-consciously I dropped my arms, glad that City Towers was one of the taller buildings in the vicinity and that no one else could see me standing on the rooftop with my arms out, wobbling my arm fat and resembling some nutcase practising a new weird-arsed dance move.

Disgusted and embarrassed by my arms' flabbiness, I was now keen to get reacquainted with the weight machine in front of me. I executed some lateral pull-downs, chest presses and bicep curls, then switched to my lower body and carried out a couple of leg extensions, abductor crunches and leg presses. Bryce also had a cross trainer, so I opted to finish off on that, running at a low level for ten minutes. That was when he came out with a horrified look on his face.

I smiled at him, but his expression didn't change. So I slowed down my strides to ask him what was wrong. 'Is everything all right?'

'I don't think you should be exercising on your own. Why didn't you wake me?'

He leaned himself up against the weight machine and crossed his arms over his abdomen.

'Because you were sleeping soundly and I thought that since I need to get used to waking at different hours, I'd get up and do a work-out, then cook you breakfast.' I slowed to a stop, took a long swig of my water and stepped off the machine.

As I took that final step down, my legs nearly gave way and I stumbled just slightly into Bryce's waiting arms. 'What the fuck, Alexis? Are you trying to kill yourself and our child?' he yelled angrily.

'Of course not. Don't be silly,' I said, a little shocked. 'My legs just need a second to remember how to work again, that's all.'

'Exactly, you haven't worked out in a while. You need to take it easy. Should you even be working out at all?' he asked in an accusatory tone, a tone I did not like.

'Yes, it's fine. I just need to do a little, a little more often.'

'Well, from now on, you are not doing it without me, got it?'

'Bryce, you're being ridiculous.' *And annoyingly bossy.*

'No, I'm not.' He opened my water bottle and not so subtly requested I drink some more.

I snatched the bottle from his hands and released myself from his grip. 'I told you, exercising is fine. It's perfectly safe, and I'm going to continue to do it with or without you. I will not allow myself to undo the hard work I've put in over the past few years.' I walked past him and headed to the kitchen.

'Alexis, I'm just trying to keep you both safe,' he explained as he followed behind me, stopping on the other side of the bench. I'd pre-made the fruit salad, so I moved it toward him without saying a word. I then cracked a few eggs into a frying pan and toasted some bread while the eggs cooked. Thankfully, the fact I was now pissed off effectively distracted me from the possibility of vomiting.

'Alexis.'

'What?' I snapped, still refusing to look at him as I continued cooking breakfast.

I had placed some bacon under the grill on low before I started my work-out, and it was now perfectly crisp.

Pulling it out and placing it on the benchtop, I arranged it on the plate then scooped the eggs from the pan and placed them onto the slices off buttered toast.

'Honey, please look at me.' His voice had softened so I looked up. 'Maybe you should stop exercising until we speak to Dr Rainer?'

I sighed, dejectedly. 'So, this is how it's going to be, is it? You are going to completely ignore everything I say until you get Dr Rainer's approval?'

Bryce didn't say anything, so I shoved his breakfast in front of him and stormed off toward our bedroom. I had suddenly lost my appetite.

CHAPTER

3

Reeling from Bryce's blatant disregard for my knowledge of what is and isn't safe during pregnancy, I turned on the taps to the shower and removed my sweat-dampened clothes. I didn't appreciate being treated like a child. I was not a child, nor was I a naive and inexperienced first-time mum. I knew what I could and couldn't do; I knew my limits. I also knew that if I didn't watch what I ate, and stay somewhat physically active, I was bound to pile on the weight, ache all over and become mentally depressed again.

After Charlotte was born, I — like most women after having children — had stacked on the kilos and struggled to lose them for months and months. I had found myself sinking into a hole of misery and depression, and I sure as hell didn't want to find myself back there. Being in that state of mind was horrible, having felt shitty, been bad-tempered and unable to sleep well. I'd had no energy, had physically ached all over, ate nothing but crap and made really bad lifestyle choices. All in all, I was just downright horrible to myself and the people around me.

So I knew that if I didn't maintain the healthy lifestyle I had now become accustomed to, I would head down that terrible path again, and I was not about to let that happen. Bryce was just going to have to back the fuck off. This was my body, my baby — okay, our baby. But my body, and I knew how to look after it, not him. *No, that is somewhat of a lie. He looks after my body exceptionally well, especially when he combines his hands and mouth ... and ... Stop it, Alexis.*

I stepped into the shower and, shortly after, Bryce appeared at the door holding my breakfast and a cup of tea he had made.

'What are you doing?' I asked him, annoyance clear within my tone.

'You didn't eat your breakfast.'

'I don't want it,' I hissed at him. 'I've lost my appetite.'

'You *are* going to eat your breakfast, even if I have to come in there and feed it to you myself.'

'Seriously, Bryce, you are being an overbearing pain the arse. I'm not hungry right now. If I become hungry after my shower, then I'll eat.'

'Alexis, you have just had a work-out which you haven't done in a while. You need to replenish your energy levels.'

'Bryce!' I yelled, moving to the opening of the shower to glare at him.

He stepped forward so quickly I barely had time to react to the piece of toast he assertively pressed into my mouth while steadying me with his arm at the same time. I choked, spat half the contents back out and freed myself from his grasp.

I glowered at him as I wiped my mouth, stepping back under the water, retreating into territory he would not enter due to being fully clothed. 'What are you doing?'

'I told you I would feed you myself, and I will, so I suggest you eat,' he said firmly, displaying a slight smirk on his face and holding out some more toast.

You stubborn — overprotective — overbearing — sexy — domineering — son of a bitch. If you want me to eat that, then you will have to come in here and do exactly what you threatened. I turned my back to him in defiance and went to wash my hair.

Almost instantly, he had me spun round and pinned up against the wall, both my arms held above my head with one of his own. He was wearing a pair of suit pants and a shirt which were now completely soaked.

'You will eat your breakfast, my love,' he said in a calm, low, and incredibly sexy, authoritative voice.

Squinting my eyes at him, I opened my mouth to take a bite of the toast. Luckily, his shower was quite large, and where he had me pinned against the tiles was not directly in the stream of water.

I bit down on the toast and quickly consumed it. 'Let me go,' I mumbled.

'No. Not until you have eaten the whole piece.' *I hate you right now, but you are so fucking hot all clothed and wet, and the only thing I want to eat is you.*

I opened my mouth for another bite, so he obliged by placing the remaining bit of toast inside. He kept a firm grip on my hands while he pierced me with his wanting eyes, the desire he harboured for me now blatantly present. So much so I could read him like a book. This was one of my favourite forms of communication with him. I loved how we were both able to stare into each other's eyes and know what we felt, wanted and needed. Right now he wanted me, and right now I wanted him. But I could be just as stubborn and until he promised to back off in relation to exercising, I had no plans to give in to his dick-tational tease.

I opened my mouth again, prompting him to lean forward.

'Do you want this, Ms Summers?' he whispered as his lips delicately brushed over mine. *Yes, fucking hell, yes.*

'No,' I breathed, not breaking our stare and letting him know that I was now in control. I licked my lips very briefly. 'I want more food.'

His eye twitched and he pressed his body harder against mine then, slowly, he let go of my hands and dragged his fingers down my arms, stopping and hovering them just over the top of my breasts. Without the slightest touch, he quickly slammed both his palms onto the tiles on either side of my shoulders and pushed himself back from the wall, fire and lust burning in his eyes.

He ran his hands through his hair and smoothed away the wet strands from his face before turning around and walking over to the plate he had placed on the hand basin. He picked up a piece of bacon and the cup of tea he had made me then stepped back into the shower. Slowly, he made his way over to where I was positioned with my hands still above my head, having deliberately kept them there with the sole intent to force him to feed me like he had threatened. He must have understood my intention, because he placed the hand holding the bacon back to its original spot, resuming his grasp above my head.

Gently putting the rim of the cup to my mouth, he tipped it slightly so that I could drink my tea. Some of it spilled from the corner of my mouth, dripping down my chin and onto my chest. Bryce quickly moved forward and licked the drip with his tongue as it fell to my breast.

I swallowed the remainder of my mouthful as his tongue sensitised my nipple, forcing my eyes to close momentarily, then open back up again. He looked up at me with a satisfied grin, then tilted the cup again, continuing to lick, suck and pull with his lips and tongue. I took in another mouthful, deliberately spilling some from the opposite side of my mouth in an attempt to have him please my other nipple, equally. He smirked at my not-so-subtle trick and moved across my chest to do what I wanted him to, tantalising me with his hungry mind-blowing mouth, right up until I finished drinking my cup of tea. *Best damn cup of tea EVER!*

Continuing to metaphorically bite my tongue, I refused to speak as he placed the empty cup in the hand that held mine above my head, swapping it for the piece of bacon he had picked up from my plate. He tormented my mouth with the bacon, wiping it across my lips and prompting me to stick out my tongue to taste its saltiness.

Aggravated by his teasing, I bit down on it with a stubborn scowl.

Bryce pushed his pelvis into mine and kept licking and kissing the edges of my mouth.

'I want more,' I whispered hungrily, forcing a growl from within him as he kissed around my mouth with heightened intensity. 'No ... more bacon,' I explained.

Trying not to smile while raising my eyebrow at him was near impossible, but I succeeded in my attempt.

He let go of my hands and stepped back. 'What else do you want?' he asked, knowing I was not going to give in until he heard me out.

I put one of my hands out to indicate he give me the bacon. 'Give me the bacon and I'll tell you.'

Bryce stepped closer, lifted my hand back up to the other, and placed the piece of bacon in my mouth. 'Well?' he asked, raising his eyebrows at me and holding my hands in place.

I deliberately paused while staring deep into his eyes. The pause was not for dramatic effect, but more so to convey my sincerity in what I was about to say. 'I want you to back the fuck off and understand I have done this before. I know what I am and am not capable of when it comes to carrying my own child. You need to stop treating me as if I'm ignorant, because I am not,' I asserted before biting down aggressively on the bacon which was now slightly wet and tasted like shit.

'Honey, you need to understand that I haven't done this before, and the thought of anything happening to you or our baby scares me to death. So, will I back the fuck off? No. You are just going to have to deal with it.'

I released my hands from his and pushed him back so that he was at arm's length. 'You will have to deal with me putting my foot down then,' I said with assurance as I licked the last of the bacon's saltiness from my lips and watched as he looked down at them and licked his own.

Bryce smirked and began to unbutton his shirt. 'In what way?'

I went to answer him, but choked from the sight of his now bare chest as well as on the rogue bit of bacon that had been floating around in my mouth. In an effort to gain my composure, I watched with anticipation and subdued excitement as his shirt fell to the floor of the shower.

Looking at it for the smallest of seconds, I then slowly raised my gaze to his hands which were undoing his pants. I followed those as he pushed them to the ground together with his underwear. *Don't look up, Alexis. Whatever you do, don't look up.*

'Well? How do you plan on putting your foot down?' he repeated.

Desperately trying to keep my stare fixed to the shower floor, I noticed his feet take a step forward so that his erection was now in my line of sight. I closed my eyes. *Yeah, close your eyes, Alexis, and pretend that Mr Fucking-Sensational Clark with his rock-hard cock is not standing directly in front of you, tempting you, teasing you and practically calling your bluff.* I swallowed heavily. *Don't let him call your bluff, tease him back.*

Opening my eyes and smirking back at him, I put my finger in my mouth and pulled it out again. His eyes were focussed on my action so I pushed it back in then retracted it completely, dragging it down my body until it reached my clit. I slowly began to massage my sensitive spot while watching his eyes stare hungrily.

Revelling in his expression, I pushed my finger further down until it was enveloped by my pussy. This made him clench his fists in what seemed like frustration and desire. *Good.* I raised my leg and pressed my foot against the tiles while massaging my nipple with the other hand, continuing to finger-fuck myself in an attempt to make him cave. He seemed somewhat aggravated, but the look on his face also indicated he was enjoying my tease — which was great — but my intent was to torture him so that he would give in and tell me he'd back off from being overprotective.

Dropping my gaze back to his hands, I noticed that they were now placed at the base of his cock. *Mm, I love watching him take hold of himself, his large hands clenched tightly around his shaft. Stop it, Alexis. Torture, torment, tease — remember?* Bryce slowly began to pump himself as he watched my hands explore my own body. I let out a moan for him and he growled in response. So I brought my finger to my mouth again, licked it slowly and went to insert it back inside me, when he grabbed my hand.

'Are you going to back the fuck off?' I asked with a smile.

He paused while gently gripping my hand, then, with his sexy-as-hell smirk, inserted my finger back inside me as far as it would go, making me gasp against his mouth. *You sexy fucker, I hate you.*

Slowly, and with deliberate control while breathing hot and heavy against my lips, he slid my finger back out again and placed it in his mouth, forcing me to shudder. *Holy fuck in a can. Damn it!*

I couldn't help but watch intently as he appreciated my flavour before gradually dragging my finger out from between his lips. And, without removing his heated gaze from my equally heated one, he kissed the tip of it then placed it upon his chest, directly over his heart.

Bryce leaned in and put his forehead against mine. 'I will never back the fuck off where you are concerned. You are my everything and will remain my everything for as long as I walk this earth.' He grabbed my face and kissed me passionately, then reluctantly pulled away. 'Now, as much as I like to watch you please yourself, quit it. It's my fucking job to bring you undone and mine alone.'

CHAPTER

4

I hated giving in to Bryce or, more to the point, I hated giving in full stop. But when the man of my dreams had me pinned to the shower wall, telling me that I was his everything and always would be and explaining that it was his sole responsibility to bring me undone, then who was I to argue?

I grabbed his head, vigorously pulling it forward to mine so that I could taste the inside of his mouth. He groaned wildly and lifted me up, indicating I should wrap my legs around his waist — and like always, I happily obliged.

Bryce gripped my arse as he held me perfectly in place to penetrate me with his glorious cock, forcing my eyes to close and my head to tilt back as he slid inside me. Then, pressing his lips to my neck, he pulled himself out to the tip and slammed back in again. I gasped at his sexy ferocity, causing him to stop and pull back.

'Shit!' He went to set me down. 'Was that too hard? Are you okay?' he asked with concern.

I searched his panicked face. 'Hey. I'm fine.'

'I'm sorry. You just make me so fucking wild.'

Grabbing his hair, I yanked it back and forced him to look deep into my eyes. 'Don't you dare go all soft on me. I'm fine and no, it was not too hard. So stop worrying and fuck me. Fuck me hard, and do it now.'

His eyes lit up as he laughed. 'You're killing me. You know that, right?'

'The feeling is mutual, trust me.' I leaned in and kissed him, which very quickly turned hot and desperate again as he re-entered me and slammed his cock in to the hilt.

I could sense a slight hint of hesitation on his part, but I didn't say anything. He obviously had concerns, and I could see he was trying to overcome them where he could. Plus, I was more than overflowing with sexed-up hormones and probably putting far too much pressure on him.

Bryce continued to drag his length out to the tip, then slam right back in again until my nails were digging into his shoulder and my body was shuddering against him. He, too, jerked as he reached his own release while gripping my arse with one hand and steadying himself against the shower wall with the other. I moved my hands to his head and wiped the wet strands of hair from his face so that I could see his piercing blue eyes as he came down from his climax.

'How did I get so lucky?' I asked.

'Lucky? I never used to believe in luck,' he said as he smiled and regained his breath.

I traced my fingers around the edges of his face, studying his perfect profile. I was now curious and a little bemused as to why he wouldn't believe in luck. 'Really? Why?'

'I used to think luck was suggestive of having no control. I believed that we — ourselves — determined our fortunes and misfortunes. But ... I had no control over you applying for a job at my hotel, so how can I continue to believe there is no such thing as luck? I'm the fucking luckiest man on earth, and you being here, naked in my arms, against my shower wall and carrying my baby, is fucking proof of that.'

* * *

Bryce and I showered properly after our argument and subsequent compromise-sex. Come to think of it, I don't recall a compromise having been reached. If I recalled correctly, he seemed to have gotten his way — as per usual.

We both headed to our desks, having no choice but to get stuck into the pile of work that awaited our attention. It was Easter this coming weekend, and the three hotels were pretty much fully booked. I could see with my own eyes just how much work was involved in the running of the City Towers complex, but to have numerous hotels around the world and plans for future developments was simply mind-boggling. I knew Bryce had a large number of very capable employees running his hotels abroad but, at the end of the day, Clark Incorporated held his name and he was very much involved in the entire operation.

I had plans to pick the kids up from school, as I wanted to drop by my old home and collect the last of my things. I hadn't slept there for nearly two weeks and I did not plan on sleeping there again. Rick was coping just fine, as far as I was aware, having accepted our separation and come to terms with the fact our marriage was over. Sadly, we weren't the best of friends any more and, unfortunately, I didn't think we ever would be. There was far too much betrayal and hurt for that to ever be the case. So far, though, we were civil and supportive of each other in our new lives, and we were there for one another where the children were concerned.

* * *

I drove my Ford Territory into the driveway, having chosen my car over one in Bryce's collection for its rather generous storage capacity. I had to collect the last of my clothes, shoes and toiletries, plus a few other things I wanted from around the house.

As I stepped inside the house, I found it to be clean and tidy, an indication that Rick really was coping and moving on with his life. The notion made me smile. I put my bag and keys down on the buffet like I had for many years — second nature, I guess.

Rick and I hadn't yet discussed dividing our assets. We just hadn't had the time nor the desire to do so. I had pretty much everything I needed at the apartment and Rick ... well ... he had five million dollars in his bank account. Therefore, dividing up our bits and pieces was not a priority for either of us. To be honest, I didn't want the material things: I couldn't care less about the TVs, couches, caravan and household furniture. What I wanted were the things that held sentimental value for me, the things that made me smile and had happy memories.

I made my way to the spare room, pulling out a suitcase and dragging it toward my old bedroom, when Claire walked out. We both screamed simultaneously from shock, not expecting each other to be there.

'Jesus! Fuck! You scared the shit out of me,' I said as I put my hand to my chest and looked her up and down, quickly noting that she was wearing one of my dresses together with a towel wrapped around her wet hair.

'Shit! Sorry, you scared me, too,' she answered with an instant blush of awkwardness across her face.

'Are you wearing my dress?' I asked — or rather, accused.

She looked down at the dress and then back up to me. 'Um ... yes. I didn't have anything else to put on.'

At that point in time, I'm not quite sure I really know what came over me. All I remember was seeing red — as in screaming bloody murder red. I can only imagine it looked as if I was a bull in Pamplona's infamous running of the bulls and Claire was one of the shit-scared runners. I basically chased her out of the house, steam surging out of my nostrils, and if I'd had horns like one of those bulls I could guarantee you they would have pierced the bitch's arse.

After yelling at her to get out of my house, shoving her handbag into her chest, snatching back my towel and slamming the door in her face, I started angrily packing up everything I could see. *How dare she come in here and start wearing my clothes, eating from my fridge, showering in my shower and more than likely sleeping in my bed. Bitch!*

I grabbed my clothes and shoved them in the suitcase. I picked up every last bottle of perfume and every toiletry that I could find. I grabbed my photo albums, pictures from the walls, potted plants, and even my KitchenAid and Aldi coffee machine. I stomped around the house looking for things I couldn't bear for her to touch, like my decorative couch pillows. Okay, so I only paid five dollars each for them at K-Mart, but they were pretty and I liked them, and I was not about to leave them there and let her get comfortably cosy with them. *Fuck her.* I forcefully squished as much as I could into my car and took off to get the kids from school.

* * *

Nate and Charli had been excited to see me waiting for them when the bell rang, but my presence at the school probably made the whole gossip-about-my-love-life problem worse, as I was clearly in a feral mood and my car was noticeably filled to the brink with all kinds of shit. One could have easily mistaken me for living out of my car, and I'm sure the rumour mill would soon reflect that.

Tash and Steph had asked me what was wrong, but I was in no mood to elaborate, so I promised them I was fine and that I would soon have them all over for coffee and a tour of my new home.

* * *

My mind was miles away as I drove toward the city, thinking about Rick, Claire, my house and the fact I now wanted to speak to my lawyer, who just happened to be my old boss. Charlotte had been talking nonstop about her friend Addison's sleepover party in a few weeks' time. I hadn't really been listening to much of what was coming out of her overzealous mouth, when my phone rang.

The Bluetooth feature in my car automatically answered it.

'Hello,' I answered with a loud, clipped bark.

'Hi, beautiful —'

'Hi, Bryce,' interrupted Charli.

'Charli!' I snapped. 'Don't interrupt.'

After a moment of silence, Bryce's voice came through the speaker again. 'Alexis, is everything all right?'

I didn't normally yell at Charli for something as minor and innocent as saying hello, and Bryce was fully aware of that.

'Yes, I'm fine. I'm just tired and I have a headache and —'

'She's been busy packing our house into this car,' Nate interjected, looking at the lampshade that was poking over the back seat.

'Right. Where are you?' Bryce asked, his tone seeming softer and somewhat concerned.

'I'm about ten minutes away. I'll see you shortly.'

'Okay, honey. But pull over if your headache gets any worse, and I'll send someone to come get you.'

'I'll be fine,' I replied before ending the call.

I put my hand to the bridge of my nose and sighed. 'Charli, I'm sorry for snapping. Mummy's head is killing her.' I quickly glanced in the rear-view mirror and smiled apologetically.

'Well, you should tell it to stop killing you.' She rolled her eyes, as if that was simply the cure to a headache.

'Duly noted, sweetheart.'

* * *

I pulled into the basement car park where Bryce was standing, waiting for us. As I stepped out of the car and closed the door, he eyed the visible contents.

Charlotte ran up to him and hugged his waist.

'Hi, Charli. How was school?'

'Good. I start swimming lessons tomorrow. Do you want to come and watch?'

He seemed slightly taken aback at her invitation, but recovered quickly. 'Sure. I'd love to come,' he smiled. Charli looked over at me then motioned for Bryce to lean down so that she could whisper in his ear. Whatever she had said to him provoked a smile to appear on his face, piquing my curiosity.

He winked at her then spoke to Nate. 'Mate, can you take Charli up to the apartment? I need to speak to your mum in private for a minute.'

Nate nodded, and both kids stepped into the elevator.

When the doors closed, I wasted no time in questioning him. 'What did Charli say to you?'

'She told me to make sure your headache didn't kill you because she loves you and, if it tried, could I please kill it first.' He raised his eyebrows at me. 'Are you feeling okay? How bad is your headache? Do I need to kill it?'

I smiled and scoffed casually. 'It's just a small one. I'm fine,' I lied. The last thing I wanted was for him to haul me over his shoulder, bundle me into the Crow and fly me to the nearest hospital.

Turning around to prevent him reading my dishonest face, I quickly distracted him by opening the tailgate to my car. Three bags and my couch cushions tumbled onto the ground. 'Shit.'

'What's all this?' Bryce asked dubiously, obviously sensing my fragile state.

'*My* stuff,' I hissed ever so slightly.

'Honey, there's a vacuum cleaner in there.' He leaned in and pulled it out.

I could hear a very small hint of amusement in his voice, which helped snap me out of my ridiculously angry mood. 'I know. It's my Dyson. It's a good vacuum.'

'So I've heard. But ... we have housekeeping. You, um ... don't ... really need it.'

I turned around to find him cautiously smiling at me. 'I know,' I conceded. 'I just didn't want *her* to touch it. These things are mine. I worked for them, I chose them, I used them; they are mine, not hers.'

'Hers?'

'Claire's. She was at the house when I showed up. She was wearing my dress and had just taken a shower. I got angry and went a little crazy.'

'Oh,' he smiled, stepping closer and wrapping his arms around me.

'I'm not angry at her for being there with Rick. Really, it's not that at all, they can have each other, I honestly couldn't care less. It's just ... I don't know ... those things were mine, are mine, and ... and ... she can get her fucking own. Anyway, I've decided I need to see my solicitor. I'm going to make Rick pay me out for the house —'

'You don't need to worry about money, Alexis. What's mine is yours.'

'It's not about the money, Bryce. I know you want to share what you have with me, and I will let you do that eventually. It may take me some time to get used to that, but I'm sure I will. No, this is more about ... and I know this is petty ... but,' I sighed and slumped into his chest, 'it's just ... he doesn't deserve to get everything we both worked for. It's a matter of principle,' I blurted out, shrugging out of his grip to pick up my cushions. I brushed them down. 'Some of this stuff is special and stupidly sentimental, and yes ... some of it is obviously just downright stupid, I get that. But what I want to do — what I *need* to do — is see my lawyer and change my will, divide our assets and put final closure on Rick's and my life together.

'I know we have to wait a year before we can get a divorce, but finalising these things first will maybe help me deal with it a little better. I have been civil to him and I have been pleasant. But it is getting increasingly hard to keep that shit up.' I closed my eyes, willing the throbbing in my head to dissipate. 'If it weren't for the kids, Bryce, I would have unleashed hell upon him. I think I just need the formality of separation from Rick as his wife. Maybe that will help with my building anger.'

'It's not petty, Alexis. If that's going to make you feel better, then do it. It's your call, your decision.' He turned to face me. 'Speaking of changing wills, you should know that I have already changed mine. I don't want you to ever have to worry about any of that.'

I looked at him, shocked. 'What do you mean you have already done that?'

'I had a meeting with my lawyer the day after you told me you were having our baby and I sorted it.'

'Oh,' I nodded, warily. I don't know why I was dubious. It sort of made sense he would do that. I guess I just didn't expect him to do it that soon.

'What's this?' he asked holding up a lopsided ceramic mug.

'It's *mine*.' I grinned as I snatched it from him. 'I made it in high school.'

'It's lovely,' he said sarcastically.

My mouth dropped, and I smiled at his audacity. 'Shut up. It's art, kind of abstract.' I rotated it in front of me, secretly thinking my statement was bullshit.

He picked up a photo of me and the kids which had been taken on my birthday the year before. 'When was this taken?' he asked, as he studied the photo. 'I like it.'

'Last year, on my birthday.'

'I'm keeping it,' he said matter-of-factly, continuing to look through my stuff.

'Get out. Stop touching.' I playfully shoved him out of the way then gathered up a few things. He, too, grabbed my suitcase and a few things more. The rest I would come back for later.

* * *

The elevator doors opened to the apartment and, as I stepped out, the sight before me had me frozen with fear.

'Alexis. Bryce. Finally, I've been waiting for you.' Gareth or Scott — I'm not really sure and I didn't really care — had been sitting on the sofa casually chatting away to my children. *How the fuck did he get in here?*

Bryce stepped out in front of me. 'Gareth, what are you doing here? Who let you in?'

He gestured to Charlotte. 'This beautiful young lady here did.'

My heart literally plummeted to the ground. *Charli-Bear, how could you be so stupid? You know about stranger danger.* Like every parent, I had explained to Charlotte that talking to a stranger, let alone letting one inside your house was extremely dangerous. Obviously, I hadn't done a very good job of it.

'Gareth, in my office! *Now!*' Bryce said sternly.

'Now wait a minute, you don't need to be like that. I've come here to take my meds in front of you just like you asked me to. I've been doing it every day like you said.'

'Gareth,' Bryce warned.

'Hang on and hear me out. I want to apologise to Alexis, explain a few things. We seem to have got off on the wrong foot, and I want to make things right, especially now that she and her children are living here.'

I couldn't be quite sure, but I thought I noticed the faintest evidence of falseness in his explanation. Then again, maybe this was Gareth and he was being genuine. No, regardless of that, I wanted him as far away from Nate and Charli as possible. He was unstable and I did not trust him, not for a minute.

I glanced at my kids who were still sitting on the sofa, now looking nervous. 'Nate and Charlotte, please go to your rooms. I will be up soon.'

Nate sensed my unease and took hold of his sister's hand, both of them making their way upstairs very quickly. When they were out of sight and the door to the bedroom had shut behind them, I addressed Gareth.

'Okay, so apologise.' I put down the items I still had in my arms and walked over to the sofa my kids had been sitting on. Bryce did the same.

'Look, I know Bryce has explained my situation, and I'm glad he has. Hopefully that will help you understand and be, um ... forgiving of my flaws, so to speak.' He seemed very calm and informative, but I picked up on a tinge of arrogance in his expression. The whole apology seemed forced. Then again, I had no experience whatsoever with someone who had Dissociative Identity Disorder. I couldn't say for sure that this *wasn't* Gareth trying to make amends, so I went along with his attempt.

'The day I attacked you ... well, *I* didn't attack you, Scott did ...' he said angrily, seemingly angry with Scott, who was also Gareth, but not angry with himself. *Oh, my god, this is surreal.* 'The day Scott attacked you, I had lost control of myself. I had no idea I had even seen you, let alone touched you. That was until Bryce told me what I had done. I'm so sorry, Alexis, please believe me,' he pleaded.

I wanted to believe him, but deep down I just couldn't.

'I have been taking my medication and seeing my doctor three times a week. I have been fine. I feel fine. I really want to get to know you if you'll let me. If Bryce loves you as much as he appears to, then I know I will love you too.' He smiled at me.

That smile, mixed with those last few words had me feeling sick to my stomach. I couldn't help it; it was all just a bit too much. My head was in no state to be deciphering anything, let alone whether a DID alter was currently putting on an Academy Award-worthy performance.

'Gareth, I appreciate what you are trying to do and I appreciate you wanting to apologise for Scott's behaviour and actions, but I've had a horrible day and this is just a bit too much for me to take in right now. Look, maybe if we spend a little more time in each other's company we might just be able to be friends. But for now, I really need to go lie down. I have a horrible headache.' I stood up quickly, feeling a bit dizzy. Bryce noticed my slight imbalance and shot up to my side.

'Are you all right?' He searched my eyes for any signs of distress.

'I'm fine. I just need to lie down and sleep off this headache. You stay here and catch up with Gareth. I'm going to go upstairs.' I stretched up and kissed his cheek while watching Gareth for any indication that it was, in fact, Scott.

Gareth looked away momentarily, making me think that it was Scott all along, but then he offered some get well wishes as I left the room. I slowly climbed the stairs, watching the two cousins sit and talk. It was clear Bryce somewhat held back in his interaction, but at the same time, it was also clear that deep down he cared and respected Gareth. It was terribly sad.

CHAPTER

5

After checking to see if the kids were okay and interrogating them as to what Gareth had said, I decided a long talk needed to be revisited: a talk to remind them never to let complete strangers anywhere near them. Charlotte had cried knowing she had done the wrong thing by opening the door and Nate, too, had sulked, knowing that he should have called my phone the second Gareth entered the apartment. I felt terrible for not having been there to stop the whole scenario, but instilling a little fear into them had to be a good form of deterrence against repeating the same mistake, right? *Oh I hope so. I hate deliberately scaring my kids. But this is for their own good; they need to be on high alert where Gareth is concerned.*

I planned to speak to Bryce about the security of the apartment, especially now that my children lived here for the better part of each week. I didn't like the fact that his family or company employees could have such easy access to his office.

'Is he a bad guy, Mum?' Nate asked as I was leaving his room. 'You seemed really scared of him. I know I should have called your mobile when I saw that Charli had opened the door, but I thought he was okay because he's Bryce's cousin and cousins are family, and isn't Bryce going to be in our family soon?'

'Oh, sweetheart, just because someone is family doesn't mean you should automatically trust them. Trust has to be earned. I know it's hard to understand but you don't know Gareth, therefore you can't really trust him yet, right?' I searched Nate's confused face. 'Look, Gareth is not very well in here,' I explained while pointing to my head. 'He gets confused a lot, and when that happens he can be dangerous. That's why I looked scared, because I don't know when he is going to get confused, and it's also because I don't trust him. Listen, I want you to stay away from him, okay? Never be alone with him, and *never* let him inside this apartment, *ever*! I don't want to scare you, it's just better to be safe than sorry, that's all.'

I blew Nate a kiss and left the room, heading directly for bed. My head now hurt with conviction and I needed to rescue my mind from its state of unrest and whisk it away to a place where it could relax and be subconsciously entertained, my pillow being a great help.

* * *

The next morning saw me recovered from the horrid feeling of a miniature person somehow climbing inside my head, unleashing hell and pounding frantically against the inner confines desperate to get back out. I think the terrible headache I had experienced was the result of shock from Gareth's appearance and apology, together with the stress of having to divide Rick's and my assets. Just lightly touching on those two issues in my thoughts was spurring another head-pounding session. The fact Charlotte was overexcited that she had her first swimming lesson, and more so that Bryce and I were going along to watch, didn't help. Her motormouth was in overdrive as she explained her take on how humans float.

Pinching the bridge of my nose, I smiled. I couldn't help finding her demonstrations amusing.

* * *

As all four of us drove toward the school in the Lexus, I found myself unenthusiastically anticipating a rather excited — let's just say floored — reaction to the sight of Bryce by the other mothers at school. I was resigned to the fact that their goggling was inevitable, but would I ever get used to it? I guess I was going to have to.

We pulled up at the school as the bell rang to signify the beginning of the day. Once out of the car, both the children happily said goodbye and ran off to class. 'See you in a minute, Bryce,' Charli called out as she went. *Oh, yeah, don't worry about me. Apparently being your mother and allowing my stomach to be sliced open in order for you to be born into this world means nothing any more. I'll just hug and kiss myself, will I?* I shook my head and smiled.

'What are you smiling at?' Bryce asked, after waving to Charli and looking back to me.

'Nothing really, it's just ... you seem to be a massive magnet to all things.'

He smirked. 'You say that like it's a bad thing.'

'It can be,' I smiled truthfully.

Just as he was about to add to our conversation, I heard my name being shouted from a distance. 'Alexis.' I turned to where Tash stood, beckoning me, then quickened her pace and closed the distance. 'Hey, how's things?' She gave me a hug.

'Yeah, good.'

'Well, helloooo, Bryce,' she sang adoringly as she smiled at him.

I raised my eyebrows and shook my head again. *I was saying?*

My group of friends were aware of the fact I was completely separated from Rick and now living with Bryce. I had met up with them for a coffee date and filled them in on the whole-truth-and-nothing-but-the-truth scenario regarding Rick, Claire and RJ. With the exception of adding that I was pregnant, of course. That was just going to have to wait.

'So how's things with you, Tashy?'

'Yeah, good, hon. It's always good on my day off work.'

'You don't like your job?' Bryce asked, with a trace of concern in his voice.

'Who does?'

'I do,' both Bryce and I answered simultaneously.

Tash scoffed. 'Yeah, I can see why.'

'Do you want a job at one of my hotels?' he offered, without so much as a second thought.

Tash smiled sheepishly. 'You're kidding, right?'

'No. If you want one, give me a call and I'll see what we can arrange.'

'Really? Oh ... um ... that would be good.' She looked at me warily.

I just shrugged. 'Tash worked in security for years, Bryce. She is a part-time events supervisor now,' I explained.

Bryce's amused smile indicated his curiosity. 'Security? Really?'

'Yes, really. So if you do anything to hurt Alexis, I'll kick your arse.' I choked. 'Tash.'

Bryce laughed. 'Good, I'll remember that. Maybe I could hire you as Alexis' bodyguard.'

'Like fuck you will,' I admonished in a hushed voice, glaring at him.

Tash tutted. 'I pretty much already do that for free,' she replied, rolling her eyes playfully.

The second school bell sounded from the speaker not too far from where we were now standing.

'So, what are you both doing here?' Tash yelled over the loud ringing.

I cringed at the ear-piercing noise and waited for it to end. 'Charlotte has swimming lessons this morning. We thought we'd come and watch her.'

Tash draped her arm around my shoulder. 'Great! Thomas has his lesson this morning, too. We can be spectator buddies.'

We walked past the gymnasium to the swimming centre. There were numerous parents sitting poolside, waiting to watch their children. A small group of known bitch-faced mums were chatting quietly and quite obviously stopped their — one could accurately assume — verbal diarrhoea when we walked in.

As we passed them to take our seats, Bryce gently placed his hand on the small of my back and acknowledged the women with his sometimes annoyingly aggravating charm. 'Good morning, ladies.'

I took note of their wide-eyed expressions and the fact that only two of them managed a 'Mornin'.'

'You're having fun, aren't you?' I asked him under my breath as we sat down.

'Yes, I always have fun when I'm with you.'

I playfully glared at him. 'That's not what I mean and you know it.'

'No, I don't know it. Now shh, Charlotte just walked in.' He raised his eyebrows at me and gave Charli a little wave. Tash spotted Thomas, so we all gave him the thumbs up too.

We watched Charlotte's entire lesson and how she over-enthusiastically volunteered for every demonstration. At one point when she performed a torpedo stroke, she deliberately — I think — kept her face down in the water for what seemed like close to a minute or more, completely freaking me out.

When the lesson finished, I blew her a kiss before she skipped off to the change rooms.

'She's pretty good,' Bryce said, impressed.

'Yep, Charli is definitely a doer, that's for sure.'

'I'm seeing that. She obviously takes after her mum.'

I laughed. 'You are soon going to find out that is not necessarily a good thing.'

Tash leaned in. 'She's a mini-Lexi, Bryce. So you're pretty much fucked.'

Playfully shoving Tash out of my personal space, I muttered, 'Bitch.'

We stood up and walked back past the staring women. Just when they thought we were out of earshot, one of them spoke. 'What's so good about her? I've heard she's a bitch.'

I tilted my head to the side and closed my eyes for the smallest of seconds to regain my semblance of composure. *I'm a bitch, all right. I've had my bowl of bitch-flakes and glass of don't-mess-with-me juice this morning. And if I weren't at my children's school right now, I would be ever so gracious as to show you just how fucking bitched-up I can be.*

I was about to politely tell them to mind their own business when Bryce gently removed his hand from my back and turned toward the trolls — sweet, calm and as charming as always.

'The word "good" does not even come close when describing this woman. So, to answer your question, ladies, she is beyond "good". She is exquisite, sensational and her very presence forms the air that I breathe. Is that "good" enough for you?'

One of them nodded, the others just sat there, stunned. He gave them a false and obviously forced smile, then replaced his hand at the small of my back, directing us out of the building.

To say that I was astonished, not only at what he had just done, but also at the beautiful words that had come out of his mouth, would be a complete understatement. The way he had defended my honour without the slightest hesitation was nothing short of amazing; so much so, I found myself openly gaping at him.

He ignored my gobsmacked state and turned to Tash. 'Okay, you are hired as Alexis' bodyguard. She obviously needs one. When can you start?'

'Shut up,' I retorted, playfully punching his arm before linking mine around it, squeezing it tight and never wanting to let go.

'I need to warn you, Bryce,' Tash continued, answering Bryce's stupid joking statement and ignoring me, 'I don't use a subtle approach when it comes to protection.'

'That's fine. I'm more than happy for you to use a more physical remedy when protecting her,' he replied.

'Seriously you two, shut up! I'm more than capable of looking after myself and if you both don't stop joking around, you'll be the ones needing bodyguards ... not me!'

* * *

After a quick goodbye and a promised invitation to have Tash and her family over for dinner, we headed back to the office. The Australian leg of the Formula One Grand Prix was to be held in Melbourne the weekend after Easter and as City Towers was one of the event sponsors and the main accommodation venue, the work that awaited our arrival was enormous.

There was to be a charity breakfast held in the Queen Victoria Ballroom on the first day of the weekend event, and I had been communicating with Joyce, the head of media liaison, and Allison, the events coordinator, to finalise the list of auction items for Ozkids Melbourne.

Bryce had to sign off on the list, which I would normally email to him, but he had been in his office for hours and I had hardly seen him so I thought I would take the opportunity to deliver it to him personally, together with the chargrilled king salmon and herb salad I had ordered for lunch.

I picked up the list as soon as Sebastian pushed the food and beverage trolley through the elevator doors. 'Good afternoon, Sebastian.'

'Good afternoon, Ms Summers.'

'Just leave that here. I will take it into him,' I explained, kindly.

As always, the shy food and beverage attendant hated it when I broke protocol by relieving him of his duty to take the trolley in to his employer. 'I promise it's fine, Sebastian,' I said reassuringly, winking at him.

He reluctantly smiled and went on his way, which was when I gently knocked on Bryce's office door. Almost instantly, he called out for me to enter, so I opened the door and pushed the trolley through.

Bryce looked up from his computer, smiled for a split second then frowned only slightly. 'You really should let Sebastian bring in the trolley, Alexis. It is his job after all.'

'Oh, shush. What's the point when I'm coming in here anyway?' I argued, stopping the cart right next to the conference table. 'Unless you don't want me to come in here,' I said in a slightly pouty voice as I turned my back to him and placed the cloches on the table, deliberately hoping he'd fall for my obvious attention-seeking ploy.

As expected, he was behind me instantly, pressing his body up against my back. His hands had a tight grip on my hips and his lips were already kissing my neck. 'I've missed you, my love,' he murmured as he trailed his mouth down to the top of my shoulder.

I felt his fingers take hold of the zip at the top of my dress and the unmistakable sound of him slowly undoing it filled me with eager longing for his hard and delectable cock.

I sucked in a breath as he dragged his hands back up my bare back, pushing the dress off my shoulders so that it fell to the floor, leaving me in nothing but my black lace bra, G-string and garter. He walked around to my front and eyed me from top to toe. 'You've got new underwear.'

'Yes, Clarissa helped me find some maternity lingerie that was not hideously ugly.'

'Hmm.' He stepped forward and unclipped the front of my bra at the strap, so that it fell forward exposing my breast.

His face lit up, and I couldn't help laughing out loud.

'I like maternity bras — easy access,' he admitted, before bending down and tonguing my nipple. *Holy fuck! I like them, too.*

Reaching up, he unclipped the other side then gently squeezed and rolled that nipple between his fingers, compelling me to moan which only intensified his actions. I gripped his head and flexed my fingers through his sexy hair. He growled, then let me go and walked straight to his office door. *What? Where the fuck are you going? Get back here now, goddamn it!*

I was just about to hurl abuse at him and jump on his back to prevent him from leaving the room, when he locked the office door and turned around slowly. Then, prowling toward me with a sexy-as-hell stride, he loosened his tie and unbuttoned his shirt. *He is just so fucking hot I can barely breathe.*

He laid his shirt and tie over the back of the sofa that was in the middle of his office and continued his sexy striding to where I was standing. Reaching for my face, he cupped my cheeks in his hands and then slammed his mouth to mine. I grabbed his arse and wrapped my leg around his waist, pulling him closer to my pelvis. He reached down and secured it by placing his hand behind my knee then gently laid me down on top of the table.

'Are you comfortable?' he asked.

'Sure.' *Sexy and sweet, I'm luckier than a leprechaun.*

I propped myself up on my elbows and watched him disappear down my body until he had his fingers hooked into my underwear, pulling them down. He scrunched them up, and I watched him place them in his pocket. *Oh, I'll be getting those back Mr G-string Thief so don't even think about it.*

He rolled one of the chairs around the corner of the table then casually took a seat. I smirked at him, amused at his positioning. *Taking a seat does make sense, I guess.* Grabbing both my ankles, he placed each foot on the armrest of his chair, leaning forward with a salacious grin before tongue-fucking my clit.

My head fell back and my nipples hardened. 'Fuck ... Bryce,' I exhaled.

'That comes next, honey.'

'You're so ba—'

He inserted his fingers, in between licks of his tongue, the glorious sensation inexorably cutting my sentence short. 'Bad, you're so fucking bad.'

Suddenly the phone rang and, as casually as one would normally answer it, Bryce reached over and hit speaker. 'Bryce Clark speaking.'

'Bryce, it's Arthur. Have you got a minute?' *Santa! Seriously, your timing is impeccable.*

'Sure, how can I help you, Arthur?' Bryce answered nonchalantly. I pulled my head back up and mouthed, 'What the fuck?'

'I've been speaking to the corporate partners coordinator in relation to the marquee at the Grand Prix.' Arthur said. Bryce leaned forward again and dragged his tongue slowly across my pussy. I nearly shrieked, but instead, I flinched and clenched my thighs together, capturing his head in between them.

He eyed me greedily.

'The entire proposal for the marquee's function has been submitted.' *Jesus, Santa. Spit it out.* 'Are you happy for me to okay the specifics of the proposal? I'm sure you'll be more than satisfied,' Arthur asked.

Bryce stuck out his tongue and flicked at my clit, sending my body into a subdued frenzy as my orgasm bordered explosion. I bit my lip.

'Bryce?' Arthur asked a little impatiently.

'Yes, Arthur, that is fine. I'm happy for you to sign off on it.'

'Sorry, am I interrupting you?'

'I'm just eating my lunch,' Bryce answered, while eyeing me devilishly. My mouth fell open, and I sat up.

'Oh, sorry, I'll let you go then.'

'No, that's not necessary. Alexis is here with me, though, and just to let you know Arthur, you're on speaker.'

'Oh. Hello, Ms Summers. Sorry to interrupt your lunch. I won't hold Bryce up for much longer.'

My face was flushed and my lips were pursed. Bryce had a vice-like grip on my hips, knowing I'd try and leave.

'Hello, Arthur,' I said through gritted teeth. 'There's no rush. Bryce is the only one eating and anyway, he is finished now.' I raised my eyebrow, which was the stupidest thing I could've done because, almost instantly, Bryce thrust his fingers into me with such force I gasped. I quickly covered my mouth and glared at him while my body thoroughly enjoyed his finger-fuck.

Bryce continued the conversation, mischievously smiling and placing kisses down my thighs, while continuing to move his fingers in and out of me. 'So, Arthur, how is Geraldine now? On the mend?'

I mouthed the words 'I hate you.' He shook his head and mouthed the reply, 'No you don't.' *Grrr, No, I don't.*

'She is much better, thanks. I have booked a holiday as you suggested ...' Arthur stated. Bryce pushed up from his chair and dragged me toward him. He spun me around and gently pushed me forward so that I was now leaning over the table. *Oh. Shit. Crap. Balls.*

'We will be going to Tasmania in three weeks,' Arthur continued enthusiastically. 'Ms Summers, have you ever been there?' *Santa, I'm slightly busy right now.*

'Yes, I have. It's beautiful. Have you been there?' *Fuck, Alexis, don't ask him questions.*

Bryce very quietly unzipped his pants and I felt the unmistakable warmth of his crown push into my now overly wet pussy. *Fuck! I'm not a quiet fucker. I moan, and scream, and pant, and howl. Fuck!*

'Yes,' Arthur answered. 'A few times, but most of those were for business.'

'So how long are you going for, Arthur?' continued Bryce, as he slowly began to push into me. I dropped my head to the desk and placed my arm in my mouth, probably resembling a freakin' dog biting a bone.

Bryce leaned forward, removed my arm from my mouth and pinned both arms to the table as he increased his pace. *I hate him ... but I love him ... holy shit!*

'We are hiring a motorhome and driving around for two weeks. I'm really looking forward to the wineries and dairy farms. Do you suggest we go anywhere in particular, Ms Summers?'

Please, Santa, shut up! 'Strahan,' I mumbled, between subdued pants.

'What? Sorry I didn't hear that,' Arthur stated.

Bryce let out a chuckle, and I swear I could've killed him.

'Strahan, Arthur. Make sure you go to Strahan and take a Gordon River cruise,' I blurted out as quickly as I could. *Seriously, Santa, fuck off and go and deliver some presents.*

'Yes, I've heard that is a must-do. Thank you. Anyway, back to my original reason for calling. I'll sign off on the marquee's specifics and send you a list of VIP attendees. Will you be coming this year, Bryce?'

He was pounding into me now, and the sheer willpower I was desperately exercising in order to supress any sound from escaping my mouth was quickly dissipating.

'I don't know, Arthur. Alexis, do you like the Grand Prix?'

I dropped my head. *You'll pay for this, Mr Fucker Clark.* He slammed into me as I was about to answer and I let out a high-pitched, 'Yes.'

'Have you been before?' Bryce asked, with a satisfied but quiet grunt, knowing full well that I had. He slammed into me again.

'Yes.'

'Do you want to come?' *Oh, you fucking know I want to come.*

'Yes,' I practically screamed, losing it and tipping over the edge, my orgasm rippling through me as I shuddered on top of the conference table.

Bryce followed, tightening his grip on my hands as he found his release. 'Yes, Arthur. We're *coming*,' he said, trying to sound normal and less breathy than he actually was. 'I'll let you know my final numbers later today.'

'Certainly, I'll wait to hear from you. Now, please continue your lunch. Good day.'

Arthur hung up.

I was still slumped over the conference table. 'Bryce Edward Clark. I fucking hate you,' I declared breathlessly.

He leaned forward and kissed my cheek. 'No, you don't. You fucking love me.'

I cracked up laughing. 'Yes, I do.'

CHAPTER

6

I pretty much smiled for the rest of the day as memories of Bryce's and my lunch date floated in and out of my head. *God, I hope Santa didn't hear my arse being ball-slapped by Bryce. I will definitely be on the naughty list if he did.* I giggled to myself. The things Bryce had me do were just so wrong, yet so goddamn right.

Danny had collected the kids from school while Bryce and I were kept busy with his back-to-back appointments for the rest of the day. Most of them were related to the Grand Prix, including the appointment with Chelsea. Her annoying helicopter piloting skills were once again required for VIP transfers to and from the hotel. The fact that she barely made any effort to acknowledge me during her visit to the penthouse office only heightened my dislike for the stuck-up bitch. She made me uneasy as I had never met anyone quite like her. She just didn't get that Bryce was no longer interested in her. I wondered if he'd ever spoken to her, set her straight like he promised he would; she needed to be put in her place once and for all. She needed to know that she had absolutely no chance with him. She needed to be told — up close and personal — that he loved me and that she was just a friend.

Regardless, I was no longer worried about Bryce where she was concerned. I wholeheartedly trusted him and I had no doubts about his feelings for me whatsoever. I just didn't trust her and that would probably never change, even if he had already set her straight. I realised that it still bothered me that she was alone in his office with him, because I was feeling sick. But only because she was a lip-licking, devious, sneaky moll and I hated her.

* * *

After we managed to pry ourselves away from the office, Bryce had reluctantly taken a walk with Nate to McDonald's to pick up our dinner. We had stupidly asked the kids to make the choice of what to eat and, of course, they chose that. I had to laugh at his efforts to not only eat the greasy burgers he was not very fond of, but to also place himself in the vicinity of the Ronald McDonald statue he feared terribly. Maybe the curly red-headed clown was growing on him.

Charli hadn't felt like going along with them. She had been a little glum since finding out we were going to the farm on the weekend for Easter, and because of that she would have to wait to see her dad. I had told her that she would see him on Easter Monday, but this was the first time we would be separated on a celebratory holiday and it had obviously really upset her.

I wanted to cheer her up, so I scrolled through my iPod and put on one of our favourite *Glee* songs, turning it up as loud as I could.

Rachel's version of 'Don't Rain On My Parade' began to play, and Charli's eyes widened while a broad smile crept across her face. Grabbing her hand, I started to sing the first line in the song, emphasising the no sitting and puttering. This made her giggle, so I pulled her up to dance around the room with me.

She performed a pirouette on the spot and flung her arms out in an over-exaggerated move which made me laugh. My daughter had just as much love for music as I did, so getting her to prance around the living area with me would surely lift her gloomy spirits.

She happily followed me like a shadow, copying my moves and singing along to the Broadway musical's song. There was a part I knew was coming and it referred to a hat, so I quickly skipped to the beat of the music and grabbed my sunhat which was hanging on the hook near the entryway wall. As I sang about the hat, I placed it on her head and curtsied to her.

Smiling, she returned my curtsy with one of her own and gracefully nodded her head.

I took off again, but stopped abruptly after only a few steps which made her bump into my back. She looked a little surprised, but realised I had done it on purpose so that I could tap my finger on the tip of her nose when the song suggested it. She responded to my nose tap by performing a cute little wrinkle and swipe of her own, then ran around me and stepped up onto the sofa with her arms flung out, mimicking a plane.

I knew only too well what she had planned because this was not the first time we had danced and performed to this song. So when she fell forward, I caught her and spun us both around in a dizzying circle.

Pausing for the smallest of seconds, we gathered our bearings after my over-exuberant twirling.

While my head deciphered which way was what, I figured I'd remain in character, acting as if I was in the middle of a Broadway drama by draping my arm across my forehead, over-exaggerating my exhausted state. Charli laughed, then joined in on the act and pretended to pat down my head and fan her hands at me.

Keeping with the dramatised theme, I sprang up unexpectedly and danced to the kitchen, grabbing an apple as the song mentioned life being juicy and having to have a bite. I pretended to take a bite of the apple, but screwed my nose up at it before tossing it to her. She completely missed the catch and the apple hit the floor and rolled away. Her smile faded to a look of shock and then she said, 'Oops'. *She is just so adorably cute.*

I danced up to her, grabbed her hand and winked, then led her back into the living area as I knew our favourite part was coming.

Sneaking a glance at her getting ready for the move, I took in her excited face and it warmed my heart. We both stopped dancing simultaneously and pointed our fingers at each other like guns, shouting 'BAM!' and, as always, I let her imaginary bullet get me by faking a clutching of my chest followed by a dramatic stumbling around.

After a quick recovery and a few more spinning leaps, the song was about to come to the end where Rachel held the word 'parade' for a long time. We both belted it out, raising our hands to our invisible audience and giving each other smiling glances to see who was going to run out of breath first. I noticed her suck in another breath while keeping her mouth open, pretending she hadn't done just that. I laughed while still trying to hold the note, and not succeeding, so I pointed at her accusingly, making her giggle.

When the song finished, we dropped our hands and flopped back onto the sofa laughing and taking deep breaths.

'Feel a bit better, sweetheart?' I panted.

'Yep, thanks, Mum.' Her smile was genuine so I pulled her close for a hug.

Suddenly, we heard clapping from behind us and spun around to see Bryce and Nate standing at the elevator door, McDonald's bags tucked under their arms. Nate was shaking his head and rolling his eyes while smiling and gently clapping — this performance was not a first for him to have witnessed.

Bryce, on the other hand, was clapping loudly with the biggest smile on his face. 'Wow! I've just found the two newest members of our band.' He walked over and kissed my head from his position behind the sofa.

'Really? Can I really be in your band?' asked Charli, excitedly.

'Sure.'

'Oh. My. God! I'm so gonna go and practise now. Mum, can I borrow your iPod?' She was bordering on hysterical!

My eyes widened at her enthusiasm, so I grabbed her hands to hold them still instead of flapping about. 'Yes, but you "so" need to eat first.'

* * *

We sat together on the balcony eating our burgers and fries. The kids and Bryce cringed when I dunked my fries into the chocolate sundae — the sundae I had subtly threatened he not return home without. *What? There is absolutely nothing wrong with potato being deep-fried in oil, sprinkled with salt and covered with vanilla flavoured soft-serve ice cream and hot chocolate sauce. I'm not seeing the problem here.*

I popped another into my mouth and hummed.

Bryce smirked.

Nate rolled his eyes.

Charli just scoffed her Happy Meal down like a hungry little piggy then grabbed my iPod and ran upstairs. She was bound to get indigestion.

* * *

For the next hour all Bryce, Nate and I could hear as we sat on the living room sofa trying to watch TV was Charli's voice intermittently coming in over the top of Rachel's as she practised singing more *Glee* songs in her room.

Nate's body language suggested a high level of irritation as he endured it, occasionally screwing up his face while looking over his shoulder at his sister's bedroom door. 'Urgh,' he grumbled, 'now look what you've done.'

Bryce and I laughed. 'Leave her alone, Nate. She's learning to sing,' I said, willing his compassion to surface.

'She needs to learn faster,' he huffed, and walked into the man cave. I'm guessing he went for the sanctuary of sound-proofed walls. *Okay, maybe there is no compassion for his little sister's singing abilities.*

Turning to Bryce, who was comfortably seated next to me, gently trailing his fingers along my legs which he'd laid across his lap, I posed a question. 'You do realise you are going to have to let her sing a song with your band now? She will not forget your promise.'

'I know. I have every intention of letting her sing a song at one of our gigs. In fact, we have one coming up in a few months. She can do it then.'

I laughed. 'You're crazy. You might want to run it past the other members of Live Trepidation first.'

He scoffed. 'I don't run things past anybody ... you know that.'

'You are such an arrogant fuck,' I teased, while looking over the sofa to make sure neither of my kids heard what I had just said.

'Yep, and proud of it.'

'We'll see how arrogant you are on the weekend when you have to deal with an entire house filled with Blaxlos. My family are not timid, you know. You might not be so cocky then,' I warned with a secretive smile. He leaned over and pulled me onto his lap so that I was straddling him.

'Bryce, stop it. The kids could come back out here.' I tried to hop off, but he held me there.

'You "Blaxlos" don't scare me. You're putty in my hands.'

'Ha, you haven't met my brother Jake, yet.' I pushed off him and got up, making my way to the toilet for probably the tenth time that day.

As I walked away, I looked over my shoulder at his still arrogant, albeit sexy, face.

* * *

The morning of our trip to the farm, Bryce had quite suddenly become rather quiet and slightly anxious. For most of the morning he seemed to be lost in thought and distracted, to the point where I stopped asking him questions because I had to repeat them again when he didn't answer me the first time. The kids had been miserable, knowing their dad would not be joining us. He was spending the holiday with Claire and RJ instead.

On our way down to the basement car park, I asked Bryce which car we were going to take. Again, he hadn't been focussed enough to answer me, only giving me a, 'Huh?' So when the elevator doors opened, I gently grabbed his wrist.

'What's wrong?'

'What? Nothing, why?' he answered dismissively.

'Bryce, you've been away with the pixies this morning and, because of that, I have been having conversations with myself.'

'What are you talking about?'

'For example, "What car are we taking?"; "Huh?"' I sarcastically mimicked him.

He looked over the cars parked in the garage, let go of the suitcase he had been dragging and scratched his head.

'I don't know,' he answered softly. 'I'm not sure which one is best.'

Suddenly, I noticed just how nervous he really was. I looked between his worried face and the kid's sullen expressions and sighed. *Ah, fuck it. Take one for the team, Alexis!* 'Actually, do you mind if we take the chopper?'

Bryce shot an astounded look at me, and Nate's and Charli's faces lit up.

'Can we? Really?' They both glanced between me and Bryce.

'If it's okay with Bryce, and Poppa gives us the all clear to land without spooking the cattle, then yes.'

My suggestion appeared to lessen Bryce's agitated demeanour. 'Sure, if that's what you all want to do.'

I could see he was trying to make it seem that he would take the helicopter only because that's what we wanted. I could also see he was now over the moon at not having to choose which car would impress my family the most without it being over the top. Instead, the over the top arrival in a helicopter could now be blamed on me, not him, which was exactly my intention.

'Okay, let's head back up. I'll ring Dad to find out where to land.'

* * *

We made our way to the apartment, and while Bryce prepared the Crow for departure, I called my dad to get the all clear and instructions as to a suitable landing spot.

Mum and Dad had over sixty head of cattle spread across their numerous paddocks. They farmed beef cattle and always had mothers with calves or pregnant heifers among their herds. Dad was a bit shocked by my request at first, mumbling something about 'What's wrong with a bloody car' and telling my mum to 'Shh' as she stood in the background and asked what I was talking about. It wasn't until I explained we were flying as a way to cheer up Nate and Charli over not being able to spend Easter with Rick that Dad dropped the annoyed and put-out attitude, instead instructing us to land in the paddock next to the shed.

Bryce buckled us all in and handed out the headphones. Charli automatically started shouting in a tone that resembled a banshee, making my ears curl up and cringe. Nate was using every word of the month he had ever come up with, speaking in what sounded like an entirely new language.

'Sick! I'm stoked. This is gonna be totally epic!'

As Bryce prepared the chopper for take-off, I tried desperately to calm down my kids. 'Okay, Nate, please speak English. And Charli-Bear, lower your voice a little. The headphones do actually work, you know?'

'Yep, yep,' she squealed again and bounced a little in her seat as Bryce began raising the chopper.

'Charli, quiet down while Bryce brings up the collective.'

'This is so sick!' Nate prattled with excitement. 'What's a collective?'

I automatically answered my son, as I had secretly researched a little of helicopter avionics. 'It's that stick thing Bryce is pulling up in his left hand. It controls the squash plate —'

Bryce interrupted with a loud laugh. 'It's called a swash plate. Not squash plate.' He kept chuckling.

'That's what I said,' I snapped. *I'm sure that's what I said. Stupid swash/squash plate/bowl helicopter lift thingamajig.* I decided to shut up after that. Bryce was in a far better position to explain things to my son — who now seemed very interested in piloting a chopper.

Bryce had looked over at me numerous times during the forty minutes it had taken us to fly to my parents' property, obviously still amused at my attempt to gain more knowledge of how helicopters fly. I had stubbornly tried glaring at him in response, but the cheeky loving grin he had on his face was hard to be pissed at for long. It wasn't until I pointed to the spot where he needed to land on the farm that our facial expressions traded places. Now I was the one smirking smugly at him, and he was the one displaying agitation, together with wiping his palms on his jeans every so often and muttering under his breath, 'Friggin' sweaty palms.'

As he placed the chopper down with perfection, I waved to my family, who were standing not too far from the shed. Bryce jumped out and gave a kind, but subtle wave in their direction and, as he did, I noticed my mother's wider than normal grin. She may have been sixty-two, but she was still a woman. I watched him walk around the front of the chopper — his eyes meeting mine for a second, forcing a shy smile across his face.

He opened the back door and let Nate and Charli out. They ran towards my parents and wrapped their arms around them while Bryce came around to my door and unbuckled my belt. He shot a quick glance toward my family which I found to be incredibly adorable. I placed my finger under his chin and directed his face to look at me.

'Hey, I thought you said us Blaxlos were going to be putty in your hands, so why the nerves? Everything is going to be fine; they are going to love you.' I leaned forward once my buckle was undone and gave him a quick kiss.

He reached in and placed both his hands on my hips then lifted me to the ground. 'I'm not nervous.'

'Liar. Come on.' I grabbed his hand and led him to my smiling family.

As we approached, Olivia was singing 'riding in a copter, wocka wocka wocka.' She put her arms out, so I took her from Jen as I kissed my sister on the cheek.

'Hello, Livy, did you see the big copter?'

She excitedly pointed to the helicopter. 'Dere, dere.'

'Yes. And what sound does a copter make?'

She bounced up and down in my arms. 'Wocka wocka wocka.'

I laughed. 'Good girl.' I leaned in and gave a Steven a peck on the cheek as well. 'Hi, Steven. Steven, this is Bryce. Bryce, my brother-in-law, Steven.'

They shook hands. 'Nice to meet ya, mate.'

'Likewise,' Bryce said with a smile.

'And you remember Jen.'

'Hi, Bryce, it's nice to see you again. It would appear you don't like driving,' she said with a silly grin. 'Hey, I'm just kidding.'

Bryce went to explain. 'I could've —'

I interrupted. 'The kids wanted to fly, so we flew to cheer them up.' I raised my eyebrows at her. 'Anyway, why drive when you can fly?'

'Yeah, fair enough,' she replied.

I gently placed my hand back in Bryce's, his grip tightening to let me know he appreciated my closeness. We moved along the receiving line my family had created while Olivia kept singing 'wocka wocka' into my ear.

I stopped in front of my mother. 'Hi, Mum.'

She wrapped her arms around me, squashing Livy at the same time. I pulled back after kissing her cheek. 'Mum, this is Bryce. Bryce, this is my mum, Maryann.'

She practically pushed me aside and wrapped her arms around him. 'It's so lovely to finally meet you, Bryce. Alexis has told me so much about you.'

You're such a liar, Mum. I haven't told you SO much about anything.

Bryce raised his eyebrows at me, obviously pleased to hear of my so-called 'bragging'. 'It's a pleasure to meet you too, Mrs Blaxlo,' he said.

'Oh, you're so sweet, but please, call me Maryann.'

I passed Olivia to Mum and then approached my dad who was still eyeing off the helicopter. 'Bryce, this is my dad, Graeme.'

Bryce shot out his hand. 'Nice to meet you, Graeme —'

'Please, call me Mr Blaxlo,' Dad said, in a stern and mildly intimidating voice.

'Dad!' I smiled at my father's not so funny joke. 'He's kidding, Bryce,' I said as I gave my dad a hug. 'You're not funny, Dad.'

Dad held out his hand to Bryce, while chuckling to himself. He shrugged his shoulders. 'Nice to meet you, Bryce.' They shook hands. 'Thanks for letting us land the chopper in your paddock. I hope it didn't spook your cattle.'

Dad seemed pleased with Bryce's concern for his beloved bovines. 'Nah, it's all good, although you can do me a favour.'

'Sure, what is it?'

'I wouldn't mind an aerial view of my property while you're here.'

'Of course, not a problem. Do you want to go up now?' Bryce asked, enthusiastically.

I butted in. 'No, not yet. Let's get settled in and then you can go joy-riding.'

* * *

After the formal introductions were complete — apart from my brother who had no sense of appointed time — we settled in. Bryce got better acquainted with my family over a coffee and some of Mum's scones. He was impressed with her baked masterpieces. So much so he asked her what she had put in them. I watched her as she put her finger up to her lips, indicating it was a secret ingredient, but then dragging him into the kitchen to reveal what it was.

Amused, I observed his expression of disbelief and was now curious as to what it was, too, but she refused to tell me ... and so did Bryce. *I'll remember that.*

Mum had also put out a platter of cheeses. I would normally dig in to the blue cheese, but I knew it was on the 'not safe to eat while you're pregnant list', so I avoided it and selected the cubed cheddar instead. Unfortunately, blue cheese had a powerful and god-awful stench, and my superhuman smelling ability honed in on that stench, triggering my vomit-express to begin its journey from stomach station to its destination — my mouth. In my panic, I quickly covered my nose and mouth with my hand then, realising being sick was inevitable, I shot up and ran for the toilet.

I made it just in time, but gagged every time I pictured or thought about cheese. *No, I love cheese. It's not fair! I could so knock back a freakin' glass of gin right now!*

I sulked for a bit, then opened the door to the bathroom. Jen was standing just outside and, as I opened the door, she pushed her way in, locking it behind her.

'Hey! It's fine, I'm fine. The cheese just smelled awful. Could you smell it?' I asked with a major case of exaggeration. My acting was far from Academy Award-worthy.

Jen placed her hands on my shoulders and pierced me with her all too knowing eyes. 'No, it smelled fine, but then again, I'm not the one who is pregnant, am I?'

Look away, Alexis. Look away. Fuck, she knows.

'No, you're not ...' I replied. 'I am.'

CHAPTER

7

'Alexis Elizabeth Summers,' was all Jen could say as she pulled me in for a hug, then pushed me out again to search my eyes, then pulled me back in again.

'It wasn't planned, Jen,' I mumbled into her chest. 'I completely forgot to take my pill during that week I spent with Bryce. I know it's no excuse, but I was so head-fucked at that point that it just completely slipped my mind.'

'Does he know?' she asked, concerned.

'Who? Bryce? Or Rick?'

'Oh shit, Lexi! Whose baby is it?'

'Calm down, Jen. It's Bryce's baby, and yes, he does know. He couldn't be happier. We are both really happy. Obviously, I had no plans at this stage of my life to have another baby. But it happened, and we are both really excited.'

She stood there stunned for a moment, then smiled brightly. 'Well, in that case, congratulations.' She hugged me again. 'How far along are you?'

'Approximately nine weeks.'

'Are you planning on telling Mum and Dad anytime soon? Because if you keep doing that ...' she pointed to my hand which I had subconsciously placed on my belly in a circular rubbing motion, 'then you are going to give yourself away.' *Oh, shit!*

'No, not yet. We are going to wait a little while longer. The kids don't even know. Only you and Bryce do.'

'Okay, well in that case stop doing it.' She pulled my hand away from my stomach. 'Oh, wow, Lexi, you're having another baby.' She took hold of my other hand and held both of them in front of us. We both beamed at each other and did a stupid little run on the spot while squealing, just like we had when she found out she was having twins. 'You are seriously going to have one of the cutest babies ever!'

I laughed. 'I know.'

Jen and I composed ourselves before leaving the bathroom, and I suddenly felt terrible for leaving Bryce alone for such a long time. My concern about him feeling awkward without my presence, however, appeared to be seriously unwarranted because when I made my way back to the kitchen area Bryce was in the middle of helping Mum prepare the roast chicken. Well ... help was probably the wrong word. He was actually in control and giving her lessons in what appeared to be the stuffing process.

Bryce looked up and caught me smirking at him, but that soon changed as I took in the sight of his hand inside the carcass, and my vomit-express threatened another departure from stomach station.

'Are you all right?' he asked, trying to sound concerned, but knowing very well why I was sick.

'Yeah, I'm fine. I think it may have been a bit of delayed motion or travel sickness from the chopper ride. I felt a bit yuck when we were in the air.'

'You're supposed to grow out of that, Alexis,' Mum grumbled. 'We could never take her anywhere when she was younger, Bryce,' she explained.

I screwed my face up at the molested chicken. 'Um ... I think I might go outside for some air. Where are the kids?'

Mum shook her head in mock playfulness. 'Where they always are ... on the tractor with your father.'

I nodded and pointed to the door, indicating I was hauling my arse out of there and away from the gut-wrenching chicken.

* * *

After Bryce had helped Mum in the kitchen, he offered to take both her and Dad up in the helicopter for the aerial view Dad had requested. Jen and Steven were sitting on the front porch with me, the twins were still blissfully asleep along with Olivia, and Nate and Charli had taken the quad bikes out in one of the paddocks.

Sitting on Mum and Dad's veranda on an autumn afternoon was simply divine. Our childhood home. A large, solid brick, ranch-styled house, with a tin roof and a veranda that circled all the way around it, sat atop the highest point on the property and, since it was situated on a hill, allowed us to experience a most stunning panoramic view of the valley. It really was picturesque and peaceful. Well, peaceful until the loud hum of an engine roared in the distance, sounding louder as it approached the house.

I knew the noise of the engine did not belong to the quads or the chopper. 'Jake is here,' I said, lifting my eyebrow while taking a sip of my cup of tea.

'Is he alone?' Jen asked, sarcastically.

'Can't see,' I replied, 'probably not.'

My older brother Jake was not married and, unfortunately, I didn't think he ever would be; he was just not the 'settling down' type. He was a truck driver and constantly on the road, not liking to tie himself down to anyone or anything, and he seemed more than happy to have a new girlfriend on his arm each time we saw him. And I use the term 'girlfriend' very loosely.

His Harley Davidson Fat Boy roared up the gravel driveway along-side Nate — who was on his quad — leaving a dust cloud behind them. Charli was following on her quad with her mouth closed and a not too impressed look on her screwed-up face. Jake jumped off the bike and removed his helmet, then laughed at Charli who was choking on some dust.

'Now that is what I call "eating my dust", kiddo.'

'You could've waited, Uncle Jake. I had to close the gate,' she sput-tered between coughs.

He walked over and patted her on the back. 'If I had waited, I wouldn't have won, would I?' He smiled, gave her helmet a light tap with his hand then headed in our direction.

'I didn't know it was a race,' Charli called out, unimpressed.

'Ah, my two baby sisters,' he stated with a cocky smile while enthusiastically leaping up onto the veranda. 'Your favourite brother is here.' Jake then uncomfortably squeezed in between me and Jen, putting his arms around our shoulders and pulling us in for an embrace. 'Hey, Steve,' he nodded towards Jen's husband, who was reading the paper.

'Jake,' Steve acknowledged, in a brief and unperturbed manly kind of way.

'So, where are your rug rats?' Jake asked Jen.

'Asleep.'

'Too easy,' he replied, retracting his hands from us and crossing them behind his head. Jen elbowed him in the ribs. 'Hey, I'm kidding,' he winced with a chuckle. 'So, Lex, where's that good-for-nothing son of a bitch husband of yours?'

'Jake, shh,' I hushed him, looking around to see where Nate and Charli had gone. 'Don't speak about him like that around the kids.'

'It's the truth though,' he responded angrily. 'I'll fucking kill him.'

'No, you won't. And regardless, Rick is still their father and they love him, so please be careful what you say around them. Anyway, he is spending Easter with Claire because I told him to. I didn't think having him here while I was introducing you all to Bryce was a very good idea.'

'Oh, yeah! So where is this Bryce?' He tilted his head back to look inside.

'Up there,' Jen said as she pointed to the sky.

'What? On the roof?' Jake stood up and walked to the edge of the veranda looking up, confused.

My brother was not the sharpest tool in the shed, but he looked intimidating. He had a big build, quite solid. He had tattoos up both his arms and across his chest. His hair was a colour in between my blonde and Jen's brown, and he always had a few days growth of beard on his face. But it was his kind, gentle blue eyes that gave away his softer side.

'No,' she mocked him, 'in that helicopter flying around. Dad wanted an aerial view of the farm, so Bryce has taken Mum and Dad for a ride.' Jen's grin widened as she noticed Jake's expression.

'Fuck off. He's flying that thing?'

'Yes,' I butted in sternly, 'he is a helicopter pilot. We flew here to cheer the kids up. They were miserable about not seeing Rick.'

Jake pulled a 'not bad' face, then put his hand to his forehead to shield the sun's blinding rays from his eyes. 'So, am I gonna like the guy?'

'I don't care if you like him or not. I like him *a lot*, and that's all that matters.'

'No, it's not. You know you need your brother's approval.' He pulled out a cigarette from the squashed pack in his pocket.

'I do not need your fucking approval. Now behave, it's hard enough for him to try and fit in as it is. It's not easy having the stigma of "billionaire" following you around.'

'Oh ... poor him,' Jake pouted, his smoke hanging out of his mouth. 'Shit, I'd just hate to be a billionaire, too.'

'Shut up, Jake, you know what I mean. All I'm saying is he's normal just like you and me, so treat him that way.'

'Yeah, normal all right, just ignore the shitload of money he has,' he mumbled as the chopper approached to land.

* * *

Watching Bryce walk with my parents from the chopper as the rotor slowed down was kind of heart-warming. It was clear Mum was a fan of Bryce's, not only because of her cooking lesson earlier, but by how she let him hold her arm as they walked, guiding her along. Dad seemed pleased as well, talking nonstop, his mouth and hands moving in unison at a rapid rate.

I stood up and grabbed my brother's arm, gripping it tightly. 'Please be nice,' I said, under my breath. I then turned my back to Bryce, but looked Jake in the eyes. 'I'm in love with him, Jake. I mean *really* in love with him,' I confessed before tugging my brother along as we stepped down from the porch.

Mum patted Bryce's arm as an indication to let go so that she could embrace her son. 'Jake, darling.' She pulled the cigarette from his mouth and stubbed it out on the ground.

'Mum!' Jake protested.

She completely ignored him and wrapped her arms around her big boy.

Dad kept walking past and slapped Jake on the back. 'Good to see you, son. I'll need your help in the stockyards in a minute. Some of the herd has pinkeye again.' Dad continued on into the house, probably to prepare the ointment that he had to wipe into the cows' eyes. Just the thought of it had my stomach churning again. *Eww, big cow eyeballs with oozy ointment.* I gagged, and I swear I spewed a little in my mouth.

'Are you okay?' Bryce whispered, looking concerned.

I smiled at him and whispered back. 'Yeah, I'm just a little extra queasy today.' I wrapped my arms around his waist, and he gently moved a piece of hair away from my eye.

He leaned forward and kissed the top of my head. 'Do you need anything?'

Still whispering, I answered, 'Hmm, I could think of a few things.' I smirked at him and his eye involuntarily twitched, making me giggle.

'Ahem.' Jake cleared his throat.

I turned, squinting my eyes at my brother. 'Jake, this is Bryce. Bryce, this is my brother, Jake.' I kept my tight grip around Bryce's waist.

He reached an arm out to shake Jake's hand. 'Nice to meet you, Jake.'

'Same. So, is that your ride?' Jake motioned to the chopper.

'Yeah, is that yours?' Bryce motioned to the Harley.

'Yeah, sure is.'

'Fat Boy Lo 2010, right?' Bryce pried my hands away from their comfortable position on his firm, sexy arse and started to walk toward Jake's bike. I pouted at the loss, but more so because I could feel a massive sexual urge creeping up on me. I was terribly tempted to sneak him into the shed and take him in amongst the hay bales. *Hmm, that's a thought.*

'Yeah,' Jake answered, impressed. 'You like bikes? You've probably got a few, right?'

'Just a couple,' Bryce said modestly, obviously trying to play it down in the hope he did not come across as boastful. I knew he had a couple of motorbikes in his garage, although I'd never seen him ride them, nor did he ever talk about them. I made a mental note to ask him why at a later point in time.

Jake and Bryce soon became embroiled in a heavy discussion about 'Knuckleheads' and 'Ecosses', so I left them to it, deciding to take a walk.

* * *

I had wandered down the hill from the house and across the creek into the farthest paddock on the property. Nate had followed me on his bike as far as the creek, but decided to turn back when I said I was heading to the hay shed. When he was younger, I had put the fear of God in him, telling him the shed was full of snakes, which technically it probably was. He had refused to go there ever since, so my not-so-false lie had worked a charm. The hay shed wasn't really my destination; the gum tree that was only ten metres from the shed was. When I was younger, I would often climb up a few branches high and perch myself comfortably in the gum's inviting arms, reading my books for hours.

I always knew it was time to head back to the house when I heard Mum's voice echo across the valley, shouting for me to return home. Her voice probably carried for quite a long way. I loved it on the farm; it was my one true home, and I loved that my children got to experience it as well.

I made my way to the gum's large trunk and traced my fingers along the etchings I had made over the years. 'Alexis tree home 1987': I scratched that one when I was ten. 'Mum and Dad suck': I'm pretty sure I was twelve years old when I engraved that one because they'd said I couldn't go to the school disco and their decision pissed me off. 'I love Johnny Depp': yep, I was definitely fourteen when I lovingly tattooed that to my tree. And finally, 'Rick and Alexis were here 1995'. I poked at the letters as tears welled in my eyes, memories flooding back of the two of us sitting in this very spot studying for our school exams — my head on his shoulder as he quizzed me about the Fair Trading Act. I wiped my tears and moved around the trunk some more, smiling when I got to the spot where I had marked Nate and Charli's birthdates.

Hearing the sound of an approaching bike distracted me from my etchings. I looked out past the shed to see that Bryce had jumped on Dad's quad and was making his way to where I was standing. The sight of him had me smiling at how quickly he could settle in and feel at home. It made me happy to see him so comfortable, not only at my parents' property, but comfortable with my family as well.

Pulling up beside the gum, he switched off the engine and gave me a curious smile.

'Hey, you going to buy one of those now?' I asked, pointing to the blue Polaris quad bike.

'I'm thinking about it. I don't have one,' he answered with a smile. He jumped off and walked toward me, his eyes speaking many things. Automatically, my body started to react by tingling in the spots that wanted Bryce's touch.

'What are you doing?' he said softly, as he cupped his hands on my cheeks and pulled me in for a kiss.

I started to answer, but couldn't as his lips were pressed firmly against mine. One of his hands slid to the back of my head, the other dropping to my hip, pulling me further into him. I opened my mouth, inviting his tongue to caress my own and, when it did, I moaned with desire and went slightly limp in his arms. He groaned in response, as his hard cock pressed into the base of my stomach.

My body began to express its desperate need for Bryce — my pulse was racing rapidly and my breathing quickened. I pulled him around to the other side of the tree and frantically pulled at his jeans, undoing them and unleashing his erection in my hands. Closing my eyes, I surrounded his shaft, feeling its warmth on my fingers.

Bryce gently stepped me up to the trunk of the tree and mouthed my neck. 'Your touch sets my body on fire, Alexis. The way you stroke my cock is fucking sensational.'

I smiled as he gently licked and nipped at my neck, adoring that my touch had the same effect on him as his had on me. I brought my thumb to my mouth, licked the tip, then swirled it over his crown. He growled harshly. *Fuck! That sound never gets old. I love it.*

Bryce pulled away and lifted my top, showing signs of frustration with it being there.

I noticed him grip it tightly in his hands. 'Don't, Bryce. Don't you dare rip my top. I can't fucking explain that to my family when we get back.'

He growled again, aggressively yanking down my bra and sucking my nipple into his mouth, tugging it delightfully with his lips. *Holy fuck!* I gripped his head and dug my nails into his scalp.

Moving his hands down to my shorts, he quickly unzipped them, forcefully pushing them to the ground. Then, teasing me with not only his hovering digit but his wanting eyes, he slid his finger along the seam of my underwear. My mouth opened as my head dropped back at the anticipation of his touch.

'Open your eyes, honey.' *Oh, fuck, not this again. I barely managed it last time.*

'No,' I said firmly, but with a smile.

He moved his mouth to the side of my head and breathed hot into my ear. 'If you want me inside you, you *will* open your gorgeous fucking eyes.'

Instantly, I flung them open and was rewarded when his finger slid deliciously into my wet pussy. 'Oh, god!' I moaned.

'God isn't finger-fucking you, my love. I am.'

'Oh, Bryce,' I moaned, correcting myself with a giggle.

He chuckled ever so slightly as well, but turned serious when he grasped my leg and wrapped it around his waist. I leaned in and kissed him forcefully as he slid himself inside me.

For some stupid reason, I suddenly had the tune of 'Home among the Gumtrees' in my head. *What the fuck, Alexis? Shut up!* I smiled with smugness, thinking I was sort of sexually patriotic. I must've started humming in between moans of pleasure while he slid his cock in and out of me.

'Are you humming?' he asked incredulously, in between thrusts.

'No,' I answered quickly, delightfully lapping up his rhythm.

'You were. What were you humming?' he asked, as his breath spiked.

'Nothing. I wasn't humming anything. Either shut up, or talk dirty to me.'

He laughed. 'I know you were humming and until you tell me what it was, I'm not going to let you come.'

I glared at him. 'You wouldn't dare,' I sighed as he slowed right down, unbearably dragging his length out to the tip. A bike engine came to life in the distance, and my eyes widened at the prospect of it being either Nate or Charli coming to look for us.

Bryce must have been thinking the same thing as he demanded an answer to the question again. 'So, what were you humming? You'd better hurry and tell me. It sounds like we might get some company.'

I tried to lean over and peek around the tree, but he held me tight.

'Please, Bryce,' I moaned.

'Are you going to tell me, honey?' He pushed back in and slowly pulled out again while groaning and making me gasp. His pace increased along with my near-orgasm.

The bike engine noise slowly got louder, indicating someone was definitely heading in our direction. I was so close, my body heating and my fingers clenching, when he stopped — just freakin' stopped.

'Tell me.' His gaze was intense and the smallest sign of a smirk crept across his face. He twitched his dick, persuading me further.

'All right, all right!' I shouted. 'It was fucking "Home among the Gumtrees".'

He practically mashed his mouth to mine and thrust into me hard, deep and fast, until I was shouting again, only this time it had absolutely nothing to do with a stupid song. Bryce, too, groaned with his release as the bike approached only a minute or so away. He pulled out of me and zipped up his jeans while I reached down and pulled up my shorts, fastening them in no time at all.

He began to laugh.

'What? It's not funny, you're not funny. Don't ever threaten me with not coming again.'

'"Home among the Gumtrees"? Really? That's fucking awesome.'

I couldn't help but laugh. 'Shut up.'

Just as I smoothed my hair down, Nate rounded the corner on his bike with Charli on the back. *Fuck, that was close ... too close.* He cut the engine and they both climbed off.

'Hey, ratbags. What ya doin'?'

'Nanny said that dinner will be ready soon.'

'Okay.'

Suddenly, I had an idea. 'Hey, you two come here.' I motioned them over to the tree. 'Find yourself a stick like this,' I said, holding up a pointy branch. 'You too,' I instructed Bryce. He frowned a little in question, but did what he was told.

I started scratching my name into the tree trunk.

'What are you doing, Mum?' asked Charli.

'I'm adding a new entry to my tree diary,' I answered. 'Scratch your name here.' I pointed to a spot close to where I had finished writing my name. 'You too,' I said to Nate and Bryce. All three of them stood there and tattooed their name to my tree. I finished off by writing, 'were here 2013'.

I smiled.

Charli happy-danced.

Nate said, 'That's kind of dumb.'

And Bryce hummed 'Home among the Gumtrees' as he kissed my head and subtly placed his hand on my belly.

CHAPTER

8

Family dinner at the Blaxlo house was always eventful, this particular night being no exception. Every time Jen or Steve placed food in their mouth, the twins would cry, having some kind of baby radar that said, 'Mummy and Daddy are having me-time. Quick, intervene'.

Livy sent everything that was a shade of green from her plate onto the floor, and Nate unsuccessfully tried to roll his Brussels sprout onto Charli's plate unnoticed — 'try' being the operative word. Charli then vocally expressed that it wasn't hers and not so subtly tossed it back onto his plate. I had to laugh when Dad performed the same manoeuvre as Nate, rolling his onto Mum's plate. But where Nate had failed to do it inconspicuously, Dad succeeded, then basked in his victory. Mum was none the wiser.

I honestly didn't know why she persisted in cooking the things, because Steve had passed his to Jen — who grudgingly ate them — and Jake had also pushed his aside. Mum and I were the only ones who actually liked them, together with Bryce who happily ate three.

Jake, mouth full and all, voiced his appreciation of Mum's new style of roast chicken. 'Good chook, Mum. What'd ya do, buy it from the shop already cooked?' He gave her a teasing smile.

'No,' she defensively snapped. 'It's Bryce's recipe, thank you very much. He showed me how to do it.'

Jake stopped his fork midway to his open mouth. 'You cook?' he addressed Bryce, a hint of a mocking smile creeping across his face.

'Yes, he does,' I interjected before Bryce could answer, 'and he's very good at it. Maybe you should get a lesson. You might actually succeed in keeping a girlfriend if you, too, possessed such a skill.'

Steve, Jen and Dad burst into laughter.

Mum gave Jake the 'your sister has a point' look.

Livy threw another piece of broccoli on the floor; thinking we were laughing at her.

'Olivia. No, naughty girl,' Jen scolded.

And the twins began to cry again.

* * *

Not too long after dinner, Jen and Steve took the kids to bed, clearly wanting to get their three children safely into the land of nod.

'See you in the morning,' she called from the bedroom door. 'Don't forget to set an alarm.'

'I don't need to,' I answered. Then, registering her baffled look, I pointed to my tummy, indicating that baby Clark and my frequent toilet visits were the reason why.

'Ah yes, baby bladder,' she smiled.

'Jen!' I whisper-growled.

'Sorry,' she whispered back, then happy-danced and quickly closed the door.

I shook my head and headed to my room.

Our family home had three spare bedrooms, all of which belonged to us kids when we had lived here. So Jen, Steve, and their kids slept in the room that was once Jen's. Jake slept in his old bedroom, and Nate, Charli, Bryce and I were accommodated in mine. Bryce and I had been sharing a room for quite some time now, so it was no longer awkward for Nate and Charli to see us share a bed.

While the kids brushed their teeth, Bryce and I got changed into our sleepwear, me in my usual long satin nightie and Bryce in a pair of boxer shorts.

'So, this was your bedroom when you were young?'

'Yes,' I replied, smiling after registering his adorably sneaky grin.

He looked around, scanning the area and taking in every surface. 'I wish I'd known you when you were young. I would've snuck into your room and had my fucking way with you.'

My body heated at that thought of it. 'I'm not sure my dad would've liked that.'

'No ... he wouldn't have.' Bryce winked at me just as Nate and Charli entered the room.

'This is just so cool,' Charli squealed while jumping onto her make-shift bed on the floor. 'We are having a slumber party. I know, I know! Let's play truth or dare!'

'No. That's for you and your friends to play,' I answered, smiling at her attempt.

'No, it's not,' Bryce answered. 'I'll play.' He had an elated smile on his face which was infectious.

'It's your funeral, then,' I warned him.

Charli happy-clapped and sat cross-legged. Nate, who was now lying in his bed, propped his head on his hand with an amused look on his face.

'Well,' I gestured to Bryce, 'what will it be, truth or dare?'

'Dare,' he said confidently, standing beside the bed in all his boxer shorts glory.

Nate scoffed and put his hand over his eyes. 'You're nuts, Bryce.'

Charli happy-clapped again.

'Slap yourself across the face,' I commanded, smiling with the knowledge that he would do it.

He smiled back and obliged, giving himself a decent whack. I burst into laughter and fell back on the bed as he raised his eyebrow satisfactorily, then pulled back the bed covers, climbing in beside me.

'It's your turn, Mum.' Nate said, sitting up and crossing his legs like his sister. *Crap! How did I get roped into this again?*

'Fine,' I contemplated my choice for a split second then decided I would follow Bryce, not wanting to be outdone, of course. 'I choose dare,' I huffed.

'Fart,' Nate blurted out, my typical nine-year-old son seeming quite pleased with his suggestion.

'No, I can't,' I shrieked, embarrassed and honestly telling the truth. Suddenly a bottom rumble sounded within the room. Nate and Bryce looked at me, their eyes widening. 'That wasn't me,' I exclaimed, hands in the air in surrender. Bryce chuckled so loudly that I had to playfully punch him in the arm. 'It wasn't me, I promise.'

'No, it was me,' Charli chimed in. 'I took Mum's dare.'

'What?' I asked, astounded, and now laughing as hard as Bryce. 'This game is stupid.'

'No, it's not. If you can't do a dare or tell a truth, someone else can do it for you. So, I did it for you, Mum. Us girls have to stick together.' Charli was the only one deadly serious and not laughing.

'Oh ... thanks, sweetheart,' I choked out, trying to be as serious as she. 'So ... what happens next?'

Quite proudly, she answered. 'You get another turn.'

'Oh, okay.' I breathed in and purposely looked at her. 'Fire away.' *And I mean from your mouth, not your rear end.*

'You have to pick truth or dare, Mum.'

'Oh, sorry. Truth, then.'

Charli smiled. 'Are you going to marry Bryce?'

Charli-Bear, we've been over this. I looked at Bryce who had placed both his hands behind his head, a smug smile plastered on his face. 'He has to ask me to marry him first.'

'Bryce, are you going to ask —'

'Hey, hey,' I interrupted, 'that's cheating. It's not his turn yet, it's yours. Truth or dare, which one?' I successfully diverted her questioning.

'Dare,' she answered excitedly.

Nate quickly jumped in again. 'Fart.'

'Nate!' I exclaimed. Charli let off another one. 'Jesus, Charli!' *How does she freakin' do that?*

Bryce was laughing hysterically, while looking between me and the kids. I placed my head in my hands, amazed at Charli's now apparent talent for breaking wind on cue.

'My turn.' Nate shuffled on the spot. *I had the urge to demand he fart, but that would only be to the detriment of us all in the long run.*

'All right, truth or dare?' I asked him.

'Truth,' he replied confidently.

Excellent, I may just like this game yet. 'Did you eat that Brussels sprout, or did you give it to Bryce when I wasn't looking?'

He quickly glanced at Bryce and answered, 'Noooooo,' in a very drawn-out, slow voice. I turned in Bryce's direction, catching him frantically moving his head from side to side, telling Nate to say 'no.'

'Liar!' Charli shouted, pointing at Nate. 'You have to do it again.'

Nate huffed.

'Okay.' I looked at Bryce and squinted my eyes with a silent message that he was about to get found out, then I looked back at Nate, opening my eyes wide in warning that he'd better not lie. 'Did Bryce say that Danny could drive you to school in the limo?'

Nate's open eyes broadened, then he screwed up his face.

'Nate?' I probed.

He closed his eyes then nodded twice.

I pointed to Bryce. 'Ha, I knew it. I knew it.'

He tried to grab my finger in an attempt to bite it, then winked at Nate. 'My turn and I choose truth this time.' He looked directly at Charli with a knowing smile.

She didn't hesitate and quickly jumped in, asking the question she attempted moments ago. 'Are you going to ask Mummy to marry you?'

'Yes,' he snapped out before I even had a moment to break their alliance.

'When?' she blurted out quickly.

'Soon,' he answered, just as fast.

'How soon?'

'Charli!' I interrupted.

Nate laughed.

'Soon soon,' Bryce continued.

'Bryce!' I poked him. *He is just as bad as both of my kids.*

'Are you going to have a baby?' Charli continued. *Whoa! Okay, game over.*

'I think that's enough of truth or dare for tonight.' I switched my voice to the game's-up-I'm-now-serious tone.

'Aw,' they all whined.

'Maybe. Would that be okay?' Bryce asked, answering Charli's question and ignoring my request that we end the game before the baby-in-my-uterus cat was let out of the bag.

'Yeah. That would be awesome,' Charli added. 'I love babies, but only if it's a girl baby. Boys are crap sometimes.' She poked her tongue out at Nate who responded by throwing his dirty socks at her. 'See what I mean? They are disgusting. Yuck!'

'What about you, Nate? Would that be okay?' Bryce queried my son. *Oh, shit! Do I want to hear this answer?*

'I guess ... but aren't you too old, Mum?'

'No, I'm not too old, and anyway, it's bedtime. Come and give me a kiss then hop back into bed.'

Both Nate and Charli climbed onto our bed and gave me a kiss. Charli even climbed over to Bryce and placed a peck on his cheek then bumped fists with him in a modern style of high five. I shook my head at the realisation that he had successfully been able to infiltrate my children's brains in order to have them side with him and gang up on me. I shot a baffled smile at him, turned off the light and snuggled into his chest.

He wrapped his arms around me, lightly kissed my neck then whispered into my ear. 'I had a really great time today. Thank you for sharing your family with me.'

I smiled, although I knew he couldn't see it. 'What's mine is yours, remember?'

His grip tightened.

* * *

Lying in bed the following morning, I got to thinking about what Bryce had said before we drifted off to sleep. I realised that the reason he'd confessed to having such a great time the day before was because he had missed out on having similar family experiences for himself. Where I took our family gatherings for granted and saw them as everyday events, not giving them much emphasis, he had thrived on the experience, enjoying the contented feeling that came from the privilege of being surrounded by family.

I hugged him incredibly tightly, loving him for being in my life; loving him for having such a great relationship with my kids; loving him for loving me, and loving him because he deserved it. My tight squeezing stirred him from his sleep, filling me with the joy of gazing on him as he returned to the conscious world. Usually it was the other way around. I thoroughly enjoyed watching him wake, watching his face come to life when his eyes met mine.

'Hey, Mr Clark. Fancy helping me be an Easter bunny?' I whispered.

'Sure. As long as we can breed like one,' he whispered back.

I giggled. 'We already have.'

He smiled with his eyes closed. 'Mm.'

'Come on, you.'

We snuck out of the room to help hide the Easter eggs that Mum, Jen and I had stashed away. Jen artistically hid foil-covered chocolate bunnies in potted plants, on chairs and under tables. Jake arranged two chocolate bunnies on top of each other in a compromising position, and Bryce and I tossed handfuls of small foil-covered chocolate eggs out onto the lawn. When we were all satisfied that our Easter bunny duties were complete, we sat down at the dining table with well-earned cups of coffee and tea, then waited for the sleeping children to wake up.

'Why is it that on Easter, Christmas and birthdays our little rascals sleep in?' Jen huffed. 'I might as well go back to bed.'

It was as though those words had been sent as a subliminal message to the twins because they started crying. She stood up and stretched. 'Ah, they are just like clockwork.' She turned to Bryce and smiled at him, raising her eyebrows. 'Bryce, do you want to give me a hand?' *Jennifer, don't you dare do anything stupid.* I shot her a warning look.

'Sure,' he replied.

Steve grinned and leaned back on his chair, glad he had been let off the hook. 'Sweet,' he uttered, happily.

'Don't tell me you breastfeed, too, Bryce,' my smartarse brother teased. I grabbed an apple from the fruit bowl and launched it at him. He caught it and, laughing, took a bite. 'Thanks.'

I looked to Bryce. 'Whatever you do, don't change Jack.'

'Who said anything about changing them?' he answered, appearing to now regret his acceptance.

'Come on.' Jen put her hands on his shoulders and ushered him toward the waiting bundles of cuteness — and their inevitably soiled nappies.

Moments later, Jen returned to the room, smiling and holding the 'blue one'. Bryce followed shortly after, his face half displaying adoration of the 'pink one' and half distaste.

'Was that a set-up?' he asked me.

Jen cracked up laughing.

'Was what a set-up?' I questioned, slightly confused.

'Elise's nappy was far from clean,' he blurted out as he bounced her on his hip.

'Oh. Sorry, but shit happens ... literally.' I giggled at my lame joke and walked over to him, stopping to take Elise into my arms. 'Did you give Uncle Bryce a nice Easter present?' I babbled to my niece.

The entire room fell silent at my choice of words, and I very quickly felt as though I had five pairs of eyes burrowing into my back. I looked up at Bryce who was standing directly in front of me, his expression overjoyed.

'Yes, she did. So next time, I choose Jack.' He kissed me on the top of my head and proceeded to sit back at the table, unperturbed at the fact I had just declared him a surrogate uncle. My family, too, continued their discussions and all was well.

Nate, Charli and Olivia woke up shortly after and scoured the gardens surrounding Mum and Dad's house for treats the Easter bunny had left behind. When they were sure every trace of foil-covered chocolate had been found, everyone sat down and enjoyed another meal together, this one just as entertaining as the night before.

After lunch, we sadly said our goodbyes with kisses to the cheeks, warm embraces and promises to see one another soon. Jake had shaken Bryce's hand and warned him — in a friendly manner — to take care of me, and not because he would have to answer to my brother if he didn't, but because he'd have to answer to me. Apparently, I was the scariest of us all — Bryce tended to agree.

* * *

Easter Sunday night was spent at the apartment with Lucy, Nic and baby Alexander. Bryce was so natural when it came to handling a baby, it was an incredible turn-on. I couldn't help but formulate a picture in my mind of him holding, hugging, kissing and fussing over our baby. And as a result of this beautiful piece of imagery foresight, I had a ridiculously large smile plastered on my face.

'You seem happy,' Lucy said, smiling as she gave me a nudge while we made a cup of coffee.

'I am, very happy. Your brother is essentially all one could ever wish for in a man, and I can't for the life of me remember making that wish or being lucky enough to deserve it being granted.' I looked up from the bench while stirring the mug, noticing Bryce enthralled by a game of peekaboo with Charli and Alexander.

'True love is not the result of a wish, Alexis. It is found by those who have open eyes. Unfortunately, so many people are blind and — because of that — will never experience it.' She put her mug to her lips and blew gently. 'I will be forever grateful to you for opening your eyes. My brother deserves the love he has found with you.'

I turned to face her, a small tear in my eye. I also stupidly placed my hand on my abdomen. Her eyes twinkled and her mouth opened, and that's when I realised what I had done. So I said the first stupid thing that came to my mind.

'Oh, I think I have a bit of wind.' *Nice, Alexis! After that heartfelt declaration, the first thing she hears you say is you need to fart.*

She squinted her eyes at me mildly, then sipped her coffee. 'Better out than in I've always said.'

Lucy picked up Nic's cup, smiled at me and walked back into the lounge area. *Shit! Crap! Balls!* I picked up Bryce's mug and followed her, feeling like a bloody idiot with a flatulence problem. I handed him the mug and sat down beside him on the sofa, red-faced and mortified. Lucy was still smiling at me. *Fuck, I think she knows.*

I averted my guilty 'you've busted me' face and addressed my kids. 'I hate to break up your game, but Charli and Nate, your father will be here bright and early in the morning to pick you both up. So it's bedtime. Say goodnight and get yourselves ready for bed. I will be up to tuck you both in shortly.'

'Is RJ going to be there? Because if he is, I'm not going,' Nate said with conviction.

'No, he's not. But you are going to have to meet him soon, Nate. You can't avoid it forever, and besides, you will probably really like him.' I kissed my son on the head before he fist-bumped Bryce.

'I doubt it,' Nate murmured.

'He likes caramel and so do you. And he barracks for the Bombers like we do,' Charli offered. I winked at her and gave her a kiss, again before she and Bryce fist-bumped.

'Whatever.' Nate shrugged his shoulders and headed upstairs after saying goodnight to Lucy, Nic and Alexander, with Charli right behind him.

* * *

The next morning, Rick was at the apartment at the crack of dawn like he said he would be. I had barely registered the daylight when the buzzer to the foyer sounded. Nic, Lucy and Alexander were still sound asleep. The kids were finishing packing their bags for their stay with Rick and Bryce was in the shower.

I opened the door, still in my satin nightie and robe. 'Hi,' I said as I let him in. 'Since when did you become a morning person?'

'Since you left me.' His response was flat, with a cutting tone.

I glared at him. 'Well, it doesn't agree with you.' *Bite me and I'll bite back.*

'So what the hell was that the other day?'

'What?' I asked, bemused.

'Kicking Claire out of my house.'

Oh, yeah. I forgot about that. I walked into the kitchen, motioning him to follow me. I didn't need anyone else hearing this conversation, which was obviously about to get nasty. Once he was around the corner and I was satisfied that we were alone, I answered him.

'For starters, Rick, it is not *your* house until you pay me for it.' He gave me a hostile look. 'And secondly, she was wearing my fucking dress. How did you expect me to react?'

'Oh, I don't know ... maybe like an adult. You didn't even let her get her shoes.' *Really? Oh! Bahaha, that's fucking funny. No, Alexis, it's not.*

'She surprised me, Rick. I was not expecting her there. I just wanted to get the rest of my things.'

'You took the couch cushions, Alexis. What the fuck is wrong with you?'

'Nothing, they are my couch cushions. I chose them. I bought them.'

'You're acting like a child.'

'Yeah, well, you'd know all about that,' I yelled at him.

'Are you finished?' he asked quietly.

'With you? Yes. I don't even know you any more, Rick.'

'I'm not the one who has changed, Lexi.'

'Yeah, I guess you're right. Maybe I just didn't know the *real* you in the first place.'

'Don't label us and our marriage as not "real". You're mad, I get that, but you and I were "real". You can be angry with me all you want — I deserve it — but you can't take it out on Claire like you did. You've moved on, clearly. I'm just trying to do the same.'

I moved to the kettle and switched it on. 'Well, I've made an appointment to see Berny. I suggest you find a lawyer as well. We both can't truly move on until we've legally gone our separate ways.'

'If that's what you want, Alexis, fine. I'm done.'

'Good. I was done a long time ago. I just didn't know it.'

Rick and I were staring each other down when Bryce walked in with Nate and Charli behind him.

'Hi, Dad,' Charli said with a small smile, while looking from Rick's face to mine. We both snapped out of our showdown and switched personalities.

'My princess, I've missed you.' He lifted her up. 'Ready to go to Grandma and Grandpa's?'

'Yes,' she said excitedly.

I blew Charli a kiss and cuddled Nate. 'Have fun. I'll see you after school tomorrow.'

'Wednesday,' Rick interjected, 'after school on Wednesday, if that is okay. I would really like to have them for the extra day this week considering I missed out over the weekend.'

I breathed in deep and closed my eyes momentarily. Bryce moved up behind me and put his hands on my shoulders. I exhaled.

'That seems fair,' Bryce added. He gave my shoulders a gentle squeeze. 'We'll both pick you up after school on Wednesday. How does that sound?' he asked Nate and Charli.

'In the limo?' Nate suggested.

'No,' I said at the same time as Rick. *Hang on a minute, where does he get off saying 'no' to the limo. I should say 'yes' now! No, Alexis you're just being bitter.* 'We'll see you Wednesday.' I kissed Nate's head.

As they walked out into the foyer, I waved, then headed upstairs to my shower — my emotion-venting, steamed-filled, head-clearing shower.

CHAPTER

9

Riding a rollercoaster of emotional highs and lows had been a regular occurrence for me over the past month — mainly riding the lows. Rick and I had continued to take nasty stabs at each other which afterward left me feeling pained and angry, and even more, incredibly hurt. The beautiful relationship we once shared was gone, seeming never to return and it saddened me. I tried desperately to get back that calm feeling I had felt in the beginning when I had found out the truth about him and Claire, but for some reason I was just so angry now. Surely it was my hormones, it had to be.

Rick and I hadn't properly spoken to each other since our exchange on the day of our fourteenth wedding anniversary when he had sent me the following text:

What do I say to you on a day like today? — Rick

My response had been:

Nothing. What can you say? — Alexis

I'd never meant it to come across as nasty or harsh, instead, my intent had been more along the lines of 'it is what it is, so maybe not say anything at all'.

Rick had obviously taken it the wrong way and replied with:

I can't fucking win with you. I don't know why I bother — Rick
It had made me feel completely awful the entire day, having been pissed off to the point where I had taken it out on Bryce, which was completely uncalled for. After I had explained the significance of the day — which was no excuse for taking it out on him — we had made up with fiery sex on the stairs. Needless to say, his ability to make my mind stop thinking about Rick and our anniversary was incredibly successful.

* * *

Gareth had also triggered my emotional rollercoaster, because during the past week he had been unbelievably kind and, I supposed, somewhat normal. Normal to the point that sometimes when he was in my presence, I would forget that he suffered from DID. I was starting to think that maybe his medication and visits to Jessica were really helping him. And deep down inside, I knew that was what I really wanted because, regardless of Gareth's alters, Bryce really did love his cousin and felt that he owed him infinitely.

Even given the ups and downs with Rick and Gareth, and even Bryce to an extent — yes, he had still been overbearingly protective and aggravating — I knew the main reasons for my feeling uptight, frustrated and angry were mainly due to the fact I was fourteen weeks pregnant and still keeping it a secret. It was increasingly stressful and difficult to do, especially around the kids.

Thankfully, the time for our baby secret to be revealed had come. Tomorrow was my birthday and Bryce had organised a party for me at the apartment, inviting our close friends and family. He had also arranged hotel rooms for everyone to stay in, which was not only convenient, but wonderfully thoughtful. We planned to announce our happy news at the party, but not until we had first let Nate and Charli know that they were going to have another brother or sister.

I don't know why I was so terribly nervous about telling them, especially after the positive reaction they gave us when Bryce had tentatively asked them during that stupid game of truth or dare. I guess it was just that deep down inside I admitted there was a possibility that the news could disappoint them in some way. Regardless, the time had come, and we had come up with the best idea of how to reveal the information.

'Nate and Charli, come here. We need your help with something,' I called from where I was standing at the bottom of the staircase. Both of them came out of their rooms simultaneously. I motioned them down the stairs. 'Remember how we came up with that idea a couple of months ago of a treasure hunt for children staying at City Promenade? Well, we want to test it out on the two of you before we make it into a permanent thing. So ... we thought we'd have a little practice in the apartment. Does that sound good?'

'Cool! I love treasure hunts. What's the treasure? Is it gold?' Charli asked, excitedly.

'Is it money?' Nate queried, hope in his eyes.

'No, you silly duffers, it's just a practice. Here, this is your first clue.' I handed them a card which Nate began to read.

'Say it out loud, Nate, I can't read,' Charli huffed, putting her hands on her hips, frustrated that reading was a skill she was still learning at school.

Nate slowly read the note out loud. 'Your first clue is feeling unfit. You can find it on the place where you exercise while you sit.' He screwed up his face then, instantly, realisation dawned on him. 'The exercise bike,' he yelled, before taking off in that direction.

'Wait for me,' Charli called out after him.

Bryce and I followed. 'So far so good,' he whispered and placed his hand at the small of my back as we walked out onto the balcony, following the kids.

Nate had already torn the envelope from its sticky-taped position on the exercise bike. He ripped it open and pulled out a photograph, holding it up and looking at it strangely.

Charli snatched it from his hands. 'It's you and Bryce, Mum. It's a picture of you two.'

'Give the photo to Bryce and he will give you your next clue,' Nate said, reading the instructions that were attached to the picture. Charli skipped over to Bryce and handed him the photograph, he in turn handed her another card. She passed it to Nate who again read it out loud. 'Go and play pool ... but don't get wet.'

Charli walked over to the swimming pool and looked into the water for the next clue. 'How do you play in the pool without getting wet?'

'Not that pool, the pool table,' Nate explained as he grabbed his sister's hand. They hurried off into the man-cave, only to come back out, shortly after entering, to where we were standing in the lounge area. Charli now held a wooden letter R. She gave it to Bryce, who once again handed over another clue. Bryce placed the letter R next to the picture of the two of us. I smiled.

'Your third clue is hungry and wants something to eat. Go to the place where you'll find something sweet.'

This time Charli took off heading straight for the kitchen, yelling, 'Lollies. The treasure is lollies.'

Nate ran after her. 'Wait, we have to share.'

'Do not. Not if I find them first,' she teased, looking over her shoulder and screaming as she noticed that he was gaining on her.

Bryce laughed as I took a seat on the couch.

'They're going to be disappointed when they realise the treasure is not edible,' I said, suddenly feeling like maybe I should've organised some form of tangible reward.

They both came back into the lounge looking a little glum. I laughed at them. 'So, what did you find?'

'A stupid word that says *having*,' Nate declared. Charli sulked as she passed Bryce the cardboard card with the word 'having' written on it. He then placed it down next to the letter R.

At this point I thought Nate would catch on by reading the clues placed next to each other, but he didn't. Instead, he moved right along and read the next card.

'This clue is in a hurry and doesn't want to go slow. You'll find this clue waiting for a ride in the Crow.' Nate threw the card and spun around heading back outside. Charli grumbled and sat down.

I gently squeezed her knee. 'What, sweetheart? Don't you like this game?'

'Yes, but I'm too slow.'

'Don't worry. I reckon you'll find the next clue before Nate.' I winked at her.

Nate came running back in, puffing and out of breath. He passed Bryce the wooden letter A.

Charli scratched her head. 'Another letter?'

Bryce handed Nate the final card then came and sat next to me, leaning back on the couch in that sexy position that I love. I stared at him and licked my lips. *Crap! That was involuntary.*

'Starlight is asleep. Go wake her.' Nate took off again toward the observatory.

I fell back into Bryce's side. 'I told you he'd go there.'

Charli frowned. 'You said I'd find the next clue. Nate probably already has it.'

'No, he doesn't, Charli. What did Nate just read out?'

'Starlight is asleep. Go wake her.'

'Yes, now think about it.'

She screwed up her face, then her eyes widened and a large smile appeared.

'Ah, see? Go and wake her up.'

Charli laughed and ran upstairs to her room. She came back moments later holding her baby doll, Starlight.

'I found it Nate,' she called out as she handed Bryce the baby. Nate came bounding down the stairs, and I cringed as I watched him, predicting a stumble and one or two broken bones.

'Please don't run down the stairs, little man. You're giving me a heart attack.'

'What was it?' Nate asked, ignoring my plea.

'Starlight, my baby,' Charlotte answered. She looked from Bryce to me. 'So where is the treasure?'

'Read the clues,' Bryce suggested.

I waited with bated breath as Nate read the clues out slowly, trying to piece them together.

'Photo, R, word "having", A, Starlight,' he said. 'That's just dumb.'

Shit! Crap! Balls! That didn't work.

'Who's in the photo?' I asked.

'You and Bryce.'

'What's the letter?'

'R,' they said together.

'What's the word say?'

'Having.'

Next letter?'

'A'

'What is Starlight.'

'A doll.'

Bryce cracked up laughing.

'No, she's a baby. Now read those all out again.'

'Mummy and Bryce, R, having, A, baby,' they both said together.

Nate's eyes widened, and I held my breath.

Charli said it again, still not quite catching on. 'Mummy and Bryce, R, having, A, baby. A baby … really? A real baby?'

I stood up and rubbed my belly. 'Yes. There's a baby growing in here. Your baby brother or sister.'

Nate smiled. *Oh, thank fuck.* Charli stepped closer and touched my tummy. 'Can she hear me?'

'I think so,' I answered.

'Hi, I'm Charlotte, your sister,' she yelled like a banshee into my stomach.

Bryce and I laughed, and a tear of joy rolled down my cheek. Bryce leaned forward and gently rolled up my top a little. I still wasn't overly showing, but when I was standing there with nothing to cover my bump, it was visibly protruding just a little bit.

'You don't need to yell, Charlotte. Just talk like this.' He placed his lips to my stomach and gave it a soft kiss. I swear I felt a little flutter.

'How do you know it's a girl?' Nate questioned. 'It could be a boy.'

'Are you a girl or a boy?' Charli asked in a lower voice, smiling at Bryce as she spoke into my belly. For some reason we all stayed quiet, appearing to be stupidly waiting for an answer.

'We will find out in just over a month if you have a baby sister or brother.'

'A month? Is that when she'll be born?' Charlotte was pirouetting in front of me. 'I can't wait. Can I pick her name?'

'Settle, petal. No, we will find out if the baby is a boy or a girl when Mummy has an ultrasound, then you can help pick a name.'

'What's an ultrasound?'

'An ultrasound is a special camera that can look inside your tummy.'

Nate walked over and hesitantly touched my bare stomach. 'I can't feel anything.'

I placed my hand on his head and gave it a gentle rub. 'You won't be able to, little man. Not yet anyway. Maybe in a few more weeks you might feel the baby kick.'

'Kick?' Charli asked. 'Why would the baby kick you?'

'Because there is not a lot of room in there, so babies push and kick at their Mummy's tummies. You used to do it *a lot.*'

'That would be weird,' confessed Nate. And he removed his hand, all the while looking slightly distressed.

Bryce placed both his hands on my belly. 'I can't wait to feel the baby kick.' He flexed his fingers gently. I looked down at him, my eyes suddenly piercing his with an ignited yearning. He registered my gaze and twitched his eye. *Fuck, I love this man. This incredibly sexy, sweet father of my unborn child. I want to undress him and show him just how much I crave, lust, love and appreciate him. I want to show him with my tongue, my hands, my mouth, my wet, sleek —* My tummy rumbled, snapping me out of my inappropriate head-porn. *These hormones are driving me freakin' crazy. One minute I'm horny as hell, the next I'm vicious, angry and short-tempered, then after that I could cry a river and eat pickles with chocolate.*

'Was that the baby? Did she growl? Is she angry?' Charli blurted out, starting intently at my stomach.

I laughed. 'No.'

'Are you hungry, honey?' Bryce asked.

'Yeah, a little.'

He stood up. 'What can I make you?'

'Um ... I could go some of that yogurt you made the other day, the one with the raspberry sauce.'

'Sure. Anything else?'

'Um ... yeah, maybe one of those turkey baguettes with the Swiss cheese. Oh, oh, and a chocolate brownie. I feel like a chocolate brownie with caramel. Does the hotel kitchen make brownies?'

He raised his eyebrow and smiled, then kissed me on the cheek. 'They will today, my love.'

* * *

Bryce had arranged for the hotel's kitchen to make me a freshly baked chocolate caramel brownie, together with a turkey baguette. He had also organised for Sebastian to collect a hot white-chocolate with a marshmallow from Gloria Jean's. That was just lunch. For dinner, he made a steak and mushroom pie with sautéed vegetables. I laughed when he dished up my plate which had, as a side, rice cakes with peanut butter — one of my pregnancy cravings.

* * *

Bryce worked in his office after dinner, finishing up paperwork from the F1 Grand Prix, which had been held weeks ago. While he worked, the kids and I had cuddled in bed, opting to watch the movie *Madagascar 3*. When the film finished, I tucked them into bed while all of us sang 'Afro Circus' and laughed — that bloody song was going to be stuck in my head for quite some time.

Completely drained and exhausted from the constant stream of baby related questions from Charlotte, I had a quick shower and lay down in bed with my book: a new adult-style story about a boy and girl in college who were insanely perfect for each other, but weren't privy to this vital detail because they couldn't keep their shit together for long enough. *Oh, young love is so aggravatingly simple, or so it seems when you are reading it.*

I must have unintentionally fallen asleep because, for a split second, I entered that realm where I was tentatively trying to distinguish the difference between dreaming and reality. It wasn't until I moved my hand down between my legs and ran my fingers through Bryce's hair, that I realised I was in reality, but living my dreams — this being strongly evident when his tongue slid up, then down, my sleek clit. *Oh! Hello, Mr Tongue Twirling Clark.* My hips instantly bucked, drawn magnetically toward him.

I practically purred. 'Oh, fuck.'

'Did I wake you?' he asked, wickedly.

'I don't know. I think I might be dreaming.'

He chuckled, then slid two fingers inside me, my eyes fluttering open while I gasped. 'No, I'm definitely awake.'

'Yes, you are.'

He deliciously moved his fingers in and out as he twirled his tongue over my sensitive spot.

'Did you finish your work?' I moaned.

'No, not yet.'

'Oh?'

'My work is not done until you are coming all over me, honey.'

Oh, fuck. I squirmed from the mix of sensation and hearing his dirty words. 'Mm, best you get to work then, Mr Clark.'

He growled and blissfully mauled in between my legs until I was clenching my thighs around his head. He had turned the lights off and lit a few candles, giving the room a sensual, amber glow. I gazed at his hungry, sexy eyes as he released himself from my legs and prowled slowly up my body, stopping to kiss my stomach.

Propping myself up on my elbows, I watched him spend this moment bonding with his baby, who was none the wiser as to what its parents were getting up to. He continued on with a knowing smile, stopping at my breasts, both of them eagerly anticipating his attention.

My head fell back as he teased my nipples with his lips, tongue and teeth. *Holy shit, he is mind-blowing.* He lifted his head at the same time as I brought mine back up to watch him. Then suddenly, our lips were together, his mouth pressing hard against mine, our tongues reuniting after hours of being apart. I simply adored kissing him, tasting him, feeling the wet warm roll of his tongue against mine.

I nipped at his chin and chiselled jawline, then dragged my lip back up to his mouth, hungrily deepening my insatiable need to taste him and groaning at my desperation to devour him entirely.

'Fuck, Alexis. Your need for me is the sexiest fucking thing I've ever seen and felt.'

'Good, because I *need* you; I *need* you in my mouth now.'

An irresistible grin appeared across his face as he continued to crawl up my body until he was kneeling directly in front of my face, his erection prominent and gloriously close to my craving mouth. He placed his palm at the base of his shaft and slowly dragged his hand up, then back down again. *Jesus! He is downright sexually dangerous.*

Slowly, I extended my tongue, lightly teasing his tip with a small swirling action. The hand he had wrapped around his cock flexed, sending a shock of excitement right through me. I opened my mouth and pressed my lips onto his warm crown, a bead of moisture already visible, evidence that I had the exact same effect on him as he had on me. I sucked at it, then ran my tongue over my teeth while watching the fire in his eyes as he took pleasure from my tease.

His hips jerked involuntarily then, sliding my lips over him. Moving forward, I took him into my mouth, as much of him as I could possibly take. He growled my name and his entire body tensed deliciously — his pecs, biceps, abdomen, and that luscious, muscled V-shape at the top of his pelvis. *I don't know what those muscles are called, and to be honest, I don't freakin' care.*

With my free hand, I reached out and traced my fingertip along the V, trailing it from his left hip, down into his groin, across the front of him then back up the other side. *Oh. My. God. That thing is fucking insanely attractive.* My eyes flickered, aroused by the feel of him in my mouth together with taking in his exquisite form.

'Fuck, I need to be inside you, honey. I can't fucking watch you stare at me like that any more and not come.'

I opened my mouth and he pulled away before moving back down the bed. He lifted my legs, placing kisses up my calves until my heels were rested on his shoulders. Tilting my pelvis, and angling it toward him, he eased himself in slowly. I could feel the walls of my pussy clench around him.

His eyes lit up at the tightening of my muscles. 'You like it like this, don't you?'

'Is it that obvious?' I smiled.

'Yes.' He began to rock into me, the amatory look on his face feeding the journey my orgasm was taking. I bit down on my lip as I felt him delve deep. He rocked in and out, in and out, gripping my hips and flexing his fingers.

'Fuck.'

Bryce shook his head at me and smirked as his rocking increased, my orgasm building with his intensity. My fingers clawed into the bedsheets as the sensation of heat rushed to my head and, as he slammed his pelvis against my arse, I let go, my orgasm rolling out of my mouth in the form of unmuted, explicit, sexual filth. I fucking loved it ... and I fucking loved him.

CHAPTER
10

The next morning, I woke up thoroughly sated and smiled constantly throughout the day. I loved and hated the way that Bryce had that power over me, the power to make me forget everything but him and how he made feel.

My family and friends arrived at City Towers for my birthday party, although my actual birthday was not until the day after. Bryce had taken it upon himself to organise the gathering — whether I had wanted it or not — convincing me to agree by saying it was a great way for the special people in our lives to see where we lived and how happy we were as a family. He had also convinced me that it was the perfect time to tell friends and family that we were expecting a baby. I tended to agree with him that one big announcement was much more appealing than many small private ones, with the exception of my mum and dad and, of course, Rick.

Regardless of the fact that my soon-to-be ex-husband and I had been at each other's throats in recent times, and as much as I was still angry at him for having an affair, I still felt he deserved to know about my pregnancy in private — directly from me. Not in a room full of people we all knew. I respected him enough to allow him that.

Bryce had sent our guests text messages informing them to check in upon arrival and make their way to the penthouse suite at six p.m. I'm guessing Lucy had a hand in getting Mr Creepy-Research Clark everyone's contact details. I had to hand it to them; the brother and sister duo were well organised and a force to be reckoned with.

My parents arrived earlier in the day at my request, as I couldn't wait any longer to let them know about their newest grandchild. Mum had been beside herself when we told her our exciting news, congratulating us both over and over and rubbing my tummy every few minutes. Dad, on the other hand, had been a bit shocked at first, smiling mildly and sitting in silence. It wasn't until I explained to him that I had no doubt that Bryce was the father, not Rick, that he seemed to relax a little. He hadn't said much to me about Rick's and my separation and break-up, but I could tell he was furious with his son-in-law for breaking his daughter's heart. I could also tell he was happy I had left Rick.

Dad had given me a tight hug, saying he would have a nice number of little grandchildren-farmers to help him with his jobs around the farm soon enough, and perhaps he could retire early and watch them do all the work for him. Bryce's brow had furrowed when Dad mentioned wanting to retire early, and I had a good idea of what Bryce was thinking at that particular moment. I made a mental note to speak to him about it at a later date. As much as Bryce always had all the money in the world and was more than willing to share it with me and my family, my dad was still a very hardworking, proud man, and I'm not sure if he would take kindly to Bryce meddling in his private financial affairs, good intentions or not.

* * *

The evening rolled around quite quickly and deciding what to wear to my birthday party had been somewhat challenging. Firstly, I didn't want to choose something that was over-the-top glamorous. Wearing labels like Versace was already singling me out among my friends and family, which I hadn't really wanted. I wished for this gathering to be intimate and comfortable, where regardless of our surroundings we could all feel relaxed and enjoy ourselves. Secondly, I had to choose a dress that was not tight-fitting. Although I was not obviously showing at this point in time, a tight dress could reveal our secret and, having someone guess my pregnancy before we made the announcement would kind of be a buzz-kill.

Clarissa had been a godsend, helping to find extra pieces of clothing for my wardrobe that were perfect for my soon-to-be swelling waistline. She was such a wonderful help and we had become good friends in the process. So, with Clarissa's amazing fashion know-how, I was finally convinced to wear a mid-length, black strapless Versace. It was loose enough to inconspicuously hide my secret, and it was perfectly simple and elegant. I loved it.

Since the dress was black, I could pair it with pretty much any shoe I wanted, and I really wanted to pair it with the Gucci Sofia Etoile peep-toes that had been patiently sitting in the walk-in stadium, waiting to be loved by my feet. I longingly stared at them every time I passed, fighting the desperation to put them on and wear them just for the hell of it. The thing is, with these shoes, they had to be respected, and wearing them 'just for the hell of it' would have broken that cardinal rule.

However, my birthday was absolutely the perfect opportunity and I didn't hesitate in choosing the gold-pailletted beige heels. As I slipped them on, I swear a heavenly beam of light shot down from the sky, illuminating them at the same time as an angel sang 'ah-ahh-ahhh' at me. *Okay, maybe not.*

Charli was excited that we were having a party and had put on her prettiest dress: pale pink chiffon with a layered tutu-style skirt and a rose on the lapel. She was also very excited that my friends' children — especially Lil's daughter, Jasmine, Charlotte's close friend — were coming along for the celebration. Bryce had organised for the hotel's nanny service to be in charge of the kids for the evening, supervising them at the arcade centre in the entertainment complex. He had even arranged for it to be closed to the general public for the evening, making it a private event just for the kids which Nate had said was 'totes sick' as it was going to be him and his 'mains'. *Wtf? I need a freakin' Nate dictionary.*

All in all, with an amazing venue, children supervised and accommodation taken care of, we had the foundations set for an incredible night.

As part of getting ready, I'd set aside time to give both myself and Charli mini-makeovers, pinning her beautiful blonde curls into a bun. I even let her wear some pink lip gloss. She looked gorgeous.

Nate had dressed as quickly as Bryce and wore black trousers with a navy shirt, while Bryce was in a charcoal suit and black shirt.

When Charlotte and I appeared at the top of the stairs, both Nate and Bryce were waiting patiently for us in the lounge area, looking incredibly handsome. Charli made her way down the staircase first and was taking slow steps, as if she was walking down the aisle, the biggest smile radiating from her little face.

When she reached the bottom, Bryce knelt down and handed her a single rose. 'A pretty rose for a pretty girl, Miss Charlotte,' he said.

She took it from him and blushed, twisting her body from side to side. 'Thank you, this is my first flower from a boy.'

Bryce chuckled. 'Oh. Well, I'm glad it was from me then.'

I smiled at them from the top of the staircase before I began my descent, Bryce raising his eyes to meet mine. He stood upright, and swallowed heavily while continuing to eye me from top to toe as I took each step closer to him. When I stopped at the bottom, he held a rose in front of me and gently dragged it down the bridge of my nose.

'Your beauty floors me, Alexis. It literally strips me of all cognitive function; I'm absolutely useless.'

I smiled seductively at him. 'Oh, you are definitely not "useless". I can vouch for that ... many times.'

His eyes sparkled at my compliment and he placed his hand at the top of my arse, passing me the rose with his other hand and pulling me to him. 'Happy birthday.'

Bryce pressed his lips firmly to mine and I could feel the fire igniting and burning in my core, but against all my will, I doused it and pulled away.

'It's not my birthday yet,' I breathed heavily.

'I know. I just wanted to be the first to say it.'

I lovingly scoffed at his charm. 'You, Mr Clark, are too sweet. Thank you. Oh, and thank you for organising this party for me and for putting up my family and friends in the hotel. It's the best birthday present ever.'

He cocked an eyebrow at me. 'This is not your birthday present, honey.'

'I'm looking forward to *that* present later.' I mirrored his raised eyebrow, but added a naughty smile.

He looked confused, but then realisation dawned on him. 'No. *That* is not your present either. *That* is inevitable. You will have to wait till tomorrow for your birthday present.'

'Bryce! I hope you didn't get me anything.' *Of course he freakin' did!* 'This party is more than enough. I don't want anything else.'

'Yes, you do.'

I gave him a strange look, ready to question him further, when the buzzer to the apartment rang. My inquisitiveness changed to one of excitement at the knowledge that my guests were beginning to arrive; so much so that I put his mysterious birthday gift at the back of my mind.

One of the hotel's catering staff politely opened the door and a wide-eyed Carls walked through. 'Well, fu—' she began to say, and cutting herself short after noticing Nate and Charli within earshot, '—far out,' she corrected, 'far freakin' out. This place is incredible.'

I walked up to her and gave her a huge hug. 'Hey, Carls.' I hadn't seen her since the week I'd spent at Mum and Dad's house after finding out Rick had lied about cheating on me, and that Bryce had offered Rick five million dollars to let me spend that week with him. Carls had come to my rescue and spent time with me, helping me forget about the pain and betrayal I'd felt at the hands of the two men. She was my best friend and had been since we were young kids. I loved her, adored her and, at times, like all best friends, could kill her.

'This place is amazeballs, Lexi!' *Amazeballs? Has she been speaking to Nate again? Where the fuck she does come up with this shit?*

I shook my head at her and smiled. 'Yeah, it's not a bad little place to live, eh?'

'Pfft, yeah, you could say that.' She held me at arm's-length and looked intently into my eyes, then drifted her stare down my body and back up again. 'You look amazing. Shacking up with a rich studmuffin does wonders for you. Speaking of the sexy studmuffin, I need to formally thank him for his hospitality.'

With her hands still on my shoulders, she gently moved me aside and headed directly for Bryce. His expression was one of amusement.

'As long as you only thank him, Carls. That studmuffin belongs to me.'

'Not until there's an engagement ring on your finger ... wait!' She paused and turned back to me. 'Show me your hand. Is that why you are looking so good?'

I rolled my eyes at her. 'No! There is no engagement ring on my finger.'

'There will be soon,' Bryce confidently stated. *Oh, shit! Is that the present he is talking about? I hope not. But ... I do want him to propose. It's just a bit too soon. Shit!*

Carls smiled mischievously then continued, reaching Bryce and wrapping her arms around him. 'Thank you.' She hugged him tight and squeezed his biceps ... then squeezed them again.

He playfully grinned over her shoulder at me. 'You're welcome, Carly.'

Pouting, she reluctantly let him go and made her way back to me. 'So, Lexi, the soon-to-be bigamist.'

'I am not a fucking soon-to-be bigamist.'

'Mum!' Charlotte waltzed into the room. 'You just f-bombed. You know the rules. Now I get to bomb you.'

Ah, crap! Who made up this stupid game? Oh ... that's right, me. Stupid me. 'Um ... I know, Charlotte, but you can't bomb me. Not now.'

Without comprehending why I was not about to let her play 'stacks-on', she automatically replied, 'A rule is a rule, Mum.'

'Charli.' I subtly tried to raise my eyebrows at her. 'You can't.' I slightly exaggerated the *can't* bit. 'You could hurt me. You don't want to *hurt* me, do you?'

She gazed at me dumbfounded with her hands on her hips, suggesting she had been cheated or swindled. Then, she caught on. 'Ooh, I could hurt the baby,' she blurted out and slapped her hand to her head. 'Okay, Mum, I'll let you off this time.' She walked up to Carly. 'Hi, Aunty Carls.'

Charlotte and Nate had always referred to Carly as their aunty. Carls was like a sister to me anyway.

Staring at me with her mouth wide open, a smile tugging at its corners, Carly looked wonderfully stunned. She nonchalantly gave

Charlotte a quick hug, while keeping her amused expression fixed on me. 'You're pregnant?'

'Yes, I am.' I shot her a warning look. 'Charlotte, please don't tell anyone else. Bryce and I want to make it a surprise and tell everyone later tonight.'

Stupid me hadn't even thought to tell motormouth Charli to keep our baby news a secret.

'Oh, sorry, Mum.'

'It's okay, sweetheart. But don't tell anyone else, all right?'

She skipped off. 'Okay.'

I turned back to Carly and smiled while placing my nurturing hand on its favourite spot — my stomach. 'Yes, Bryce planted his seed,' I smirked.

He came up behind me and placed his hands on my shoulders. 'What can I say? I just like gardening,' he explained.

I leaned back into him and laughed.

'Wow ... that's ... wow! I'm assuming it wasn't planned,' Carly said with a hesitant look.

'No. It definitely wasn't planned,' I answered.

She looked up at Bryce, then her expression changed. Curious, I tilted my head to glance at Bryce as well. However, whatever had prompted that strange shift in her was lost on me, because he peered down into my eyes, displaying nothing but love and happiness, filling me with butterflies.

'So you're both happy?'

We answered her simultaneously, without removing our eyes from one another. 'Of course we are.'

'In that case, congratulations.'

With impeccable timing, a waiter appeared next to us with glasses of champagne on a tray. Carly grabbed two glasses and went to hand me one. She paused at the same moment Bryce opened his mouth and objected.

'Uh-uh.' He grabbed the slightly pink-coloured glass that was still sitting on the tray. 'You, my love, get this one.' He handed me the drink. 'The pink glasses are yours. All waitstaff have been briefed and know only to give you these ones.

'You've got to be kidding.' I furrowed my brow at him. 'What is it?'

The buzzer to the apartment sounded again, and the door was opened to allow entry to the members of Live Trepidation. Bryce began to make his way over to them when he answered my question. 'No. I'm not kidding. I never kid where you are concerned. You, my love, are drinking non-alcoholic rosé wine tonight.' *Shit. Crap. Balls.*

Carly shrugged her shoulders and, rather than put one of the two glasses she had in hand back on the tray, she happily took sips from them both.

'Suffer,' she said, with a childish grin.

I narrowed my eyes at her, then smiled toward the newly-arrived guests. Carly quickly tilted her head down and lowered her voice, speaking into the glass. 'Who the fuck is that sex-on-a-stick?' She took an inconspicuous sip.

I followed her line of sight. 'That is Derek, Bryce's best mate. He's also the lead singer of the band. He was at the pub in Shepparton, remember? When the band played 'November Rain' and Bryce performed the guitar solos for me.'

'Is that him? Oh, my god, he looks different.'

'Well, you were slightly preoccupied with the barman. Plus, Derek has shaved his head since then. Maybe that's why you don't recognise him.'

'Fuck, Lexi. He is beyond hot. His hotness factor is through the bloody roof.'

I laughed at her choice of words. 'It's funny you should say that, because he is a firefighter.'

She grabbed a hold of my arm and pretended to go weak at the knees. 'Please tell me he's single, Alexis, because I have a fucking ferocious fire in between my legs that he needs to put out.'

I cracked up laughing. 'Yes, Carls. He is single ... as far as I know.'

Derek was extremely good looking. He was the same height as Bryce, approximately six foot five. He had tanned skin and clearly defined biceps which, from memory, were artfully decorated with a few tattoos. His eyes were a bright blue and his once caramel-coloured hair was now closely shaved to his head.

Bryce and the rest of his band, bar Lucy, which consisted of the aforementioned Derek — lead singer and guitarist — plus Matt, the bass guitarist, and Will, the drummer, all made their way over to where Carls and I were standing. As they got closer, she squeezed my arm tighter and dramatically said under her breath, 'Quick! Quick! My vagina is burning. Please *come* to my rescue.'

I laughed and murmured back: 'Mr Firefighter Derek, please douse my friend's fiery hole with your fire hose. Nobody likes a burnt burger.'

Carly nearly spat her champagne. She was good at that.

With great difficulty, we both managed to subdue ourselves and act like the adults that we were by the time the men reached our position in the room.

Bryce placed his arm around my waist securing me to him. 'Alexis, you remember Derek, Will and Matt.'

'Yes, of course I do. It's nice to see you all again. Thanks for *coming*.'

Carly giggled at my choice of word, forcing a childish giggle from me, too. *Carly Josephine Henkley, stop that.*

'Happy birthday, Alexis.' Derek handed me a small package. *Oh, god, a present. How embarrassing. I really don't need presents.*

I sheepishly took it from him. 'You really shouldn't have.'

He smiled and shrugged his shoulders. Bryce looked at him in wonder.

'Is it your birthday, Lexi?' Carly asked, knowing it was. 'Because I didn't get you jack shit.'

I gently shoved her shoulder. 'Sorry, this rude bitch here is my best friend, Carly. Carly, this is Will, Matt and Derek. They are members of the band Bryce plays in.'

'Yes, I know. I saw you guys in Shepparton. You were all fantastic.' She pointed her glass at Derek. 'And you,' she drawled, 'have a voice to die for.' *Oh, god, Carls, the epitome of obvious.*

I smirked at her as I unwrapped my present, discovering a Live Trepidation CD. 'I love it! Thank you.' I really did love it. Now, I could cruise around in my car and listen to my sensationally talented, sexy rock god playing his guitar chords. I looked up at Bryce with a big smile. 'You didn't tell me you had a CD.'

'We've only just recently produced it. It appears you would be one of the first to own a copy.'

'Oh, lucky me. Can you all sign it?'

'I think track four already has your name on it,' Matt said as he took hold of a beer from the tray a waiter was balancing beside us.

'A track that has my name on it?' I repeated, confused.

The buzzer to the door sounded again and, this time, the people entering seemed to be never-ending. Bryce quickly interrupted my train of thought and excused us.

'Your family is here.' He gently guided me toward the apartment's entryway door.

* * *

I spent the first part of the evening as a tour guide, showing my friends and family around the apartment, Tash being the only exception; she had already visited after taking Bryce up on his offer of a job at the hotel. She was due to begin her first shift as an event supervisor starting this coming Monday.

Lil, Jade and Steph, together with their husbands, also seemed quite impressed with my new home. *Honestly, how could you not be? This place is a palace. I still feel like royalty when I am here and I love it. I might make all my friends curtsy upon entering.*

My brother Jake playfully tutted every time I showed him a new room, and Jen ... well, she was just about ready to move in, having taken a liking to Lucy's room containing the cot.

The evening had gone rather smoothly, with everyone happily talking among themselves to low-volume background music. The kids were having a great time at the arcade, allowing parents to relax and enjoy each other's company together with food and drinks. Rick was even contentedly mingling with our mutual friends. However, he was clearly avoiding my family, especially Jake.

Even Gareth had cheerfully arrived with Samantha by his side and he appeared to be enjoying his surroundings and company. Seeing him and Sam look somewhat jovial and happy eased my concerns in regard to their relationship. However, I still felt Sam deserved to know the truth about Gareth's diagnosis so that she could decide for herself if his condition was one she could overlook. Deep down, I knew I should tell her. I had basically made that decision the moment I became aware of Gareth's Dissociative Identity Disorder and had had an apprehensive sensation in the pit of my stomach which told me one way or another I would enlighten Sam. I just hoped it didn't reverse Gareth's clearly positive progression of late.

The time to make a speech and deliver our exciting news was fast approaching, so I decided I would take the opportunity to speak with Rick privately on the balcony. He was in deep discussion with Dean — Tash's husband — about the Grand Prix when I politely interrupted.

'Excuse me, guys. Sorry, but could I talk to you for a moment, Rick?'

He gave me sceptical look. 'Sure. I'll be right back, Dean.'

I motioned him to follow me out to the balcony and around the corner, where the Crow sat silently in the night's darkness. Leading us both over to the balustrade, I hoped the twinkling city skyline would provide a calm and serene atmosphere. It didn't seem to work, because I suddenly felt nervous as fuck, knowing the news I was about to deliver was going to hurt and anger Rick. And regardless of what he had put me through, I didn't want to hurt him.

'Um ... so are you having a good time? I know coming here, especially on your own, could not have been easy. I appreciate that you did decide to come though. It means a lot to me that we can still share these types of moments in our lives, regardless of what has happened.'

I had made it clear that Claire did not form part of the invitation and that his 'plus one' could be anyone else but her.

'Yeah. Although Jake keeps giving me a death look, but apart from that it's been all right. No matter what we've been through, Lex, we were friends before we became lovers, and friends are something I want us to go back to ... no matter what. I don't want us to be bitter any more.'

'Good. I'm glad you think that, because I don't think you are going to like what I'm about to tell you,' I said hesitantly, biting the inside of my cheek. He turned to me, his face taking on a look of angst.

Closing my eyes for a split second to muster the courage, I then opened them and let it out. 'Bryce and I are having a baby. I'm due in November. We are announcing it tonight ... shortly. I wanted to tell you in person rather than spring it on you in front of our family and friends.'

He blinked a few times, then turned to look back out over the city. He was deadly silent for what seemed like minutes on end.

'Rick?' I prompted him to say something.

'Could it be mine?' he asked quietly, his voice barely audible.

'No.'

'How can you be sure? A November due date puts conception pretty fucking close to when we were last together,' he hissed.

'No, Rick! You are *not* the father of my baby. I've had tests and conception was weeks after we had sex for the final time.'

'Had sex,' he muttered angrily under his breath.

'Look, I knew you'd be angry, but it is what it is. At least I didn't fall pregnant with Bryce's baby while we were still together.' *Shit! I just can't fucking help myself, can I?*

The look he bestowed upon me was one of offence and hatred. 'I want a paternity test. The timing is too close.'

'You know what, Rick? Fuck you! You have no right to demand this. You cheated on me. You had another child with someone else. This child is not yours, it's Bryce's. You have two choices: either calm down, realise I'm telling the truth and rejoin the party, or go home and continue to act like a selfish prick who is grasping at straws. What's it going to be?'

He pushed off the balustrade and glared at me. 'I want the paternity test.' Then he turned, walked back inside and exited the apartment.

CHAPTER
11

After watching Rick storm away from me, I turned around to take in the still night air that moved gently over the surrounding buildings. The sounds of city traffic echoed quietly from forty-three floors below, capturing me briefly in their humming lull. My focus shifted from the city ambience when I heard footsteps coming my way.

I'm not sure if it was the sound his strides made, or the likelihood that it was him looking for me, or even just the unmistakable feeling I would get when he was in my presence ... regardless, I knew Bryce was making his way toward me, and when I felt his warm, strong loving arms embrace me from behind, I felt at peace again: calm, content, happy and relaxed.

He rested his hands gently on my belly where our child was safe and sound. 'Did you tell Rick?'

'Yes. Couldn't you tell by the way he stormed out of the building?'

'Are you okay?'

'I'm fine. I knew he wouldn't like the news, but I never expected him to think the baby was his and then demand a paternity test.'

Bryce spun me around to face him, nearly sending me spinning vertically into the air from sheer rotational lift. 'He said what?'

'He wants a paternity test. He said the timing is too close for him to just take my word for it.'

'He's fucking lucky he *has* left the building. There is no way I will let him stake a claim to *my* child.'

'Bryce, settle down,' I said calmly. 'No one will be staking a claim to our baby except us.'

He wasn't looking me in the eye. Instead, he was killing a focal point somewhere beyond my head with his murderous glare.

I reached up and touched his face. 'Hey, look at me. This baby is yours. I am one hundred percent certain of it. So despite Rick's pathetic attempt at whatever it is he is attempting to achieve by his demand, it doesn't matter. He is wasting his time.' I tenderly rubbed his cheekbones with my thumbs, helping him let go of some of his anger. 'I'm yours, Bryce,' I reassured him while placing his hands back on my stomach. '*We* are yours.'

He sighed dejectedly. 'You were once his.'

'You know what? Looking back, I don't really think I ever was Rick's. I mean, on the surface, maybe, and on paper ... yes. But deep down, I was waiting for you to come along and show me what it is to truly belong to someone: mind, heart, body and soul.'

He threaded his fingers through my hair, gripping the sides of my face and pulling me to him. The kiss he placed upon my lips and mouth was just about the most passionate, emotional and possessive kiss I had ever experienced and, after he pulled away, I literally had to be forced back to the present moment. I was standing there, my head supported by his hands, which were still firmly placed on either side of my face, and my mouth was open, confused by whether or not it still functioned.

Slowly, I opened my eyes, finding his equally impassioned expression.

'I love you,' he whispered.

'I love you, too,' I whispered back.

He growled lasciviously. 'Come on. The kids are on their way back from the arcade. It's time for your cake and for me to tell the world that I'm the luckiest man alive.'

I smiled at him. 'Oh, good, because I have been desperately waiting ... waiting for ... cake.'

He raised his eyebrow at me. 'Cake? Is that all you have been desperately waiting for?'

'Oh, Bryce, you have no idea how much I love cake.' I stepped us up against the balustrade and pressed my body against him then, hovering my mouth just over his and breathing onto his lips, I continued. 'I love how sweet it is, how it rises, and I love it when it's full of cream.' I licked my lips.

His eyes flared with desire. 'That's good. Because I have a huge cake for you.'

I reached down and cupped his erection which was now pushing against his trousers. 'How huge?'

'Fucking enormous.'

I giggled as I gently squeezed him. 'Can you feed me your cake?'

His eyes fluttered, then closed. 'Yes,' he groaned.

'When?' I whispered into his ear.

He eyes shot open. 'Now.'

With lightning fast speed, he scooped me into his arms, making me squeal as he walked briskly to the chopper. He opened the door and carefully placed me down. I scooted backward along the seat as he climbed in and prowled toward me. *Oh, fuck. He is going to screw my brains out in the Crow with our friends and family only metres away.*

I would normally object to such a high-risk sexual encounter, but the look in his eyes made it impossible to say no, together with the fact that my sexed-up hormones were currently going crazy.

He placed his hands on my calves and dragged them up my legs, taking my dress up with them. I pressed against the door opposite to the one we got in by, panting with excitement, my chest rising and falling while watching his passionate desperation for me. He reached my underwear and paused looking up at me.

I didn't hesitate. 'Do it. Do it now, Bryce. I want to feel you in between my legs. I can't wait.'

He growled and tore my underwear apart, then leaned forward and stroked my damp clit with his tongue. *Oh, god. Yes!* I pressed my hand to the window and it slipped from perspiration. I giggled seeing what I had just done.

He looked up. 'What's so funny?'

'I just did a Rose, from Titanic.'

He looked at my smudged handprint on the window and chuckled then mumbled something about being 'king of the world'. I laughed, but suddenly swallowed the amusement as his tongue hit that perfect spot, flicking away and sending luscious pulses right through me.

'Oh, fuck, Bryce.' A sweet orgasm rippled through me as he flicked his tongue and sucked my clit. I reached for his head and lifted him to my face, feeling and tasting my desire for him then, leaning in, I pushed him back against the seat and unzipped his pants. He shuffled them down just enough to free his ready and waiting cock.

I grasped it between my hands, dragging them up to his tip, and gently massaged the moist crown with my finger before climbing onto his lap and greedily engulfing him with my pussy. He groaned as he gripped my arse and helped me pump his cock.

'You have no idea how fucking happy I am right now,' he breathed.

'I think I do.'

'No ... you don't.'

I smiled and kissed him, only to hear what I thought to be Tash's voice. 'Oh, sweet Jesus! My eyes, my bloody eyes.'

Followed by Jade's. 'Is that ...? Are they ...? Fuck me, where's the popcorn?'

I quickly glanced out the window and spotted Tash pushing a reluctant Jade back toward the apartment, all the while giggling and cursing at her. 'Jade, get your arse out of here now.'

I didn't care though because I was having my cake and cream ... yes, I was having the cream too. Bryce jerked, groaned and gripped me tightly. *Oh, fuck. I really do love cake and cream.*

Dampened with sweat and unable to stop my giggling, I quickly climbed off him. 'Oh my god, they saw us. I'm never going to hear the end of this.'

'I hope not. We just fucked in the Crow. I have wanted to fuck you in the Crow since the day Alexander was born.'

'Really? Little do you know I wanted that too,' I admitted. We sat for a small moment, blissfully absorbing the peaceful, happy aura surrounding us.

I remembered back to that first time he buckled me into the front seat. 'You have no idea how hard it was for me to keep my legs closed that time you were fishing for the set of headphones.'

'You have no idea how hard it was for me not to have pried your legs apart and kissed that sweet pussy of yours. I nearly fucking did, you know.'

I laughed. 'I'm glad you didn't.' I raised my eyebrow at him. 'I'm glad you didn't, because that very first time I felt your tongue on me was pure unadulterated bliss. I'll never forget it.'

'Neither will I, honey.' He leaned over, grabbed my hand and brought it to his lips. 'Are you ready to do this?' He was staring at me, waiting like a kid on Christmas morning.

'No,' I replied. His smile plummeted, so I quickly added, 'I need to get cleaned up. I'm not going out there in front of my family and friends, fully fucked and pantyless, with come dripping down my legs. I need underwear.'

He climbed out of the chopper and helped me out the other side. 'Come on then,' he said, as he playfully smacked my bum and placed his hand on my hip, holding me to him as he led me to his office.

* * *

After a sneaky trip via the private elevator to our bedroom to clean up, Bryce and I rejoined the party and positioned ourselves behind a small table which had been set up on the step that looked down into the lounge area. The room had been decorated with hundreds of silver and blue metallic helium balloons with matching spiralling twine that dangled from each balloon's securely-tied lip. There were also approximately twenty large bouquets of white and blue roses placed meticulously around the room. *Trust Bryce to find a way to have blue roses for me.* I smiled at their brilliance, which was nothing in comparison to the man standing next to me. The room looked magical, but it was still very simple and elegant, and I was grateful Bryce had stayed true to his word when he promised he would not go overboard. I really did not want that.

I had been appreciatively taking in the surrounding scenes and, because of that, had not noticed the enormous three-tiered cake that had been placed on the table before me. It was perfectly centred and looked stunning and delicious. It also kind of looked like the Empire State Building. No shit! It stood about one metre high with long rectangular panels of white chocolate secured to each side of the three square tiers, and each tier was topped with fresh raspberries. It was simply spectacular and looked utterly delectable.

'I told you my cake was huge,' he whispered to me.

I shook my head at him and giggled. 'You're not wrong. You really are something else, Mr Clark. White chocolate and raspberries, you honestly think of everything.'

He pulled me into his side as a number of waitstaff quickly passed out glasses of champagne to our guests. 'I think of you, Alexis. You, our families, and no one else.' He kissed the top of my head, then gently tapped his glass in order to gain the room's attention and hush the verbal communication flowing between the guests.

When the conversations passed to silence, Bryce began to speak. 'Firstly, I just want to thank you all for coming today, to celebrate Alexis' birthday. We both really appreciate you taking the time to share this evening with us.' He let go of my side and placed his hand on the champagne flute he was holding, peering into it. 'Look ... I'll start by addressing the elephant in the room by saying that it is no secret Alexis and I found each other under somewhat controversial circumstances.' He moved his gaze to me, a hint of guilt flickering in his eyes. I winked at him, encouraging him to go on.

'Controversial or not, the truest crime of all would have been to ignore true love. From the moment I laid eyes on this beautiful woman standing next me, my heart decided to once again function as it was designed to. And, if I'm going to be completely honest, the feeling that came over me shortly after meeting her for the first time literally shocked the shit out of me.'

Everyone in the room let out a chuckle which seemed to relax Bryce.

'So, there I was, my heart going berserk, telling numerous parts of my body that my true love — my soul mate — had just entered my life. And knowing that it was criminal to ignore what I was feeling, I had no choice but to act. To say that I deliberately pursued Alexis is indeed correct. Do I feel guilty about that fact? Well ... at the time, yes, yes I did. But knowing that she, too, felt the same way about me, but refused to let herself accept it, enabled me to push aside that guilt. Look, I guess what I am trying to say is that sometimes in life you know you are going to do the wrong thing. That what you are about to do goes against everything you stand for. But there are also times in life when you have to ignore the morality of the problem that faces you and go with your heart. Because at the end of the day, your heart is what truly makes you happy. And Alexis is my heart, entirely.'

The room was completely silent, but the loud thudding noise my heart was making as it pounded in my chest was deafening. I had tears streaming down my face as I looked up at the man who fulfilled every part of my being.

He noticed me crying and gently wiped away the salty menaces that were trickling down my cheeks. I helped him rid my face of the moisture and choked back the tears threatening to fall. I looked out over the room of smiling faces, and some were even crying — my mother and sister being two of them — and some were playfully scoffing at Bryce's romantic declaration, my brother and Derek being two of those.

I cleared my throat. 'Wow! I can't really top that, can —'

'Yes, you can,' he interrupted, smiling at me.

I knew exactly what he meant. 'Actually, yes, I can.' I took in a deep breath and felt my face stretch into an enormous grin. 'Tomorrow I turn thirty-six years of age, and during those thirty-six years, I can honestly say that I have experienced *a lot*.

'I have learned what it is to be a daughter, sister, friend, wife and mother. I have learned about commitment, devotion, loyalty, love, hurt and loss. But I think what I have learned most in my life's journey is that no matter what difficult situation you face, there is always some sort of reprieve, always a light at the end of the tunnel. Even if at first that light seems dim and not worth trying to reach, there is a light and it is worth reaching. It's worth grasping and doing everything you can to brighten it. All of you — my friends and family — you are my light, and I truly appreciate having every one of you in my life.'

I placed my hand around Bryce's hip and leaned in to his shoulder. 'As most of you are aware, I have recently had to fight for a reprieve during a very wounding, lightless time in my life, yet it was a fight worth winning because the path that lies ahead of me now, at age thirty-six, is the most exciting path I will ever walk. It's a path I plan on taking with you, with my two beautiful children, with this wonderful amazing man who I now know to be my soul mate and with our precious little miracle who is growing strong as each day goes by.' I gently caressed my stomach.

There were gasps around the room and a couple of people even clapped. I choked a little and continued. 'Yes, Bryce and I are expecting a baby and we couldn't be happier.' I looked up at him, but he did not give me time to focus before his lips were touching mine. I placed my hand on the side of his face and savoured his embrace.

'Jesus, you two, there's already a bun in the oven, no need to try and make another one.' My brother's voice cut through the room, prompting a laugh from everyone, including me and Bryce. We broke apart.

'I'm going to be a dad,' Bryce said to the room. He picked up Charli and sat her on his hip, and I reached for Nate who was standing not too far from my side. 'We are going to be a family.' Bryce raised his glass to the room. 'To a life of fulfilment.' Everyone raised their glasses and said cheers.

A waitress lit the candles on my cake and everyone started singing happy birthday. Bryce placed Charli on the ground next to me, so I knelt down to her height and kissed her on the cheek. As I looked through the candle flames out into the room before me, I spotted Gareth standing next to Sam, his look unreadable and, for the first time in a while, I had a chill go up my spine.

CHAPTER
12

I shook the eerie feeling Gareth's obscure expression had given me and focussed on the rest of our guests.

Lucy was the first to greet us after our announcement. 'I knew it! A little bit of wind, my arse,' she exclaimed. I momentarily looked at her dumbfounded then remembered my embarrassing cover story to her on Easter night.

'I'm so sorry,' I laughed. 'I had to fake it. We wanted it to be a surprise. I would never have forgiven myself if I ruined it by admitting I was pregnant to you that night. "Wind" was the first thing that came to my mind!'

Lucy shook her head in amusement. 'I didn't buy it, you know.'

'Shit! I felt awful. You had just finished opening your heart to me, and there I was pronouncing I had wind.' I put my head in my hands. 'Kill me now.'

Bryce and Nic both shrugged their shoulders, having no idea what Lucy and I were babbling on about.

'On that Easter night, Alexis not so subtly caressed her tummy when she and I were making coffee and talking,' she explained to Bryce and Nic. 'I knew straightaway she was pregnant, but she tried putting it down to having wind. It was hilarious watching her face turn a shade of pink.'

Lucy grabbed her brother and hugged him tightly, saying something quietly into his ear, something I couldn't hear. He nodded his head at her, an expression of triumph and self-satisfaction on his face while answering her with a 'Thanks'.

'Congratulations! You both deserve to be happy ... and Alexander deserves a cousin his age to play with.' She bounced baby Alexander on her hip. 'How does that sound? A cousin to boss around,' she said in playful tone to her son.

Bryce smiled as he let his nephew grip his finger. 'Speaking of cousins, where is ours?'

We all turned our heads, scanning the room, looking for Gareth. 'He was here a moment ago. I spotted him during our announcement,' I answered, concerned for where he was at that moment, and even more concerned about his frame of mind.

'How did he seem?' Bryce asked.

I didn't know whether to say good or not good. To be honest, I didn't know if his expression was, in fact, bad. It looked it though, and it had left me feeling unsettled, like it used to months ago. 'Honestly, I'm not sure. He didn't seem overly happy for us, but he didn't seem heartbroken either.'

'I probably should've told him in private, like you did for Rick.' He looked out over the room again, while running his free hand through his hair in exasperation. 'Shit! I wasn't thinking.'

'Bryce, don't worry, he'll be around here somewhere. Go find him and talk it over,' I offered, as he seemed quite concerned.

'Yeah, that's probably a good idea,' Lucy added. Alexander tried desperately to put Bryce's finger in his mouth, Bryce playing a little tug of war with him.

'We are going to head up to bed. Al needs a feed and a sleep. I just need a sleep. Do you mind if we stay?' Lucy asked, looking at me and waiting for an answer.

'Of course not.' *Why is she asking me? I'm pregnant with Bryce's child, not ruler of his universe.* 'Why would you ask that?'

'Because this is your home now, not ours. We don't want to intrude,' Nic replied.

'You're never intruding,' Bryce answered, finally freeing his finger from Alexander's tight grip. He kissed my cheek. 'I'm going to find Gareth.'

I watched him walk away in search of his cousin. *Shit, I hope Scott hasn't returned. Shit! I hope Sam is okay. Shit! I really need to tell her about his illness.* I hugged Lucy and Nic goodnight while contemplating how I would inform Sam of Gareth's condition. I wondered if she were the type to take that kind of information in her stride, or whether she would run for the hills. *Unfortunately, I think hill-running is more Sam's style.*

Just as I was about to turn around and mingle some more, I felt a pair of arms wrap around my shoulders, and an unmistakable, unmelodious voice sing Creed's 'With Arms Wide Open' into my ear. I laughed, turned, and gently pushed Tash back. 'You're an idiot, you know.'

'Geez, tough crowd! If you're not a Creed fan, I could try a little Ed Sheeran.' She started singing 'Small Bump'. Lil, Jade and Steph joined in.

I stared at them, amazed. 'Shut up!'

Laughing, they embraced me in a big group hug, congratulating me.

'Thanks, bitches. And I say that with love,' I said sarcastically, as they all pulled away from me.

'That better be your hormones speaking,' Jade playfully warned.

'Speaking of hormones,' Tash said, lowering her voice, 'remind me to never say yes to a ride in the Crow. I'm scarred for life now.'

'I'm not. That was fucking hot, Lexi!' Jade winked at me.

'What did I miss?' Steph asked.

'Lexi and Bryce were —'

'None of your business,' I interrupted, the smirk on my face betraying me. We lowered our gazes — kind of like a Western stand-off — and sipped our drinks. *Hmm, this non-alcoholic rosé shit ain't all that bad.*

Lil broke the stand-off. 'How'd Rick take the news? Not well, I'm guessing. I saw him storm out before your announcement.'

I closed my eyes momentarily as I swallowed my drink. 'No, not well at all. He thinks the baby is his.'

'Could it be?' she instantly asked.

I replied just as quickly. 'No.'

'Are you sure?'

'Yes, Lil, I'm sure.'

'Well, then relax, luv. He can think it all he likes. Don't let it stress you out. You don't need stress right now.'

'I know. It's fine. I'm fine. I'm not worried about Rick. It will sort itself out. I'm a hurdler, remember.'

Tash sighed. 'How many hurdles can one jump in such a short space of time though? Fuck.' She looked concerned.

I hugged her. 'Really Tashy, I'm fine. Hurdles were made to be jumped over. Though if you can't jump them gracefully, kick the fuckers down with your foot and step over them. Either way, the hurdles are goin' down.' I motioned for a waiter to come my way when I noticed his tray was adorned with macaroons. *Pistachio macaroons. I'll take about four of those, thank you very much.* I loaded my napkin up with the delicious treats.

Jade raised an eyebrow at me.

'What? I'm eating for two, and I happen to know that Baby Clark likes pistachio macaroons.'

Jade put her hands in the air. 'I'm not saying anything.'

'Baby Clark?' Tash questioned.

'Yes. Why? Got any better names?'

'Well, since you like collective names, what about Bark?'

'No, Tash. No! Definitely not.'

'I know, what about Boaab?' she asked excitedly.

The rest of the girls and I snorted at the horrid name. 'Seriously, Tash? What the fuck?'

'BOAAB. Baby Of Alexis And Bryce. BOAAB. Shit, I'm smart.'

I screwed my face up. 'How much have you had to drink?'

'Clearly, too much,' Lil interjected.

I agreed.

Shaking my head with a smile, I momentarily diverted my attention and scanned the room, looking for Bryce, Gareth, or both of them together. There was no sign of either. I did, however, spot Carls in the middle of the lounge room, flirting as she spoke to Derek.

I grinned and then got a great idea. 'Hey. Want to help me stir up Carls? Bryce has me drinking non-alcoholic wine and it's depressing me. I need to punish someone. I owe Carls about a thousand pay-backs, so she is my victim.'

The girls smiled. 'What did you have in mind?' Steph asked, while stealing one of my macaroons. I gave her the mother of all deadly looks which prompted her to gingerly place it back in my hot little hand.

Shooting daggers at Steph one more time, I turned to Tash. 'I need some songs about fires.' I gave her a mischievous grin, knowing full well my human jukebox of a friend would come through for me.

After Tash rattled off a few 'fiery' songs, we were set to put our plan into action. Trying to keep a straight face and looking completely casual and inconspicuous, I slowly walked past Carly while softly singing 'All Fired Up' by Pat Benatar. I stopped in front of a waiter who was only a metre from where Carls and Derek were standing, grabbed a glass of pink rosé shit — or whatever it was called — then made my way back to the girls, singing the chorus slightly louder as I strolled past Carls. Tash then did the same thing, only her song of choice was 'Light My Fire' by The Doors. As she made her way back to me, she raised her voice and danced while gently patting at her snatch, as if it was alight. I cracked up laughing and noticed Carly turn slightly in our direction with an unsure look on her face.

Quickly looking down and avoiding eye contact, I desperately fought back the hysterics, knowing that if our eyes did meet, I would crumble.

Phase two in the let's-get-Carls-all-fired-up game consisted of the five of us walking over to the waiter and staying put, this now giving us the excuse to remain in Carly's earshot so that we could continue to sing rather than walk away. As we stood in a circle with our drinks, I started us off by humming 'Girl On Fire' by Alicia Keys. Tash joined in moments after and hummed along with me right up until the pause before the chorus. I nodded my head at her and the other girls, then we sang the lyrics in the chorus together, rather loudly.

Now, if you're not familiar with the song, the chorus is what you would describe as a 'belter', meaning, one: you have to be relatively good at singing — which we weren't. And two: you needed to belt it out really loud — which we did. Needless to say, it got everyone's attention, mainly due to the fact we sounded awful.

Before I knew it, Will had grabbed a couple of forks from a serving platter and started drumming the beat on the top of the bar, assisting our charade. I smiled at him as I laughed and continued to sing the song. I think the drumbeat actually helped our tone.

Carls had caught on to our game by that point and was pinching the bridge of her nose and screwing up her face. Derek just seemed highly amused at our apparent flash mob performance. This behaviour was not out of the ordinary for us girls so after we had finished, we received a small round of applause then the room went back to its normal small talk and chitchat.

I hadn't noticed Bryce return until we had finished our singalong. He was standing next to Jake looking pretty comfortable and relaxed. I walked up to him and wrapped my arms around his waist.

Jake shook his head at me. 'Are you sure you want her to have your baby?' he asked Bryce, pointing toward me with his beer. 'She's slightly crazy.'

Bryce kissed my head. 'I like crazy.'

I pulled away and gently elbowed him in the ribs. 'Did you find Gareth?'

'No. He's obviously taken off. I'll speak with him tomorrow.'

I shot him an apologetic look.

'Alexis, it's not your fault, so don't —'

'What's not her fault?' Jake asked.

'It's nothing, Jake. Gareth is just not a fan of me and Bryce as a couple.'

'Why? Does he have a thing for you, Lexi?'

Um, no, not me … the sexy father of my child. 'It's a long story, Jake. I'll fill you in another time.' Now was not the time to enlighten Jake that Gareth was Bryce's mentally ill cousin who had an alternate personality, one that was in love with Bryce and wanted me out of the picture. *No, now is definitely not the time.*

'Fair enough,' Jake sighed, seeming to let it go. Knowing my brother, though, he would revisit it at some point in time. 'I'm gonna hit the sack. I have a late run up the Hume Highway to Sydney tomorrow. If I get my shut-eye now, I will be able to do the round trip without stopping.'

'Drive safely, okay. I hate it when you do long trips.' I gave my brother a big hug.

'Of course. This little tacker in here ...' he said, while gently placing his hand on my tummy, 'must be dying to meet its uncle. I have no choice but to stay safe. Wouldn't want to disappoint the little rugrat when it's born.' He removed his hand and shook Bryce's. 'Congratulations, mate.'

'You are so full of yourself, you know that, right?' I teased.

'Yep, full of shit-hotness! Don't forget it.'

'Eww. Go. Go to bed.' I nudged him toward the door.

'Night,' he called behind him.

'Night,' we replied.

The kids had already taken themselves to bed. Mum, Dad, Jen and Steve followed shortly after, leaving only Live Trepidation, the girls and their husbands, and their kids, who were beginning to turn feral. And, of course, Carls. Carls who was on the warpath heading directly for me.

'Shit! I think I'll take you up on the security guard offer,' I said quickly as I wrapped myself in Bryce's arms for protection.

He seemed a little concerned. 'What? Why?'

'It looks like Carls wants my head on a platter.'

She stormed right up to me, her face desperately trying to hold tight. 'You are hilarious,' she said sarcastically.

'I know,' I answered honestly.

'No. That wasn't funny. I was so fucking embarrassed.'

'Relax. He had no idea.'

'Who had no idea?' Bryce asked.

'Derek,' we both answered.

Bryce looked over at his lead singer, slightly confused. 'What does he have no idea about?'

I jumped in before Carls had a chance. 'He has no idea Carly has a burnt burger.' I cracked up laughing.

'You're a bitch, Alexis Summers.'

'No, I'm not, Carly Henkley. Your burger is burnt and you need it thawed out. I was simply trying to begin that process.'

'I can thaw out my own burger, thanks,' she hissed under her breath.

Bryce took a step back. 'I'm not fucking sure if you are talking about a barbecue or something entirely different. Either way, I don't want to know about Carly's burger, so please excuse me.' He headed toward the other men in the room.

'There is nothing wrong with my burger, Bryce,' she called out after him. 'Just so you know, it's a good burger.'

'Carly!' I playfully hit her on the arm. 'Don't offer your burger to my man.'

'Why? Is he a vegetarian?'

'No! God, no!' I laughed. 'The man is a carnivore through and through.' I bit my lip as I remembered our encounter in the Crow.

'I hate you, you know,' she admitted, while taking in my hungry expression.

'You should. Every woman should. I've scored big time.'

'Good. I'm glad you know it, hon.'

'Oh, trust me, Carls. I know it all right.'

CHAPTER

13

The next day our family and friends checked out of the hotel at staggered times of the day, most of them popping up to the penthouse to wish me a happy birthday and to thank us and say goodbye. Mum and Dad took Nate and Charli back to the farm with them as it was school holidays for another two weeks. The kids were so excited; they adored the farm and spending time with their grandparents.

Rick had arranged to be off work for the second week of the holidays so that the kids could stay with him. I assumed that was still the case, but after last night's heated exchange, I couldn't exactly be sure. I would have to contact him sooner rather than later to find out. I was still kind of reeling from his outburst and accusation, and feeling like I now had to prove my innocence, so to speak. That feeling really pissed me off. I did not have to prove anything to him. I did not have to prove my child was Bryce's, and I did not have to prove that I had done nothing wrong.

Anger over the whole situation was simmering away deep within me, and I could feel myself begin to get worked up, so I thought I would take out my frustration and stress on the cross trainer. I quickly changed into a pair of knee-length gym pants, a singlet top and a pair of runners before making my way downstairs.

Bryce was sitting on the lounge with his guitar, strumming some chords and writing down what I assumed were notes. *Fuck, he looks sexy holding a guitar, too sexy for his own good.* I almost changed my mind about taking my frustration out on the cross trainer, instead thinking I could take it out on him — sexually. He just looked so goddamned tasty.

'Havin' a work-out. Just thought I'd let you know in case you wanted to hold my hand.' I gave him a sarcastic, cheeky grin as I waltzed past him.

He raised his eyebrow at me and put his guitar down. I continued out through the bifold doors and onto the balcony where the home gym equipment was situated. As I stepped up on the cross trainer, I watched him casually stroll up to me with his hands in his pockets, stopping at the weight machine and leaning up against it.

'Can I help you?' I asked him, playfully.

'No.'

I began to stride. 'You're not seriously going to stand there and watch me, are you?'

'Yes, I seriously am.'

'Bryce, I was only kidding about the whole hold-my-hand thing. Go away.'

'Can't do it, honey.' He lifted one foot and propped it back against the machine, hands still in his pockets and looking as comfortable and as sexy as ever.

'This is not funny. I'm not kidding, you know.'

'Neither am I.' He pushed off the machine with his foot and walked over to a chair. Sliding it out from the table, he spun it around and sat on it backwards, facing me with his arms crossed on the backrest.

He's fucking serious. I stopped my strides and glared at him. 'Bryce!'

'Don't bother. I'm not moving. You won't listen to me and stop exercising on your own, so I will make sure you are not on your own. I'm not going anywhere.'

'You are fucking unreal.' I started striding again, trying damned hard to ignore him. It wasn't working.

Even though I was no longer making eye contact with him, I could feel his stare bore into the depths of my body. His scrutinisation was arousing a sexual response, compelling my heart to pound vigorously.

Well, you are exercising, Alexis. That could explain the increase in heart rate. My nipples twinged, tickling and firming as I moved. *No, it's Bryce's stare, definitely Bryce's stare.*

A bead of sweat trickled down my forehead, so I grabbed my towel from where I'd draped it over the handle of the machine and wiped my brow while catching a glimpse of Bryce, who was smirking at me. 'Are you enjoying yourself, you overprotective arse?'

He laughed. 'Yes. I'm especially enjoying the view. You are fucking hot when you sweat. Although, I like to be the one who makes you sweat.'

I narrowed my eyes at him. 'Yeah, well, best you enjoy watching me sweat. Because it's the only way I'm going to sweat for you if you insist on being a domineering dick.'

He laughed again. 'Sorry, did you say I have a domineering dick?'

'No.'

'Yes, you did.'

'No, I didn't. I —'

'My dick likes domineering your mouth and your —'

'Your dick will be domineering nothing if you keep this shit up.'

He chuckled. 'You're sweating again, honey.'

You infuriatingly sexy son of a bitch. I slowed to a stop, wiped my brow and stepped down from the machine. Bryce watched me intently as I walked over to the exercise bike. He swivelled his chair around so that he could continue to face and taunt me.

I dropped my head back in surrender and groaned. 'URGH!'

'I love it when you groan. Do that again.'

I lifted my head. 'No. Piss off.'

He laughed and rested his chin on his folded arms. 'You're sexy when you're angry.'

'Bryce Edward Clark!'

'Fuck, I love it when you say my name in full.'

He had an amused, cocky grin on his face. I rolled my eyes and groaned again.

'Ah, that groan, Alexis. It's like you are fucking me from a distance.'

I dropped my head to my arms which were crossed over the bike's display monitor, smiling behind the screen as I pedalled harder and faster out of frustration. Frustration over him taunting me, but more so because I was enjoying it and really wanted to go over and bite that naughty mouth of his.

'Alexis, slow down.' His voice was no longer playful.

I ignored him and pedalled harder. *Who's got the domineering dick now, ha? Um ... clearly not me! Um ... never mind.*

'Alexis, I'm serious. Slow down.'

I raised my head and looked at him. 'No.'

He stood up quickly, pushing the chair away, and walked over to the bike. 'Alexis!'

'Bryce!' I mimicked.

He switched the power off, forcing the bike to lose momentum.

I gripped the padded handles, squeezing them tight and screamed my irritation at him. 'Who do you think you are? You can't boss me around like this.' I stepped off the bike and poked him in the chest. 'Back off. I mean it.'

'Fuck, you drive me wild.' He bent down and wrapped his arms around the base of my arse, gently hauling me up and over his shoulder. Then he turned to walk back inside.

I slapped at his arse. 'Put me down.'

'I will when we get to the bedroom.'

'No. Forget it, you bloody control freak! I'm not fucking you.'

'Yes, you are.' He practically bounded up the stairs, not showing any signs of strain. Apparently my weight was not much heavier to him than a feather.

'No. I'm not.' *Yes, I am. Who am I kidding?*

'Well, I'm fucking you. You can just lie there and enjoy it.' He walked into our room and gently placed me on the bed. I went to get up, but he grabbed me and held me down, pressing both arms firmly into the mattress. He climbed over me so that he was straddling my hips, but I noticed he was bearing his own weight so that he did not crush me or the baby.

'Get off,' I half-arsedly hissed.

'Do you really want me to get off?' he asked seductively, then leaned forward and dragged his tongue from my collarbone to just below my ear.

The warm, wet, lubricated slide of his tongue made me shudder. 'Yes,' I whispered, blatantly lying.

He trailed kisses from one side of my neck to my jaw, then across to the other side of my neck, barely skimming my mouth. 'Are you sure?' he breathed again. 'You can have a work-out with me, now. I'll make you sweat like never before.' He trailed some more kisses across my neck and back down to my collarbone, dipping further so that his lips were pressing into the top of my cleavage. 'Are you really sure you want me to get off?' he murmured, before dipping his tongue in between my breasts. I moaned in response, letting him know that he'd won, and that I wanted nothing more than for him to continue.

'I didn't think so, honey.'

* * *

After giving in to Bryce and taking my frustrations out on him in the bedroom, I pouted for the rest of the afternoon, glaring at him every so often. I found myself to be slightly bored and not having much to do. It was a Sunday, my children were away, and I no longer had to worry about housework. I never really minded doing my housework. I used to get some sort of self-satisfaction cleaning my house and my things. It made me feel appreciative of what I had. Don't get me wrong, I didn't *love* housework, and I was more than happy with the fact that I didn't have to do it any longer. I just sort of felt a little useless now.

Bryce had been in the man-cave for most of the afternoon, and I assumed he was working on some songs. I could hear a faint beat sounding through the walls but couldn't make out what it was. It sounded very different from the style the band usually played. I was tempted to go and watch him, possibly even stalk and annoy him like he had me, but I figured he was working on something important, so I left him to it.

Instead, I picked up my book and immersed myself in its fictional world. I was about ninety percent finished with the story, where the two lead characters were narrowly cheating death in a school fire. I was thoroughly engrossed and hoping to god that this second chance would lead to them getting their shit together, when Bryce took my book from my hands and placed it down on the coffee table. I watched it change location from my hands to the table, like it had grown legs and moved there itself.

He grabbed my hands and helped me rise. 'Come on, get up.'

'Hey, I was reading that.'

'You need to get ready. I'm taking you out for dinner, birthday girl.'

'Oh, where are you taking me?'

'You'll find out soon enough. Go and get ready. I've laid something out for you on the bed.' I smiled, loving it when he picked something out for me to wear; it was like a surprise present in itself.

* * *

Bryce took me out for dinner to Seaspray, a lovely modern seafood-inspired restaurant by the beach at St Kilda. The head chef was a friend of his and had been somewhat of a mentor to Bryce over the years, teaching him all he knew about cooking. My tastebuds would be forever grateful to Chef Daniels and his exceptional culinary teachings ... forever grateful.

After our delicious grilled rock lobster, seared Moreton Bay bugs and VIP treatment from the restaurant's staff, we headed back home. As we stepped into the elevator, I latched my arm around his and rested my head on his shoulder, smiling contentedly.

'Thank you for dinner ... for everything. You really do spoil me. But that's not why I love you, you know.'

'I know. You love my domineering dick.'

I raised my head to catch his arrogant smile. 'I do love your domineering dick, but no ... that's still not why I love you. I love your passion and devotion, and I love how you love with everything that you have. You're incredible, Bryce, and what we have is incredible and I thank my lucky stars for it every day. I'm kind of waiting for my bubble to burst though.'

'No bubbles are going to burst, honey.' The elevator doors opened to the apartment. As we exited, he stepped in front of me and produced a blindfold from his pocket. He placed it over my eyes, his serious yet sneaky smile disappearing as my vision turned black.

'What are you doing?' I asked, taken aback.

'Getting you ready for your present.'

'Bryce, I really don't need another present. You've spoilt me enough as it is,' I said, as he led me to the couch. I had my arms out like a zombie, braced and ready for god knows what.

'Relax. Here, sit down.' He guided me to a sitting position. 'I have to give you this present, Alexis. I kind of promised you.'

I furrowed my brow, trying to remember a time where he had promised me something.

'You have no idea, do you?'

'No. None at all.'

'I should just let it go then. I really didn't want to do it after I followed your instructions and googled it.' He let out a regretful huff and bounded up the stairs. 'Wait there,' he called back.

'I'm not exactly in a position to go anywhere, Bryce. Where are you going?' I yelled. He didn't answer me.

The room grew silent as I sat awkwardly on the edge of my seat, alone and in darkness. I felt very self-conscious and slightly anxious at not being able to see what was going on around me. For some reason, time felt longer with a blindfold on.

I was sure many minutes passed before I heard Bryce come down the stairs again. 'Finally. What took you so long?'

'If I'm going to do this, I'm going to do it right. And trust me ... I don't think I'll be doing it again. My arse is very fucking uncomfortable right now. I have a new-found respect for you, honey.'

'What?' I laughed. 'What are you talking about?'

'Shh,' he breathed, unbearably close to my mouth. His sudden proximity startled me, together with the feel of his lips as he brushed them across mine, the sensation heightened because I could not see it coming. 'You're about to find out. When you hear the music, take your blindfold off.'

My mouth was open, ready for his lips and tongue. I moved my neck forward, searching for his lips that were no longer there. *Hang on, what? Music?*

The deep drum and bass sounds of 'Pony' by Ginuwine filled the room. I flinched at first, wondering what the hell the noise was, but when I realised it was Bryce's sound system playing that sexy R&B song, I grabbed at my blindfold and tore it down. My eyes needed a second to adjust to the light that was now streaming into them, but when they did, I found Bryce at the top of the step, standing with his legs apart and his hands behind his back, wearing a baseball cap, a hoodie, very baggy tracksuit pants and white runners. Visions of

Channing Tatum in *Magic Mike* played across my memory, together with me telling Bryce, after a bet he lost, that he would have to perform a 'Channing' for me.

My eyes widened when he rolled his neck around in a slow, sexy and seductive way and I gasped, throwing my hands over my mouth. *Holy fuck, he's really going to do a Channing.* Realising what he was about to do for me, I squealed then kicked my feet up and down on the ground.

'Oh! My! God! Bryce!' I shrieked.

He unzipped his jacket as he took a step toward me, sliding to the beat. I squealed again as he got closer, bouncing on my seat, my smile feeling as if it was about to spread wider than the edges of my face.

He moved his hips to the beat as he removed his jacket and dropped it on the floor, a smirk appearing at the corner of his mouth. *Fuck, where the hell did this dancing god come from? He's got moves!*

He rolled his body back a few times as he raised his eyebrow suggestively at me, prompting an instant squeezing of my legs together. My pussy abruptly woke up, beckoning his touch, a touch I wanted desperately, but not until he'd finished Magic-Miking for me. This was just too fucking good.

He slid my way a little more then ran his hands down his chest which was covered in a tight, white singlet top. My mouth went dry and I swallowed slowly. *Oh, fuck. I'm about to sexually combust.* I could feel the blood rushing to my head as he got down on his hands and knees and crawled toward me, then slid backward in a dry-hump of the floor kind of way. I threw my head back and laughed, as that particular move was my favourite part of Magic Mike's striptease in the movie, and Bryce pulled it off perfectly.

He smiled at me, then with total ease did a backflip. I screamed, unprepared for his talented acrobatics and for fear he was about to land on his head. He didn't though. He landed perfectly on his feet then stripped off his singlet triumphantly, revealing his delicious chest, abs and that freakishly fantastic V muscle.

I gripped the edge of the couch, needing to restrain myself from tearing across the room and clawing at him like a sexually-crazed wild animal. I couldn't entirely rule that scenario out ... the sight of him was stirring an uncontrollable, heated primal feeling within me.

The chorus kicked in, and Ginuwine sang about a ride on his pony and, as those lyrics filled the room, Bryce thrust out his cock and pointed at it, forcing my jaw to drop. Yes ... it dropped to the freaking floor, followed by the rest of my body.

I was on my knees in front of the couch, sitting back on my heels, salivating. *Fuck!* I desperately wanted to ride his pony. I wanted to freakin' ride it immediately.

He did a 360° spin and stopped, standing over me, only centimetres away. He pulled his tracksuit pants down at the front, only slightly, revealing what looked like red underwear. *No! He hasn't ... he didn't ... fuck, I think he did!* My eyes widened and I knelt up higher to sneak a peek at what I thought was a red G-string, just like Magic Mike's.

He grabbed my hand and twitched his finger at me, as if to say 'nuh-uh', then he gently pulled me up so that I was once again sitting on the edge of the couch.

Eye-fucking me heatedly, he slowly crouched down to his knees and placed his head between my legs. I shuddered. *Oh, holy fuck.* Then, almost instantly, he lifted me and stood up, my pelvis covering his face and my legs wrapped around his neck. I screamed at my change of elevation and because Magic Mike did the same thing to some random chick in the movie.

He walked me over to the step and gently knelt down, laying me flat on my back. I laughed and covered my face with my hands.

'You're crazy!' I shouted at him over the music.

He didn't say anything, just pretended to dry-hump me as Ginuwine sang about being horny. I couldn't stop laughing at his smirking face when he hovered over my mouth and teased me with his lips. I tried to kiss him, but he pulled away and slowly crept down my body, eyeing me devilishly and stopping momentarily to nip at the damp spot between my legs. My thighs instantly closed around his head, holding him tightly, but my strength paled in comparison to his as he opened them with ease, releasing himself to stand above me once again.

'You're insane,' I giggled, and he waggled his eyebrows in response, while removing his shoes and socks.

Propping myself up on my elbows, I eagerly watched him pull down his tracksuit pants. My eyes widened, and I fell back, putting my hands over my mouth to subdue the laughter that wanted to burst from within me.

To my absolute delight, I had been right in my assumption that he was wearing a red G-string, just like Mike.

'Happy Birthday, honey,' he said with conviction.

I covered my eyes, laughing hysterically, but peeking through my fingers at the luscious eye-candy above me. I kicked my legs up and down with excitement as I knew what he was planning next. He crouched down over me, facing my feet. Then, hovering his crotch over my face, he pumped his pelvis to the music to pretend-fuck my face. I squealed again and tried to bite at his cock.

'Hey, easy,' he laughed.

I ignored him and gripped his delicious arse, pushing his package into my face.

The music died down and Bryce rolled off me, all the while trying to pluck the thin material from between his arse in an awkward fashion. I couldn't hold it in any longer and burst into hysterics.

'I can't believe you,' I said in between laughs and gasps for air.

Chuckling, he finally replied, 'Believe it, because I ain't wearing this fucking arse-flossing red piece of shit ever again.'

CHAPTER
14

I've often wondered: if you fell asleep with a smile on your face and woke up with that same smile, had it stayed on your face the entire time you were asleep? Evidence of overpowering elation you experienced before your mind went into rest?

If that notion was at all possible, then I was pretty sure the smile I had just woken up with was the same smile I had worn when I fell asleep the night before — a result of Bryce's striptease.

My eyelids had not even opened, yet I was thoroughly beaming, remembering the birthday present my Mr Magic-Mike Clark had given me. *Oh! My! Freakin'! God! He was hot.*

I giggled then snapped out of my euphoric state, opening my eyes completely to scan my surroundings. Bryce wasn't lying in bed next to me. In his place were a blue rose and a note telling me he had a mountain of work to do and for me to sleep in, take my time and come down when I was ready.

Picking up the rose, I held it to my nose and inhaled its scent, still smiling from ear to ear. I then eagerly climbed out of bed and hopped in the shower without hesitation. I wanted to go and see the sexy dancing studmuffin as quickly as I could and hoped that maybe, just maybe, I would get him to do an encore performance.

Continuing my pathetic adolescent giggles, I started humming 'Pony' while swaying my hips from side to side as I washed myself. I realised that Ginuwine's song and the visuals of Bryce creeping along the floor to me, were going to be permanently etched on my brain and inner eyelids. *Awesome! Best birthday present, EVER!*

Shaking my head in disbelief at his devotion to pleasing me — and the fact that he was a pretty good dancer — I quickly showered and got myself ready to help him get through the mountain of work in any way I could. I put on my purple Versace jersey wrap-dress, which adapted quite nicely to my slightly thicker waistline, and paired it with my divinely gorgeous purple Manolo Blahnik Kilis.

I hopped along, putting my heels on as I walked to the top of the stairs, making sure they were secured firmly before I started to make my way down. As I took my third step, I felt a sudden surge of terror, a feeling of imbalance and dread as if my senses knew what was happening to me before my brain had a chance to convey the message. My heartbeat seemed to cease, and my breath stopped as I realised I was falling forward.

My first instinct had me turning to the side to prevent tumbling face first, while reaching out and securing my hold on the railing with both hands. But as I gripped the safety rail, I felt a shocking surge of pain in my ankle, forcing me to let go and slip further down. The battle to stay upright was lost, and I slammed into the stairs, hitting my head and instantly feeling really strange, before everything went black.

Bryce

I really needed to hire more staff. Ever since Alexis strolled into my life like an angel, I had been up to my fucking neck in work. Why? Because she was a major distraction in every possible kind of way and, because of that, I kept pushing my work aside just to spend time with her. I couldn't help it, and it was only going to get worse, especially when the baby arrived.

I didn't want to spend day after day working while the love of my life and our happy little family spent time together without me. No, fuck that. I had every intention to back off work and devote more time to what was more important. I had worked my arse off for a long time and I was now ready to reap the benefits.

I picked up the phone and dialled Arthur.

'Arthur Gordon speaking.'

'Arthur, it's Bryce.'

'Good morning, Bryce. What can I do for you?'

'I need to set up a board meeting. Topic of agenda will be making you senior vice-president.'

Arthur cleared his throat. 'That is certainly not what I expected you to say. Can I ask why?'

'Arthur, Alexis is pregnant. I'm going to be a father. I need to relinquish some of my duties and free up some time so that I can be the best father and partner I can be. I can't do that without your help.'

'Oh ... well ... I see. Congratulations, Bryce. Good gracious, that was quick.'

I chuckled at my late father's best friend, my close friend, and the only man I had ever looked up to, apart from my dad. 'Thanks. It wasn't planned, but we are beyond thrilled. I'm going to sign over an additional six percent stake in the company to you, giving you fifteen percent in total. You will hold the title of senior vice-president, Gareth will still remain vice-president with his ten percent stake and his duties will go unchanged. Your duties, however, will increase.

'If you require a personal assistant to help with the additional work-load then we will hire one. What do you say? I don't trust anyone else,

Arthur. Please say yes.' I waited for his answer. 'Listen, think about it and —'

'No, Bryce. Of course I'll do it. I am honoured, thank you.'

'Thank you, Arthur.'

'So, you're going to be a dad. I couldn't be happier for you, Bryce, and I know your parents are somewhere up above, incredibly proud and smiling down on you.'

I almost choked at the old man's words. I respected Arthur and looked up to him more than he'd ever know, and his kind words and thoughts of my parents pierced my heart in a big way. 'Thanks, Arthur. I hope you're right. Listen, I've got to go. I will speak to you about the changes in a few days, okay?'

'Of course.'

I ended the phone call, stood up from my desk and walked over to the window, taking in the view of Port Phillip Bay. Would my parents be proud? I hoped so. I'd never really given much thought to the notion that they could be smiling down on me, but I liked the idea. I liked thinking that they could somehow see me and Lucy grown up and happy, with families.

I looked at my watch and noticed it was past 10 a.m. *Alexis, you little sleeping beauty.* The thought of her asleep on her stomach, her bare back visible and longing to be touched, stirred my need to go and see her. *Fuck, the things she does to me. No wonder I am so far behind in work.* I honestly didn't care though. She made me so fucking happy, all I wanted was to be around her.

A devilish smile appeared on my face as I made my way to the apartment door, already running ideas through my head on different ways I could wake her.

* * *

Walking into the apartment, I headed for the stairs. At first, I didn't register the sight before me, because it was so fucking terrifying that it just couldn't be real. But it was.

'Fuck! Jesus! Fuck! Alexis! No!'

I ran the fastest my legs could carry me and skidded to my knees where her crumpled body lay at the base of the steps. 'Please don't be dead! Fuck! No!'

Adrenaline was coursing through me, and the first thing I did was check for a pulse. 'Thank god.' She had a pulse and she was breathing. Gently, I lifted her head and noticed blood on my hand. 'Fuck!'

She made a murmuring noise, one of pain.

'Honey, you're going to be okay. I'm going to call an ambulance.'

I grabbed my phone and dialled triple-O.

'You have dialled triple-O emergency. Do you need Police, Fire and Rescue, or Ambulance?'

'Ambulance, I need an ambulance now. My girlfriend has fallen down the stairs and she is unconscious. She is fourteen weeks pregnant. Her head is bleeding, and ... oh, fuck, I think her leg is broken.'

I'd seen some pretty horrific shit in my life, but the angle at which her foot lay to her leg was not normal.

'Is she breathing?' the operator asked, in a calm voice.

'Yes. Yes, she is breathing. My name is Bryce Clark, and I own City Towers. We are in the penthouse. I have a helipad. Please send a chopper, now!'

Alexis murmured again. I gently ran my hand down the side of her face. 'It's okay, my love, I'm right here.' I leaned over her, wanting to pick her up in my arms and hold her to me, but I knew not to touch her. I didn't know if anything else was broken, she could have fractured her spine for all I knew.

Looking over her with a bit more detail, I took in the blood staining her dress in between her legs. 'Oh, god. No.'

The operator was still talking on the other end of the phone, but I couldn't focus on a word she was saying. I stared down at Alexis and I lost control, taking hold of her hand and kissing it, crying and telling her that the paramedics were coming and that she was going to be fine. After that, it was all kind of a blur.

* * *

Once at the hospital, my incoherent state of mind still remained. I remembered seeing her being wheeled away from me and into the emergency department, then feeling that my life had once again ended.

'Mr Clark?'

I turned as a nurse lightly touched my arm. 'Yes.'

She very cautiously guided me to a seat. 'I'm so sorry that your wife is hurt.'

I didn't correct her mistake. To me, she was my wife; she was my life, and as soon as it was legally possible, I was going to marry her. We just had to get through this first. We *had* to.

'Your wife is stable and she will be fine.' *Oh, thank fuck.* 'She is on her way to radiology to have an X-ray of her ankle, which is clearly broken. She will also have a CT scan to check the severity of her head injury. Now, Mr Clark ...' she placed her hand on my shoulder, 'I'm so terribly sorry to have to tell you this, but upon examination of your wife by the paramedics, they found evidence of an incomplete miscarriage.'

I dropped my head into my hands, already knowing that was the case. I had noticed the blood stains on Alexis' dress, kind of making it unmistakable. It wasn't any less painful to hear though.

The nurse — I didn't even know her name — gently squeezed my shoulder with the hand she had placed there. 'I'm so sorry. Is there anyone I can call for you?'

I lifted my head. 'No, that's okay. I will call Alexis' mum. Thank you.'

'There is a waiting room, just down there.' She nodded down the corridor. 'Please help yourself to a drink. I will be at the nurse's station if you need anything. As soon as your wife is out of surgery, I will come and let you know.'

I thanked her again then turned and headed for the waiting room, grabbing my phone out of my pocket. I dialled Chelsea's number.

'Bryce, hi. It's so nice —'

'Chelsea. I need you to take a chopper and fly to the coordinates I'm about to send you. I need you to pick up Alexis' family, then fly them directly to the Royal Women's Hospital as soon as possible.'

'Is everything okay? Are you —'

'Chelsea, can you do that for me? Please.'

'Of course, I —'

'Thank you. I'll send the coordinates now and the clearance to land when I have it.'

I hung up from Chelsea and dialled Maryann.

'Hello?'

'Maryann, it's Bryce.'

'Hi, Bryce. Is everything okay?'

'No. Alexis is in hospital. She fell down the stairs.'

'Oh, my goodness. Is she all right? Is the baby all right?'

'She has a head injury and a broken leg. I'm not sure if anything else is broken, or the extent of her head injury.'

'Oh my god. Um, I —'

'A friend of mine is on her way to pick you up in a chopper and bring you here. I'm not sure the kids should come at this stage though. I ... I really don't know if it's a good —'

'No, you're right. We won't mention anything to the kids. Bryce, is the baby all right?'

I paused, not knowing if I could actually open my mouth and say the words. I had to though, so I sucked in a deep breath and said it out loud for the first time. 'No, Maryann. The baby did not survive the fall.'

I heard her gasp and subdue a sob. 'Oh, I'm so sorry. Oh no. My poor darling girl.'

'Chelsea is the pilot's name. I've sent her details to land where I did at Easter. She should be there in approximately forty minutes.'

I hung up the phone and stood completely still, the past hour's events only just now having sunk in. My adrenaline levels had plummeted and I felt the sudden urge to hurl my guts up. I noticed an exit sign and a door which led outside and, without hesitation, I slammed my hands against the glass panels and pushed it open. I took a few steps and vomited into the garden.

CHAPTER
15

I was almost certain when I began to rouse that falling down the stairs had been a nightmare and I was simply waking up from it. I was almost certain that the constant beeping sounds and white noises, which had been filtering in through my ears, were part of that unconscious realm. I was also almost certain that the unpleasant aroma intermittently plaguing my sense of smell was, again, part of my dreamlike state. The thing was, I wasn't dreaming and my brain had only just now begun to decipher the reality surrounding me, decoding what was real as opposed to a delusion. The facts as opposed to the fiction became clearly apparent.

My foot was throbbing with pain, and my head had the sudden urge to explode — that was fact. I could hear voices and noises close by and in the distance — fact, yet again. I could smell the unmistakable scent of sterilising lotion — that was also a fact. And I had a dry, scratchy-like irritation at the back of my throat, together with a horrible metallic taste in my mouth — once again, fact.

I willed my brain to force my eyelids open, but instead my hand contracted and grasped at the hand underneath it.

'Alexis. Alexis, it's me, honey. I'm right here.' Bryce spoke, his voice penetrating my ears, filling me with a sense of calm. 'Maryann, I think she's trying to wake up again.'

His hand tightened around mine.

'Jen, get the nurse,' my mum said, her voice growing louder as she spoke.

I felt a finger graze my cheek and it startled me, forcing my facial muscles to twitch.

'Lexi, sweetheart. It's Mum.'

My eyelids were stubbornly refusing to open, so this time rather than willing them, I demanded they open with everything I had in me. They obeyed and fluttered, filtering in flickers of light and a spectrum of colour. I blinked a few times, gaining strength and control of my eyelids.

Almost instantly I saw Bryce standing to my left, an expression of mixed emotions on his face. He looked happy and relieved, yet at the same time exhausted and concerned. My mum was to my right, brushing hair away from my face and smiling warmly at me.

'Is she awake?' my sister Jen asked, as she burst into the room, which I now confirmed was a hospital room. The cream walls and clinical equipment surrounding me were a clear indication of that.

A nurse in lilac-coloured scrubs walked in after Jen, making her way over to me with a calm and reassuring look on her face. She started checking the monitors that were set up beside my bed. 'Hello, Alexis. My name is Estelle. I'm a nurse here at the Royal Women's Hospital. You were brought in this morning after you fell down some stairs and hit your head.'

I tried to talk, but only garbled words and noises came out of my mouth.

'You might find it a bit difficult to talk at first. You were put under anaesthesia and intubated, so your throat may feel a little sore or irritated.'

I nodded and tried to speak again. 'Mm ... my ... foot ... f-f ... feels —'

'Yes,' she interrupted, 'your foot will feel quite sore. When you fell you fractured your fibula. You've had surgery to repair the break and your ankle is now set in a cast.'

Nurse Estelle checked my wound dressing. I looked down at my ankle which was slightly elevated and surrounded by a plaster cast. Just looking at it heightened the pain.

'I will go and get you some painkillers and water, okay? I won't be long.' She patted my arm gently and gave Bryce a reassuring smile.

He nodded at her, then sat down on the chair next to my bed, still clasping my hand in his. Leaning over me, he kissed my forehead, his lips lingering on my skin for what seemed like a long time. 'I love you,' he whispered, then I heard him sob and take in a breath. The agony in his gasping inhalation was unmistakable.

All the pain I had felt moments ago — my foot, my head, even the spot on my hand where the IV was injected — was as nothing in comparison to the unbearable hurt I felt in my heart when I realised why he was sobbing and why I suddenly felt empty.

I shook my head. 'No.'

Bryce didn't remove his lips from my forehead when he responded. 'I'm so sorry, honey.'

'No, no, no,' I cried. 'Please, no.'

Mum placed her hand on my leg. 'Sweetheart, there was nothing they could do. When you fell, your placenta detached.'

My heart was pounding and my chest felt incredibly tight, strangling me from within. I closed my eyes to stop the tears from flowing and tried to return to the moment before I fell, desperate to reverse the series of events that had led me here: bruised, battered and completely heartbroken. 'Oh, god, I'm so sorry,' I sobbed.

Bryce pulled away from my head and placed his hands on either side of my face. 'You're sorry. Alexis, what are you talking about? You have no reason to be sorry.'

'I fell. It's my fault. Our baby is gone because I fell.'

'This is not your fault. It was an accident.' He leaned forward and kissed my head again.

Jen turned her back to me and looked out the window, her shoulders shaking as she quietly reeled in her sadness.

Mum dragged a seat to the side of my bed and placed my hand in hers. 'Bryce is right, Alexis. It was an accident, you cannot blame yourself.'

It didn't matter what they said though. I fell. I didn't protect my baby. If I had been more careful my baby would still be alive and growing inside me. *My baby is gone.* A wave of excruciating heartache hit me again, and I cried like never before.

Mum, Jen and Bryce tried desperately to reassure me that I wasn't at fault, but after their attempts failed, they stopped trying and just let me cry. I cried on and off for hours. I cried till there were no more tears left to cry.

* * *

The next morning I felt somewhat better. My tears had run dry, my drowsy, sleepy state had lifted a little, and I was allowed to eat a light breakfast of semolina and yogurt. Bryce had taken one look at my first meal in over twenty-four hours and wanted to leave the hospital and get me something that did not look like 'vomit' — his words, not mine. I had to insist he stay with me, which ended up being easy. He didn't argue, not one bit. *Weird.* To be honest, I didn't feel like eating all that much anyway; I still had a headache and still felt nauseous.

My head injury had only been minor, resulting in instant concussion, subsequent soreness, nausea and headaches. Apparently, I was lucky. *Lucky?* That one particular word from the mouth of a nurse who had just come in on a change of shift threw me back into a state of devastation. I had cursed at her and told her that if the 'definition of luck was falling down the stairs and killing your unborn child then I was the fucking luckiest bitch alive'.

Bryce had asked her to leave the room, while following her out, furious at her lack of tact. Needless to say, I did not see her again, but looking back now, it really wasn't her fault. Her choice of word was poor; at that time it had cut me like a knife.

* * *

Shortly after my outburst, a hospital counsellor came by to have a chat to me and Bryce. She spoke to us about what we may or may not feel in the coming days and weeks, which I found slightly irritating. I hated being told what I 'may or may not feel' by someone who did not know me at all and could not possibly know how I would feel. She kind of made me angry, but then again, she said I 'may or may not feel angry', so I guess she did sort of know what she was talking about. Regardless, I was not sure I liked her, so I mainly just listened on and off.

She went through the various options that were available to us for when we were ready to farewell our baby. Options that I could not comprehend, let alone make a clear decision about. I didn't really want to think about it; I didn't want to think about anything. I just wanted to sleep.

I didn't have much to say to her anyway, not being the type to talk to a stranger about my innermost feelings, irrespective of her training and university degree. Bryce appeared to feel the same way, but I expected he would eventually talk to Dr Toffee-nosed Carrot-top Jessica, which was fine. He could obviously confide in her and was comfortable with her professional skills. And, to be honest, I was glad he would have someone to share his grief with other than me.

She must be one hell of a good psychologist despite her demeanour, because she had helped Bryce in the past. And she dealt with Gareth and his illness on a weekly basis. One thing was for sure, I wasn't going to confide in her — no way. She'd made it very clear when we first crossed paths that she did not like me.

* * *

Later that night when it was quiet, Bryce and I finally had a chance to talk. We were lying next to each other in my rather large hospital bed in my rather nice hospital room that I'm fairly sure Bryce had a hand in organising.

'You should go home and get some proper rest,' I said softly, as he rested his head on mine and gently stroked my arm with his thumb.

'No. I'm not leaving you here alone. And, anyway, I don't want to be alone either.'

I tilted my head to look up at him, tears filling my eyes. 'I'm so sorry.'

'Honey, don't. Don't do this to yourself again. It's not your fault,' he said sternly.

I tried desperately to choke back my tears. 'But it is. *I* fell. *I* was rushing to come and see you, to help you. It is my fault. The thing is, I'm sure I put my heels on properly ... but maybe I didn't ... I can't really remember, my memories are all mixed.'

I kept thinking about it, though, replaying it over and over in my head, recalling things that I didn't think happened, but I couldn't be sure. The uncertainty scared me so I tightened my arm which was lying across his chest.

'What do you mean, your memories are all mixed?' he asked, curiously.

'Well, I keep having these flashbacks or visions where I stop and look at my shoes before I go down the stairs. They are secure on my feet. I know they are, because I look at them the whole time I fall.'

I closed my eyes in an attempt to 'get back' the visions I had been seeing over the last couple of days, with no success. I reopened them and looked sorrowfully up at Bryce. 'I don't know how I slipped ...' Tearing my eyes away from his, I dropped my head back down to his chest, feeling stupid for saying it. 'I know ... it's crazy. It's probably just my subconscious trying to help me to feel less guilty. I don't know ...' I sighed. 'If that is the case, it really isn't working.'

'Honey, your mind will play many kinds of tricks on you. It's life's cruel way of getting you to sort through your grief, your guilt and your sadness so that you can move on. It's one of those fucked-up lessons we have to learn.'

I squeezed him tighter, appreciative, but equally saddened by his knowledge of despair. He, of all people, knew how to deal with grief and loss and what steps to take in order to heal. He also knew how to bear guilt.

'Thank you. Thank you for not hating me, because god knows I hate myself.'

'Alexis, I could never hate you. I love you so much, it's unfathomable. Seeing you lying lifeless at the bottom of the stairs scared the absolute shit out of me.' He took a deep breath and exhaled shakily. 'I keep fucking replaying it in my head, and each time it makes me ill. I thought you were dead. Then I saw the blood on your dress and I knew ... well ... I just knew.' He shook his head as if to shake away the horrifying vision. 'I don't want to think about it. You're safe, and you'll heal. We both will.'

He tightened his grip on me gently, without causing any pain. I was still tender and bruised on the ribs and lower abdomen.

We fell asleep that way, holding each other, comforting each other, supporting each other, allowing one another to grieve in a manner that only we knew how. A small part of both our hearts had been torn away and would be lost forever.

I knew deep down that time healed the wounded and heartbroken, and I was confident that time would do just that for us. I knew this, because at the end of this tragedy we had each other and that would never change.

* * *

Day three was kind of a blur. Dr Rainer came to the hospital to explain the details of my miscarriage. She said the force of my pelvis hitting the steps had detached the placenta and ruptured my cervix. She also explained that while I was under anaesthesia for the surgery on my ankle, a dilation and curettage was performed in order to remove the baby and placenta from my uterus.

Dr Rainer also informed us that the hospital had an area named The Garden of Angels. She explained that we could have our baby cremated and that we could sprinkle the ashes in the garden if we wanted. I remembered the counsellor having mentioned this the day after my surgery, but at that time I could not even consider the notion. Now, I liked the idea. It seemed kind of nice; a place where other baby angels were, a place where our baby could rest in peace.

* * *

Mum and Jen visited again before heading home. When Bryce had stepped out to take an important phone call, Mum explained that he had arranged for Chelsea to fly to Shepparton to pick both her and Jen up not long after the accident occurred. She also said that Chelsea was flying them back later that afternoon. I didn't know what to think of that.

The kids were still with Dad at the farm, and both Nate and Charli were none the wiser about my fall. I wanted it to remain that way, at least for the time being. I had no idea how I was going to explain to my children that the baby we had just told them about — the baby they were excited about, the baby that we had all grown to love — was now gone. How was I going to explain that?

I spoke to them briefly on the phone, telling them I missed them and loved them and could not wait to see them both. I told them I was bored, but also busily working. I hated lying to my children, but I'd had to. I'd had to pretend I was good and not in any way hospitalised. Nate would have panicked.

* * *

My orthopaedic surgeon also paid me a visit that day, explaining that he had fixed two screws and a plate to my fibula and that the cast which reached to my knee would more than likely be on for a couple of weeks then eventually replaced with a moon boot, rather than another plaster cast. After that, I would be required to undergo physiotherapy rehabilitation and walk around on crutches for another five to seven weeks. Just the thought of it had me depressed and worried. So much had happened to me and it was all just a bit overwhelming.

* * *

By the fourth day, my brain and physical self were once again starting to work in unison with each other. I was finally able to get out of bed to have a shower, which I was relieved about, but also silently dreading. Bryce, being Bryce, helped me every step of the way.

'Here, take a seat.' He guided me to the plastic chair where I sat down. I watched him strip down and, like always, I admired the view. I was, however, in no mood for anything intimate; nor would I be for some time. I still admired the view though.

'Now, the nurse gave me this cast protector to put over your leg so that you don't get it wet.'

He held out the big plastic cover, bent down and started to put it over my leg. He was so cautious and gentle, it really was adorable.

I stood up with his help, balancing on one leg.

'You okay?' he asked, as he steadied me carefully.

'Yeah, I've had worse pain.'

He brought my hand to his lips. 'I'm sure you have, but if you are in pain, you need to say so. They can give you more medication for it.'

He reached behind me and untied my backless hospital robe then gently pulled it away.

'I know, but really, I'm fine. The pain is sort of a welcome reminder.'

Bryce placed his hands on my shoulders and gazed into my eyes with a look of worry, possibly searching for that slight bit of crazy my last response seemed to indicate. He must not have found it, because he ended his search and turned to get the shower ready.

As I stood there on one leg, braced against the wall, while he adjusted the water temperature, I looked down at my leg and snickered.

'Are you laughing?' he asked, astonished.

I giggled this time. 'Yeah, I think I am.'

He stepped up to me and wrapped one arm around my waist, pressing me to his bare skin and easily lifting me just slightly. Regardless of the trauma I had recently experienced, my body reacted to his just like it always had. My nipples hardened and that electric tingle he charged me with was also present.

He slowly stepped backward with me still attached to his front, stepping us over to the water and holding me tightly as it cascaded around us.

'Why are you laughing?' he asked softly.

'I have a rather large leg condom on,' I replied.

He looked down to inspect my cast cover then looked back up at me, a smirk on his face. The smirk quickly turned into an outburst of laughter. 'Yes, you do. But fuck, you look hot in a leg condom.'

I laughed with him and it felt good. Good to be naked in his supporting arms and laughing with him again. It gave me hope.

Dropping my head to his chest, I subdued my laugh to a soft giggle.

'We will get through this, you know,' he said as he kissed the top of my head, 'and if you want to — and there is no pressure — we can try again.'

I tilted my head and looked into his eyes. I could see he meant no pressure, but at the same time, I could see that he desperately hoped I would want to try again. *Do I want to try again? God, I don't know. I don't know if I can.*

'We don't have to discuss this now. I just wanted you to know that, okay?'

I couldn't give him an answer, not yet anyway. I nodded and cuddled into him again.

Bryce positioned me against the wall, where I held onto the arm supports. 'Okay, my love, let's get you clean.'

I think I fell in love with him all over again as I watched him slowly wash me, kissing me and telling me how much he loved me and could not live without me. I knew then that I would eventually try again. For him, I would do anything.

CHAPTER

16

On the fifth and final day in hospital, Bryce wheeled me down to The Garden of Angels in a wheelchair so that we could scatter our baby's ashes. The garden was beautiful, with an array of different coloured flowers and little handmade wooden signs with words of prayers and love. It really was a magical place that was both sombre and heart-warming at the same time.

The weather was mild with a very light breeze, perfect for what Bryce and I were about to do. We knew we had to do it, but allowing our baby to become an angel in this little garden kind of made the whole miscarriage final, and that was incredibly difficult to accept. I knew I had to accept it though, so I took a deep breath while trying to still my hands, which were shaking uncontrollably as they gripped and tipped the small urn.

As I tipped, the breeze picked up slightly, carrying the ashes across the garden. I matched the whisper of the breeze with a whisper of my own. 'You will be forever in our hearts, little angel. You will always be remembered, cherished, treasured and missed. We love you.'

Tears fell down my cheeks as Bryce and I watched our precious baby's ashes magically flow through the air, once again becoming a part of life — a part of nature. It was terribly hard to do, but at the same time it gave me a sense of calm, knowing that so many other little spirits were surrounding us, helping us, and welcoming our precious one into their midst.

* * *

After saying goodbye to Baby Clark, I was handed a small envelope by a nurse. She explained that when I was ready — if I wanted to open it — it contained a picture of my baby and the details of his or her gender. I didn't know what to do with it, so I handed it to Bryce, then was discharged and allowed to go home.

We pulled into the basement car park in the Cadillac ATS Coupe. I knew straightaway why Bryce chose the Caddy. It was probably the most comfortable of all his cars, and it definitely had the most leg room.

Quickly climbing out of his side of the car, he made his way to my door, opened it and helped me twist around. Then, without any hesitation, he placed one arm behind me and the other under my legs, lifting me up.

'Bryce, I have crutches,' I said, half rolling my eyes and half smiling.

'I know, but I have arms and I enjoy it when you're in them.'

'I need to get used to the crutches, you know.'

'Honey, I'm carrying you. You've got six weeks to get used to those crutches.'

I groaned. 'Don't remind me.'

Deciding not to argue with him at that particular moment was not going to benefit me. Clearly I was not going to win, so I rested my head on his shoulder and watched him close the car door with his foot and head for the elevator.

* * *

When the doors to the apartment opened and we entered, I felt strangely disconcerted upon looking at the stairs. I couldn't explain it. It just made me feel ill, to the point where I felt they were evil, which was incredibly stupid. First of all, stairs are not evil: Freddie Kruger is evil, and so is that hunter who killed Bambi's mum. Secondly, I fell down them: they didn't secretly trip me up.

After staring at the stairs for several seconds, another flashback entered my head. Again, in my recall, I hopped along the walkway that led to the top of stairs, bending down and putting my heels on as I stepped. I recalled stopping, bracing myself on the railing, and wiggling my foot into my shoe, making sure it was perfectly secure. I recalled smiling and looking out over the lounge area in search of Bryce. I recalled taking my first step without a problem. I recalled taking my second step, again without any difficulties. The third step however, I was falling forward — fast — but not tripping. I definitely did not trip.

Bryce's voice broke through my recall. 'Alexis, are you with me? What is it?'

'Um ... sorry, did you say something?' I stuttered, coming back to the present time.

'Yes, I asked where you wanted me to take you. Are you okay? You look a little pale.'

'I just remembered something. I didn't trip, Bryce. I know I didn't trip. My shoes were on just fine. I must've had a problem with my balance or something, but I know I didn't trip.' I was speaking fast, desperate to voice what I had just visualised.

'It's okay, honey. Like you said, maybe you were momentarily off-balance. Either way, it still wasn't your fault. Stop torturing yourself, you can't change it.'

I nodded at him then looked back at the stairs, not wanting to go near them. 'Please don't carry me up them.'

'I wasn't going to,' he said softly, as he kissed my head. 'Where do you want to go though?'

'I don't know. I might just stay where I am,' I raised my eyebrow at him.

'Suits me just fine.' *Of course it does. I wouldn't put it past you to actually carry me all day.*

'No, I'm kidding. Anyway, what are your plans for today? Do you have to work?'

'No, I'm all yours. Arthur has taken on more responsibility, so don't worry about my work. Whatever you want or need, I'm here for you. I'm at your beck and call.'

He remained standing there, holding me in his arms and waiting for my instructions.

'Oh ...' I said, bemused. *I really shouldn't be bemused. This is Mr Perfect-Loving-Caring Clark we are talking about.* 'Well then, in that case take me wherever you want to take me. I'm basically as useless as tits on a bull at the moment.'

He raised his eyebrow. I didn't think he meant to do it seductively. He was kind of being a perfect gentleman. The thing was, this man could not raise an eyebrow without it being seductive.

'I doubt that is true, Alexis. I can think of many things we can do without the use of your leg.' *Okay, he definitely meant it seductively.*

'I'm sure you can, but don't forget, I can't have sex —'

He laughed. 'I haven't forgotten, and no ... I wasn't insinuating that.'

'Oh. What did you have in mind?'

His mischievous, almost childlike grin appeared, and he carried me into the man-cave, placing me gently onto the sofa.

I grabbed his face. 'You are not going to carry me around everywhere.'

'You do not have a choice if I choose to leave your crutches in the car.' He stood back up and winked at me before heading for the door.

'Bryce, what if I need to pee ... or even worse?'

He didn't look back, just laughed. 'I'll carry you,' he asserted.

'Bryce, you can't —'

He exited the room. *Grrr, talk about taking advantage of my inability to walk.*

I shuffled uncomfortably on the couch, feeling the effects of my painkillers wearing off. I quickly calculated when I could take some more. *Two, four, six hours ... now. Good!*

Pulling my phone out from my pocket, I sent Bryce a text:

Seeing as u wish 2 b my immobility-bitch, can u please bring me some water & painkillers ♥ — Alexis

I received a reply straightaway:

Did u just call me a bitch? — Bryce

I giggled. *Shit!*

Yes ... yes, I did. I kinda like the sound of it, don't u? — Alexis

No. U do realise u r going 2 have 2 pay 4 that — Bryce

Pfft, what's he going to do?

Oooh, what r u going 2 do about it? Break my leg? — Alexis

Ok, bad joke. *Really bad joke, Alexis.*

Never mind. I take it back — Alexis

I quickly sent another text:

PS I take back the break leg bit, not the bitch bit. You're still my bitch — Alexis

I typed another, I was now in apology-mode.

PPS I love u by the way — Alexis

I waited for a response. I didn't get one, so I typed again:

Bryce? I'm only kidding. You're not a bitch, I am — Alexis

I still hadn't received a reply minutes later, and after agonisingly waiting yet another minute, I got concerned. I was just about to roll off the sofa and perform some kind of caterpillar manoeuvre in order to go find him — becoming some form of wiggly looper — when a single rose was placed over my head in front of my face. I clasped it as his warm breath caressed my ear.

'One, you're not a bitch. Two, I love you, too. And three, yes ... you will pay for that.'

He gently nipped at my ear lobe then kissed my neck.

I shivered with delight. 'I look forward to "paying", Bryce, but that is going to have to wait for a few weeks.'

He walked around to the front of the sofa and put down a tray which contained a hot white chocolate, an espresso, two muffins, some Tim Tams and a bowl of popcorn. He turned to me and got down on his knees so that his face was level with my own.

'Let me tell you something. When you are ready to make love to me again, you will not be "paying" for anything. I will be the one "paying", paying a considerable amount of attention to making you come in every possible way.'

I swallowed dryly as I processed his words. In the hospital, I'd had a moment of concern as to whether or not I'd be able to have sex again so soon after miscarrying, for fear of ... well ... just, fear. But sitting on the sofa at that very moment, looking at Bryce with eyes full of nothing but want, need, love and worship, I knew that when the time came, I would not hesitate to make love to him again. How could I? Fuck, I wanted to now.

'How do you plan on making me pay then?' I whispered, as I leaned forward and kissed his lips.

He chuckled, broke free and walked over to the stone fireplace to switch it on.

'Well?' I asked again.

He didn't answer, just made his way to the Blu-ray player and popped in a disc. I watched him smile as he sat down on the sofa next to me, then he gently took hold of my perfectly good foot and began to massage it.

'No-oo,' I giggled and cringed.

'Yes! We are sitting here and watching the *Lord of the Rings*, and you, my love, are going to have a foot rub.'

'I hate you,' I said, like I always did.

He looked over at me, and I sensed a slight bit of doubt on his face. I motioned my finger, telling him to come closer to me. He obliged and leaned in further so that our lips could touch.

'No, I don't,' I whispered against his mouth before I kissed him.

* * *

Bryce and I watched *LOTR: The Fellowship of the Ring* before he carried me to the kitchen to watch him cook a kick-arse beef stroganoff. It amazed me. He didn't even put paprika in it and yet it still teased my taste buds with its tasty awesomeness. What also amazed me was that I watched him cook the damn dish and it was so easy, yet it tasted heavenly.

I swore he added a secret ingredient.

He swore he didn't.

I swore he was lying.

He swore that I was going to 'pay' again.

I swore I'd kick him with my cast.

He swore I wouldn't.

I just swore.

* * *

After dinner, we watched *LOTR: The Two Towers*. I must've fallen asleep across Bryce's lap, because the last thing my brain processed was the people of Rohan fleeing to Helm's Deep.

The next thing my brain processed was being laid down in our bed.

'Shit, I fell asleep, sorry,' I said, feeling a bit groggy as I woke up.

'We are now even,' he assured me.

'Yes, we are.' I smiled, remembering when he fell asleep while we were watching *Lady and the Tramp* during our trip to Uluru.

I felt his hands settle on the top of my waistband then, gently, he pulled down the loose yoga pants I was wearing, being extra careful when sliding them over my cast.

His eyes travelled up my legs to my underwear, which were still feminine and pretty. Broken leg, head concussion, heartbreaking miscarriage and subsequent bleeding — I still insisted on having nice underwear. This habit of mine would never be broken. I'd rather wear nothing than wear nanna-knickers.

I could tell Bryce, too, appreciated this habit of mine, because his sight lingered on the navy satin lace brief I was wearing.

Propping myself up on my arms, I watched him crawl up the bed to me, helping me sit up so that he could remove my t-shirt and expose my matching bra. I leaned back on my hands and smiled as he took me in.

'You might want to look away, Mr Clark. Because that look on your face normally means one thing. And that one thing is not going to happen tonight.'

'Honey, there are other things that can happen, starting with this.' He grabbed my face and kissed me softly, yet passionately, causing my arms which were supporting the upper part of my body to go weak and shaky, and slowly collapse, lowering me to the bed.

His lips stayed attached to mine as I lay flat on my back, Bryce now lying by my side. I held him to me as his tongue gently brushed against mine, caressing it delicately over and over as he dragged his knuckle down the side of my cheek to under my chin.

I savoured his touch and our kiss, equally stroking, licking and nipping at his mouth. The sheer love, lust and connection we felt for each other was as ever-present in our kiss as it had always been, and it reassured that we were on the path of healing and would eventually be fine. It also conveyed that we needed each other more than ever.

He broke away from my mouth and pressed his lips to my forehead quite firmly. 'Go back to sleep,' he whispered as he pulled himself back. 'I just want to hold you in my arms and be grateful that you are still here with me.'

'Of course I am still here,' I whispered back as my eyelids got heavy. 'I'm not going anywhere.'

* * *

The following morning, Bryce had to leave for an appointment with Jessica. I asked him if he was okay and reiterated that if ever he felt he needed to talk, I would always be there for him: to listen, to advise, to share. He assured me that he would talk to me if he needed to and that the reason he was seeing Jessica was simply to get an update on Gareth. But I suspected our recent heartbreaking loss was going to be a topic of discussion, which kind of irritated me. It shouldn't have, though, because Dr Jessica Carrot-top was his psychologist and had been for a long time. Therefore, it shouldn't bother me that he would talk to her and tell her things that he would not tell me.

But I couldn't deny that I was jealous.

I think it was probably because she was a stuck-up, toffee-nosed bitch more than anything. Regardless of my immature insecurities and dislike for Dr Jessica, I was glad he talked about his feelings rather than bottled them up. I appreciated that fact.

Bryce kissed me deeply before leaving, just as the doors to the elevator opened and Lucy entered the apartment. He broke away from me slightly breathless, winked and walked toward her. She gave him a long embrace while talking quietly to him and intermittently rubbing his back. Tears filled my eyes at seeing her love and support for her brother. It really was touching.

'I won't be long,' he said to her as he stepped into the lift.

'Go, it's fine. She'll be fine. I've got this.'

'Thanks.'

He turned to me and blew a kiss as the doors closed. It was then that it dawned on me that he had arranged for Lucy to visit and babysit me while he was gone. *Caring, over-protective arse.* I was capable of babysitting myself for an hour or so.

Lucy made her way over to where I was on the sofa. 'Alexis, I am so sorry. I can't imagine what you are feeling right now and I'm not even going to begin to try. Just know I am here for you, whatever you need.' She sat next to me and leaned in for a gentle hug.

'Thank you, Lucy. I'm okay. Just you being there for your brother is all that I need.'

'Don't worry. I'm keeping my eye on him.'

I let out a breath. 'Good, I'm relieved to hear that. So far he has been open about the whole ordeal, but I worry about him, being that he is a controlling stubborn arse at times.'

'Yes, he is that, and more, Alexis. But he and I have both learned from past experiences that it is best to be open about our feelings rather than to close them in and pretend they do not exist. Don't worry. He'll talk to me if he needs to.'

I smiled at her sorrowfully. Not because I did not believe her, but because it was obvious she knew exactly what she was talking about due to their sad history — and that was sad in itself.

'I hope so. He desperately wanted this baby and I think he may be keeping it together for my sake. The thing is, I'm coping. I'm okay. Obviously, I'm devastated, but life does go on. I can't bring my baby back. I can't reverse the clock and decide to take the elevator instead of the stairs. I just can't. All I can do is move on and treasure the time I had when my baby was a part of me. All I can do is remember and be grateful.'

'You are a strong woman, and Bryce is a strong man. You were both meant for each other. You'll see. He'll be fine, too, just like you. Knowing my brother, he will break at some point, then he will find the strength that you obviously already have. Now, I am going to make you a cup of tea. Sit back and relax. I'm here to wait on you hand and foot — Bryce's orders.'

Lucy made me a cup of tea and we talked about the things we had always talked about. I asked her how Alexander was, and at first she tried to change the subject. It was obvious when I asked her if he had rolled over yet and she dismissively said, 'Yes, two days ago,' as though it was nothing, and then proceeded to talk about politics.

'Luce, it's fine. I can talk about babies, especially your adorable little son. Is that why he's not here with you? Because you thought seeing him would make me upset?'

She nodded apologetically. 'He's at home with Nic, but he's sick and miserable and very clingy. He had a slight temperature last night.'

'Luce, go home then. I'm fine. You should be with Alexander, not here babysitting me.'

'No, it's okay, Nic is with him. She'll cope.' Her voice did not sound confident.

'Lucy Clark. Go home, now! Bryce will be back soon. My arse is pretty much stuck on this sofa, so GO!'

'Are you sure? Bryce will kill me,' she said, as she bit down on her thumbnail.

'I'll handle your brother, don't you worry.'

She smiled. 'I know you will. That's what I love most about you. You have an uncanny form of control over my brother. No one else has even come close to having that type of power over him — no one.'

I smiled at her words, because at times I felt I had no power over him at all. He had made it quite clear on numerous occasions that he holds the upper hand. Speaking of which, I realised I needed my crutches.

'Can you do one thing for me before you go, though?'

'Sure. What is it?'

'Get my crutches from the basement car park. Your control freak of a brother left them down there so I would have no choice but to let him carry me around.'

She burst out laughing. 'He's good, I'll give him that. Sure, I'll go get them now.'

* * *

Lucy found my crutches and placed them next to the sofa before she left.

I was just about to start my new book about a young girl who discovers her true identity, when the buzzer to the door rang. *Fuck! Of course, as soon as I'm alone and in the mood for a fictional happily-ever-after, I get a visitor. Just my luck.*

I slowly got up and, with the assistance of the crutches, hobbled over to the door.

The buzzer sounded a few more times during my journey there. *Okay, okay! Hold your fuckin' horses, you impatient pain in the arse.*

I pressed the buzzer and in a frustrated tone, answered. 'Yes?'

'Alexis, it's me.' Rick's voice spoke back to me.

Shit! He still doesn't know about my accident. Shit, shit. I can't deal with him right now.

I pushed the buzzer and spoke again. 'Rick, now is really not a good time.'

Almost instantly, he responded. 'Open the door. We need to talk.' His tone seemed slightly more irritated.

I pushed the button again. 'Are you still having the kids next week for the holidays?' I asked, figuring that I'd better clarify this while the opportunity presented itself.

'Yes, of course. Why? Open the door. Why aren't you opening the door?' he asked again with annoyance and a tone of confusion.

'Good. That's all we needed to talk about then. Now please, Rick, go. I can't get into an argument with you right now.' *Please just go. Please just go.*

'Alexis. Stop being a fucking child and open the fucking door. You could be carrying my baby and we need to talk about it,' he shouted, angrily.

My heart started pounding, and I felt dizzy. I braced myself against the wall as tears started to flood my eyes and face.

I pushed the button again, clearly speaking through sobs. 'Please, Rick, just leave me alone. I can't do this.'

'Alexis, you can't avoid me. This is too serious. You can't honestly tell me that there is absolutely no chance that the baby could be mine.' His tone had softened a little, but he was still persisting.

'Yes, I can,' I struggled to say through whimpers and gritted teeth.

'How can you possibly fucking know?' he shouted again.

At that point, I couldn't take it any more, I was beyond upset. He was not going to let this go, so I slammed my fist onto the button and screamed into the intercom. 'Because I am no longer carrying a baby, you fuck! I fell. I lost it. I fucking lost my baby. Now fuck off and leave me alone.'

There was silence for what felt like minutes as I propped myself against the wall crying and reliving my horrific memories, guilt and grief flowing back through me.

'Alexis,' he said, his voice not much louder than a whisper. 'Alexis ... fuck, I'm so sorry. Please open the door. I need to know you are okay. Are you alone? Where is Bryce?'

I slumped against the intercom and pressed it with a heavy hand. 'He is at an appointment. Just go, Rick, I'm fine.'

'Alexis. Open the door, now ... please ... I'm begging you.' His tone was now full of concern, and he was pleading, so I surrendered and opened the door.

He practically burst through, ready to hug me when he saw my foot was in a cast.

Rick put his hand over his mouth and the other through his hair. 'Jesus! Shit! What happened?'

I wiped my face and glared at him then turned and made my way back to the sofa. 'I told you. I fell.'

He put his hands around my shoulders, trying to help me walk. 'Where? How? When?'

I shrugged them off. 'Don't. I can do it myself.' I reached the sofa and sat down.

Rick didn't hesitate and sat right down beside me. 'Alexis, I'm sorry. Talk to me. What happened?'

'I fell down the stairs. I knocked myself out. I broke my ankle and I lost my baby. That's it,' I answered dryly.

He placed his hand on my back and gently rubbed. 'When did this happen?'

'A couple of days after my party. I was in hospital for five days after that, I got out yesterday.'

'Do the kids know yet?'

He seemed really concerned. I think he also knew that Nate and Charli would be devastated.

'No, they are still at Mum and Dad's house. Bryce and I were going to pick them up tomorrow so that they were ready for their time with you on Monday.' My tear-bank broke again and I sobbed harder this time. 'I don't know how I'm going to tell them, Rick. I don't think I am ready to tell them, but they'll know. They are both smart kids.'

He wrapped his arm around my shoulder and pulled me to him. 'Don't worry about that. You obviously need more time. I will drive to Shepparton tomorrow and pick them up. That way you can have this week to sort through everything that you need to sort through. I know I can't do much for you, but I can do that. I can give you the extra time you need.'

'Thank you, Rick.' I hugged him back.

At that moment, the elevator doors opened and Bryce walked in.

CHAPTER
17

'What the fuck are you doing here?' Bryce hissed at Rick as he stepped out of the elevator.

I began to speak. 'Bryce —'

He stormed over to the sofa. 'Get your hands off Alexis, and get the fuck out of my home,' he growled.

He was furious.

Rick stood up. 'Bryce, settle down, I'm consoling her. Clearly she is upset. And who are you to tell me not to touch Alexis?'

'Rick —' I tried to talk again, but no one seemed to be listening to me.

'*I* will console her, not you. You have no right to fucking help her grieve the loss of our baby, *my* baby.'

Oh, no, this is why he is so upset. He thinks I was letting Rick grieve.

'Bryce, it wasn't —' I began to explain, but I was cut off yet again.

'Who said it was your baby, Bryce? It could've been mine.'

'Rick! It wasn't your baby. I told —'

Before I could finish what I was saying, Bryce had thrown a punch which connected perfectly with Rick's jaw.

I screamed. 'Bryce! Stop! No!'

Rick recovered quickly and barrelled into Bryce's stomach, with his head down and his arms wrapped around Bryce's waist in an attempt to take him to the ground.

I screamed again.

Rick was obviously no match for Bryce, not only in size, but also in combat, self-defence and fighting skills, as Bryce was able to get Rick in a headlock and subdue him gently, slowly squeezing the air out of him.

I tried to stand up, putting pressure on my foot, forgetting that I had a broken leg. I cried out in pain.

'Alexis!' Bryce let go of Rick — who fell to the floor — and dashed over to me. 'Shit! Are you okay?'

'No!' I screamed at him, now in a considerable world of pain. 'I'm not fucking okay. I'm not okay at all.'

Rick was on his hands and knees coughing, attempting to get his breath back.

Bryce didn't even look over at him. Instead, his eyes were on mine. 'What can I do, honey?' His voice had softened and it was laced with regret and concern.

'Nothing! You've done enough.' I turned to look at Rick. 'Rick, are you okay?'

'Yes,' he spluttered.

'Good. I think you should leave.'

He looked up at me, registering that I just wanted him to go. 'Fine, I'll ring Maryann and Graeme and tell them I'm coming to get the kids. Don't worry about them. Like I said, that's the least I can do.'

Bryce looked at Rick then back to me, suddenly comprehending that the encounter he walked in on was about Nate and Charli, nothing else.

He dropped his head. 'Fuck! I'm sorr—'

I cut him off. 'Don't.'

Rick got up. 'I'll let myself out.' He stopped midway to the door. 'Alexis, again, I'm sorry for your loss.'

I looked up at him and nodded. 'Can you get the kids to FaceTime me? I really need to see their faces.'

'Sure, not a problem,' he replied, then he left.

* * *

I started crying again, then quickly reeled myself in, shuffling up to reach my crutches. Bryce snatched them away.

'Give them back,' I hissed.

'No. Where do you want to go? I'll take you,' he pleaded.

'No, you won't. I just want to be alone.'

'Honey, I'm sorry. I just saw you both together hugging, and you were crying, and I fucking lost it. I thought you were both —'

'I know what you thought, Bryce. And if you had given me a chance I would've explained.' I tried to push myself up to a standing position, but he dropped to his knees in front of me and placed his hands on my hips, holding me down.

He surrendered and slumped his head onto my lap. 'I thought Rick was grieving the loss of my baby like it was his. He has no right to grieve what I lost.'

He broke at that moment and sobbed into my lap. *Lucy said he'd break at some point. This must be it.*

'Oh, Bryce.' I placed my hands in his hair, and his hands slid to my arse, gripping it tightly, and hugging me like he would never let go.

We stayed like that for minutes. I let him cry and I cried along with him.

* * *

Bryce and I allowed some uninterrupted time to comfort each other. We promised we would be honest and upfront with one another about what we were feeling and why we were feeling it. This assurance alone seemed to help with our grieving and healing process. Although we also kind of kept our distance from each other for much of the day, Bryce spending time in his office and the kitchen, while I read my book in between taking long gazes out across the skyline of the city of Melbourne.

I decided I would ring Mum as she had texted me numerous times since heading back to Shepparton. I knew she was worried about me — she was a mum, of course she was worried — so I figured I'd better ease her mind with a phone call.

'Hi, Mum.'

'How are you coping?' she asked, without delay.

I sipped the cup of tea Bryce had made me prior to ringing her. 'I'm doing okay, Mum. More so if I don't think about it. I know that's not a healthy approach, but it's working for me at the moment, so I'm sticking with it.'

'As long as you don't bury what needs repair, Alexis. Life's problems cannot be resolved if they are buried. We bury what is finished, obsolete. We bury what we cannot restore. Grief can be overcome. It can be addressed and alleviated. Remember that.'

'I'm not burying anything, Mum. Bryce and I have talked, and I know I have you, Jen and my friends if I need you. I just don't right now. I'm coping; life goes on. What has happened cannot be reversed. Moving forward is my only option.'

'Okay, sweetheart. How is Bryce coping?'

Mum knew when to let things go.

'Clearly, he is devastated.' I paused for the smallest of seconds. 'I have decided to try again, Mum, but I haven't told him yet. I'll tell him when the time is right.'

'Are you sure, Alexis?' she asked, sounding neither enthusiastic nor apprehensive.

'I want to give him a child, Mum. He deserves a child of his own.' I sipped my tea, which was now lukewarm.

'Answer me honestly. Are you trying to give Bryce another baby because you feel guilty and responsible for losing the one you had?'

I replied in a calm voice. 'No, Mum, I am not doing this out of guilt. I'm doing it because I want to. I want another baby. I want Bryce's baby.' I took in a breath and let it out slowly. 'Being pregnant again felt so good, so right. At first I was hesitant about having another child, but I grew to love the idea. Knowing that I was going to hold another baby that I created filled me with so much joy and happiness. I desperately want that back, so I am going to get it back. Why? Because I can and because I want to.'

I heard her sigh down the phone, but it wasn't a bad sigh. I think it was a content sigh.

'Very well, darling. I just want you to be happy.'

'Don't worry, Mum. I will be, eventually.'

I hung up from Mum after having a quick word to the kids. Apparently Nate had helped Dad deliver a calf.

Dad was overly proud.

Nate said he never wanted to do it again.

And Charli had reinforced the decision that she definitely did not want to be a veterinarian any more.

I smiled at the thought of my kids witnessing and participating in a Blaxlo farming rite of passage, then dialled Carls' number.

'What up, Duffy?' she answered, with a playful, carefree tone.

I dropped my head. Strangely enough, I did not feel sad at her pregnancy stab. This was Carls, after all, and she was renowned for putting her foot in it.

'Not up the duff any more, hon. I lost the baby,' I said sadly, but not sadly enough to make her feel bad. I didn't want to make her feel bad. Carls was Carls and I loved her just the way she was.

There was silence on the other end, then I swear I heard her sob.

'Carls? You there?'

'Uh huh,' she said.

'You all right?' I asked.

She scoffed then sniffed. 'I just shamefully make a joke about you being pregnant when you're no longer pregnant, and you ask me if I'm all right? What's fucking wrong with this picture?' She sounded angry with herself.

'Carls, how were you to know?'

'It doesn't matter,' she sulked. 'I'm a bitch, a horrible best friend.'

'You are not ... well ... you are a bitch, but you are definitely not a horrible best friend.'

'Yeah, well ... I disagree. So what happened, Lex? Do you want to talk about it?'

'Sure. There's not too much to say really. I fell down the stairs, broke my ankle and miscarried,' I explained, insipidly.

'Jesus, fuck! When did this happen?'

'Monday, just past. I was in hospital pretty much all last week.'

'Right. I'm coming over there.'

'No. I actually just want to be with Bryce, Carls. But thank you.'

'Oh, poor Bryce. He was really looking forward to being a dad. How is he?'

'He's coping. Anyway, hon, as you can imagine, I need to call a few people, and next on my list is Tash. I will need a moment to prepare myself, so I'd better get going.'

Carls laughed, mildly. 'I understand. Okay, if you need me for anything, please call. I love you, you know.'

'I do know. I love you too. Bye.'

I hung up and wiped a tear from my eye. Carly Josephine Henkley never cried.

Realising that I was just a bit too emotional to call Tash after calling Mum and Carls, I decided I would ring her later after I had gathered some semblance of composure.

I propped myself up on my crutches and hopped back into the kitchen where Bryce was cooking something that smelled insanely fucking good. Twitching my nose like a sniffer dog, I sat myself down on the stool at the bench.

'How did it go?' he asked while stirring a pot. *Man, he makes cooking look damn sexy.*

'Sorry? Oh, two down, one to go. I figured I needed to brace myself before calling Tash. I will do it after dinner.'

'That's probably a good idea,' he agreed.

'What are you cooking?' I stretched my upper body so I could peek into the pot.

'Well, I know you like Thai food, so I thought I would try a massaman curry with coconut rice.'

'Is this your way of saying sorry for earlier?' I probed.

'Honey, my methods of apology normally involve you moaning. This is an alternative.'

I sniffed in a big breath and licked my lips. 'Oh, trust me. I'm pretty sure that it will make me moan.'

His eye twitched and I smiled.

As we sat down to eat dinner, the door buzzer sounded. Bryce got up and answered it, letting Samantha into the penthouse. She was holding an enormous bunch of flowers.

'Hi, Alexis. These came for you just now.'

'Oh.' I manoeuvred my chair backward, so that they would fit on my lap.

She handed them over. 'I'll get going, I don't mean to interrupt. And Alexis, I'm very sorry for what happened to you.' She smiled sheepishly and quickly made her way to the door. Bryce let her out.

By the time he made his way back, I had found the card:

I'm so sorry, Lexi. Am I still a bitch? — Carls ♥

I smiled, replaced the card back into the bouquet and sniffed the pink roses.

'Who are the flowers from?'

'Carls,' I replied while reaching into my pocket for my phone. I pulled it out and typed her a one word in response:

No — Lexi ♥

After dinner, I called Tash. She had been angry, sad, quiet, shocked, sad again, and eventually numb. I'd run through all those emotions again with her, feeling her deep sincerity at my loss. We cried together, and she insisted on coming to see me. But again, like I had with Carls, I informed Tash that I just wanted time with Bryce. She reluctantly respected my decision, but made me promise that when I was ready for visitors to let her know.

I promised her I would.

After hanging up from Tash I sat on my own in silence, my mind wandering, allowing more memories of my fall to filter through and present themselves for deliberation. I couldn't erase the visions and, as a result, I couldn't shake the feeling of something sinister being involved in the whole ordeal.

At first, I thought it was my mind's natural defence mechanism kicking in, reassuring me once again that I was not to blame; something or someone else was. But the more vivid the feelings and senses became, the more I felt they were not a result of my guilty conscience. Instead, they were more the result of a physical warning — an alarm, even.

I couldn't fathom what they really meant, so I just pushed them to the back of my mind.

* * *

The following day Bryce and I went for a walk together through the shopping precinct. I really liked the idea of getting out of the apartment, but I could not walk far. My skinny, muscleless arms were not fond of supporting crutches.

I persevered though, and enjoyed my new surroundings.

'Do you feel proud when you walk through this complex?' I asked, personally impressed with his accomplishments.

He looked down at me. 'Yeah, of course I do. Look at the place. It's fucking awesome.'

I laughed at him and looked around once again. 'Yeah, it kind of is.'

During the scan of my surroundings, I noticed a shop attendant in Prada quickly look away, pretending she had not just been caught staring at me. *Um, hello, you stick out like dog's balls. Own it.*

I ignored her, but it bothered me.

We kept walking — or in my case, hobbled — and I soon became aware of more people watching us. I hated it.

My hands had become sweaty, and I started to feel a little clammy.

'Alexis, what's wrong? Are you okay?'

'I'm fine, I'm just hot. Are you hot?' I removed the light scarf I had around my neck, but it didn't help.

'No, honey,' he replied, concerned. 'Let's go to the lobby and take a seat.'

We made our way to the City Towers front office and Bryce made me take a seat next to the water feature that sat in the middle of the extravagant lobby. I took deep breaths, but felt a sudden surge of helplessness course through me.

'I think you're having a panic attack. Just breathe.' He began rubbing my back and I noticed him motion Liam over.

'Yes, sir?' Liam asked. He awaited Bryce's instruction while looking at me with concern.

'Can you please get Alexis a glass of water?'

'Of course.' Liam hurried off.

Almost instantly, Abigail was crouched down at my side, Samantha standing beside her and Chelsea next to Bryce.

'What's wrong, dear?' Abigail asked.

I couldn't answer her. I tried, but my mouth wouldn't open. I honestly felt that everyone was staring at me, secretly thinking that my losing the baby was a result of karma, and they thought I deserved it. It filled me with such dread that I started to feel light-headed then, all of a sudden, there was black — nothing.

* * *

When I came to, I was lying on the sofa in our apartment. Bryce, Abigail and Janette were standing in the lounge room, not too far from me.

I opened my eyes. 'What happened?' I murmured, confused.

Bryce came over and sat on the seat next to me, gently moving the hair out of my eyes. 'You had a panic attack. Your blood pressure dropped and you fainted.'

I tried to sit up.

Janette moved closer. 'Stay there, with your feet up. At least until your blood pressure returns to normal. It is still a little low. I will take a reading again shortly.'

I closed my eyes, briefly remembering what happened downstairs. 'Everyone was staring at me. I didn't like it.'

Bryce dragged his knuckle along my jaw and my eyes reopened. 'No, honey, they weren't.' He smiled at me. 'Then again, you are incredibly beautiful, so you could be right.'

I gave a weak smile in return. 'I thought they were judging me,' I explained.

'Why would anyone judge you?' Abigail asked.

'I don't know.' I brushed off her question. I didn't want to answer it honestly in front of anyone.

The door buzzer sounded.

'I'll be right back.' Bryce kissed my forehead before he stood up to go to the door.

I tilted my head and watched him leave when Janette stepped into my line of sight. 'Okay, let's take your blood pressure again.'

She pressed the stethoscope attachment into the crook of my arm and began pumping air into the pressure cuff wrapped around my bicep. The cuff tightened, then slowly relaxed and loosened again. 'Good, it's going back up. You can sit now, but do it slowly. No fast movements or actions, okay?'

I sat up just as Bryce entered the room, opening the door for Jessica. *Oh, fuck no. Why not invite Chelsea, Gareth and the bitchy mum from school. They can have a 'We hate Alexis convention'. She had better be here to see Bryce.*

They made their way toward me; it was quite obvious she was not here to see Bryce.

My eyes widened and pierced Bryce's. 'No, Bryce,' I said sternly. 'Definitely not.'

'Alexis, clearly you need to speak to someone.'

'Okay, I will, but someone else. No offence, Jessica.' *Actually, yes offence. Plenty of offence for you.*

'Alexis, please let me help you,' she said kindly. *Oh my god. She is like a mix of Glinda the Good Witch of the North and Cruella De Vil.*

'I don't need any help. I'm fine!' I snapped.

I hadn't noticed that Abigail and Janette had already been escorted out of the room by Bryce.

'You are blaming yourself for the miscarriage, are you not,' she asked, or more accurately, stated. Her tone was still kind though.

'Not,' I answered quickly, while looking around for my crutches. *Where the fuck are my crutches? I'm going to fucking kill my Mr I'm-Carrying-You Clark.*

'You feel guilty.'

'No.'

'You're scared.'

'No.'

'You think you deserve punishment.'

'Yes,' I answered honestly, by accident. *Shit!* 'No, I mean no. Bryce, where are my crutches?'

He shrugged his shoulders.

'Don't fucking play this game with me. I want my crutches, now!'

He looked down at his hands.

'Bryce, please,' I begged him.

'I'm sorry, Alexis. I love you and want you to talk, to heal. Jessica can help.'

'No, she can't.'

'Yes, she can.'

'No,' I screamed at him.

'Give her a fucking chance, Alexis,' he shouted back. 'I don't want to see you lying unconscious any more. I can't handle that, it fucking kills me. Please just talk to her. Fuck!' He got up and stormed to the elevator then turned back to face us. 'Jessica, make her talk to you. Do what you have to. I don't fucking care what it takes.' He slammed his hand on the button. 'Alexis, I fucking love you.' He stepped into the lift and left the room.

I sat there stunned for god knows how long, then moved my gaze to Jessica. She was staring at the elevator doors, smiling fondly. I'm guessing her fondness was for the man who had just angrily left the room. It pissed me off even more. *Get that look off your face now, before I hop over there and wipe it off.*

I'd had just about enough.

'I'm so proud of him,' she said in awe. *What?*

I didn't answer, but she continued to talk.

'He has come so far since the death of his parents and his brother. At one point, I thought I would never again see the bright, intelligent young man my best friend gave birth to and raised.' She turned to me and smiled. *Best friend?*

'Stephanie adored Bryce. She was always doting over him. He was her pride and joy. She loved all three of her kids equally, but Bryce had a special connection with his mother.'

I was speechless, so I sat there and continued to listen.

'Stephanie and I went to college together. She was a social sciences graduate and her philosophy on life was truly unique. We hit it off instantly. After she married Lindsay and gave birth to Bryce, her priorities changed, but her outlook on life never did. She was a fantastic mother, and Bryce was a real mummy's boy.'

I smiled. *Yeah, I can actually imagine that.*

'She brought Bryce up to be passionate, outgoing, ambitious and charming. All the qualities a young man would require to go far in life. She was so proud of him. When she died, something in Bryce died too. His passion diminished, he was no longer outgoing, his ambition turned to determination and his charm faded considerably,' she said sadly as she stood up.

She walked across to the grand piano and ran her finger along it. 'Has he played the piano for you?'

'No, I've never seen him go near it. He has always played the guitar for me.'

She raised her eyebrows at me, knowingly. 'He's very good, isn't he? This might break doctor-patient confidentiality, but he did just say "Do what you have to. I don't fucking care what it takes", didn't he?'

'He did,' I agreed.

'Well, he loves that you love watching him play the guitar. When he told me about the first time he played for you, he was beyond happy. He was boasting.' *Oh! My! God! He told her about that. I'll kill him.*

I blushed.

'Oh, don't worry. He didn't give me the details.' *Thank fuck.* 'Alexis, Bryce has come a long way over the years. But it wasn't until he met you that he got that spark back. Whatever had died in him, you managed to resurrect. I have never seen a person so devoted, so in awe of their love, so *in* love before. At first I thought it might be unhealthy, but over the past eight months I've come to realise that he absolutely adores you and wants nothing more than your happiness.'

Tears began to fall down my cheeks. 'I know,' I admitted.

'If you're not happy, he is not happy.'

'I know, I feel the same way.' I was sobbing again.

She came back to the couch and sat next to me, handing me a tissue.

'He is absolutely terrified of losing you. Not just physically, but mentally. He knows what it feels like to lose someone both physically and mentally.'

I looked up at her. 'Gareth?' I whispered.

'Yes, Gareth,' she confirmed. 'Alexis, please let me help you get through this. I want to help you, not only for Bryce, but for you. I have a deep respect for the woman who snared Mr Bryce Clark's heart.'

I stared at her wide-eyed. 'Okay.'

Dr Jessica was not so bad after all.

CHAPTER
18

Nate and Charlotte FaceTimed me the following day. I had missed them terribly, having only briefly talked to them on the phone a couple of times since last seeing them. I desperately wanted them to come home, but I had to regain a good frame of mind before I let them see me, and before I explained to them what had happened over a week ago. The good thing was, I had a positive outlook now and truly believed Jessica would help me get to the good frame of mind that I needed. It had felt nice talking with her and I looked forward to talking to her again. We had arranged to meet every day for the coming week, and I felt terrible that I had made the wrong assumption about her. A book's cover did not always reflect its contents.

* * *

Bryce and I had made up when he returned after his false-imprisonment ploy. He had been right in doing it and he had the best intentions, though, so I could not stay mad at him. We were starting to get on each other's nerves, however, and we would deliberately bait each other over the smallest things. I was starting to think it had more to do with sexual frustration than anything else.

One of the things I did that was getting on his nerves was trying to scratch underneath my cast. It was so goddamned itchy, and I couldn't wait until the following Monday to have the cast removed and the moon boot fitted. In the meantime, I was desperate to relieve the horrid irritating sensation on my leg, and I was doing it using any means possible. This was pissing Bryce off, and the fact that he was trying to stop me from doing it was pissing me off.

* * *

I woke up Tuesday morning fidgeting, trying to scratch a really deep spot down near my ankle which was practically impossible to reach.

'Alexis, for fuck's sake, stop scratching,' he groaned into his pillow.

'That's easy for you to say. You don't have a tube of plaster attached to your leg irritating the shit out of you.' I stuck my finger back down into the cast, but it fell way short of the spot.'

'You have been tossing and turning all night,' he growled.

'I know. I'm the one who has been doing the tossing and the turning.'

I got out of bed, hopped to the bathroom and opened the vanity cupboard. *Excellent.* I grabbed Bryce's comb and wedged it down into my cast, relieving the annoying tingling.

'Oh yeah, that's what I'm talking about,' I purred with relief.

'What are you doing?' he called out from the bedroom.

'Nothing, mind your own business,' I called back, smiling and lapping up the respite by happily pulling the comb up and down my leg.

'Honey, stop that.' He was out of bed and standing in the doorway. 'The surgeon said not to poke things down into your cast.'

'No! I don't care what the friggin' surgeon said. He is a hypocrite. He put this stupid, heavy, irritating, ugly piece of shit on my leg. He does not get to tell me not to itch.' I scratched a little more, desperately trying to push the comb in deeper.

'Alexis, give me that. Hang on a minute, is that my comb?' he questioned, with eyebrows raised.

'Yes, it is.'

He put his hand out.

I yanked the comb back out and threw it at his chest. 'I hate you.'

He laughed. 'No, you don't.'

I hopped past him. 'Right now? Yes, yes, I do.'

* * *

Bryce and I had been working sporadically over the past week. He'd told me that I didn't need to, and that Abigail and Lucy were sharing my workload. It's just, I wanted to work. It helped keep my mind from travelling back to the events of the accident. I still couldn't stop the flashbacks, and Jessica was working on methods to help me with it.

She had helped me immensely throughout the week. Her covert talent in making me open up to her completely was obviously a good thing. I was functioning again, thinking clearly and not stepping off my path to recovery, or not as much: I still had moments of self-defeating behaviour. Now that I was back at work, sporadically or not, I enjoyed the distraction, but I still kind of felt useless, a hindrance, a burden even.

Ever since I had taken on the role of PA to Bryce, I had brought nothing but dramas to the job; mostly as a result of his inclusion in my life, but regardless, I still felt someone else could do the job better than me. I didn't want to disrupt his business life as I had disrupted his personal life.

Jessica had told me to tell Bryce everything I was feeling when I was feeling it. I had also told myself this before having my talk with Jessica, but I guess her being a professional and instructing me to do it pushed the thought into an action.

I hit the button on my phone and buzzed Bryce in his office.

'Yeah?' he answered in his sexy, I'm-a-busy-billionaire-businessman voice.

'I think you should replace me,' I said quite frankly.

'Excuse me?' he replied, uncertainty in his tone.

'I suck and I'm a nuisance. There are plenty of other women who are better than me,' I explained.

'Alexis, can you come in here for a moment, please,' he said softly, but still businesslike.

'No, I can't.'

'Alexis!'

'Bryce! I quit.' *There, I said it. That wasn't too hard now, was it?*

His door opened suddenly and he walked out into the foyer.

'You want to talk?' he asked.

I shook my head.

'You want me to talk?'

I shook my head again.

'You want me to come over there, pick you up, carry you upstairs and spank your sexy arse?' he said, quite casually.

I thought about it. *Hmm, actually yes, that does sound like a good idea.*

He noticed my pause and made his way to my desk.

'No,' I said quickly, with apprehension and playfulness in my voice. *Shit! Too late.*

I grabbed hold of my desk just in time, as he bent down and put his arms gently behind my back and under my legs.

'Let go,' he demanded, a look of dominance and desire in his eyes.

I bit my lip and shook my head quickly, feeling my control dwindle.

'If you don't let go of this desk now, I will pick it up, or drag it along with us,' he breathed in my ear. 'Your choice.'

I believed him, so I let go.

He lifted me up and carried me directly to the elevator.

'Are you really going to spank me?' I asked curiously as we ascended.

'Do you want me to?'

'Maybe. Do you think I deserve it?' I raised my eyebrow at him.

'Oh, yes. I found one of my drumsticks wedged in your cast last night after you fell asleep on the sofa, so you definitely deserve it.' *Oh, shit! Remember to hide the evidence, Alexis, you fool.*

'Damn it,' I said ruefully.

He carried me to the bedroom and placed me down on the bed, then very carefully climbed on top of me, holding his weight and securing my hands above my head.

'You are not quitting. You are not a nuisance and you do not suc—' He cut himself off. 'Well, you do suck, but in a very, *very* good way.'

I rolled my eyes at him.

'So, tell me what's going on in that head of yours, or I will call Jessica or spank it out of you.' He leaned forward and kissed my neck. *Oh, god that feels good. How long has it been since we've made love? Fuck, I can't remember.* 'Well?' he said, waiting for me to divulge.

I moaned a little. 'I'm a walking disaster,' I breathed out.

He dragged his tongue down my neck and kissed my collarbone, my chest rising to meet his lips.

'No, you're a limping miracle,' he said with a husky voice as he made his way back up my neck to my ear lobe.

I clenched his hands in mine and moaned again. 'I'm hopeless.'

He released one of my hands and placed it on the outside of his pants so that I could feel his hard cock. 'Clearly you are not, honey.'

Mm, clearly you are a god, Bryce.

I had the sudden urge to have his delicious erection in my mouth. I needed to feel him, taste him. I needed to feel I was in control of something. I knew I had nothing but control when my lips were around his cock. I could control his orgasm and his relief and the feeling I now had at the thought of what I was about to do filled me with a sense of value.

'I suck,' I exclaimed, as I tried to lift my head from the pillow to meet his.

He leaned back, refusing my request for his mouth. 'No, you don't.'

'No, I do and I want to suck right now.'

His eyes changed within a second from endearing and heavy, to hot, hankering and alive with expectation.

Dropping his head to mine, he finally allowed my tongue to find his, kissing me passionately.

'Are you sure, my love? We can wait longer if you want.'

I pushed him off so that he rolled onto his back, lying next to me.

'Yes, I'm sure. I want you in my mouth. I don't want to wait any more.'

Positioning myself onto my side and making sure my ankle was comfortable, I undid his pants and unleashed his hard cock into my hand. Just the sight of it so gloriously close made me smile.

I cupped his balls, then dragged my hand from the base to the tip, licking my finger and swirling it over his crown.

'Fuck!' he groaned.

I gave him a salacious grin before I wrapped my mouth around him, taking in as much as I could and gently clamping my lips down. I could feel his soft, warm skin beneath them. He felt and tasted so good, I couldn't get enough.

Bryce placed his hand on my head, gently clenching his fingers in my hair. 'So good, honey,' he slurred.

My smile at his enjoyment and praise circled his shaft and I began to escalate my movement over him, repeating the consumption of his length over and over.

He moaned and growled explicit words which made me feel hot and empowered, helping me take charge even more and forcing the taste of his enjoyment into my mouth. I dragged my tongue up and down, flicking the spots I knew were sensitive to him. He bucked his hips and pushed himself further into my mouth, and I accepted his offering by sucking him deep.

'Fuck, I love you,' he hissed as he reached his climax, jerking into me.

I lapped him up and savoured the moment of being, once again, in control of a part of my life that I enjoyed. A part he obviously enjoyed, too.

* * *

Shortly after I literally blew Bryce's mind, and after he spanked my arse for quitting my job, we had a visitor. The joy and sense of self I had felt after sharing an intimate moment with Bryce had not lasted long, ending abruptly when Gareth entered the apartment.

'I just wanted to personally come by and offer my condolences to you both. I heard about the fall and subsequent miscarriage, and the broken foot. I'm terribly sorry. I also wanted to apologise for skipping out on your birthday party. I felt very ill quite suddenly and needed to lie down,' he said immediately, sitting down on the couch opposite me. It felt like no time at all before my chest started rising and falling dramatically and the heat in the room also seemed to be rising quickly.

Bryce had made his way over to the bar to fetch us all a drink.

'I need something strong,' I said as I locked eyes with Gareth, desperately trying to calm myself.

'Do you want a gin then?' Bryce asked.

Removing my stare from Gareth, I switched it toward Bryce while wiping my sweaty hands on my pants. 'Yes, gin is great,' I replied rather quickly.

'So, Alexis, how are you feeling?' Gareth asked.

'Fucking awful,' I honestly replied. 'How do you expect to me feel?' My tone was defensive and angry, I couldn't help it.

Bryce sat down next to me and handed me my drink, a worried and curious look on his face. 'Here.' He placed his arm around my neck and rested his hand on my shoulder.

'I'm sorry, Alexis. I didn't mean to sound insensitive.'

Gareth leaned forward and placed his drink on the coffee table when I caught a hint of his aftershave. It washed over me, triggering my visions and flashbacks. I saw myself hopping along the walkway as I'd seen in my head time and time again, only this time I smelled Gareth's aftershave as I took my first step. It was a deep woody, earth-like aroma. I didn't like it. In fact, I hated it; it made me nauseated.

'Alexis! Alexis, hey are you all right?' Bryce was lightly shaking my shoulder with his hand in an attempt to get my attention.

I looked at him, then to Gareth. My breathing spiked and I could feel my body temperature rising. I turned back to Bryce and shook my head at him.

The last thing I remember is Bryce leaning forward to put his drink down and saying, 'Shit! Not again.'

* * *

This time when I came round, I noticed that Bryce had swivelled me into a horizontal position and propped my legs high on the arm of the sofa. The second thing I noticed is that my blouse was drenched and smelled of gin, and the third thing I noticed was Gareth standing next to Bryce — rather close — and that Bryce was on the phone.

'Yes, Janette, she's coming round now, her eyes just opened.' He smiled warmly at me. 'No, I'll call Jessica. You stay where you are and sort out your incident. Thanks for your help. I'm thinking I will have to give you a raise in salary very soon.' He chuckled back at her response and then hung up the phone, dialling Jessica instantly.

'Hi, Jessica. Alexis has had another panic attack and again she passed out.' He walked over to the sofa and knelt down beside me. 'No. No, she's been fine other than that.' He picked up my hand and kissed the top of it quickly. 'Yes, please. I'd appreciate it. Thanks, I'll see you soon.'

I noticed, from the corner of my eye, that Gareth fidgeted.

'Jessica is on her way, honey. How do you feel now?'

'Okay, I guess. I'm a bit soggy, but I'm okay.'

He went to get up. 'I'll get you another top.'

I grabbed his arm. 'No, don't leave me,' I begged, while glancing at Gareth.

'Okay, I won't leav—'

Gareth butted in. 'I have to go, got a lot of work to do. I'm glad you're all right, Alexis.' He nodded at Bryce then hastily left the room.

* * *

I had moved out to the balcony to get some air when Jessica arrived. She followed Bryce out and stood next to me at the balustrade. I had rugged myself up in a thick coat and Jessica — thank goodness — had done the same.

'So, what happened?' she enquired.

'I'm not quite sure,' I answered dishonestly while glancing quickly toward Bryce.

Jessica noticed my subtle eye movement and proceeded to remedy the situation.

'Bryce, I would like to speak to Alexis alone if you wouldn't mind.'

He let out a breath in a stoic manner. 'Sure. I need to go and check the progress of the Metropol renovations anyway.' He kissed my forehead. 'Call me when you're done, okay?'

I nodded.

He turned and walked inside.

'Thank fuck,' I blurted out while looking around my vicinity, desperate for something to poke into my cast. 'Where are all the long pointy things? I swear he has removed everything and anything that could be used to scratch my leg, damn controlling arse that he is.'

I was just about to hop over to the yucca plant and tear off a leaf when Jessica smirked at me and handed me her pen.

'Oh, you are my saviour.' I gripped the railing, balancing myself and shoved it directly into my cast. 'I hate this thing. I hate it with a passion. I hate all orthopaedic surgeons and I want to wage a war against plaster and fibreglass.'

'That would be an interesting war,' she murmured. 'People have fought and died for much less.' She continued: 'So, would you like to tell me what happened now that Bryce has gone?'

I nodded and grabbed hold of my crutches. 'Let's go inside first, I think it's about to rain.'

We both made our way inside and sat opposite each other on the lounge.

'Would you like a drink?' I offered.

'No, thank you, dear.'

'Are you comfortable?'

'Yes, I'm just fine.'

'Can I get you anything at all?' I offered again.

'Alexis? Are you being overly polite or are you trying to delay the inevitable?' *Grrr, you smart, smarty-pants doctor of smarts.*

'Okay, Gareth is what happened,' I admitted with defeat, while continuing to scratch my leg with the pen.

The mention of Bryce's cousin — her patient — got her full attention.

She snapped her eyes to mine. 'How so?' she asked probingly.

I shrugged my shoulders as I nonchalantly rattled off my reasons. 'He came by to visit. Scott and I have a history. I don't really know how to act around him. He makes me feel uneasy. And his aftershave triggered a flashback.'

She raised her eyebrow, then frowned at me. 'Tell me all about it. I want to know what happened from the moment he walked in to the moment you passed out.' She patted her pockets, looking for a pen. I reluctantly offered hers back.

'Never mind, I've got another one.' She reached into her briefcase and pulled out another pen. *Brilliant, I probably would not have relinquished this one anyway.*

I repeated everything that had transpired like she asked me to, while she sat there and took her notes.

'Alexis, we've been through the possibility of your flashbacks being a result of your inner guilt —'

I cut in. 'But I don't feel guilty any more. I've honestly accepted that the fall was not my fault. So why would my mind persist on trying to convince me of something I am already convinced of?'

'That's a good question. And my answer is that this recent attack may just be a result of your anxious feelings toward Gareth. It may be completely separate from your fall altogether.'

I shrugged my shoulders. Maybe she was right, although I wasn't quite sure.

'I can prescribe a mild antidepressant drug for you, if you'd like. But, honestly, I don't think you need it. I think we should continue our talks. I also think you need to get back to your normal everyday life. You've been working again, which is good. How about your friends? Have you seen any of them?'

'No, not yet,' I answered, quickly.

'Why's that?'

'I've just wanted time with Bryce, alone. It's too soon to see them.'

She nodded. 'That's okay, Alexis. You can see people when you are ready to see them. I'm glad you're consciously making that choice.' Her voice sounded soft and reassuring. 'Think of it as a process, a routine, a cycle as such. As time moves on and you go back to doing the things you have always done, you will find that you are moving on out of habit. Now, if that doesn't happen for some reason, we will look at other methods to help that eventuate.'

She put her notepad down and picked up her phone. 'Now, if Gareth triggers another attack I want to know right away. That, in itself, is perplexing, but as I said it may just be a result of your dislike for him —'

'It's not that I don't like him. I just get the feeling he doesn't like me and that makes me feel uneasy.'

'Fair enough. It might be best to just avoid him though, or practise the breathing techniques I taught you for when you do come across him again.' She started typing into her phone. 'When are you planning on seeing your children next?'

'Tomorrow,' I answered with a smile.

'Good. After you explain to Nate and Charlotte what has happened, you may find you feel less anxious and that a weight of relief has been lifted from you, a weight you did not know you carried.'

'I'm fully aware that I am carrying that particular weight, Jessica.'

'Of course you know you are carrying *that* weight, Alexis. But that weight could also be linked to you being anxious and fearful in general, not just over telling your children. Do you understand what I'm saying?' She rested her hands on her lap.

'Oh, yes. Maybe you're right.' I deliberated that notion for a second.

'Getting back to being intimate with Bryce may also help relieve your anxiety. Do you have any concerns about that?'

'We have been intimate.' I quickly correct myself, slightly stuttering. 'We have obviously not made love yet ... but we have had intimate moments.' *Oh my god! I'm talking to Jessica about having sex with Bryce. Once upon a time I would have considered this an adynaton. Maybe I need to look out the window and see if a pig flies past.*

'That's good. Like I said, getting back into your normal routine can only help your situation. Now, if you are planning to try again to have another baby, then you should wait a couple more weeks, but I'm sure your doctor talked to you about that.'

'Yes, she did.'

'Okay, good. So, how do you feel now, after our chat?'

'Do you always ask that question at the end of your "chats"?' I asked flatly.

'Yes.'

'So it's a habit?'

'Yes, but I want to know your answer.' She packed up her briefcase and stood up.

'I feel better.'

'Good, as long as you don't feel worse, then we are on the right track. Now, stay there, don't get up. Bryce is on his way.' She walked toward the door.

'How do you know?'

'I sent him a text.'

I rolled my eyes. 'Am I the only one who doesn't do what he says?'

She smiled back at me. 'Yes, I think so.'

As she turned the handle to the entryway door, the elevator doors opened and Bryce entered the room.

'I'll speak to you tomorrow, Alexis. And Bryce, Gareth missed his session last week and he is not returning my phone calls. You know what is coming up, so if you see him again today, please tell him I want to see him as soon as possible.'

'Sure, thank you for letting me know.'

He walked over and held the door as she passed through it.

After Jessica left, Bryce made his way to the lounge and sat down.

'That makes sense you know,' I said.

'What makes sense?' he asked as he rubbed his hands up his arms. 'Are you cold? I can put the fire on.' He got back up and made his way to the fire without waiting for me to answer. 'Sorry, what makes sense?'

'Gareth wanting to leave so quickly when you mentioned Jessica was on her way here.'

'Yeah, I did pick up on that too. I will track him down shortly. He knows he shouldn't be missing appointments with her, especially this time of year.' He sat back down and pulled me to him.

'Why? What's this time of year?'

'The anniversary of the accident. It's a week from Monday,' he answered, emotionlessly.

I snuggled into him as I watched the flames from the fire pick up. 'Do you do anything to mark the day?'

'Yeah, we normally go to the cemetery. Would you like to come?'

I tilted my head to look up at him. 'I'd love to.'

'Good, I've always hated going on my own.'

'Didn't you just say "we" normally go to the cemetery?'

'Yeah, Lucy, Nic and Gareth.'

'Then you were never on your own, were you?'

'Yes, I was.'

I squeezed him tightly, understanding what he meant. 'Well, you aren't any more.'

CHAPTER
19

I never quite liked feelings of impatience, even if they went hand in hand with an outcome of joy — a reward for enduring the waiting. I hated the obsession with time, flicking to my watch every few minutes in the hope it would display a passing of hours instead. I hated the feeling of disappointment when I was so sure my wait was over, only to realise it wasn't and having to be patient once again.

On this particular day, my impatience was a result of having to wait for Nate and Charlotte to arrive home. I was so eager to wrap my arms around them both, see their beautiful, adorable faces and hear their sweet voices. But as excited and eager as I was, I was also terrified, because I soon had to explain why my leg was broken and why I was no longer pregnant. It was a surreal type of impatience and I hated it even more.

* * *

The buzzer to the door sounded and I jolted excitedly, kicking the coffee table.

'Shit! Crap! Fucking balls!'

'Alexis, for fuck's sake, be careful. As much as I have enjoyed carrying you around these past two weeks, I don't want you to re-break your foot.'

'They're here, Bryce!' I shrieked with a huge smile. 'I haven't seen them in two weeks. Do you know how hard that has been for me?'

He smiled back at me. 'Of course I do, honey.'

I stood myself up on one leg, arranging the crutches into position. Bryce went to the door and opened it, letting Rick and the kids in. I hobbled over to where they were all standing and watched as the colour drained from my children's faces.

'Mum, what happened? How did you break your foot?' Nate asked, looking as if he wanted to hug me, but was not sure how to go about it without hurting my injured leg.

'I fell down the stairs, little man.'

'Are you okay?'

'I wasn't okay at first, but I am now.'

He stepped forward and gently squeezed my waist then let go and stood back, still looking overly concerned.

'Mum, did it hurt?' Charli enquired curiously while staring at my cast.

'Yes, sweetheart, it hurt like hell.'

'How did you fall, Mum? Were you running? You shouldn't have been running. You keep telling us not to run, and now look what's happened.' She placed her hands on her hips, with an expression that basically branded me a hypocrite.

'No,' I laughed at her. 'I was not running. I just kind of lost my balance when I was coming down the stairs. It was an accident, Charli-Bear. A horrible, horrible accident.'

Charli glanced at my tummy. 'Did you hurt the baby when you fell? I bet she didn't like being bumped around in your belly.' *Oh, god. This is going to be harder than I thought.*

I compelled the tears to remain at bay and forced a fake smile. 'No, she didn't like being bumped around, but I'll tell you about that later. Right now, I need to sit down. These crutches are hurting Mummy's arms.' I quickly turned my back to them, giving myself a second for composure.

'Can I have a turn of your crutches, Mum?' Nate asked with raised eyebrows.

I grinned. 'Yeah, when I'm not using them though. Come on.'

As the kids and I headed for the kitchen, Bryce pulled Rick aside to apologise for hitting him a week earlier. I stopped at the doorway and noticed Rick also make amends for something, although I couldn't hear what. Both of them ended their discussion with an unemotional handshake and a light pat on the back. It was a step in a direction that led to god knows where. I just hoped that wherever it led, it was a good place.

We sat down around the dining room table, and Bryce ordered sandwiches from the hotel's kitchen. It was a strange and surreal feeling sitting around the table with my estranged husband and my new partner. But the atmosphere was no longer hostile or territorial. It was a strange type of calm.

'Charli, are you going to tell your mum what we did during the week?' Rick suggested with a nod.

'Oh, yeah, Dad took us to see the Crusty Demons. I want to be a Crusty Demon. They go upside-down and everything. They even let go of their bikes in the air and they jump over fire and do flips. It was soooo cool!' she babbled at rapid speed.

My eyes widened as I stared at her obsessively crazed face, then I turned to Nate with a questioning look.

'Yeah, it was awesome, Mum, but Charli *REALLY* enjoyed it. She screamed and clapped every time they jumped.'

'Don't they jump ... a lot?' I asked.

'Yeah,' Rick said quickly, 'they do.'

Oh, god, Charli-Bear a Crusty Demon, shit! I think I may need to take her to Disney on Ice *or something.*

'So, Nate, do you want to tell Mum and Bryce who you met yesterday?'

Nate shrugged his shoulders, and Charli went to open her mouth to spill the beans, but Rick put his finger to his lips to silence her.

'Go on, Nate, tell them.'

'I met RJ. I went to his soccer game,' Nate said quietly.

'And?' I asked, a smile creeping across my face.

'He's kind of funny.'

Rick started laughing and scruffed Nate's hair. 'What about when he kicked that goal?'

Nate giggled. 'Yeah, he did a forward-flip and a cartwheel, Mum. It was hilarious.'

'I liked it when he pulled his t-shirt over his head and bumped into one of the other boys because he couldn't see where was going,' Charli added.

* * *

Rick left the apartment after lunch and I thanked him for keeping the kids busy, happy and completely oblivious to the events that had transpired in their absence. I also explained that I was going to tell them about the miscarriage tomorrow morning, because I just wanted a happy evening with them, one without heartbreak and a lesson on life's sometimes cruel happenings.

He apologised to me for his behaviour the week before, for being inconsiderate and insensitive. He also told me to call him if I felt he could help with the kids and their reaction to the news I would soon give them. I thanked him again and said that I would if I needed to. It was such a nice reprieve to not have to worry about my on and off again issues with Rick. Hopefully from now on we could move on in a civil and friendly manner.

Shortly after Rick left, Bryce received a text from Lucy asking if practice was still on for this evening. Before my accident, Bryce had arranged a practice session and a fish and chips dinner at the apartment with Lucy, Nic and the members of Live Trepidation.

After I lost the baby he had completely forgotten to reschedule them and was about to cancel when I insisted that he didn't. Cancelling was the last thing I wanted. I wanted things to go back to normal, and fish and chips on a Saturday night was normal, so I convinced him that the change in atmosphere was just what I needed.

An hour later, I was sitting on the sofa in the man-cave with Charli at my foot gently drawing pictures on my cast. So far, I had a rainbow and a unicorn, and she was now attempting a Crusty Demon. Lucy was at the keyboard practising, and Nic was sitting next to her with Alexander on her lap. He was practising too, slamming his little hands down on the keys and having a wonderful time. Nate was playing pool with Derek and Matt, and Will was lightly tapping out beats on the drums. Bryce was sitting on the arm of my chair, playing the guitar and strumming chords that every now and again sounded familiar.

When he started playing the riff in 'Sweet Home Alabama' by Lynyrd Skynyrd, I casually lounged back, putting my hands above my head, deciding I'd join in and sing along. Before I knew it, he changed the song. I removed my hands from behind my head and pouted at him because I really liked that song. He smiled at my protruding bottom lip, but kept playing the new tune. It didn't take me long to figure out that the new song was 'Layla' by Eric Clapton, so I chimed in and sang that one instead. Then, like clockwork, he switched the song yet again. I glared at him, but he only smirked back at me. I listened to his new choice and caught on that it was 'Wanted Dead or Alive' by Bon Jovi, so I blurted out the opening line while smirking back at him.

Suddenly, the rest of the band were gathered around and were watching me play the guessing game with him, as Bryce would switch to a new song and I would quickly try and guess which one it was before he switched again. I thought I was doing a decent job, guessing songs like 'Dr Feelgood', 'Enter Sandman', 'Back In Black', 'Foxy Lady' and 'Johnny B. Goode'. But then he'd decide to try and make it a little harder, by playing stuff I hadn't heard of and completely random songs like 'Just A Girl' by No Doubt and 'Mister Sandman', which I laughed at, because he pulled a stupid face as he played it.

It wasn't until I guessed with much enthusiasm that he was playing 'Eruption' by Van Halen that he gave up the game and said, 'You win.' I tried to do a happy-dance but obviously couldn't, so went with the happy-clap instead, and I was rewarded with a quick, soft kiss on the lips. It was in that moment that I decided I wanted to surprise him and learn to play the guitar, so that I could play for him. I thought that maybe he would appreciate me learning something he was so passionate about. It was also a gift I could give him, a gift I could give a man that appeared to have everything.

* * *

He'd disappeared for a short time with Lucy and Charli to cook the fish and chips. So I took that opportunity to approach Derek and see if he wouldn't mind giving me some secret lessons.

I motioned for him to come over to me then spoke in a hushed tone. 'Um, Derek, can I ask you something?'

He looked around the room in a sneaky type of way with a cute grin on his face. 'Yeah, why are you whispering?'

'This is going to sound completely crazy, but I was hoping you'd do me a favour.'

'Okay, sure. Fire away.'

I giggled. Yes, giggled like an idiot at his choice of the word 'fire', remembering Carly's burnt fiery hole that she wished he'd put out with his hose. I had to rein myself in again, much to my embarrassment and his amusement. 'Aren't you going to ask what the favour is before you agree?'

He chuckled. 'No, how bad can it be?'

I raised my eyebrow at him and he sat back just a little. 'Nup, still can't be that bad. So, what can I do for you?'

I leaned over so that I could whisper in his ear. I didn't want anyone else hearing my plan. 'I want to learn to play the guitar as a surprise for Bryce and I was wondering if you'd teach me.'

He shot back away from me. 'Seriously?' He sounded somewhat amused.

'Yes, seriously. There's not much I can give a man that has everything, but this is something I can give him. I think he'd enjoy it.'

He scoffed, but in a good way. 'Yeah, I think he would too. Of course, I'd love to teach you. When do you want to start?'

'As soon as possible. I'm kind of bored shitless at the moment and Bryce is due to go to Sydney in a week's time for work, then to Brisbane for the rest of that week. Lucy and Nic are going to stay here, so I'll fill them in and swear them to secrecy.'

'Sure, I like a challenge and you look like a challenge,' he said, in a mildly flirty way.

'Hey, I might just surprise you and be your best student.'

'Well, considering you'll be my only student then, yeah, you just might.'

'Give me your phone. I'll program my number into it.' I put my hand out for his phone and he obliged, so I entered my number into his contacts. 'As soon as you've got some spare time, give me a buzz.' I handed him back his phone.

Bryce walked in moments later and placed the large platter on the coffee table. He walked over and handed me my own dish of sauce, saying loudly, 'Alexis double dips.'

'And proud of it,' I announced as I glared at him playfully and snatched it. I then proceeded to dip my finger in my dish and suck off the sauce.

His eye twitched and I couldn't help but smile wickedly at him.

My phone buzzed in my pocket as Bryce went to fill a plate with seafood for me. I pulled it out to find a text from an unknown number:

Don't worry, I double dip too. But don't tell anyone — Derek

I looked up at Derek standing next to the table. He gave me a wink then dipped his prawn back in the sauce.

I burst into laughter.

* * *

For the remainder of the evening the guys and Lucy practised some of their original songs and a few they planned to cover at the upcoming gig. I adored their rendition of 'Hurricane' by Thirty Seconds to Mars and 'Fader' by The Temper Trap, and I soon became really excited at the prospect of seeing them play again on stage, together with playing a guitar myself.

I found myself staring between Bryce and Derek, watching them intently as they strummed the guitars. They made it look so simple. *Fuck! What have I got myself into? I'm so going to suck and Derek is going to find it hilarious, if not aggravating — possibly even infuriating.*

'You might want to be careful where Derek is concerned,' Nic whispered into my ear, breaking me out of my regretful thoughts.

I turned to her, confused. 'What do you mean?'

'He is a very flirty guy, just be mindful of that. You've kind of been staring at him.' *Have I? Oh, shit! I have, but not like that.*

I screwed my face up at her, slightly offended at her not so subtle accusation. 'Yes, I have been staring at him and at Bryce, for a reason. I am going to learn the guitar as a surprise for Bryce, and Derek has agreed to teach me. For your information, Nic, I've been watching them both play.' I turned my head back to Bryce, who had picked up on my change of demeanour, so I smiled at him.

'Oh, I didn't mean anything by it, Alexis. I just noticed you getting friendly with Derek and thought I better warn you that he can get quite friendly in return. Sometimes too friendly.'

'Do you speak from experience?' I asked her, snidely.

'No,' she replied sharply.

I turned back to her. 'Then what are you talking about, Nic? I am in love with your brother-in-law. We have just lost our baby, and I want to make him happy again, give him something special to show him how much I love him. That is why I want to learn the guitar. I can't exactly ask Bryce to teach me, can I? So in comes Derek. He is going to help me, that is it.'

She lowered her voice even more. 'Sorry, I honestly didn't mean anything by it.'

'Yeah, you did, Nic,' I answered without looking at her.

The music stopped and everyone seemed to be pleased with their form.

'I'm going to take Alexander upstairs to bed,' Nic announced to Lucy.

'Okay, I'll be up in a minute.' She gave Nic a look of concern. She obviously picked up on the unpleasant discussion happening between me and her girlfriend. Or, maybe in addition to her humongous IQ and computer hacking skills, she could also lip-read — I honestly wouldn't put it past her.

'Nate and Charli, it's getting late. You can say goodnight too, okay?'

Both my kids did their new fist-bump style of high five/thumbs-up/goodbye salute with everyone in the room. I shook my head and got to my feet, grabbing my crutches.

Bryce made his way to my side. 'Here, give me those.'

'No, I can manage,' I said playfully, but trying to assert my authority at the same time.

'Are you challenging me, honey?' he asked in a daring tone.

I felt my face redden, so I quickly looked around the room.

Lucy smiled and shook her head and Nate quickly sided with Bryce.

'Mum, you are so gonna lose. Bryce always wins.'

Bryce kept his eyes on me, but extended his fist toward my son, my son quickly bumping it with his own.'

'Really?' I asked, looking at Nate and now standing on one leg with my hands on my hips.

'Yeah, really,' he replied, then snatched up my crutches and ran off.

'Nate, you little traitor,' I yelled out after him just as Bryce bent down and swept me off my feet.

As he carried me out of the room, I looked over my shoulder to Lucy. 'And you think I have control over him. Ha, you're crazy!'

She just shrugged her shoulders.

* * *

Bryce helped me put the kids to bed, which involved tilting me in their direction so that I could give them a kiss goodnight. Charli didn't ask anything further about my fall, and I was kind of glad. Being able to explain the next morning seemed like a better option. I was still dreading it though and Bryce picked up on my unease.

'Do you know what you want to tell them yet?' he asked as he carried me to our room.

'No. I guess I'll just tell them the truth. Um, where are we going? You still have guests downstairs.' I tried to peek over the half-wall banister, which stretched from the top of the staircase to the end of the walkway.

'They'll let themselves out. They always do,' he said casually.

'Bryce. You can't just abandon them to put me to bed. And anyway, who said I was ready for bed? It's still early.'

'Yes, I can. And trust me, you are ready for bed,' he exclaimed as he buried his head into my neck with an animalistic growl.

I squealed in excitement. 'Bryce!'

CHAPTER

20

I dragged myself out of bed the morning after Bryce very deliciously put me to sleep by way of kissing nearly every surface of my body — nearly every surface. As I made my way into the kitchen, I found him and the kids creating works of waffle-art for breakfast. There were numerous toppings of whipped cream, sprinkles, marshmallows and chocolate sauce. I liked his way of making what would be a horrible heart-wrenching moment somewhat better with sugar and aerated cream. My feelings told me it was not going to work, but I appreciated his effort nonetheless.

All four of us were seated around the dining table when I decided to get it over and done with. Stewing on the inevitable was not something I enjoyed doing.

'Nate, Charli. Bryce and I need to tell you something.'

Bryce dropped his hand and placed it on my thigh, giving it a gentle squeeze.

I sucked in a deep breath then slowly let it out as I opened my mouth to speak. 'Charli, remember when you asked me if the baby was hurt when I fell?'

'Yeah, Mum. I hope she is not angry at you, because it was an accident. You didn't mean to hurt her,' Charlotte said with the sweetest
sincerity.

'No, Charli-Bear, I didn't mean to hurt her. But ...' I sighed and
closed my eyes briefly. 'She did get hurt and unfortunately, because of
that, she stopped growing and the doctors had to take her out of my
tummy.'

Nate stopped eating and gave me a strange look. I could see him
putting two and two together. Charli, on the other hand, put her fork
down and smiled from ear to ear.

'Where is she? Can I see her? Can I hold her?' *Oh, shit! No, I didn't
mean it like that, fuck!*

I blinked a couple of times then brought myself back together,
opening my mouth to speak. 'No, Charlotte, sweetheart. You can't,
because she didn't survive.'

Her smile faded and she scratched her head. 'What do you mean?'

'She means the baby died, Charli. When Mum fell, the baby got
hurt, bad.' Nate got up from his seat and made his way over to me,
wrapping his arms around my shoulders. 'Sorry, Mum. That must be
really sad for you.'

I clasped his arms with my hands holding him tight, but I could
not respond.

'Nate is right, Charlotte. The baby stopped growing, and her heart
stopped beating,' Bryce explained, knowing my voice had temporarily
seized up.

Charli's bottom lip dropped and it began to tremble, breaking my
heart for the umpteenth time. 'Oh, sweetheart, come here.' I freed
my arms from Nate, holding them out for her. She slid off her seat
and walked toward me, bursting into tears before she made it to my
embrace. I wrapped myself around both my children and squeezed
them tightly.

'She's in baby heaven now, playing with lots of other baby angels.'

'Are there other baby angels?' Charli asked, weeping and pulling
away while wiping her eyes.

Bryce put his arms out for her so that she could sit up on his lap
and be level with my face. 'Yes, Charlotte, there are lots of baby angels.
Some babies are not lucky enough to be born into this world, and

some babies are born, but then don't live for very long. When that happens, they all go to baby heaven and become good friends,' Bryce explained as he reassuringly stroked his hand down Charli's head.

'Do you think she has made friends yet?'

I smiled through my sadness. 'Of course she has. I think she has lots of friends, darling.'

Charlotte nodded and returned a small smile to me. 'So, Mum, I was right then. She was a girl.'

I looked at Bryce, then back at Charli. We had decided to open the envelope a few days ago to see if our baby was a boy or a girl, but I had chosen not to look at the picture. I was not ready for that yet.

'Yes, Charli, you were right.' A tear fell from my eye.

Nate left my side and returned instantly with a tissue.

'Thank you, little man.' I kissed his head and tucked him back into my arms.

'Mum, what was her name?' Charli asked quietly.

Bryce took a deep breath. 'Well, your mum and I thought that you could choose her name, Charlotte.'

She looked up at Bryce, then gave him a hug. 'Okay, I will pick the prettiest name ever.'

He hugged her back. 'I know you will, Charli.'

We finished our breakfast together and answered more of Charlotte's questions. Bryce was incredible and seemed to have the most amazing explanations for her, ones she would understand almost right away. Seeing her expression change from nervous curiosity to understanding made me feel so much better, and the weight of apprehension I had felt prior to this encounter lifted, just like Jessica said it would.

'Are you all right?' Bryce asked as the kids made their way upstairs.

'Yeah, I am. That was probably one of the hardest things I've ever had to do, but it just proved to me how wonderful and special my children are. I'm so unbelievably proud of them both. And you ... you just blow me away. Your ability to handle difficult situations is remarkable. I'm so blessed to have you,' I said as I wrapped my arms around his waist.

While I was appreciating the man I encircled and never wanting to let him go, Lucy and Nic walked into the kitchen with Alexander.

I couldn't look Nic in the eye. I was still slightly pissed that she had accused me of flirting with Bryce's best friend. It was none of her business and she had jumped to the wrong conclusion. *I mean, fuck! I was only talking to the guy and watching him play the guitar. I wasn't salivating or flashing him my tits.*

'How'd it go?' Lucy knowingly asked Bryce.

'Yeah, okay, those two children are pretty bloody awesome, just like their mum.' He gave me a loving wink. Lucy smiled.

'There're some leftover waffles if you both want them,' he said as he pointed to the plate on the bench.

Lucy took a seat at the breakfast bar. 'Thanks, but your eggs Benedict are my fav,' she sang, batting her eyes at him in the hope he'd cook them for her.

He raised his eyebrow and smirked at her.

Interpreting that expression as an acceptance of her request, I unwrapped my arms from around his waist and took a seat at the breakfast bar. Bryce confirmed my interpretation by turning to the fridge and taking out a carton of eggs.

Sitting one seat away, I leaned in and baited her. 'Tell me again, who has power over him?'

She looked up through her lashes at Bryce and answered quietly, 'My methods are different from yours.'

'Yes, I know,' I replied.

'So, big bro, what time does your flight leave next week?'

I slumped over the bench, having been reminded by Lucy that Bryce was flying to Sydney for business then to Brisbane and I would not see him for an entire week.

'Nine a.m. Why?' he asked, as he blended egg yolks, lemon juice and water together.

'You're going to miss Alexis' appointment with the surgeon to have the plaster removed.'

He looked at me apologetically. 'I know. I can cancel if you want me to come.'

'No, don't be silly, I'll be fine. Anyway, you've neglected far too much of your work for me lately. You can't keep doing that.'

'No, you can't,' Lucy interrupted. 'So, as I was saying, seeing as I'll be the one taking her, I will need to borrow one of your cars.' She smiled naughtily at her brother.

'No, you won't. You have your own car,' he accurately pointed out.
'It's broken.'

He raised an eyebrow at her as if to suggest her reason was pathetic and unbelievable, which clearly it was.

'I'll take the McLaren,' she said without looking at him.

'No, you won't.'

'Fine, I'll take the Ferrari.'

'No. You. Won't.' He was very carefully pouring melted butter into the blender. 'You can take the Jag.'

'I don't like the Jag,' she said, like an ungrateful child. 'Lexus or Trans Am. That's my final offer.'

He smirked at her and she smirked back, both of them indulging in a war of smirks. I sat there watching them, trying not to laugh. Nic, too, stifled a smile while rolling her eyes.

'You can take the Lexus. It has more leg room than the Trans Am.' He switched off the blender.

'Deal,' she said with a victorious grin.

Bryce finished off the eggs Benedict by sprinkling some chives on top. He leaned across the bench and went to hand it to Lucy, but quickly snatched it back and took a bite, teasing her.

'Arsehole,' she said playfully.

I burst into laughter.

'I was about to give this back to you,' he said. 'But now I'm just going to lick it.' He held the slice of baguette up to his mouth, again teasing her. She went to grab it, but he was too quick.

'You are so aggravating at times,' she growled as she pushed her stool back and launched herself around the island bench, now in frustrated pursuit of the half-eaten baguette. I watched her chase him around the bench a couple of times when I noticed another slice on the plate with a perfectly cooked egg and silky hollandaise sauce to match. I looked up at the brother and sister duo still running rings around me, then leaned forward and picked up the abandoned baguette. *Hmm, don't mind if I do.*

I bit down on it with a huge grin on my face. *Yum!*

Nic laughed and smiled at my munching. Her smile also held an apologetic undertone. She jiggled Alexander in her lap as she spoke to him. 'Aunty Alexis is a clever cookie, isn't she?'

I swivelled around on my stool to face her, making sure I kept my leg out of the way of Bryce and Lucy. I thought I'd offer my own form of acceptance of her apology, offering her some of the eggs Benedict. I held it up toward her. 'Want some?'

She nodded cheekily, then stood up from the dining table and quickly walked to the bench to avoid getting run into by Lucy, who still hadn't noticed the spare slice.

Nic took a bite and let out a loud, 'Mm.' Lucy ceased chasing Bryce, and both stopped in their tracks.

Nic and I froze.

'Are you for real?' Lucy asked, exasperated.

We both shook our heads. Bryce laughed harder, then shoved the last piece he was holding, into his mouth. I quickly did the same.

'You all suck!' she said. 'Not you baby boy. Mummy still loves you.' She wrinkled her nose at Alexander. 'But you, you and you,' she pointed at each of us. 'You all suck!'

She went to walk out of the room.

'Luce,' Bryce said, as he scooped out two perfectly poached eggs that had been hidden in the pot. She turned around, spying him placing them down on another sliced baguette. 'Remember that thing you did for me a few weeks ago, where you said I owed you?'

'Yeah?'

He poured the remainder of the sauce over each plate. 'Well, we are even.' He smiled triumphantly as he pushed a plate toward her and one toward Nic.

Lucy stepped forward and took hold of the plate with an equally triumphant grin. 'Whatever.' Then she left the room.

* * *

Nic and Lucy had taken Alexander to the shopping precinct for the afternoon. Bryce had taken off in search of Gareth to have a word to him about skipping his appointments with Jessica, and Nate and Charli were in their bedrooms. Nate appeared at the top of the stairs just as I was about to head up there to see what they were doing. The sight of him at the edge of the top step terrified me immensely, causing me to panic.

'Nate, be careful!' I shouted in a loud voice.

He startled a little at my outburst and gripped the railing rather tightly. 'Mum! You scared me. I was being careful,' he called down to me.

'Sorry, mate. Just make sure you hang on to that railing at all times, please.'

He nodded and made his way down slowly, timidly walking up to me and giving me a hug.

'Promise me you'll just be very careful, okay?'

'Okay, Mum.'

'What's Charli doing?'

'Writing girls' names on her notepad with coloured markers. There are a lot of names on that list, Mum.'

'I'm sure she'll pick the right one.' I loved Charli's dedication to a task that was set for her, although I knew she felt this task was a special one.

'Mum, can you have another baby?' *Oh, shit! That came out of nowhere.*

'Yes, I can.'

'When?'

'Not right away, mate. Mummy's body needs to heal first.' I smoothed his hair away from his face. 'Why?'

'I was sort of looking forward to it.'

I pulled him to me and hugged him tight, kissing him on the side of the head. 'Do you want to know something?'

'Yeah?'

'I'm going to ask Bryce real soon if he would like another baby, but it's a secret, so don't tell him.'

Nate nodded his head, but had a dubious glint in his eye.

'What, little man?'

'What will happen if the next baby dies too, Mum?'

I sighed. 'Sometimes these things just happen, for no reason. We can't stop them. All we can do is accept and try again. I can't promise you that our next baby won't die, too, because I don't control that, sweetheart. But what we can do is be hopeful and look after each other.'

'Mum, I'm going to look after you.'

'I know you are, because you are totes the sickest son ever!' I said in Nate's style of lingo.

Nate just shook his head at me.

* * *

One week later, Bryce and I were snuggled next to each other in bed. He was due to fly to Sydney the following day and the thought of being away from him for a week was beyond depressing. He'd arranged for Lucy and Nic to stay with me while he was gone, which at first I had not been happy about. But after realising that it would not only be easier for me if I were to need help, that it would also put his mind at ease while he was away on business, I relented and let him have his way. *Didn't I always?*

'I'm going to miss you,' I said as I traced small circles around his abs.

'I'm going to miss you, too, but I have to go, honey. It's just shit timing.'

'You have to do what you have to do, Mr Clark, being the big billionaire hotel owner that you are,' I retorted playfully, trying to lighten our dull moods.

'It's what I do, Ms Summers.'

I giggled. He hadn't called me Ms Summers in a while and I kind of missed it.

'What else do you do, Mr Clark?' I tilted my head up to look at him through my lashes.

A small but sexy growl resonated from his throat right before he slid out from beside me and propped himself up on his side. His eyes found my lips, and I couldn't help but squeeze them together and drag my top row of teeth across the bottom one. That small uncontrollable reaction to his stare was all he needed to lose his restraint and move forward, rapidly seizing my mouth.

I broke away moments later, breathing heavily, trying to catch my breath. He moved his perfect lips down my neck, gently licking and nipping at my skin. My fingers made their way into his luscious dark-blond hair, where I gripped his head with the intention of stopping his lips teasing me any further. I had to stop him, because his mouth had the ability to divinely torture me into wanting more and more, which I could not have for at least another week.

I was about to tell him to stop, when he came back up to my mouth and I felt his tongue once again.

'I know what you're thinking right now,' he said through heavy breaths in between kisses. 'You're thinking I want to make love to you, and you're thinking you don't want to say no.' *Yes, your thinking is one hundred percent correct.* 'Well, you're right. Of course I want to make love to you, but ... you have so many other body parts that need my attention, that need me to make love to them, that need to be fucked by my mouth.'

He caressed my tongue with his own then pulled away from my lips, eyeing me salaciously as he changed course and trailed kisses along my neck and up behind my ear. I sucked in another breath as his glorious lips kissed and sucked my skin.

His hand slid down from my cheek, along my neck and stopped at the seam of my bra, all while his lips, teeth and tongue continued to tease the very sensitive spot under my ear lobe. My skin began to heat, and my pelvis automatically rose away from the mattress.

Bryce groaned mildly then slipped his finger underneath my bra, gently grazing my perked nipple. I gasped and tried to roll my hips into him.

'Hmm, that's right, honey. That piece of you right there wants to be fucked, doesn't it?' he breathed into my ear, before dragging his teeth down my neck then trailing his tongue back up to my ear lobe, teasing and tricking me into thinking he was going to fuck my nipple.

'Oh, god,' I moaned, desperate to feel his wet, warm tongue on my breast.

He gently bit down on my ear lobe again and squeezed my nipple between both his fingers.

'Bryce! Yes, please fuck it.'

He chuckled against my skin as he made his way down to my nipple. 'I have every intention to,' he admitted, as he undid my bra and removed it, eyeing my breast before he slid his tongue across my nipple. It hardened at his touch, forcing my chest to arch toward him, pushing my nipple further into his mouth.

Groaning at my response, he flicked his tongue quicker, sending my body into a meltdown. I was climbing to a climax in a weird kind of way. Not strange weird, but different weird, good weird. It was a new sensation, and I was enjoying it.

He released my nipple from his lips and made his way down my stomach. *No, reattach, goddamn it!* The things the man could do with his touch were utterly mind-blowing. I had not previously known the kind of passion my body felt since being with Bryce, and I was so grateful that I finally had. It really felt so fucking good.

Now trailing the tip of his tongue across my stomach, he gently dipped into my belly button and back out again while continuing to move until his teeth were gently nipping at the curve in my side. *Holy fuck, that feels good.* I flinched and gripped his head.

'Does this spot right here want to be fucked, too?' he murmured.

'Yes. Yes, it does,' I begged.

He reached up to grab my entire breast in his hand as he continued to lick, suck, nip and kiss the sensitive skin at my side. *Oh, god. I'm going to come from kiss-fucking. Is kiss-fucking even a word?*

My breathing started to spike, and my back began to make its journey away from the mattress yet again.

'Not yet, honey. There are more parts of you that want to be fucked and I intend to fuck them all.' *Shit! Are there? Okay, go ahead and fuck them.*

'Sure, knock yourself out,' I mumbled with my eyes closed, more than happy to let him place his mouth wherever he felt necessary.

He chuckled and I felt him move lower, till he was just above the seam of my underwear, his lips pressing into my lower stomach.

My fingers automatically tensed in his hair, remembering that the last time he did that the kiss was not for me, but more so for our baby. I took in a deep breath as he nuzzled the spot for the smallest of seconds then continued down to the place he wished to fuck next — my legs.

Bryce trailed kisses along the insides of my legs, close to my knees while running his hands up and down them — it was simply divine.

My orgasm began to climb again as he teased with his mouth.

'Bryce, I need you,' I moaned.

'I know, honey. I need you too.'

He moved back up to my breast and sucked my nipple, tugging it gloriously long.

I gasped again, only this time I knew I was about to come.

Bryce flicked his tongue at a rapid speed, mouth-fucking my nipple with sensational self-assurance until I released and called his name. It was a different kind of release, but it was a release all the same.

He instantly moved up to my mouth, kissing me ferociously all the while pumping his cock with his palm against my side. My eyes were still closed, encasing me in a new world of sensation, sensation created in a way I never thought possible. As I forced my way back to equilibrium, I heard him groan fiercely.

I opened my eyes and watched him reach his release, too, amazed and in awe of his abilities to please us both sexually. His body tensed, his muscles tight and hard, his hand in complete control as he squeezed his cock — it was sexy as hell.

I moved closer, pulled his head to mine and kissed him again.

'As soon as we can, Bryce, I want to try again. I want to have your baby more than anything.'

CHAPTER

21

The next morning, Bryce got up early to leave for his flight. I was still comfortably snoozing when I felt his warm lips touch the side of my neck and his suggestive voice whisper into my ear.

'I've got to go, my love. I'll call you as soon as I can, and you can tell me all about your moon boot. I want a picture of you in nothing but the moon boot.'

I giggled at his request as I opened my eyes. 'You can be strangely sexy sometimes.'

'I mean it. I want a picture. I need to see every inch of you before I go to bed. I won't be able to sleep until I do.'

He trailed his finger delicately down my bare back, sending the electric tingles that I loved right through me.

I rolled over, so that I was facing him. 'I'm not sending you a naked photo of me in a ridiculous-looking moon boot. Forget it.'

His finger did not stop its journey over my skin, still swirling around and finding my nipple. He rolled it between his fingers. *Oh, fuckity fuck. His fingers are just so ... fuck!*

Instantly, my breasts firmed and both my nipples said 'hello'.

'I want a picture,' he said firmly, but with a husky voice.

I closed my eyes, taking in the glorious feeling he was giving me. 'No,' I repeated.

I felt him take my other nipple into his mouth, so I grabbed his head, digging my nails in and holding him against me.

He growled and engulfed my breast more hungrily. 'I'll send you one.'

My eyes shot open. 'You'll send me a picture?' I asked, a large smile appearing across my face.

'Sure.'

I started to get visions of different pictures he might send me, pictures of his body and its stunning parts. 'I'll think about it,' I compromised.

'Hmm.' He leaned down and pressed his lips to mine, then pulled away regretfully. 'Don't be surprised if I'm not back here tonight and you are in my arms. I don't think I have it in me to stay away.'

'Go!' I placed my hands on his chest and lightly held him at bay. 'Do what you do, Mr Clark. I will speak to you later.'

I watched him walk out the door, staring at his perfectly defined arse in his Versace pants, permanently etching the picture on my brain so that I could recall the sight when needed over the next few days — and boy, would it be needed.

Moments later, I got out of bed, showered, and made my way downstairs via the elevator to see the kids before Danny chauffeured them to school.

'Bye, ratbags. Have a great day,' I called to them as they grabbed their schoolbags and made their way to the elevator.

'Bye, Mum. Bye, Lucy. Bye, Nic,' they called back.

Lucy and Nic were having breakfast and both waved to Nate and Charli as the kids left the apartment. Nic pushed a cup of coffee across the breakfast bar toward me as I uncomfortably shuffled onto the stool with great difficulty.

'I cannot wait to get this big, heavy, white piece of shit removed from my leg today.' I growled.

'What time is your appointment?' Lucy asked as she spooned some Weet-Bix into Alexander's mouth, his tongue gently pushing half of it back out again.

'Two p.m.'

'Alexander has his six month maternal health check appointment at midday, so I will be back in time to take you.'

'Sorry, Luce, I feel like such a burden.'

'Don't be silly. It's no problem at all. I want to help, and anyway, why do you think we are staying here while Bryce is gone?'

'Because he told you to stay.'

She laughed but with an ironic tone. 'Yeah, he did. In fact, he told me not to let you out of my sight. But no, you are family now and we help out our family.'

I shook my head at Bryce's conscientiousness then smiled meekly at her over the rim of my coffee cup as I took another sip.

'So what are your plans today, Alexis, other than your appointment?' Lucy asked.

'Well, I was going to ring Derek and see if he was free to start giving me guitar lessons.' I gave Nic a don't-even-go-there look.

Lucy did the same. 'Yeah, I heard about that. I think it's a brilliant idea. Bryce will flip out —'

Nic interrupted, 'Hey. About that, Alexis, I really am sorry. I didn't mean to imply you would deliberately cheat on Bryce with his best friend. I was just trying to give you a friendly warning as to Derek's forwardness.'

'Nic, just forget about it. All I'm going to say is I love Bryce and would never do anything that would jeopardise that. He is not just my lover, he is my soul mate. We belong together. As for Derek, well, I barely know the guy, but from what I can see, he is lovely and a great friend to Bryce. And anyway, I have plans to set him up with my girl-friend, Carly.'

Lucy laughed. 'Yes! They would be a match made in heaven.'

'Not sure heaven is the correct place to match Carly up in,' I responded.

Lucy agreed and laughed again.

* * *

After breakfast, I gave Derek a call to see if he was available for my first lesson. He was a firefighter with the Metropolitan Fire Brigade and worked shifts. I was in luck as he was not due to start work until this evening.

Within an hour of my call, the buzzer to the door sounded.

'I'll get it, you take it easy,' Lucy said, as she placed Alexander on the floor under his play gym. She walked briskly to the door to welcome Derek and, by the time she got back, Alexander had barrel-rolled to the edge of the lounge. 'Hey you, roly-poly,' she chuckled and picked him up.

'You may need to get a kiddy pen,' I suggested.

She cringed. 'I think you may be right.'

'Derek, thank you so much for doing this,' I said as he walked past both Lucy and Alexander, stopping briefly to playfully wiggle Alexander's nose.

'No sweat,' he stated then sat down on the sofa opposite me.

Derek opened up his case and pulled out a black, shiny acoustic guitar, then jogged to the man-cave and returned with one of Bryce's acoustics for me.

'I'm sure he won't mind you learning with this one,' he said with a sly smile as he handed me the guitar.

Lucy's eyes widened. 'You reckon?' she said mockingly.

'It's Alexis, Luce. Come on, he'd hand me my balls on a plate if I taught her on anything less.'

'Ha! Yeah, you're probably right.'

'Okay, let's get into it, shall we?' he said, as he positioned his guitar on his right leg. 'I hope you're right-handed?'

I nodded to him, smiling excitedly.

'Okay, hold your guitar like this, and try to keep the headstock of the guitar horizontal to the ground, not up or down,' he explained, demonstrating the movement for me.

'What's the headstock?' I asked.

Derek raised his eyebrows, obviously trying to suppress an outburst.

'What?' I sulked, suppressing my own outburst.

Lucy laughed.

I dropped my head and pouted. 'Oh, my god, I suck already.'

'No, that's okay. I'll start from the *very* beginning then.'

He took a few moments to point out and explain all the parts of the guitar. I already knew a lot of them, but that section at the end of the neck ... well ... I didn't know that part was called a headstock. Now that I know, well ... yeah ... it was freakin' obvious.

After Derek had patiently explained the anatomy of a guitar, I was now more comfortable with the instrument sitting on my lap. I'd also learned terms like tuning pegs, position markers and frets.

'Okay, as you can see the guitar has six strings starting with number one being closest to the bottom and up to number six at the very top. Now, pluck each string to hear its sound.'

I did what I was told.

'Do you know the basics of sheet music?' he asked.

'Kind of, I took singing lessons in school. We had to learn beats and rhythm, but I don't really remember. I remember something to do with face though. You know "f-a-c-e" and "even good boys do fart" or was it "every good boy doesn't fart". Shit! I can't remember.'

Derek lost control and threw himself back on the couch laughing hysterically. Even Lucy couldn't restrain her amusement and rolled on the floor next to Alexander.

'What now? Oh, I give up. This was a bad idea, anyway.' I went to put the guitar down next to me.

'No, Alexis. No, I'm sorry,' Derek chuckled before composing himself. 'It's not a bad idea. It's a great idea and Bryce will love it. I just think we will need to practise as much as we possibly can. That's all.'

Lucy stood up. 'I have to go. Don't give up, Alexis.'

She laughed and mumbled something to herself as she headed upstairs.

'Now where were we? Oh yeah, the boy who farted.' He chuckled again, so I glared at him. 'What you are referring to is the mnemonic for the notes and spaces on the treble clef. It's actually more commonly known as "Every Good Boy Does Fine".' *Oh, Alexis, you stupid, stupid idiot.*

'Oh,' I giggled. 'Fair enough.'

He continued on and cleared up the basics of sheet music, including the time signature, measures, and half, quarter and whole notes.

Before I knew it I was strumming notes in rhythm and in beat, tapping my foot as I went.

'You're actually a quick learner, Alexis.'

'Thank you. I might get my mnemonics mixed up, but I recover gracefully.'

'You do,' he smiled.

'What's the time?' I asked, as I didn't have my watch on.

'Nearly a quarter past one.'

'Shit! That went quick. Luce should be back soon to take me to my appointment. I'm getting this horrid thing off today.' I pointed to my cast. 'Do you want a drink or anything?' I went to get up.

'Yeah, but I'll get it. Can I get you one?'

'Yes, please. Just some water is fine.'

He headed over to the bar to pour us a drink.

Just as I was thinking Lucy better hurry up, my phone rang. I hopped over to my bag to fish it out and, speaking of the devil, it was Lucy.

'Hey, where are you?'

'I'm stuck in traffic. A truck lost its load on the Bolte Bridge. Shit! I'm not going to be able to get you to your appointment on time. I'm so sorry.'

'Don't worry, it can't be helped. I'll just ask Danny to take me or get a taxi. It's no big deal. I'd better go and organise it though, so I'm not late. I'll see you when I get home.'

I hung up and flicked through my phone in search of Danny's number.

'Is everything all right?' Derek asked as he handed me my glass of water.

'Lucy is stuck in traffic and can't take me to my appointment. So I need to track down Danny and see if he is available.' I found his number and went to press dial.

'Never mind Danny, I'll take you.'

'Don't be silly. I'm sure Danny can quickly drop me off and pick me up later.'

'Alexis, it's fine. It really isn't a big deal. And anyway, I've got nothing better to do.'

I stewed on it for a second. 'Well, if you really don't mind then, thanks, I appreciate it.'

'Okay, let's go then.' He swung his keys round his finger. 'Hope you've got a helmet.'

'What?' I shrieked.

'My ride is a Ducati.'

'Absolutely no way. Thanks for the offer, but I humbly decline.' I went to dig my phone back out of my bag.

'I'm kidding,' he joked.

'You'd better be,' I retorted.

He nodded and gently placed his hand on the small of my back as I hobbled past him on my crutches and through the front door.

* * *

Derek's ride was actually a bright blue 2012 Ford Ranger, pretty much the perfect height for me to get in and out of without assistance.

During the quick ride to the hospital, I'd found out that Derek and Bryce had gone to school together and that's when they started up the band. Derek also came from a wealthy family. However, he'd had no inclination to follow in his father's footsteps as a shipping magnate. I'd also ascertained that he was single, and I could not wait to put my Alexis matchmaking skills into action. If my plan worked, Carly's fiery hole would be doused sooner rather than later.

We both took a seat in the waiting room of my surgeon's consulting clinic. There were many other surgeons who practised at these particular offices and their patients were also waiting.

'Thanks for doing this. Hopefully we don't have to wait for long,' I said as I looked around the room.

A doctor came out of his office and announced a patient. 'Asoka Andrews.'

Derek muttered under his breath, 'Asoka?'

I smiled at him. 'Yeah, I think that's what he said, why?'

'Isn't that a character in *Star Wars*?' he explained.

I laughed. 'I think you're right. Ask Nate next time you see him, he'll know.'

'I will.'

I leaned forward and picked up a magazine from the coffee table next to me. I needed something to keep my eyes focussed on for when I asked my next question. Matchmaker Alexis was about to come to life.

'So, why are you single, Derek? What's wrong with you?'

I noticed from the corner of my eye that he'd swung his head round in my direction, so I tried desperately to keep my stare fixed on the pages. He didn't answer so I chanced a glance up at him. He actually looked quite adorable with his shaved head and blue eyes, and especially the way he'd furrowed his chin in a for-me-to-know-and-you-to-find-out kind of way.

'What?' I asked. 'That's a fair question. You're young, intelligent, good-looking and obviously athletic. You're a firefighter and a lead singer in a band. I don't buy it. Something has to be wrong with you.'

'Okay then, you tell me what you think is wrong with me,' he challenged.

'Um, then maybe I asked the wrong question before. You might not have a girlfriend, but maybe you have a boyfriend?' *Shit! I hope not. Carls' hole will burn to a crisp if that's the case.*

He laughed. 'No, not gay. I have nothing against being gay, I'm just not gay myself. Next,' he challenged again.

'Third nipple?' I asked, unperturbed by my outrageous suggestion.

He laughed harder this time. 'No. Want to check?' He went to pull down the collar of his t-shirt.

I hit him in the arm. 'No, I believe you.'

'Next,' he said again.

'Small dick?'

'No. Wanna chec—'

I cut him off before he had a chance to finish.

'Alcoholic?'

'No, don't drink ... much.'

'Drugs?'

'No, hell no!'

'Bad in bed?'

'Now you are just insulting me,' he said playfully.

'Well? You tell me then.'

'Why do you want to know?'

'Because I may have a friend.'

He smiled. 'This friend of yours doesn't happen to be blonde and incredibly cute, does she?'

'Maybe,' I answered still flicking pages. 'So, are you an axe murderer?'

'No, and my dick works just fine in bed. I just want to clear that up for when you tell Carly.'

I snapped my head toward him with a huge smile on my face. 'So, do you want me to tell her then?'

'Sure, why not? I liked her.'

I may have been smiling on the outside, but on the inside I was in full-blown happy-dance, happy-clap, party mode, singing and chanting to the tune of the conga in my head, 'No more fiery hole, yeah. No more fiery hole, yeah.'

Another doctor walked out and called for Spiros Soggianis.

Derek leaned in closer and whispered, 'Did he just say soggy anus?'

I cracked up laughing, dropping my head into my hands. 'Yes, I think so.'

* * *

Shortly after Mr Soggy Anus got called in for his appointment, I got called in for mine.

My surgeon helped me up onto the trolley bed and assessed my cast. 'So, Alexis, how have you been? How has the pain been?'

'Yeah, not too bad. It hurt at first, and if I avoid doing stupid things like forgetting and putting all my weight on it or bashing it against the table, then it's fine.'

'Good. And pain relief?'

'I've just been taking a couple of mild painkillers when needed. Other than that, it's been really good. The worst thing has been the bloody itchiness.'

'Well, lucky for you, that's all about to get better. Okay, let's get this cast off and have a look, shall we?'

He slid across the floor on his wheeled stool to a machine, grabbing what looked like a small saw and sliding back to my bed.

'What the crap is that?' I asked, my eyes as big as saucers. 'Sorry, but what the hell?'

'It's a cast saw. It cuts through the fibreglass casing,' my surgeon explained.

'What if it cuts through to my leg?'

He gave me a reassuring smile. 'It won't, I promise.'

'I can't watch. Can you knock me out or something? I can't watch. You're about to put that sharp, spinning wheel of death right against my leg. I need to be unconscious.'

'Alexis, it's fine. I've had it done before, you'll be fine,' Derek placed his hand on my shoulder and lightly flexed his fingers. It was nicely comforting, but I wished he was Bryce standing there reassuring me and calming me.

I covered my face with my hands. 'Do it, just do it.'

I heard the saw start up, and I swear I nearly passed out. 'Oh my god. Oh my god,' I said in a muffled voice through my fingers.

Within minutes my leg was free, but I was still covering my face, breathing deeply.

'Alexis, it's done.'

I opened my eyes and peeked though my fingers. It was done, and as my surgeon pried the cast apart and away from my leg, I cringed. It looked shocking. My skin was dry and peeling and there was still minor yellowing from the bruises around the incision marks.

'Yuck, it looks hideous.'

'It does not. It actually looks really good. It's healed nicely. Now, can you push against my hand?'

I tried to push his hand away with my foot. I could do it, but only weakly.

'That's good. How does that feel?'

'Okay.' It did feel okay. Just getting some air to my leg was nice.

Derek drove me home after I was fitted into a moon boot. It was much heavier than the cast, but it was much better because I could take it off as long as I kept my foot completely still. I could also scratch as freely as I liked. I thanked Derek for his help and organised another lesson for the following day.

* * *

Later that night, after I'd just settled in bed, my phone rang.

'Do you miss me?' I answered, after seeing a picture of my Mr Hotness Clark appear on the screen.

'Do you need to ask?' he replied, and I visualised him smirking. 'So how'd you go at the surgeon's clinic today?'

'Good. I'm wearing astronaut's foot attire. It's rather sexy. And, best of all, I can itch and scratch as much as I like. Mind you, he cut my cast off with a friggin' saw, Bryce. A sharp, fast and incredibly scary saw. I was terrified.'

'Aw, honey, I'm sorry I wasn't there. At least Lucy was though. I'm sure she would've held your hand.'

'Actually, no, she wasn't. She got held up in traffic. Derek took me instead.'

'Derek?' he questioned rather quickly. 'Why did Derek take you?'

Oh, fuck! How do I explain this without giving my secret away? Shit! Crap! Balls!

'He called in to pick up something just as Lucy rang to say she was not going to make it. Seeing that I was without a ride, he offered to take me and bring me back.'

'Right,' he mumbled. 'That was nice of him.'

There was an awkwardly silent pause. *Shit!*

I had to think of something to break our hiatus. 'So, about this naked picture ... I was thinking real time would be better.' *I hate myself sometimes. I am my own worst enemy. Stupid, stupid Alexis.*

'What did you have in mind?' he asked. Bryce's tone now sounded curiously intrigued and excited; my suggestion obviously successful in sidetracking his thoughts from Derek.

'FaceTime me.'

Almost instantly, I had a request come through to my phone for a FaceTime chat. I hit accept and was pleasantly greeted with my handsome man's sexy face.

'There's my gorgeous lady.'

'There's my yummy man.'

'Just seeing you makes everything better,' he admitted.

I sighed.

'Show me your moon boot, and you better be naked.'

'Hang on,' I giggled and put the phone down. *I can't believe I'm doing this.*

Stripping my nightie off completely, I laid back down on the bed, positioning myself in my most sensual pose. 'So, Mr Clark, I'll show you mine if you show me yours.'

All of a sudden, I was staring through the phone at a chandelier, all the while hearing the unzipping of his pants. Squinting my eyes at the phone, trying to make out exactly what he was doing, the scene changed again and Bryce's handsome hankering face was staring back at me. 'What do you want to see first, Ms Summers?'

Hmm ... cock? Arse? Pecs? V? 'I think I'll start with your chest.'

He held the phone out and positioned it in front of his body, giving me a view of his delectable chest. Even the sight of him via phone call was enough to begin my path to lubrication.

I cleared my throat.

'My turn. I want to see your boot, then I want you to bring the phone slowly up your body,' he said with authority.

I did as I was told, showing him my boot and moving the phone up my bent leg and across my pussy.

'Slow down, Alexis,' he demanded, with a dominant growl that escalated my heart rate. Again, I did as I was told.

'Fuck, honey, you have no idea how badly I want to run my tongue across you and taste your pussy. I fucking miss how good you taste. It's been far too long.'

'Lucky for you, tasting is now back on the menu.'

'I can see that.'

I had a sudden surge of confidence and dragged my finger down to my clit, so that he could see it swirl my sensitive spot.

'Alexis, you're fucking killing me. I should hop on a plane right now and come and do that myself.'

'I wish you could,' I moaned as I removed my finger and placed it in my mouth, moving the phone along with it so he could watch. I then sucked it and returned it to my pussy, gently playing with my entrance. 'Your turn, I want to see you stroke yourself.'

He obliged, and I was instantly rewarded with a close-up view of his cock being caressed by his clenched hand, slowly gripping from his base and stopping just short of his tip.

'Swirl your thumb over your head.'

He did.

'Pump it ... Start slow, then increase your speed.'

Again he did as he was told while I continued to tease myself with my finger. I watched him pick up his pace when I noticed his crown start to glisten.

'Slow down,' I growled, mimicking his dominant instruction.

'You sound so fucking sexy right now, honey.' *I actually didn't give a shit how sexy I sounded. I wanted to see him milk himself and I wanted to see it now.*

'Bryce, I want you to come for me,' I pleaded.

He didn't waste any time and began pumping himself vigorously. I could see the muscles in his lower abdomen tense, together with his upper thighs and forearm as he spilled out his orgasm, jerking with each thrust.

I licked my lips as I watched him. 'Mm, thank you.'

'Now, put your phone back down to your finger, honey.'

I obeyed.

'Flick your clitoris and do it fast.'

I twitched my finger quickly and took pleasure in my movements, closing my eyes and imagining it was Bryce between my legs.

'Alexis, I want to see your face when you come undone.'

'Uh huh,' I answered as my climax began to rise.

'Put your finger inside you, make it wet, then flick your clitoris again.'

I inserted my finger into my warm, wet pussy, sliding it in and out a couple of times. Then, I went right back to flicking my sensitive spot, ready to come for him. I sucked in a deep breath, arching my back as I lifted the phone to my face.

Staring at him intensely as I spiked, I let out a moan of pure relief then slowly came back down from my orgasm with deep controlled breaths.

'I'm not going to last five days, honey. I can fucking guarantee it.'

CHAPTER

22

The number of times I had woken up with a smile since being with Bryce was probably ridiculously unheard of, yet it continued to happen pretty much on a daily basis, this day being no exception.

I picked up my phone and stared at the screen, willing the vision of my first phone-FaceTime sex with Bryce to reappear. It was incredibly hot and satisfying, and in lieu of him actually being here with me, was my new favourite form of release. Another reason why I was smiling as I got myself out of bed and into the shower was because I would be continuing my guitar lessons with Derek today. I had a long way to go, but he'd seemed pleased with my progress after just one day, therefore my aim to play at least part of a song for Bryce was promising.

Another thing on my to-do list for the day was speak to Samantha. From the moment I found out about Gareth's DID diagnosis, I'd had this underlying feeling that I had to warn her about it. Call it a gut instinct, I don't know, but I just felt she had a right to know who she was really dating. Our encounters in recent times had been obviously brief, having only spoken to her momentarily at my party and again when she delivered my flowers from Carly. It was obvious she felt uneasy in my presence, and I'm not sure if that was result of my accident or if Gareth had told her an untruth about me. Either way, it was time to get to the bottom of it.

* * *

I finished my shower and made my way to the lounge room where Lucy was putting together the kiddy playpen she had bought yesterday.

'Look what Mummy bought for you, roly-poly. It's your own personal jail,' she said in a droll tone to Alexander as she clicked the walls in place.

I corrected her as I sat myself down on the sofa. 'It's not a jail, Luce.'

'It is. Look at the bloody thing, it has bars. I feel terrible putting him in this.'

'It's for his own safety. As long as you put some toys in there with him, he'll love it. Plus, you can now go to the toilet without taking him with you. I'm thinking that action in itself is far more detrimental to him than the kiddy pen.'

'Well, yeah, probably, I guess.'

I laughed at her confusion. 'Hey, I've been meaning to ask you something.'

'What?'

'Do you know if Gareth is still seeing Samantha?'

'I think so. I don't exactly ask him about his love-life. Why?'

'Because I think Samantha has a right to know about Gareth's condition. It has been bugging me for a long time.'

'She may already know.'

'See, that's the thing. I honestly don't think she does. If she did, I'm guessing she would re-evaluate her relationship with him.'

Lucy shrugged her shoulders.

'Look, I'm not calling her shallow or anything. I'm just thinking that she is young and naive and not the type who could handle a condition such as Gareth's. I am hoping to be wrong, you know.'

'So what are you planning? Clearly you plan on doing something.'

I sighed, thinking about the precarious situation. 'I don't know. A part of me is saying: "Yes, tell her, she has a right to know." But there is also a part of me that is saying: "Stay out of it, it's none of your business. Your interference could undo Gareth's progression of late." And believe me, Luce, the last thing I want to do is contribute to Gareth reverting back to a dark place.'

'Alexis, normally I would say stay out of all things that involve Gareth. But I know Samantha is your friend, and I also know that you are as stubborn as the best of them. What I will say is tread carefully. Say only what you need to and nothing else.'

'Will you help me?'

She sighed. 'I hate getting involved where Gareth is concerned. I've been on the receiving end of his alter Scott, and let me tell you ... it was terrifying.'

'What happened?'

'Gareth has an alter, Scott. I know you are aware of him. Bryce mentioned he has made himself known to you a couple of times.'

'Oh, yes, I've met Scott. I met him in the office and at the Tel V Awards.'

I hadn't mentioned to anyone about my third encounter with Scott, which was after the board meeting a few months back.

Lucy continued. 'Well, it was shortly after I'd gone off the rails and Bryce had — for the umpteenth time — come to my rescue. He'd let me stay here while I was detoxing and I'd been an ungrateful, selfish bitch to him in front of Gareth. Jessica said that my harsh outburst and unappreciativeness would have been the trigger to Scott's appearance.

'At that stage, we'd known that Gareth had developed post-traumatic stress disorder, but he had not yet showed any signs of the DID.'

Lucy had started gently combing her hair nervously and, if I wasn't mistaken, she appeared to be quite agitated.

'I had been sitting on the sofa watching TV. Gareth was at the dining table reading the paper, I think. Bryce had told me that he was going to get Uncle Charles to have some of my assets frozen, because I had been squandering my inheritance on drugs. As he left the room to go into his office, I screamed at him calling him a "fucking controlling prick." Shortly after his door closed, I felt a terrible pain on my head and soon realised Gareth was pulling me by the hair from behind the sofa.

'He had lost it, completely lost it. I remember him speaking in a cold, hateful voice as he yanked me up and over the back of the sofa to the ground. "You ungrateful, self-centred, fucking brat. He deserves so much better than the filth of a sister that you are." It was just so unlike Gareth and he sounded like a completely different person. At first I yelled at him to let me go, asking him what the fuck he thought he was doing. But it was his eyes that told me something was not right; also, his tone of voice was quite wrong. I screamed for Bryce at that point, because I was terrified and I felt at any moment he would rip my hair from my head.'

Sitting there, listening, and realising the extent of Scott's obsession with Bryce, had me in complete shock. 'Lucy, that sounds absolutely dreadful.'

'It was, but thankfully Bryce had heard my cry for help and came running into the room, grabbing Gareth and pinning him up against the wall. He'd asked him what the fuck he thought he was doing laying a hand on a girl, let alone his own cousin. Bryce was absolutely furious. But it was what Gareth did next that showed us there was something seriously wrong.'

She leaned over and teased Alexander with a soft squeaky toy, gently touching his nose with it, then moving it away, only to touch his nose with it again. Alexander thought it was a brilliant game.

'What did Gareth do, Luce?'

She took a deep breath. 'He said to Bryce, "The name is Scott, and you have no fucking idea how long I have waited to be pinned up against a wall by you," then he leaned forward and kissed Bryce.'

I shrieked and replaced my hands over my mouth.

'He only got so far as a peck, but it was enough to shock the shit out of us, especially Bryce, who then punched Gareth directly in the nose, knocking him out.'

'Jesus,' I blurted out.

'Yeah, Jesus all right. On the floor was Gareth out cold with a broken nose, Bryce standing over him running his hands through his hair, just staring, and I was still crumpled on the ground. That's when we discovered Gareth had DID and why he got it. Bryce was devastated and blamed himself. He also decided that from then on his martial arts training would be put to better use teaching women to defend themselves when being attacked, starting with me. So, although I can confidently say I can defend myself from my cousin and his psycho alter, Scott, I still try to avoid anything that could trigger his appearance.'

'Oh, Luce, I completely understand. Don't worry about me and my telling Samantha. I can handle it.'

'I hope so. The last thing you need right now is more drama, especially where Gareth is concerned.'

* * *

I deliberated over what Lucy said and agreed that I did not need any more drama in my life, but I had a conscience, and I desperately had to get the nagging Samantha-Gareth issue out of my head. Finally, I took the plunge and asked Abigail to send Samantha up to the penthouse to collect Bryce's brief, which at this point in time was non-existent.

I was sitting at Bryce's desk when Samantha knocked on the door.

'Come in,' I called out.

She opened the door and walked in, closing it behind her and gingerly making her way toward me.

'Hi, Alexis, how are you feeling? Oh, sorry, you don't need to answer that if you don't want to. Shit, sorry, I'm really not good with these types of things.'

'Sam, it's okay. I'm fine.' I smiled reassuringly at her.

She could barely look at me.

I pushed myself up from the desk and hobbled over to the sofa in Bryce's office. 'You got a moment for a chat?' I gestured to the other sofa opposite the one I sat on.

'Sure,' she hesitantly answered.

'So, what's been happening, Sam? I miss you. I feel like you avoid me now.'

'I don't mean to. It's just when I heard about your fall, I didn't want to say the wrong thing and upset you.'

'Don't be silly, I'm okay. I'm getting stronger both mentally and physically as each day goes by. It happened and it can't be changed. All I can do is move on.'

She smiled feebly at me.

'Oh, I've been meaning to ask you. I didn't get to say goodbye to you at my birthday party. What happened?'

I figured I'd play dumb and get her side of the story before I mentioned anything to her about Gareth.

'Oh.' She displayed an expression of confusion. 'Didn't Gareth say goodbye?'

'No,' I answered, with a dumbfounded expression.

'That's strange. As I was exiting the bathroom shortly after your announcement ... oh, shit, sorry, I didn't mean to mention the —'

'Sam, it's fine. Keep going.'

'Sorry, um ... where was I? Oh yeah, when I walked out of the bathroom, Gareth took my arm in his and said we were leaving. He was actually in a pissy mood if I remember rightly. He said the party was winding up. Sorry I never said goodbye, but Gareth told me he'd already done it on my behalf.'

'Maybe he did, I can't quite remember,' I said, brushing it off.

I had a sickly feeling in my stomach at the confirmation that Gareth had, in fact, lied about why he left the party. Something was not right and I had a feeling I knew what it was: Scott was pretending to be Gareth. I couldn't be positive though, and I had no idea how I would prove it without baiting him and putting myself or my children at risk. I would have to think about it a lot more, but first, I needed to tell Sam the truth. If my feelings were correct and Scott was disguising himself as Gareth, Sam deserved to know and she deserved to know immediately.

'Sam, I need to tell you something. It might come as a shock, but you deserve to know the truth.'

She tensed in her seat and looked at me intently.

'Has Gareth mentioned anything to you about his medical condition?'

She tilted her head to the side. 'Well, yeah, he suffers from horrible migraines, poor bugger. I can't stand a mild headache let alone a severe migraine.' She appeared to relax a little.

'Has he told you why he gets the migraines?' I probed further, causing her relaxed position to tense up again.

'No, and I didn't want to pry.'

'Hmm,' I mumbled.

'Alexis, what is it? Look, I know you are not a fan of Gareth, and clearly he was not a fan of yours, but he has been trying to make amends for that.'

'Sam, Gareth has Dissociative Identity Disorder with positive symptoms of schizophrenia.'

Her mouth dropped and she blinked.

'I'm not sure if you are aware, but Bryce's parents and brother were killed in a car accident when he was nineteen. Gareth had been in the car and was the sole survivor. He suffered severe head injuries and as a result developed DID.'

She looked at her hands which were entwined with each other. 'I ... um ... I had no idea.'

'I didn't think so. I'm sorry, I just thought you had a right to know. It's my understanding Gareth has many alternate personalities. Scott is the personality that does not get along with me.'

'I'm sorry, what?'

It was clear Samantha had no idea as to the complexity of Gareth's condition.

'Sam, his personality changes. One minute he is Gareth, the next he can be Scott, or Deirdre —'

'Who the fuck is Deirdre?' she blurted out.

'Deirdre is one of his alters, Sam. I have not yet met her. I've only met Scott.'

She dropped her head in her hands. 'I don't know if I can ... I mean ... what do I say or do with this?' She lifted her head, displaying a look of complete stupefaction.

'I don't know, hon. It might help to research the condition before you do anything rash though. I can tell you that he sees the family psychologist for therapy weekly, and takes medication daily to supress the alters from dominating him.'

'Why didn't he tell me?' she asked in an angry tone.

'I don't know. Maybe he was scared, or maybe because, as part of his treatment, he is encouraged to live his life normally and telling everyone he comes in contact with about his DID would hinder that.'

'Right,' she answered, still looking completely lost.

'I'm sorry, Sam. I just thought you should know the whole truth.'

She smiled mildly at me. 'No, that's okay. Thank you for telling me, I appreciate it. I just have a lot to consider now.'

'I know you do. But make sure you consider everything, okay?'

Sam stood up, then helped me up to stand with her. 'So, how long are you in that stylish thing?' she pointed to my moon boot.

'Five to seven weeks,' I answered with a pout.

'Well, it could be worse ...' She froze and her eyes widened. 'Oh, shit! Sorry, I didn't ... see what I mean? I'm hopeless, absolutely hopeless.'

'Sam, seriously ...' I placed my hand on her shoulder as I picked up my crutches. 'I'm sure you are not the only one who mouth-farts at the wrong time. We all do it.'

After Sam left the office, I felt only mildly better. Better because she was now aware of Gareth's situation and could make her own informed decision about what to do with regard to their relationship. But I also felt terrible, because I could see Sam's heart break as she realised her partner was not who she thought he was.

* * *

Derek stayed for dinner after knuckling down and giving me my day's guitar lesson.

'How's she coming along?' Lucy asked him as we ate our meals ordered from the hotel's kitchen. I missed my smirky chef and his culinary wizardry.

'She's a natural. Or am I the bomb when it comes to teaching?' He shot a smile at me. 'Yeah, I'm thinking I'm just that good.'

I rolled my eyes, so did Lucy.

'So, Alexis, how do you plan on springing your new-found guitar talent on my brother?'

'I don't know. I was just going to sit him down and play something, I guess, when the time was right,' I explained, as I popped a forkful of food into my mouth.

'That's boring, and plain ... just ... boring. You need to do it in a way that says "Look the fuck at what I have learned for you."'

I laughed, 'And how do I do that exactly?'

'At our gig in a few months,' she said proudly.

Derek choked on his food, and Nic screwed up her face.

'I'm singing at that gig you know,' Charli added.

'You are, are you?' Derek asked. Obviously this was news to him.

'Yep, Bryce said I could. I've been practising.'

'He did, and she has,' I confirmed.

'Yeah,' Nate moaned, 'she has been practising *a lot.*'

I narrowed my eyes at my son, a warning to be nice or else.

Lucy stood up and took her plate to the sink. 'Perfect, a family gig. Nic, do you want to join in, too?' She raised her eyebrows at her partner.

'Do you want to change Alexander's nappies for a month?' Nic counter-offered back.

'Point taken,' Lucy replied in a sweet voice. 'So what song are you going to play for him, Alexis? Do you need help choosing? The gig is in three months. You might want to start practising it.' *Um, shit! I only just picked up the bloody guitar. Steady on.*

'I haven't really thought about it, Luce, maybe "The Only Exception" by Paramore. I don't know.'

'Actually ... that would be doable, Alexis. It's a very basic song to learn on the guitar for the most part, and I could play what you might not be able to learn in the available time,' Derek said as the cogs in his brain started to turn.

'Yes, great song choice, Alexis, and perfect for your voice,' Lucy added, her brain cogs turning too. *I'm sorry, did you just say my voice?*

'What do you mean, perfect for my voice?'

'It's the perfect song for you to play and sing to Bryce at our gig. Oh my god, he is going to die when you perform this for him,' she declared with increasing excitement.

'I dunno, it's one thing doing it in private for him, but up on stage at one of your gigs? I don't think I can do that.' *Already I felt clammy and nervous.*

'Alexis, how much do you love him?'

'Lucy, that's unfair.' *You sneaky little guilt-tripper.*

'Well? How much?'

'More than anything.'

'Then you should do it, because I can tell you this would absolutely blow his mind.' *Really?*

'Can you sing?' asked Derek.

'Not —'

'Yes, she can,' Lucy interrupted.

'I can hold a tune, that's different from being able to sing,' I corrected.

'Pfft, I know for a fact you can sing.'

'How?'

'How did Bryce say you put it? Oh, yeah ... creepy research.'

Oh, for the love of ...

CHAPTER

23

So, it was set. In approximately three months' time when I was no longer supported by crutches and a hideous-looking boot, I would be performing 'The Only Exception' for Bryce at one of Live Trepidation's gigs. *How the flying fuck did they talk me into that? Oh, yeah ... it was because it was 'going to absolutely blow his mind'.* How could I have possibly refused when Lucy put it like that? And, after giving it more thought, Bryce had gone above and beyond when it came to doing things for me: helicopter rescue, Tel V Awards, 4Life, Kings of Leon, Uluru, Brylexis, and the list went on. I really had no choice, and I had to perform the absolute shit out of it because he deserved nothing less.

For the past few days, Derek and I had been practising as much as we possibly could, and my lessons had gone from learning how to understand and play music, to listening, copying and winging it — which had been working nicely. Already, I was getting used to the 6/8 time signature and the introduction of the capo on the second fret. I was also getting used to different methods of strumming the strings.

Bryce was due home the next day, and I was beyond excited. I couldn't wait to touch him, inhale him and taste him. *God, I sound like a Mr Clark-devouring monster.* The thing was, I was a greedy little monster when it came to him. I could not wait to have him in close proximity again. He was my drug of choice and I had suffered withdrawals for the past week. As much as I was looking forward to seeing him, I was also grateful for the time he was spending away as it was giving me more of an opportunity to practise with Derek. I didn't see how that was going to continue after Bryce returned — apart from sneaking off to rehearse with Derek behind Bryce's back. I hated that idea. I knew too well that that kind of behaviour could only lead to bad things; things like lying, deceit and wrong assumptions.

* * *

Derek and I had been practising for a couple of hours and my fingers were sore. I wanted a rest, so he had me watch him play the verse and chorus of the song over and over, because essentially — where the chords were concerned — the verse and chorus were one and the same.

I was lightly singing the words and watching him strum when the door to the man-cave opened and Bryce walked in. His sudden appearance gave me a fright, but the shock soon disappeared when that natural wave of guilt at being caught out washed over me, setting in panic and making my response to his arrival plainly not what it should've been.

'Hey.' I smiled gingerly at him. 'You're back early.' *Shit! What do I tell him?*

'Yes, I am,' he replied, as he eyed Derek with a suspicious scowl.

'Hey, mate. I was just picking up the new music composition,' Derek said casually, as he put his guitar down.

I propped myself up and grabbed my crutches so that I could make my way over to Bryce, embrace him and, hopefully, remove that betrayed look clearly plastered across his face.

I stopped in front of him and balanced my arms on the tops of the crutches.

'Did you get everything finish —'

He grabbed my face in his hands and kissed me hard before I could finish my question. His kiss wasn't a sensual, loving caress. It was possessive and angry. I pulled away from him and caught a look of distrust in his eyes, and it stabbed me right through the heart.

'I'll get going, let the two of you get reacquainted,' Derek said, just as casually as before. He packed up his guitar and slipped past us. 'I'll let myself out.'

'Best you fucking do that,' Bryce replied, his voice dripping with accusation.

My mouth fell open and I glared at him. Derek stopped on his way to the door, just a few feet from where Bryce and I were standing and turned slowly. The tension in Bryce's face was at boiling point, and I sensed that he was almost ready to rip Derek to shreds. I was almost certain Derek would've put up a decent fight.

Placing my hand on Bryce's arm to calm him down, I farewelled Derek. 'Bye, Derek, and thanks again,' I said apologetically.

'No sweat, Alexis,' he replied while eyeing Bryce, before he turned back around and left the room.

When the door closed behind Derek, Bryce stared at it for a few seconds, as if he was ready to knock it down and go after Derek.

I reached up and turned his face toward mine. 'What the hell was that all about? You were so rude to him,' I complained.

'You tell me, Alexis. What the hell did I just walk in on?' he replied with an icy tone.

'Are you serious? Please tell me you are not serious.'

'Oh, I'm very fucking serious,' he hissed, as he eyed me fiercely.

My mouth dropped again and I turned away from him, hobbling on my crutches toward the door. 'What you just walked in on was Derek calling past to collect whatever it was he needed to collect.'

I wrenched the door open and proceeded through it to the lounge. Lucy was at mother's group, Nic was at work, and the kids were still at school.

'Why did he have his guitar with him if he was only picking up sheet music?'

'I don't know,' I replied, exasperated. *Fuck!*

'Doesn't make sense, Alexis. What the fuck are you not telling me?'

He followed me out of the room, and I swivelled around to face him.

'Nothing! What are you insinuating?' I shouted defensively while pointing my crutch at him.

The fact he would think what I thought he was thinking pained my heart. How could he possibly assume there was something going on between me and Derek after all he and I had been through? How could he think that?

'Is something going on between you and Derek?' he asked me, outright.

A tear rolled down my cheek. 'What, so you think that just because I was tempted by you, I would also be tempted by the next person who came along? Fuck, Bryce, you don't know me at all.'

I continued on toward the elevator. He followed and gently grabbed my waist, spinning me around and pinning me up against the entry-way wall, the very spot that held memories of so many heated, passionate and now anger-fuelled moments.

Both my crutches fell to the floor.

He pressed his body firmly into mine. 'What was he doing here, and why were you sitting with him, watching him play the guitar?' His tone had softened and his face was only centimetres from mine.

'Let me go, Bryce. I have nothing to explain.' I turned my head to the side, not wanting to look at him.

He gently placed his hand under my chin and turned my face back to him. 'Alexis, answer me.'

'Why? It's obvious you don't trust me.' More tears fell down my cheeks as I stared into his eyes. 'Is this how it's always going to be between us? No trust, because I gave you a small piece of me when I was still with Rick?' I whispered.

'No, honey ...' His voice surrendered and he dropped his head. 'I just know when I'm being lied to.' He raised his gaze back to mine. 'And you're lying to me, aren't you?'

'So you immediately think the worst. Did you not stop to think that I could be lying for a reason? One that did not lead to me having it off with your best friend?' I gave him a questioning look and the look he returned was one of remorse. 'Obviously not.' I sighed and turned away once more. 'Let me go.'

He turned my face back to him yet again. 'So you admit that you are lying?'

'Yes.'

'Are you going to tell me what you are lying about?'

'No.'

'Why?'

'Because I don't want you to know. Not yet, anyway.'

'Alexis, that doesn't cut it,' he said, through gritted teeth.

'Do you trust me?' I asked imploringly, as I ran my fingers down his distraught face.

He searched my eyes for a moment, a moment longer than I would've liked or expected. 'Yes,' he finally said.

'Then do that and trust me. When I want you to know why I need Derek to help me, I will tell you.'

He continued to hold me against the wall as he peered into my eyes, into my soul, my answer obviously causing him distress.

I smoothed his hair away from his face. 'Bryce, I promise you that I love you, only you. And I promise you that no man has made me feel what you make me feel, and no man ever will. I promise you I will never betray you, not in any way. I love you. *You.* I'm only going to say it once, so either accept it and take me to bed ... or, just take me to bed. It's your call.'

I waited a split second before his lips met mine, this time the anger gone and intense love and passion once again present. I wrapped my leg around his waist and struggled to lift the other, my muscles all but depleted. He noticed my strain and gently lifted it for me as he walked me into the elevator.

'I've missed you,' he said through tongue and lips. 'I couldn't wait any longer to see you again, to touch you again. I just don't function without you any more.'

'I know, and that's not healthy.'

'Fuck being healthy,' he growled, as he walked me into our room.

I giggled as he tenderly placed me on the bed, my amusement stopping when he reached for the button on my jeans. Just that one action indicating his motives, had my pussy aching for his touch. So much so that I lifted my pelvis automatically in order for him to pull my jeans down with ease. He did just that, but stopped at the freakin' moon boot.

Slowly, he undid the velcro straps. 'How is it?' he said as he gently lifted my foot from its brace to inspect it.

'Good. Apparently really good. I started physiotherapy just the other day and, already, I'm gaining strength.'

'That's great, honey.'

Bryce carefully removed my jeans completely, leaned over and placed a soft kiss on my healing ankle. My body reacted and shuddered in response as he continued to kiss up my leg, stopping when his lips touched the material of my underwear. He looked up at me through his lashes and grinned as he bit down on the seam and aggressively dragged them off with his teeth. *Oh, holy fuck, he's a sexy animal.*

Crawling back up my legs, he bent my uninjured one over his shoulder, his head now perfectly positioned in between them. I sucked in a ragged breath as he touched my clit with the pad of his finger, my body bucking with sensation.

'Oh god, I've missed you ... I missed this,' I breathed out as I tilted my pelvis to get closer to his mouth while his finger kept teasing me, tracing my wetness up and down and swirling at my entrance. 'What are you waiting for?' I panted.

'I'm admiring the view. Your pussy is pretty fucking nice to look at.'

'It's also pretty fucking nice to taste, so stop admiring and taste it.'

He chuckled, leaned forward and pressed his nose into me, then, pausing for a second, breathed hot and dipped his tongue. I clenched his hair and dug the heel of my foot into his back.

'Mm,' he growled, so I clenched and dug deeper. I loved his growls.

Bryce pleased my pussy with his sensational tongue and fingers, flicking and sucking at my clitoris while sliding his fingers in and out of me. I could feel every insertion and every retraction as he repeated the motion, while altering the pace. His movements had the ability to trick and tease my mind and body.

'I want you, Bryce, all of you,' I pleaded.

He pulled away and crawled on top of me. 'I'm all yours, honey.'

It had been weeks since we were last with each other, and I desperately wanted to feel him inside me again. I needed to feel him for so many reasons. Reasons that were solely for pure carnal necessity, but also reasons for wanting to reconnect with him after both of us losing a piece of our hearts.

'And I'm all yours, don't forget that,' I whispered.

He leaned down and pressed his warm lips to mine, gratifying me with his delicious tongue.

I pulled away. 'Oh, and please don't forget my ankle is exposed, unprotected and highly fragile.'

'Your ankle is safe with me, I'll be careful. Now shut up and let me fucking make love to you,' he growled with a smirk on his face.

I grabbed the back of his head and pulled him to me, hungry for the man who fulfilled my every need. He reached up and unbuttoned my blouse, pushing each side away and exposing my chest. His hands felt smooth as they glided across my skin, removing the unwanted material.

Reaching down, I took hold of his belt buckle, unlooping the leather strap and gaining access to his pants. I unbuttoned those too, and found his erection ready for my grasp.

A rumble of relief resonated through him as I placed my hands on his cock, slowly gliding them up and down. I delighted in the feel of him tensing under my touch. It gave me a sense of empowerment and reassurance that his cock belonged to me.

Clenching it tightly, I positioned it at my entrance and, before he pushed into me, we had a silent moment, our eyes communicating as perfectly and as clearly as they had always done. I could tell he was checking to see if I was okay, and ready to make love for the first time after losing the baby.

I was. I was ready to move ahead in the hope that once again I would carry his child, our child.

I touched his face, smiled softly and nodded, causing his eyes to sparkle and fill with love as he pushed forward, easing himself inside me. His rhythm was slow, soft and sensual, and I took great pleasure in every rock of his hips.

He was controlled in his delivery, fashioning our lovemaking to last a long time so that we could savour each other without a care in the world. I wanted to roll him over and slide my tongue down his neck and chest and follow the happy trail to a happy place. But I couldn't. I couldn't move without hurting my ankle. So I accepted submission and let him take control of my body, which he did with a blinding talent. He owned every part of me and made it known by leaving no surface of me untouched.

'I hate not being able to move, Bryce. I want to climb on top of you and ride the fuck out of you,' I said breathlessly.

He lowered his head and tongued my neck just below my ear. 'I love it when you ride the fuck out me, too. But right now, you *will* lie here, and you *will* let me love you.'

I dragged my nails down his back as he escalated his pace, feeling my own orgasm on the verge of explosion. 'You feel so good,' I moaned.

He grabbed my hands and held them above my head. 'Tell me you love me and only me,' he demanded, as he dragged his length out to the tip.

'Bryce!' I pleaded, closing my eyes and wanting the feel of him to return.

He slowly slid back inside me, then pulled out again just as brutally slow. Grazing his teeth on my lobe, he breathed into my ear one more time. 'Tell me. I want to hear it again.'

I arched my neck and moaned louder. 'You know I love you and only you.'

He leisurely slid back in, then out. 'Again,' he growled, his long strokes pure bliss.

'You, Bryce,' I breathed languidly.

Another long delicious stroke followed by an animalistic groan. 'Alexis.'

'You,' I replied more aggressively.

He increased his pace, sliding in and out, harder and deeper.

'Only you,' I cried out and released as he spilled into me while jerking and kissing my neck. 'Only you, Bryce,' I repeated as I gasped for air.

His mouth found mine as he let go of my hands. I instantly grabbed his face and pulled his head back, looking at him intently. 'I love you and only you.'

'So you fucking should,' he smiled, before seizing my lips.

We lay there bathed in sweat for several minutes, entwined in each other's arms. I was limp, exhausted and thoroughly sated. I was also relieved to once again feel I had jumped another hurdle in my life. Although this particular hurdle wasn't one I wanted to forget, or put behind me. There were hurdles or roadblocks in my life that I wanted nothing more than to make a distant memory of, or disregard even, but my miscarriage was not one of them. Yes, I wanted to move forward and carry on with my life, but I wanted to acknowledge what I'd lost and remind myself daily of what I already had, and what I could still attain. I wanted to be always grateful. If I had learned just one thing in life, it was that pessimism hurt those who could not, or did not, want to be optimistic.

* * *

Bryce and I decided we would go to Nate and Charli's school and surprise the kids by picking them up ourselves. I also needed to see my friends and break through the initial awkwardness that always plagued a terrible situation. I accepted that those types of reactions were natural responses to a sad event and were inevitable. But it didn't mean I liked to let that awkwardness linger and settle in, or drag on and on before things went back to normal.

We pulled into the school car park in the Lexus, and I spotted Tash, Lil, Jade and Steph. Tash had not long left City Towers herself to pick up William and Thomas, and I loved that Bryce had been so wonderful when organising her role as an event supervisor. She now had a flexible job she loved and was able to work hours where she could still drop her kids off and pick them up. He'd mentioned she was always thanking him for it.

'Wait there, honey, and I'll help you,' he said, as he switched off the engine.

He exited and gave the girls a wave as he crossed over the front of the car and opened my door. I went to grab my crutches when he lightly gripped my arm and pulled it toward him.

I automatically protested. 'No, you are not carrying me in the car park of my kids' school. I absolutely and unequivocally put my foot down, Bryce.'

'You can't put your foot down, remember?' he said with a tinge of arrogance. *Smartarse.*

'Bryce, I mean it,' I said sternly.

'Okay, okay,' he chuckled. 'Your friends are coming over here, anyway, so I won't need to carry you.' He nodded toward the girls who were making their way to the car. 'Just let me help you out, honey.'

'Okay,' I said, as I abandoned my stance.

Bryce took hold of both my hands and slowly pulled me up and out of the passenger seat so that I was standing on one leg. I put my hands on his shoulders for support when he took advantage and placed his hands on my sides, lifting me flush against his chest and quickly wrapping his arms around my arse.

'You lying arsehole, put me down,' I said through gritted teeth, while scanning the car park for onlookers.

'Settle down, I'm only carrying you to the bonnet. Although, we can stay just like this if you'd like.'

'Bryce Edward Clark —'

He gave me a wicked smile. 'Bonnet it is, then.'

As he placed me down on the hood of the car, I glared at him with a smile that I tried desperately to suppress but couldn't. He was just so aggravatingly adorable and I had to secretly commend him on his efforts.

Standing there facing me with his back to my approaching friends, I looked up at him and let out a long, frustrated breath.

'I hate this part,' I said, with a regretful groan.

'What part?'

'The sympathy and sadness part.'

He lifted his hand and put his knuckle under my chin, tilting my head up. 'It goes hand in hand with progression.'

'I know. I just hate it.'

He winked at me encouragingly as Steph stopped beside him.

'Lex, how are you?' she asked as Bryce stepped aside.

She moved forward and wrapped her arms around my neck, giving me a squeeze.

'I'm getting there, luv,' I replied, while smiling reassuringly over Steph's shoulder to the others.

'That's good, hon. One step at time,' Lil said, always calm, supportive and first to offer encouragement. Jade agreed and gently squeezed my thigh. I placed my hand on top of hers as a gesture of thanks, that being all Jade and I needed to exchange. She was like me in that way; sometimes less is so much more.

Tash stepped up to me next, pausing before she leaned and hugged me tight, sending me a message through her body-hugging squeeze. The beautiful bitch brought a tear to my eye.

'Don't you dare start singing,' I warned, as I choked back more tears.

I heard her sniffle next to my ear. 'I won't ... I'm just ... so sorry, Lex.'

I whispered back. 'I know, hon.' I patted her back to let her know I was grateful for her thoughts, but that I was all right.

She pulled away and wiped a tear. 'If you need anything, you know where I am.'

I nodded. 'I know, Tashy.'

'You know where we all are,' Lil reaffirmed.

'Yes, I do.' I smiled then quickly changed the subject. 'And as soon as this boot is off and my foot is dance ready, we are going out.'

Tash playfully rolled her eyes. 'You can still dance with crutches, Lex. You'd pull off a decent zombie in 'Thriller'.' She proceeded to slump her arms and twitch her shoulder and neck.

'You idiot,' I giggled. 'No, I'm not going out in public and dancing with crutches, forget it.'

Bryce asked Tash how the job was going while I talked to the girls about the surgery and when I was expected to be walking properly again. I also reminded Lil and Steph that Charli's birthday was approaching and that she wanted to have a sleepover with her friends, which included Lil's daughter, Jasmine, and Steph's daughter, Katie. Both Lil and Steph were over the moon at the prospect of relinquishing their daughters into my care for the evening. Me ... not so keen. I remembered all too well how loud, fun ... and loud, a sleepover of young girls could be.

The bell sounded and children began finding their waiting parents. Nate spotted us first and excitedly jogged our way.

'Bryce!' he shouted, right before he kicked the football in his direction. Bryce was quick and took off, marking it before it hit any cars.

'Nate, not near the cars,' I rebuked.

'Sorry,' he called back.

I noticed Charli skipping happily toward us when a girl I did not recognise walked up beside her and said something Charli did not like, causing her to stop and turn toward the girl. I noticed Charli's fists ball at her sides and I knew that was not a good sign.

'You're just mean,' she yelled at the girl.

The little girl shoved Charli, nearly causing her to fall backward.

'Hey,' I called out ready to hop my way over there when Nate saw the commotion and went to Charli's aid in my stead. The little girl saw him coming and ran off.

'What did she say?' Nate asked Charli as they walked closer.

'Nothing, she is just a bully. I hate her,' she answered.

Charli walked right up to me and pressed her head into my stomach before wrapping her arms around me.

I placed my hand on her head and spoke softly. 'What was that all about?'

'Nothing, Mum, she just sucks and she smells like cheese.' *How a child smells like cheese, I wasn't sure.*

'Charli, why did you yell at her?'

'Because she said babies are dumb. They are not dumb. My sister wasn't dumb,' she said angrily, her head still pressed against my abdomen.

Tash put her hand to her mouth, Bryce looked in the direction the little girl took off in and I just held Charli tightly.

'Little girls that smell like cheese are dumb, Charli. Not babies.'

'I hate cheese,' she said as Bryce opened the car door for her.

'No, you don't, silly rabbit.'

* * *

We sat around the breakfast bar watching Bryce make dinner after we got back to the apartment. It had taken a while to douse Charli's raging anger toward the cheese-girl, who Charli refused to identify by her real name. I decided to let it go because, like me, she was incredibly stubborn and I knew from my own experience that constant probing would only make her clam up more.

Switching my attention from an uncooperative Charli, I offered to help Bryce with the dinner preparations instead. He refused, so I turned my offering into demanding and was rewarded with dicing the onions. I made a point of telling myself never to offer or demand again, as the onion fumes singed my eyeballs, forcing tears to spill onto my cheeks.

'So, Charli-Bear ... goddamn it! My eyes ...' I wiped my sleeve across my face. 'Urgh! Have you thought of a name for ... who invented onions anyway? Stupid smelly things.'

Bryce was laughing as he chopped carrots.

'Laugh all you want. I'm never offering to help you again.'

'Good,' he arrogantly replied.

I glared at him, but it must've resembled a wincing, screwed-up, ugly glare as I could not yet open my eyes without them burning like fuck.

'Sorry, Charli. Have you thought of a name for your sister yet?'

'Yes,' she said happily.

'Well? Let's hear it, sweetheart.'

'Bianca,' she said confidently.

As soon as she said it I loved it. 'That's a beautiful choice. Why did you choose Bianca?'

'Because it's pretty, and I like it, and it has all our initials in it.'

Bryce stopped chopping and just stared at Charli. I was speechless, too. She had put so much thought into it, much more thought than a six year old should have. It was so endearing.

She noticed our pause and continued. 'And anyway, I didn't like Blanche or Cinba.'

I looked at Bryce and smiled, trying not to laugh and also thankful she had not chosen Cinba — it reminded me too much of *The Lion King*. He put his knife down, picked up Charli and sat her on the bench so that she was his height.

'Bianca is perfect, Charlotte. Thank you.' He leaned in, kissed her on the head, then went back to chopping the carrots.

I noticed a tear in his eye as I wiped my own. 'I'm chopping onions, what's your excuse?' I said to him lovingly.

'I don't have one,' he replied.

CHAPTER

24

I've never liked cemeteries, even as a young teenager, when it had been 'cool' to sneak into the local one at night and pretend to call upon the dead. I'd hated that game and, at the time, I'd hated my brother for blackmailing me and Jen to go along with him and his idiot friend. I can't say that as an adult my dislike for cemeteries had decreased, because it hadn't, and as I hobbled along the gravel path in between row upon of row of headstones, that became hugely apparent. It wasn't that cemeteries gave me the creeps — unless I was at one during the night with said stupid brother and idiot friend. No, it was more that they held such sadness and the loss of people who were dearly missed.

As reluctant as I was about being at Melbourne General Cemetery, I wouldn't have wanted to be anywhere else other than with Bryce at that very moment. I had promised him I would be there to support him on the anniversary of the accident that claimed the lives of his parents and little brother, Lauchie. It was also the accident that subsequently led to Gareth suffering from Dissociative Identity Disorder.

Gareth, Lucy and Nic were walking a few metres ahead of us. Lucy was carrying three large lilies, Nic carried Alexander and Gareth held a book called the *The Hunger Games*.

Bryce was by my side as I hopped along on my crutches, crutches I dearly wished to burn on a celebratory bonfire. He was quiet; they all were, but not in a bad way. I guess doing this annually for the past sixteen years had made each year that little bit less harrowing ... then again, possibly not. Maybe they had just found a mutually agreed way to deal with their emotions and communicate on this particular day. Either way, I was still glad to be by his side, supporting him.

'Hey, you all right?' I said in a low voice.

He looked over at me. 'Yeah, but it doesn't get any easier, you know?'

'I don't think it's supposed to get easier. I think you just learn to accept that you are supposed to believe that it does.'

Bryce scoffed mildly. 'Yeah, we do tend to fool ourselves more than we fool those around us.'

'Uh huh, we do. It's one of life's great delusions,' I said, with some degree of disappointment.

He placed his hand on the small of my back. 'I'm glad you're here with me.'

I looked up into his sad but appreciative eyes. 'Me too.'

There was silence for a minute then Bryce slowed his pace, forcing me to do the same. 'I need to warn you.'

'Warn me of what?' I asked curiously.

'There's a very good chance you could meet Deirdre today.' *Deirdre? Oh ... Deirdre.* Deirdre was one of Gareth's alters, an alter that was not only female, but elderly, and a mother hen type, so to speak. From what I had been told, she kind of held the other alters in check and tried to keep the peace.

He struggled to retain a straight face, but I could see a trace of humour creeping in. 'Let me just say she is ... um, how do I put it? Pushy ... and forward ... and ...' he leaned in closer, 'fucking annoying.'

'Bryce!' I whispered back, my eyes darting from him to the back of Gareth's head.

'She is, you'll see.' *Oh god. I hope Deirdre doesn't want to hurt me like Scott does.*

The thought of Scott wanting to hurt me entered my mind, causing a wave of dread and a vision of my fall again. *Alexis, stop linking the two together. Scott was not there in the apartment. You would have seen or heard him.* I had to keep telling myself that. He couldn't possibly have been there that morning, could he? No, he didn't have access to the apartment. Bryce had made sure all key card access numbers were changed after his last uninvited visit.

'We're here,' Bryce said, snapping me out of my thoughts and compelling me to halt before I ran right up the back of Gareth.

I looked up and noticed Lucy and Nic on their knees and placing the lilies on each of the three graves. Lindsay and Stephanie Clark's headstones were on either side of Lauchlan Clark's headstone, and I found it both touching and fitting, as if they were both still nurturing and protecting their young son even after death.

Gareth moved forward and propped the book up against Lauchie's headstone. 'This one's a good one little mate, you'll like it,' he said, his voice soft and tender, and obviously holding an enormous amount of love for his young cousin. It was heartbreaking, but also enlightening to see this side of him. He stood back and took in the grave before him.

Bryce noticed me staring and leaned closer to my ear. 'Lauchie loved books, and so does Gareth. He brings him a new one every time he visits.'

Gareth removed a weathered paperback that I'm assuming he'd left here the last time then stood back up while gazing down at Lauchie's grave with a lost expression. Bryce moved forward and placed his hand on Gareth's shoulder, giving it a tight squeeze before putting his hand back in his pant pocket.

'God, I miss them,' sighed Lucy as she traced her finger along the letters of her mother's headstone.

Nic wrapped her arm around Lucy's shoulder, pulling her head closer to gently touch her own. Alexander squealed at his mother's sudden closeness while trying to grab at her hair. I hopped two steps forward so that I was standing next to Bryce again, then I slid my hand into his pocket, taking a hold of his and removing it so that I could encase it in my own and let him know I was there for him. He looked down at our interlaced fingers then up to my eyes. His eyes were moist, and the hurt and pain he felt was clearly visible, a small piece of me destroyed at the sight of his distress. In that moment I decided I absolutely hated the man who ran the red light and caused this overwhelming feeling of grief, hurt and loss. I hated that man.

Lucy laid out a blanket next to her mother's grave and put her hands out for Nic to pass Alexander to her. 'Come here, my big boy,' she cooed at him. 'Let's tell Nanna what you have been doing lately.' Her sad demeanour was pushed aside so she could forge a happy alternative to replace it.

'Yeah, tell Nanna how you keep rolling around everywhere and so Mummy bought you a jail,' Nic said while clapping Alexander's hands in her own.

'Don't,' Lucy groaned. 'I already feel bad about the stupid kiddy pen.'

'Mum would absolutely freak if she saw that thing, then she'd throw it right over the balcony,' Bryce interjected with a knowing smile.

He took a seat on the grass next to Lucy, then stretched out his arms to gently pull me down into his lap.

'What is so wrong with a playpen? I used one with both my kids, and they don't have a jail complex,' I said defensively.

'I don't know, they just kind of look punishing. Maybe if they replaced the bars, I'd feel better. Hey ...' she addressed Bryce, lightly flicking the back of her hand on his leg. 'Remember that time when Mum's friend Ros came over, and her son, Jacob, had one of those child restraint things on —'

'Yeah,' Bryce smiled as he traced his finger up and down my leg. 'Mum took it off him and threw it straight into the fireplace.'

'How shocked was Ros,' Lucy giggled.

'It did look like a leash, Luce. Mum was appalled.'

'I know. That was so funny,' she reminisced, lightly shaking her head.

I looked at Nic, who shrugged her shoulders as if to say, 'I don't know. I haven't heard this story before.'

Bryce caught our exchange and offered an explanation. 'Mum was a strong believer in free will: no restraints, no restrictions. And that included kiddy restraints.'

I raised my eyebrows. 'No restrictions?' I teased. 'So that's where you get it from?'

He gave me a playful glare.

'If I remember rightly,' Lucy added, 'Ros asked Mum what the hell she thought she was doing, and Mum replied with something along the lines of "freeing Jacob from the confines of madness".'

Bryce shook his head and smiled as he recalled that particular memory of his mother. 'Yeah, and then Ros yelled, "How is keeping him safe madness?" and Mum yelled back, "Because *you* are supposed to keep him safe, not a dog lead! He is not a dog!"'

'Well, she was correct,' Gareth added, his feminine-sounding voice grabbing my attention. 'This Ros woman was the boy's mother, was she not? Therefore, it was her responsibility to teach him to obey without the use of a restraint. When my son was a young boy, he did as he was told. No ifs, buts, or maybes.'

Bryce whispered in my ear. 'Alexis, meet Deirdre.'

Gareth turned in our direction. 'Bryce, my dear boy, look at how handsome you have become. And who is this injured young lass on your lap?' Deirdre asked.

I was dumbfounded, stunned, at a loss for words. Gareth was staring me in the face, but it wasn't him, having lost his Gareth mannerisms. Instead, he now had a set of new ones, feminine ones, ones that suited an elderly woman such as Deirdre.

'Well,' she said with a hand on hip, 'aren't you going to introduce me?'

'Sorry, Deirdre,' Bryce said with dry amusement. 'This is Alexis, my girlfriend. Alexis, this is Deirdre.' *Fuck! What do I say?*

'Well, aren't you just a modern-day beauty. It's a pleasure to meet you, dear.' He extended his hand, or was it her hand? *Oh, god! I'm so freakin' confused right now.*

'And Lucy,' she squealed in a higher-pitched voice, 'you look simply exquisite and ... oh, don't tell me ... is this ... is this little bonny boy your son?'

Gareth gracefully pranced over to Lucy, smoothed his pants down as if he was wearing a dress, and sat on the blanket next to Lucy, legs together and folded to the side.

'Yes, Deirdre. This is my and Nic's son, Alexander,' Lucy happily replied.

Deirdre gave Nic a sideways glance, wrinkling up her nose. 'I don't see how that's possible,' she said in a pompous tone.

She turned back to face Lucy, fussing over Alexander.

Nic looked at Bryce and me and deliberately went cross-eyed. I burst into laughter.

'Something funny, dear?' Deirdre asked as she played with Alexander's finger.

'Oh no. Nothing's funny,' I answered, like an adolescent child trying to cover up a secret.

'One does not laugh unless one deems something funny, dear Alexis.' *One needs to get the fuck out of here before one puts her broken foot in it. Help!*

'I told her a joke,' Bryce added quickly, sensing my inability to find my maturity and act responsibly in this bizarre situation.

'Let's hear it then,' she probed with an encouraging flick of her hand.

'Dyslexic man walks into a bra,' he said, stony-faced and in an extremely flat tone.

Again, I couldn't contain myself and burst into laughter. Nic and Lucy followed suit and Bryce couldn't help but chuckle along with us.

Deirdre just looked downright confused. 'How does one walk into a bra? Was it hanging out to dry?'

* * *

We stayed at the cemetery for a couple of hours longer, Bryce and Lucy recalling moments of their childhood, a childhood which sounded just like most: innocent, fun and full of love-filled moments. Gareth — or Deirdre, I should say — continued to nosily extract little pieces of information about our lives. She was actually an endearing, yet overly inquisitive alter, and it wasn't long before I relaxed around her and took her, not at face value, but at character value.

'So, Alexis dear, how did you break that ankle of yours?' Deirdre asked as she tilted her head to the side to study my boot. 'That's quite an odd-looking contraption you have there.'

Bryce pulled me to my feet and helped me balance while getting my crutches.

'Well, I fell down the stairs ...' I paused, standing on one foot, feeling slightly uncomfortable in explaining to Deirdre the series of events that led to my fractured bone. I couldn't help shake the feeling that she already knew.

Bryce handed me my crutches which I secured in place under my arms.

'And how did you fall, dear?'

'I don't know,' I said, rather sharply.

Lucy placed her hand on Gareth's shoulder. 'It's time to leave, Deirdre,' she said softly, as she turned him around to face Lauchie's grave. I noticed him put his hand to his head for a moment.

'Deirdre normally leaves and Gareth returns about now,' Bryce whispered into my ear.

Moments later, Gareth turned to face us and, almost instantly, I could recognise *his* demeanour. It was so surreal. He lowered his gaze, appearing embarrassed, I'm assuming because he realised what had happened. I tried to ignore him and act as though nothing had happened, thinking that was the best thing to do.

Lucy and Nic had already started walking to the car, so Bryce and I turned to follow, Gareth behind us.

Bryce stopped. 'Shit! Give me a second,' he said, then turned back toward the graves, walking past Gareth. He knelt down and placed something small at the base of his father's headstone.

Gareth slowly walked up to me as I watched what Bryce was doing. 'You didn't have to tell her,' he said quietly, sounding partly angered and partly dismayed.

I looked up at him. 'Sorry?'

'Sam. You told her about my condition, and now she is "taking a break" to clear her head.' He held my gaze.

'Gareth, I'm sorry, but she deserved to know.'

'I liked her, Alexis. *A lot*,' he bit out as he leaned in closer, giving me an uncomfortably chilly feeling.

Unpleasant as it was though, I could see the sincerity in his eyes. *He really does like her.* I tried to reassure him.

'Gareth, give her some credit. She may just need some time to come to terms with it.'

'That's just it, I do give her credit. She's smart and, because of that, she'll stay away from me,' he sighed. 'For once, just once, I wanted to be selfish and have a normal relationship.' His shoulders slumped and he walked away as Bryce approached. *That's just it, Gareth, it wasn't normal. Hiding something like that is not normal.*

'Is everything all right? What were you and Gareth talking about?'

'Nothing,' I dismissively answered.

'Alexis, don't keep things from me. Not where Gareth is concerned.'

I sighed in defeat. 'I told Sam about the DID and he is unhappy about it.'

'Fuck!' he said quietly, as he looked up after Gareth.

I felt I needed to defend my actions and it annoyed me, but deep down I knew this was not so black and white. 'She had a right to know. It was killing me.'

'You should've told me of your intentions first.'

'Bryce, I've never run anything about my life past anyone for approval. I'm not about to start doing it now.'

'Gareth's situation is complex. You know this,' he said, with a huff of irritation.

I turned and began to head toward the limo. 'Of course I fucking know this. Have I not just been having a conversation with Deirdre for the past hour? That was probably one of the most complex situations I have ever found myself in.' I approached Danny who was waiting by the open door, but before climbing inside, turned back to face Bryce while lowering my voice. 'Listen, I had to tell Sam. I would not have forgiven myself if anything happened to her. And again, she had a right to know.' I gave him an end-of-story look before I awkwardly climbed into the limo.

Things were, of course, a little tense during the ride home. Gareth had stared out the window and hastily left us when we arrived back at City Towers. Lucy and Nic had focussed their attention on Alexander the whole time until we dropped them off at their house. And Bryce had been pondering quietly, but still tenderly touching some part of my body at all times, whether it was my shoulder, my arm, or my leg.

As soon as we were back in the apartment, I got dressed in my gym attire as my physiotherapist was due to make a house call in a matter of minutes. Bryce had made his way to his office, but not before making me a heart-shaped sandwich and setting it on a plate in the middle of the dining table. I smiled at his sentiment. Even in his frustration and sometimes anger toward me, he could still find a way to let me know he loved me.

The buzzer to the door sounded as I bit into my sandwich of love. 'Coming,' I called, my voice muffled with my mouthful.

I grabbed my crutches and headed for the door, opening it up to let in Tim, my physiotherapist. I'd had a couple of sessions with him already and found him really easy to get along with. He was also quite helpful and extremely professional. Tim was in his mid- to late-twenties, tall, shoulder length caramel hair, dark brown eyes and athletically built. I'd also found out during our last session that he had a fiancée and a two-year-old son.

'Hi, Tim. Come in.' I hopped backward, clearing the doorway to let him through.

'How's the foot?'

'Good. Although my upper thigh is tight and sore.'

'Yeah, that will happen. You're no longer using those muscles like you should be,' he explained as he made his way down into the lounge. 'I'm going to start you riding the exercise bike today, to build up strength in your leg muscles and to get your blood flowing properly again.'

He dropped his bag on the floor and opened the bifold doors. 'Come on, let's get to it.'

I spent fifteen minutes on the bike on a low setting, then with Tim's assistance and guidance, did some weights to strengthen my upper legs. After that session was complete we went back inside.

'Now, before I go, I'll get you to lie down on this mat here, and I'll stretch your legs for you.'

Tim rolled out the yoga-style mat and helped me position myself on my back. He knelt down at my feet and took hold of my foot, removing the moon boot. 'Have you put any pressure on it yet?' he asked as he gently felt the tender area. *Argh! Stop touching my foot, I hate it. Why didn't I break my finger, or nose even ... okay, maybe not the nose.*

I winced. 'No, not really.'

'In that case, this week I want you to put a very small amount of weight on it a couple of times a day, but not so much that it hurts. Pain is not gain in this situation.'

He shuffled forward, having one knee pushing against my arse and his other foot out beside my body to steady himself — kind like he was about to propose. Then, lifting my leg into the air, he pushed his body against it, stretching my hamstring. 'Feel the pulling?'

'Yep,' I struggled to say, feeling the strain on my leg. I ignored the stretched ache of my muscles by continuing to talk. 'So, how's your son?'

'Good, although he thinks his bedroom wall is a giant piece of paper,' he answered with a roll of his eyes.

I laughed. 'Tell your fiancée to get some Magic Erasers. They live up to their name.'

'Sweet. I will.' He pushed my leg closer to my head just a little bit more. 'You feel that? Is it a good stretch?'

'Yeah,' I awkwardly mumbled again.

Just as I answered, Bryce stepped out from behind Tim, his hands in his trouser pockets.

'Hi,' I groaned, while straining as my leg was pushed into my abdomen, making it difficult to speak.

'Hi,' he answered sternly, while holding his hand out to Tim and introducing himself. 'Bryce Clark, Alexis' partner.'

Tim let go of my leg, but pushed his body harder into me so as to not lose the tension in my stretch. He reached his now free hand out to shake Bryce's. 'Tim,' he answered as he gripped Bryce's hand, 'Alexis' physiotherapist.'

I noticed Bryce's eye twitch as he looked down at our position on the floor. *He's jealous. My Mr Possessive Clark is jealous.* Then again, I wouldn't blame him. If Tim and I weren't wearing clothes, or on the floor for the sole purpose of stretching, one could think we were attempting the art of the *Kama Sutra*.

Hmm. Kama Sutra *and Bryce mixed together in a big ball of sexual Play-Doh. I must try that.*

I smiled up at him, letting him know I was aware of his unease. I didn't do it to rub salt into his wounds, I did it to reassure him that everything was fine and that I felt his jealousy was cute. He didn't see that meaning behind my smile and glared at me.

Bryce took a seat, resting on the sofa in his sexy, laidback couch position, one arm stretched across the back of the seat and his foot crossed over the top of his knee. I met his eyes and they told me he was tense, needy and desperate. He openly clenched the hand that rested on the back of the sofa and burned me with his stare. That's when my mouth broke into a seductive smile and I noticed his dick twitch in his pants.

My breath caught and I let out a small gasp.

'Is that too hard, Alexis?' Tim asked, his voice sounding worried. His concerned tone brought my attention back to his actions. *Hard? No, but what's pushing against Bryce's pants is hard and I want it.*

I looked at Tim and honestly replied. 'No, you can go harder if you'd like.'

Bryce swapped his leg over the other.

'No. I don't want to push you. Not yet, anyway,' Tim replied.

'How often should she stretch like this?' Bryce asked, still looking intently at my face.

'Daily, a few times if she can. It will loosen the tension in her legs and promote blood flow.'

Bryce nodded.

'Okay, Alexis, swap legs.' Tim shuffled backward and slowly brought my leg back down. 'How does that feel?'

'Good,' I deliberately purred.

Tim then gently set my foot down and lifted the other. 'Now you should get a bigger stretch out of this one. I should be able to push you harder.' He looked down at a spot on the floor, concentrating as he pushed into me, stretching my leg a lot closer to my head this time. While his stare was fixated on the ground, I seductively flicked my eyebrows up and down at Bryce, his response being a crack of his neck to either side. *God, I love that.*

I ran my tongue over the top of my teeth while eye-fucking him, driving him wild.

'All right, Alexis, remember what I said: a little bit of weight on the foot, but no pain; exercise bike daily, but only ten minutes; and stretch your legs out nice and hard.' He re-attached my moon boot and got to his feet, helping me up also. Bryce stood up and passed me my crutches, giving his pants a subtle readjustment.

We both walked Tim to the door.

'Thanks, Tim, and don't forget to tell your fiancée about those Magic Erasers,' I said as he walked out of the apartment.

'I won't. See you in a couple of days,' he called back.

I closed the door behind him and was instantly pinned up against it, Bryce's hard body pressed up against mine. I could feel his heart beating through his chest, and the heat that radiated from him was a mixture of burning passion, burning anger and burning need — all of which I absorbed.

My breasts swelled as they pushed into him and the friction against my nipples felt delicious. 'Do you have a problem with my physiotherapist, Mr Clark?'

'I have a problem with him pressing his cock into your leg.'

I bit the inside of my lip in order to subdue a smile. 'He was stretching me, Bryce.'

'Yeah, well I'm about to fucking stretch you, and I won't be fucking stretching your leg.' He scooped me up and I squealed as he carried me off to bed.

CHAPTER
25

After a few weeks of physiotherapy sessions every second day, my foot and ankle had improved dramatically. I was now able to put the majority of my weight on it by limping around with a walking stick, which was awesome, obviously, except now I felt like my late grandmother. I still had to wear the moon boot, but I could take it off when I was resting, during sleep, and during sex — so, a lot.

From the moment I told Bryce that I wanted to try for another baby — and from the moment we were in a position to actually do it — he had taken that confession and exploited the shit out of it, taking me against every available surface during any available moment of the day. When I looked back over the amount of times we had made love in recent weeks, I kind of felt like a sexed-up whoreasaurus, but not in a bad way. In a good way ... a very, *very* good way.

Things had started to go back to normal again, 'normal' being an under-appreciated word in my life. Normal, in the sense that the kids were happy and healthy, Bryce and I were happy and healthy — with the exception of my foot — and work was, as per usual, Bryce busily running his company and I busily running his errands and office. Even my relationship with Rick was on the mend, to a point where

I had felt comfortable enough to have a coffee with him and Claire after dropping the kids off at my old house. Yes, him *and* Claire! She and RJ had moved in with Rick and he seemed relatively happy. I say relatively, because I nonetheless picked up a very small vibe that Rick still loved me and wanted me back. I could see it buried deep behind his eyes in a place he thought was hidden, but wasn't, or not from me anyway.

There were things that he had been proficient in hiding from me, but either I had become more astute in their discovery or he no longer had the ability to successfully hide them. Either way, that ship had long sailed. I was Bryce's and he was mine, and I had never been more sure of anything than I was of that.

We can stumble upon a connection in life, a feeling, an instinct even, having an uncontrollable desire to act upon it. All the while knowing that acting upon it may or may not be the right thing to do. The thing is, it's in that action where we prove our initial feeling to be right or wrong. I had done just that, acted on my connection with Bryce, and it had paid off. We were in love — made for each other.

During these past weeks, I'd also covertly kept up my guitar lessons with Derek. Some were by way of FaceTime in the man-cave while Bryce was working, and others were when he was out of the office at appointments. It was tedious, and I hated sneaking around behind his back — especially after he had thought I was seeing Derek on the side — but I did it because I knew the outcome would be worth it. I was actually becoming quite good at playing the guitar considering the short amount of time I'd had to learn. Lucy was right; Bryce was going to absolutely love it. I couldn't wait. Well ... I couldn't wait to see his reaction, but I could definitely wait to get up in front of an entire roomful of people. That scared the absolute shit out of me. The gig was only just over a month away and I knew it wouldn't be long before I was taking that plunge and performing for him.

Those nerves, together with the frustration of still having to wear a stupid Velcro space-inspired foot brace, were dampening my recent good spirits. I'd had enough of my broken ankle and I didn't want it to be the reminder of my fall and miscarriage. I'd lost and endured so much more, but my ankle seemed to dominate and it kind of irritated me. I wanted out of this moon boot completely and back into my heels. I wanted to forget about falling down the stairs, but not forget about Bianca. She was far superior to my shattered ankle and she was deserving of my recollection so much more than my fall and subsequent fracture.

* * *

Feeling a little flat and wishing the next few weeks would pass by rather quickly, I sat on the circular ottoman in the middle of the walk-in stadium, my knees raised and my head resting on top of them. I sulked as I looked over my rainbow wall of heels, heels I missed terribly. It would be months before I could wear any of them again, and, pathetic as it may sound, it saddened me.

'Stop staring at your shoes and get out of there,' Bryce called from the bathroom.

'No! I can't do anything else with them at the moment, apart from stare, so I'm staring,' I grumbled.

The buzzer to the front door sounded. 'Perfect timing,' he mumbled.

I grabbed my walking stick and headed out of the room, momentarily stopping in my tracks at the sight of Bryce. He was not long showered and casually dressed in dark denim designer jeans which hugged his arse perfectly. He also had on a plain long sleeved black V-neck t-shirt which clung to his muscled arms and chest. He looked simply gorgeous.

'Where are you going?' I asked curiously and somewhat disappointed that he was going out without me.

'Catching up with the guys over a few drinks.'

He approached the top of the stairs and stopped, holding out his hand to me knowing I was still apprehensive about them, especially walking down on my own. I didn't know if this fear would ever leave me, but until I could walk properly again, it was either assistance from Bryce, or the elevator.

I took hold of his hand. 'When were you going to tell me about this? I kind of wanted to snuggle and watch a movie tonight.'

'We can do that tomorrow, honey.'

He smiled, but his smile betrayed him, displaying evidence of something hidden.

'What are you up to?' I asked, my face now smiling in response.

'You're about to find out.'

He led me down the remainder of the steps and to the entry door of the apartment. 'Are you ready?' he said mischievously, as he opened the door and stood aside, letting in Tash, Carly, Lil, Jade, Steph and Jen.

Tash walked in first, holding up a DVD of *Dirty Dancing*. 'Nobody puts Alexis in the corner,' she dramatically stated as she kissed my cheek.

My mouth dropped open in shock. Carls stepped up to me next and plonked a cake in my hands. She quickly kissed my forehead before heading straight for Bryce. I looked at the cake and smiled. She'd attempted my favourite, Lemon-lime Meringue Cake ... I must reiterate the word *attempted*.

Jade followed, holding a game board. 'Celebrity Head,' she said, grinning while dancing her shoulders up and down. She knew I loved games.

Steph playfully bumped Jade aside and gave me a quick hug then looked down at my foot. 'Thought as much,' she said, quite sure of herself. 'You need a pedi.' She held up her make-up bag, which contained some bottles of nail polish.

Lil was next, holding a big bunch of assorted brightly-coloured roses. 'This is your official cheer-the-fuck-up-party, luv. You didn't want to go out dancing, so we have come to you.'

Jen giggled and waved her Michael Jackson *Thriller* CD in the air.

I was speechless for a second then found my voice, although it was hesitant. 'What? When? Who?'

They all pointed to Bryce.

Normally he would shrug his shoulders or play dumb or dismiss it, but he didn't. He just strode toward me and grabbed my face with his hands, directing my lips to his. I fell into the kiss, heavily, greedily and completely mesmerised. My walking stick fell to the floor and I held out the cake, indicating someone better grab it before I dropped it. Someone did and, as soon as my hands were free, I placed them around his neck and threaded my fingers through his hair.

'Get a room,' Tash groaned.

'No, this is hot,' Steph replied.

'Where's the fucking popcorn?' Jade asked.

'I'm getting a drink,' Lil declared.

'I miss my husband,' Jen sighed.

And Carls just asked to join in.

I ignored them all, I was totally invested in the man in my arms, drinking him in and savouring his mouth. 'I love you so much,' I whispered against his lips.

'The feeling is mutual, my love.' He kept his eyes locked on mine. 'Now have a great night. Relax, drink; drool over Patrick Swayze, but just this once though,' he smirked.

'Don't you worry, he's got nothing on you. I've seen you dance ... in next to nothing, remember?' I raised my eyebrow seductively at him.

'What. The. Fuck!' Steph screeched. 'He dances ... too? Alexis, I officially hate you. H.A.T.E you.'

Bryce kept his eyes on mine, love pouring out of them. It literally made me weak at the knees. 'I'll see you later.' He kissed me again then left the apartment, this time his kiss leaving my lips tingling, swollen, confused and sad at his departure.

'Come on you. It's party time,' said Jen encouragingly as she threaded her arm through mine and led me to the lounge.

We sat down and watched *Dirty Dancing* while eating the delicious tapas that Bryce had arranged one of the complex's restaurants to deliver to us. He amazed me with his attention to detail and I pined for his return even more, so that I could show him my appreciation.

'Alexis Elizabeth Summers, get your head out of cloud-Clark and pay attention,' Tash snapped.

'What? Sorry.' I adjusted my Celebrity Head headband and took another swig of my gin. 'Is it my turn?' I asked.

They all barked. 'Yes!'

'Okay, geez! Um, am I male?'

'Sometimes I think you are,' Tash added sarcastically.

I launched my cushion at her.

'Yes, Lex, you are a male,' Lil clarified.

'Am I fucking hot?'

'Yes,' Steph said bluntly.

'Are you serious?' Lil was wide-eyed. 'No, Lex, he is not.'

'Yes, he is,' Steph corrected her. 'Don't tell me you wouldn't want that between your legs.'

'No, I wouldn't.'

'You're a lesbian, aren't you? Admit it, I'm totally fine with it, Lil. I love lesbians.'

I laughed at Steph's ability to deliberately bait Lil. Lil picked up her beer bottle and wrapped her lips around it suggestively, then took a drink.

'So am I fucking hot or not?' I shouted, over the top of the two of them.

Jade blew at her toes, which she'd just painted with polish. 'Debatable. Ask another question.'

'Am I an actor?'

'Yes. A very fucking good actor, in more ways than one,' Jen said, as a hint of anger crept across her face. *Hmm, interesting.*

'Do I have a big cock?' I asked as I tried to swallow my gin, the swallowing not working too well.

'Yes,' Steph said, in a manner that suggested she was picturing said big cock.

Lil gagged. 'Bet you it's tiny.'

Steph scowled at Lil. 'His hands are huge. Enough said.'

'That's a fucking myth,' Lil bit back.

I automatically found myself thinking of Bryce's large, luscious hands and his equally large luscious cock. *Myth or not, my Mr Huge-Hands Clark is not an exception.*

'Alexis! Stop thinking about wrapping your lips around Bryce's man-rod,' Tash said with her hands on her hips.

'Why? It's a pretty good man-rod,' I giggled.

'How good is it?' Steph asked eagerly.

'Oh ... real good.' I raised my eyebrows and opened my mouth suggestively. *Alexis, how many gins have you had?*

'I knew it. I knew you swallowed,' Carls piped in, concentrating really hard on painting her toes.

'So do you. And again, for the record, you can stop telling me all about it,' I reminded Carls.

'Pfft! Well, yeah, of course I do. It's full of protein, you know!'

Jen shivered, 'Na, yuck. I'd rather eat friggin' egg.'

We all looked at Jen and burst into laughter.

'What?' she said defensively. 'Do you all swallow?'

We all searched each other's eyes with sly smiles on our faces, no one else giving anything away, except for Tash, her lips beginning to purse.

I pointed at her. 'Tash, you little whoreasaurus, you swallow, too.'

'Alexis, how old are you?'

'About as old as you,' I drunk-giggled.

'Lexi, can you please pull yourself together and ask another fucking question or I'm quitting this stupid game,' Lil threatened.

'All right, all right. Have I been in a lot of blockbusters?'

'Yep,' they all answered.

'Well, if they are blockbusters, I'm guessing they are action movies.'

'Yep,' they all answered again.

I stewed on it for a second, then put two and two together. 'Will he "be back"?' I said in my best Austrian accent.

Steph rolled her eyes. 'Yes,' she groaned.

'Does he say "It's not a tumour" really well?' I asked, again in my horrible Austrian accent.

Jen cracked up laughing. 'You suck.'

I happy-danced a bum wiggle in my seat. 'Am I Arnold Swarzaschnitzel?'

Tash laughed and gave me a knowing smile.

'Don't you mean Schwarzenegger?' Jade asked.

Tash giggled. 'She can't say Schwarzenegger, so she says Swarzaschnitzel.'

'She can't say parallelogram, either,' Carls chimed in, now finished with painting her toes.'

'Say it,' Steph prompted.

'No!'

'Say it!' they all begged.

'Urgh! Fine.' I sighed frustratingly. 'Pall ... arello ... agram,' I mumbled, truthfully struggling to say the stupid word. Not to mention the added difficulty due to liquor consumption.

They pissed themselves laughing.

'That's gold, Lex. Say it again, please,' Jade pleaded.

'Fuck off,' I giggled.

Tash jumped up. 'Okay, this game sucks. Let's dance.' She grabbed Jen's Michael Jackson CD and turned herself in a 360° spin. 'Where's the CD player?'

'Ooh, in here,' I answered like a naughty kid, excitedly pushing myself up from my chair and limping to the man-cave without my walking stick. *Stupid thing.* I turned around just before opening the door to see the girls lined up behind me in single file, excitement plastered across their faces. It was hilarious.

'This room is known as the man-cave,' I slurred and sniggered. 'It's where men do manly things.'

I opened the door and we all filtered in. 'Don't touch the instruments,' I ordered.

Steph pouted. 'Aw, you're no fun.'

'Awesome, a pool table! Rack 'em up, bitches,' Tash hollered as she frisbee'd the CD to Jen.

I grabbed a pool cue knowing that I was in no position to play, let alone wield a long pointy object, but when you are powered by alcohol, anything goes. 'I'll break,' I confidently decided.

'You'll break something if you don't stop twirling that pool cue around,' Jade pointed out.

Just as I was about to attempt a twirl of the cue around my head, the howl of a wolf sounded through the speakers around the room, followed by the beats of *Thriller*. Lil whistled, and Tash and I started jerking our shoulders like we had an involuntary twitch, both of us taking slow steps toward each other, my limp fitting in perfectly with the act.

One minute we were casually standing around the man-cave, the next we were possessed by Michael Jackson's zombies. Jen let out an MJ holler and threw her hands up in the air, dangling them like claws. Jade and Lil then proceeded to stomp around the room, Tash and Carls joining in. But it was Steph who attempted a moonwalk, failing and falling backwards onto the sofa. It seemed we all had our own *Thriller* dance moves.

I'm not sure if I resembled the best zombie due to already hobbling around like one, or because I was slightly intoxicated but, either way, I was in full blown *Thriller* mode, zombie-dancing all over the room.

Squatting down with my back to the door, I then proceeded to pivot my body around slowly to the music when my eyes met four pairs of the male variety, one pair of those belonging to Bryce. *Oh, for the love of god, not again. How many freakin' times is he going to bust me dancing or singing like an idiot?*

I did what any half-cut, thirty-six-year-old woman would do. I waved then pivoted back around and continued acting like a zombie with my friends.

As the music started to fade out, Bryce, Will, Derek and Matt entered the room, amused grins on their faces. Derek smiled at me then moved his sights to Carly, who was still twitching her shoulders like a zombie, not having noticed his arrival. When she did look up her face was stark with mortification. She gave him a sheepish grin and spun around, allowing him a view of the back of her head. I thought it extremely funny, knowing that Derek would think the same.

Picking up the pool cue while eye-fucking Bryce, I ordered Tash to get our game underway. 'Trashy Tashy, break those balls,' I commanded.

'Consider them broken, sexy Lexi,' she fired back.

He stalked toward me and slid his hands around my back, settling them on my arse. 'Sexy Lexi, I like it,' he said, with a charmed expression.

'I like you,' I said, with a stupid smile and snort outburst to match. *Oh fuck! I just snorted like a pig. Was that me? Maybe it wasn't. Maybe it was Tash.* I looked at Tash. *Yes, it was her.* I looked at Bryce, who was on the brink of uncontrollable laughter. *Shit! No, it was definitely me.*

'I like you, too, especially when you make animal noises.' He grinned before pulling me to his mouth.

I could have given him a cluck, or a bleat, or even a donkey heehaw, but I held myself together and just kissed him back. *You will thank yourself for that decision in the morning, Alexis.*

* * *

The rest of the evening went well, with unskilled games of pool, additional crazy dance moves, a couple of impromptu jam sessions, and Derek and Carly hitting it off. I even spotted some playful flirting and light body touching, which surprised me, because Carly was not normally shy or bashful when it came to letting a guy know she was interested. I sensed she really liked Derek — *really* liked him.

Bryce had arranged hotel rooms for my friends. I loved living in a hotel, with the hotel owner. It was really convenient.

As the girls were leaving, I pulled Carls aside. 'So, Carly Josephine Henkley, is your fiery hole about to be put out?'

'Lex, he is so putting a scorching heat between my legs, it is not funny.'

'Need I remind you that he is a firefighter ... let the guy put it out. Apparently that's what he's good at.'

'I'm terrified,' she whispered.

I whispered back. 'What the fuck? Carly does not get terrified. Why is Carly terrified?'

She continued the whispered conversation, now referring to herself in the third person. 'Because Carly really fucking likes Derek.'

I dropped my hand to hold hers by our sides conspicuously. 'Oh, Carls, that's great. Do you want to know a secret?'

'What?'

'He likes you, too,' I whispered with an impish grin.

'How the —' she blurted out, then looked around sheepishly and continued in a more quieter tone, 'fuck do you know?'

I kissed her forehead. 'Because he told me.' I then turned her shoulders around and playfully smacked her on the butt, ushering her out the door.

CHAPTER

26

I've always considered myself a quietly confident type of person. Not cocky or arrogant, but grounded and self-reliant. My parents had brought me up to be assertive in all that I did, instilling me with the mindset that you should always attempt what is attemptable. If you succeed in your attempts, you will have experienced something profound, but if you fail, try again. And if you fail once more, learn from your failure, but appreciate why you failed in the first place.

I think it was that piece of advice that gave me the confidence to agree to do a lot of things in life. It was either that or my lack of willpower to withstand peer pressure that had me doing things I would not normally do, like performing at a local pub in front of ... let's say ... an easy one hundred or so people.

This day was a perfect example of that, being the day where I was to perform 'The Only Exception' for Bryce at an inner city bar. I'd been learning the basics of guitar for the past few months with the intention of surprising Bryce and giving him something personal after our devastating loss. I'd told myself that I wasn't doing it because I felt responsible for that loss, but I guess if I was going to be completely honest with myself, there was a small part of me that was doing it for that reason. I also wanted to give him something back; something only I could give him.

Derek had been wonderful. Not only with his instructions, but with our last-minute secret get-togethers in order to practise behind Bryce's back. I think he also enjoyed the one on one time so that he could get information out of me about Carly. They had been on two dates already and I assumed they were taking things slowly as Carly had not yet mentioned anything about his physique or stamina, or his cock's look, feel, taste and ability — things she often filled me in on right away.

* * *

Nate, Charlotte, Carly and I were waiting patiently while Live Trepidation set up for their gig on the rooftop at Bar 22. Carls had come along to see Derek perform, and I wasn't sure whether I appreciated that or not. If my performance for Bryce was acceptable, then great, she was there to witness it. But if it was a complete flop, then fuck, she was also there to witness that, and have the ammunition to never let me live it down.

It was a perfect spring Saturday afternoon, the temperature sitting nicely in the mid-twenties. Mind you, I felt rather hot and slightly clammy and guessed it was a result of my intense anxiety. I scanned my surroundings, taking in the contemporary rooftop bar, with wooden bench seats running along the boundary walls. Walls which were wood panelled to about halfway up, then stopping to support an ornamental garden containing lights. The lights nestled in the garden lit up the painted feature walls that spanned the space from the garden top, all the way to the veranda-styled roof. The roof protruded from each wall like a wave of corrugated iron, but failed to congregate in the centre and provide perfect coverage by leaving a rectangular opening to view the sky. There were also mirrored Art Deco pieces hung on the feature walls that grabbed the light beam from the garden and bounced it back into the room.

The bar sat opposite the stage, which was placed in front of the furthest wall when you walked onto the rooftop. The rectangular space in front of the stage and bar was filled with matching square-shaped wood-panelled tables and groovy white and red tub chairs. We were seated in those chairs around a table, the closest to the stage.

'Alexis?'

Carly's raised voice snapped me out of my scrutinising.

'Yeah?'

'Are you all right? You've been off with the pixies ever since I arrived.'

'Sorry, I'm just ...' I leaned in closer to her. 'Nervous.' I sat back and couldn't help the terrified expression on my face.

She screwed up her face in puzzlement, then leaned closer to me. 'Why are you nervous?'

I looked at Charli and Nate who both had their heads down, attention fixed to their iPods. 'Derek has been teaching me how to play the guitar, and I'm going to surprise Bryce with a song. I'm freaking out. I've only been playing for a few months.'

'Fuck off!' Carls said out aloud.

I glared at her then subtly flicked my eyes in the kids' direction, although they hadn't even flinched.

'Are you for real? Oh, my, god! That's awesome. So, why are you nervous?'

'Oh,' I deadpanned for the smallest of seconds, 'let me guess ... 'cause there's a whole rooftop full of freakin' strangers.'

'Who cares?' Carls said bluntly as she picked up her glass of wine and sipped it.

'I do!' I blurted out as I picked up mine, sipping it not quite as calmly as Carly seemed able to do.

'Why? Who are you performing for? Them or Bryce?'

I tilted my head to the side in frustration. 'Bryce.'

'So just play it for him. Don't even acknowledge anyone else.' She sipped her drink again then focussed her attention on Derek, having convinced herself that her advice was my solution. 'We haven't had vanilla yet,' she added.

'Oh.' I gave the kids another quick glance, checking to see they were still occupied with their handheld devices and not catching on to the fact that their mother and Carly were now talking about sex. 'Why not? That's unlike you. You normally devour vanilla, then jump right in to chocolate or even rocky road.'

'I do not,' she scoffed.

'Yes, you do. There's not many flavours you haven't tried.'

'I like strawberry, Aunty Carls. Do you like strawberry?' Charli asked, not taking her eyes from her iPod. *Charli, you eavesdropping little rabbit.*

'Yes, Charli, I love strawberry. It's my favourite.' Carls pressed her lips together as if to say 'Mm.'

'Mum, what's your favourite?'

I don't know. Are we talking about sex or ice cream flavours? 'I like vanilla with sprinkles and topping and chocolate chips,' I answered quickly. *There, I think that about covers everything.*

'Yeah, me too,' she smiled. 'Can I have some now?' *What?*

I looked at Carly, her amused face revelling in the fact I had to somehow dig myself out of this dilemma. 'What Charli? What do you want?' I asked flustered.

'Ice cream.'

'Um, sure.' I dug out my purse. 'Nate?'

'I'll have what she's having,' he replied unperturbed, and like Charli, not even removing his eyes from the little screen. *This is the weirdest conversation ever.*

Carls was laughing. I shook my head at her.

'Here, Charli, go up to the bistro desk over there and order two ice cream sundaes.' I handed her the money and pointed her in the right direction. 'Nate, go with her, please.'

'Huh?'

'Go with Charli to order your ice cream, or I'll change my mind,' I threatened, in a joking manner.

'Oh, okay. Thanks.' He placed his iPod in his pocket and walked off with Charli.

When they were gone, I turned to Carls. 'Why haven't you fucked Derek yet? Carls, what's wrong with him?'

'Nothing. It's not him. It's me.'

'What's wrong with you then? Is your fiery hole singed?' I said, as I choked on the wine I had just swallowed.

'You're such a bitch. No, I really like him and I don't want to screw this up.'

'You're not going to screw this up, Carls,' I said quietly, as I pulled her hands into mine and squeezed them with reassurance.

'How can you be so sure?' she groaned.

'Well, I can't, hon. But I know you and you're awesome. Derek seems to like your awesomeness as well, so just be yourself and go with the flow. Don't try to change who you are.'

'It's not that simple,' she whinged.

'Carly?'

'Yes,' she replied, her tone laced with hostility.

'Do you want to fuck Derek?'

'Yes,' she sighed.

'Well, that's fucking great, because I want to fuck you, too,' Derek said as he stepped up beside Carly. 'How 'bout tonight? My house. I'll even cook you dinner first.'

Carly looked as though she had shrunk about two sizes.

'I won't bite, Carls,' he bent down and leaned closer to her ear, 'unless you want me to.'

Her eyes widened and a small, embarrassed smile appeared on her face. I couldn't help smiling along with her.

'Sure,' she answered, shakily.

'Good.' He stood back up as if he had not just blown Carly's mind. 'Alexis, how you feeling?'

'As nervous as fuck,' I answered, continuing with his blasé attitude and ability to easily change the subject. I held up my hands to see if they were shaking. Surprisingly, they weren't.

'Don't be. The last time we rehearsed you were fine. I will pick up the chords if you falter. Now, Lucy is going to call Charli up on stage as soon as our set finishes, then you'll be next.'

'Okay,' I nodded.

Carls still hadn't moved, still slightly stunned, but now staring greedily at Derek.

'Hope you like chicken. I make a mean satay,' he declared before he kissed her quickly, then headed back to the stage.

I watched Carly come back down to earth in the seconds after Derek left.

'I don't,' she said as she finally made eye contact with me.

'You don't what?'

'Like satay,' she admitted.

I laughed.

'But fuck! I'll eat it for him. I'll even eat it off him if he wants.' She dropped her head to the table in surrender.

* * *

Charli and Nate returned shortly after, eating their ice cream sundaes while we watched the band kill some popular covers and play some of their own songs. I hadn't yet had a chance to listen to the CD that Derek gave me for my birthday, but after hearing the two songs they played, I was going to make it a priority — they were great songs.

'When do I get to sing?' Charli asked excitedly. *Geez, I wish I had her enthusiasm.*

'Derek said when they finish this first set of songs, Charli,' Carls explained. 'So what are you going to sing?'

'I'm going to sing 'True Colours'. Lucy has been helping me to practise. I like that song because it's about rainbows.' *Oh, my god! When has Lucy been helping her practise?*

Just as I was about to ask, Lucy called her up on stage. She jumped up like a grasshopper and made her way toward Lucy. Bryce took a seat beside me and placed his hand on my thigh.

'We have a very special guest here today to perform a song for you,' Lucy said into the microphone as she adjusted her seated position behind the keyboard. 'I'd like to introduce you all to Miss Charlotte Summers. She is going to help me sing 'True Colours' by Cyndi Lauper.'

Charli took a seat next to Lucy and moved the microphone down so that it was positioned perfectly in front of her mouth. 'Hi, everyone,' she said happily, addressing the room's occupants with confidence.

Lucy started playing the keyboard, making my heart beat heavily in my chest, excitement and anticipation radiating through me. I sat straight up and beamed at my brave and beautiful little girl, waiting for her voice to fill my ears.

When it did sound over the rooftop, it brought a tear to my eye. She was so confident and smiled as she sang each and every word. Lucy joined in on the chorus which made Charli smile even brighter and, before I knew it, I was dabbing my eyes more often.

Bryce squeezed my leg and whispered into my ear. 'She has been practising a lot.'

'When? How?' I asked, dumbfounded.

'Sometimes it's easier to hide something blatantly than it is to hide it furtively.'

I shot him a quick glance. *Shit! Did he know about my surprise?* I smiled timidly and turned back to Charli. She was more than halfway through the song and had displayed no hesitation, just confidence and poise, loving what she was doing. Her ability to take that stage and sing to a room full of people made me so proud of her. It also gave me the nerve I needed to do the same for Bryce; that, plus Carly's advice to just sing it to him.

As the song wound to a close and Lucy slowly pressed the final keys on the keyboard, the room erupted into a round of applause. I got to my feet — thankful that I no longer needed any form of walking aid — and clapped the loudest.

'Thank you very much,' Charli said as she positioned herself in the middle of the stage and curtsied. I laughed at her brazenness and winked at her as she made her way toward me.

Meeting her halfway, I knelt down and wrapped my arms around her, giving her a tight squeeze. 'That was absolutely beautiful, Charli-Bear. I am so proud of you.'

'That was so cool, Mum! I want to be a singer when I get older.'

Normally I would say 'add it to the list', or 'that's nice', knowing she would more than likely change her mind the very next day, but I could see the determination in her eyes this time. 'You can be anything you want, darling.' I gave her a quick squeeze then noticed Derek grab Bryce's guitar.

Lucy stepped down from the stage and squatted next to us. 'Well done, Charli. That was perfect. Now it's Mummy's turn, and she is going to be perfect, too.' She gave me a reassuring grin. Charli looked at me, confused.

I winked at her and put a finger to my lips. 'Shh, it's a secret for Bryce.'

Standing back up, I smoothed down the front of my pink floral-patterned dress. I'd pinned my hair up on purpose, making sure it was neatly secured and out of my way.

'You'll be fine,' Lucy said as she stood, giving my hand a quick squeeze. She then proceeded to direct Charlotte back to the table. I continued on and stepped up on the stage, taking a deep breath before turning around. When I did turn around I found Bryce's eyes and his eyes only, causing an overwhelming calm to roll across me. I smiled at him and his brow furrowed.

Derek stepped up to the stool I was standing by and handed me Bryce's guitar, having prepared it for me moments ago. I put the strap over my head and took a seat on the stool, adjusting the microphone comfortably.

As I repositioned it, I spoke to the crowd, but my message was for one person. 'Hello, everyone. I have to let you in on a little secret. You see, for the past few months, I have been learning to play the guitar for the sole purpose of performing here today as a surprise for someone who means the world to me.' I allowed my eyes to find Bryce's again. 'This special someone and I suffered a great tragedy recently, and in the midst of that tragedy I came to realise that I couldn't live without him. He always finds ways to support me and give me everything that I could possibly want or need. So I wanted to give him something back, something only I could give him. Bryce, this is from me to you.'

His face was emotionless, but not in a bad way. I think he was in shock in some way or another. I looked down and positioned my fingers and began strumming, counting the 6/8 time signature. Derek joined in, playing his part and smiling encouragingly at me. I looked up again, deliberately finding Bryce as I sang the opening line. He adjusted his seated position, leaning forward with his elbows balanced on his knees and his hand covering his mouth. He shook his head in disbelief, which made me smile through the lyrics as I continued to play the song.

When I got to the chorus, I emphasised that he was my only exception by looking deep into his eyes and singing the words to him and him only. He repeated the shaking of his head at me, shock and disbelief still plastered across his face. Lucy gave a loving nudge to his shoulder but he didn't take his eyes from mine.

As I began the second verse, I relaxed a little and swayed to the rhythm, closing my eyes and letting the song absorb me. I sang like this until the song escalated into the chorus, which was when I reopened my eyes to find Carly, Nate, Charli and the rest of the band smiling and swaying along with me. The fact that I had naturally closed my eyes stunned me, and I instantly worried that I may have stuffed up my playing in one way or another. Ironically, worrying if I had stuffed up or not caused me to then accidentally miss a chord, but luckily, it was the chord that Derek played along with me, so my mistake would've gone unnoticed to the majority of the room. I gave Derek a knowing look, but he just continued to smile reassuringly.

His encouragement prompted me to step it up a little, so I held the final note in the chorus, deciding I would do what I had informed Derek I wanted to do. I stood up and removed my guitar, gently placing it on my stool. Then I grabbed the microphone from the stand with the intention to concentrate more on my vocals. As the song escalated during the bridge, I started to make my way down off the stage, just like Bryce had done when he played the guitar solo for me.

I watched his expression change from awed disbelief to amusement as I slowly stepped toward him singing the lyrics in the bridge. I stopped just in front of him and held the longest note before the final chorus then dropped my hand from the microphone to touch his face as I once again told him he was the only exception. He placed his hands on top of mine and pressed them to the side of his face then pulled me to him, forcing me to sit on his lap. I giggled a lyric as he helped position me comfortably on top of him, wrapping his arms around my back and across my lap.

Looking into his eyes, I sang the final line, no longer able to hold in my emotion and letting a tear fall to my cheek. Bryce reached up and wiped it tenderly with his finger then pulled me down to kiss him. The crowd then broke into applause, some even sounding a few wolf-whistles, but I didn't pull away, my lips were stuck on his — perfectly attached. He threaded his fingers through my hair and tightened his grip as his tongue found mine, lovingly caressing it with passionate strokes. Eventually, he loosened his grip and released me from his kiss.

'You are incredible. I'm ...' He shook his head and looked down, his eyes level with my chest. 'I'm just so ...' He looked back up to my face. 'I ... thank you —'

I interrupted him, seeing that he was struggling for words. 'You're welcome. Sometimes it's easier to hide something furtively than it is to hide it blatantly,' I said with a sneaky smile, reversing his earlier explanation.

'Nice work, Alexis,' said Will, while tilting his beer in my direction. 'Now we can finally get rid of Derek.'

Derek stopped by the chair Bryce and I were sitting on. 'I heard that, arsehole.'

I climbed off of Bryce's lap and stood up, giving Derek a hug. 'Thank you so much. But, oh my god, I'm glad that is over,' I whispered into his ear.

He chuckled and pulled away. 'You did great.'

I rolled my eyes. 'I did miss that chord.'

'What chord?' he said with a shrug of his shoulders, obviously trying to dismiss my mistake.

Bryce stood up and shook Derek's hand. 'Thanks, mate, although I'm not too sure what to think about you being able to spend so much time with my woman behind my back and without my knowledge.'

Derek patted Bryce on the back. 'You *should* be worried about that, mate,' he said playfully, before he moved away to pull up a chair next to Carly.

'Mum?'

I turned to Charlotte. 'Yes, sweetheart.'

'Do you want to be in my band?' she offered like quite the bargaining professional. 'You can play the guitar and help me sing the songs. I'll be the lead singer though.'

I laughed and ran my hand down her head. 'Sure. I'd love to.'

Bryce insisted I take a seat back on his lap while the band finished their drinks before getting up to perform their final set. He made his possession of me quite obvious through touch, whether it was his hand placed on my lap or his fingers that gently caressed my lower back. Every now and again I would catch him staring up at me, or at my hands, and when I did catch him staring at my hands I would move them to seize his, breaking his trance.

'Are you all right? You seem a bit lost in thought?' I whispered as I leaned back into him.

He inconspicuously moved my hair away from my neck and in a voice no louder than my own, breathed out, 'I'm just thinking about the ways I can show you how much I fucking enjoyed that performance, how fucking perfect it was and how fucking perfect you are.'

I took a sip of my wine and swallowed heavily.

'If you are not already carrying our next child, my love, you will be by the end of the night.'

I leaned forward and put my glass down then turned back to him. 'Well, best you hurry up and finish this set. We have work to do.'

CHAPTER

27

Bryce, Derek, Will, Matt and Lucy played the remainder of their gig, and I watched the ease with which they all complemented each other. None of them were serious, die-hard musicians in the sense that they had to live and breathe performing; they just seemed to casually enjoy getting together and playing for a group of people. I wondered if, at any stage during the past, they'd wanted to become a professionally-signed band. My curiosity would have to be addressed later.

Now that the gig was coming to a close, I found myself starting to think about my impending conversation with Rick, the one I planned on having with him when we dropped Nate and Charli off at the house. A year of separation between the two of us was fast approaching, and I needed to discuss with him my wish to apply for a divorce. I didn't really know how he would react to my request, and it worried me that it would ruin the good progress we had made with each other of late.

'Ready to go?' Bryce asked, as he slid his hand across my back, resting it on my hip.

'No, Alexis and I need the ladies room,' Carly insisted. *Do I?* I gave Carly an unsure glance, her expression enforcing that I did. *Oh, okay ... I do need the loo.*

'Be back in a minute. I'll meet you at the car.' I gave him a quick peck on the lips and followed Carly to the bathroom.

As we pushed through the door, I gave Carly my questioning stare. 'So why the last minute toilet trip?'

'Because I need to go,' she answered flatly.

Okay, well I guess I'll go too. I entered the cubicle next to her. 'Why else?' I probed further as I awkwardly relieved myself.

'Because I'm still shitting bricks,' she divulged. *Not the best choice of words while in the toilet, Carls.*

'Literally or figuratively speaking, Carls? We are in the loo, remember?'

'Figuratively, you idiot! I'm terrified of having sex with Derek, and clearly he wants it ... tonight!'

'Carls, for god's sake just screw the man. What is wrong with you? I've never seen you this apprehensive about intimacy, ever!' I flushed the toilet and made my way to the sink.

Carls followed shortly after. 'I don't fucking know. I hate this feeling. What ... the ... fuck is this feeling?'

'I think it's lurrrve,' I purred, like an adolescent idiot.

She shrugged it off. 'Pfft. It's not love. I barely know him.'

I flicked water at her head, getting her attention. 'You love him.'

She wiped her head and made a spitting noise at me. 'You're disgusting.'

'Well, you are falling for him at least. That's the only explanation.'

She looked at her reflection in the mirror as if she were trying to catch herself in a lie. 'Urgh! You're right. I think I'm falling in love with him, and I haven't even had sex with him yet. This is insane.'

I moved to the hand dryer, raising my voice over the loud hum. 'No, it's not. It's exciting and wonderful, and the first time you have sex with him is going to be great.'

A smile teased at the corner of Carly's mouth as she joined me to dry her hands.

'Go home, Carls. Shave your legs, arms, pussy and toes if you have to —'

'I don't have hairy toes. Who has hairy toes?'

'Shave whatever needs shaving, then moisturise and do all the fucked-up shit we think we have to do before we let a man see us naked. Then make sure you practise your alphabet to loosen the muscles in your face.' I started emphasising the letters 'A' and 'O' opening my mouth wide, suggestively. 'When was the last time you sucked cock? It's been a while, hasn't it? You would've told me otherwise.'

She sheepishly looked away. 'Fuck off.'

'Yeah, I thought as much.'

'Well, I'm not telling you any more.' She walked past me and pushed the door open to return to the rooftop.

'Oh, yes you will. I want a phone call first thing tomorrow morning.'

* * *

Bryce and I drove to my former home to deliver the kids into Rick's care for the next few days. He invited us in for a drink which we accepted. It was slightly strange sitting at my former dining table, in my former house with my former husband. Strange as it was though, it was exactly that ... former. The past. History. And in order to move on, I needed to get the wheels of my divorce in motion. I just didn't know how to break it to Rick. Letting my nerves get the better of me, I decided to chicken out and tell him another time.

As we made our way out of the house, Rick must've picked up on my withholding of information. He was always good at sensing my reluctance.

'Lex, you got a minute?' he asked, as Bryce and I stepped out the front door. I'd already kissed the kids goodbye, and they were now out playing in the backyard.

'Sure,' I said hesitantly.

Bryce gave Rick a courteous nod. 'I'll wait in the car.'

Claire had remained inside.

Once Bryce was in the car I turned back to Rick. 'What's up?'

'You tell me. We may no longer be happily married, Lex, but I can still tell when you are stewing on something.' He leaned his weight on the doorframe and crossed his arms confidently.

'Um ... I just didn't want to do it like this,' I said sadly as I twiddled my fingers.

'Just say it, Lex.'

'After Christmas, I'm going to get Bernie to prepare an Application for Divorce.' I looked at him hesitantly, but he didn't flinch. 'Once the application is complete, the process is fairly straightforward and a hearing date will be set. You don't have to attend the hearing if you don't want to.'

'No, it's all right, I'll attend. Just let me know what you need,' he said calmly.

His placid demeanour kind of threw me off a little. I'd half expected him to fly off the handle with anger then compose himself shortly after and apologise like he normally would. But he didn't, he just casually accepted my information.

A confused smile started to creep across my face, forcing one on his. 'Lex, I think you said to me a while back ... "It is what it is."'

I nodded. 'Yeah, I did.'

'Well, you were right. It is what it is. I lost you and you lost me. We can't change that, nor should we try. You are happy now, I can see that. And I'm becoming happy, too. Hopefully, before long you will also see that.'

'I can see that already, you know.'

'I'm getting there, Lex.'

'Good, Rick, because despite the past year, I want you to be happy.' I stepped up to the doorjamb and wrapped my arms around him. 'Thank you.'

He hugged me back and the hug cemented that we held nothing more than mutual respect for each other and a love that held no romance, just a deep friendship. It was nice.

When I got into the car, Bryce reversed the Lexus out of the driveway. 'Everything okay?'

'Yeah, I just asked Rick for a divorce.'

He turned his head to me and paused, mid-reverse. 'Are you sure he understood that?'

I laughed. 'Yes, he has moved on, and so have I. I just want to make it official.'

He continued to drive and casually asked, 'So, when will it be official?'

'Shortly after Christmas.'

The smile that plastered his face gave me butterflies.

* * *

We arrived at City Towers and, entering the private elevator, found that Bryce's key card would not activate it.

'Fucking stupid piece of shit,' he said as he typed in his security code.

'You're pretty hot when you're angry,' I declared while watching him frustratedly push a numerical sequence. 'Here try mine.' I handed him my card. It didn't work either.

'Fuck!'

'Maybe you should just get a key like the rest of the world,' I teasingly taunted him.

He lifted his head to meet my gaze, then turned in my direction.

Automatically, I detected carnal need rolling off of him in sexually-charged waves, causing me to back up until my arse was pressed against the railing inside the elevator car. He strode toward me, then stopped and pressed his delectable frame against my chest. I took in a sharp, suspense-filled breath as he placed his hands on the wall on either side of my face, our eyes desperately searing one another's.

My tongue gently moistened my lips, then my teeth grated against them, as I knew that I would soon be tasting him. He growled harshly as he pushed his palm into a panel and reached for the phone, all the while keeping his hungry stare on me.

'Sam, my private elevator has malfunctioned. Have Dale look into it, please. Thank you.' He hung up the phone.

'So, are we stuck here ... together ... for a while?' I asked innocently.

'Yes,' he replied as his gaze dropped down to my chest, my chest automatically rising toward his stare.

'What are we going to do, Mr Clark?' I purred, as I placed my hand over his groin, feeling his hard, thick erection.

His eyes closed momentarily, then shot open as I squeezed mildly. 'I'm going to fuck you, honey. I'm going to show you how much I adore you. I'm going to show you just how much I appreciate you being in my life. I'm going to ensure that you will never want to leave it. Ever!'

'Mm-mm,' I hummed, enjoying his possessive words while trailing my hands up his chest, across his white t-shirt and up to his neck. He dragged my dress up to my stomach and hauled me into his arms where I eagerly wrapped my legs around his waist, enjoying the fact I could easily do that again.

Bryce gripped my arse and thrust his tongue deep into my mouth. His passion and ownership of me ignited a hungry need, driving me to desperation. A desperation that had me biting down on his plump lip and gently pulling it, before letting it go again.

He growled and carried me into the basement garage, my flip-flops falling off in the process. 'Tell me where you want it, or I'll fuck you right here like this,' he mumbled around my tongue.

'Harley,' I breathed out as I threw my head back to take in some much needed oxygen.

He pressed his lips and tongue to my neck as he carried me toward the black and chrome motorcycle.

'Oh fuck, Bryce. I want you so bad.'

'You've already got me bad, honey.'

I giggled. 'I know.'

He walked up to the side of the Harley, where he placed me down on its black leather seat. Impatiently, he yanked my long cascading dress back up to my waist and wrenched my white lace G-string down my legs, dragging it as he followed its descent.

Then, dropping to his knees, he lifted my legs, propping one foot on the exhaust and the other on the engine, spreading me wide for him to devour. He slid his hands up my thighs, as he closed the gap between my pussy and his mouth. I sucked in a breath, anticipating his tongue and desperately waiting for that warm wet feeling his mouth granted me.

Forcing me to crave his touch, he paused before sliding his tongue along my sensitive clit the bundle of nerve endings responding delightfully.

'Oh god,' I moaned as he dragged his tongue up and down and buried his face into me. My head fell back in exquisite pleasure as he repeated the motions, while tightening his grip around the tops of my thighs.

Bryce released one hand and dragged his finger through my wetness, finding my opening and delving in deep. 'Shit, honey,' he groaned as he leaned forward again and flicked his tongue against me.

I clenched my fingers into the leather of the seat, feeling my body climbing to orgasm with each stroke and flick of his tongue in perfect rhythm with the slide of his finger.

'Let go,' he coaxed, sensing my stubbornness to hold on.

'I want to let go when you let go,' I whimpered.

'You will,' he growled, as he sucked my clit into his mouth.

'Oh, fuck!' That was all it took to push me over the edge, my hips bucking underneath his face, my hand finding his hair and my nails finding his scalp. I gripped tight, holding on in fear I'd fall for failing to have the strength to stay on top of the bike as my orgasm spread in waves through me.

As the pleasure waves decreased, he stood up, pulling me to stand with him and lifting my dress completely over my head. I reached for his jeans and undid them with ferocity, helping him drag them down and away from his perfectly sculpted legs. He kicked them free, together with his shoes, then straddled the bike and leaned back on the seat.

His cock was prominently positioned, asking for my lips and mouth and, never being one to refuse its blatant invitation, I accepted quiet happily. I straddled the bike in front of him and leaned forward, engulfing his warm, solid shaft into my mouth.

'Fuck,' he groaned, as my lips slid down then sucked right back up to his tip, over and over. I loved the feeling of him filling my mouth and touching my throat, the feeling of my tongue subtly teasing his soft, velvety skin.

I looked up at him through hooded lids, at the way he was arched back in the motorcycle's seat. He looked so fucking sexy, his head tilted backward, his neck taut and rigid. I had the urge to lick that masculine neck and then take his tongue in my mouth again. I also had the urge to ride his cock on this stunning machine.

Giving him one last suck, I let go. He lifted his head to meet my voracious crawl toward his face, his mouth.

'So fucking beautiful,' he uttered before I reached him and pressed my lips to his.

Placing my feet on the exhaust on either side of the bike to give me a platform to balance myself, I lifted and hovered over his cock. He stroked himself with both hands and positioned it upright, allowing me to lower myself perfectly on top. As I felt him slide inside me, I let out a pleasured sigh, my pussy clenching and hugging him tightly with grateful acceptance. Bryce groaned at the sensations and gritted his teeth, urging me to wrench his t-shirt over his head and reveal his mouthwatering chest.

He leaned forward and unclasped my bra, tearing it from me and releasing my heavy breasts, his hands kneading my sensitive flesh, his thumbs gently rubbing my nipples. I reached behind me, finding the handlebars and, pushing my tits in his face, I braced myself to ride the fuck out of him. He was in so deep, and I could feel every inch of him as I carefully pushed up and down.

'Fuck, you feel so good and look so fucking sexy riding my cock right now.'

I smiled at him and tilted my head back, revelling in the feel of him, hard within me.

A sudden surge of pleasure rippled through me as the pad of his thumb found my clit, rubbing in small circles as I pumped him slowly. 'Oh god, Bryce, I'm close.'

He leaned forward, secured my arse and laid me down against the fuel tank. Bryce was tall enough to place his feet on the ground on either side of the bike, allowing him perfect balance and control. He positioned his cock at my entrance once again and pushed in aggressively, holding my legs as he repeatedly slammed into me. It wasn't long before I was screaming my second orgasm, he grunting his first. It was so intense and delicious and my breath had all but left my body, my lungs desperately trying to suck in some more.

'Great choice,' he breathed out as he continued to slowly push into me, easing my orgasm. He leaned forward and sucked on my nipple, then dragged his tongue up my neck till he found my mouth.

I savoured him while I regained my composure, then broke away and let my body surrender completely against the motorcycle. 'We need to do that again. This motorcycle is far too hot to be sitting idly in this garage. Maybe we can go for a ride down the coast on it.'

His body tensed slightly, then he pulled out and bent his legs, lowering himself onto the seat. 'Yeah, maybe.'

'There's a reason you don't ride any more, isn't there?' I asked, as I sat up and faced him.

His eye twitched mildly. 'Yes.'

Reaching forward, he grabbed my hips and lifted me on top of him. I wrapped my arms around his shoulders and my legs around his waist.

'Are you going to tell me why?'

He nuzzled my nose. 'If I have to.'

I tilted my head up to kiss his nose. 'Yes, you do.'

'I used to go riding with my dad. It was just something he and I did. When he died, I stopped riding. It just didn't feel right.'

'Do you think you'll ever ride again?'

'With you in my life, I'm pretty sure I can do anything.'

* * *

We dressed ourselves after that ride of a lifetime and walked hand in hand the long way around to the lobby of City Towers.

'Alexis, you look fabulous. It's nice to see you getting around freely again,' Abigail said as she stepped out of the Concierge Attendant's office.

'Thanks, Abigail. It's so nice to be able to get around freely. We really do take the ability to walk around for granted.'

Samantha stepped out of the office and gave me a shy smile before ducking away quickly.

'Please excuse me for a second, Abigail. Hey, Sam,' I called after her, 'wait a second.' She stopped hesitantly and spun around, putting on a fake smile.

'How are you doing?' I asked, cautiously.

'Yeah, I'm good.'

'Has anyone ever told you that you suck at lying?'

She bit the inside of her lip. 'Yeah, my dad.'

I chuckled slightly. 'Have you spoken to Gareth since you told him you needed space?'

'No. I just need more time.'

'Okay, I'm not pressuring you in any way. I just want to let you know that if you have any questions, ask. Again, no pressure, but Gareth really likes you, and he understands your need for distance.' *I can't believe I am sticking up for Gareth.*

She let out a long breath and nodded her head. 'Thanks. Look, I gotta go. We are being briefed on the hotel's Christmas festivities.'

'Okay, I'll talk to you soon.' I watched her walk away, knowing that she was torn about her feelings for Gareth. Unfortunately, there was really nothing I could do about it. Sam had a decision to make, and she had to make it on her own.

I sighed dejectedly and turned back around to find Bryce chatting away to a blonde who I recognised as none other than Chelsea. I took in her close stance next to him and her blatant flirting. The woman just didn't let up. I still hadn't confirmed with Bryce whether or not he had ever put her in her place about their friendship being just that — a friendship. Regardless, it seemed quite obvious that she needed a reminder. I'd had just about enough of her disregard of Bryce's and my relationship.

I confidently walked up to them and threaded my arm through Bryce's. 'Sorry, I just needed to tell Sam something,' I smiled apologetically at him, then turned on artificial-Alexis for the bitch in front of me. 'Hello, Chelsea. How are you?'

'Wonderful,' she answered, batting her eyelashes at Bryce. *Are you for fucking real?* 'I see your ankle has healed?'

'Yes, thank you. I'm back to my old self.'

'How nice,' she answered dryly. 'Bryce, I've been meaning to tell you about the new Bell that Dad's looking at acquiring. You really should come down to the heliport and have a chat with him.'

'I'm sure he knows what he is looking at,' Bryce answered politely. *This bitch needs the opposite of politeness. She needs a face full of rudeness, unashamed and deliberate.* 'Excuse us, Chelsea. We need to see Dale about the elevator.' He went to lead me away.

I let go of his arm. 'You go. I need to have word to Chelsea. I won't be a second.'

He gave me an unsure glance, but turned and headed for Dale's office.

When he was out of earshot I turned to face Chelsea. 'This stops now,' I hissed. 'Whatever you think you and Bryce have is over, so enough of the disrespectful flirting. Back the fuck off.'

She looked in his direction, a lascivious glint in her eye, then turned back to me. 'You are no longer carrying his child, nor do you have a ring on your finger. Until then, he is fair game.'

Before I knew it, my hand connected swiftly with her face, the echo from my skin slapping hers sounding loudly throughout the lobby.

'Don't you dare mention my child, you fucking bitch!' I hissed quietly. I was furious. She stood there stunned, holding her hand against her pink cheek. 'Get this through that thick head of yours: Bryce. Is.

Not. Interested. In. You. He wasn't years ago and he isn't now. I am the one he is looking at when he says "I love you". I will be the one he gets down on bended knee for and, before you know it, we will be married and you'll be working for me. So pull your fucking head out of your arse, or you'll find yourself unemployed.'

I gave her the once-over with a critical glare, then left her there to dissect my words.

CHAPTER
28

There is no right or wrong way to grieve. It is an emotion so intense that it takes control and overpowers your senses, leaving you feeling at a loss entirely. Without grief, we would never appreciate the joy we had beforehand. We would never value what we lost. We would never be truly grateful.

If all had gone to plan and what was written in the stars was for me and Bryce to be the parents of a newborn baby girl, then Bianca would be in my arms this day. But life did not always go as planned. It was full of ups and downs, twists and turns, love and loss. And life would not be worth experiencing if it weren't just that. You can't have the good without the bad; you need to somehow learn to accept the bad and adjust to it in a way that it can be endured and overcome.

Bryce was busy with overseeing the precinct's setting up of the Christmas Extravaganza that was held every year. I'd asked Lucy to fill in for me in the office as I was not in the right frame of mind to work. I needed some time to myself to clear my head, not only from the wave of grief I had been feeling on and off since waking up this morning, but from the dreaded sensations of my fall that kept torturing me. I still suffered flashbacks on occasion, but had learned to acknowledge them, then let them go. It was quite possible I would never be rid of them. Then again, maybe one day I would. For now though, accepting them and moving on was what Jessica had encouraged me to do and I was doing that.

* * *

I popped my Live Trepidation CD into the Charger's player, wanting the songs to distract my sorrow-filled thoughts as I drove to the hospital. Remembering what Matt had said at my birthday party, I pressed track four, and the sound of an acoustic guitar riff filled the speakers in my car, automatically provoking a smile at the recognition of Bryce's musical genius. The tune was sweet, yet the twang of the strings plucked in quick succession indicated the intricacies of the music. Derek's smooth voice filtered through the speakers shortly after, singing lyrics of awakening and coming to life, about the concept of a revelation that one can be lost then found. I liked the song and automatically connected with it. It was not just a connection because Bryce was the sole instrumentalist, but it had significance for my life's recent journey; it was entirely appropriate.

Derek's vocals rose along with Bryce's strumming, singing the chorus which instantly triggered a sense of déjà vu, the lyrics being ones I had seen before.

You're all that I want and nothing else,
I've fallen hard and will never get up.
I cannot let go ... I won't,
You're infectious, my love.

Oh, my god, it's the song Bryce was writing when we first got together. I quickly turned it up and listened in surprise and wonderment. Having Bryce's declaration enshrined in the form of a song captivated me and left me stunned, but it also warmed my heart immensely.

When the song finished, I smiled. *Is it naive to believe that Bryce loves me as much as he appears to love me?* I shook my head, feeling that I had to pinch myself daily where he was concerned, having once believed that a love like ours was a love only found in fairytales. I was wrong and he had proved that time and time again. His devotion for me was evident in everything that he did.

As I parked my car, I reached into my handbag and pulled out my phone in order to type him a text.

I just listened to track 4 on your CD. If anyone is infectious, it's you, my luv — Alexis

I hit send, sighed contentedly, then looked out the window, taking in my surroundings and thereupon losing my smile. It is amazing how your heart can play tug-of-war, fighting between happiness one second and sadness the next, then somehow finding that in-between to keep it sane. My heart was currently in that predicament as the last time I was here I'd had to say goodbye to my daughter.

I proceeded to get out of my car, and before I had even locked the door, my phone beeped with a reply.

It's how I feel, honey. You rule me entirely. Where are you? — Bryce

I probably should've told him where I was going, but he was busy, and I figured that if he wanted to come along we could always come back later in the day.

I typed my response:

So everyone keeps telling me. I think it's the other way round though, you rule me. I'm at the hospital ... I wanted a moment to feel close to Bianca — Alexis

I hit send and waited for the reply I knew would come swiftly. It did:

R you all right? — Bryce

I didn't want him to worry. I was all right.

I'm fine. Thought I would spend some time in The Garden of Angels. I'll see you later, luv u ♥ — Alexis

Again, his reply was instant.

Luv u more — Bryce

I tucked my phone back into my handbag, pulled out a fluffy pink smiley-faced star I'd found at the shops and headed to the garden.

* * *

It felt quite different from the last time I was here as I stepped out onto the path and looked at the vivid blue blossoms of the jacaranda which formed the centrepiece of the garden. Maybe that was because it was now summer, the garden awash with colour, sunlight and a happy aura that only summer could bring.

Slowly, I walked along the winding cobbled path around the entire garden, taking in the abundance of toys, teddy bears and brightly-coloured wooden creatures staked into the ground There were also homemade plaques situated in amongst the shrubbery, against the trees and propped along the edging of the path; plaques containing baby's names. I stopped and took the time to read each and every one, acknowledging all the angels that shared my little girl's home. It gave me an idea to ask Charlotte to make one for Bianca and bring it with her the next time we visited as a family.

After reading all the plaques, I sat down on the wooden park bench directly across from the spot where we sprinkled Bianca's ashes and said our goodbyes. I had the pink star on my lap and was tenderly stroking it and hugging it as if it could replace the one thing I wanted to hug and caress the most — my daughter.

As I sat there with my eyes closed, visualising a life with Bianca in it, I felt the seat shift and a comforting hand rest on my shoulder. I didn't have to open my eyes to see who it was, but I did, because his presence still surprised me. He was puffed and slightly glistening, his face a little pinker than usual.

'That was quick,' I said with a smile as I nestled into his side.

'I didn't want you here alone for a second longer,' he said with strained breath as he tightened his grip.

'I'm fine. I just needed to be close to her today.'

'Why didn't you tell me?' He sounded a little disappointed.

'You were busy, and I just thought I'd come on my own.'

'I'm never too busy for you, or Nate and Charli. Remember that you come first. Always.'

I knew he meant it, but he was still an extremely sought-after person in his work life, and I didn't want to interfere with that. There were some things I would have to do on my own, and I was okay with that. I needed my independence. I liked it.

I looked up at him and noticed him staring at the garden ahead. 'I think she would've looked like you,' I said softly.

'Me, too ... the force is strong in my family,' he playfully replied.

I lovingly shoved him. 'Yeah, don't I know it.'

'I think she would've had blonde wavy hair like her mother, my blue eyes, your button nose, and the sweetest little dimples like

Charli. She would've had Lucy's smarts, Nate's determination, and your kindness.'

I was staring at him, tears rolling down my cheeks.

He turned his head to me and wiped them away. 'No doubt she would've sent me to an early grave.' He smiled sadly.

I giggled. 'I know. I can imagine her having your stubbornness, your drive and your "no restraints or restrictions" attitude.' I broke free of his embrace and leaned forward, ready to put the pink star in the garden. 'I guess we'll never know,' I said regretfully.

He grabbed my hand and gently took the star from it, smiling as he identified its significance. He ran his fingers along it, then passed it back after taking my hand and pressing it to his lips. 'You're wrong, honey, we do know.'

I gently caressed his sad face then moved forward and placed the star in the garden.

Happy with its perfect position, I moved back into Bryce's safe, secure and comforting embrace.

* * *

The following weekend was Charlotte's birthday. She was a Christmas baby and hated it. I remember her saying to me not too long ago that it wasn't 'fair' and that she had to wait an entire year to celebrate. I'd tried explaining that we all had to wait a year to celebrate, but that just frustrated her even more.

'Charlotte, are you ready? Your friends will be here in any minute.'

'Yes, Mum,' she called from her room, 'I'm coming.'

Charlotte appeared at the top of the stairs dressed in a purple and blue Young Versace dress that Bryce had bought her with Clarissa's help. At first I hadn't known what to think of my now seven-year-old daughter in a designer label. Then the more I thought about it, an unshakeable feeling of hypocrisy bubbled in the pit of my stomach, so I shrugged and let it go. Plus, she did look unbelievably sweet in the flowing, pleated floral dress.

I beamed at her. 'Look at you, sweetheart. You look beautiful.'

'Like mother, like daughter,' Bryce said as he looked up from his newspaper at Charli. He was seated on the sofa next to me, barefooted, in jeans with his legs stretched out and resting on the coffee table, this now being my favourite sexy couch position of his.

Charlotte gracefully pranced down the stairs, a large smile covering her face. 'Thank you. I love my new Versace dress,' she said in a posh voice, enunciating the word Versace. *Oh god, I've created a little designer-Charli monster.*

As she twirled around the lounge room — making me laugh — the buzzer to the door sounded. The refined poise she had just displayed evaporated into thin air, a squealing, jumping noisy banshee replacing it.

I got up and followed Charli to the door, opening it to find both Lil with her daughter, Jasmine, and Steph with her daughter, Katie.

'Come in,' I smiled.

Charli embraced both her friends with high-pitched giggles and a lot of bouncing — lots and lots of bouncing. Steph and Lil remained in the foyer.

'You coming in?' I asked, confused.

Steph laughed sarcastically. 'Nope, are you kidding? They're all yours.'

'We are heading to the shops. Have fun.' Lil twiddled her fingers in a faux wave, then linked her arm with Steph's as they skipped away.

'Bitches,' I called out jokingly. 'We will have fun.'

As they skipped through the foyer, they passed Addison and her mum, Addison's mum giving both Steph and Lil a strange look.

'Hello, Addison.'

'Hello, Mrs Summers.'

'Come in, sweetheart.'

Charli, Jasmine and Katie noticed Addison and all squealed again. I cringed at the noise.

'I hope you have a set of earmuffs,' Addison's mum said as she stuck her finger in her ear.

'We have a soundproof room,' Bryce called out from his sexy, sprawled position on the couch.

'Oh, my,' I heard Addison's mum say under her breath as she looked in his direction. She quickly covered her slip by answering his remark with a nervous stutter: 'Um ... even better.'

'Would you like to come in?' I asked.

'No, I won't stay. I have a few things to do,' she said red-faced. 'Addison, I'll pick you up in the morning.'

Addison didn't take any notice of her mum and just answered, unfazed. 'Okay, Mum.'

'Actually ...' Bryce said as he strode in our direction. *Fuck, he looks extremely hot today. Why does he look hotter than his normal hotty hotness?* 'Danny, my chauffeur, will drop the girls at home tomorrow in the limousine, if that's all right?' he asked with a charming tone that no sane woman could refuse.

The girls screamed.

I licked my lips.

And Addison's mum just stared.

'I think the girls would like a ride in the limo, wouldn't you?' he asked them as he pulled me into his side.

'Yes,' they squealed.

'Mum!' Addison screeched, snapping her mother out of her Bryce-induced trance-like state.

'Yes, yes. Sorry. Yes, that is fine, sorry. Thank you. Okay, I'll see you tomorrow.' She quickly kissed Addison on the forehead and hastily made her way out the door.

I closed it behind her and wrapped my arms around my man. 'You do that on purpose.'

'What?'

'Hmm,' I mumbled, while narrowing my eyes at him.

He chuckled, leaned forward and kissed me on top of my head. All the girls sounded a drawn-out 'ooooooh'.

I laughed and rolled my eyes, prying his hands from around my waist. 'Okay, you four, what will it be first: cupcake making or makeovers?'

'Makeovers,' they screamed and clapped. With perfect timing, the buzzer to the door sounded again. Bryce walked over and let in two of the hotel's spa centre staff, who were both pushing a garment rack containing five fluffy robes and a case which I assumed contained many beauty makeover products.

'This is Bridget and Emily, Alexis. They will help makeover each and every one of you.'

All four girls happy-clapped and bounced on the sofa.

'Hi, pleased to meet you,' I said.

'Great! Now that Bridget and Emily are here, that is my cue to leave. I'll be in my office if you need me.' He placed two fingers on his lips and blew me a kiss. I sighed. *Did I just sigh out loud? Shit! What is wrong with me today?*

Emily and Bridget spent the next hour applying facial masks to me and the girls while 4Life played through the speakers in the background. We each had our hair in buns with headbands keeping the loose strands of hair back, a greenish-tinged poo-coloured mud mask was spread across our faces and slices of cucumber balanced lightly on our closed eyes.

All four of us were lying back on the sofa with our robes on and our feet up on the coffee table.

'How long does this mask have to stay on?' I asked Bridget or Emily, unable to see either of them. Quite frankly, I couldn't see shit through these circles of cucumber.

'Another five minutes,' one of them replied with a slight giggle. *Glad you find this funny!*

I nodded very carefully. I honestly couldn't wait to get this shit off my face. I was only indulging in this incredibly expensive mud mixture — it was probably dug up from down the street — because Charli wanted me to.

The sound of a camera shutter broke through the only piece of silence I'd had since the girls arrived.

'Was that a camera?' I asked awkwardly, as the mud around my mouth was dry and made it difficult to move my facial muscles to talk.

'Yes,' Bryce answered with a cocky tone.

I shot up, the cucumber slices falling into my lap. Blinking for a second, I spotted Bryce standing on the opposite side of the coffee table holding up his phone.

He smiled satisfactorily. 'This photo is going on my desk.'

'Like fun it is,' I said as I stood up. 'Give me your phone.' I held out my hand.

'Sorry, honey.'

'Bryce Edward Clark.' I put my hands on my hips.

Bridget, Emily and the four girls started laughing.

'You know I can't chase you,' I said angrily, but with a subdued laugh.

'I know.' *Grrr.*

'You do realise I look like a clown. Would you like me to put on a red nose for you? Maybe even a coloured wig,' I warned.

He raised his eyes to meet mine. 'Point taken. I'm deleting it now.'

I squinted my eyes at him — I must've looked atrocious. 'Good,' I said triumphantly as I took a few steps toward him. 'Now give me a kiss.' I reached out to grab his t-shirt, pursing my crackly skin and lips, but he was too quick and jumped away.

The girls all laughed — again!

* * *

After our makeovers were complete, two dozen cupcakes were baked and artfully decorated then consumed. Pizzas were devoured and movies were watched, and we all made our way to bed.

'My fucking ears are ringing,' I complained. 'I must have a permanent high-pitched squeal noise going on in there.'

'No, they are all still screaming,' Bryce grumbled as he turned over and placed the pillow over his head. 'A house full of young girls. Whose idea was that again?'

'I don't know, but please, someone shoot me.' I flopped onto the bed, just as another round of loud giggles echoed down the hallway. 'Grrr.'

'You're so sexy when you growl into a pillow.'

I growled back. 'Shut up.'

CHAPTER
29

The end of the calendar year was fast approaching which meant one thing: Christmas! I loved Christmas. I loved all things Christmas. I loved Santa. *Not the Mr Gordon-Santa variety; he interrupts too many of my fun sexed-up moments.* No, I loved the dressed-up Santa, his big round belly and big black boots. I loved the fantasy and joy behind the concept of Santa and his elves, who joyously made the toys in the North Pole. I loved the reindeer and the Christmas tree, the sleigh and the presents. I loved the sense of family and togetherness, of giving and being grateful. Oh, and I loved the food. Damn, did I love the food.

We decided to have Christmas at the hotel, since it was a convenient place for everyone to stay. I was terribly excited that we were hosting both our families; so much so I had gone just a tad overboard in my decorating. I'd twirled tinsel around the staircase banister, bought a sleigh which was about two metres long and one metre high and came with an entire set of Santa's reindeer. I'd also put up twinkling lights on every doorframe and window frame I could find. But I think my truly over-the-top craziness was when I'd gone absolutely gaga on sighting the huge hanging snowflakes and baubles dangling from the hotel's lobby. They were gorgeous, and each one was approximately one metre squared.

The next thing I knew, Bryce was having them hung from the ceiling in our lounge, three levels high. He'd also organised a ginormous Christmas tree to be put up, the tip of it being the perfect height for Nate and Charli to adorn it with a star — from the top of the staircase. The apartment looked like a Christmas wonderland ... I absolutely loved it!

* * *

'Charli, don't touch that bauble, missy,' I barked at her as she gave my perfectly colour-coordinated Christmas tree decoration a tap with her finger.

'Alexis, calm down. Everything is perfect,' Bryce said, reassuringly.

'It doesn't matter, Bryce,' advised Nate. 'No one touches Mum's Christmas tree. She goes nuts if you do.'

I was tidying up the lounge area, making sure it was as baby-proof and toddler-safe as I could get it. 'Listen to your brother, Charlotte, or that rather large present toward the back of the tree with your name on it will no longer have your name on it,' I said flatly, without removing my attention from what I was doing.

'When is everyone going to get here?' Charlotte groaned impatiently.

'Soon, Charli. It's only 7.30 in the morning.'

'Urgh! I wish they'd hurry up. I want to open some presents.'

'Alexis, come and sit down and we'll open our presents before everyone gets here,' Bryce suggested.

I raised my head and noticed him looking just as eager as the kids. He really was adorable at times. 'I've got to go and set the table,' I argued.

He stood up and strode my way, then bent down and picked me up, throwing me over his shoulder.

'Presents! Now!'

'Bryce! All right,' I squealed while smacking his arse.

Both the kids laughed.

'Me first, me first,' Charli squawked.

Bryce set me down next to the sofa then pulled me onto his lap, my back to his front and his arms securing me to him.

'Go on, get the big one at the back,' I said to Charli. 'Nate, you can get that one over by the wall.'

Both the kids launched themselves into demolishing the wrapping paper I had so precisely applied.

'Sick! A telescope,' Nate said, as he stood back to admire the rather expensive telescope Bryce had picked out for him.

'We can set that one up in your room, Nate,' he said with excitement on his face. I loved how they both shared this fascination with space — just the two of them.

'Awesome, thanks.' Nate got up and gave us both a hug.

Charli's shrill voice sounded next, securing all our attention. 'Oh! My! God! My own karaoke machine.'

'Oh, geez! Charli, please be careful with that,' I said while cringing as she tried to lift the state of the art model Bryce had insisted on getting her.

He gently squeezed my waist and dug his chin into my shoulder blade. 'Stop stressing,' he whispered into my ear.

'I'm not stressing. I just know how much both those things cost.'

He wrenched me around and dipped me to the side, making me scream in surprise. 'Honey, you seem to forget that I'm made of money.'

'I don't,' I giggled as he nuzzled my neck, tickling me. 'I've just learned to respect it and appreciate it and —'

'I appreciate that I have a lot of it, and I also appreciate that I now get to spend it on you three,' he mumbled into my neck, unfazed by his wealth.

'I know you do, and I also know you have given generously to so many charities lately. It's very sexy.'

'Ew! That's gross,' Nate grumbled.

Bryce ignored my son's unease. 'It's what I do, Ms Summers,' he said with a perfect smirk.

I laughed at him as the buzzer to the door rang. 'Yes, it is, Mr Clark, and you do it so well.'

Nate and Charli jumped up and made their way over to the door to open it. When they did, it was like a never-ending freight train of Blaxlos, Summers and Clarks: Lucy, Nic and Alexander; Rick, Claire and RJ; Mum, Dad, Jen and Steven and the kids; and lastly, Jake and his new girlfriend, a tall attractive redhead, who was not his normal type.

I scrambled off Bryce's lap as they all filtered into the apartment.

'Are you two ever not all over each other?' Jen asked as she approached to give us a hug.

'No,' Bryce said as a matter of fact. *I can't really disagree with him either.*

Jen passed Jack to me. 'Here, Merry Christmas, he's my gift to you. He spews, shits, cries and doesn't sleep. Enjoy.' She kissed me on the cheek then moved over and hugged Bryce. 'Merry Christmas.'

I jiggled Jack on my hip as I greeted everyone else, leaving my brother till last. As I approached him and his scarlet companion, I lifted Jack and gently pushed him into Jake's arms. 'Here, Merry Christmas, he's my gift to you. He spews, shits, cries and doesn't sleep. Enjoy,' I said, repeating what Jen said to me.

Jake had no choice but to accept. 'Geez, just what I've always wanted ... a smaller version of myself.'

The scarlet one let out a snorting laugh. 'You're so funny,' she complimented adoringly. *Oh god! She's a Jake groupie.*

'Alexis, this is Johanna. Johanna, Alexis, my little sister.'

'Clearly, I'm not little,' I said as I rolled my eyes at my brother. 'It's nice to meet you, Johanna.'

'Nice to meet you too, Alexis.' Johanna said politely, putting her arms out to Jake, wanting to hold baby Jack. My brother more than happily obliged, passing him over.

'Hello, you big handsome boy,' she cooed at him, as she walked toward the rest of our family, Jack now bouncing on her hip.

I linked my arm around Jake's. 'So, how long is this one going to last?' I murmured with a low voice.

'I dunno, hopefully a while. I like her.'

'Didn't you like the others?'

'Not really.'

'You're such a man-whore.'

'Correction: was a man-whore. I like this one.'

'Well, if you want to keep said "one" stop referring to her as a number.'

Jen walked over to us while giving Johanna unsure glances.

'Who gave my son to a stranger with a funny laugh?'

Jake pointed to me and I pointed to him.

'I re-gifted,' I explained.

'So did I,' retorted Jake.

'Jake, she'd better be clean and sterile.'

'Listen, you two, be nice. She is clean and sterile, although we did shag before we came here.'

I punched his arm. 'Eww.'

'That's it! Get my son, someone get my son. She's kissing his cheek and I have a fairly good idea where her lips have been.' Jen turned around and headed for Johanna.

I smiled sweetly at Jake. 'So she gave you head before our Christmas lunch? She's so nice,' I said stretching out the 'nice' part of my statement.

'Alexis, give her a chance.'

I looked at him askance, insulted. 'I will. I was being genuine, she does seem nice.'

He glared at me.

'I'll do you a deal. Be nice to Rick, and I'll do the same to Johanna.'

He raised his head and spotted my estranged husband. 'No can do. The man cheated on you with that little bitch hanging off his arm,' Jake said angrily.

'Hey, I know. We both made mistakes, and anyway, I'm better off now. I'm happy and I've forgiven him, so you can do the same.'

He huffed. *Yes, my brother huffs.*

'Deal?' I offered again.

'Hmm.'

I hugged him. 'I love you, Jakey Snakey.'

We walked down into the lounge area to mingle with the rest of our families. I noticed Dad and Bryce come out of Bryce's office, Dad giving Bryce a manly slap on the back, both of them looking quite pleased. *God, I hope Dad didn't just agree to let Bryce buy him a helicopter or something.*

I let go of Jake's arm so that I could embrace Bryce. 'What are you getting up to with my father?' I inquired as I slid my arms around his waist. 'He didn't just agree to sign his life over to you, did he?'

Bryce chuckled. 'Kind of.'

I scowled at him with curiosity. 'I know you want to share your wealth with me and my family, but you need to keep me informed about it. I hate shit being said and done behind my back.'

He leaned forward and kissed my nose. 'Okay. I'll let you know.' Then he unwrapped my arms and headed to the kitchen.

I stood there and shook my head at him, then turned to find Rick staring at me. He met my gaze, smiled mildly, then returned his attention to Charli who was showing off her new karaoke machine. It dawned on me in that moment that he had not yet seen me and Bryce physically affectionate toward each other. It also dawned on me that it must be hard on him to observe such moments. So I made a mental note to tone it down, not wanting to ruin anybody's Christmas, although he would have to start getting used to it sooner rather than later.

* * *

Bryce had offered to cook the Christmas turkey and ham, but I had insisted that he didn't do so, wanting him to have a break and enjoy the day without any work involved. He'd worked enough as it was lately. Besides, he had a perfectly good chef downstairs in the hotel's kitchen who was more than happy to cook our Christmas lunch for us.

Chaos surrounded the dining table as both our families dished up their lunches. I smiled warmly at the four highchairs lined up next to each other, hoping that one day soon another would be added to the adorable sight before me.

Bryce approached from behind, having noticed me staring at the babies.

Resting his chin on my shoulder momentarily, he whispered into my ear. 'You want to sneak off and try to make one of those now?'

I chuckled quietly in response and tilted my head to touch his. 'You're a sex fiend, you know that?'

We enjoyed our Christmas lunch along the extended table, which was covered in a white damask tablecloth and topped with a white bone china dinner set and silver cutlery. I'd placed Christmas crackers at every place setting and sprinkled gold and silver glitter stars over the table top, stars now being one of my favourite things.

Charli had made place cards out of gold and silver cardstock, having matched my theme and cut them into star shapes.

I'd sat Rick next to me to keep him away from my grudge-holding family and, surprisingly, it had not felt weird sitting in between him and Bryce.

Bryce was faced the other way, chatting to Lucy, and I had not yet cracked open my Christmas cracker, so I turned to Rick — my cracker pointing directly at him — and offered the challenge.

'Don't cheat like you always do.'

'I don't cheat,' he said with a wicked grin.

'You do. Look, you're holding it wrong. That's cheating.'

'How am I supposed to hold the bloody thing?'

I shook my head at him. 'You're such a liar,' I blurted out.

Noticing that the room had gone a little silent at my choice of words, I quickly continued our harmless argument to reassure the family eavesdroppers. 'Ha! You know exactly how to hold it, Rick. Like this.' I rearranged his hand into the correct position. 'Ready?' I smiled. 'Go.'

We both wrenched our ends of the cracker, creating a loud snap and tearing the giant, foil, lolly-shaped novelty apart. The contents — the winner's prize — went hurtling into the air and across the table, smacking Jake right in the middle of the face. Everyone held their breath, except for Olivia who pointed at her uncle, saying, 'Ouch.'

I bit down on my lip in order to supress an outburst of hysterics while Rick raised his hands in surrender.

'Accident, mate.'

Jake was still stony-faced, and for once I couldn't tell if he was about to lose his shit or laugh at the funny side.

It wasn't until scarlet-Johanna snorted a laugh at him that everyone else followed suit, including Jake. Nate picked up the bundled prize that had rolled in his direction after bouncing off Jake's nose. He unfolded the paper hat and fitted it to Jake's head, then read out the festive joke.

'"What do you call a dog in the desert?"' Nate announced slowly.

Most of us shrugged our shoulders.

Jake deadpanned. '"A hot dog."'

Johanna snorted.

'No,' Nate groaned.

Charli laughed.

And Olivia threw something and said 'Ouch' again.

Nate waited until we were quiet, then happily announced, '"Sandy Claws."'

We all groaned.

* * *

You know you've had a good Christmas feed when your stomach is full to the brim with seafood cocktail, roasted turkey, glazed ham, golden crisp potatoes, pumpkin and steamed greens. If that wasn't enough to satisfy your hunger, you would then indulge in Christmas pudding and custard, pavlova and trifle, and every few seconds you'd pop chocolate-coated nuts and lollies into your mouth. By the time you eventually stopped eating, you'd have that increasing urge to undo your pants, followed by a developed waddle and a hand lightly placed on your bulging gut, together with a screwed-up look on your face that said, 'Urgh! I won't ever eat again.'

Most of us were showing those signs as we moved back into the lounge area to exchange our gifts.

'Best Christmas meal, ever!' Jake exclaimed as he rubbed his gut and let out a belch. 'Excuse me. See what I mean?'

Scarlet-Johanna was the only who found that funny.

'So my Christmas dinners have been shit, have they?' Mum asked defensively.

'Na, Mum, not at all. This one was just better.' Jake winked at her.

'Can we open presents now'? Charli asked anxiously.

'Yes,' I sighed in surrender, sending the kids haywire with the ripping and shredding of Christmas paper.

Jen and Lucy spent the next few minutes removing bits of that paper from their babies' mouths and clenched hands, while everyone else was deep in discussion of some kind or another.

I sat back and watched the excitement and rejoicing and, crazy as it was, the scene before me was one of the reasons I loved Christmas so much: everyone just seemed happy. All resentment, bitterness and dislike were checked at the door, replaced by contentment, laughter, joy and cheerfulness — it was bliss.

Bryce had placed envelopes under the tree for my brother, sister, mum and dad. He'd even put one under there for Rick. I was curious as to their contents, hoping to god it wasn't money.

Instead, he'd organised Clark Incorporated-Hotel Family Cards, so that my family could stay at any of his hotels around the world, on any day, at any time. I was completely stunned.

'Mum, there's a big present right at the back. It says "Honey",' Charli struggled to say, while on her knees with her bum in the air and her head deep in the depths of the Christmas tree, reaching for the present.

'Ooh,' I beamed, finding Bryce's knowing smile as I quickly got up from the sofa.

'It's big,' she whined as she dragged it out.

Once it was free from the confines of the tree, the odd shape of the box kind of gave its contents away. My face lit up as I lifted it and carried it back to the couch, sitting down next to Bryce. I couldn't help butt-wiggling as I opened it, while letting out my own high-pitched squeal.

I lifted and opened the box to find a guitar case and, turning to Bryce with a smile so bright that the muscles in my face stretched under the strain, I mouthed thank you.

Running my hands over the case, I unlatched it and took hold of my guitar, *my* very first guitar. As I lifted it out of the box, I noticed a pretty design on the front with a bird and some flowers — it was gorgeous.

'Nice!' Lucy commented. 'Is that a hummingbird?'

I studied the bird a little more closely. 'Oh, so it is. The bird is a hummingbird. How sweet.'

Lucy and Bryce laughed at my discovery, exchanging expressions of a private joke.

'Yeah,' Bryce answered. 'True Vintage.'

'Of course it is,' she acknowledged.

'What?' I asked. 'Am I supposed to understand what the two of you are referring to?'

'Nope,' Bryce replied and pulled me in for a quick kiss.

'Well, thank you, anyway. I love it, it's perfect.'

'I've got something for you too,' I said sneakily, then whispering into his ear I added, 'This is a decoy. You'll get your real present later.'

He eyed me suspiciously as I handed him the box.

'No pressure,' I said as he opened it.

He laughed and lifted out the motorcycle helmet.

'I couldn't see that you had one, so I figured that if you were going to take the plunge, you'd need a helmet.'

'Thanks, and you're right, I don't have one.' He leaned closer to me. 'What about you? You'll need a helmet too.'

I raised my eyebrows. 'I'm one step ahead of you.'

Later that night in bed, I asked Bryce why he gave Rick a Hotel Family Card.

'You didn't have to give Rick one, you know. You already gave him five million dollars.'

He sighed. 'Honey, can we not talk about my paying Rick? I might not regret offering him the money and having a hand in forcing the truth out of him, but I do regret bribing him with something I had a good idea he could not refuse.'

'No, I don't mean it like that. What I mean is, because of you he can afford to stay anywhere in the world as it is, so why give him a card?'

He stroked my face gently, 'Because it's a Family Card, and he is your family and always will be.'

'Yes, he will be,' I honestly replied.

He would always be family. We shared two beautiful children and many memories, but we'd both moved on with our lives and, in just a few weeks, would be officially divorced.

* * *

A few days later, I knocked on the door of my former house, my children behind me with their suitcases.

'Mum, how long are you going to be in Italy for?' Nate asked. 'I want to come.'

'Next time, sweetheart, I promise. This trip is for work and it's only for a few days. I'll see you both next weekend.'

Nate slumped his shoulders.

'I'll bring you back a Ferrari?' I offered, enticingly.

'A real one?'

I thought about my answer carefully, knowing he meant a full-sized one and I meant a scaled version. *A toy one is still real if it's from Italy, isn't it?*

'Yeah,' I answered.

'Sick!'

Rick opened the door and let us in. 'You still have your key, Alexis. You can use it.'

'I know. I'm still not going to let myself in, though, especially after last time.'

He gave me a sardonic grin.

'What? I honestly didn't know she had no shoes,' I defensively answered, remembering back to when I'd kicked Claire out of the house due to my crazy anger.

'Sure,' he teased.

I followed him into the kitchen, still feeling a little nostalgic about my surroundings. 'Where are Claire and RJ?'

'RJ had a friend's birthday party,' he explained.

'Right.' I took a seat at the dining table. 'Listen, I have the, ah ...' I opened my handbag to pull out the Application for Divorce, 'the divorce papers,' I said nervously.

Rick walked over casually and pulled out a chair opposite me. 'The time has come, has it?'

'Yeah, Rick, it has.' I slid them across the table to him.

He grabbed his reading glasses from the fruit bowl in the middle of the table.

I laughed. 'You still put them there? They don't belong in the fruit bowl.'

He looked up at me over the rim. 'I always know where they are, that's why I put them there.'

I shook my head.

He dropped his gaze back down to the papers in front of him, studying their content with precision. I took that moment to take him in, noticing how much he had changed in the past year, not just mentally, but physically. He now wore his dark brown hair a little longer, taking a few years off his age. His five o'clock shadow was clean-shaven and he'd toned up, looking a lot healthier overall.

He looked over the top of the reading glasses again, displaying a mischievous smirk. 'Having second thoughts?'

'What?' I said, snapping out of my Rick analysis. I lifted an eyebrow and smiled. 'No. I'm not having second thoughts, smartarse. I was just taking in how good you look, how healthy and happy you seem.'

'You look good, too.'

I scoffed. 'Separating has done wonders for us, hasn't it? Maybe we weren't as good for each other as we thought we were.'

'Lexi, we were good for each other.'

I looked down at my keys which I still had looped over my finger. I found the key to the house and started removing it from the ring. 'Rick, are you happy ... honestly?'

He took his glasses off and placed them on top of the papers. 'Yes, Lex, I'm happy. Claire is great. She's matured and she really does love me. I'm lucky to have her after the way I treated her. And RJ? Well ... he is just awesome, he's so good and sweet ... and ... he's just perfect. Nate and Charli are happy and healthy and they obviously really like Bryce. He seems to really like them, too —'

'He loves them,' I interrupted, correcting him.

'Yeah, I can see that. I can also see just how much he loves you. I could never compete with that.'

'Rick, it was never a competition. I loved you. I loved you very much, but there was just something missing in our marriage, and I think you can agree with me in saying that we didn't realise that until we had no other choice but to realise it.'

'No, you're right, I do realise that. I loved you, too. I still do. I always will. But you deserved a much greater love than what I could give you, and I truly am happy that Bryce is the one who can give it to you. Believe it or not, I do respect the fucker.'

I laughed. 'Funny, that. I think in a weird fucked-up way he respects you too.'

Rick shook his head in amusement. 'Okay,' he said as he put his glasses back on and collected all the papers into a bunch, tapping them on the table, then lying them back down again. 'Let's get this shit signed.'

CHAPTER
30

The last time I was in a private jet, I was flying back home from spending the most amazing few days in Uluru with Bryce. The jet I was standing in at this moment, however, was slightly bigger. In fact, it was much bigger and much more private. When I stepped into this aircraft I noticed it was not open-plan like the one we were in last time. This one had walls and rooms.

As I made my way inside, I was met with a sitting area containing chocolate-brown leather seats with a table in between them, and a flat screen TV. There was also a three-seater sofa against the plane's side that spanned the length of that particular room. I continued my inspection, opening the door ahead of me and walking into a spacious master bedroom with an inviting queen-sized bed, a wardrobe, drawers and a desk with another chocolate-coloured leather seat. It was indulgently decadent, that decadence rolling through into the large bathroom.

'Wow! Just wow!' I muttered, stunned. I had no idea an aircraft like this existed. It was basically a luxury motel room with wings.

'Yeah, it's not bad,' Bryce replied with a deliciously handsome smile.

I turned to him, my hand finding my hip. 'You're so fucking arrogant at times.'

He smirked at me then pulled me onto the bed, securing me on top of him. 'Admit it. You love it when I'm arrogant.'

I shook my head and pursed my lips. 'No, I don't. It makes me mad.' *I lie. He is hot — arrogantly hot.*

He raised his eyebrow in amusement. 'I like it when you're mad.'

'Do you just?'

'I do.'

I dropped my arms and fell to his chest, my lips landing against his. He ran his hands up the sides of my face and into my hair, then he swiftly rolled me on my back, pinning me to the bed.

'I'm going to fuck you senseless on this bed when we are 30,000 feet in the air.'

He pushed against my mouth, dipping his tongue vehemently and taking my breath away.

'I can't wait,' I said through husky breaths as he moved his mouth down my neck.

'We have seventeen hours till we land in Rome, and we are going to make the most of every single one of them.' *Holy fuck! Seventeen hours with Bryce in a private jet en route to Rome ... it doesn't get any better than this.*

The captain's voice sounded through the aircraft's speaker. 'Excuse me, Mr Clark and Ms Summers. We will be taking off in less than five minutes. If you could make your way to your seats, Amy will secure the cabin.'

'Is that Captain Paul, from last time?'

'Yes, I request him whenever I fly. I trust him completely. And Amy.'

'So they just drop everything to be your flight crew?'

'Yeah, pretty much.'

I shook my head at him.

'Honey, stop shaking your head at me or I'll rip this dress off you and spank that perfect arse.'

'Is that a threat?' I challenged him.

'No, it's a promise.'

I deliberately shook my head again. 'Ooh, so nasty.'

He pushed up off me so quickly that I barely registered he'd done it and, before I knew it, I had been turned onto my stomach, Bryce now straddling me and facing my feet.

He wrenched up my dress and exposed my G-string wearing arse, a cool breeze now touching my tense cheeks. 'Mm, so fucking tight,' he murmured as he rubbed his hands across each buttock.

I clenched automatically, but also in suspense as to when he would spank me like he said he would. I felt his weight shift, then the drag of his warm wet tongue along the bridge of my arse. *Oh, fuck!*

I arched my back, rising to meet his tongue.

'You want me to spank you, don't you?'

'Yes,' I whimpered.

Not a second later, I felt the sting of his hand against my soft flesh, the sound of his slap sharp in the air. It hurt, but with pleasure, making me gasp and clench my core.

His hand found the tender spot and he rubbed it slowly, affectionately. Then I felt his finger trail down between my cheeks, pausing momentarily at my puckered opening, only to continue to my wet pussy.

He teased my entry, then plunged his finger hard and deep. 'Fuck, you did like that, didn't you?'

Slowly, he began to move his finger in and out when there was a knock at the door.

'I'm sorry to interrupt, Mr Clark, but we have clearance to leave now,' Amy said through the solid mahogany door.

I lifted my head and turned to face Bryce, only to see the back of his head.

'Thank you, Amy. We will be right out,' he answered with frustrated yet friendly authority.

He climbed off me, so I rolled onto my back, catching sight of him putting his finger in his mouth to suck off my arousal. I drew in a deep frustrated breath, got up and walked toward the door.

I felt his hands grip my hips, halting me. 'We will finish this later, my love,' he whispered huskily, his hot breath caressing my ear.

I shivered at his promise. 'I know.'

He gently placed his hand over the spot he spanked and gave it a light tap, then he walked me out of the room.

* * *

Bryce fucked me senseless like he promised, shortly after reaching our cruising altitude. I kind of felt different now — a member of the mile-high club — superior in some way.

'I love seeing that look on your face, that look of satisfaction.'

I gave him a smug smile as I flicked through my magazine. 'You love the fact that you put it there.'

'Of course I do.'

'So, when we land in Rome, what's the plan?' I asked while putting down my copy of *Better Homes and Gardens*, now curious as to our itinerary for the next couple of days.

Bryce's eyes seemed to twinkle with excitement before he answered me. 'Well ... we'll fuck in my hotel room first. Then we'll sleep to catch up on the hours we have already lost. Afterward, I have a meeting with my hotel managers, and then when that is finished, we'll order in and fuck again. Tomorrow, we can go sightseeing, then I'll take you out for dinner later that night and we'll fuck like crazy after that. The following day we can sleep in and eat breakfast off each other's naked bodies. I will then need to oversee some of the construction of the new complex, and after that, I'll take you shopping, we'll fuck again, and then we'll fly home. Sound good?'

My mouth had dropped open, astounded by his organisation, not to mention the number of times he'd said he planned on fucking me. Oh, and that we were going sightseeing and shopping.

'Alexis, do you want to add anything to that?' he asked, with a sexy confidence, knowing I'd be more than happy with his suggestion.

'No, sounds perfect.'

I picked up my gin and swallowed, giving him an appraising wink over the rim of the glass.

* * *

When we landed in Rome, the Eternal City, we were met on the tarmac by a limousine and driver. The transfer to Opulenza Della Città took less than half an hour. It was cold and raining, as it was winter in this part of the world. But when looking out the window at the enchanting ancient city, I felt the rain added to its character.

When we pulled up to the Opulenza Della Città, we were greeted by the valet who stood outside a cream-coloured, historic-looking beautiful building, no taller than ten storeys high. It was so different from City Towers.

As we stepped into the lobby, it felt like I was walking into a grand ballroom from a fairytale. The chequered marble flooring caught my eye first, but the curtains hanging exquisitely from the floor-to-ceiling windows, together with the large crystal chandeliers, had me speechless. *Oh my god! This place is truly breathtaking.* I'd stopped in my tracks, my mouth open, taking in my surroundings, when I felt the gentle grip and pull of Bryce's hand in mine.

'Do you like it?' he asked, clearly boasting.

'Like it? I'm awed, it's simply stunning,' I answered, wide-eyed.

'You're simply stunning, my love. This is just a building.'

I removed my gaze from the large Renaissance painting hanging on the wall to meet his stare. 'Just a building? If you weren't being so terribly sexy and romantic right now, I'd try and slap you. This is not "just a building". Give yourself more credit.'

A tall, dark-haired, exotically beautiful man interrupted us. 'Excuse me, *Signor* Clark. *Benvenuto*, it is so nice to see you again,' he said with a thick accent and charming smile.

'*Buon giorno*, Antonio. Yes, it has been a while. I'd like you to meet Alexis.'

Being innocently uncultured, I stuck out my hand to shake his in greeting.

He chuckled and pulled me closer, kissing both sides of my cheeks. '*Bella*, Alexis. It is my pleasure.'

Bryce raised his eyebrows then hugged me to him.

Noticing Bryce's statement of claim, Antonio politely took a step back. '*Signor* Clark. Your suite is ready for you.'

'*Grazie*, Antonio.'

Bryce placed his hand at the small of my back and led me toward the elevator.

'He was very friendly,' I teased.

'He's supposed to be. Just not with you, and not in front of me.'

Bryce swiped his card through the security pad at the entrance to the suite's door, which was situated on the top floor.

He pushed the door open at the sound of the click. 'After you, my love.'

I beamed and stepped through the door, being hit straightaway with mustard and terracotta hues, gold fixtures and fittings, big ornate mirrors and fake stone columns. It was very ... well ... Roman.

The suite had a lounge with a stone, rough-textured fireplace which was lit and already cosy and inviting. On the floor in front of the fireplace was a beautifully patterned rug, and atop it was a Victorian-style, deep-buttoned chaise longue.

As I continued to walk through the suite, I took in its opulence, the master bedroom being no exception. It was enormous and followed the range of hues used for the suite, except the palette in the master bedroom had a subtle mustard shade, which complemented an elegant king-sized bed backed with glorious, thick golden drapes that hung from a pelmet and fanned out like a triangle, framing the bed.

A knock at the door pulled me out of my mesmerised state. I walked back into the lounge area of the suite to see Bryce greet a bellhop delivering our luggage and an attendant pushing a trolley containing a bottle of wine and a food cloche. He politely thanked them both and closed the door behind them.

'Don't you tip your staff here?' I asked, as he set the cloche and bottle of wine on the table next to the chaise longue.

'No, not in Italy, but I do take note of all my staff and their demeanour, and I make sure they are commended appropriately before I leave.'

I stepped up to him, placing my hands on his shoulders. 'You are a very generous employer. I can vouch for that.'

'Mm,' he groaned, running his hands underneath my heavy coat and pushing it off my shoulders. I did the same for him and removed his suit jacket, both of us tossing them onto the chair not too far from where we were standing. I reached up, grabbed the nape of his neck and pulled his lips to mine, lips that I could never get enough of. Plump, warm and sensationally talented at pleasing whatever they touched.

His hands found the zip at the top of my black Burberry shift dress, which went falling to the floor once the zip met its end. I stepped out of it, now standing in my black underwear, garter, stockings and my Louboutin heeled boots.

'You're a fucking goddess, Alexis. A vision of the highest order.'

I dropped to my knees and unfastened his trousers while eye-fucking him wickedly. He cracked his neck from side to side, causing a rippling sexy sensation to surge right through me. I dug my hands deep into his pants releasing his thick, hard cock from its now snug confines. It sprung free, positioned with authority and deliciously resting at the tip of my mouth.

Wrapping my hands around its base, I gripped tightly, dragging them up and pumping a glistening drop over his smooth crown. I licked its saltiness, then ran my tongue over my teeth, allowing Bryce to see how much I enjoyed tasting him.

He caressed my face lovingly, pure adoration pouring from his eyes and radiating through his touch. 'You are everything to me,' he said as he gently pulled the clip out of my hair, releasing my blonde waves to cascade and frame my face.

I smiled at his ownership, gently teething his shaft.

His fingers flexed into my scalp, urging me to clamp my mouth down and suck him vigorously. 'Fuck!' he growled as his hips bucked.

He rocked forward some more, before stopping. 'Alexis, I need to be inside you. Now!'

Sliding his cock out of my mouth, he then lifted me to my feet, scooping me into his arms and placing me on the chaise longue. The fire crackled and flames flickered into the air above it, giving the room not only warmth from the outside chill, but a romantic ambience to complement our first sexual union in Italy.

Bryce walked around to the foot of the chaise and ran his hands through his hair. 'You have no idea how irresistible you look in that lingerie and reclined on that chair.'

Leaning forward, I snagged him by his tie. 'Pants. Lose them. Now!'

He smirked at my dominance, then pushed his trousers to the ground and stepped out of them.

Yanking fiercely on his tie, I gave him no option but to crawl on top of the chaise and on top of me. I opened my legs, allowing him to settle between them and, wasting no time, I aggressively tore open his shirt, dislodging a couple of buttons.

He growled as he leaned into me, his mouth finding my neck, my hands finding his cock. I pulled my G-string aside, exposing my wet flesh and, with quick precision, guided him into me.

'Oh, god!' I moaned with pleasure as he slid so perfectly into place.

I wrapped my legs around his waist, securing him deep and tight as my pussy clenched down on him in acceptance.

'Fuck, I love it when you squeeze me like that,' he said through gritted teeth, his words sending a fiery passion into my ears and right down to my stomach.

'I love you so much, Bryce,' I moaned, as he rolled his pelvis into me, over and over.

He thrust hard and deep. 'I love you, too, Alexis.'

With my orgasm teetering, ready to wash over me, I dug my finger-nails deep into his flesh and waited for that surge of pleasure. When it rolled through me I dragged them down his back uncontrollably, forcing an animalistic growl from Bryce that vibrated right through me. *Holy fuck of all fucks.*

Panting, I shuddered with sensation, closing my eyes and going limp. Bryce did the same, relaxing some of his weight on top of me. He was heavy and making it more difficult to breathe, but I didn't care. There was nothing I wanted more in that moment than to feel his moist, warm body against mine.

We needed a nap after making love, not really having the energy to do anything else. Bryce had then gone to his meeting as scheduled and come back in time for dinner. We were suffering the effects of jet lag and overexertion from our many sexed-up encounters, so we'd gone to bed early in the hope we'd be fresh for our sightseeing the next day.

* * *

When I woke up the following morning, there was a rose on my pil-low together with a note informing me that he had gone to the hotel's gym. It gave me some time to clear my head and think about an excit-ing yet terrifying prospect, one I had deliberately been ignoring over the past week. The longer I ignored it, the possibility that it was true only excited me more, but I was too scared to take the plunge and find out, scared to be disappointed.

As I stood in the bathroom, naked after dropping my robe, I looked down at my belly and lightly rubbed my hand over the precious spot I hoped housed another baby. My period was a week overdue and I was apprehensive about confirming why. However, the longer I left it, the more nervous I became. I decided I would wait until we got back home to buy a test, not wanting to be sad on our trip if the result was negative.

Sighing with mixed feelings, I stepped into the shower.

Not too long after, Bryce appeared in the bathroom, sweat-stained and gloriously glossy, his work-out towel draped over the back of his neck and his pants hanging low on his hips. *He is simply gorgeous.*

He stripped off and joined me, telling me about the steam room and how he wanted to get one built at City Towers.

'Actually, I might get a private one built out on the balcony. Making love to you in a steam-filled room is definitely on my list of things to do, and soon.'

I laughed. 'Sounds hot!'

'You're punny,' he said, cleverly.

I lightly smacked his chest. 'Come on, we've got so much to see today.'

The hotel was situated in the middle of Rome's high-end shopping district, but as tempting as shopping in Rome sounded at that moment, I was keen to see Vatican City and the Colosseum.

We finished our shower and dressed warmly, although it was not bitterly cold and, surprisingly, once the sun came out, it would be a beautiful fresh day. A limousine waited at the front of the hotel to take us the short distance across the Tiber River to the Vatican. I was beyond excited at the prospect of seeing famous places and landmarks up close and in person, giving me the ability to decide for myself as to their brilliance and stature.

As the limousine approached, I spotted the top of St Peter's Basilica, and tingles of exhilaration prickled over me. When the limousine finally stopped, I wrenched the door open and let myself out, breaking protocol and surprising the driver.

'Alexis,' Bryce chuckled, 'you might want to wait for me.'

'You snooze, you lose,' I called back with a smile as I headed for St Peter's Square.

The sound of the limo door shutting came quickly, and then the sound of his footsteps gaining on me. I squealed when I felt his arms scoop me up. 'I'll never let you get away.'

I placed my hands on his shoulders as he helped slide me back onto my feet. 'I'll never want to,' I whispered to his lips. 'Now let me go. We have sightseeing to do.'

Walking around a place so rich with history, art and religion was not only a wonderful experience, it was made even more wonderful by sharing that experience with Bryce. We held hands as we strolled through the Apostolic Palace. The Sistine Chapel gave us sore necks as a result of time spent craning our heads back to really appreciate Michelangelo's painted masterpiece on its ceiling.

After a quick lunch at a café and an espresso to keep me awake for days, we headed to the Colosseum. As we approached the ancient ruins, I couldn't help but wonder what it would've looked like in its prime. Of course, I'd seen illustrations and movies depicting it whole and vibrant, and full of spectators watching a brutal battle of gladiators, but to see it in the flesh in all its glory would have been amazing. I was surprised at how much of the amphitheatre had collapsed and it saddened me. Unfortunately, preventing destruction by natural forces had been impossible.

* * *

We arrived back at our suite in the late afternoon.

'Are you feeling lucky today?' I asked Bryce as I slumped on the bed.

'What?' he shot out, as if I'd sprung him doing something suspect.

I lifted my upper body from the bed, propping myself up on my elbows. 'Maybe you're not feeling so lucky then.'

'Sorry, I was just thinking about something,' he said dismissively. 'Am I feeling lucky? I hope so. You have no idea how lucky I hope to feel, why?'

'Because ... I was going to let you rub my feet. They are fucked.'

He walked toward the bed, removing his shoes in the process. 'It must be my lucky day then.'

He had a grin so wide, it made me mockingly roll my eyes. 'Whatever floats your boat, Mr Clark.'

He took hold of my foot, the one I'd broken, and gently removed my shoe. I watched him delicately trace his fingertips over my scar. 'How does it feel?'

I lowered myself back down to the mattress with a thud. 'Good, although I gave it a good test today.'

'Well, we won't be walking tonight.'

'Tonight?' I queried, feeling a little too exhausted for anything.

'Yes, I have a special reservation.'

'Where? What are we having?'

'Italian.'

I playfully kicked him with my other foot. 'Der!'

* * *

I was pleasantly surprised when we stepped out of the hotel to find a scooter instead of the limousine. Bryce handed me my helmet and put his on — the one I bought him for Christmas.

'Scooter? Really?' I asked, astonished and unsure if I was excited or not.

'We are in Italy. It's the best way to get around.'

'I'm going to ruin my hair.' I said, while looking at the helmet.

'Nothing about you can be ruined, honey.'

I tilted my head to the side and gave him a cynical grin. 'If only that were true.'

Sliding on the helmet, I positioned myself behind him on the scooter, thankful I was wearing pants.

Bryce had laid out clothes on the bed for me like he'd done so many times before, and it now dawned on me that he had chosen my dark denim skinny jeans, Dolce & Gabbana blouse, Louboutin boots and my trench coat for a very good reason.

I hugged him tightly, clenching my thighs around his hips and shouting through the helmet. 'It's not the Harley, but it's a start.' I gave him another squeeze as he took off, my initial squeal being left at the curb.

We pulled up to Ristorante Di Tony, a cute little restaurant in a quiet part of the city. It was not the type of restaurant he would normally choose, as this one seemed far from fancy. Don't get me wrong ... it was lovely, quaint and, from the sidewalk, appeared homely. It was just very different from Bryce's usually extravagant taste.

I waited for him to dismount and remove his helmet before I headed to the front door of the building.

'This way, honey. I have my own private entrance,' he said casually as he took hold of my hand and led me toward the alleyway next to the restaurant. There was something in the way he said it, or maybe the strikingly handsome smirk on his face, that triggered a sense of déjà vu.

I giggled as he pulled me along. 'Do you know the owner?'

He smiled at me. 'Yeah, I just bought the place.'

'What? Why on earth would you buy —' As we rounded the corner, the sounds of 'Bella Notte' filtered into my ears, once again triggering my sense of déjà vu. The music, I soon discovered, was being played by a duet who were seated off to the side of a lone round table, topped with a red and white tablecloth, a candle and a single red rose.

Surrounding the table were several potted plants, shielding the table from the musical duet, and also from the general area behind the restaurant. The plants created a backdrop to what I assumed was our dining spot. Many candles in jars were lit and placed along the ground, romantically paving a walkway to our seats. It was in that moment that I realised my feeling of déjà vu was sparked by standing in the middle of a scene from *Lady and the Tramp*.

'Oh! My! God!'

CHAPTER
31

'Bryce! Oh, my god, when did you —'

'Never mind about the when, honey, come and take a seat.' He placed his hand at the small of my back and ushered me toward the table.

I let out a surprised laugh. 'You are amazing. This is amazing.'

'It's what I do, Ms Summers,' he said with a smirk, while pulling out a chair for me to sit in.

As he sat down opposite me, I was struck by just how handsome he looked in the candlelight. His dark-blond hair was styled back and away from his face, as if he had just run his hands through it and it had obeyed. He was wearing a charcoal coloured shirt with the top two buttons open, a black suit jacket and his sexy light-wash jeans.

'Does your mind ever take a break?' I asked, as he wiped his palms on his pants while he settled into his seat.

'No. A mind functions simply by functioning. If it takes a break, it ceases to exist.'

'Have I ever told you that I find your intelligence a major turn-on?'

'No. I thought you wanted me for my body.'

'Well, yeah, that and your cooking.'

A waiter stepped out from behind the screened potted plants. '*Buona sera, Signor* Clark *e la Signora* Summers.'

'*Buona sera,*' Bryce replied, his accent rolling off his tongue like liquid sex.

Unable to speak Italian, I just nodded and smiled in response.

'Can I get you both a drink?' he asked, switching to English but with a heavy accent that was adorable.

Bryce raised his eyebrows at me in question.

Feeling a little daring, I thought I'd try my luck and ask for something a little unorthodox. 'I don't suppose they serve a Cock 'n Balls, do they?'

Closing his eyes slowly, Bryce twitched his head ever so slightly, clearly fighting a battle not to laugh. He opened them again and looked our waiter dead in the eyes. 'Is it possible to get my girlfriend a Cock 'n Balls?'

The waiter flushed bright red. 'I'm so sorry, *signor*, we do not serve such a drink.'

'Never mind,' I said sweetly. 'How about Salty Balls or Big Balls?'

The table started shaking, and I soon realised it was from Bryce chuckling. 'Honey, I don't think they serve any form of balls here.'

'Ha, I bet they serve meatballs.'

'Yes, *signora*, we serve meatballs,' he replied happily, now able to serve me some form of balls.

I started laughing and touched the waiter apologetically on the arm. 'Thank you, but I'll have a glass of Chianti Classico, please. And *Signor* Clark will have a Scotch on the rocks.'

He nodded sheepishly and made his way into the restaurant.

'They serve meatballs, Mr Clark. Did you hear that?'

'Yes,' he answered, still chuckling. 'I did.'

I shuffled in my seat and grabbed my napkin, laying it over my lap. 'So, you said on our way in that you bought this restaurant. Why? It doesn't fit your normal real estate acquisition criteria.'

'I like it. The place has character.'

'You're such a romantic.'

'Honey, you have no idea.'

'I think I'm starting to. You blow me away.'

'No, Alexis, you blow me away.'

'No, I just blow you,' I said with certainty, eye-fucking him.

One of the members of the duet missed a note, clearly mucking up the tune.

I bit my lip and sank down a little in my seat, whispering, 'I think they speak English.'

Bryce leaned forward and took hold of my hands. 'They do,' he said with amusement.

Just as butterflies started to flutter in my stomach at the look of love in his eyes, our waiter appeared with our drinks and, behind him, another waiter with a large plate of spaghetti and meatballs.

We both sat back as they placed the large dish and our drinks on the table. '*Buon appetito.*'

'*Grazie,*' Bryce and I replied simultaneously, my accent nowhere near as sexy as his.

The duet started playing 'Bella Notte' again, this time a little more pronounced. The heightened sound of the accordion and the large plate in front of us — which we were about to share — made me giggle.

'You don't miss a thing, do you? Although, if my memory serves me correctly, Butch passed Lady a meatball with his nose.'

Bryce leaned forward with a playful grin and poked his nose into the plate, nudging a meatball in my direction. I couldn't help but burst into laughter, not only from his daring move, but also due to the fact he now had Bolognese sauce on the tip of his nose.

I leaned forward and licked it off, then quickly patted his nose dry with my napkin. 'Why, thank you, kind sir.'

I kept laughing as I picked up a piece of spaghetti, giving him one end while I took the other. Then, just like the movie, we both started sucking it in, grinning at each other as our mouths moved closer to one another's. When the spaghetti disappeared, our lips were touching, massaging, kissing while we both swallowed our halves of the noodle. I thanked him with a flick of my tongue, then sat back down in my seat.

Forking some spaghetti into my mouth, I figured I'd be just as daring as he was and slurp up a long noodle like Lady had in the movie, forgetting that the sauce would flick all over the place. My natural instinct had me closing my eyes to avoid the spiralling sauce from entering them.

After I'd finished my marathon slurp, I opened one eye and spotted Bryce sitting still, his chest heaving and his expression mixed with want and something else.

'Fuck it, I can't wait any longer. You are just too fucking adorable and sexy, and I'm not waiting any more.' He stood up quickly, startling me, just as it started to rain. *Oh, god! We can't have sex here. Can we?*

'Oh no,' I said, looking up at the droplets now falling around me and thinking he was about to have his wicked way with me on this very spot.

Bryce walked around to my side of the table and, just as I was about to get up and out of the rain, he bent down on one knee before me. 'Alexis, from the moment I first laid eyes on you my heart held a secret, a secret I later found out to be true love. You ensnare me completely with your beauty, your wit, your humour and your kindness. And you wake in me every single emotion that I hold.

'Honey, I don't want to live another day without you, I don't want to take another breath without you, and I don't want to wait another second to ask you to become my wife.'

I watched him through drenched eyes and cheeks as he reached inside his jacket pocket and pulled out a small velvet box. My breath caught and my heart became motionless within my chest as the heavens opened and showered rain down upon us.

He opened the lid of the box, revealing a diamond ring. *Holy, f… f… f… fuck!* I was stunned beyond all imagination, seeing a huge twinkling chunk of diamond before me.

He looked up into my eyes, sincerity saturating his handsome face, together with droplets of rain. 'Alexis Elizabeth Summers, will you marry me?'

My mouth was open as I stared from his face to the ring and back to his face again, warm tears streaking down my cheeks and mixing perfectly with the cool of the rain.

'Yes,' I said, barely able to speak. Then, as if reality just up and smacked me in the face, I started nodding profusely. 'Yes. Yes. Yes, Bryce! I will marry you.'

He slid the ring onto my finger, then kissed my soaked hand. I grabbed his face and leaned into him, pressing my mouth to his like I had so many times before, except this time, it felt indescribable.

The passion, the love, the lust and resolution poured out of us both through hands, mouths, lips and tongues.

He stood up and, as if I were a feather, picked me up and held me to him, not separating his mouth from mine, not even the slightest bit.

I wrapped my legs around his waist, securing our bodies together and feeling the wet, soggy clothing between us. The cool of the rain, together with the heat from our passion, hardened my nipples and left me panting with pleasure.

He gripped my arse ferociously as he lapped deliciously at my mouth, then my neck, then chest and the top of my breasts.

'Bryce,' I said breathlessly, 'our meatballs are getting wet.'

'Fuck the meatballs,' he groaned as he carried me back down the alleyway toward the scooter, the duet still happily playing 'Bella Notte' in the rain.

* * *

The ride back to the hotel was both exciting and downright scary. My adrenaline was sky-high, but the wet slippery roads together with Roman crazy drivers had me on edge. I clung tightly to Bryce out of fear as well as infinitely overflowing love.

He led me hastily through the lobby, both of us leaving a wet trail behind us. When we were in the elevator car and the doors had closed giving us privacy, the hungry desperation returned.

He lifted me up, placing my arse on the railing that bordered the elevator walls. I let my hands find his hair, his face, his back and his arms, touching as much of him as I could touch. He tore my shirt apart, exposing my damp chest and, not waiting any longer than he saw fit, wrenched my bra down and took my perked nipple into his mouth.

We both groaned in succession, our lustful need spilling out of us at a rapid pace.

'Mm, you're mine,' he growled, as he greedily swapped from one breast to the other.

I threw my head back in pleasure. 'I've been yours for a while, Bryce.'

'I can't wait to make you my wife.'

'I can't wait to be your wife,' I breathed, as I took his tongue back into my mouth.

The elevator dinged and the doors opened to reveal our suite. Carrying me inside, he headed straight for the lounge, or more precisely, the open fire. We continued to kiss each other feverishly and desperately, as if our mouths knew nothing else, all the while frantically peeling our wet clothes from one another.

Bryce set me on my feet then dropped to his knees, lifting my leg onto his lap.

'I like you on your knees. So far only great things have come from your mouth while on your knees,' I lovingly admitted, as I looked at my ring, then back at him, my eyebrows rising with a smile.

He smirked devilishly at me as he unzipped my boot and removed it, then switched legs and did the same with the other. As he unbuttoned my jeans and stripped them from my body — together with my G-string — I quivered with excitement. His tongue slowly made its journey up my leg, finding my pussy wet with desire, desire for him, desire for my fiancé. *Holy fuckaroo, Bryce Clark is my fiancé.*

'You are my fiancé,' I exclaimed, my voice appearing to sound as though I had only just let the notion sink in.

He flicked his tongue across my clit, then paused. 'Yes, I am.'

'We are getting married,' I exclaimed again.

'Yes,' he mumbled against my pussy before inserting his finger.

The feeling of fulfilment nearly had me buckling at the knees, so much so that I stumbled back against the large floor to ceiling window. Bryce stood up and faced me, pressing me against the thick glass panel with his warm, hard body while the Italian winter air kissed the window with its ferocious chill, shocking my skin at its icy feel. I gasped.

Reaching down, he wrapped one arm underneath my arse, lifting me against him while the other hand stayed pressed against the glass pane. I opened myself to him, his erect head not needing any guidance into my pussy. He was hard, full and ready to be pumped.

He slammed into me with intense fervour, then pulled out and repeated the motion. At first I thought his enthusiasm might be too much for the window, but the sheer carnality of his actions had me forgetting my surroundings, instead focussing on him and him only.

Bryce pounded me against the window over and over until I was screaming out his name and digging my teeth into his shoulder. Then, barely recovering from my orgasm, he pulled out and spun me around, forcing me to splay my hands against the glass. I watched his reflection in the rain-streaked window as he slid his arm around my waist, compelling me to lean forward and spread wide for him.

Finding the strength to get up on my tiptoes for him, I bent slightly and waited for him to drive back into me.

The feeling of fullness I experienced weakened my stance, causing my head to drop and my hands to lose their grip against the glass.

'I've got you,' he said softly, yet with dominance so profound that I knew he did have me. He had me entirely.

I lifted my head to resume watching his magnificent reflection, a reflection of a body that I would get to admire forever. I greedily took in his flexing muscles as he increased his rhythm. His thrusts became rapid, then deep, strong, slow and hard, stripping me of any vigour I had left.

He growled with such intensity as he came, strong and deep within me, leaving me limp and pretty much suspended across his arm.

Bryce pressed a kiss to my shoulder then shifted me so that he could scoop me up. 'So, was that a good first date?' he asked with a cocky tone.

His cheeky question hung playfully in the air. I giggled as I closed my eyes and leaned into his chest.

'It was all right,' I teasingly answered, as he walked us to the bedroom. 'You weren't kidding when you said we were going to "fuck like crazy" after going out for dinner though, were you?'

'No, and I wasn't kidding when I said I was going to eat breakfast off your naked body.'

'Mm,' I mumbled, as my mind caught up to my body, shutting down and taking a well-earned rest.

* * *

The following morning I woke to the aroma of coffee and Bryce eating *fette biscottate* off my stomach.

'Good morning, my beautiful fiancée. Sleep well?' he asked, as he licked a crumb from around my navel.

I squirmed at the ticklish feel. 'Good morning, my handsome fiancé. Yes, I slept perfectly thanks to you.'

He pulled himself up closer to my head, poking the breakfast bread into my mouth. I bit down, finding that I was very hungry after only eating a few bites of dinner the night before.

Snatching it from his hand, I took another bite. 'Yum, this is delicious.'

I could see his face start to break into a cute little protest when his phone started ringing.

He rolled over and picked it up from the bedside table. 'Good morning, Lucy,' he answered with a smirk. I cuddled into his chest so that I could hear her through the phone's speaker.

'So,' she said impatiently, 'did you ask her?'

'Yes,' he answered, keeping his emotions flat, not giving anything away.

'And?' she said, her impatience palpable.

'I said yes,' I yelled up at the phone.

The next thing I heard was squealing through the speaker. Bryce frustratingly removed it from his ear, all the while smiling at his sister's happy reaction.

'Congratulations,' she sang, happily.

'Thanks,' we answered simultaneously.

'Okay, I won't keep you. I just wanted to know if my brother had manned up or chickened out. Go back to celebrating.' She blew a kiss into the phone, then hung up.

He put the phone back down and pulled me on top of him.

Sitting naked, straddling his glorious hips, I sighed. 'Can we just send out an email and tell everyone?'

'No, that's boring,' he said as he kneaded both my breasts in his hands. 'And anyway, your dad already knows. I had to get his permission first.'

My eyes widened at the knowledge he had been planning this for a while. 'When did you ask my dad?'

He squeezed my tender flesh meticulously. 'Christmas Day.'

I automatically lifted my arms and twisted my long hair into a bun holding it up on my head then thought back to Christmas Day and the sight of him and my dad leaving his office. 'Mm, you're sneaky,' I purred. 'Okay, how about we text everybody with emoticons instead?'

He rolled both my nipples between his thumbs and fingers and pinched mildly. 'No, that's still not good enough.'

I closed my eyes and began to rub my pussy against his expanding cock. 'Good old-fashioned letter?' I suggested, hopefully.

'I was thinking more along the lines of hiring a skywriter, or making a guest appearance on a morning television show.'

My eyes shot open. 'You wouldn't?'

He grabbed me and wrestled me to the bed. 'I would.'

After another mind-blowing orgasm, a skinny latte and some more *fette biscottate*, Bryce headed out to check the progress of construction work on the new Clark Incorporated hotel.

I was beaming, cheerful and joyously happy. I kept glancing at my ring in wonderment, now in a position to fully take in its brilliance. It was a large, square-cut diamond — large probably being an understatement — in a halo setting of twenty-five smaller diamonds, with another fifteen smaller diamonds around the band on either side. *Yes, I counted them, all fifty-six of them.*

Bryce had said he was going to be out for an hour or more, so I decided that rather than waste a beautiful day I would go for a walk along the main street.

The streets of Rome were beautiful and full of character, the buildings graced with tradition and charming cobblestone roads. I was deliriously happy as I skipped along the path. *Did I just skip? Oh my god, I think I actually skipped.*

I'd stopped myself momentarily, questioning my sanity, when I noticed I was in front of a pharmacy. My mind went straight to the strong possibility that I could be pregnant, but did I want to find out now ... today? I stared at the shop front and bit down on my thumbnail, a smile blossoming across my face. Yes, I did want to find out today, because even if the test was negative, nothing could possibly ruin my happy spirits.

I pushed open the door and went inside.

Half an hour later I was back in the hotel suite, a pregnancy test in my hand. I'd peed on the stick, enclosed it in the plastic cap then turned the results window down in my hand, not looking at the final outcome. I didn't want to do it alone; I wanted Bryce here with me. The problem with that idea was that my hand had started to cramp up. *Shit! How do I let go without seeing? I could close my eyes. No, I might drop it, then what?*

Just as I was about to make the decision to continue to grip or let go, and probably resembling a fretful person holding a ticking time bomb, Bryce walked through the door.

He strode right up to me and wrapped his arms around my waist. 'Longest fucking two hours of my life.' He took my head in his hands and kissed me with intention.

I didn't hug him back. Instead, I held my arms outstretched as if the pregnancy test contained a highly infectious disease.

'What's wrong, honey?' he asked, concern on his handsome face. He looked at my enclosed hand. 'What's that?'

'A pregnancy test,' I blurted out.

He was stony faced, not knowing whether to smile or frown. I knew how he felt.

'Are you —?'

'I don't know, I haven't looked. I was waiting for you to come back. I'm over a week late.'

'Fuck! Why didn't you ring me?' He grasped my hand and moved it so that it rested in between our two bodies.

I slowly began to loosen my fingers.

'Wait!' he said, staring down at my hand.

I froze.

He lifted his gaze to mine. 'If it's negative, that's fine. We can keep trying.'

I lifted my other hand to touch his obviously anxious face. 'I know, my love. If it's negative we'll keep trying and trying until it's positive.' I placed a soft, calming kiss on his lips. 'Are you ready?'

He nodded, and we both looked down as I opened my hand.

'What does that mean?' he asked.

A rush of elation rolled through me. 'It means we are having another baby.'

CHAPTER
32

The rest of our time in Rome was kind of surreal. After the pregnancy test revealed two pink lines, we had stared at it for minutes, rotating it and making sure it wasn't playing a cruel trick on us. When we were satisfied that it wasn't, we both hugged each other, kissed each other and wiped away each other's happy tears. Then, my Mr Over-protective Over-domineering-Arse Clark returned, marching us both back to the pharmacy to get some folic acid and pregnancy vitamins.

Satisfied that I was happy and healthy, he'd finally allowed us to continue our day and finish our sightseeing plans by walking to the Spanish Steps, the Trevi Fountain and the Villa Borghese gardens. We'd then done a little shopping on our way back to the hotel and stocked up on some souvenirs, not forgetting my promise of picking up a real Ferrari for Nate. Unfortunately, I couldn't find a rude piece of cutlery for Tash — Italy had no crude-looking monuments.

* * *

We departed Leonardo da Vinci-Fiumicino International Airport later that night, basically sleeping the entire way before waking up during our stopover in Hong Kong. Bryce had gone back to gently caressing my stomach and I adored that paternal side of his that just naturally took over.

'So, when do you want to get married?' I asked him as we lay side by side in the luxurious queen bed on the private jet, only hours from landing in Melbourne.

'When are you officially divorced?'

'In a few weeks time.'

'Well ... in a few weeks time then,' Bryce answered, carefree and unconcerned.

'Can we wait till after the baby is born?'

He rolled back to get a better look at my face and, before he could object, I explained.

'It's going to be a few weeks before the divorce is final, then we have to submit the marriage application and that takes at least three months —'

He interrupted. 'There are ways around that.'

I rolled my eyes at him. 'I don't want to be pregnant while saying my vows to you.'

'Alexis,' he sighed, 'you're even more beautiful when you are carrying my child. Wrap you up in a wedding gown and I couldn't think of anything else more perfect.'

'You're deliberately word-fucking me. I'm on to you, I know how you operate.'

He laughed. 'It's what I do.'

'The reason I want to wait until after we've had the baby is because I'd like *all* our children to witness us pledge forever to one another. I think it would be nice.'

I could see the cogs of his mind working hard. 'Well, when you put it like that. How can I refuse?'

I smiled. 'Simple ... you can't.'

He growled in loving frustration. 'Don't I know it.'

* * *

As we stepped into the elevator on our way up to the apartment, I groaned. 'Why is it that we've just spent many long hours on a plane, sleeping and relaxing, yet I feel completely drained?'

He pulled me to him, engulfing me in his perfectly comforting arms. 'Because we didn't just sleep and relax,' the elevator doors to the apartment opened and we stepped out, 'and because you are carrying my —'

'Surprise!'

Bryce and I looked into the lounge room where our family and friends were standing with congratulatory signs, Lucy at the forefront of them.

Bryce still had his hand resting on my lower abdomen when he finished his sentence in a shocked tone. '— baby.'

My mouth dropped at the sight of all the smiling faces looking at us, those smiles now even wider.

'You're pregnant again?' Lucy asked, looking as if she was ready to burst at the seams with happiness.

All I could do was nod.

'Oh my god! That's wonderful. Engaged and preggo.' She stepped forward and wrapped her arms around us both, hugging us tightly. 'I'm so happy for you both.'

Mum and Dad were by our side next. 'How far along are you?' Mum asked, smiling but wary.

'I'm not too sure, maybe six weeks. It's only early days.'

'Oh, sweetheart.' She put her hands on either side of my face. 'I'm happy for you, for both of you, but I worry that too much is happening too fast. You need to slow down. This past year has been so ... so crazy for you. Your emotions have taken a battering.'

'Mum, it's okay. We are not getting married straightaway. We've spoken about it, and we are going to wait until after the baby is born. Believe me, I know how crazy my life has been this past year, and I know now is the time to take a step back and enjoy each day as it comes.'

She kissed my forehead. 'Good girl.' She then moved to Bryce, smoothing his hair and giving him a hug.

Dad stepped aside to let Mum fawn over her future son-in-law.

'Did he bribe you?' I asked my father, jokingly.

'Who? Bryce?'

'Yes, when he asked for your permission to marry me.'

'Somehow, I don't think my permission mattered,' Dad replied, honestly.

I took hold of Dad's hands. 'Maybe not, but it would have meant a lot to him.' I gave him a kiss on the cheek.

'I could not say no to a man who clearly loves you more than his next breath. That's all a father wants for his daughter; someone who would move heaven and earth just to make her happy.'

'He does make me happy, Dad.' I looked over at Bryce who was now shaking hands with Steve and shaking fingers with Elise. 'Very happy.'

'Move over, Dad. I need to see this ring. It practically blinded me when she walked into the room.' Jen grabbed my hand and lifted it to inspect my engagement ring. 'Jesus! It's —'

'I know. It's perfect,' I interrupted her, staring longingly at my hand.

'I was going to say huge.'

I giggled. 'Yeah, there's that, too.'

'So, you're having another baby.' She rested her hand on my stomach. 'It's natural to feel a little worried and uncertain, especially after what you suffered.' She grabbed my hand and looked intently into my eyes. 'This is a new pregnancy though ... and it won't do you any good to be apprehensive. So think positive thoughts, okay?'

She pulled me in for a quick hug.

'Thank you, Jen. You always know what is buried deep down inside of me.'

'I'm your sister, it's my job.'

Then, eventually, our friends greeted us with well wishes and congratulations.

'So, Lexi, let's talk about me being your personal bodyguard. That rock needs protection,' Tash said in an authoritative tone as she stood by me, looking around.

Before I could answer, she protectively put an arm around me while ushering Steph back. 'Step away, please,' she said to Steph. She then put her hand to her ear, pretending to talk into an imaginary earpiece. 'Yes, the bird is safe, the rock still secure.'

Bryce laughed, so I glared at him.

Noticing my reluctance, she persisted. 'I can even go all Whitney and Kevin on you,' and, taking my hand, she started belting out 'I Will Always Love You' from the movie *The Bodyguard*.

I walked away and shook my head, smiling but not letting her see it.

Carly and Derek were on the balcony, and I couldn't contain my elation at seeing them publicly show their affection for each other. However, I was slightly pissy that she had not yet filled me in on her 'fiery hole' status — something told me it was no longer fiery.

'Carly,' I addressed her sternly, but not hiding my playful undertone.

She looked at me warily, then glanced at Derek, then looked back at me. 'Alexis?'

'Carly. Hole status? Affirmative or negative?'

She flushed red and narrowed her eyes at me. 'Affirmative,' she said, through gritted teeth.

I raised an eyebrow. 'I thought as much.'

Bryce came up behind me and automatically threaded his hands across my belly.

Derek put a hand out for Bryce to shake. 'Congrats, mate.'

Bryce released one hand and shook it. 'Thanks.'

Carly and I were having a silent conversation with our eyes, hers telling me Derek was well endowed. *Well ... at least I think that is what she is saying.* I leaned forward, concentrating on her eyes, which were looking at Derek's package then looking back at me wide open. She repeated that motion a couple of times. I looked around the outdoor area trying to find a size comparison, spotting a cylinder candle. I flicked my eyes to it, asking the question. She screwed up her face and shook her head as if to say no. I bit my lip in frustration.

Carls then lifted her hands and separated them approximately seven to eight inches wide, then quickly clasped them together. I smiled at her and gave her the 'not bad' face, then put my hand to my eye in a circular shape, pretending to look into it like a telescope, asking her for an indication of girth. Her hand shot out faster than lightning and she picked up the candle. My mouth dropped. She just grinned.

'Did you just explain to Alexis how big my cock is?'

Carly, still grinning at me like a giddy schoolgirl, shot her head up to look at Derek. 'Um, no, I was just expressing my appreciation of the fact that Bryce and Alexis use candles. Global warming is a serious issue, and cutting down on our greenhouse gas emissions is very important. Every little bit helps, you know,' she blurted out. *Oh, high-the-fuck-five for you, Carls. Save of the century.*

'Bullshit, you just sized my cock,' Derek bragged, not believing a word she said. *Okay, maybe not.*

I laughed.

'Na, you're wrong, mate,' Bryce said while kissing the top of my head. 'If she had been sizing your cock, she would've held up her pinky.'

Derek gently shoved Bryce's shoulder. 'You're going to force me to prove you wrong,' he said as he began to unbutton his jeans.

'Um ... excuse me, Alexis,' Sam interrupted, as her eyes fell to Derek's pants. She quickly moved them to my face.

'Sam! I'm so glad you're here.' I greeted her with surprise, giving her a hug. 'Are you here with Gareth? Oh, that's wonderful —'

'I was here with Gareth, but that's what I wanted to talk to you about. Something happened and he left. He was furious and he kept muttering, "This ends here." I'm not sure if he meant us, or something else. I don't know what I did wrong.'

Bryce let go of my waist. 'It's not you, Samantha. You did nothing wrong.'

I turned to face him, worry saturating my face and voice. 'I have a bad feeling about this. Something is wrong.'

'I know. I feel it too. I want you to stay away from Gareth. I have a feeling Scott has returned.'

'Bryce,' I said shakily, 'I think he never left.'

Scott

Look at these fuckwits standing around with their stupid fucking congratulations signs. Just because he has put a rock on the bitch's finger doesn't mean jack shit. It can just as easily come off.

I looked around the room at Bryce and Alexis' family and friends, some of those friends having once been mine. *Hmm, Derek, if you weren't such an arrogant prick I'd consider 'blowing' your mind ... among other things.*

'Gareth, isn't it wonderful that they are getting married? It's happened so quickly. It's just ... so romantic.'

I looked down at Sam hanging off my arm, her pretty little strawberry-blonde head full of love, butterflies and rainbows. *Stupid bitch.* I thought she'd done a runner after finding out about me, and as a result having to then put up with Gareth fucking pansy moping around like a soft cock. That was the last thing I needed. I wonder what changed her mind? I guess it doesn't matter. Solves my sooky, lala Gareth problem, so who gives a fuck?

'Okay, they just arrived,' Lucy announced, clapping like a fucking seal.

I tilted my head back and rolled my eyes, spotting the top of the staircase. A wonderful memory entered my mind, bringing me back to when I snuck in here months ago and pushed Alexis down the stairs. The bitch didn't see it coming, just tumbled down those steps like a rag doll.

I should've stayed around to make sure I'd done the job properly, but hearing Bryce in his office made me nervous. He could never know I was the one who had killed her. It had to look like an accident. Fuck, my only regret was that I hadn't killed her. Now I have to rethink and rework my plan to get rid of her for good.

The ding of the elevator snapped me out of my reverie, only to see my Bryce and the bitch walk into the room.

'... and because you're carrying my —'

The room erupted into cheers of congratulations.

'— baby,' Bryce said with his hand on her stomach.

Are you fucking serious? Not again. Fuck!

I felt my body fill with rage, my limbs going rigid.

'Gareth, did you hear that? She's pregnant again.'

I stared Alexis down, wanting to set her alight with my murderous gaze.

'Gareth, are you okay?'

'What?' I snapped at Sam.

'Are you okay?' she repeated, looking scared.

Fuck it, I can't do this any more. I can't pretend to be Gareth and I don't want to. I want this to end. I want it to fucking end. If I can't have Bryce, then neither of us will.

'No, I'm not okay, this ends here,' I hissed at Sam. Pushing past one of Alexis' stuck-up bitch friends, I left the apartment.

This fucking ends here.

CHAPTER
33

Our friends and family made their way home shortly after having the afternoon tea Lucy had organised. Bryce had waited for them to leave before heading out in search of Gareth, both of us being concerned about the erratic behaviour Sam had mentioned.

He'd come back over an hour later after having no luck in finding his cousin, and I could tell he was deeply worried about the entire situation: about me and my safety, but also about Gareth. I think he realised that the meds and the therapy were no longer working, and the alternative form of treatment was not something he wanted to entertain.

Exhaustion had eventually overcome him, seizing his mind and body and inevitably leaving him asleep with his head on my chest and his arm across my belly.

* * *

Bryce left early the next morning to have a meeting with Jessica about Gareth's state of mind while I tackled the workload that being personal assistant to Mr Bryce Clark provided me. He was worried about leaving me alone, but I assured him that I'd be fine. After all, he was only

going to be gone for a short period of time. Being the over-protective
arse that he was, he made me do my work from his secured office. I
secretly appreciated this demand.

Just as I was finishing a phone call with Chris from Marketing, I
heard a loud clanging noise reverberating from the apartment. *That's
strange, Bryce isn't due back yet.* Curious who could be making the noise,
I walked over to the door and typed in our security code. When it
opened, I walked through, stepping into the dining room only to be met
by the unmistakable stench of gas. The smell was incredibly strong. *Shit!
Did Bryce leave the stove on?* Panic washed over me, knowing that the
gas's potent smell meant the vapours had to be thick and in abundance.

I made a choice to enter the kitchen and see if I was correct, thinking to be able to turn it off. As I approached the island bench that
separated the kitchen from the dining room, Gareth shot up from his
squatted position down near the oven.

I froze.

You know you're in trouble when you get that undeniable feeling deep down in the pit of your stomach, that feeling telling you
to be alert instinctively. I had that particular feeling and, as I took in
Gareth's appearance, I sensed he was not the one before me. Instead,
Scott was present and the gas smell a result of his doing.

'Gareth,' I said shakily. 'What are you doing?' I tried to keep my
voice neutral and kind, but I was terrified, and my adrenaline was
pumping, causing my brain to switch into survival mode.

He put both hands on the bench and smiled at me with a grin so
malicious it was revolting. 'Just the person I was hoping to see,' he
stated, in a tone laced with satisfaction. I noticed him clench his right
hand and rub his thumb over whatever he was holding.

Alarm bells were sounding internally as my eyes automatically
scouted the kitchen, noting that the burner knobs on the stove were
turned on but with no flames, and the oven door was also wide open.

'How did you get in here?'

'I have a code,' he said cockily.

'That's strange. We changed the codes after the elevator malfunctioned.'

He sneered, saying, 'Why do you think the elevator malfunctioned?
Lucy is not the only one in the family who is good with computers.'

The pit of my stomach dropped, but I forced myself to remain calm. 'Oh ... so what can I do for you? Do you want to go and sit in the lounge, or in Bryce's office?' *Get out of this kitchen, Alexis.*

'Do you think I'm stupid?' he said calmly, still displaying his evil smile.

'No, Gareth. Why would I think you're stupid?' I playfully laughed.

'You're fucking doing it again,' he screamed at me, making me jump.

Tears stung my eyes as my fear hit a new-found height. I began to tremble. 'What? What am I doing?'

He pointed his hand at me, revealing that what he held was a lighter. 'You're fucking treating me like a fool. Gareth is a fucking fool, not me.'

'Scott? Oh, I'm sorry Scott. No, you're not a fool,' I sobbed.

'Aha.' He laughed sadistically. 'Now you understand. Now you want to be honest with me.'

'I have been honest,' I argued.

'Fucking bullshit,' he spat back.

He took a step back toward the stove, leaning over and checking the knobs. I wanted to run out of the kitchen, but my legs were weighted heavily to the ground, riddled with my fear and unfortunately forcing me to stay put.

Reasoning with him was my only option. 'Scott, talk to me. Tell me what you want.'

'I want you dead,' he replied flatly.

Those words and the manner in which he said them sent a chill through my body. It was so terrifying that I nearly passed out.

'I don't understand. Why do you want me dead?' I asked, now crying.

He stepped toward the island bench, hatred and pain rolling off him in waves. 'Because he fucking loves you, that's why!'

'And you love him, don't you?' I stuttered.

He closed his eyes for the slightest of seconds. 'Yes.'

'So why do you want to hurt him by killing me? Surely you know that if you kill me, it will kill him.'

'He'll get over you,' he said quickly, while grabbing the bridge of his nose. 'It's me he will mourn the most.'

Stupidly, I opened my mouth again. 'Why would he mourn you, Scott?' I asked, confused, and not understanding why he would mourn Scott if I were the one dead.

His eyes shot up and locked on mine, pure loathing coursing out of them and cutting right through me like a knife. *Shit! I didn't mean it like that. Shut up, Alexis, just shut up. No, keep talking, it's buying you time.*

'Because when I fucking kill us both, he will be devastated.'

Oh, god, he's completely lost control.

'Scott, you don't have to do this —'

'Yes, I do. If I can't have him, neither will you.'

'But Scott, I'm pregnant with his child,' I pleaded.

'It didn't matter last time and it won't matter this time,' he said, as he laughed to himself in a manner that suggested he was disappointed. 'I should've fucking pushed you harder, or better still, tossed you over the railing.' He let out a deep breath. 'That doesn't matter, though. I will not make the same mistake twice.'

My knees went weak and my body trembled profusely. I'd subconsciously known he was to blame for my fall, but hearing it aloud horrified me beyond belief. Bile rose in my throat and the sudden urge to vomit washed over me.

He started tapping the lighter on the bench, taunting, forcing me to watch it slowly and take in its every detail.

Hearing the tap of the plastic hitting the benchtop over and over momentarily removed my mind from the present torture, and an idea materialised in my head, an idea that could quite possibly buy me more time and inevitably make Bryce aware of my predicament.

'Scott, why don't you ring him, talk to him?'

He stopped tapping the lighter. 'I would like to hear his voice again. Just one more time.'

'I'm sure he'd like to hear yours as well,' I said, with a faux smile, lying and grasping the only lifeline I could.

He pulled a phone from his pocket, pressed a button and put it up to his ear. My heart pounded in my chest as I watched his face change from radiating psychotic vengeance to displaying enlightened sadness as he listened to Bryce's voice on the other end.

'If only that were true, Bryce. I'm where I always am, right under your nose.'

As he spoke into the phone his posture slumped, indicating he was exhausted and deflated. He was sad and I couldn't doubt that, as delusional as it was, Scott really did think he loved Bryce and that Bryce was his.

'I'm past talking,' he murmured disappointedly.

His body language and words were quickly demonstrating that he was going to go through with his plan and blow up the room with both of us in it.

I wanted to run, flee, at least get out of the kitchen. If I could manage to get into the lounge area, surely it would give me more of a chance of survival. It was a more open-plan room and less flooded with gas fumes. I made a small step toward the door.

'I don't fucking want Samantha, Bryce. I want you. I've always wanted you,' he screamed down the phone, forcing me to a halt once again.

Scott started to sob painfully and his hand began to shake and rotate the lighter. 'I'm ending it and I'm taking her with me.'

His precise confirmation propelled me to cry out and say my goodbyes. 'Bryce, I love you. I'll always love you. Tell the kids I love —'

Scott cut me off. 'Shut up, bitch. You don't get to say goodbye.'

I cried out, petrified, now realising I was going to die and never see my kids again, never see Bryce, my family, my friends.

Scott paused for a second, as if he were deliberating something Bryce had said, giving me just the tiniest glimmer of hope.

I held my breath.

'No. You're lying. I can see how much you love her.'

I closed my eyes and slowly let out the breath. It was no use.

'No, you don't. Goodbye, Bryce.' Scott laughed painfully. 'You won't have to.'

He pushed a button, gently set the phone down on the benchtop, and tilted his head to the side. 'You fucking brainwashed him. You ruined him.'

I felt sick, my nausea at its peak, and I soon realised it was partly due to fear and partly due to the gas I was inhaling. I could also see the fumes having an effect on Scott as he kept grabbing the bridge of his nose and shaking his head.

My sight drifted past his face, finding the many photos stuck to the fridge. I focussed in on the one of Bryce and me at Uluru, then to the photo of Bryce and the kids sitting next to the Ronald McDonald statue, and the one of all four of us taken the night of my birthday.

Drinking them in, I filled myself with the vision of those memories, the happiness that was captured when they were taken and the people who were in them. I didn't want to say goodbye. I didn't want to die and, as I cemented those thoughts within my head, something came over me. Call it strength, willpower, the uncontrollable urge to survive. Whatever it was, it made me realise I had to do something. I had to change tack. It was my only chance.

'Gareth, I know you are in there, I know you can hear me. Fight him, show him once and for all you are in control —'

'Shut the fuck up!' Scott growled, grabbing his nose again.

I continued, not knowing what else to do. 'Gareth, fight him! Do it for you. Do it for Bryce. Do it for Lauchie. Don't let Scott ruin your life,' I begged.

'Argh!' he moaned, pushing his hands into his forehead. 'Fuck!'

'Gareth, please,' I screamed in desperation.

He was clenching his head so aggressively, his eyes closed so tight.

'Alexis, I'm sorry,' he groaned, his tone noticeably different.

'Gareth, is that you?'

'Argh! Alexis run!'

It was him, it was working. My heart started beating faster and my adrenaline picked back up. 'Gareth, no, fight him, please. You can beat him.'

'I can't. Go! Go!' he begged while opening his eyes and clearly conveying to me that it was now or never.

In the back of your mind, you think that there could come a time in life where you may be faced with the decision to fight, or to take flight. I think all of us like the notion that we would choose to stay and fight if we had to, but in hindsight, that may not always be the best choice. If I didn't have family that loved me, children I adored and who depended on me, and a life growing deep within that I was blessed with protecting, I may have stayed and helped Gareth fight. I wanted to, but I didn't. I chose flight and ran, ran as fast as I could.

I scampered through the lounge and straight to the elevator, thinking it was the quickest way out of the apartment, all the while hearing Gareth cursing and fighting in the kitchen. His cries of misery and anguish deeply pierced my heart as I pressed the button, hoping to god the car was at this level of the building. *Come on, please come on.*

Panicked, frantic, and knowing I couldn't waste another second waiting for the elevator, I went to abandon it and try the stairs. Thankfully, as I turned around, the doors slid open.

I ran inside and hysterically pressed the button to close the doors. 'Go, go, go!' I shouted, willing the doors to slide shut and swiftly take me to safety. My agitation and fear were increasing at the sound of Gareth's outbursts getting louder and I knew he was losing, losing his internal fight. 'Please!' I screamed, as I backed up slowly to the far end of the car.

The doors began to slide shut, painstakingly slowly, but just as the elevator finally started to descend, there was an enormous explosion. I screamed as the car shook violently, thinking that it would plummet forty-three floors to the ground, but it didn't. It dropped only slightly, then shook violently again, knocking me off my feet.

I felt a surge of pain through my head as I hit the hand railing and, almost instantly, I recognised that feeling of sleep, that feeling of losing control. I felt that feeling of unconsciousness and watched my sight tunnel into darkness with no power to stop it.

CHAPTER
34

Bryce

As I made my way back to work, I realised Gareth's prognosis wasn't good even though he'd been taking his meds daily. I'd fucking made him take them in front of me like a goddamned child and I hated doing it like that, but I had to — there was no other choice.

It worried me that Jessica had mentioned he'd missed a few sessions, which was never a good thing, and now the evidence before us suggested he would need to be admitted to a psychiatric hospital ward. I hated that, too. I hated having to commit him to such a place. When all was said and done, I fucking loved the poor guy. He was my cousin, my brother.

Deep down, I knew it had to be done, though. Alexis was pregnant again and she was in far too much danger. Not only that, Nate and Charli could be in danger too, and I was not about to let anything happen to any of them. They were my family now, and I had to do everything in my power to protect them.

Fuck! I needed to call my uncle and tell the miserable old bastard that his son would be spending some more time in the hospital. Not that he'd give a shit. It made me furious knowing he wouldn't care, he never had. He only cared about one thing and that was money. It's ironic how miserable bastards like him only ever seem to care about things they don't have, can never have; explains why they are so fucking miserable in the first place.

I went to request that the Bluetooth on my car dial my uncle's number, when an incoming call came through the speaker. It was Gareth. *Thank fuck for that.*

'Gareth, where are you? I've been looking for you everywhere.'

'If only that were true, Bryce. I'm where I always am, right under your nose,' he said sarcastically, but with a tone of sadness.

My stomach clenched, my instincts immediately telling me something was wrong.

'Are you okay? Do you want to talk?' I offered, sincerely.

'I'm past talking.'

His voice was flat and that just reinforced my unease. *Fuck! I've neglected him lately, pushed him aside.*

'Listen, I know I have been distant with you lately, so much has happened, but I promise that will change. Things will get better.'

I had a horrible feeling I wasn't talking to Gareth and, instead, talking to Scott. Remembering what Jessica had told me many times before, I spoke of things that would make Gareth happy.

'You're taking your meds again, mate, and you've been doing good. You've also got Samantha. She cares about you and was really worried last night.'

'I don't fucking want Samantha, Bryce. I want you. I've always wanted you,' he screamed down the phone, hurt and pain sounding throughout my Aston Martin.

Painful sobs then followed, filling me with dread. *It is Scott. I should've known better. Fuck!*

'Scott, what are you doing?'

'I'm ending it, and I'm taking her with me.'

It took me a second to comprehend those last words and, when I did understand his threat, my chest pained immensely.

'Bryce, I love you. I'll always love you. Tell the kids I love —'

Alexis' terrified voice hit me like a ton of bricks.

'Alexis!' I shouted, frantic with fear.

'Shut up, bitch. You don't get to say goodbye,' Scott hissed with such hatred.

She cried out, her petrified weeps echoing right through me.

Oh god, he's going to hurt her. I have to do something.

'Scott, please don't hurt her. I beg you. I'll do anything. I'll leave her and we can be together.' *Yes, lie to him. Trick him. Make sure she's safe then have him committed. Shit! He's worse than any of us realised. Fuck! How could I let this happen? I've fucking let her down again.*

Scott paused for a second as if he were deliberating what I'd said. 'No. You're lying. I can see how much you love her,' he answered dryly.

Feeling utter dread pass over me, I whispered to the speaker of my car. 'I love you more, Scott.'

'No, you don't. Goodbye, Bryce.'

Terror hit me with force in that moment. 'Scott, don't be fucking stupid. I swear to god if you hurt any hair on her head, I'll kill you. I'll fucking kill you myself,' I yelled, hysterical, now more desperate than ever to get to her.

Scott laughed, painfully, almost masochistically. 'You won't have to.'

What the fuck? I'd lost him. He was going to kill her, kill them both. This didn't feel like a threat, it felt real — sounded real.

I had to get back to the apartment. 'Scott!' I yelled. 'Gareth, don't —'

The line went dead.

'Fuck! Fuck! Fuck!' I roared with fear.

I looked out the window of my car, just barely able to see the top of City Towers as I pulled into the street and desperately headed for the building's entrance. Alexis was up there, held hostage by my mentally ill cousin. She was terrified, carrying my baby and wearing a ring on her finger that held a promise I had made to her, a promise I fucking intended to keep.

With my heart thudding like fuck, I dialled Dale, my head of security, then I did something I thought I would never do in my life. I put my foot down and sped dangerously through the traffic, desperate to get to the apartment to save her.

After a couple of rings, Dale picked up. 'Yes, sir.'

'Dale, get up to the penthouse now!' I demanded.

'I'll send Brett, he's on level forty doing a —'

'Just fucking do it. Alexis is in danger. Gareth has fucking kidnapped her. And stay on the line.'

I sped into my basement garage and screeched to a stop just shy of the elevator doors and leapt out of the car, running toward the elevator as fast I could, hoping to god Scott hadn't already hurt her in any way. *Fuck!*

Just before I reached the button to call the elevator, a loud roar echoed up above and the ground shook mildly. 'What the fuck was that?' *Oh, no. Fuck, no.*

'I'll call you back,' Dale said quickly, before hanging up.

My heart increased its painful thump in my chest, adrenaline coursing through my body. I pressed the button in rapid succession, watching the light remain lit on level forty-two. 'No! Fuck! No!' I yelled, while spinning and heading for the stairs.

The sound of my building's fire alarm rang continuously, reverberating through the stairwell as I launched myself up the stairs, taking two, three, even four steps at a time.

In no time at all, I reached the exit to the lobby and wrenched open the door to find subdued panic on the faces of staff and guests who were looking up at the ceiling.

'Mr Clark,' Abigail called out, uncertainty and fear on her face.

I didn't have time to reassure her. 'Put Emergency Plan B into action,' I ordered, as I kept running toward the elevator. I had no idea what I was running to, but I didn't care. All I cared about was getting up to the penthouse.

My phone started ringing in my pocket, and a glimmer of hope flowed through me at the prospect of seeing Alexis' name on the screen. I fumbled, my hands trembling as I wrenched it out only to see my head of security's name instead.

'Dale, talk to me.'

'There has been an explosion on the penthouse floor. From what I can see on the emergency system, it's localised to that floor only.' *Jesus fucking Christ! Alexis, please be okay.*

'Abigail,' I shouted, 'cancel Plan B action. Order an evacuation and floor search of levels thirty-five and up. Explosion localised to the penthouse. As far as I know, there's no other threat.'

She nodded and with courage and a professionalism I admired, she turned and took control, shouting out commands to staff trained in the appropriate areas.

I put my phone back to my ear. 'Dale, where's Brett?'

'He got as far as the elevator.'

'What's the status on the elevators? I'm going up.'

'But, sir —'

'Just do it, Dale. Alexis is up there, for fuck's sake.'

'Okay, hang on. Right, your private elevator is jammed between levels forty-two and forty-one. It has structural damage according to these reports. The backup brakes are locked and it's not going anywhere. Elevators one, two and four and at ground level are secure, and car three is on automatic override and is on its way down now with Brett in it.'

'Good, override number one now.'

'I can get it as far as level forty-one, sir. You'll have to take the stairs after that.'

'Just do it now, Dale. Fuck! And override the security lock to my apartment access doors.'

'Okay, car one is open, go! And Bryce ... from one mate to another, be careful. I can't tell the extent of the damage. Cameras are down up there.'

I hung up, not having time for small talk. I had to get to Alexis. I had to make sure she was all right. *Fuck! I hope she is all right. No, she has to be all right.*

The doors to elevator one opened and I wasted no time in stepping inside and indicating to the surveillance camera — the one I knew Dale was watching — that the car should hurry and move. The doors closed and the car climbed with speed.

Running my hands through my hair, and impatiently pacing the enclosed space on my way to the penthouse floor, I couldn't help but replay in my mind Alexis' terrified voice. Of her crying out what she thought were her last words and telling me that she loved me and always would, that she loved her kids, kids I now loved, too.

'Fuck!' *Can't this thing go any faster?* I loved her so much, and the thought of her being ... dead ... hell, I couldn't even comprehend that. I'd already had that feeling before for the smallest of seconds and it tore me apart. It was the worst few seconds of my life.

The elevator stopped and the doors slid open and, barely waiting till they were wide enough, I squeezed through and headed for the stairwell. All I could smell when I opened the door and started to climb the stairs — again taking many at a time — was smoke.

As I approached the door to my apartment, the roar of flames deafened my hearing and smoke was now visible and thick, burning my eyes and lungs. I pulled my shirt up to cover my mouth and nose then touched the door handle. It was hot but not scorching hot, so I gripped it tighter and turned.

Without precaution or hesitation, I pushed the door forward, being met with flames, smoke, steam and water from the sprinklers. Visibility was almost non-existent.

'Alexis!' I shouted through a wall of smoke and orange heat from the flames. 'Alexis!' *Please, please answer me.* There was nothing, no response. All I could hear was the crackling of fire.

Looking up while shielding my eyes from the flames, I noticed the second floor to be smoke-filled, but not yet ferociously dominated by fire and, with hope, I turned toward the stairwell and climbed another level.

I burst through the doors to the second floor, then bent down low to avoid the thicker smoke and to get a better visual of the space ahead of me. I scampered toward our bedroom, all the while shouting her name.

'Alexis!' I repeated, painfully realising that she wasn't there. 'Alexis!'

I stumbled back out of our room, my lungs straining from the lack of oxygen, and my eyes begging for relief from the smoke. The radiant heat from the fires scorching blaze was also starting to find its way to the second floor, making my plans to continue to search a hell of a lot harder. I headed back to the stairwell door when I ran straight into a firefighter.

'You need to leave, sir. It's not safe up here —' he shouted, just as another smaller explosion sounded.

'Alexis!' I yelled while trying to barge past him, fighting his aggressive restraint. 'Fucking let me go, my fiancée is here somewhere.'

'You need to leave. We'll find her,' he said automatically, as he led me back into the stairwell.

Other firefighters were coming up the stairs in single file.

'Bryce!' I heard one of them call.

I looked up and noticed Derek lifting his breathing apparatus from his face. 'Bryce, thank fuck you're all right, mate.'

'I'm not all right. Alexis is in there.' I looked back at the door, ready to go right back through it.

He grabbed my arm, forcefully. 'I'll find her, mate.' Then he pushed past me and ran inside.

'Sir, you need to come down to the next level.'

Coughing, I followed the firefighter down to the next level where I leaned against the wall, trying to catch my breath. *She has to be all right, they have to find her. And Gareth ... fuck!* I couldn't even think about what may have happened to my cousin. Just the thought of it made me feel sick.

I lifted my head to see a few firefighters exit the stairwell and a few more take their place, but still no sign of Alexis, Gareth or Derek. *I can't do this, I can't just fucking wait here.* Just as I was about to go back up, a firefighter came out and grabbed his radio. 'Confirmation: DP found.'

It was at that point that my adrenaline levels plummeted and all hope I held left me. I stumbled back against the wall and slid down, putting my hands in my hair as I sank to my knees. The unbearable grief that overwhelmed me tore my heart, clawing at me with its vicious dreadful hand. I knew too well that DP stood for Deceased Person.

I was fucking cursed, doomed, never allowed to love and be loved. This was my penance, and I was going to absorb it and wear it for the rest of my life.

Crying and in pain, I rocked back and forth against the wall, desperately wanting to hold Alexis in my arms, feel her warmth, breathe in her intoxicating scent and taste her mouth. I wanted to press her against me, lock her to my soul, never let her go. I could hear her voice calling out for me to help her and it tortured me even further, but it was a torture I would endure.

I covered my ears and cried harder, but her cries for me only grew louder.

'Can you hear that?' one of the firefighters said to the other.

I lifted my head from my hands and stared at the two men with confusion. 'What?'

Realising what they were suggesting, my heartbeat lifted frantically, and everything turned into a deathly silence. I strained to hear what I didn't want to let myself believe I'd heard, because if it turned out to be false, I would die another thousand deaths. Then I heard it again, Alexis' cries for help. I stood up and, as if being drawn to a magnet, found myself taking steps closer to her pleas.

'Bryce! Anybody! Help!'

It was unmistakable this time, it was Alexis.

'The elevator,' the firefighter said. 'It's coming from the elevator.'

I threw myself at the doors, desperate to pry them open. 'Alexis! Can you hear me?'

'Bryce! I'm in here. I'm in the elevator,' she called out.

Fuck me, she's alive. Her voice was like fucking music to my ears.

I'd gone from feeling overbearing grief to soaring relief in the space of a few seconds and now desperate as ever to get to my fiancée.

'Hold on, honey. We'll get you out.'

She coughed and moaned. 'I'm not going anywhere.'

I couldn't help, but let out a laugh. A laugh at her impeccable timing, a laugh at her endearing sarcasm, and a laugh because I was so fucking relieved.

One of the firefighters zipped open a bag and pulled out a crowbar. 'Step aside, sir.'

Fucking bullshit I'll step aside. He wedged it in between the doors and began to pry them open. I didn't hesitate and helped pull them apart, then reached into the car. Alexis' hand touched mine, and like every single time beforehand, I felt like I'd been struck by a bolt of lightning.

'Bryce,' she coughed, as she latched onto my arm.

The elevator had stopped in between the level we were situated on and the one below, so that the floor of the car was a few feet below where we stood and she had no way of climbing up. I looked down and could see her innocent, terrified, but relieved eyes staring back at me.

'Honey, hang on.'

'Please, sir, move aside, I'm going in. Ma'am, move back against the wall.'

She did what she was told as the firefighter lowered himself into the elevator. He quickly assessed her, then boosted her up.

I secured her underneath her arms then, shuffling back on my knees and slowly rising to my feet, I lifted her free from the car. 'I've got you.'

She wiggled out till she was standing on her feet, then, wrapping her arms around my neck, she squeezed me tightly. It was the best feeling in the world.

'You're alive. You're fucking alive,' I exclaimed as I ran my hands all over her body just to make sure she was really in my arms.

She started crying and shaking and I felt her begin to go limp.

'She needs to see a medic,' the firefighter said.

I had to agree, but I wasn't about to let her out of my arms. 'I'll take her down,' I replied, just as Derek walked through the door that led to the stairwell.

He wrenched off his helmet and breathing mask and wiped his face with his hand, looking relieved, but confused. 'Thank Christ for that,' he said as he squatted down and fetched a water bottle. 'Where?'

I pointed to the elevator. Derek just shook his head then fell back against the wall.

After a moment of silence, I lifted Alexis' legs into my arms. 'You're okay, honey.'

'Gareth?' she asked against my neck, her sobs painful, her tears moistening my skin.

I looked at Derek who sorrowfully shook his head, confirming my fears and filling me with a sense of loss. 'He didn't make it,' I said softly.

She began to cry harder, which had me perplexed. 'He saved me, Bryce,' she sobbed.

I threaded my hand through her hair, pressing my palm against the back of her head and holding her tightly, my hand finding a rather large bump.

'Did you hit your head?'

'Yes, I've been unconscious.'

'Come on, you need to see a paramedic.'

CHAPTER

35

Bryce carried me in his arms down one flight of stairs, then I remember going into an elevator with him. Then I was at ground level and being fussed over by two paramedics. Soon after that, I ended up back in hospital.

I was drowsy from my concussion and my eyes still stung from the smoke, therefore I found it much easier and more comfortable to keep them closed. I could hear Bryce talking with my doctor, their voices audible, but not quite in my room.

'Physically, she is fine. She suffered a mild concussion and will be somewhat drowsy. She also suffered minor smoke inhalation and could experience shortness of breath and a sore throat for many days.'

'And our baby?' Bryce asked the youthful-sounding female doctor who had an English accent.

'Your baby is fine, Mr Clark. The ultrasound still shows a strong foetal heartbeat.'

'Thank you,' Bryce said as he exhaled the breath he'd been holding and sounding relieved, yet fragile.

'I'm more concerned for your fiancée's mental state at this stage. Her medical records indicate she sees Dr Jessica Laitan.'

'Yes, she does,' he replied.

'I think it may be wise to make an appointment for her as soon as possible. Other than that, she is ready to be discharged. Give me a moment to complete her paperwork and then you can take her home.'

Moments later, I felt Bryce's warm, comforting hand on top of mine. I clenched it tightly and slowly opened my eyes, finding him slumped over the bed, his head resting on his folded arms.

He began to sob. 'I'm so sorry.'

'Bryce,' I said, my voice raspy and my throat sore and dry. 'Don't be sorry. Please don't be sorry. None of what happened is your fault.'

'You're wrong, it's all my fault,' he answered angrily. 'I knew Scott had returned and I didn't protect you.'

I moved my other hand to touch his head. 'Look at me.'

He slowly lifted his head from his arms.

'I knew Scott had returned as well, but neither of us could've known what he had planned.'

He dropped his head again. 'I knew what Scott was capable of, Alexis. What if Charli and Nate had been there, or Lucy and Alexander?'

Just the thought of it made me feel sick again.

'Did you know he was capable of that?' I asked sternly.

'No.'

'Then stop blaming yourself.'

'I nearly lost you, Alexis. I thought I'd lost you. I thought you were dead.' He took my hand in his and brought it up to his cheek while closing his eyes.

'Open your eyes, Bryce.' I said it with authority, like the many times he'd said it to me. They shot open.

'You didn't lose me, I'm right here. I've told you before, I'm not going anywhere.'

* * *

I leaned up against the window, thirty-eight floors above the city of Melbourne, the window which now housed the view from our make-shift apartment in City Towers. It had been days since the explosion and fire that destroyed the interior of the penthouse floor, or the bulk of it, at least. There was no major structural damage, but the heat of the fire and extent of the smoke damage left the entire apartment needing a complete renovation. Until that happened, we were staying in one of the villas a few levels down.

'Alexis, are you with me?' Jessica asked softly, but firmly enough to bring my attention back to her.

I removed my gaze from the many kayakers streaming along the Yarra River below. 'Yes, sorry.'

'It's okay to dwell on what's happened. You're allowed to think about the events, just make sure you talk about them out loud.'

'I wasn't really thinking about it. All right, maybe I was. I'm worried about Bryce more than anything. He's blaming himself.'

'I know he is, Alexis, and I'm working on that. If you feel you need to constantly reassure him, then do so. But he will need to sort through his guilt and his insecurities himself.'

I turned back to look out the window, to the sun which was partway up the sky, indicating midmorning. It was hot outside and a beautiful day, but that beauty was soon going to turn glum when we made our way to the Melbourne cemetery to say farewell to Gareth.

I had on a black sheath dress with a top layer of black lace. It was conservative but also cool enough for the day ahead. I leaned into the window again, but closed my eyes to block out the vertical drop that now greeted me.

'Alexis, I am here to listen to you, to make you feel comfortable enough to open up to me and rid yourself of information and feelings you do not know how to dissect and comprehend. I'm here to help you, and I want to, but you need to tell me what you're thinking.'

Still keeping my eyes closed, I confessed what I had held onto since Scott's attempt at my murder. 'Scott pushed me down the stairs. He was the reason I fell and lost our baby. He confessed before he tried to blow up the apartment, but ... I think I kind of already knew that he'd pushed me, that he was at fault.'

'Hmm, it would appear you did. And how does that make you feel?'

'Angry,' I bit out while turning to face her, my back now to the window.

'That is a reasonable reaction, Alexis.'

'I'm not angry at Gareth, because Scott's actions were never his fault. I realise that, I do. I'm angry because Bryce will blame himself.'

She pushed her glasses back up to the top of her nose. 'He feels responsible for Gareth.'

'Yes, he does, and he will feel responsible for the death of our daughter because of that. I will not let him bear that guilt. Ever! Her death was not his fault. It wasn't my fault. Fuck, it wasn't even Gareth's fault. It was Scott's.'

'So, you've chosen not to tell him the truth?'

'Yes.'

'That's quite a secret to carry.'

'I know,' I sighed, while closing my eyes again. 'But I will carry it. I will bear it to save him more heartache. He has suffered enough. I love him so much I can barely breathe, Jessica, and I can't handle seeing him torture himself any further. Carrying this secret is nothing compared to seeing that.'

'Well, dear, that's why I'm here. You no longer have to carry that secret alone.'

Shortly after, my session with Jessica ended, and we headed to the Melbourne General Cemetery in order to pay our respects to Gareth. Bryce had been terribly quiet during the limousine ride, and Lucy had not said much more than him.

I threaded my arm behind Bryce's back as we walked over the grass to the marquee set up for Gareth's memorial service.

'I know this is a stupid question on a day like this, but are you all right?' I asked as I leaned my head against his shoulder.

'I'm fine,' he answered flatly.

I stopped us from walking any further, the marquee only metres away. 'Bryce, why are you angry?'

'I'm not.'

'You are. You're angry with Gareth, and you're angry with yourself.'

He twitched his eye ever so slightly, and I noticed his free hand fist into a ball.

I grabbed hold of it and brought it to my lips, kissing it tenderly. 'For starters, you shouldn't be angry at yourself. We've gone through this. None of it was your fault. So please, let it go. And secondly, you shouldn't be angry with Gareth. Scott, yes. Gareth, no.'

He gave me a slight roll of the eye.

'Bryce, don't blame Gareth for Scott. Gareth was a hero. He saved your brother, pulled him free of a burning car wreck without a second thought. He saved me, Bryce.' A tear rolled down my cheek. He lifted his hand and wiped it away like so many times before. 'He saved my life. He fought back, took control. He allowed me to get away. Gareth was a hero, don't ever forget that. Don't let Scott mar your good memories of your cousin. A cousin you cared deeply for, a cousin you loved like a brother. Don't be angry with Gareth, okay?' It was now my turn to wipe a tear from his eye.

'Okay,' he answered, with mustered courage then, pulling me to him, he placed a renewed kiss on my forehead. 'Let's go say goodbye.'

I gently touched his cheek. 'I love you, Bryce Clark. You are an amazing man.'

He went to say something, and I could tell by the look on his face that his response was going to negate my words to him, so I put my finger to his lips then continued toward the group of people that were slowly gathering.

We sat under the makeshift marquee in the hot summer sun, listening to Gareth's life story, a story of achievement, of loss, of sadness, but also of friendship and family. Looking around, Gareth had many friends and family who cared for him. There were a lot of people I did not know, but there were also a lot of people I did know, and it warmed my heart that they had come to pay their respects. I noticed Derek, Abigail, and Santa, together with other board members of Clark Incorporated. I also noticed Jessica, Patrick the head designer, and even Clarissa. But it was Sam who stood beside Abigail, with her head hung low and a tissue scrunched in her hand that had me catching a breath. She looked so sad, so torn, so heartbroken. It really was awful.

I hadn't spoken to her since the fire and Gareth's death. I really wasn't sure what she was thinking or how she felt toward me. It made me nervous to think that this may have a detrimental effect on our friendship, and if it did, I would try my hardest to make it right again. Sam was my friend, an unorthodox one, but she was my friend and had helped me transform from being a stay-at-home mum to being a working professional again. She'd helped keep me sane.

As if she felt me staring at her, she looked up and caught my eye. I smiled at her warily and hoped for the same response. Thankfully, I got what I thought was a sympathetic smile back, so I nodded respectfully at her, then gripped Bryce's hand as the minister began to speak.

* * *

After the service and burial, I took a moment to linger above Gareth's plot while clenching a book to my chest. I'd wanted a few moments alone to pay my respects, having an overwhelming feeling I had to let Gareth know in some way that I was aware of what he had done for me.

I took a deep breath, knelt beside his grave and looked down at his casket. 'Thank you. I know you sacrificed yourself for me, I could see it in your eyes right before you told me to run. I knew at that moment what you planned to do, and I want to let you know that I'm truly sorry I couldn't help you.'

I wiped the tears from my eyes. 'You've probably already read this, Gareth, but just in case you haven't, I thought you might like it. Plus, you kind of remind me of Samwise Gamgee.' I dropped my copy of *The Fellowship of the Ring* into his grave. 'And don't worry, I'll make sure Lauchie gets a new one every year, I promise.'

I spent a few more moments alone by Gareth's grave thinking about life: past, present and future. Bryce and Lucy were talking to friends and family, and Nate and Charli were both at school. I felt it wasn't necessary, nor was it responsible to allow them to go to the funeral. Charli was too young to understand Gareth's condition or reason for his death, and Nate was too smart for his own good and would piece together the story.

So much had happened in my children's lives this past year as a result of my actions and decisions, and although some of those changes had been good and for the better, some had been incredibly hard for them too. I didn't want to add another painful event to the list of things they would have to decipher and work through. They didn't need to know their mother was almost killed by their soon-to-be stepfather's mentally ill cousin. Instead, I had told them that the apartment had caught fire due to an explosion, and that Gareth had tried to save me. It wasn't too far from the truth. In my eyes, he was a hero after all.

EPILOGUE

I once learned that to calm your nerves, one needed to regulate one's breath. Breathe in through your nose while imagining the air to be cool and refreshing. Then, breathe out through your mouth, your exhalation warm and comforting. *Bullshit! Icy cold air in and warm soothing air out? Pfft, calming, my arse. Whoever came up with that crock of shit needs to experience a day in my life, then practise that breathe-in breathe-out crap and tell me it works. It doesn't, it doesn't fucking work.*

'Somebody get me a gin and squash, please,' I begged, as I paced the room in my Maggie Sottero wedding gown. The A-line, fitted, cap-sleeve ivory lace dress with a keyhole back and corset closure, draped gracefully down my nervous body. It had a simple elegance, and I loved it. 'Gin ... somebody ... please!' I implored.

'No, you don't need any more alcohol, Alexis. An intoxicated bride walking down the aisle is never a good look.' My mother was fixing an ivory-coloured, rose garland on top of Charli's head. 'I don't know why you're so nervous. You're never this nervous.'

'Mum, look, we are both princesses,' Charli beamed, as she tried to twirl her dress which was of the same material as mine.

'Charlotte, keep still,' Mum barked.

I turned around from my position in the lounge area, careful not to catch my heel in the fishtail train of my dress, which finished in scalloped edging and was delicately sprinkled with Swarovski crystals.

'Mum —'

I was about to argue my need for a drink when Tash interrupted.

'Aw, Mrs B, a little schnappies won't hurt,' she said mischievously, as she slipped me a small shot glass of Baileys and schnapps while singing in a high-pitched whisper, 'Schnappies!' Tash then proceeded to walk around the room and hand out shot glasses to the others in my bridal party: Jen, Carls, Lucy, Lil, Jade and Steph. All seven of them were wearing strapless mushroom-coloured chiffon dresses, the hem stopping just above their knees.

'Oh, for the love of god, please do not spill any of that on your dresses,' my mother whined, finishing with Charli's hair and taking an appreciative stance.

'Mrs B, here, down this.' Tash handed Mum a shot. 'Drink up, bitches!' she hollered, and we all knocked them back.

Mum just stared at hers.

'Go on, Mum. Trust me, it helps,' encouraged Jen.

Mum put her glass to her lips and slowly tilted her head back, all of us watching in anticipation for her reaction.

She lowered her head back down with that screwed-up, squinty-eyed, I-just-stuck-my-finger-in-a-powersocket look, then casually softened her expression. 'Actually, that was quite nice,' she said as she licked her lips.

I let out a loving giggle, then walked out onto our balcony, forty-three storeys above the ground. If there was any place that could calm my nerves, it was the balcony — or my shower, and I was not about to go and hop in there.

Two years had passed since Scott tried to kill the both of us by blowing up the apartment, and it had since been completely renovated and now felt more like our family home. Bryce had tried to convince me for months after the fire to move into a house in the suburbs, or by the beach, but I hadn't wanted to. City Towers held such sentimental memories for me, and I couldn't bring myself to abandon it. Okay, so the building also held some pretty devastating memories, too, but I was of the mindset that you didn't run away from your fears and demons, you faced them head on. You addressed them, dealt with them, conquered and quashed them. Only then could you honestly move ahead.

I'd also decided that I wanted to get married at City Towers, because again, let's face it, the place was sentimental. It was where Bryce and I first met, where we first kissed, where we both first said 'I love you', and it was the place where we shared our lives together both personally and professionally. For me, it was the perfect choice.

My friends had thought my choice was crazy, because ... well ... it was no secret we pretty much had all the money in the world, as the saying goes. But I wanted something familiar, elegant and private. I wanted something intimate. The glory and over-the-top hype that was involved with weddings just wasn't my thing. City Towers was the perfect setting, I was positive of that.

It was February in Melbourne and relatively warm, but I liked summer. It was the perfect time of year to get married.

Our ceremony was to be held in the Garden Terrace which was located in the precinct area. It was quaint and offered both an outdoor freshness and an indoor feel with the luxury of air conditioning. Always very much needed for the summer season.

I took in the view from the balcony like I had so many times, and like those other times, its serene calmness and beauty washed over me and settled my nerves. Mum was right, I was never this nervous. I guess it showed just how happy Bryce made me and, because of that, I wanted this day to be perfect.

'Lexi, your phone just beeped,' Lucy said with a snide smile as she handed me my phone, then turned and headed back inside.

I looked down at the screen and noticed a message from Bryce.

29 minutes and 13 seconds — Bryce

I shook my head a little, just as my phone beeped again.

28 minutes, 19 seconds and counting until you make me the happiest man alive — Bryce

I typed back:

27 minutes and 21 seconds until I become Mrs Alexis Clark — Alexis

I can't wait — Bryce

Neither can I — Alexis

Well then hurry up — Bryce

I love you, you know — Alexis

I do — Bryce

Aren't you supposed to say that in 25 minutes and 33 seconds — Alexis
That's it, I'm coming up there to get you — Bryce
I giggled. *Shit! He probably would.*
Okay, okay. I'm on my way ♥ — Alexis
You better be ♥ — Bryce

'You look beautiful, baby girl,' Dad's voice sounded from behind me. I turned around to see my father in a tux with a rose buttonhole pinned to his breast pocket.

I tilted my head to the side and gave my dad a bashful smile. 'Thanks, Dad, you look pretty smashing yourself.'

Dad hated suits. Hated them. He was most comfortable in a pair of tracksuit pants, overalls and Blundstone boots.

He tugged at his tie, uncomfortably. 'Hmm,' he muttered with false frustration.

I stepped forward and adjusted it correctly for him.

'I know this is your second time down the aisle, sweetheart. But let me tell you, I'm just as proud to walk you down it this day as I was the first.'

I wrapped my arms around the wonderful man I was privileged to call Dad. 'I promise this is the last time you'll have to do it.'

He nodded. 'Good! Okay, let's get this show on the road then, shall we?'

* * *

My bridal party huddled into the elevator and made their way down to the lobby, while Charli, my parents and I waited for it to return to collect us.

'Alexis, sweetheart. Take a breath,' Mum advised.

'Leave her alone, Maryann, she's allowed to be nervous.'

I clenched Dad's arm a bit tighter.

'Mum, you're my favourite princess, even more than Cinderella and she's really beautiful.'

I ran my hand over Charli's cheek. 'And you're my favourite princess too, Charli-Bear.' I winked at her just as the doors opened.

Mum, Dad and Charli stepped out before me, and when I stepped into the lobby after them I was stunned to a halt. There were potted rose bushes lining a white velvet carpet which stretched as far as I could see, wrapping around the corner and out into the entertainment precinct. Guests and staff lined the route, waiting for me to walk down it on my journey to marry the man of my dreams.

'Oh my god! Who organised all these roses and where did all these people come from? They look as if they are forming a guard of honour. How embarrassing,' I said quietly under my breath.

Lucy spun around to face me after positioning my bridal party in single file, ready to walk to the terrace. 'Get used to it, Alexis. You are about to marry the biggest control freak on earth.'

'Don't I know it,' I murmured.

Lucy spun back around and gave her orders. 'Okay, okay, ladies and little lady, let's walk.'

Charli smiled brightly and gave me the thumbs-up.

I smiled back and blew her a kiss. 'Take it away, princess,' I called back to her.

She started walking slowly along the carpet dropping rose petals from her basket, while each bridesmaid followed shortly after.

Mum gave me one last kiss and hug before wiping her tears and heading quickly to the Garden Terrace.

I sucked in a huge breath and blew it out before cracking my neck from side to side. *Not the classiest thing to do, Alexis, especially while in a wedding dress in front of so many people. But damn, that does help ease tension. I now understand why Bryce does it.*

'Let's walk, darling.' Dad said, before linking his arm in mine and leading the way.

As I walked down the carpet, I smiled brightly at the hotel's staff. Many of them I had become quite friendly with, and many had abandoned their duties throughout the hotel to pop into the lobby and see me on my way. I also smiled at the hotel's guests and waved at their children who waved back excitedly as I walked past. I was so caught up in parading through the hotel that I had not realised I was now standing at the entrance to the Garden Terrace and in a position to see Bryce standing at the altar. Derek, Will, Matt, Nic, Steve, Jake and Dale were lined up to his right, and my handsome little man, Nate, stood proudly at his very side.

Mum appeared next to me again, this time handing me my equally handsome little, little man, Brayden.

'Hello, Mummy's spunky boy. Have you been good for Daddy?'

He nodded. 'Dadda ova dere,' Brayden giggled, pointing to his dad who was as still as a statue while watching me hug our son.

'Yes, he is, isn't he? And he looks very handsome, just like you. Have you got a kiss for Mummy?'

My chubby little eighteen month old leaned forward and placed a sloppy kiss on my lips.

'Thank you,' I said, conspicuously wiping the additional slobber that toddlers seem to be able to produce away from my lips and chin. 'Now, hold on to Nanny's hand and your special pillow, and walk down to where Daddy is.'

I placed him on his wobbly feet and watched Mum lead him down the aisle, my heart thumping at the sight of his gorgeous wobbly steps toward his dad. We had waited nearly two years to get married, just so we could see our gorgeous little Brayden walk down the aisle and, although the wait was agonising — especially for my Mr I-can't-fucking-wait-any-longer Clark — seeing our son's adorable eager steps toward his father was definitely worth the wait.

Everyone in the room smiled at my blond-haired, blue-eyed little boy who seemed to charm everyone in his vicinity, just like his dad. He was sweet and playful and again, just like his dad, had stolen my heart the moment I first laid eyes on him.

A tear left my eye as I looked down the aisle at all three of my children and the man who captured my soul the very moment I met him. The sight before me was perfect.

A Live Trepidation musical piece sounded through the speakers, indicating I should begin to walk down the aisle. I wiped my tear and smiled, then I squeezed Dad's arm, prompting him to turn his head in my direction and pat my hand. I took comfort in his action, then beamed at the people around me.

I spotted Santa and Mrs Gordon first, both of them smiling and nodding their heads as I walked past. Next was Abigail, Sam and Liam, Liam fluttering his hands in front of his face in an attempt to prevent himself from crying. Moving along, I spotted Clarissa and Johanna, and I was glad Jake had been truthful when telling me that he liked her, because obviously he had — she was still very much a part of his life and his house.

Taking my final steps to the altar, I came upon Jessica wiping her eye with a tissue, and something told me her tears were a result of happiness and sadness; sadness that her best friend — Bryce's mother — could not be here to witness her son get married. I smiled sympathetically at her, and she thanked me with a brighter smile in return.

The last set of guests I laid eyes on before turning to my father were Rick, Claire and RJ. Rick looked happier than I had ever seen him. He was fit and healthy and very much in love with his heavily pregnant fiancée, Claire.

'Okay, darling. This is where I leave you and hand you over to a man I know that this time will love and care for you until his dying day.'

I smiled lovingly at my father. 'How do you know that?'

Dad nodded in Bryce's direction. 'Just look at him.'

Dad then leaned in and kissed me on the cheek before I turned and faced Bryce.

Okay, I have to agree with you, Dad.

Bryce's eyes were glued to me as if in a trance, his mouth slightly open and his hands by his sides showing signs of fidgety agitation.

I stepped up to the altar beside him and mouthed the word, 'Hi.'

He looked at the celebrant. 'Can I kiss her now?'

The terrace erupted into a chuckle.

'I'm sorry, Mr Clark, not quite yet.'

The windows to his soul were wide open as he stood before me, exposing his undeniable love and indisputable devotion. 'I love you,' he mouthed, as he eyed me adoringly.

'I love you, too,' I mouthed back, drinking in his passion.

He was handsome, smouldering and sexy at the best of times, but standing in a long-lined black tuxedo with an ivory-coloured vest to match my dress, the man simply made my knees weak.

I handed my bouquet of roses to Jen before turning to face Bryce. He subtly wiped his palms on his pants before taking my hands, and giggled at this sign of his nervousness. As our fingers stroked one another's, the excitement that his touch always generated filled me entirely. Then, against all rules, he lifted my wrist to his mouth and placed a kiss on it, while fixing his deep blazing gaze on me. The man never did what he was told, never followed the rules.

The celebrant — an amused smile on his face — cleared his throat. Bryce just happily smirked.

'We are gathered here today ...' the celebrant began and, as if I were in a daze, I concentrated on the man before me. We had connected from the moment I met him and I knew we belonged together. Against all odds, here we were, about to eternally pledge our commitment to each other.

'Bryce Edward Clark, do you take Alexis Elizabeth Blaxlo to be your wife? Do you promise to love her, cherish her, honour and keep her, in sickness and in health as long as you both shall live?'

'I do,' he pronounced with certainty.

The celebrant then repeated 'The Asking' to me.

'I do,' I answered honestly.

He nodded to Brayden. 'Now I believe this young man right here has the honour of handing over the rings.'

Mum whispered to Brayden and set him on his feet and, like all toddlers do, he surged toward his older brother who had bent down to make sure he did not go tumbling to the ground. Nate caught him in his arms and took the pillow from him which contained our rings.

'My pillow,' Brayden complained as Nate handed it to the celebrant.

'Hang on, buddy, you can have it back in a second,' Nate said, as he placed his hands on Brayden's shoulders, positioning him at his front.

The celebrant untied the rings and handed the pillow back to Brayden. He happily accepted it and made his way back to Mum and Dad.

'Bryce,' the celebrant said as he handed over my ring, 'I believe you have something to say.'

'Yes, I do.' Bryce took the ring then lifted my hand in his. 'Alexis, you're a thief,' he said boldly.

I laughed. *What?*

'You stole my heart and you stole it good. You kept it, joined it with yours and never gave it back. But, honey, I want you to keep it. It's yours, it belongs to you and it always will. I've waited all my life for a thief like you —'

I laughed again and so did our family and friends, Brayden laughing along with them.

'I live for you, breathe for you. I form part of this world simply for you. With this ring, I vow to be everything you need and want. I vow to be your life, your breath and the reason for your existence.' He lifted my hand again and pressed it to his mouth before sliding the ring on my finger.

Tears were streaming down my cheeks and I looked at it through blurred vision, perfectly placed it was beside my engagement ring. And Brylexis right next to it.

Bryce gently wiped my tears away. I leaned in to his touch before taking his ring from the celebrant.

'Bryce, if I'm a thief, then you're my ultimate loot —'

This time he laughed along with the occupants in the room.

'— my greatest treasure. You are my knight in shining armour. The person who opened my eyes, heart and soul to a love I did not know existed, a love so deep that it's effortless, raw and pure. I vow to be all that you'll ever want or need. I vow to be your life entirely. I vow to love you so profoundly that you'll realise I am no thief and your heart was never yours, it was always mine.'

Just like he did, I lifted his hand and placed a kiss to it before sliding his ring onto his finger.

'Can I kiss her now?' he asked almost desperately through gritted teeth.

'With the power invested in me,' the celebrant began to say, 'by the Commonwealth —'

Bryce did not wait for him to finish before taking me in his strong arms and pressing his lips to mine. His hands were on my back, and I was deliciously pressed against him as we merged our mouths together for the first time as husband and wife. I melted into him, then suddenly felt myself being lowered and turned to the side in a dip.

The room cheered and I heard Brayden squeal in happiness, forcing both Bryce and I to stop and instinctively find our son. We both turned our heads to see him sitting on my dad's lap, clapping his hands and bouncing up and down. We both let out a laugh before we turned back to each other.

'Mr Clark, you can lift me back up again.'

'Not just yet, Mrs Clark,' he said with a smirk, then leaned in and kissed me again.

The End? ... Not really.

Attainment

Book 3.5 in The Temptation Series

A companion novella...

PROLOGUE

How do you know when you are truly happy and that your life is ultimately fulfilled in all aspects imaginable? Is that even possible ... ultimate attainment? Some people measure their happiness on their level of success, while others measure it on their fortune or ability to live an unencumbered or inhibited lifestyle. Some people even fool themselves into believing that they are truly happy when, in fact, they are just filling a void with a bullshit pretence.

Not too long ago, I was one of those people; deceiving myself into believing my life was what it ought to be. But as I sit here now, looking out the window of my City Metropol building toward my penthouse apartment at City Tower, I feel nothing but ultimate attainment. Today, I can finally say that I have achieved everything I have ever wanted in life. Today, my family becomes complete. Today, I marry the love of my life; Alexis. It is today, after setting eyes upon her three years ago, that I will finally be able to call her my wife.

From that very moment when I first saw her, she stirred something within me that had lay dormant — happiness. But it wasn't until our lips first touched that I knew I would stop at nothing to have her completely. There was just something in that kiss which told me she was the one, something in that instant shifted in me — I needed her; I wanted her.

Wholeheartedly knowing at that point that we were both put on this earth to be together, I realised how I would make that happen. I would show her what she was missing in life. I would show her how it felt to truly be desired and loved. I would show her what her life was supposed to be like — I would show her me ... us ... forever.

PART 1

My life has just begun

CHAPTER

1

Glancing ever so slightly toward Alexis who is sitting in the passenger seat of my car, I notice her perform an awkward shuffle of her arse. It is obvious she is uncomfortable — again.

Over the past six months, I have watched what she endures on a daily basis from being pregnant. And during those times, I couldn't help but find myself wondering just what it would feel like. You know ... to be pregnant; to carry a small human being inside your abdomen. Would it feel like you've just eaten one huge breakfast? Or would it feel like you constantly want to squeeze the baby out from between your legs, the same feeling you get when you can no longer hold onto that shit you've been putting off having all day? I guess it could ... it does make sense. Or perhaps it just simply feels like you've swallowed a watermelon ... whole. A watermelon with moving limbs ... and hair?

I shudder at the thought.

Speaking of hair on a baby's head, apparently our little angel has a decent amount of it. According to Alexis, that is the reason why she is burping so much, or, as she puts it: 'Indigestion'. Can hair on your unborn baby's head really make you burp? To me, that's like saying the socks I chose to wear today make me fart. It's just ridiculous and completely far-fetched. I don't understand why Alexis feels she needs an excuse to burp, and even when she does belch unexpectedly, I still find her sexy as hell. Probably even more so because she blushes then comes up with her little pregnancy-fib. *Yes, I'm not stupid. Hair on a baby's head cannot make you burp.*

Initially, most of the stuff she told me about being pregnant I had put down to being a pregnancy-fib. Some of it resulted in confusion, or had made me laugh in disbelief, or it had just scared the absolute shit out of me. Like when she'd said that a father could experience 'a sympathetic pregnancy' or more technically put — couvade syndrome.

What. The. Fuck?

I remember her telling me while displaying that cocky, fucking adorable smirk on her face. 'Bryce,' she'd said with one eyebrow raised, 'there's a very good chance you could experience morning sickness, weight gain, sore breasts —' she rattled off. At that point, I'd had no choice but to interrupt her, saying 'I don't fucking own breasts, Alexis. How the hell can I get sore ones? You're yanking my chain, honey.' But no, she was adamant it was true. So, of course, I googled it. Well, fuck me, she wasn't lying. A father could actually experience symptoms of pregnancy.

Now, I've said it before and I will say it again. I will do absolutely anything for Alexis ... anything. Because let's face it, I worship the ground this woman walks on. But experience sore breasts, breasts I don't even have, and labour pain? Screw that. I was born with a dick, and not experiencing childbirth firsthand is a perk of owning said dick.

Alexis' voice slowly becomes audible, tearing me away from my nightmarish thoughts of couvade syndrome.

'Bryce, earth to Bryce,' she says in a singsong tone.

'Yeah?' I ask a little stunned, before gathering my bearings.

'Are you with me?'

'Sorry, I was faraway.'

'It would appear so. Where is faraway?'

I take off my seat belt and turn to face her, noticing her concerned expression. 'Never mind, I'm here now, honey. And it appears that we are here now, too,' I say as I glance around the underground car park of Dr Rainer's consulting rooms.

'Yes, we are,' Alexis murmurs, still displaying an expression of concern. 'You sure you're all right?'

'Really, I'm fine. And,' I say, now directing the conversation to my baby while leaning over to press my lips to Alexis' stomach, 'today we are going to find out if you need a blue room or a pink room —'

'Oh no, we are not!' she interrupts, and gently pushes my head back.

I move against her shove, returning to her stomach. 'Yes, we are.'

'Bryce, I want it to be a secret.'

'Fine, I'll keep it a secret from you.'

'You can't,' she pleads.

'Yes, I can.'

'No, I mean you can't do this to me. It's not fair that you will know the sex and I won't.'

I take her hands in mine and smile at her beautifully distraught face. 'Honey, I'm not waiting to find out what we are having. I want to know. I want to be prepared. If you want it to be a surprise, I promise I won't tell you. In fact, I think I will enjoy not telling you.'

Alexis abruptly removes her hands from mine and shoves me back over to my side of the car. 'I hate you,' she grumbles.

I laugh. 'No, you don't.'

'Grrr,' she growls as she quickly tries to exit the car.

Hurrying out of my side, I meet her and hold her door open as she steps out. 'You fucking love me and you know it,' I say, leaning against it with my ankles crossed while pretending to brush something off my shoulder in a show of cockiness. I really shouldn't bait her, it's just ... I can't help myself. Her little fightbacks are always such a turn-on.

She slowly stands up straight, giving me a little Alexis-attitude. 'Yeah, well that can change.' *Like fuck it can change.*

I waste no time and bend down, gently sweeping her off her feet and placing her on the bonnet of the car. 'No. It. Can't. Change,' I reaffirm, before taking her head in my hands and pressing my mouth to hers.

The remnants of her toothpaste coat my tongue as I thrust it into her mouth, taking possession of her tongue like it's mine. Well ... it kind of is mine; she is mine. My possessiveness forces a moan to escape her which brings a smile to my face. I love how she reacts to my touch.

Sliding one hand to the back of her head, I pull her closer, prompting her tongue to delve deeper. *Fuck!* I want to take her here ... now ... on the Lexus. I know how much she loves being fucked in, on and against my cars.

My cock springs to life, encouraging thoughts of making love to her before our appointment. But I know we can't, we shouldn't. Well, not here, anyway. The thought of anyone seeing her in the throes of passion does not sit well with me. Only I get that privilege.

I reluctantly separate our conjoined mouths and rest my forehead against hers. 'Come on, we need to leave before I strip you naked and run my tongue right down your centre. Believe me, the thought is crossing my mind.'

Her mouth drops open, but she then shuts it again and smiles, refusing to budge by displaying a cheeky grin on her face.

'I'm serious. Come on,' I say, taking hold of her hand and shaking my head in amusement. Alexis, when pregnant, is insatiable ... horny as fuck ... as randy as a rabbit. Hell, she almost wears me out ... almost!

* * *

Before too long, we are in Dr Rainer's office and Alexis is lying flat on the examination table with an ultrasound image of our baby swirling around on the monitor. Her hand is gripping mine with an intense clasp as we wait for the sound of a heartbeat.

She won't admit it, but I know this is hard for her. How could it not be? It wasn't long ago that we were both here staring at a similar image, that image being Bianca. If fate hadn't decided to be cruel and malicious during that time, Bianca would now be approximately four months old.

I take a deep breath, push aside my sad thoughts and smile at my fiancée. I have to be strong for her, because god knows she is forever putting on a brave face. What Alexis has experienced in the past eighteen months is more than most would experience in a lifetime. Her continual strength and resilience blow me away, together with her ability to take on life's ruthless challenges and not only meet them head on, but somehow find a way to conquer them. When all is said and done, Alexis is simply amazing, and I thank my lucky stars every day that she has agreed to become my wife. Not only that, but she is carrying my second child, and her two children — Nate and Charlotte — have accepted me as their stepfather. I couldn't be more proud.

The rhythmic sound of popping filters through my ears, bringing my gaze back up to the screen. It really is such a wonderful tone, a reassuring one.

Hearing our baby's heartbeat, Alexis lets out the breath she has been holding and tilts her head to flash me one of her earth-shattering smiles.

I lean down to give her a quick kiss. 'Everything is fine, my love.'

She nods.

Dr Rainer records a few measurements on the screen then turns to me and Alexis. 'Baby's heartbeat is still strong at 140 beats per minute. And his or her measurements are consistent with gestation —'

'His? Or hers?' I ask, probably a bit too eagerly.

'Do you really want to find out?' she questions with a curious smile, seeming to know that I do and Alexis does not.

'Yes, although Mummy here,' I gesture to my not so happy looking fiancée, 'does not. So you can whisper it in my —'

'All right! All right!' Alexis blurts out, clearly frustrated. 'I want to know, too.' She crosses her arms over her chest in a show of reluctant surrender.

I have to smile, because she looks so damn adorable. I knew she would eventually cave in. She hates secrets with a passion, especially when I'm the holder of the secret in question.

Gently grazing my knuckles down the side of her face, I smile at her triumphantly. 'You know, you really don't have to find out. I promise I won't tell.'

'Screw you, Bryce Edward Clark. I'm finding out the sex of our baby.'

I laugh out loud. 'There you go, Dr Rainer. We both want to find out.'

'Very well. I'm fairly certain I know baby Clark's gender already. However, I want a better angle just to be sure. Alexis, I'm going to move the ultrasound wand further down and apply a firm pressure. This will help get a better view of baby's genitals,' she explains.

Dr Rainer does as she has just informed and pushes into Alexis' lower abdomen, causing her to wince.

'Are you all right?' I say with concern, glaring at Dr Rainer.

Alexis squeezes my hand. 'Yes, I'm fine. I just need to pee ... desperately.'

I let out a sigh of relief and am thankful Dr Rainer didn't see my unwarranted look of displeasure.

'I'm sorry, Alexis, I know this is uncomfortable for you.'

'Yeah, you can say that again.'

'Okay, nearly done. You do know this is not one hundred percent accurate, don't you?' Dr Rainer informs us, her eyebrow raised.

'Yes,' we both answer simultaneously.

'Good, okay. There we go.' She presses a few buttons which freezes the image on the screen. 'Say hello to your son. You're having a little boy.'

Alexis gets up on her elbows while I lean in closer to the screen. *Fuckin' oath, that's a boy. Check him out!*

'There,' I point to the screen. 'He sure is, and he takes after his father.'

'Bryce, that's your son's leg,' Dr Rainer states in a dry, condescending tone.

Bullshit! He doesn't have three legs ... I quickly re-count. *One leg. Two legs ... that's definitely not a third leg. He most certainly takes after me.* I smile proudly with a knowing nod of my head.

'Bryce,' Alexis says, grabbing my attention, choking on her words and trying to push back her tears. 'We are having a boy. That's our son. Look at him.'

I glance back at the screen. *My son! That's my fucking son! That little blurry image is my living, breathing baby boy.* I turn back to lay eyes on Alexis' beautiful face and realise that life doesn't get much better than this.

* * *

On our way back to City Towers, I start to think about the things I can organise, change and get ready ... like our son's room. The renovations and rebuild of the penthouse are not far off completion, and it's probably only a few more weeks before we can move back in. After our ordeal with Gareth, I'd tried to convince Alexis to consider moving into a house by the bay, or in the suburbs — wherever she wanted.

But she'd wanted to remain at City Towers, assuring me that it just 'felt right', that it was 'home'. Our home.

Not wanting to argue with her decision — because let's face it, it was a fucking brave one — I instigated repairs, renovations and a rebuild almost instantly. In the meantime, though, we have been residing in the presidential villa.

Sadly, pretty much everything on the first floor of the apartment was ruined by the explosion and subsequent fire. The upstairs bedrooms had sustained water damage, but no clear structural impairment. Mainly, the devastation was cosmetic, although Charli was absolutely shattered that her 4Life memorabilia was destroyed. Little does she know that I have arranged replacements and plan to surprise her with them when the refurbished apartment is unveiled.

'What are you thinking about?' Alexis says, once again breaking me out of my trip to "faraway".'

'Our son. Our home. Our future,' I honestly answer.

'And ...?'

I quickly glance at her, curious of her questioning tone.

'And ... I have a lot to do. The apartment should be finished in a few weeks and I want it to be perfect before we move back in.'

She reaches over and touches my face. I love her soft touch. 'Bryce, it will be. I have no doubt. Please stop worrying about that.'

I release one hand from the steering wheel and take hold of hers, pressing my lips to her wrist. 'I love you.'

'I know you do,' she smiles. 'And I love you, too.'

Feeling bold and knowing she is in a very good mood, I broach an off-limits topic. 'Are you sure you don't want to get married sooner? I know you want to wait, but —'

'Bryce, we've talked about this. You know I can't wait to be your wife. But after everything that has happened, and with BB on the way, I just think we need to slow down a bit and enjoy the ride.'

'BB?'

'Well ... yeah ...' She coyly hesitates. *Damn, she's cute.* 'BB ... as in Baby Bryce.' She gently caresses her stomach, filling me with so much fucking love for this woman that I can barely breathe.

'Baby Bryce?' I repeat, unable to contain my grin.

'Yes.'

I continue to drive, silence now swirling around us. Every couple of seconds I glance at her, knowing she is watching my reaction.

'You know, Mr Clark,' she says, her tone now lowered and sounding sexy as hell, 'when you smile like that it makes me want to climb onto your lap.'

'Honey, you are a threat to road safety. You really need to get in control of that.'

'Then stop grinning that sex-on-a-stick grin. I just want to lick it.'

'I can't stop. You have that effect on me.'

'I know. So it appears we have a predicament.'

'We do.'

She leans over and slides her hand across my thigh, stopping on top of the hard mound in my pants.

'Alexis,' I growl in warning. *Bloody hell, she drives me wild.*

She gives me a firm squeeze while answering in an innocently sweet voice. 'Yes?'

Swallowing heavily, I rein in the serious wood that is forming beneath her hand. 'You'd better start thinking of all the ways you want to be fucked. Because when we get home, we are going to be performing each and every one of them.'

CHAPTER

2

Experiencing conflict with one's self, when you think about it, is kind of absurd. But despite that absurdity, we subject ourselves to this illogical torment at more than one point in our lives. Why? Well, I would probably put it down to stubbornness, or the ability to be unyielding, even if that means you go to war with yourself.

I'm no stranger to being at war — figuratively speaking — having fought and won many battles in my life. Battles in business, against family, and even against morality. But fighting a battle against one's self is not a battle you intend losing. The thing is, if you are defeated, then you have only yourself to blame.

* * *

'Bryce, I know this is hard for you. But you have to talk about your feelings of guilt if you ever want to get past them.'

I look up from my seated position. Jessica — my psychologist and family friend — is sitting across from me with her notepad rested on her lap. She has her reading glasses perched on the tip of her nose and a troubled expression on her face. It's quite obvious to me that her concern is due to the fact I am not openly discussing what happened with Gareth as she wishes I would.

We are both sitting in her office, which is situated on Bourke Street in the CBD of Melbourne. It's a quaint office, furnished with soft colours, unobtrusive ornaments and feel-good artwork, purposefully placed to make her patients feel comfortable, relaxed and, unbeknown to them, unguarded. I have been here many times and am aware of my deceptive surroundings; they don't fool me.

'What if I don't want to get past my guilt? What if I don't deserve to?' I respond with determination.

'Guilt is felt not only by the guilty, but more so by those who feel they deserve it when, in fact, they don't. Guilt can be a humble, yet deceitful emotion.'

'Jessica,' I sigh, deflated and tired as a result of this session's conflict. 'I know you are trying to help. I know you are trying to make me see that Gareth's death was not my fault. The truth of the matter is ... it was. I abandoned him when he really needed me and, on top of that, I nearly lost Alexis in the process. I deserve this guilt. Please, just let me bear it.'

She places her notepad on the seat next to her and removes her glasses. 'Gareth's death was not your fault. If it was, then it would equally be mine. Actions have consequences, consequences have results and sometimes those results are devastating, as in Gareth's case.'

Leaning back in my chair, I close my eyes and run my hands through my hair, the pain and memory of my mentally ill cousin's demise still too brutally raw.

'Bryce, look at me,' Jessica says with a soft, but authoritative voice.

I open my eyes and meet her gaze.

'I'm going to ask you to think about something and then I want to discuss it next week.'

'Sure,' I respond flippantly, with a tinge of arrogance. My intention is not to be an arsehole. After all, she means well. It's just that I'm exhausted and want to get home to Alexis and find solace in her warm embrace. Alexis keeps me grounded; she always has and I hope she always will.

'What you're experiencing is known as "unhealthy" or "inappropri-ate" guilt. I want you to look at the situation from a different point of view, put someone else in your shoes. Take Lucy for instance. What if it were her? Would you find her just as responsible for Gareth's death? After all, she too is his cousin. She knew what you knew. She had just as much influence as you —'

'Jessica,' I snap, 'leave Lucy out of this. It —'

'Bryce!' she interrupts, as abruptly as I had. 'Just think about what I'm saying and we'll talk about it next week.'

I stand up, not happy with her request to 'pretend' to put Lucy in my place. Gareth's death had nothing to do with my sister. 'Fine, I will see you next week. When is Alexis due to come in next?'

'Alexis and I have arranged monthly visits now. She tends to listen to my advice and not be so sceptical of what *you* may feel are unorthodox suggestions.'

My eye involuntarily twitches and I clench, then release, my fist. *Bloody hell, she is on a tirade today.* 'I'm glad to hear my fiancée is dealing with the situation and finding a way to put it behind her. Thank you. The last thing she needs is to feel any stress in her current state.'

Jessica stands and makes her way toward her desk. 'Well, she is not the only one.'

'Goodbye, Jessica,' I respond, contemptuously. 'I will see you next week.'

'Bryce,' she says, not looking up, 'you know that, despite your stubbornness, your mother would be proud of you.'

I sigh. 'You tell me this every time.'

'Well, it's true. She would, and you need to hear it.'

I head for the door without looking back and give her the reply that I always do, 'Thank you.' Except this time, I don't really mean it.

* * *

A few weeks later, we are standing on the threshold of our newly refurbished apartment with my hands covering Alexis' eyes.

'Are you ready?' I ask, drawing out the unveiling of the renovations.

She urges me forward. 'Yes! Yes! Come on, let's go in.'

Releasing one hand from her eyes, I turn the handle on the door, opening it for us to walk inside. 'Keep them closed until I say, all right?'

She huffs. 'Yes, okay, you are such a control freak.'

'And your problem is?'

'Bryce Edward Clar—'

'Okay, okay,' I chuckle, while holding her back against my front and slowly shuffling us along the entryway of the apartment.

Leaning down, I slowly and softly whisper into her ear. 'You can open them, my love.'

I tilt my head around to get a clear view of her reaction, watching her eyelids flutter and the expression on her face morph from anticipation to amazement. It's not as if she was blind to what the newly refurbished apartment would look like, because she did, after all, help redesign it. But I guess seeing it in actuality for the first time, together with the extra little bits and pieces I organised without her knowledge, is the cause of her happy astonishment.

She steps forward and gazes over the lounge area. 'Oh, Bryce, it's ... it's ... wow! It's wonderful.'

The layout of the apartment is still much the same, except now there is no step down into the lounge. Alexis wanted to minimise the number of steps in consideration of the rolling, then crawling, then walking little person on his way. The other noticeable change is the softer colour palette throughout the lower level, and the now child-friendly furniture — no sharp, sleek lines or edges.

Where there had been shades of grey, white, black and deep blue, there are now cream, beige, fawn and chocolate brown. I'd arranged for new family photographs to be enlarged, framed and displayed on the walls, together with replicas of the cushions Alexis went a little cuckoo over when she left Rick. I'd even arranged for some Twister carpet to be laid in my new recording studio, although it was no longer really fitting to label it a 'recording studio'. You see, it is now a larger room containing many new toys. Not man toys ... but child toys, including the carpet.

Before Alexis has a chance to move further into the apartment, I seize her hand gently and spin her around, stepping her backward until she's stopped against the entryway wall, my prurient intentions now made clear by the pressing of my raging hard-on against her hip.

'I believe we need to break in this freshly rebuilt wall,' I suggest seductively, pinning her arms above her head and grazing my lips across her ear.

Thoughts of the first time I had her pressed to this very spot flit across my mind, and it's obvious to me that I want her now just as much as I wanted her then ... probably even more.

She takes in a sharp breath, pushing her plump tits into my chest before exhaling slowly. 'What did you have in mind?' she purrs.

Fuuuuuck, I love it when she teases me with her sultry voice.

'I think a complete rehash,' I murmur as I lightly lick the crook of her neck, 'of our first time together is a very good start.'

'Start?' she questions, her voice still low and sexy. 'We have to pick up the kids from school soon, Bryce,' she adds, lacking conviction.

Pulling away from her, I look at my watch then lean back in, stopping only centimetres from her mouth. 'There's a lot I can do to you in the space of an hour,' I say as I watch her lips and how she has no control but to moisten them with her tongue.

'Good,' she smiles, 'I'm looking forward to it.'

Not wanting to waste any time, I slide my tongue into her mouth, relishing her luscious warmth and silky feel. An uncontrollable growl resonates from within me, intensifying our fervour and increasing my need to bury myself inside her. To say I'm completely attuned to her body's needs is an understatement. I know what she wants ... likes ... needs.

Now feeling her legs weaken, I release one of her hands and hold her hip to steady her and, almost instantly, her newly freed hand finds the back of my head. The tightened grip on my hair fucking exhilarates me.

'Would you like sex up against the wall again?' I ask in a whisper.

'Yes, I'm fucking thirsty.'

I pull away, entertained by her response. Obviously, I was not referring to one of our favourite cocktails, the one which inspired this passionate position in the first place.

She notices my paused state, giggles, and pulls me back in for a kiss. 'I'm kidding,' she mumbles. 'Now, get on your knees. If memory serves me correctly, you were all about tasting, not admiring.'

I shake my head at her sassiness and begin to unbutton her silk blouse, finding her perfect tits with my hands. Kneading them with heightened hunger, I allow my fingers to massage the plump flesh right before pulling down the cup of her bra and taking her nipple into my mouth. The soft peak hardens at my touch, eliciting my desperate urge to flick it with my tongue.

A sharp, uncomfortable yet fucking sensational ache ripples through my head as she suddenly grips my hair and tugs ferociously, indicating her approval of my tongue's pursuit.

'You like that?' I murmur around her wet nipple.

'Uh huh.'

'What else do you like?'

Her hands glide down my shirt as she makes her way to my belt, their journey south such a turn-on. She finds the buckle and, wasting no time in unlatching it, has my cock in her hands within seconds. 'This ... I like this,' she answers.

Fuck! The feel of her warm hands on my shaft stimulates me even further. 'So you fucking should,' I growl, a determined new hunger rolling out of me. I allow her to caress my cock for only a few seconds longer before my impatience wins over and I strip her of her clothes.

Taking a step back and stepping out of my own pants, I hungrily take in her gorgeous pregnant form. Her swollen belly is so fucking beautiful that it has my dick twitching with excitement, knowing that in mere seconds my hands will be caressing what I see in front of me.

I raise my eyes to her chest. The rhythmic rise and fall has me intoxicated, together with her eyes which have now become heavy with desire. It is almost the exact same look she pierced me with the first time we were in this position.

'You still, and always will, fucking take my breath away,' I say as I cup her cheek.

She turns into my hand and closes her eyes, and it's this small sign of pure love that has me dropping to my knees before her.

Alexis' hands find my hair, the corners of her mouth lifting in a provocative grin. *Fuck! That look does me in every time.*

'You want me to taste you, don't you? To run my tongue in between your legs while you tug on my hair?'

'Yes,' she breathes out, 'yes, I do.'

Grabbing my head, she threads her fingers through my hair and coaxes me forward, her yearning desperation now eagerly prompting me to spread her legs and nudge her clit with my nose.

Alexis sucks in a breath and then exhales. 'Oh, Bryce,' she breathes, as her head drops back against the wall. 'Yes, I do want that. I want it now.'

God! I fucking love it when she moans my name. The sound of her quivering approval of my actions always gives me assurance.

Sliding my tongue out, I drag it across her soft skin, sampling her already aroused pussy, the taste — fucking delightful. I could eat her slowly all day. The taste of her at the tip of my tongue is sensational.

Her fingers dig into my scalp in response and, at the same time, my grip tightens on her hips. I swirl my tongue and coax her hips to roll against my mouth. She obliges and lifts her leg, draping it over my shoulder, prompting me to increase my tongue's ferocity as it laps and flicks at her. I could seriously devour her sweet flavour for hours. Listen to her pant for hours. I could, quite simply, stay like this for hours.

'Bryce, I ... I ... oh, god,' she cries out as her body tenses, then shudders while I hold her tight as she comes on my face — one of my favourite things imaginable.

Sucking her clit into my mouth one final time, I follow it with a tender kiss then proceed to stand.

'I need you inside me, now!' she demands, her desperation evident.

Given no time to taste her nipple again, she impatiently grabs my face and directs her mouth to mine, getting a taste of her own arousal on my lips. Being a man who loves to eat pussy, there's just something so incredibly sexy when a woman tastes herself on my face and, when Alexis does it, I could honestly die a happy man.

Separating from her hungry kiss, I spin her around and splay her hands on the wall, then gently coax her into a bent position. My cock throbs with expectant release as I open her up, driving deep inside her. Slowly, I slide back out, tantalising her with my hard length. I know she loves a good tease.

'Does that feel good?' I question between slow thrusts.

'Yes.'

'Do you want it harder?'

'Yes.'

'Are you still thirsty?'

She laughs. 'No.'

I snigger, then proceed to slide in and out of her at a faster pace. In and out, in and out, the warm walls of her pussy massaging my shaft as I glide back and forth.

'You feel so fucking good,' I rasp before reaching forward and cupping her bouncing tits.

Noticing her arms weaken as she holds herself up against the wall, I release one breast and wrap my arm around her waist, supporting her.

'I've got you. Just relax.'

Her body slackens just a little, and her head drops back onto my shoulder. I let go of her breast, brace my hand against the wall, and seize her mouth with my own.

My efforts to refrain from ejaculating become impossible as the sensation is just too great, and I explode into her, filling her as I pulse with pleasure. Our climax melts into one as I continue to roll against her, slowing down and steadying not only our stance, but our breathing as well.

I slide out of her and turn her back around to face me, catching the elated joy radiating from her in the form of a satisfied smile. She wraps her arms around my neck and rests her forehead against mine.

'Why are you so happy?' I question, already pretty sure of the answer.

With a sexy as hell lift of her eyebrow, she takes a hold of my tie and tugs me toward the lounge. 'One room down, at least five to go.'

CHAPTER

3

One hour was not enough time to complete Alexis' plans for the five rooms. It was, however, enough time for both the recording studio and the master bedroom. Never would I ever say no to her, but damn, was I glad we only had an hour. Any longer and my dick would've fallen off.

In the beginning of the pregnancy, Alexis' sexual appetite was non-existent, and it was completely understandable considering what happened during that time — she was traumatised for a few weeks following Gareth's death. The thing about Alexis, though, is she has an incredible ability to put on a brave face and deal with life's hurdles, as she puts it.

During those initial weeks, we comforted each other, both of us trying to move past the explosion, and I say the term 'move past' with some reservations, 'moving past' not being easily achievable. It wasn't until approximately a month afterward — and in amongst our comforting — that our sexual urges returned, our intimate moments helping heal the unspoken words of the tragic event. Then, for the weeks that followed, Alexis' morning sickness reared its ugly head, halting our recently restored libidos. *Why it is called morning sickness bloody stumps me. It's never just the mornings.*

Shortly after her constant need to vomit disappeared, her sexual desires increased tenfold. Now, don't get me wrong, I'm certainly not complaining. Her physical presence still drives me wild. It's just ... my dick fails to let my brain know that at times it is fucking whacked and in need of a rest.

* * *

'I can't believe you had Twister carpet put in,' Alexis laughs while watching the passing traffic on the Tullamarine Freeway. She turns to face me with a mischievous grin. 'You know, as soon as I've popped out BB, I'm challenging you to a game ... naked.'

We are on our way to collect Nate and Charlotte from school and then surprise them with the completed apartment.

'Why wait till after you give birth to challenge me?' I ask, curiously. I'm surprised that considering her current sex drive she hasn't penned in a game for this evening.

'Because you will have an unfair advantage.'

'How's that?' I chuckle while noticing her eyes spark wide.

'Because I can't easily twist and manoeuvre with a child growing within my womb.'

Before I can answer her, she shouts at the top of her lungs. 'Hey! Quick! Pull into 7-Eleven.'

Her sudden outburst shocks the shit out of me and has me veering into the service station. In a slight panic, I bring the car to an abrupt halt. 'What! What's wrong? Is everything okay?' I ask, fear gripping my insides as I reach over and place my hands on her stomach to inspect her for signs of distress.

'I need a Slurpee. A big one! Ooh, I hope they have bubblegum flavour,' she says with excitement while patting my slightly trembling hands before unbuckling her seat belt and climbing out of the car. Just before closing the door, she pokes her head back in. 'You want anything?'

Letting out a long sigh of relief, I respond. 'No. I'm all good.'

As I watch her lightly waddle through the shop doors, I drop my head to the steering wheel in exasperation. *Jesus fucking Christ! She will be the death of me.* Talk about giving me a heart attack and all for a frozen, crushed ice drink, saturated in sugar syrup. *Bloody pregnancy cravings.* When Alexis was pregnant with Bianca, she preferred potato chips dipped in ice cream and, as disgusting as that had been, I could stomach the notion and satisfy that particular craving for her when required. However, the shit she has been eating this time around nearly has me dry retching. I mean, who the hell eats pickles on toast with cheese and mayonnaise? And did I mention I caught her dipping a carrot into her glass of chocolate milk last week?

She walks back to the car, happily sucking on her Slurpee.

I smile. She is just so incredibly cute. 'Happy now?' I ask as she sits back in the car and buckles her seat belt.

Alexis sucks her straw, slurping loudly, then smiles back at me. 'Yep.'

'Good.'

She tilts her drink toward me. 'You want some?'

'No. That shit is basically liquid sugar.'

'And your problem is?' she asks while stirring the mixture around, seemingly unperturbed by my factual health statement.

I glance over at her, the sides of my mouth rising in a smug grin. 'My problem is that it's not good for you.'

'BB likes it. Look ...' she points to her stomach, her expression happily cocky, 'he just high fived me.'

Wearing a pair of maternity jeans and a tight fitting grey top, she is all baby-belly.

'Wait for it ...' she says in anticipation.

I humour her and wait, staring at her tummy.

'Ha! See?' she giggles as her tummy jerks ever so slightly, showcasing my son's movement. 'You like Slurpees just like Mummy does, don't you, BB?' she coos in her mummy-baby voice.

Seeing her stomach move like that fills me with a feeling of complete awe, love and astonishment. I could watch it all day. I remember back to the first time I felt BB kick. *BB? Bloody hell! I can't believe she has me referring to my son as the letter B squared.* Annoyed at myself for allowing such a ridiculous nickname for my unborn son, I decide I really need to do something about it sooner rather than later.

Bringing my gaze back to her happy face, I go to complain about the absurd name but am halted as I take in the joy radiating from her while she rubs her tummy.

'Mummy likes the bubblegum and cola flavour, BB, but next time we will try grape. What do you reckon?'

Her hand jerks again and we both laugh. I decide now is not the time to bury the nickname BB and, instead, return to my recollection of when I first felt my son move. It was shortly after we found out that he was a boy. We were lying in bed after just having a bath together, and Alexis was playfully singing 'Kiss You All Over' by Exile, because I had only just moments before kissed her all over. She'd started the chorus then paused mid-word .... 'He kicked!' she'd blurted out, looking at me as though being internally booted was extremely pleasurable. 'Quick! Quick! Give me your hand.' She'd then grabbed my hand and pressed it against her stomach. The wait for movement was the weirdest anticipation I had ever felt. I knew what a baby kicking my hand was like, because I had experienced Alexander do it to Lucy. But waiting to feel the first movement of my own child was ... well, it was surreal. Exciting, but strangely tense.

When that first bump finally nudged my hand, a sensation of sheer fucking joy had spread through me like wildfire. My child was alive, growing and playfully moving around inside the woman I love. I'd felt the joy from the smile plastered across my face travel to the heart pounding in my chest and right down to my feet which had been twitching with excitement. *Best bloody experience, ever!*

Sitting in the car at the 7-Eleven car park and fixing my stare toward Alexis' stomach where my son is happily practising his martial arts skills, I reach over and gently lay my hand across her bump. She looks up at me and her expression changes from cheeky playfulness to one of heartfelt love.

Placing her hand over mine, she asks our son to move again. 'Daddy wants a high five, BB.'

We wait for what seems like minutes when, in actual fact, it was probably only seconds. Our hands jerk in unison, causing my heart to pound with excitement. *Ah, there it is.*

'Good boy,' I praise him then gently fist-bump her tummy.

Alexis interlaces our fingers together then rests our hands on the centre console of the car and, with her free hand, lifts the Slurpee to her mouth, smiles and takes another loud gulp. I shake my head and grin, clenching her hand a little tighter to indicate a sense of amused affection. It's the little things like this without spoken words that I cherish with her. We fit each other so perfectly.

* * *

After picking up the kids from school, we head home. As we step into the elevator, I hit the penthouse button and stand back. Instantly, Nate questions my choice. The kid doesn't miss a beat; he is so switched on.

'Are we going to check the renovations?' he asks, curiously.

'No, even better,' I reply, waggling my eyebrows.

Nate wrinkles his forehead, then delighted understanding appears on his face in the form of wide eyes. 'It's finished? Are we moving back in?' he asks, looking from me to Alexis then back again.

Charlotte pauses in her dancing to non-existent music and shoots her head up. 'What?'

'I don't know, Bryce. Do you think they are ready to see their new home?' Alexis teasingly asks.

'Hmm, not sure,' I respond, going along with her charade. 'They may not like it.'

'Is my room pink?' Charlotte squeals, jumping up and down. 'Oh, I hope it's pink ... even pinker than last time. I love pink. Wait! I like purple too. Is it purple?'

'You are just going to have to wait and see, Charli-Bear,' Alexis states with a smile.

'I don't care what colour my room is, as long as it's not pink ... or purple ... or maybe even yellow,' Nate adds.

'Good, 'cause yours is white and blue, little fella,' I say proudly. 'Carn the mighty Cats!'

I watch his face as his eyes search mine for the slightest telltale sign that I'm bluffing. Nate is a one-eyed Bombers supporter like his mum.

'Mum,' Nate says hesitantly, 'please tell me he's joking.'

I glance at Alexis, trying not to laugh and give myself away. I wonder for a moment if she'll play along and tease Nate, or if she'll cave and stay true to her beloved football team. The inner struggle is evident on her face, and I can't help chuckling at her attempt to prevent it from screwing up.

'Nate, my little man,' she says with gritted teeth, while giving me that sexy fucking determined glare. She stands straight and smiles satisfactorily at me before turning her head to face her son. 'Would I ever let Bryce decorate your room in anything other than the Bombers colours?'

Nate sighs with relief. 'No. You wouldn't.' He then turns to me, and a spark of satisfaction appears to surge through him as he fires a shit-eating grin in my direction. 'When you least expect it, Bryce, you may find a clown sleeping in your bed.'

Alexis bursts out laughing. I, on the other hand, do not find that little threat funny at all.

'Really?' I ask Nate.

He just nods. *Yeah, I wonder who he gets his cockiness from.*

'Bryce,' Charlotte interrupts, her sweet angelic voice laced with concern. I feel her hand gently clasp mine. 'Clowns aren't real, you know. And neither are ghosts, or witches.' Her look of sincerity is both adorable and ... well ... humiliating. Here is a seven-year-old girl telling a thirty-seven-year-old man not to be afraid of clowns because they aren't real, when in fact they freakin' are. In this moment my testosterone levels sink dramatically. *I'm a fucking coulrophobic pansy.*

I pull her to my side and give her a hug. 'Thanks, Charli.'

Alexis, who is still trying to refrain from laughing at my awkward I-have-no-balls moment, winks at Charli. Fortunately, the doors to the elevator open. We all step out and Alexis and I hang back, my arm around her shoulder and hers around my waist. We watch excitement filter through the kids as they explore their new surroundings.

'It's just like before, but it's not,' Nate says, displaying an expression of slight confusion.

'I don't know about the brown, Mum,' Charlotte says with aversion.

'What's wrong with the brown?'

'Brown is poo colour.'

Alexis laughs. 'It's also chocolate colour.'

Charlotte spins around slowly with her hands on her hips. 'Yeah, but it's not pretty.'

'We don't want the lounge area to be pretty,' I explain.

'Why not?' *Because it's a goddamn lounge, not a fairy palace.*

Alexis squeezes my hip, then lets go. 'If you want pretty, Charli, go see your room.'

Charlotte squeals that high-pitched, burst-my-fucking-eardrums squeal that she is good at, then makes her way upstairs. Nate, Alexis and I follow behind.

The new staircase spirals round in a large curve, deliberately designed that way so it feels like you are walking up a hill rather than a steep incline. Alexis was adamant when we discussed the new designs that she did not want a vertical staircase. And I honestly can't say that I blame her. I think her fall from a year ago still plays on her mind. It probably always will.

Nate calls out from his room, 'Sick!' and I know immediately what he has just found.

'Oh my god!' Charlotte squeals and, again, I know why.

I turn to Alexis, stopping her in her tracks. 'You take Charli. My ears can't handle her vocal range. I'll take Nate,' I say, before hurrying off to Nate's room. His surprise is far more appealing to me than Charli's replacement 4Life memorabilia.

When I walk through his door, he is already opening the boxes. 'These are awesome!' he says, sheer delight covering his face.

I'm fully aware of how awesome they are, having wanted to try one out for days. 'These are the Walkera HM Airwolfs,' I explain to him.

Nate rotates one of the boxes, taking in the picture. 'Sweet!'

He has no idea just *how* sweet these babies are.

Nate and I sit on the floor of his room, wasting no time in putting the remote control helicopters together. Nate hangs on every word that I say as I instruct him in the assembly of the aircraft. Appreciation and fondness fill me when I look at him, as I see his mother's determination and intelligence, not to mention he has her blue eyes. From the moment I met Nate — that time he came to visit his mum's place of work — I found it easy to form a bond with him. He has so much of Alexis flowing through him and possesses an uncanny ability to read most situations. He really is a smart and loving kid.

'Spin that rotor blade there, Nate,' I instruct.

He does what he's told, then smiles as it spins effortlessly. 'It works!'

'I think we are done,' I say in response and get up from my seated position on the floor.

'Thanks, Bryce. I like doing these things with you.'

The honesty in his words and on his face pulls at my heart. I have no doubt that I love him like a father does. But at the same time, I am fully aware that he has a father, a father who loves him dearly. One thing that I never want to do is step on Rick's toes where Nate and Charli are concerned, but that doesn't mean I cannot love them and show them that in my own way.

'You're welcome, mate,' I say as I scruff his hair with my hand. And, as always, he jerks his head away playfully. 'I like doing these things with you, too. Now, let's get these babies up in the air where they belong.'

We place them down on the desk and take a step back, pointing the radio transmitters in their direction. With a hum and a buzz, both of them hover off the desk. I take control instantly, circling it around the room. Nate, however, requires a little longer to perfect his new piloting skills. Surprisingly, though, he takes a lot less time than I expected he would need and before I know it, we have them flying beautifully out of the room. Nate follows me into the passageway, our eyes trained intently on the hovering choppers.

Alexis and Charli duck out of our way with a scream.

'Shit! Sorry,' I smile apologetically.

'My bad!' Nate chimes in, a little less remorseful.

Alexis shakes her head and pulls Charli to her side. 'I knew those things were a bad idea. Did you have to buy two of them?'

'Actually,' I reply with a smirk while keeping my vision solely on my helicopter and slowly walking past Alexis and Charlotte, 'I bought four.' I head for the stairs, Nate in tow.

'Four! Why four? I don't want one,' Alexis exclaims, with a little disgust.

'It's not for you.'

'Who's it fo—' She cuts herself off and sighs. 'Bryce, BB's not even born yet.'

CHAPTER

4

The buzzer to the door sounds, indicating Rick's arrival to pick up Nate and Charli for the weekend.

Standing in the kitchen, I finish preparing a spinach, cheese and tomato omelette for Alexis' lunch, the dish full of protein, folic acid and magnesium, which I found out is not only good for her but also good for our baby.

I wipe my hands on the tea towel and toss it on the benchtop before heading into the lounge. When I walk into the room, I spot Rick behind Alexis, his hand on her shoulder and the other pushed firmly into her lower back.

Neither of them seem to notice me at first, and as I stand there watching him place his hands on her, assisting with whatever the fuck he is assisting with, it makes my blood boil.

'Is it there?' Rick asks her.

'Yeah,' she winces. 'It's not as bad as when I carried Charli, but it still hurts.'

'Thought as much. I could tell straight away when I walked in that it was bothering you.'

Not being able to stand there any longer and watch their exchange, and wanting to know what is hurting Alexis and why Rick knows about it and I don't, I make my presence known. 'Is everything all right?' I ask, desperately trying to curb my resentment.

Rick drops his hands and takes a step back just as Alexis straightens and stretches, arching her back and poking out her tummy. The discomfort on her face is obviously present. *Where the fuck has this soreness come from?*

'Yeah,' she murmurs, unaware of the fact that what I just witnessed between her and Rick has unsettled me.

'Bryce,' Rick says with a nod of his head while extending his hand.

The last thing I want to do is shake the fucker's hand, wanting to break it instead for providing relief to my pregnant fiancée's back. I really can't help it. Seeing him with her pisses me off, infusing me with jealousy. But at the same time, I know deep down inside that my response to their interaction with one another is completely unreasonable. Regardless, he still irritates me.

I honestly hate feeling this way. I'm not normally the jealous type. And I'm not afraid to say the reason for this is probably due to the fact I always get what I want. I'm never in a position to be jealous in the first place, so this feeling is somewhat foreign to me, only having felt it one time before — when Alexis was married.

Begrudgingly, I shake Rick's hand as I stand by Alexis and instantly place my hand on her lower back, wanting to remove his touch and replace it with my own.

'Not long to go now,' Rick suggests, nodding toward Alexis' stomach.

'No. Four weeks and two days,' I reply, wanting to reiterate that I know exactly how long.

'Well, yeah, if she delivers on her due date. Alexis tends to go into labour early.' He smiles at her knowingly, and it takes every bit of restraint I have to not knock him the fuck out.

'Dad!' Charli yells, as she comes around the large central pillar that leads to the stairs.

'Princess! Come and give me a big hug.'

Charli drops her shiny pink suitcase and launches herself at Rick.

He lifts her up and places her on his hip, grimacing playfully. 'You've grown again since I saw you last.'

'Well, yeah, Dad!' Charli rolls her eyes. 'I slept four times since then, so I've grown four times. Miss James says you grow in your sleep. Did you know that?'

'I do now. Where's my kiss?' Rick asks, puckering his lips like an idiot.

I notice Alexis smiling at their exchange and it irritates me even more.

'Nate, come on,' Rick yells. 'We've got the footy this afternoon.'

'Coming. Geez, don't go all loco on me,' Nate answers while entering the room.

'Loco?'

'Don't ask, Rick,' Alexis says before giving both Nate and Charli a kiss goodbye. 'Now be good, and I'll see you after school on Monday.'

They hug their mum before fist-bumping me and then walking out the door.

I waste no time in finding out what the hell is wrong with Alexis' back. 'Want to tell me what's wrong with your back?' I ask, my tone deliberately snappy.

She gives me an unsure look. 'I get back spasms. Why? What's wrong? Why are you angry?'

'Because this is the first I'm hearing of it. Yet *he* seems to know all about them.'

I hate speaking to her with such anger in my voice, but I can't help it. Her ex-husband just pisses me right off. Look, there's not a day that goes by where I don't feel a slight bit of guilt for moving in on Alexis when she was married to the scumbag. After all, I'm not a heartless bastard. I think what angers me the most where Rick is concerned, is what he did to her — cheating on her right after she gave birth to Charlotte when she was at her most vulnerable. The thing is, if he hadn't fucked up on an epic scale like he had, she may still be married to him. So it's bittersweet in a way.

'Really, Bryce? You're angry because Rick knows that I get back spasms?' she asks with a roll of her eyes.

Her blatant dismissal of my unease at being kept in the dark angers me even more. 'I'm pissed off because *I* don't know about them.'

'Well, sorrrryyy,' she says, sardonically drawing out the word. 'I didn't realise I needed to tell you absolutely everything. How about I make you a list?' She places her hands on her hips. 'Number one ...' she begins, raising her hands and pointing to a finger. 'My feet have begun to swell and look like little bloated piglets. See?' She kicks off her shoe, sending it hurtling through the air and into the lounge. 'Feel free to oink at them, they may respond.'

The notion that her feet can resemble piglets makes me want to laugh, and I feel my anger toward her slipping away.

'Two ...' She points to another finger, clearly not finished with her defensive tirade. 'My nipples are dry and sore and starting to leak colostrum. Would you like to hear more?' she asks, pausing only for a second. 'Good, 'cause I'll give you more,' she continues, not allowing me the option to refuse. 'I have the constant need to urinate. I feel like I could shit a brick. I have heartburn from hell. And I am so hungry I could eat a horse.'

Colostrum? What the fuck is colostrum? And why is it leaking from her nipples?

I don't answer her for a minute as I try to process the list she has just heatedly rattled off, a list I need to get onto. The fact she could eat a horse stands out to me as the first problem I can solve.

My absent reply — I can only assume — frustrates her further as she huffs and starts to turn away. 'They are just back spasms, Bryce. I didn't think it was that important.'

I soften my voice, feeling like an absolute piece of shit for making her upset. 'Honey, everything to do with you and our baby is important.'

She stops, turns back around and sighs, exhaustion clearly present. 'Honestly, they come and go. They haven't bothered me until recently. I used to get them a lot when I was pregnant with Charli, which is why Rick caught onto it straightaway. I'm not deliberately keeping my ailments from you.'

I take the remaining steps between us and place my hands on her shoulders. 'I want to know everything, EVERYTHING that is happening with that body of yours. I can't help if you don't tell me what is going on.'

Wrapping her hands around my waist, she closes the remaining distance between us as she pulls herself to me, the gorgeous bulge in her belly preventing our complete unity. 'Okay, but you can't help me shit a brick, or stop me from constantly peeing.'

'No, but I can dish you up a horse.'

She laughs. 'I know my cravings are crazy, but steed sandwiches are definitely a no-no.'

'What's colostrum?' I ask, my thoughts back to her nipples.

She pulls away and smiles, then lets out an adorable giggle. 'It's pre-breastmilk.'

Pre-breastmilk? I can't help but look at her breasts.

Suddenly, I feel a slap and a push to my chest and she is no longer in my arms.

'I'm not going to drown you in it, you know,' Alexis deadpans as she walks away.

'What? I ... I didn't say that.'

I quickly take off, capturing her and holding her back to my front.

'You didn't have to,' she says in a sulky voice. 'You looked at my breasts as though they were ready to shoot at you like a fire hose.'

I laugh out loud. 'I did not. Although ...' Feeling her struggle to free herself from my arms, I hold her tighter, her freedom not even an option. 'I'm kidding. No, seriously, I just thought they couldn't leak anything until after BB is born. And speaking of BB, can we please discuss names? I really cannot bring myself to call him that any more.'

'Why not? It's cute.' She drops her head back onto my shoulder and looks up at me with a smirk. 'I was actually thinking of calling him that officially.'

I squint at her, narrowing my gaze and trying to assess whether she is bluffing or not. 'Don't kid a kidder, my love.'

'I'm not.'

'You better be, because there is no way in hell we are naming our son BB.'

She bites the inside of her bottom lip and smiles. 'Fine, but I at least want his name to begin with B.'

'Why?'

'No reason,' she shrugs.

Leaning forward, I plant a quick kiss on her forehead, causing her eyes to close momentarily. I love how her eyelids fall heavy for the smallest of moments when I kiss her. It shows her vulnerability to my touch. 'Okay, the letter B it is. It's a good letter.' I confidently grin at her.

'Hmm, I know,' she moans, arching her head back further, her lips reaching for mine.

Lowering my head so that I can give her what she wants, what I want — what I always want, to taste her — I savour the feel of her sweet, warm mouth and the soft, silky glide of her tongue against mine. She tastes like the most delectable form of oral consumption known to man, and I am the lucky son of a bitch who exclusively gets to consume her.

Regretfully, I separate my mouth from hers and pull away. 'I have a little work to do. Your lunch is ready and waiting for you in the kitchen.'

She pouts, and it's so fucking lovable. 'Thank you ... and fine, you important businessman. I have a date with a very naughty priest anyway.'

What naughty priest? This is the first I've heard of Alexis being religious.
I pull my head back from her in slight disbelief. 'Priest?'

'Yes, Father Stearns.'

'Are you Catholic?'

'No. But after reading this book, I'm thinking of possibly converting.'

'What book?'

She laughs and gives me a little shove. 'Never mind. Go, go and do what you do.'

I take a few steps backward in the direction of my office, still confused by this Stearns bloke.

Still laughing, Alexis blows me a kiss. 'Don't look so concerned.'

'I'm not. I'm not scared of a priest.'

As I turn and open the door to my office, I hear her mumble something barely audible until I hear the word clown.

I pause.

'I love you,' she calls out, giggling.

'Hmm,' is my only response.

* * *

I spend the next hour looking up baby names beginning with the letter B. Let's just ignore the fact that I am supposed to be finalising the complex's involvement in the upcoming AFL Grand Final celebrations, because the thought of giving my son a name is far more important.

'Bailey,' I say to myself. *Nah, too much like Irish cream.* 'Bane,' I voice with a wishy-washy tone. *Hmm.*

I decide to check the meaning behind that particular name. 'Son of a farmer.' *No, that won't do, although he is the grandson of a farmer.*

I keep scanning.

'Beaver?' *Are you fucking for real, who would call their son Beaver?* 'Bowel?' *Now that's just cruel.* I shake my head and keep reading down the list. 'Boyd.' *Maybe.* It does say that Boyd means blond-haired, and I'm fairly certain our son will be blond.

Scanning further down the list, I spot my name. Curious as to its meaning, I read on. 'Ambitious and quick-witted.' I smile and nod. *Fuckin' oath, I am.*

My phone rings, breaking my attention from the name searching. I pick it up and notice Derek's goofy-looking face on my screen. 'Hey, mate. What's goin' on?'

'I was thinking 'bout the intro song for the next gig. How 'bout "Birth" by 30STM?' Derek suggests, apparently forgetting the courtesy of a greeting.

'Yeah, nice! Have you spoken to Will about it? That song has a killer beat.'

'Yeah, Will's on board.'

'Good. I guess we open with "Birth" then,' I reply, still gazing at the list of names on the screen in front of me.

'You busy?'

'No, not really, just looking up baby names.'

'Call the little tacker Derek.'

'Fuck off, dickhead. I'm not calling him Derek.'

'Why? It means "big knob".'

I roll my eyes even though he can't see it. 'Yeah, you can say that again.'

Ignoring my insult, Derek continues. 'He who owns largest cock. Almighty and powerful with massive dong.'

While he's spinning bullshit into my ear, I look up the real meaning of his name. 'You are bloody shittin' me,' I say out loud.

'What? You just looked up my name, didn't you? What's it say? It says big cock, doesn't it?'

'No. It says full of shit,' I answer, closing the subject when really it had said 'the people's ruler'. I'll be damned if I'm going to tell him that, he loves and worships himself enough as it is.

'What did it say? I wanna know.'

'Look it up yourself. Hey, while I've got you, Alexis wanted to know if you and Carly could come round for dinner tonight.'

'I'll check with the missus and get back to you. It should be fine though. Hey, you cookin'?'

I smile at his reference to Carly as his 'missus'. Derek has never been the settling down type. For some reason though, Carly has managed to whip his playboy ways into submission.

'Yeah, I'm cookin'. Ain't I always?'

'I want that pasta stuff you made a while back.'

I know which 'pasta stuff' he is referring to because he helped himself to about four servings. 'No can do. It has ricotta in it. Alexis can't eat that. It could be harmful to the baby.'

'Ah, shit!' he groans.

'I'll do a lasagne. That all right?'

'Done.'

'Good. Talk to Carly and let me know. Dinner is at 6 p.m.'

'Will do, mate.'

We disconnect the call, and I return my attention back to the names in front of me. So far I've jotted down Boyd and Billy. I lean back in my chair and run my hands through my hair, feeling frustrated. *How can you name your son when you haven't seen him yet? What if he doesn't look like a Billy or a Boyd?*

I decide to give up my search for the time being and discuss it with Alexis later ... in bed ... where I hold all the power.

Locking my fingers together behind my head, I smile satisfactorily to myself, now visualising her on the cusp of climax, her orgasm teetering on the very edge, ready to wash over her in sensational waves. The mental picture I now have affords me a sense of total domination, not to mention a stiff dick. Because it's in those moments when she is lying underneath me that she will do and say anything I ask. It's in those moments where I hold the supremacy. Those moments are my favourite form of control.

CHAPTER

5

'Mm, that smells delicious,' Alexis moans from behind me as she wraps her arms around my waist.

Just the sound of her moan — whether or not it holds a sexual undertone — stirs my dick within my pants. How she manages to do this to me so often has me perplexed ... but not in a bad way.

'Here, have a taste.' I turn to face her and hold up a spoon containing some of my Bolognese sauce for her to try.

Watching as she gently blows on the spoon through her sweet plump lips, my dick now decides that he too, wants in on some of her blowing action.

She takes the spoon into her mouth, her lips pressing together around the stainless steel implement, and I can't help but watch like it's the most intriguing sight to be seen by anyone, anytime. Suddenly, the lids of her eyes spring apart, and her intently focussed and astonished stare finds mine. Appreciation radiates from her face as I drag the spoon back out of her mouth, deliberately wiping some of the remnants across her lips and chin as I remove it. She raises her hand to wipe my apparently clumsy smear when I gently grab it midair.

Our eyes lock, ignite and burn each other with intense passion, love, yearning and lust.

Slowly shaking my head at her and indicating that she not wipe her face, I bring her hand to my lips, pressing a soft kiss on her wrist. She smells like flowers and musk, and her skin delicately caresses my face as I drag my cheek and lips across it.

As I softly place each kiss up the inside of her arm — gradually making my way to my destination — her breathing becomes rapid, her chest rising and falling in short bursts. I notice her eyelids flutter with each press of my lips, together with the subtle shade of pink forming across both of her cheeks.

Smiling with a sense of fulfilment as a man who knows how to satisfy his woman, I let go of her hand as my mouth reaches her neck, nibbling and sucking her most sensitive spots.

'You are so good at that,' she says with praise, as she draws in a ragged breath.

'Honey, I'm fucking good at a lot of things,' I mumble into her skin.

Threading her hands into my hair, she grips it tightly. 'Don't I know it.'

Alexis tugs my head mildly, yet with enough assertiveness to send a searing jolt of wicked excitement right through me and down to my twitching cock. A cock which is aware of its impending duty to stiffen and take form, rubbing the satin of my boxer shorts and hardening against my denim jeans. The now confining space in my pants gives me an increasing urge to unleash my erection and slide it into her warm wet pussy.

I know she's wet; it never takes me long to have her drenched with arousal. *Fuck!*

'Alexis,' I growl, as I push my hips against her and raise my lips to the corner of her mouth. With a quick glide of my tongue, I remove the sauce I deliberately planted there.

She doesn't allow me long to linger at that spot, seizing my mouth with her own in an aggressive, yet passionate attack. We taste each other, suck each other, lick each other and moan one another's name.

Alexis reaches between us and undoes my fly, the sound of the zipper's release assisting my already hardened state. She yanks down my jeans and boxer shorts in one swift move, allowing my cock to spring free with relief, only to be surrounded once again, this time by warm and possessive hands.

Frenzied and visibly hankering, she grips my shaft and then slowly glides both hands up it as though she is praying in thanks for the privilege. Little does she know the privilege is all mine.

'Honey, I fucking love it when you stroke me like that,' I groan into her mouth before licking her bottom lip, teasingly.

She runs her tongue over the spot I have just tasted and pulls away slightly. 'What else do you fucking love me doing to your cock?' she asks, wicked intentions blaring from her.

Alexis is my angel, the most pure light in my life. Yet when I stir sexual desire within her, the sinful, carnal and unashamed amatory devil emerges. I have the best of both worlds and I fucking love it.

'Well?' she asks, her voice saturated in innocence.

The sensation that her hands are applying to my cock renders me momentarily speechless, as if she has cast a spell of lip-paralysing pleasure. I try to respond, but then she sticks her pointer finger in my mouth and caresses my tongue before taking her finger back out again. I watch eagerly as she reaches back down between us and swirls the now moist digit over the top of my crown. *Jesus fucking Christ!* 'Tell me, Bryce. Do you like it when I make it wet? Kiss it? Lick it? And suck it?' she asks, the intent behind her eyes unmissable, despite her innocent grin.

'Yes,' I hiss, leaning back against the counter.

Alexis goes to kneel in front of me and, as much as I find it incredibly sexy seeing her on her knees, I can't find it within myself to let her kneel on the floor in her current condition.

I gently stop her by placing my hands on her shoulders. 'Wait!'

'What? What's wrong?'

'I can't have you kneeling on the floor, my love,' I inform her, as I sweep a loose tendril of hair away from her face.

Hoisting myself up on the benchtop, I provide a more comfortable height and position for her to take me in her mouth. 'Better?'

She smiles lovingly at me and steps between my legs, taking hold of my cock once more. 'Aw, such a gentleman,' she drawls.

'Do you like it when I'm a gentleman?'

'Yes ... and sometimes no.'

'What do you want me to be now?'

Smiling seductively, she lowers her head. 'I want to you shut up and let me suck your cock,' she replies, mumbling the last couple of words as she envelops my hard length with her mouth. *Fuck me! She sucks better than a Dyson. I swear all vacuums would bow at her feet if they were aware of her talents.*

Her lips glide up and down my shaft as her hand slowly pumps my base, the building pressure in the head of my dick nothing short of sensational. I love it when she takes me in her mouth, the feelings she elicits with her lips and tongue. But what I love most of all is watching her head bob continuously while her mischievous eyes fuck me, those eyes and the passion within them ruling me completely. Let's face it, it's moments like this that cement the fact I would walk to the ends of the earth for Alexis. Yes, it's only a blow job, but I am a bloke after all and, truth be told, it's a fucking awesome blow job.

She cups my balls, making my cock tighten and my jaw clench, bringing me one step closer to exploding with release. I notice her lips dance a playful smile which makes me instantly aware of what she is about to do, this expression always leading to her favourite move. She tongues the tip of my crown like a lollipop, causing me to jerk uncontrollably. *Bloody hell!*

Just as I'm about ready to blow, the buzzer to the door sounds. Alexis pauses, looking like a deer in the headlights, except this little doe has a rock-hard cock protruding from her mouth.

'That better not be Santa,' she mumbles around my dick. *Santa? As in Father Christmas?*

'Who's Santa? Apart from the obvious,' I ask.

'Never mind,' she mumbles once more.

The buzzer sounds again, and the look in her eyes asks me what she should do. Sitting and staring at her beautifully compromised face, there's no question what I want. There's no question what any man would want. *Finish me off! Only the inhumane would leave a man on the brink of ejaculation.*

She nods, appearing to nod more to herself than me, and then pumps me vigorously as she sucks with sheer intention. I climb with the building sensation in my dick once again, and this time spill over the edge and into her mouth.

Seconds later I am zipping myself up as the buzzer rings for the third or fourth time, I'm not quite sure. I hand Alexis a tissue, pour her a glass of water and ask if she needs anything else.

'I'm fine. Go answer the door.'

I grab her and kiss her, caressing her beautiful face. 'I fucking love you.'

'Yes, I know,' she smiles, as she gives me a quick peck on the lips and then takes a drink.

Jogging out of the kitchen and toward the entry door, I can't help but grin the satisfied grin of a man well looked after.

'What took you so long?' Derek asks as I open the door to let him and Carly inside. They both stare at me for a couple of seconds as though they want an answer and, just as I'm about to reply with 'None of your fucking business', Derek slaps me on the back. 'On second thoughts, no need to enlighten me,' he says with a cocky grin on his face before walking past me.

'Hey, Bryce,' Carly greets cheerfully, giving me one of her flirty hugs.

I've come to realise that Carly will always be quite willing to allow her hands to linger on my biceps just that little bit longer than necessary. But, I must admit, her level of flirtation has significantly dropped since she hooked up with Derek, this being a good thing. Not only for Derek, but also for my biceps.

'Where's Lexi?'

'Kitchen.' I nod in the direction from where I just came ... *literally.*

Carly smiles and disappears around the corner.

'Speaking of kitchen, smells awesome as usual,' Derek says as he looks around the apartment. 'Wow! This place looks different. Not so much the bachelor pad anymo—'

'You did!' Carly screeches from the kitchen, interrupting our conversation. 'You little whore!'

I furrow my brow. The thought of Alexis being called a whore does not sit well with me, but, for some reason, coming from Carly, I manage to let it go.

Derek just shakes his head and smiles. 'That girl of mine's mouth needs a filter ... then again ...' he ponders, 'I do love it dirty.'

'I don't want to know about Carly's dirty mouth,' I say with certitude, all the while thinking of Alexis' sweet mouth and the sublime thing she just did with it.

'You just got your dick wet, didn't you?' Derek pokes.

Ignoring the pervert's question, I change the subject. 'Want to see the new recording studio?'

Derek rubs his hands together greedily, dismissing my digression. 'That's what I thought. It doesn't normally take that long for you to answer the door. Plus, you have that I-have-a-happy-cock look on your face.'

I continue to ignore him as we make our way to the recording studio. His reaction to my newly refurbished room will be retribution for his perverted probing.

Opening the door, I wait for it with keen anticipation.

'What the fuck? Dude, this isn't *Playschool*,' he says with a crooked grin on his face and his hands resting on top of his head.

I knew the boys would find the new addition of soft teddies and toy trucks amusing, so I inwardly chuckle to myself. 'No, but when the baby is born, he'll need some toys to play with.'

I walk over to the computer equipment and switch it on.

'Doesn't he have his own toy room? Ya know, other than in our recording space?'

'Of course he does, but I want to spend as much time as I can with him after he's born. They grow so quickly, you know. Look at Alexander. He's already one and a half.'

'I know how old Alexander is,' he grumbles while taking in the new surroundings.

'Look, I don't want to miss a thing if I can help it.'

'I get that. But I don't know, man. Won't it be too loud for him? Baby's ears are kinda small.'

I laugh at the stupid fucker. 'Of course they are small, and anyway, I'm one step ahead of you.' I make my way over to the wicker basket on the floor near the rug and pick up a pair of tiny, fluffy, earmuffs. 'See? It's covered.'

At that moment, Carly and Alexis walk in carrying a couple of beers and wine — Alexis drinking her non-alcoholic rosé.

'This is, um, interesting,' Carly stutters as she takes in the toys.

'You can say that again,' Derek mutters, then turns his back and starts typing on the keyboard.

Scanning the room and its surroundings, I feel proud and excited, knowing my son will — in matter of weeks — be sharing this space. It couldn't be more perfect.

Alexis passes me my beer and stands beside me. 'Yes, I know. I told Bryce that putting toys in here was going a little overboard, but he insisted.'

With my free hand, I slide it behind her back, stopping to rest just above her arse. As always, she snuggles into my side.

'Overboard?' Carly questions a little sarcastically. 'There's a freakin' coloured-ball pit over there. And is that Twister carpet?'

'Sure is. Alexis' idea,' I say proudly before swigging my beer. 'Isn't it great? We have it in many of our family-friendly rooms over in the City Promenade building.'

Carly makes her way over to the colourful spotted carpet. 'It's awesome! I want some.'

'That can be arranged,' I inform.

'I reckon the school would benefit from some as well. Alexis, you could seriously be on to something here.'

I take another swig of my beer and gently caress Alexis' lower back. 'That's what I told her.'

'What? No, it's just a bit of fun.' She dismisses our praise and takes a casual sip of her drink.

'Ah, Bryce, here it is.'

I reluctantly step away from her warmth and walk over to Derek to see what he has found. 'Here's what?'

'Backing music for "Birth". Unless you want to hire a friggin' orchestra and some taiko drums.'

I raise my eyebrow at him.

'Well ... shit, Bryce!' Derek shrugs. 'I never know with you. I wouldn't put it past you to hire the bloody Melbourne Symphony Orchestra.'

'Good on you, I'm not that bad. Backing music is fine. Although I think Will may have a taiko.'

'Sweet! And Luce can handle the electronics on the board. So it's set then, we are opening with "Birth".'

'What else are you going to play?' Alexis asks.

I turn and watch her fiddling with some of the soft toys in the play area, her hand gently caressing a pale blue teddy bear's head. She places it back in the wicker basket then finds my eyes when she realises I haven't answered her question. We have a moment of unspoken words, something we do often, even more so lately than ever before. Right now I'm telling her that she looks fucking beautiful while pondering our son's imminent entry into our lives, and her return stare tells me that she knows what I'm thinking and how I feel about her.

'You two make me gag sometimes,' Carly complains, breaking our silent moment.

'You're just jealous,' Alexis retorts as she closes the gap between us.

'Am not,' Carly mumbles and turns her back to Derek, her face displaying a shade of crimson.

Clearly she is.

Leaning against the pool table, I watch Alexis approach me and drape her arms over my shoulders. My hands automatically find her belly, and I tenderly rub the precious spot.

Ghosting my lips with her own, she asks the question again. 'So, what else are you going to play?'

'What do you want me to play?'

A very subtle moan sounds from the back of her throat; at the same time she delicately licks her lips, lustful desire rolling from her. I love the way my playing the guitar has such a positive affect on her, her reaction always such a turn-on. I must admit though, watching her play the guitar has the same lust-fuelling affect on me too, not to mention the reason why she learned. It still blows me away.

I remember her surprising me, playing at one of our gigs while singing 'The Only Exception'. I was completely stunned and in awe of her capacity to gain this new skill without me even knowing, together with how completely amazing she looked, performed and sang. In that moment, up on that stage, no one except her had existed, her voice carrying a superb musical message which was for my ears only. It was something I would never ever forget, because it was her way of letting me know that no matter what we experienced together in life, we would always pull through.

Since that day, Alexis has been learning more of the basics and is a natural with a guitar. In fact, she is a natural musician. I've given her a few private lessons myself, but the both of us never really get far when I'm teaching; instead we end up on the floor in a sexually charged tangle of body and limbs. Unfortunately, I'm thinking that if she is serious about learning the guitar properly, maybe it's best Derek continues to teach her. After all, he has done a good job so far.

'I'd love to see you all do a Kings of Leon song,' Alexis purrs, bringing me back to the present. She lowers her head and whispers into my ear, her warm breath tickling my lobe. 'You know what their music does to me.'

And there it is, her ability to so easily drive me wild, my cock now wanting out of his pen and into hers. All it took was the sound of her suggestive voice.

'Oh, yeah?' I swallow and grip her tight arse. 'What did you have in mind?'

'"The End",' she says with a salacious smile.

Derek interrupts our moment by singing the first line of the song while playing air guitar like a member of an eighties hair band. Not surprisingly, the talented fucker actually nails the tone and lyrics of the song. Alexis smiles and turns her head toward him, at the same time baring her neck which is only centimetres from my mouth. The smooth, soft skin before me begs to be stroked by my tongue, the fresh floral notes rolling off her, mesmerising me. I lean in and whisper into her ear, 'Do you want me to play it now?'

She turns, her lips just touching mine. 'You know it?'

'I do.'

'Then, yes, Mr Clark, play it for me.'

I push off from the pool table and bend down to kiss her stomach then head for my Gibson ES-137.

Slinging it over my shoulder, I hand Derek the bass and raise my eyebrow at him. 'Lexi wants a quick demo.' I plug the amp in, tune it with a few strums and wait for Derek to count himself in.

As I play my first chord, I take in the sheer worship and adoration in the sparkle of Alexis' eyes. It's one of the best fucking sights imaginable.

* * *

Later that night in bed, I gently caress her tired body.

'I shouldn't have attempted to play Twister,' she groans.

'Not your brightest idea, my love,' I agree with a smile as I sit up on the bed. 'Where are you sore?'

'My piglets are hurting and my back needs to man-up,' she replies almost sulkily, her gloomy pout so damn cute.

'Here, let me show some love to those piggies.'

'No!' she snaps.

'Alexis, let me rub your bloody feet,' I state, my tone displaying that I'm not in the mood for her objecting to her feet being touched.

She growls then surrenders, placing them on my lap. 'Fine.'

Taking a hold of one foot, I lightly pinch her big toe with my fingers, giving it a gentle wiggle. 'This little piggy went to market ...' I begin.

Knowing she will try to kick me, I quickly secure both her feet tightly, but not tight enough to cause any discomfort. The ankle she broke just over a year ago still gives her a little grief.

'You're mean,' she pouts.

Chuckling, I place a soft kiss on the ankle in question and start to lightly massage the bottom of her foot. 'So, I looked up some baby names —'

'Did you?' she smiles. 'And ... any you like?'

'Nothing that screams "my son". Anyway, how can we name him without seeing him first? The name we pick may not suit him.'

'Pfft, I picked out Nate and Charli's names when I was nine years old.'

I swap her feet, gently placing one down and picking up the other. 'What?'

'Sure did. Jen and I were playing in our cubbyhouse with our dolls. We got to talking about who we were going to marry when we grew up and how many kids we were going to have. That's when I chose those names.'

'You didn't change your mind at all?' I ask, both shocked and a little unconvinced.

Alexis yawns and closes her eyes. 'Nope, I loved those names when I was young and I still love them to this day.'

'What if Rick hadn't liked them?'

She shrugs her shoulders, eyes still closed. 'It would've been stiff shit ... a deal-breaker,' she explains, the corners of her mouth lifting into a smug smile. 'He liked them though, so it was easy really.'

Lightly tickling the side of her arch, I watch her lying there peacefully. 'You are incredibly stubborn, you know.'

'I know someone who gives me a run for my money,' she murmurs.

'So, who did you decide you were going to marry when you grew up?' I ask, curious as to her childhood crush. A sudden dread passes over me, fearing her answer to be Rick. I really don't want to hear that.

'Tom Cruise,' she sighs then opens her eyes and props herself up on her elbows. 'It was because I thought he was a fighter pilot in real life,' she says, while waggling her eyebrows and grinning like the Cheshire cat.

'He's got nothing on me, honey.'

She laughs and drops her head back before bringing it upright again. 'I know, he's not even good enough to be your wingman. So, what names did you look up?'

I screw up my nose, still not overly happy with my results. 'Boyd, which means blond-haired. I figure BB will be blond.' *Fucking BB, she has brainwashed me, I swear.*

'I think that's safe to say,' she smiles. 'What else?'

'Billy.'

'What does Billy mean?'

'I can't remember.'

'So why did you choose it?'

'No reason.'

She narrows her eyes at me, and I can't hide my sly grin.

'Bryce, you're lying.'

'I am not.'

'Yes, you are. Why Billy?'

Realisation spreads across her face 'Oh ... hang on a minute. No way. If you are suggesting Billy because of Billy Brownless, you can forget it. No way is my son going to be named after a Cats player. No way in hell. Pick another name.'

I laugh. She knows me too well. 'You pick one then.'

'Fine. Brayden.'

I repeat the name in my head a few times. *Brayden? Brayden?* The more I say it, the more I like it.

'I was going with Bracken,' she continues, ''cause it has all our initials in it, like Bianca did. But I just don't like the sound of Bracken as much as I like Brayden. Plus, Brayden means brave. Bracken means "Braccas's Town" and that's just stupid.'

'Brayden ... I like it. But I still think we need to see if it will suit him first.'

'Whatever,' she huffs happily, while laying back down and closing her eyes. 'I'm telling you, it won't matter. Babies don't look like any name in particular when they are born. They grow into their names.'

I shake my head at her stubbornness once again. 'How do the piglets feel now?'

'Better, thank you.' She yawns again.

'What about a middle name?' I ask.

'I've already picked that one.'

'Is it a deal-breaker?' I probe, playfulness in my voice. *Nothing is a deal-breaker for us where I am concerned.*

'No. But I think you'll approve. At least I hope you will.'

'Uh huh. Well ... what is it?'

She opens one eye and screws up her face, reluctant to answer.

'Tell me. But before you do, if you say Hird or Lloyd or any other Bombers player's name, we will have to forge a deal of the century.'

'Lauchie,' she says softly, her eyes searching mine for approval.

Lauchie ... after my little brother. My heart hammers in my chest and emotion fills my entire body. This woman never ceases to amaze me. Just when I think I can't possibly love her any more than I already do, she does or says something else that has me worshipping her further.

I climb back under the covers and bring her close to me, kissing her lips passionately. 'It's perfect, my love. And so are you.'

CHAPTER

6

I know I've said this before, but honestly, I love watching Alexis sleep. To stare at her naked back while she dreams, taking in every tiny bit of the beauty she projects during her peaceful slumber. For the past three months, though, she hasn't been able to sleep on her tummy. Therefore it hasn't been the sight of her naked back that I have lovingly absorbed. Instead, I have been privileged with a view of her angelic face and her perfectly rounded stomach — a stomach that makes my heart beat like fuck every time I see it.

Carefully shifting in bed next to her, I make myself more comfortable, supporting my head on my hand and lightly trailing my finger around her protruding belly. My touch is deliberately featherlight, as I don't want to chance waking her; she needs all the sleep she can get.

Last night was exhausting for her, especially after playfully jamming with me and Derek, followed by an awkward attempt at Twister carpet with Carly. If I wasn't mistaken, my best friend — and shameless pervert — found their gently tangled position highly amusing, and not in the funny ha-ha kind of way.

I have no doubt that last night's antics, together with Alexis having gone back to numerous piss-stops throughout each night, is a result of her overtiredness. Obviously, this is bad for her, but not so much for me. Why? Because I can't help but find her midnight toilet runs entertaining. I know that sounds horrible, but it's true. The grumble of annoyance she makes as she awkwardly rolls and shuffles herself in the bed is fucking adorable. Not to mention her not so hushed cursing of her 'pathetic, weak and sad excuse for a bladder'. It gets me every time. *She's just so funny ... and beautiful ... and adorable ... and fuck ... I'm one lucky son of a bitch!*

Whenever I feel the bed shift during the night, I pry an eye open and smile and wait for the sound of her mumblings before jumping up to help her. I genuinely love helping her, whether it's during the day, evening or middle of the night. Of course she tells me not to and says she can manage on her own, and sometimes she even tries to get out of bed very slowly in order not to wake me. The thing is, it's pretty fucking impossible for her to move without the entire bed moving along with her.

These past few weeks she's repeatedly told me that 'she's over it' and 'thank fuck she's not an elephant' because, apparently, elephants are pregnant — on average — for nearly two years. Don't get me wrong, because I do sympathise with her lack of comfort and sleep, but I can't help finding her frustration over some parts of her pregnancy some-what comical. *I mean, really, how bad can it be?*

I'm glad I just said that in my head. I'm also glad she is still asleep. Shit! Could you imagine the death stare she would graciously give me if that had, in fact, dribbled out of my mouth?

Obviously, I have no idea what it's like to carry a baby, and I never will — cheers to owning a dick. And while our metaphorical glasses are still raised in a toast to my gender, I think a 'cheers' to my abilities in evading the evil curse known as Couvade Syndrome is also war-ranted. *Clink!*

Now, seeing as I am the proud owner of a dick, I am left with no choice but to accept that my role during the whole baby-baking process is to acknowledge that everything Alexis complains about is justified: the sore back, the swollen feet, the aching tits and our little precious one practising his soccer skills by bending it like Beckham with Alexis' ribcage. I know when he does this, because Alexis screws up her nose and rubs her abdomen in an annoyed yet nurturing way.

It's fucking adorable, and it makes me smile ... which makes her mad ... *really* mad. At the same time though, I do give her my sympathy and jump to her aid, because let's face it, at the end of the day it's the least I can do.

Alexis takes in a sharp breath and her chest rises, pushing out her full luscious tits, taunting me. I'm desperate to press my lips to them, take her soft, perked nipples into my mouth and ravish them with my tongue. *Fuck!* I have a hard-on right now just and contemplate trying it, but wonder if I did, would she wake. *Should I? Of course I should.* Then again, her threats of late are becoming quite believable, so a rethink of that course of action is probably wise.

Last week, Alexis made it very clear that her nipples were no longer allowed to find their way into my mouth. She told me they were now 'off limits' because colostrum had appeared. I was no longer allowed to ravish them with my tongue ... well, at least until our son was drinking from a bottle.

Much to my disappointment, I admitted this news did seem fair to me ... until she then told me that he would more than likely start to drink from a bottle when he reached the age of one. *One ... really? Fucking bullshit, age one. There's no way in hell I'm waiting that long to suck her nipples. He can drink from a bottle long before his first birthday.*

I shake my head at the absurd thought and lean in closer to Alexis' tummy to have a one-on-one discussion with my boy. I do this often, especially when his mother is asleep: secret Daddy business.

'I know you are awake in there,' I whisper. 'I can see you moving around. Listen, you know I love you and will do absolutely anything for you, give you anything you need, right?' I wait for him to acknowledge me with further movement.

He does.

'Good, because I need you to understand that your lease over the use of your mother's nipples is for a term of six months and no longer,' I inform him.

Glancing up at Alexis, I confirm that her eyes are still closed, then return my attention to her stomach. 'You might think the duration of your lease is unfair, but I can tell you I am being very reasonable.

So, that being said, do we have a deal, baby boy?' I lightly fist-bump Alexis' tummy. 'Good boy,' I whisper with a satisfied smile on my face and gently nuzzle her skin with my nose. *God, she smells good.*

'I can't believe you just made a deal with our son over his use of my breasts,' Alexis says quite casually without opening her eyes. *Shit! I could've sworn she was still asleep.*

'He needs to know who's boss,' I defensively answer while shuffling closer to her face.

She opens her gorgeous eyes and rolls onto her side, facing me. 'I think you are the one that needs to know who's boss, and I can confirm, Mr Clark, that it is not you,' she says with a contented, cocky grin on her face.

'Honey, you know that is not true. Technically, I am still your boss,' I assert, as I caress her tummy.

She growls, filling me with a devious happiness.

'I need to get up and have a shower,' she adds, now snotty at the truth of my correct words.

I raise my eyebrow at her then get up on my knees, resting back on my heels and giving her full sight of my morning glory. 'A shower ... now? Are you sure?'

'Yes,' she says with a faux yawn, trying to keep her obvious want of me at bay while she begins her practised shuffling to the edge of the bed.

Smiling to myself, I take a hold of my cock and slowly drag my clenched hand along its length, prompting her to swallow heavily.

She stares at me and licks her lips.

I've come to realise over the past year that this action of hers is involuntary. I love it, it reveals her uncontrollable surrender.

'Alexis,' I say, in a low predatory tone as I crawl over her body, stopping her from getting away and placing myself in a spooning position behind her back. 'Are you saying you don't want this?' I ask, continuing to tease her while pressing my cock onto the soft apex of her arse.

Instinctively, she pushes into me, but refuses to look over her shoulder in my direction.

'Uh huh,' she moans, giving me a lazy rub with the rotation of her hips.

I lean forward and lick the skin just below her ear. 'You're lying.'

'I am,' she giggles, then tilts her head back and welcomes my mouth to hers, my tongue to caress her own. *My god, she tastes wonderful.* I could fucking kiss this woman till I run out of breath, and I'm positive there have been moments when I nearly have.

Slowly, I trail my hand down her front and slide two fingers inside her amazing pussy, enjoying the warm wet softness as I penetrate.

'Fuck, Bryce,' she moans, as I swirl them around inside her.

My cock twitches, indicating he too wants a piece of her inner sanctum, so I pull my fingers out and take hold of her thigh, opening her wide and placing her foot on the bed behind my legs. I position the head of my dick at her entrance and slowly push into her. *Jesus, she feels good. How is it that she always feels this fucking good?*

Alexis reaches behind us and grips the back of my head, making me groan and flex my fingers into her hip. *Bloody hell!* I know she likes it controlled and tortuous in the beginning, so I rock my pelvis deeper and harder, but keep my rhythm slow before building my pace.

'Oh, god,' she moans, reassuring me of my thoughts.

Her hand moves away from my head and is transferred to my arse, her nails digging into my now tense cheek — a clear indication of her climbing orgasm.

'I love you so fucking much,' I growl out loud, my momentum picking up with a passionate vigour.

'I love you too,' she replies breathlessly.

I can never get enough of hearing her say that to me, those three words making me the happiest man alive and surging me with adrenaline every time.

Moving my cock in and out of her quickly and relentlessly, I feel the pressure start to build in my shaft. She pants heavier now, and her inner muscles clench around me, assisting my release and tipping me over the edge.

'Fuck,' I growl into the crook of her neck, drowning out her cries of gratification.

I trail kisses along the tops of her shoulders and down her arm as I rub out the end of our climax, taking my time and enjoying her body. When both our breathing returns to a normal level, I straddle her lower thighs and hover over her.

'Do you still want your shower?' I say seductively, arrogance in my tone.

'Yes,' she counteracts, 'as a matter of fact I do.'

I chuckle, shake my head, and launch myself off the end of the bed, now primed for the rest of my day. Sex with Lex in the mornin' always has that affect on me.

'Here ...' I reach out my hands as I stand in front of her, offering to pull her up. She accepts and slowly rises to her feet, while letting out an uncomfortable grumble. I'm about to mock her cuteness when suddenly, I feel a warm, wet sensation on the top of my feet. 'What the fuc—'

'Oh, god,' Alexis gasps, letting go of both my hands and clutching her stomach. 'My waters just broke.'

CHAPTER

7

I'm not sure how long I stood glued to that very spot, staring at my wet feet. I'd like to think it was only a split second, but to me it felt like an eternity. Eventually, comprehension of what was occurring right before my eyes smacked me across the face.

'Shit! Shit! Come on,' I go to grab her arm and gently drag her out of the room.

'Bryce, where are you going?' she asks, while pulling against the direction I wish to go.

'To the bloody hospital, where else?'

'I'm naked and so are you.'

I look at her superb, mouthwatering body that transformed into a sexy as hell protective house for our son, then I look at my own bare form. 'Fuck! We need clothes.'

'No shit, Sherlock,' she mocks. 'But I'm having a shower first.'

Alexis casually shrugs out of my grip.

'No. What do you mean? We don't have time.'

She turns and makes her way to the bathroom. 'Yes, we do. It's fine. Anyway, you may want to wash your feet.' *How can she be so bloody calm? Our son is on his way.*

'What?' I say, astounded.

She stops, braces herself against the doorway, then turns back to me and smiles and it is the most hypnotic expression I've ever seen. 'Come on, Daddy. Help me wash. Our baby boy is on his way.'

* * *

After showering at the speed of light and collecting Alexis' hospital bag, I finally manage to get her in the Crow and on our way to the Royal Women's Hospital.

'Are you okay, honey?'

'Yep, couldn't be better,' she answers sarcastically with a forced smile on her face.

I hold back my laugh.

'Argh! Jesus! Who invented labour pain? Who invented labour full stop?' she whines and pants.

'Are you okay?' I ask again, now concerned at the sudden escalation of her pain.

'Stop asking me that. You'll know if I'm not okay,' she spits through gritted teeth.

Right, mental note: Don't ask if she's okay again.

'We are nearly there, hang on,' I advise tediously, glancing at her from the corner of my eye.

'Hang on? You try hanging on to a baby that wants nothing more than to climb out of your vagina,' she grumbles.

This time I can't help but let out a laugh.

Thankfully, Alexis' phone rings at that same moment, distracting her from the abuse she is about to hurl my way. I'm more than glad to escape her impending vocal bullet and prepare to land the chopper on the helipad as she reaches into her handbag to pull out her phone.

She squints at the screen and blows out long breaths. 'Carls, what's happening?' she answers flippantly through puffs of air.

I smile and shake my head while setting the chopper down and shutting off the engine.

'No, I'm not fucking Bryce,' she explains while pausing for a minute and dropping her head back in amused exasperation. 'I'm not lying,' she pants. 'I'm breathing heavily because I'm in labour, you silly cow.

Argh, god!' They are getting stronger,' she groans, and for the first time shoots me a nervous look.

'Hang up,' I say calmly.

Alexis nods in agreement. 'Carls, gotta go. I'll talk to you later,' she says breathlessly, as she disconnects the call.

I exit the cockpit and, on my way round to help her out of the chopper, I quickly type Lucy a text.

Baby on the way. At hospital — Bryce

A reply comes through as a nurse pushes a wheelchair in our direction.

OMG! I will be there as soon as I can — Lucy

Sliding one arm behind Alexis' back and the other under her knees, I lift her into my arms and gently place her into the waiting wheelchair. 'Oh, for the love of f-f-frying pans,' she groans.

'That's a new one,' the nurse smiles, before introducing herself. 'We get fire trucks a lot.' *I'm surprised Alexis just doesn't swear. It's never stopped her before.*

'I don't want the f-bomb to be the first word my baby hears coming out of my mouth,' Alexis hisses, breathing out through her teeth as her contraction eases.

The nurse nods. 'That's fair enough, dear,' she says then proceeds to push Alexis toward the birthing suite.

Not even minutes later, Alexis starts cursing again. 'Shit! Shit! Shit!' she groans with puffed cheeks. 'Why? Why am I doing this again? And how did I forget how bloody painful this is?' She glares at me.

Not really knowing how to answer that question — and against my better judgement — I attempt it anyway. 'Because it's worth it, honey,' I say softly, trying to reassure her while patting her hair away from her face.

'Don't pat me like a dog,' she snarls as she swipes my hand away. *Another note to self: don't pat her.*

I go to put my hand back in my pocket when she grabs it. 'Sorry ... I'm sorry. I don't mean to bite your head off. It's just ... oh, god! It hurts,' she cries out as she clenches my hand in a death grip. *Jesus fucking Christ, that's hard! When did she get superhuman strength?*

We enter the birthing suite and she lets go of my hand: relief, together with blood flow, returns to my semi-crushed fingers.

'Alexis, dear, my name is Kate. I'm a midwife. Dr Rainer is on her way and will be here shortly, okay? Now, let's get you up onto this bed and check how baby is doing,' she says with a smile.

I help Alexis out of the wheelchair and up onto the bed, assisting her by fluffing up pillows and basically just fucking fluffing about. Obviously, I'm way out of my comfort zone and don't know what the hell I'm doing.

Kate sets up an IV and attaches some straps and cords to Alexis' stomach. 'Now, your hospital chart says you had an emergency C-section with your last delivery. Baby was in breech, right?'

'Yes, yes, she was. Charlotte liked to dance around even before entering this world. Seven years later and she hasn't changed,' Alexis answers lovingly, almost calm and serene.

I gently wipe a bead of sweat that has formed on her brow and take note that even in distress, and obviously a shitload of pain, she is still absolutely gorgeous.

Then, just like a gust of wind, her calm demeanour is swept away and a harsh, boiling disposition replaces it. 'I want an epidural, god-damn it,' Alexis growls through deep breaths while closing her eyes. 'Please!'

Placing my hand on her forehead, I then gently drag my fingers through her hair in the hope of calming her down. *Fuck, she's beautiful.* Her eyes open with lightning speed and she fires a death glare in my direction. *Fuck, she's scary.* Quickly, I panic and lean in to kiss the spot where my hand has just been, apologising for breaking the 'no patting rule'. This seems to do the trick because she smiles meekly at me.

'Your contractions are three minutes apart and lasting just over one minute long,' Kate explains. 'I'm going to check how dilated your cervix is, then we will discuss an epidural.'

Alexis nods.

I nod, too. At this point in time, I think I'll nod at anything being said. Nodding is good.

'Not another one. F-f-fruit cake,' Alexis moans and turns the shade of a tomato. 'I just had one, give me a break.'

I take hold of her hand, remembering not to pat her. 'Just breathe, honey.'

'Seriously?' she huffs.

'That's what you told Lucy to do.'

'I know, but it's bullshit.'

'I just thought —'

'Shut up!'

Another note to self: shut up.

'Bryce I'm sorry. I love you. I just don't like you right now.'

'Yes, you do,' I say with an authoritative tone.

She looks at me with knowing eyes, and mouths with exhausted defeat, 'Yes, I do.'

I bring her hand to my lips. 'I know, honey.'

She nods and closes her eyes during a long exhalation.

Kate positions herself between Alexis' legs, her expression one of concentration. 'Hmm, I'm sorry, dear, but you are nine centimetres dilated so there will be no epidural,' she explains. 'Looks like baby is nearly ready to meet his or her parents,' Kate offers as a compromise, her eyebrow raised persuasively.

'His parents,' I reply, overjoyed. 'We are having a boy.'

'Congratulations!'

'Argh! For the love of f-f-furry freakin' ferrets ... where is Dr Rainer?' Alexis screams, now clearly stressed and in much more pain, not to mention tripling her f-bomb replacements.

'She'll be here any minute,' Kate reassures her, now moving around the room quite quickly and collecting towels, mats, a trolley on wheels with sharp-looking implements that curdle my stomach, and a see-through crib with an overhead light.

Alexis screams out again. 'Fuck! I want to push. I want to push, he's coming.'

'Not yet, Alexis, just breathe through it. You can push in a minute. You're doing really well.'

'What happened to not saying fuck, honey?'

'Fuck you! You try pushing a tennis ball out the eye of your dick and see if you cannot say fuck. Fuck!'

The doors to the birthing suite open, and Dr Rainer walks in with gloves and a big smile on her face. 'Just in time I see,' she says, as she sits on a stool at the end of the bed. 'Bryce, would you like to come and stand next to me and help deliver your son?'

Deliver my son? Me? Are you crazy?

'Sure,' I answer, like it's something I do on a daily basis.

Alexis screams out again and pushes, and all I can see as I stare at her is her mouth moving at a million miles per hour. She looks angry ... and red ... and angry. I can't hear anything she is saying though, because it's like someone has just pushed a mute button and removed all sound. What I can decipher is just how beautiful she is, how amazing and strong she is, and how much I adore her. I smile at her lovingly; she simply takes my breath away.

'Are you smiling at me, Bryce?' she growls, snapping me out of my adoration and removing the silence.

'What?' I stutter.

'I said, are you smiling at me? Does this look fucking funny to you?' she yells.

Mental note yet again: don't smile.

'No. I'm —'

'Okay, Alexis. I see his head. When I say, I want one big push and —'

'Head?' I croak, and take a sneak peek between Alexis' legs. The sight before me nearly has me dying of shock. 'I can see his head, honey. Push!' I command with over-enthusiastic encouragement.

'No. Not yet,' Dr Rainer warns and gives me an annoyed look.

I ignore it.

'No. Don't push,' I add, following her instructions. She is the doctor after all.

'When can I push? I want to push. Screw you all, I'm pushing.'

Dr Rainer places her hands around my son's head. 'Now, Alexis. Push!'

'Now, honey,' I add again.

Alexis lets out a mighty big yell and pushes with everything she has. The sound of her pain and sheer determination rips at my heart, drowning my ears until I hear the most wonderful sound in my life: my son's cry.

Looking down, I see his tiny little body in Dr Rainer's hands, and I can't for the life of me begin to describe what my heart is doing in my chest. I'm stunned, yet so happy, and I want to fucking cry. I never fucking cry.

'Daddy, would you like to cut the umbilical cord?' Dr Rainer says as she hands me a pair of scissors.

I accept them and automatically go on Daddy-autopilot, snipping the cord and helping to wrap him in a blanket. *Shit! He's so bloody small.*

Alexis is now quiet and her breathing is more controlled. Her eyes are wide and damp and her neck is craning up, searching for our boy. Dr Rainer gives him a quick check, then places him on Alexis' chest.

I'm fucking floored, stumped, halted in my tracks. My fiancée is holding our son in her arms and it's the most amazing thing I have ever seen.

'Hi, little boy. It's me, Mummy,' she says as she drags her nose along the bridge of his and kisses his forehead.

Seeing that small loving gesture has my heart thumping like crazy in my chest. 'I love you,' I say softly, finally opening my mouth and finding the words. 'And I love you, too, baby boy.' I lean in to kiss my son for the first time. *Wow!* He's so warm ... and soft ... and perfect. Perfect like his mum.

Sitting on the edge of the bed, I drape my arm around Alexis' shoulder and kiss her like never before. Pouring everything I have into it. 'Thank you. You make me the happiest man alive. Thank you for our son.'

She cups the side of my face, then looks lovingly at the little miracle in her arms. 'So, Daddy, do you think he looks like a Brayden now?'

I gently wiggle his nose with my finger and his lazy little eyes find mine. 'Yes, I do. It suits him.'

She smiles through elated tears and hugs him to her chest. 'Welcome to the world, Brayden Lauchie Clark.'

CHAPTER

8

In the blink of an eye your life can change. How you feel, act, think and see the surrounding world around you. It just changes ... without your say so ... never able to go back to the way it was beforehand. Not that I would EVER want my life to revert back to how it was prior to becoming a father. No way in hell!

Standing here with Brayden sleeping peacefully in my arms and Alexis sleeping soundly beside me in her hospital bed, I feel as if my life has just begun.

I slowly take steps around the room, lightly bouncing and assisting Brayden in a lulled slumber. The swelling on his face is just starting to go down as it is only hours after he entered the world.

'Brayden,' I whisper, while placing a soft kiss on his head, 'Daddy loves you so much and I can't wait to take you home so we can spend every minute together. You and me, buddy, we are going to have so much fun.'

A gentle knock at the door sounds right before it slowly creaks open. Lucy pokes her head around and locks her eyes on me cradling my son. The smile we share in that moment is profound and one only Lucy and I can communicate.

I nod my head and indicate she come in.

As she tiptoes over to where I'm standing, a tear is already making its way down her cheek. 'Oh my god, Bryce, he's amazing!' she whispers as she places her hand on his head and wraps her other arm around my shoulder. 'Congratulations, big bro. I'm so happy for you.'

'Thanks,' is about all I am capable of saying, still semi-speechless from sheer awe.

'It's overwhelming, isn't it? Finally holding, smelling and seeing your baby in the flesh for the first time.'

Staring down at his peaceful little face, I answer. 'There are no words, Luce. No words.'

Lucy nods toward Alexis. 'How is she?'

'Yeah, she's good. Just tired and exhausted, but other than that she's fine.'

'So, it was a quick labour?'

'God, Luce! It was the longest and fastest two hours and fourteen minutes of my life. Alexis though ... well ... she was just simply perfect the whole time. She just ...' I shake my head in veneration as I glance over at her sleeping. 'She just amazes me.'

Lucy gently trails her finger down the side of Brayden's face. 'What did the doctor say about him being four weeks premature?'

'Dr Rainer did a thorough examination after Alexis bonded with him. She was happy with his vitals, and when he attached to feed without a problem, she was even more pleased, saying there was no reason why he couldn't remain in the ward with us.'

'He's a tough little cookie, then, isn't he? Determined and strong-willed already. Hmm, I wonder why that is?' Lucy mocks. 'So, does my gorgeous nephew have a name?'

'Yes, of course he does. It's Brayden ... Brayden Lauchie Clark.'

Lucy is silent for a moment, staring intently at Brayden, her expression full of emotion. She sucks in a deep breath, squeezes my arm, then nods and smiles. 'Perfect, Bryce. He's just perfect.'

'I know.'

'So, have you had anything to eat today? Gone to the loo, that sort of thing?'

'No, not yet,' I answer with contentment, the thought of eating or pissing or anything else not even crossing my mind.

She holds out her arms. 'Okay, pass him over and go and see to yourself.'

As I assess Lucy's outstretched arms, a moment of panic washes over me at the thought of letting Brayden go.

Returning my gaze back to my beautiful little boy, I politely decline. 'No, really, I'm fine.'

'Hey,' she says softly while placing her finger on my jaw to turn my face in her direction. 'It's all right. This is me, your sister. I promise I won't let anything happen to him while you're gone. Just go, take a quick breather, get something to eat and then come back.'

Debating whether or not I should leave him, I reluctantly pass Brayden over to her and, almost instantly, a sensation of loss fills me. Not only are my arms now cold, but I experience a reaction of incompleteness, feeling somewhat unsettled and powerless. *Fuck! Is this what fatherhood feels like? Helpless and vulnerable?*

I lean down and kiss Brayden on the forehead, then check to see that Alexis is still sleeping soundly. 'Okay, but I'm only going for some coffee and the loo. I'll be right back.'

'I'll have a skinny latte, no sugar.'

'Skinny latte,' I mumble to myself as I jog out the door, heading for the cafeteria on the ground level.

* * *

After what seems like the longest fifteen minutes of my life, I quietly open the door to Alexis' room. Carrying two coffees and a hot white chocolate on a tray, I walk in to find Alexis wide awake and Brayden happily breastfeeding. Lucy is sitting by her bed, pushing buttons on her phone and, it seems, keying in what Alexis is saying.

'Two point seven kilos and forty-seven centimetres long. Born at 11.14 a.m.,' she finishes.

'Thanks,' Lucy offers. 'Nic likes details.'

Alexis looks up as I walk swiftly toward her and Brayden. 'Hey, Daddy, where have you been?'

Worried that she might be disappointed in me for leaving them, I quickly place the drinks on the benchtop by the window and make my way to her side, kissing her forehead and gently stroking Brayden's temple. 'I'm sorry. I didn't mean to leave. I needed —'

'Bryce, it's all right. You can take a few moments to get a drink. We are fine, see? Look, he's such a good feeder.'

I watch him contentedly suckling away and it's one of the single most beautiful sights I've witnessed. Guilt briefly sweeps through me at the thought of telling him to give up his food source after only six months. Alexis' breasts now belong to him and he can have them for as long as he needs.

'I hope you are not planning a reduced leasing term where your agreement with our son is concerned,' Alexis warns.

I chuckle. 'No, honey, I was just thinking quite the opposite.'

'What are you two talking about?' Lucy asks as she gets up and fetches the drinks.

'Nothing,' I advise, wanting my secret Daddy business to remain just that — secret Daddy business.

Passing me my coffee and Alexis her white chocolate, Lucy flippantly responds, 'Fair enough.'

'Now, I've spoken to Mum and Dad, Bryce,' Alexis says as she gently shifts Brayden to feed from her other breast. 'They are on their way here together with Jen. Rick and the kids are also on their way. Jake and Johanna will visit us when we are back at home as Jake is currently on a run to Brisbane. Um ... Carly and Derek are coming in tomorrow for a quick visit. And Tash, Lil, Jade and Steph will also probably visit when we are back at home.'

'Right,' I state, dubiously. 'Alexis, I'm not sure you should have all these visitors so soon. Is it safe for Brayden to have so many people around him? He needs to get stronger first, build up immunity or something. I'm sure I read that somewhere.'

'Visitors are fine, providing they are not sick. I'm sure none of our family and friends would visit if they were under the weather in any way, shape or form.'

I smile half-heartedly at her attempt to ease my mind, all the while thinking that I will now have to go gather some of those surgical masks. The last thing I want is some germy fucker sneezing, or coughing, or even breathing on my baby boy.

Alexis sits Brayden upright and places his tiny head in the palm of her hand, her fingers spreading out on both sides of his cheeks. The position she has him in puffs his already puffy cheeks even more — he looks so bloody cute.

She starts gently patting and rubbing his back. 'Here, do you want to burp him? I need to pee.'

'Sure,' I answer hesitantly, as I sit on the bed.

Replacing her hands with my own as she passes Brayden over, I proceed to mimic what she had just been doing by lightly holding his face and patting his back. He lets out a teeny little burp.

I laugh. 'You get that from Mummy.'

'He does not,' she complains in defence.

'Yes, he does.'

'I burped so much during my pregnancy because of all that hair,' she says as she strokes his fair baby wisps.

'I still don't believe it. Babies having hair cannot make you burp,' I repeat. Although, I must admit, he does have a decent head of hair.

'Yes, they can, Bryce,' Lucy chimes in.

'Thank you, Luce,' Alexis says as she readjusts her breasts and winces.

I notice the obvious discomfort on her face. 'What's wrong?'

'My milk isn't properly "in" yet, so feeding kinda hurts,' she explains. 'Actually, it borders on downright painful.'

Appearing to be in the middle of typing a text message, Lucy adds to the conversation. 'She needs Lansinoh, Bryce.'

'Yes, Miss Know-it-all, I'm fully aware of what Lansinoh is. It's in her bag.'

Lucy pokes her tongue out at me and jumps up. 'I'll get it —'

'No, it's fine. I'll get it,' Alexis interrupts. 'I need to freshen up anyway. I'm going to have a shower.'

'Do you need any help?' I offer.

'No. I'll be fine. I'll yell out if I do.'

I lower my voice so that my smug little sister cannot hear. 'Am I doing this right?' I ask, indicating my method of burping.

Alexis gently brushes her lips across mine. 'Yes, you're doing just fine, Daddy. In fact, you're perfect.'

* * *

Later that day, I watch Brayden being passed around to person upon person and I really don't like it. I don't fucking like it at all.

First he is handed to Maryann, then Graeme, then Jen. Soon after, he is in Lucy's arms followed by Nic's. Then — of course — Nate and

Charli want a cuddle and, as if she hasn't just cuddled him for a good part of the afternoon, Maryann has him once again. Watching what reminds me of a pass the fucking parcel game, I start to get highly irritated, but it's not until he is passed to Rick that I can no longer hold back or bite my tongue.

Seeing Brayden in that fucker's arms makes me feel murderous, bordering on fucking insane and, feeling that at any moment my head will spin around on my shoulders — exorcist-style — I finally put an end to the show and tell.

'Okay,' I voice after a minute or two of Brayden being in Rick's arms — a minute or two of too fucking long, 'I think Mum and baby need a rest. It's been a long day. You are all more than welcome to go back to the hotel and stay. Abigail will make sure you are well looked after.'

I gently pry Brayden from Rick's arms and hold him close, protecting him from any further manhandling. He yawns and starts searching for his food source.

'He's due for a feed anyway,' Alexis announces.

'And his first bath,' a midwife adds, as she enters the room. 'Visiting hours are about to close.'

Straightaway, I like this midwife. This midwife deserves a raise, or a promotion, or an employee of the month award. In fact, I make a mental note to look into offering a personal recommendation for that particular award.

'You heard her,' I speak up. 'Out!'

'But Mum, I want to stay,' Charlotte whines.

'I know Charli-Bear, but you can't. Dad will bring you back tomorrow, won't you, Rick?' Alexis asks with a pleading look on her face.

'Actually,' the midwife speaks up, 'if Dr Rainer is happy with your recovery, there's a good chance you'll be allowed to go home tomorrow.'

'Really, so soon? Oh, that would be wonderful,' Alexis beams, an enormous smile plastering her face.

Strapping a blood pressure cuff to Alexis' arm, the midwife continues: 'I'm not sure that applies to Brayden, though.'

What? I decide this midwife needs a new career, fuck her promotion and award.

Before I can voice my objection to leaving my one-day-old baby boy here alone, Alexis does it for me. 'What? That is absurd. I am not leaving my son here alone. That is not even an option. If he stays, I stay. If I go, he goes. End of fucking story.'

'Alexis! Language,' Maryann scolds.

Jen nudges her mother out of the room. 'Mum, stay out of it.'

'I'll wait outside,' Rick adds. *Good idea, you do that.*

'Ms Blaxlo, I didn't mean you would have to leave him. The hospital has a hotel for mothers who are well enough not to need a hospital bed. Because your son is four weeks premature, he will more than likely need monitoring by a nurse. We need to be sure that he is feeding well and putting on weight before he can go home with you. That being said, Dr Rainer will assess him again tomorrow before a final decision is made. '

'I don't want to stay in the hospital hotel. I don't even want to be in a different room from him.' Alexis looks toward me with an anxious expression on her face.

'The hospital hotel is lovely and is only one building awa—'

'That's not necessary,' I interrupt. Noticing Alexis' heightened distress, I step in to calm the situation down. 'Honey, don't worry. We are not leaving Brayden. I'll sort something out, I promise.'

She nods and glares at the midwife, who quickly prepares Brayden's bath and then leaves the room.

* * *

Later that night as I lay propped up on my side, Alexis on her side and Brayden fast asleep on the bed in between us, I couldn't possibly be happier. Well ... I could. Alexis is yet to become my wife.

'Shit! I almost forgot,' I proclaim, rolling off the bed and reaching for the baby bag.

Alexis straightens and cranes her neck. 'What? What did you forget?'

'Yours and Brayden's presents,' I answer, holding the two gifts behind my back.

'Presents?'

'Yes. It is Brayden's birthday, is it not?'

'It is. So what did you get him?' Alexis asks, trying to peek around my back.

I reveal one arm and place the soft-knitted guitar next to Brayden, a hugely proud grin covering my face.

Alexis giggles. 'Aw, you got him his first guitar. How adorable.'

'Guitar's aren't adorable, honey. They are cool as shit. Brayden is now the coolest baby in this hospital.'

Laughing, Alexis kisses his forehead. 'Did you hear that, baby boy? You are cool as shit!'

He doesn't respond. He's too cool to respond.

'So, you said presents, as in plural. That means you have something else behind your back.'

Raising my eyebrow at her, I nod.

'Is it for me?' she asks with an excited smile.

'It is.'

'Are you going to give it to me?'

'I am.'

Drawing out the suspense for her — because I know she hates surprises — I slowly reveal my hand, only to put it back out of sight, fooling her. The next second, I have a punch to my bicep.

'All right, all right, here,' I laugh, rubbing my arm and producing the velvet box.

Opening it up for her to see, I watch with anticipation as she goes to put her hand in, then quickly pulls it back.

'I'm not falling for that any more. The box, hand it over,' she demands with a smile.

I laugh and hand her the box. *She knows me too well.*

Alexis opens the box and takes out the gold engraved heart pendant and chain. 'Bryce, it's beautiful,' she whispers as she reads the inscription of all her children's names. A lone tear falls from her eye when she looks up and meets my stare. 'You even had Bianca's name engraved on it.'

I lean forward and wipe the stray tear from her jaw. 'Of course I did.'

'It's perfect, thank you. But I didn't give you anything.'

She tenderly strokes Brayden's face with her finger and gazes adoringly at our son, and I realise it's the single most peaceful and amazing moment in my life thus far.

'Do you really know how much I love you?' I sincerely ask her.

She looks up and smiles. 'Yes.'

'No, I mean do you *really* know how much I love you?'

Her smile softens a little, and she blushes ever so slightly. 'Well, yeah ... I think so.'

'I don't think that you do,' I explain, as I push a lock of her hair behind her ear. 'Today, my life changed and that's all because of you. Today, I received the most precious thing imaginable and again ... that's all because of you. Today, my heart grew beyond all proportions, and you are the reason why. You, Alexis. You have given me something no one else has and ever will. You have given me the best present possible.'

She lifts herself up and over Brayden, then smiles mischievously at me before leaning in to kiss my lips.

'It's what I do, Mr Clark.'

CHAPTER

9

In the morning that followed, Dr Rainer decided to keep both Alexis and Brayden in hospital an extra day for observation, but then authorised their release the following day after I explained that we were more than happy to have a live-in nurse at the apartment for as long as needed.

She agreed, but felt a midwife would only need to make a few house calls in the week ahead. She was happy that Brayden was already doing exceptionally well, especially now that Alexis' breast milk was — in the words of the Emperor of the Galactic Empire — 'Fully operational'.

Thrilled to finally be taking Brayden home, we made our way out to the underground car park. Not seeing where our car is parked and forgetting to ask Chelsea when she handed me the keys, I lift the remote and click the button. The lights of our brand new Tesla Model S flash, revealing its whereabouts.

'What? ... How? ... When?' Alexis asks, confusion covering her face.

Smiling while holding the hospital bags and many stuffed teddies, I reveal my latest secret surprise. 'This is your new car, my love. It's the safest on the market.'

'But ... I like my Territory, and the Charger and the Lexus.'

I place all the stuff in my arms on the ground next to the navy coloured, high-performance, sports sedan with the best safety rating of any car ever tested. *This car is a wet dream ... with protection.*

'Again, this is the safest car on the market. I want you and the kids as protected as possible.'

She looks as if she is going to argue — and I'm fully prepared to put up a fight — but she refrains, shuts her mouth and just nods. 'Okay, I understand, but what about the chopper? Don't you need to fly it home? And how did you get the car here?'

Shocked by the fact that she didn't argue any further, I quickly pick up the stuff from the ground and place it in the boot. 'Chelsea. She drove the car here this morning then flew the chopper back to the hotel,' I explain while shutting the boot lid.

'Right,' Alexis murmurs, her tone now sounding obviously disgruntled.

I step up to face her and look down at Brayden cradled in her arms. 'Hey, what's the matter? Don't you like the car? I just want you to be safe. I don't ever want to lose anyone I love in a car accident ever again. Please don't fight me on this.'

'I'm not. The car is fine. I'm happy to drive it if it makes you feel better. Honestly, I understand.'

'Then what's the matter?'

'Do I have to spell it out to you?' she sighs.

I really have no idea what she is suddenly upset about, so spelling it out like a first-grade teacher is welcomed.

She searches my eyes then drops her gaze. 'Chelsea.'

'What about Chelsea?'

'I don't trust her.'

'We've been through this, honey. I thought you were okay with her working for us.'

'Us?'

'Yes,' I say firmly. 'Us.'

'That doesn't mean I have to be all cheery when you mention her name. I still don't like the bitch,' she spits out.

Shit! Where the hell has this come from all of a sudden? I'm taken aback by her vehement and unexpected insecurity. Maybe this is part of the 'baby blues' thing that the midwife mentioned. Or maybe it could be the start of postnatal depression.

Worried that it could lead to something quite serious, I make a mental note to ring Jessica when we get home.

'Alexis, I really don't want to argue about Chelsea with you. She is no more than a friend, an employee. Look, I don't want to argue with you at all, especially here ... now ... in the car park on the day we bring our baby boy home for the first time,' I say as I gently drag my knuckle down her cheek.

She gives me one of her faux smiles, places Brayden in my arms and turns for the car. 'Neither do I.'

* * *

Soon after we arrived home from the hospital, I realised that I wanted Brayden close by pretty much all the time. It had been less than twenty-four hours when I'd decided the solution to my predicament was to order more bassinets, one to be placed in the lounge area and the other in my office. Charli had asked for one to be put in her room as well, which I thought was cute. However, Alexis had felt I was going 'overboard' and soon put a stop to any more of my baby furniture purchases.

The kids had been wonderful, adjusting really well to having a new sibling. For the first couple of days, Charlotte had followed Alexis around like a bad smell, wanting to know every single tiny detail about her baby brother. Needless to say, I was impressed with her inquisitiveness — she was good at creepy research.

Nate, on the other hand, had been a little quiet at first and this had worried both Alexis and me. It wasn't until we started giving him special responsibilities, like making sure his Mum had a glass of water every time she was feeding, and helping me to bath Brayden, that he soon resembled his normal self again.

* * *

Currently inundated with work, I have no choice but to spend a lot of my time in the office. However, due to my additional bassinet purchase at the beginning of the week, Brayden can spend some of that time with me. It's a win-win situation.

'Bryce, you can't take him with you everywhere. A little separation is good, you know,' Alexis says with her arms crossed while standing at the door to my office.

I glance down into his bassinet which is next to my desk. How separation can be good for someone, let alone a newborn baby, baffles me.

'You are creating a rod for your back. Actually, you are creating a rod for my back,' she grumbles. *What?*

'What are you talking about?' I ask with a smile, her frustration mildly cute. The only rod I create is the one in my pants, which is also the one I currently want in between her legs.

'It means that what you are doing now will create problems in the future. If you continue to take him everywhere with you, it is what he will get used to and he'll want it all the time.'

I take in her form as she leans into the doorjamb. She has on a pair of yoga pants and a tight fitting t-shirt. Her baby bump is almost non-existent and her hair is in a ponytail dangling down her back, longer than it ever has been. She looks stunning as per usual.

'What's wrong with wanting that?'

'Argh!' she groans. 'You just don't get it.' *Fuck, that groan. I love that fucking groan.*

I feel like baiting her more just to hear that groan, because apparently I will have to wait a couple more weeks before I can hear it as a result of my making love to her.

'I do get it. And he's fine. He's barely a week old. He needs to know his daddy is always close. I don't want him thinking any other way.'

Her attempt to hide her grin fails as she runs her tongue over the top row of her teeth.

Just as I'm about to get up and make my way over to her to run *my* tongue over her teeth, my phone rings.

I press speaker.

'Yes.'

'Hi, Bryce, it's Chelsea. I need to make an appointment with you for later today in order to discuss the flight transfers for VIP guests at next week's AFL Grand Final. Do you have time?'

I look in my diary which is as confusing as fuck. I desperately need to get Lucy on it. 'I have some time at 3 p.m. I can see you then.'

'Looking forward to it.'

Aggravated by how disorganised my schedule is, I quickly dismiss her. 'Okay, I'll see you then.'

I hit the disconnect button on the phone and take a deep breath before looking up, suddenly remembering that before I was interrupted, I was about to taste the mother of my son.

Finding the doorway vacant, I screw up my face. I wonder where the fuck she has gone when I spot movement from the corner of my eye. Turning to the window to look onto the balcony, I find Alexis working out on the gym equipment — working out probably an understatement. She is going hard and clearly in a determined mood. *Jesus! Why is she always so fucking determined to try death by exercise?*

I pick up Brayden and walk into the lounge area to transfer him to the bassinet beside the piano. *See? Multiple bassinets ... fucking genius.*

I make sure he is still sleeping soundly before heading to the balcony. 'You might want to take it easy,' I state, a little annoyed that I have to remind Alexis once more to tone down her over-exuberant fitness training.

'Don't start this shit with me again,' she snaps. 'I'm no longer pregnant and am now fully capable of working out.'

'Alexis, I'm just saying that you gave birth a week ago. Your body is still healing and adjusting. Don't rush things.'

'I'm not.'

I notice her refusal to look at me, and it reinforces the concern I felt the morning we brought Brayden home, the morning I mentioned Chelsea.

Curious, I decide to pose that question. 'Has this got anything to do with the fact Chelsea just rang?'

Alexis presses a button, accelerating her strides on the treadmill. 'No. The flying fuck I give about that bitch just flew the fuck away,' she says sarcastically while flapping her hands like a bird.

Really? Clearly that is not the case.

'Honey, why does she make you so angry?'

'Because.'

'Because is not an answer. Alexis, talk to me.'

'No, go away.'

Bloody hell! I want nothing more than to carry her kicking and screaming up to the bedroom and force her to talk to me while my cock is planted firmly in her pussy. But I can't. That form of dominance is a no-go at the moment and it pisses me off.

Having no other choice, I reach into my pocket, take out my phone, and dial Jessica. She answers after only a couple of rings. 'Bryce, dear. How's fatherhood treating you?'

'Hello, Jessica,' I state, while watching Alexis' reaction. 'Fatherhood is wonderful. Perfect, in fact.'

Alexis closes her eyes briefly and sucks in a long, deep breath.

'Lovely. How can I help you? We are not scheduled for a session until Thursday. Do you need to see me earlier?' Jessica asks, hope in her voice.'

'Actually, yes. I would like you to come over today, if possible.'

'I can organise that. Is everything all right?'

'Well, I'll leave that up to you to decide. Alexis is ... let's just say, displaying signs of angry frustration. She won't talk to me about it, so I'm a little concerned.'

'Oh ... you didn't just go there,' Alexis hisses, her fiery glare incinerating me on the spot.

I glare back at her, determined to sort this shit out. I'm not having one of the happiest times of our life marred by her pent-up, unwarranted feelings of jealousy toward Chelsea.

'Okay, I can be there in an hour,' Jessica informs.

'Thank you. See you soon.'

I end the call and put the phone back in my pocket, my stare never wavering from Alexis.

She accelerates her strides even more, practically punching the button with her clenched fist. 'I can't believe you just insinuated I am not coping well after giving birth. Firstly, you have no right. Secondly, I am dealing with mothering our gorgeous son just fine, thank you very much. To even imply that I cannot handle him or —'

'I'm not implying that at all.'

'Then what was that?'

'You need to talk about whatever it is that is pissing you off. And if you won't talk to me about it, you can talk to Jessica. You should be exceedingly happy at the moment, but you aren't. I don't want you to look back at this time and have any regrets.'

She hits the emergency stop button on the treadmill and comes to a halt, slumping over the armrests. Taking deep breaths and looking somewhat exhausted, she wipes her brow with a towel.

After a few seconds of catching her breath and getting her bearings, she steps off, grabs her water bottle and has a long drink before walking up to me. 'I have no regrets ... none at all, none where you and Brayden are concerned. I never have and I never will,' she says quietly, hurt evident in her voice.

I watch her walk back inside before stopping at the bassinet and smiling at our son. The love she projects for him is obviously genuine and in abundance which just confuses me all the more. *Then why is she so unhappy all of a sudden?* I sigh and pray that Jessica will figure it out.

* * *

Just over an hour later, I let Jessica into the apartment.

'I like what you've done with the place,' she says admiringly, grinning at the now babyfied surroundings.

'Yeah, feels more like a home now.'

'So, where is she?'

'Up in our room with Brayden. Just go straight up.'

'You sure? I don't want to start a session with an already irate patient. It's much more work on my part.'

'It's fine, she's feeding. I'm sure she won't mind.'

Jessica winks and squeezes my arm before giving me a tight embrace. 'Congratulations, I'm so proud of you. And don't worry, I'll get to the bottom of whatever is bothering Alexis.'

'Thank you,' I reply while watching her make her way up the stairs before I head for my office.

As I sit down, I'm instantly made aware that the baby monitor on my desk is switched on as I hear the sound of Alexis' voice singing 'Baby Mine'. As her words filter through the small portable speaker in front of me, I am transfixed by the indisputable love she projects as she sings them. I could sit here forever and listen to her heartfelt words to our son. It's mesmerising.

'Excuse me, Alexis. Sorry, am I interrupting you?' Jessica says, her voice also now sounding through the speaker.

I go to switch the baby monitor off, but pause with my hand on the button, unable to bring myself to do it. It's my excessive curiosity and basically having to know every single detail which prevents me from doing so. Instead — as my conscience goes to war with itself — I sit and continue to listen.

'No, that's all right. I'm just settling him for sleep,' Alexis informs.

There's a pause for a moment and I hear some muffled sounds.

'Oh, goodness, he is just a perfect little angel,' Jessica coos.

'Isn't he just? Here, would you like a cuddle?'

'Do you not want to put him down to sleep?'

'It's fine. He basically lives in Bryce's arms, so he's used to it.'

'Well, in that case, I'd love to.'

There's another pause in discussion and some more muffled sounds.

'My, oh my, does he look like his father.'

I hear Alexis giggle. 'Yes, he sure does.'

This statement has me grinning from ear to ear when my phone rings. Annoyed by the interruption, I buzz Abigail. 'Abigail, can you please hold all my calls until further notice.'

'Certainly, Mr Clark,' she responds, the ringing ceasing immediately.

'Thank you.'

I hang up and continue to listen to the monitor.

'So how's everything going? Is he feeding well? Are you getting enough sleep?' Jessica asks.

'Now, Jessica ... you wouldn't be here to find out if I'm suffering postnatal depression at all, would you?' Alexis asks with a playful tone to her voice.

Jessica laughs and it has me a little perplexed. That is exactly why she is here.

'No, Alexis. Well, that is why Bryce asked me here. But no, I just wanted to see your handsome and incredibly adorable little son.' *Traitor! Fucking traitor!*

I'm just about to get up from my desk and march upstairs to demand she put her skills — that I pay a considerable sum for — to use, when she continues speaking.

'However, since I am here, and seeing how you are clearly not suffering from postnatal depression, do you want to tell me why Bryce is so concerned? Obviously you have given him reason to be.'

Clever woman, why did I doubt her?

'It's my own insecurities, Jessica,' Alexis sighs. 'I'll get over them.'

'Insecurities about what? You look great. You're healthy, you're —'

'I look great? Pfft, I have a long way to go to get back to the weight I was happy with. The weight I was when I met Bryce.'

She has a long way to go? Fucking bullshit! She looks as stunning as ever.

'Alexis, I'm not going to stand here and tell you that these insecurities about your post-baby body are ridiculous, because they are not. Nearly every mother to have just given birth feels this way. It's quite normal. What I will say, though, is give yourself a break. You will get back to the weight you want to be, in time.'

'I may not have time,' Alexis mumbles, so softly that I can barely hear.

'What do you mean?'

'Nothing, it's nothing. Look, I know I will never be a skinny supermodel and I never want to be. I was happy with my curves and being a size twelve. After all, I am thirty-seven years of age and a mother of three. It's just ... I want to get back to that weight as soon as possible. I don't want to risk —'

Alexis cuts herself off.

'You don't want to risk what, Alexis?'

Leaning in closer to the monitor, I strain to hear what she is so worried about.

'I don't want to risk losing Bryce,' she says sadly.

What. The. Fuck? *Lose me? Why would she lose me? She will NEVER lose me!* With my heart hammering in my chest, confusion plagues me as to why she would feel this way. As far as I am aware, I have never given her cause to believe I would abandon her. It doesn't make sense to me.

'Alexis, why do you feel you could lose Bryce?' *Yes, why?*

'Because it's happened before,' she exclaims, her voice now raised and sounding desperately troubled. 'After giving birth to Charlotte, I waited too long to lose my baby weight and Rick ... well ... he obviously didn't find me attractive any more and went elsewhere. He had an affair with a younger, slimmer, prettier woman. God, Jessica, I don't think I'd cope if Bryce does the same. It will kill me. I can't let that happen. I won't let that happen. I won't let Chelsea take him away from me,' she shouts, desperation in her voice.

Fuck! Fuck me! The pieces start to fit together.

Brayden's little cry sounds through the monitor.

'Oh, baby boy, Mummy is sorry. I didn't mean to frighten you,' she sobs. 'God, I'm so sorry.'

I hear another muffled sound together with Alexis sobbing in the background and it tears me apart. I want nothing more than to run to her and comfort her, to let her know I would never do what Rick did. EVER! And, I want to kick his fucking head in for making her feel this way.

'Alexis, Bryce is not your ex-husband.' *You can say that again.* 'He is undeniably in love with you and I can confidently say would never betray you like that. You need to trust him, but first and foremost you need to trust in yourself.'

'I do trust him. I just don't trust Chelsea. She made it very clear to me after we lost Bianca that she was in love with him. I warned her then to back off, but I know women like her; they wait like a snake in the grass. Wait for their time to strike. And she's fucking waiting, I can tell.'

I run my hands through my hair, completely dumbfounded by what I am hearing. *Am I that oblivious to Chelsea's feelings? Does she only have eyes for me? Shit!* If that is the case, no wonder Alexis is acting the way she is.

'Maybe you should tell Bryce how you feel,' Jessica suggests. 'He has known Chelsea for a long time and is probably unaware of her true character. In fact, I can assure you that he is unaware of her true character.'

Alexis sighs. 'I don't think it will matter, Jessica. Where Chelsea is concerned he is like a brick wall.'

What? Am I?

'Okay, well in that case we work on you by making you feel better about yourself. We need to build up your confidence, starting with a trip to the hairdresser. I think you should organise a girly pampering afternoon with your friends.'

'That's actually a great idea, but what about Brayden? I can't exactly take him with me.'

'I think his father will cope.'

'Oh, I know that. Bryce has been an exceptional dad so far. He's perfect. I have no qualms there. It's just, he is so busy.'

'I'm sure he'll be fine. Call Lucy in if it makes you feel better. Or speak to Arthur.'

'No. I'm not going behind Bryce's back and interfering with his business. No way in hell. That is his domain.'

Brayden's little cry pierces through the monitor again.

'Is he ready for a feed?' Jessica asks. 'I'll let you get back to it then.'

'He shouldn't be, the little guzzle-guts. But thank you. Thank you for coming and talking to me.'

'Anytime, dear. And remember what I said. Bryce is not Rick.'

'I know. I just ... I get a bad feeling about Chelsea.'

'I can see that. If talking to Bryce about it is off the cards, take matters into your own hands and build your confidence back to the level it should be.'

'I will, Jessica. Thank you.'

Brayden cries out again, except this time he is letting Alexis know he wants a feed.

'All right, hungry little piggy, I'll get them out for you. God, you are so much like your father.'

I laugh. Yes, he is like me, wanting to latch onto her nipples every chance he gets. Except that I want to for a completely different reason.

'I'll let myself out. Take care, and contact me if you need anything,' Jessica says as her voice trails off into the distance.

'Thanks, I will,' Alexis calls out.

Seconds later I hear what sounds like Alexis unclipping her bra, and then that unmistakable sound of Brayden suckling. I'm totally jealous.

'Whoa, settle petal,' she giggles. 'There's plenty of milk in there and it's all for you, buddy. No need to try and rip Mummy's nipple apart to get it.'

Loving to eavesdrop on their time together, but at the same time wishing I could see them both, I consider looking into a video monitor when I hear a knock on my office door. Knowing that it's Jessica coming to say goodbye, I quickly switch off the monitor and call for her to come in.

I play dumb as she walks toward me. 'How did you go?'

'Just fine, Bryce. She is definitely not suffering from postnatal depression.'

I nod and smile. 'That's great. So, what is the matter?'

'I can't tell you, you know that. But what I can tell you is this: open your bloody eyes, especially where certain members of your staff are concerned. And pay her attention. Tell her how much you love her. Tell her how incredible she is and, most importantly, tell her how incredible she looks.'

I continue to nod and smile. Her requests are second nature to me; making Alexis feel good about herself is one of my favourite pastimes. 'I will,' I promise.

'Good. Call me if you need me. And by the way, Brayden is superb,' she states, smiling brightly. 'If ever you need a babysitter, you know where I am.'

'Noted,' I say as she approaches the door and lets herself out.

Once Jessica is gone, I start to think about everything I overheard. Alexis' need to get back to her pre-baby weight. The fear she has of losing me. That fuckwit ex-husband of hers and how he has destroyed her confidence. And her thoughts on Chelsea's true character.

Swivelling my chair to face the view of Port Phillip Bay, I take in the scenic vision that has many times granted me clarity in determining a course of action. This time is no different from before as I decide what my next step will be. A step that involves planting a seed, and we all know how much I love gardening.

10

'You're beautiful, you know,' I say as I break the silence while watching Alexis feed Brayden. 'And I love you more than life itself. That will never change.' I walk into the room and sit next to them, picking up the soft guitar and nervously fiddling with it. I don't know why I'm so nervous. I guess I just don't want her to be angry with me any more. I feel like a complete arsehole.

Alexis gives me a critical look. 'Did Jessica speak to you?'

'No, not really. She just assured me that you weren't suffering from postnatal depression.'

She stands up and walks over to the nappy change table. 'I told you I wasn't.'

'I know you did. But I had to be sure.' I put down the guitar, wanting to help her, wanting to make things right. 'Here,' I say, stepping up next to her, 'let me.'

She moves aside and allows me to take her place.

'Hello, Daddy's boy,' I coo like an idiot, something I have absolutely no control over. Even when I try desperately not to talk to my son using my daddy-baby voice, it still comes out of my mouth that way. God only knows how much shit Derek and the boys are going to pile on me when they hear. 'Let's change this wet nappy and get you all clean and dry, yeah?'

I open the nappy to find the filthiest-looking mushy substance known to man. Fuck, I can't even begin to describe what colour it is.

After wiping his dirty arse and sliding a clean nappy underneath — just like Alexis showed me — I hold out the folded nappy-of-death for Alexis to dispose of.

I then lift Brayden's bottom to position him correctly and wipe his little fella clean. Just as I am about to secure the clean nappy, a fountain of yellow baby piss hits me square in the face.

What. The. Fuck?

I hear Alexis muffle her mouth with her hand and, even though my eyes are closed and painted with urine, I know she is about to burst into laughter.

'Did our son just piss in my face?' I state calmly.

Alexis, still trying desperately to stifle her outburst, croakily responds. 'Um ... yes, yes, he did.'

'Right. Do you want to hand me a towel, or a wipe, or a fucking tissue?' I ask, still keeping my tone calm.

'Sure.' She lets go of her bottled outburst and cracks up laughing. 'I would love to.'

Seconds later I feel her wiping Brayden's piss from my eyes, followed by my lips and the rest of my face. And, now feeling that it is safe to unseal them, I pry one eye open at a time to find one happy little boy squirming around underneath my hand.

'You think that's funny, don't you?' I ask him. 'Pissing on daddy like that.'

'You need to keep his Mr Doodle covered with either the nappy or a towel AT ALL TIMES!' Alexis reaffirms as she leans down and kisses Brayden's head. 'Otherwise this little cheeky critter will give you a golden shower. Won't you?'

'Speaking of shower, that's where I am headed now,' I declare as I walk toward the en suite.

'Bye, Daddy,' Alexis calls out from behind. I turn around to find her holding Brayden and waving his little hand at me. 'Thanks for changing my nappy.'

'You're welcome, baby boy,' I reply with a laugh. 'Anytime.'

* * *

After a quick shower, I discover it is almost time for my appointment with Chelsea. As I make my way down the stairs, I find Alexis sitting on the floor with Brayden lying on a bunny rug beside her. She is holding a brightly-coloured caterpillar-looking thing not too far from his face.

'Boo!' she coos at him, after pulling it away quickly. 'I can't wait for you to smile for the first time, BB. Something tells me you will have a smile like your daddy.'

BB? I thought we dealt with that shit.

I quietly and purposely walk up behind them. 'BB?' I question, while firing an interrogative expression her way.

She startles a little and looks up with an uh-oh, I-just-got-busted look. 'Um ... yes! Baby Brayden.'

Realisation dawns on me. 'That is why you wanted the initial B, isn't it?' I ask, impressed.

She giggles, revealing her plan. 'Maybe.'

'You never cease to amaze me,' I say, shaking my head with a smile. 'Listen, I have my appointment with Chelsea now. I want you and Brayden to come in to the office while she's here.'

'I really don't want to,' Alexis murmurs without looking at me. 'We are happy here.'

The buzzer to my office sounds and we both look at the speaker. Why we do this I'm not really sure.

'Please, I want to show off my son ... and the amazing woman who gave him to me.'

I hear her make a 'pfft' noise, and her confident demeanour from seconds ago is now gone. It saddens me.

'Sure, if it means that much to you,' she says with clear distaste, as she slowly gets up from the ground and takes Brayden to my office.

I'm ready to put Alexis' and Jessica's theory to the test. Surely Chelsea isn't as bad as they say she is.

* * *

Heading to the door I open it to find Chelsea seated in reception, brushing down her dress and fixing her hair and makeup. Instantly, I pick up on her effort to make herself presentable. Normally, I would find this preparation an honourable quality, something that employees or business associates should make a habit of doing before a meeting. This time, though, I see it more as an attempt to impress me on a different level.

My new-found insight surprises me.

'Good afternoon, Chelsea. Please come in.' I stand back and hold the office door open for her, remembering what my mother had always said about being a gentleman: 'Chivalry is only dead if you yourself kill it.'

Expecting her to walk in like I directed her to, I'm shocked when she stops and places a quick kiss on my cheek. 'Hi, it's nice to see you again. I feel we haven't caught up in such a long time.'

Okay, that kiss was unprofessional and certainly not called for, considering my fiancée is in the room and has just recently given birth to our son.

Worried because this particular experiment is now proving Alexis and Jessica's theory correct, I quickly give Alexis a glance to check I haven't upset her any further. I honestly did not see Chelsea as this brazen before now. *Shit! Have I been that blind?* I expect to see Alexis resembling a cartoon character with steam billowing out of her ears and nostrils. Instead, I see a withdrawn woman who is extremely uncomfortable.

Chelsea follows my line of sight toward Alexis. 'Oh, hello, Alexis. I didn't know you would be here,' she says with a sweet, but somewhat bitter, tone of voice.

'Well, I do live and work here, Chelsea,' Alexis replies, just as bitterly sweet, while cradling Brayden in her arms, 'and this is my fiancé's office, so I'm bound to be around, aren't I?'

'Yes, you are,' Chelsea replies curtly. She looks back at me, waiting for my instruction as to where we should sit.

Thinking that she would have acknowledged Brayden by this stage and be asking how he is — heck, even asking what his name is — I'm surprised that she hasn't. *Maybe it's because he is in Alexis' arms and approaching her would be awkward due to their obvious animosity toward each other.*

I decide to put that theory to the test, too, and take Brayden from Alexis. 'Chelsea, this is Brayden, Alexis' and my son,' I say proudly, stepping up right beside her.

'He's cute,' she replies, giving him a quick smile, then focussing back on me. 'But then again, he is your son.'

I furrow my brow, her flirting obvious and quite frankly pathetic.

At this point, I'm pissed off. Pissed off because, one: I've been so fucking blind and, because of that, Alexis has been hurt, and, two: I fucking hate it when I'm wrong. And, three: the way she just treated my fiancée and son in front of me was nothing short of appalling.

Moving away from Chelsea, I pass Brayden back to Alexis and kiss her with a purposeful show. When I'm done, I turn back around and ask Chelsea to sit in the seat in front of my desk. She does, but not before shooting Alexis a subtle scowl.

Sitting down opposite her, I steeple my hands in front of me and prepare myself to potentially lose an old friend. 'Chelsea, I'm going to have to let you go,' I say neutrally.

'Let me go wher—'

'Your behaviour, especially today in this office, is unprofessional and quite frankly embarrassing. I made it exceedingly clear that we were nothing more than friends a long time ago, and I'd honestly hoped you could work here with a proficient, friendly and skilled manner. Clearly, you can't. And that being the case, I'm sorry to say that your employment with Clark Incorporated is now effectively terminated.'

Chelsea sits stunned, mouth agape, searching my eyes for some form of reprieve or indication that what I just said was some strange ploy. Slowly, she turns to face Alexis. 'You. This is all your doing.'

I stand up and gesture that she do the same. 'I can assure you that this has absolutely nothing to do with Alexis. I had every intention of giving you the benefit of the doubt today, truly sceptical that what I had suspected was just that: an unwarranted suspicion. Unfortunately, Chelsea, you have proved me wrong, and because of that and the way you feel, I can't have you working here any more. It's not fair to Alexis and it's not fair to you.'

Chelsea stands up, fury and hurt in her eyes. 'And how exactly do you think I feel, Bryce?'

Seeing the hurt seep out of her is unsettling, and the last thing I want is for her to be upset, but I now realise she needs to be told bluntly, once and for all, that she holds nothing more than my friendship.

'I think it's obvious how you feel. Can you honestly stand there and tell me that you don't have feelings for me, Chelsea? That you haven't harboured those feelings since we hooked up all those years ago,' I candidly request.

She looks down at her hands, her bottom lip trembling. 'I can't.'

'And that's why you have to leave. Move on. You can't do that here.'

She nods slowly, but doesn't look up.

'Listen, I want you to be happy like I am. Find that special someone you deserve to have in your life ... because that someone is not me. I belong to Alexis and I always will. We have a family and we will be married in the near future.'

She looks up at this point and finds Alexis and Brayden. I find them too, taking in Alexis' tear-streaked face.

Chelsea sucks in a breath and covers her mouth with her hand. 'I'm sorry, Bryce. I ... I just thought that we ...' She momentarily shuts her eyes and shakes her head. 'You're right, I've acted terribly. God, I need to leave. Shit! I'm sorry.'

She turns and heads for the door with rapid speed. I take a step forward, my intention to chase her down. I don't want her to leave in the state she is in. Hesitating for a mere second, I pause, fearing that if I do go after her, I will give her the wrong impression.

Alexis hands me Brayden. 'Here, take BB. I'll go after her.'

I watch her run off, wiping her eyes.

Minutes later, Alexis walks back into my office. I've already placed Brayden down in his bassinet, and he is — as per usual — fast asleep.

Standing up from my seated position behind the desk, I make my way around to the front of it and lean my arse against the edge. 'How is she?' I ask, worried about the answer.

'Devastated —'

'Shit!' I run my hands through my hair in frustration. I really didn't want it to end this badly.

Alexis steps up to me and takes my hands in hers. 'Devastated ... but she'll be okay. You gave her the wake-up call she needed.'

Letting go of her hands and placing mine on her hips, I guide her closer and press my mouth to hers, the taste and feel of her body instantly healing my apprehension.

'Believe it or not,' she whispers, pulling away from my mouth, the loss of her tongue agonising, 'you did her a favour.'

I rest my forehead on hers and momentarily close my eyes. 'I know. But I feel terrible.'

'That's because you have a big heart.'

'A heart that belongs to you and only you. I wish you would realise that.'

'I do ... now.'

She tilts her head up to kiss me once again, and I welcome the invitation eagerly. No one makes me feel what Alexis makes me feel. No one ever has. It's as though we are two kindred spirits; two halves of a whole.

'Jessica told you, didn't she? You won't confess because if you do you admit she broke patient-client confidentiality. I get that.'

'No, she didn't,' I admit sheepishly. 'I heard your entire conversation through the baby monitor.'

Still secured in my arms, she leans backward and looks at the monitor, then back to me. 'Did you not think to switch it off?'

'I was going to, but when you started talking about being afraid of losing me because of what Rick did, I just had to listen. Honey, I would never, EVER, do what Rick did to you.'

A tear falls from her eye, slowly sliding down her cheek. I stop its descent as it reaches her jaw and place a kiss where it had been only seconds ago. It kills me to think that what Rick did shortly after Alexis gave birth to Charlotte has resulted in a lack of faith in herself. *Fuck! I want kill the arsehole.*

'You, my love, are perfect in every way,' I say, kneeling down before her. I lift her top, bunching it just under her breasts. 'Every. Single. Bit of you,' I reiterate in between placing kisses along her stomach.

'Even this new stretchmark here?' she asks, pointing to the pale pink scar on her tummy.

I drag my tongue along it and watch her close her eyes, not sure at this point if they are closed due to discomfort or pleasure. 'Especially this one, because this one signifies what you endured to give me the most precious gift imaginable.'

CHAPTER
11

A few weeks after we jumped Alexis' Chelsea-hurdle, Alexis is nearly back to her old self. I couldn't be happier. She has been hitting the gym quite hard though, and as much as I don't like seeing her treat her body so harshly I figure it's best to stay out of it. I don't want to dampen her improving mood.

Standing at the window in my office, looking onto the balcony where she is now using the weight machine, my dick throbs in anticipatory agony. I'm almost at the point of having to go knock the top off it just to get some relief. I desperately want to be inside her, having not made love to her for nearly four weeks due to her post-birth healing.

I suck in a breath and growl like a friggin' bear as I watch her legs open and close, her abductor muscles flexing and taunting me. Right now I wish they were closing and clenching around my head while I taste her sweet pussy, followed by them tightening and clamping around my hips as I fuck her senseless. *Jesus, fucking Christ!*

Adjusting my raging hard-on, I shuffle to get some relief, but my relief is short-lived. She stands up, then grabs her towel and bottle of water and I watch with perverted delight as she drags the towel across her forehead, over her face and down her neck. I've never wanted to be a towel so much in my bloody life.

She presses her drink bottle to her lips and tilts her head back, gulping the water and quenching her thirst. A little bit of the water misses her mouth and travels down her chin to trickle slowly between her breasts.

Now, I want nothing more than to be that droplet of water. *Fuck! I need her.*

Stalking her like she is prey I'm about to devour, I walk along the windows to my office, not taking my eyes from her mouthwatering form. My dick seems to have a mind of its own, escalating its request to explore her depths. And believe me, I'm more than inclined to grant this ardent appeal.

She turns, bends over and places her water and towel on the ground. I can't help but pause in my pacing of the window to stare at her arse which is primed and positioned for me to grab hold of ... I'm completely done for. Cock-stunned and fuck-ready.

'That's it!' I groan.

Eagerly striding toward the door which leads into the apartment, I'm halted by the ring of my phone.

'What now?' I growl at the plastic telecommunications device from hell, the bane of my existence.

Walking back to my desk, I hit the speaker button and bark like a vicious animal. 'What?'

'Bryce, sorry, have I caught you at a bad time. Is everything all right?' Arthur asks, concern manifesting in his voice.

How this man manages to find the most inappropriate times to interrupt amazes me.

'Yes, Arthur, everything is fine. But I am in the middle of something,' I say through gritted teeth, as I watch Alexis now performing knee raises on the power tower.

Her gaze travels to my window and she struggles to smile as she strains and lifts her legs.

I smile back.

'I'm sorry, but this can't wait. There has been an incident downstairs on the casino floor.'

Eyes still trained on Alexis, I watch as she blows me a kiss. *Fuck!*

I drop my head back and close my eyes in heated frustration. 'What kind of incident?'

'Armed hold-up at one of the cashier booths, sir.'

Breathing in deeply, I turn around and take a seat at my desk. 'Which one?' I ask, as I access the casino's security feed through my laptop.

'Booth six. Dale has the assailant in the holding cell, and the police are on their way.'

I find the security files for Cashier Booth Six. 'How long ago did this happen?'

'Approximately five to seven minutes.'

I click on the file date-stamped eight minutes ago and begin to watch the feed. Before long, I notice an agitated Caucasian male pointing a handgun at Selena, one of my long-term employees. Selena is a fifty-four-year-old mother of three and has been working for me for over twelve years.

'Shit! Is Selena okay?' I ask, running my hands through my hair.

'She's a little shaken, but she's fine.'

'How the hell did this creep go unnoticed?' I question, furious that our state-of-the-art facial recognition software and highly trained security officers were unable to prevent this attack.

'I don't have the details yet, but obviously we will have to review the entire event. Dale is waiting for you in the cell, but if you are busy —'

'No, I'll be there. Just give me minute.'

'Okay. See you soon.'

I hang up from Arthur and drop my head in my hands.

'Is everything all right?' Alexis asks as she makes her way toward my desk with Brayden against her chest.

The sight of both them rips my aggravation away like tearing off a Band-Aid.

'Yes, everything is fine. But I have to head downstairs for a moment. There was an armed hold-up on the casino floor.'

'Shit! Is everyone okay? God! Nobody got hurt, did they?'

Putting my arms out, I indicate I want to cuddle my son and Alexis obligingly hands Brayden over to me. The mixture of his pure, baby smell and the soft scent of Alexis' perfume has me feeling at peace once again.

I sigh a little and answer to put her at ease. 'Selena, the cashier who bore the brunt of his threat, is apparently a little shaken. I want to go and see if she is all right and gather a few more details as to how this happened.'

'Of course, I'll cancel my afternoon with —'

'No, don't do that. You deserve an afternoon of pampering with your friends. It's long overdue.'

'It's okay. It's only hair, massage and some waxing. It really isn't that important.'

'Honey,' I say, as I touch the side of her face, 'you're going. I promise this won't take long. And anyway, I'm looking forward to a bit of just-me-and-the-kids time.'

The buzzer to the door sounds, interrupting us.

A huge smile covers her face. 'You are, are you?'

Instantly, I sense her smile and tone of voice holds hidden meaning. 'What's that supposed to mean?'

She takes Brayden from me and, like always, the feeling of loss is unpleasant.

'Nothing,' she replies, clearly full of shit.

I would've interrogated her further, but she opens the door to my office and is nearly thrown back by a massive bunch of blue and white balloons.

Lil — the bearer of those balloons — awkwardly stumbles through the door. 'Hello, congratulations! Let me see, let me see,' she squawks, while letting go of the helium filled bunch she is holding. The balloons hit the roof and bob around.

Following Lil through the door is Carly and Jade, then Steph holding a big green dinosaur and a bunch of flowers. They all gather around Alexis and Brayden and coo at my little man like he is the most adorable sight to be seen. Well ... I can't really blame them. He is.

Smiling, I shake my head and get ready to head out the door.

'Where's Tash?' Alexis asks, disappointment appearing across her face. 'Don't tell me she can't make it.'

The girls laugh, except for Lil who just rolls her eyes and places her hands on her hips. 'She refused to ride in the elevator with the balloons,' Lil deadpans.

Alexis looks to the roof and cracks up laughing. 'Oh yeah ... I forgot she has a phobia of balloons. Funniest thing ever.'

A phobia is far from the 'funniest thing ever' ... I should know. But balloons? Yeah, that is pretty amusing.

Just as I'm about to kiss Alexis and Brayden goodbye, Tash enters the room and gives the spot where the balloons have rested against the roof a very wide birth while eyeing them suspiciously. 'Keep those fuckers away from me. I swear, Lil, if you pull the shit you just pulled downstairs with those evil things again, I will cut you. I'm not kidding.'

'That's my cue to leave,' I announce. 'I'll be back soon.'

I kiss Alexis and Brayden goodbye and then head out of the room. As I'm walking to the elevator, I hear Alexis ask what shit Lil pulled.

'She locked Tash in the car with them,' Steph explains. 'It was hilarious.'

'Yeah, ha ha ... very funny,' Tash responds. 'I'm scarred for freakin' life.'

I smile and shake my head, but soon frown at the thought of being locked in the car with a clown. That shit is just not funny.

* * *

After spending a little time with Selena and praising her for staying calm and following protocol, I reaffirm she was safe by reminding her that the cashier booths are bulletproof. I send Selena home on extended leave and organise some counselling for her. Despite the fact it is company policy anyway, I want her to feel well looked after.

I'm then briefed by Dale — my head of security — that the assailant is a desperate drug user and not the sharpest tool in the shed. I make it very clear that I want a full rundown of the circumstances; exactly how did a shady character — looking the way the dickhead looks — get into the casino in the first place. I then leave Dale to handle the police and manage the aftermath.

Opening the door to my apartment, I find Alexis breastfeeding Brayden while sitting around the lounge with her friends.

'I swear, I shot milk a good metre away,' Steph says proudly.

'Yeah, well, I could write Jade on the shower screen,' Jade explains as she grabs at her breasts and mimics the lettering of J.a.d.e.

What. The. Fuck?

'Yuck! You two are disgusting. I'm not having kids for that reason alone. No one should be able to write their name with liquid from their boobs,' Carly interjects.

I tend to agree with her.

'Oh, grow up,' Lil grumbles. 'When you have that much milk in your ducts, you can't help it. It just squirts out.'

Feeling the need to end this conversation before I hear something I will never be able to wipe from my memory bank, I make it known that I am standing in the room. 'Ladies, sorry I took so long.'

I head over to Alexis, kiss her forehead, then cup Brayden's head in my hand and rub his earlobe with my thumb. Hearing what sounds like a loving sigh, I look up to find Steph staring at me, all dreamy like a bloody teenager. I give her an awkward smile just as Jade elbows her in the ribs.

'Here you go, Daddy,' Alexis says, handing me my very milk-groggy son. 'He needs to burp and he also needs his nappy changed. I should only be gone for three hours. Ring me if you need anything and I'll come straight up. If he happens to get hungry again, or I'm running a little late, there's backup milk that I've expressed in a bottle in the fridge. He's got a little nappy rash, so don't forget the cream and —'

'Go!' I demand, kissing her worried face and stopping her rant. 'We'll be fine. Won't we, Bray?' I ask, giving him a fist-bump. 'Go and enjoy yourselves.'

'Bye kids,' Alexis calls out, Nate and Charli reciprocating their acknowledgement by shouting back.

Carly links her arm around Alexis' and practically drags her to the front door, Tash giving her arse little smacks on the way there. I'm momentarily jealous, wanting to be the one giving her arse small smacks, not only with my hand, but with my hips and ...

Brayden's little cry snaps me out of my light bondage fantasy of Alexis. 'Shit! Burp, that's right,' I murmur to myself. 'Sorry, buddy.'

I drape the burping cloth over my shoulder and hoist him up gently, patting his back as I walk upstairs toward his nursery. Seconds later, he lets out a noise that I'm fairly sure was not solely a burp.

'That did not sound good, Bray,' I state, a little concerned. 'That sounded wet.'

Passing Charli's bedroom, I find her lying on her stomach on the floor, colouring in. 'Hey, Charlotte. What you doin'?'

'Drawing Addison a best friend picture. Do you like it?' she asks, holding up a pink piece of paper covered in girly pictures and sparkly shit.

'Yeah, it's ... girly.'

Charlotte giggles. 'Of course it's girly, silly. Addison is a girl. I can't give her a boy picture.'

As per usual, the little lady is correct.

'No, you can't,' I say with a smile as I turn and head toward Brayden's nursery.

'Um ... Bryce?'

'Yeah,' I call back, twisting around.

Charlotte screws up her face and points toward me. 'You have baby spew on your back.'

I twist further and catch a glimpse of a white trail down my shirt. 'Gee, thanks, Brayden. Just what Daddy has always wanted. Come on, looks like we are both getting changed.'

'Can I help?' Charlotte calls out.

'Sure.'

We enter the nursery, and I automatically smile at the space theme Alexis and I agreed on. Stepping in here reminds me a little of being in the observatory. Painted on the walls and roof are constellations, planets and spaceships. Okay, so the spaceships don't remind me of the observatory, but the rest does.

Right before I lay Brayden down on the change table, he lets one rip, except like the burp beforehand, it sounds incredibly wet.

'Please don't tell me you did what I think you just did?' I groan.

He grunts a little, reinforcing that, yes ... he did.

'Er, what's that smell?' Charli whines, pinching her nostrils.

'What do you think it is?' I ask, not really requiring an answer.

'Brayden, did you just do poo-poo in your nappy?' Still pinching her nostrils, Charlotte drops her head close to his face. 'Poo-poo is for the potty.'

He widens his eyes at her closeness, seeming to adjust his tiny vision.

'He's a bit young for the potty, Charlotte.'

'Starlight's a baby and she uses the potty.'

Who the fuck is Starlight?

I look at her a little perplexed. 'Who's Starlight?'

'My baby doll.'

'Oh.' I don't really know what to say to that.

Unbuttoning his little blue onesie, I soon become horrifyingly aware that yes, the wind he not long ago broke was not wind at all. Instead, what is filling his nappy and spilling out over the sides, is my worst nightmare.

'Aw, Brayden ... what the crap, buddy.'

I lift his legs out of his onesie only to find the mushy shit has found its way down them as well. *Ah, shit! It just keeps getting worse.*

Charlotte spots the poo-splosion and takes a step back. 'That's just gross.'

'Tell me about it,' I agree wholeheartedly.

As I attempt to free his arms as well, his little hands clench the sleeves, preventing my efforts. *Why are these stupid onesies called Wondersuits? There's nothing fucking wonderful about them.*

'Brayden, let go,' I laugh at him with frustration, as I gently try to pry his fingers apart.

He does as he's told — well, technically not — and I get him free from his suit. Except now I have to tackle the singlet ... which I'm pretty fucking sure was white when Alexis put it on him this morning. Now looking at it, it's a yellowish brown and stuck to his skin. *Why do babies have to wear so much bloody clothing?*

'Shit!' I curse to myself, now beginning to stress out.

'Don't swear,' Charlotte says from behind.

I twist around to find her inconspicuously taking steps backward toward the door. 'Where are you going?' *Don't you bloody abandon me now.*

'To my room.'

'You said you wanted to help.'

'That was before I saw that,' she says, pointing to Brayden's nappy.

'You can't leave. I need all hands on deck ... Nate!' I shout, hoping for an extra set of them.

Within seconds, Nate comes into the room looking worried. 'What?'

'I have a situation with your brother,' I explain as calmly as possible.

'Don't do it, Nate,' Charlotte warns. 'Don't go any closer.'

'What's wrong? What's that sme—'

'That smell is what Brayden is covered in and no doubt soon to be covering me.'

I hate to admit it, but I cannot see any way out of becoming victim to his mess.

'Right. And what do you want me to do about it?' Nate asks, now stepping back to where Charlotte is standing.

'Pass me things.'

'What things?'

Good fucking question.

'Um ... wipes. I need wipes! But first get one of those smelly bag thingies.'

'I'll get the bag,' Charlotte pipes up.

Nate moves to my side. 'I'm on the wipes.'

'Good. Let's get this *shit* sorted.'

'Don't swear,' Charli says again.

'Sorry,' I mutter, feeling a little less overwhelmed.

Cringing like a goddamn pansy, I peel Brayden's singlet from his tiny chest, lifting it over his head and accidentally wiping some of the shit on his cheek. *Fuck! Sorry, little mate.*

'Ew, you just wiped poo on his face,' Charlotte complains.

'Sh, I didn't mean it. Don't tell your mum,' I plead like an idiot. 'Hold the bag out.'

She holds the bag out and I drop the singlet in it.

'Wipe!' I command, now sounding somewhat like an army sergeant. 'On second thoughts, Nate, make that a few wipes.'

He hands me a whole bunch of them, and I wipe the shit off Brayden's cheek then tackle his back and tummy. Soon, we seem to have the situation under control, the mushy poo-smeared nappy and clothing in a bag.

Looking down at Brayden's Mr Doodle — *bloody hell! Alexis and her stupid nicknames* — I fret for the smallest of seconds after discovering I don't have it covered and the last thing I need after cleaning him up is having piss everywhere.

Quickly, I grab a nappy and place it over the top of his unpredictable little fella, and then sigh with relief. 'Okay, Nate, grab another singlet and suit, please,' I say, and wait for the fresh items of clothing.

'What do I do with this?' Charlotte asks, standing like a statue and still holding the bag with the poo-covered clothes and nappy in it.

'Rubbish bin.'

'Mum won't be happy if you throw his clothes away.'

'Don't be silly. We can't keep those. They are covered in shit.'

'Don't swear.'

'Where has this "don't swear" shit come from?'

'Don't swear. And Nanny told me to say it. She said you and Mummy swear a lot.'

I chuckle to myself. *Bloody Maryann.*

Nate hands me the clean clothing and another wipe even though I don't need one. 'She's right, Mum won't be happy if she finds out you threw away Brayden's clothes.'

'Thanks, mate. But I don't need any more wipes.'

'Yes, you do. You have poo on your head and arm.'

Looking at my arm and now becoming acutely aware of a smear on my head, I shudder and wipe both spots. 'Thanks. Okay, baby boy, let's get you dressed.'

I place a clean nappy under his bottom and go to secure it.

'You need to put some of that white cream on his bottom,' Charli reminds me.

'Yes, yes, I do.'

Thankful for my little helpers, I take the nappy rash cream Charlotte is holding out for me and wipe a bit on Brayden's bum. I am now happy and content that I have covered all bases where this nappy change debacle is concerned, so I reclothe Brayden and pick him up, holding him in the air just like Simba in the *Lion King.*

He smiles at me.

Hold the fuck on ... he just smiled at me.

'He's smiling,' Nate says with a laugh, while pointing to his baby brother.

Leaning in closer for a better look, I smile back. 'He is, isn't he?'

Despite the past hour and the nightmare he was the cause of, his smile fills my heart with happiness. He is my pride and joy.

CHAPTER

12

'Do it again,' I probe, pulling ridiculous faces at Brayden. 'Come on, smile for Daddy.'

'It was just wind, Bryce,' Alexis deadpans from the sofa.

Lying on my side on the floor next to Brayden, I desperately try to get him to smile like he had before. 'No, it wasn't, he smiled. Nate, tell your Mum he smiled.'

'Yeah, Mum, he did. Right after he did the biggest poo in history. It was disgusting.'

Alexis laughs and looks at me sympathetically. Her hair is now shorter, much shorter, sitting just below her shoulders. She looks incredibly cute in a sexy way.

'He will only be four weeks old tomorrow. I think it's too early for him to smile,' she says with sympathy, while flipping the page of her magazine.

'He smiled,' I repeat, not having it any other way.

Alexis puts down her magazine and looks toward the kids. 'So what's for dinner, ratbags?'

'McDonalds,' they both chant.

Shit! I hate McDonalds.

I look up at Alexis and shoot her a you'll-pay-for-this look. She innocently bites her bottom lip and smiles. There's no way I can fight that smile and she knows it. It's her ultimate weapon. That, and the weapon between her legs.

Compassionately patting me on the thigh like I'm some elderly frail man, she offers me an out. 'It's okay, I'll go get it.'

God! I'm pathetic. 'No. I'll get it,' I say, shaking my head and rolling my eyes at her as if to say that I'm quite capable of going to the horrid place and that it doesn't faze me in the slightest. When, truth be told, it does; it fucking fazes me immensely. I hate with a vengeance having to go anywhere near Ronald McFucking Donald with his bright red scary hair, yellow fucktard suit, pasty white powdery skin and obscenely high eyebrows. How the hell he doesn't bother every person on this planet mystifies me.

'Charli-Bear,' Alexis says, clasping Charlotte's hand in hers while making it extremely obvious that she is trying to keep a straight face, 'I think you should go with Bryce.' She raises an eyebrow at Charlotte, hinting I need someone to hold my hand.

I know what she's doing and she thinks she is funny. She also thinks she is going to get away with it, but she's not. No. Way. In. Hell.

Charlotte looks over at me and nods her head as though I'm her new-found charity case. My balls basically evaporate.

'Come on then, Charlotte,' I say as I get up off the ground.

Charli walks over to the door and waits while Alexis swaps places with me. As Alexis bends down on her knees, I lean in to kiss her neck and gently whisper in her ear. 'I like your hair. I like it so much that I'm going to grab a fistful of it tonight while I fuck you into the next century.'

I walk toward the door and briefly look back, finding Alexis still on her hands and knees watching me with hungry eyes and a salacious grin. Her arse is perfectly poised in the air, and if it weren't for the three children in the room, I wouldn't hesitate to yank down her jeans, rip her underwear to shreds, and plant my cock so fucking deep inside her pussy, I'd be more than balls deep.

Lingering probably just a little too long on her rear end, I click my neck to the side and clench my fists, taking a second to get my shit back together before focussing on my trip to McFucking Hell.

* * *

'Why are you scared of clowns?' Charlotte asks as we walk through the entertainment precinct.

'Mr Clark,' one of my security team acknowledges as we pass by.

I nod back at him, then answer Charli. 'Because they are weird-looking.'

'Are you scared of ET?'

'No. Why?' I ask, a little perplexed by her randomness.

'Because he's weird-looking, too.'

Huh, she has a point.

'Are you scared of sloths?'

I have to think for a second about what a sloth actually looks like. 'No, I don't think so.'

'They are REALLY weird-looking.'

'I'll take your word for it, Charli.'

We turn the corner, and once again I'm greeted with the evil statue sitting on the park bench-style seat like he owns the fucking joint. *Newsflash, McFuckhead, I own it.*

I purposely keep my distance as I approach the counter. Charli, however, decides to take a seat next to him.

It makes me cringe with disgust.

'Bryce, come sit with me,' she proposes, smiling sweetly at me.

'Nope, I'm good. What do you want, Charlotte? A Happy Meal?' I ask, wanting to get this McShit ordered so I can get the McHell out of here.

All of a sudden Charlotte bursts into pretend tears. And I mean *really* bursts into pretend tears, howling loudly like she is auditioning for the cowardly lion in *The Wizard of Oz.*

I look around slightly dumbfounded, noticing others looking her way as well.

'Charlotte, what are you doing?' I whisper under my breath. Her howl gains a few decibels.

Feeling uncomfortable as it is — by having to be here in the first place — I am now in the equivalent of hell, taking in the bystanders giving me dirty looks. I realise it's because I'm just standing here while an innocent little girl is crying.

Bloody hell!

'Charlotte, come here. Tell me what's wrong.'

'No,' she faux sobs while peeking through her finger-covered face. 'You come here.'

You cheeky little shit! You are just like your mother. I'm both furious and impressed with her efforts to get me closer to the statue of Satan.

An elderly lady touches me on the arm. 'Is she all right?'

'She's fine,' I reassure the nosey woman then begrudgingly make my way over to Charlotte. I kneel in front of her and ignore the statue with every fibre of my being. 'You're making a scene, Charli —'

She drops her hands from her face with lightning speed and clasps mine which I've placed on her knees. Her eyes are wide like saucers, wide and dry ... completely tear-free.

'He's not real,' she whispers, focussing intently on my face.

I feel her lift my hand and move it toward the statue. *What. The. Fuck?*

I go to pull my hand away, but she secures it with her other hand, now having both hands wrapped around mine. Intrigued by the determination in her face — because let's face it, I could lift her up and out of this seat with my pinky finger — I play along for a second.

'I'm not touching the statue,' I say with stern words.

'Yes, you are. You need to,' she retorts, just as sternly.

'Charlotte. I. Am. Not. Touching. That. Statue,' I say again through gritted teeth, placing her hand back on her knee.

She doesn't let go of mine, and this time her faux sadness becomes real. 'I don't want you to be scared.'

In this moment, my heart fills with love. 'Sweetheart, I don't want to be either. But I can't help it.'

'But Bryce, look at him. He is just paint and,' she knocks on his leg, 'plastic?'

I drop my head, knowing she's right. Apart from the plastic — technically, he's fibreglass.

Breathing in deeply and drawing on every bit of willpower I own, I look up and place my hand on Ronald's knee. 'Is that better?'

'I don't know, you tell me,' she says with a tear-filled smile.

So much like her mother.

I stand, pulling her up with me and placing her on my hip. Then I lie. 'Yeah, much better.'

* * *

Later that night after the kids are in bed and Brayden is asleep for what we hope is at least six hours, I walk into the en suite to the sound of the shower running and Alexis humming what I soon make out is Cold Chisel's 'Flame Trees'.

Propping myself against the doorframe, I watch as she soaps her body. She has her back to me, which I'm thankful for, because it affords me a little extra time to take in the curved silky body that rocks my world.

Grabbing my t-shirt from behind, I pull it over my head and drop it to the floor quietly, so that I don't alert her to my presence. I want to surprise her.

Unbuttoning my jeans, I pull them down over my already hard dick and, taking myself in my hand, I slowly palm my length to ease the intense throbbing that has surfaced.

I'm eager to touch every inch of her, so I make way into the shower and secure her from behind, cupping her pussy with one hand and placing the other on her neck. She jolts in surprise for the split second it takes her to realise I am the one holding her captive.

'It's been twenty-seven days since I've been inside you, Alexis. Twenty-seven fucking agonising days,' I whisper harshly in her ear.

My finger flexes and massages the soft skin of her clit, while my other hand firmly clenches her neck, but not enough to make her feel uncomfortable.

She moans and her legs weaken, but being so attuned to her body, I predict this movement and support her waning frame.

'Can you feel my cock on your arse?' I question, nipping at her ear before running my tongue along the back of her neck. 'How hard I am?'

An indistinct word is mumbled from her mouth as I press my finger deeper into her wet skin. Alexis begins to rock her hips against my hand, and her head falls back onto my shoulder, baring her neck. I loosen my grip and lightly trail my hand up and down her neckline.

'Please tell me I can fuck you.'

With her eyes still closed and water streaming down her chest, she licks her lips. 'You can.'

I let out a growl, something I do often when around this woman. 'That's not what I asked you to say.'

I want her to tell me I can fuck her; I want to hear those dirty little words, beg for it.

Alexis tilts her head to face me, grabs a handful of my hair and brings my mouth to hers, all the while forcing my finger inside her pussy. 'You can fuck me,' she mutters aggressively.

My body responds to her request, tensing, magnetising to her soft, wet skin. I slide my finger in and out of her and augment it with a second, gently stretching her in preparation for my cock. The last thing I want to do is hurt her; after all, it's only been four weeks since she gave birth.

'Does that feel good?' I ask her, making sure she is enjoying what I'm doing.

Her body indicates that she does, but I want to hear her say it ... purr it.

'Yes, it feels ... so good,' she moans.

I press my mouth to hers again and stroke her tongue with my own, tasting all she has to offer. She is my delicacy; my desired flavour.

Alexis breaks away from my mouth and bends forward, placing her palms flat against the tiled wall and widening her stance. Dropping my hand from her throat, I glide it down in between her breasts, only to rest it upon her hip.

With a delectable moan slowly pouring out of her mouth, she presses her arse against the crown of my dick, allowing me to glide and swirl it around her opening.

'Fuck,' I grind out, now desperate to feel her pussy walls clenching around my cock.

Slowly, I press into her, closing my eyes in tune with the superb sensation of her warmth. It has been twenty-seven days of waiting. The air surrounding her mouth is sharply inhaled, and it worries me for a split second that she isn't quite ready even though she says she is.

Just as I am about to withdraw, she lets out the most erotic-sounding moan with enough ardour to rival the steam in the shower.

'Oh god, Bryce. I've missed you, I've missed this.

'I've missed you too, honey, more than you'll ever know.'

Encouraged by her gratification and obvious euphoria, I proceed to hold her hips and drive into her with timed precision, my glide effortless — she's so wet and primed for me.

When I'm feeling this fucking ravenous and alive with pent-up sexual tension, I need to remind myself to be careful, and not get carried away for fear of hurting her. So I pull out and spin her around to face me, which always brings me back to a safer momentum.

Lifting her back onto my cock, I impale her and press her against the wall, my sudden change of position forcing her to gasp. With her lips now parted, I ravage her mouth, seeking out her tongue with my own as I continue to drive into her, relishing the feel of her body once again joined with mine. I realise just how much I have missed being inside her, holding her, hearing the raw, carnal noises reverberate from within. I've simply missed making love to the woman I love.

Okay, I realise this can be seen as ridiculous. In hindsight, it has been less than a month since I last had sex with her. The thing is, the power of addiction is a force to be reckoned with; a dependence that can only be cured with fortitude. And where Alexis is concerned, my resolve is non-existent.

Feeling the build-up of pressure at the head of my dick, I explode into her like Mount Fucking Vesuvius and growl like a goddamn barbarian, my release too long in waiting.

* * *

Following our lovemaking from the night before, you'd think I'd be one happy, relaxed and fully sated man. But I'm not, not completely anyway. Yes, my balls now feel a little more like the billiard variety and a lot less like the bowling variety, I can't dispute that. The thing is, today I'm anxious for an entirely different reason; today is Gareth's birthday and I can't seem to get him out of my mind, or off my conscience.

Sitting here at my desk, I replay the final conversation I had with him on the morning his psychotic alter, Scott, held Alexis hostage and nearly killed her. I'd been so wrapped up and absorbed in my own life, I had not paid attention to Gareth's state of mind and body language, completely failing to see just how out of control his condition really was. I'd fooled myself into believing that he was taking his meds because I'd asked him to do so, never having thought to check that the pills he was actually taking were, in fact, the prescribed ones. Apparently, he had been popping vitamins in my presence.

Now, nine months down the track, I can clearly see — as I look back on those weeks leading up to the explosion — that his behaviour and conduct were not only irrational, but evidently disturbed. Things like the angry phone call I received after Christmas, when he accused Alexis of deliberately omitting him from our family lunch. Not to mention the numerous phone calls and emails I got while Alexis and I were in Italy — emails checking on Clark Incorporated issues that did not concern him. All these things I'd just swept under the rug, because for once in my life — ever since the car accident occurred — I didn't want to have to deal with Gareth, didn't want to be responsible for babysitting him. Except the moment I did drop my guard and responsibility, the worst possible thing happened ... I failed him.

Sitting on the edge of our bed, I watch Alexis peacefully enjoying her slumber. She has no choice but to sleep on her back, because apparently if she sleeps on her stomach she'll wake up in a puddle of breast milk. As I stare at her glorious breasts, which are hidden behind her maternity bra — a crime in itself — I yearn to caress the soft flesh with my tongue.

The imposed nipple prohibition is slowly killing me, eating at my sanity and diminishing my tenacity. Having no choice but to fight my nipple-need, I think of a distraction.

A smile creeps onto my face as an idea of something I know she loves, but something I haven't done in a while, takes form. I race downstairs and grab a yellow rose from the vase in the foyer then race back upstairs and kneel on the ground next to the bed. I am excited just like a kid on Christmas Day, all because I love waking her up with a rose.

Very lightly, I wipe the bud of the flower across her forehead, this prompting her brow to crease ever so slightly. Her rose-taunted face is adorable and I have to bite my lip to suppress a laugh.

Returning the rose to the bridge of her nose, I trail it downward very softly. Her hand swings up out of nowhere and swipes at what her subconscious is telling her is there. I quickly retract the rose before she touches it and, with a mischievous inward chuckle, wait patiently for her to settle again. She does, and as I take in her serene appearance, I melt with love. Her eyelashes are long and black, and fan beautifully atop her cheekbones. She has some very faint freckles, and the last time I counted there were about nineteen of them across her nose and cheeks. Her lips are downright irresistible, plump and semi-pursed. And her blonde hair neatly frames the most beautiful face in the world.

Swallowing the lump in my throat and smiling because I know how fortunate I am, I place the rose on her lips and sit it just under her nose, knowing that when she inhales her next breath, the scent she loves so much will filter into her senses and will begin to wake her from sleep. I watch with fascination as she breathes in a deep breath, her chest rising as her hands find her hair while she stretches. Her eyelids flutter open and within seconds she begins to decipher what is before her. When she does interpret what her eyes are seeing, her heartbreaking smile starts to spread across her face. And, as always when she graces me with that expression, I am conquered ... done for.

'Mornin',' she mumbles, and sits up on her elbows while taking the rose from my hand.

'Mornin',' I reply, leaning down to kiss those perfect lips.

She drops back onto the pillow and wraps her arms around my neck, securing me tightly to her. 'You're dressed. Why are you dressed? You should be butt-naked and underneath me.'

Wanting to be butt-naked and underneath her, I contemplate that actual scenario before reminding myself why I am dressed and ready to leave. 'I have an appointment. I'll be gone for an hour.'

'Okay,' she pouts.

'Don't do that.'

Her pout increases. 'What?'

'You know what.' I lean forward and suck on her pouty lip. 'I've to go,' I say sadly.

She unwraps her arms and places both hands on either side of my face. 'Is everything all right?'

Feeling her enquiring stare pierce deep into the depths of my eyes, I lie. 'Yeah, I'm fine. Just want to get this done so that I can get back here to my favourite people in the world.'

She nods and kisses me lightly, then lets me go and, just as I stand, movement from Brayden's bassinet catches my attention. I creep over slowly — probably looking somewhat like a fucking cat burglar — and find my little treasure trying desperately to free his hand from his tightly confining wrap. Smiling, I notice the little Houdini has already managed to release one of his hands and is sucking on it ferociously.

'Good morning, little buddy. I'm sorry to tell to you, but it doesn't matter how hard you suck on that hand, you're not going to get what you want out of it.' He lets out a frustrated cry. 'I know. Life's not fair. I want Mummy's boobies in my mouth all the time too.'

A sharp sting to the arm registers as I incur Alexis' swift slap. 'Bryce!'

I lift Brayden up, giving him a quick cuddle and kiss before handing him to his mum. 'Right,' I say with annoyance, wanting to stay with them, 'I'll be back soon.'

Making my way out of the room, I prepare myself for my visit to Gareth's grave.

CHAPTER
13

To feel contrite is a humane and moral virtue, but in order to experience this form of repentance, you must first acknowledge your sin then show remorse for your wrongdoing. Jessica has made it quite clear that she does not agree with my sense of contrition where Gareth's death is concerned, saying I have no sin to feel remorseful over in the first place, but she is wrong.

For the past nine months, Jessica and I have had session upon session where she has tried desperately to conquer my inner battle with guilt using her own personal army of professional advocacy. The thing is, not all battles are fought and then won.

A perfect battle would end in a resolution always being achieved, whether by annihilating the opposition, or forcing them to abandon their mission and surrender their forces. And that's exactly what Jessica's warfare strategy, where my battle is concerned, has been of late: the implementation of tactics to break my resolve and renounce my fight with myself. And I have to admit, it's starting to work.

I hadn't wanted to, but I humoured her and put myself in Lucy's shoes, looking at the entire situation from another perspective. Did it make me feel less guilty? No. Did I still feel contrite? Yes, I did, because at the end of the day, I could have prevented Gareth's death. However, the reason for me deciding to wave the white flag after so long was Jessica's argument during our last session about not letting the guilt 'eat me alive'. It helped me realise that for Brayden and Alexis' sake, I needed to ask for my own forgiveness. Jessica had said that if I couldn't find it within myself to see that I was not at fault in the first place, then I had to apologise and make amends for what blame I felt I had. And the first step in doing that was to visit Gareth's grave and say sorry.

Hearing my phone ring through the Bluetooth of my Lamborghini, I take note of Lucy's name on the screen. 'How's my favourite sister?' I say as I take the call, going for the buttering-up type of approach.

'Your *only* sister is fine. It's her brother she is worried about, today of all days.'

Shit! Why was she born with an IQ to rival Einstein?

'Don't know what you're talking 'bout, baby sis. I'm fine.'

'Don't pull that shit with me. We made each other a promise a long time ago, remember? Telling each other everything goes both ways, not just when it suits you.'

Inwardly groaning to myself, I click my neck to both sides then fess up. 'I'm on my way to the cemetery, Luce. I need to get a few things off my chest ...' I pause for the slightest second then continue. 'It was Jessica's idea, and for once, I'm listening to it,' I finish, with not much enthusiasm in my voice.

'Do you want me to meet you there?'

'No, really, I'm fine. I just need to get this done so that I can move on and live my life. A life I have waited so long to live unburdened.'

Lucy sighs. 'Okay, but if you need me, you know I'm here.'

'I know,' I sigh back.

I'm about to say my goodbyes when her choked voice sounds quietly through my speakers. 'I love you. I respect you. I look up to you and only want the best for you.'

Feeling that horrid thump in my chest when I know I have to rein my shit in before I cry like a kid, I take a deep breath and focus on the traffic ahead. 'I love you too, Luce. Always.'

* * *

The light spring breeze whispers across my face as I walk the gravel path I have walked many times before. It's a sombre walk, full of sadness, and no matter how many times or for how long I have done it, it still leaves me feeling partly empty.

With a bunch of lilies in my hand, I stop by Mum, Dad and Lauchie's graves first. This is the first time I have been here since becoming a father and, for some reason unknown to me, I am bearing extra emotion.

I lay the lilies down for my mother and whisper to her headstone, never really understanding why I do it. Deep down, I know I'm talking to a slab of granite.

'Mum, guess what? I have a son and he's ... he's perfect. His name is Brayden ... Brayden Lauchie Clark.'

I look over to my little brother's resting place, 'Did you hear that Lauch? Yeah, he shares your name.'

Taking a small photograph of Brayden out of my pocket, I place it at the base of Mum's headstone. 'You can have this for now. But I promise I'll bring him by soon.'

I don't want to linger too long, because I hate coming here on my own. I stand up and take a step closer to Dad's place of rest. Touching the top of his headstone, I say four words that now hold so much meaning: 'I get it now.'

As I'm about to move on to Gareth's grave, I hear footsteps on the gravel path behind me. They could belong to only one of two people, and as I feel her hand slide into mine, I have no doubt who she is — warmth and a sense of fulfilment now flowing freely though me.

'You should've told me,' Alexis whispers into my ear as she rests her head on my shoulder.

I squeeze her hand, knowing that I should've confided in her.

'It's okay, though,' she continues. 'I understand you need to do certain things on your own. But I want you to know, you are never alone. I'll wait for you over there until you're finished, okay?'

I nod and she releases my hand before kissing me softly. She then bends down and places a new book on Lauchie's grave. I notice its title: *Tomorrow, When the War Began* and smile. Unbeknownst to her, it was one of his favourites.

While Alexis stands patiently by an elm tree, I say the few words to Gareth I'd planned on saying. 'I let you down, mate, and for that, I'm sorry. I'm sorry that you were the one in the car with Mum, Dad and Lauchie all those years ago. I'm sorry that you were the one to hold Lauchie in your arms while his life slipped away from him. I'm sorry that you never got to live the life you deserved. And I'm sorry you died because of me.'

Sucking in a deep breath, I will the tears not to fall. I refuse to let them fall, I don't deserve to cry. 'Gareth, I'm sorry, but I'm a father now, and my son deserves a dad who knows how to accept responsibility for his own actions, yet also forgive himself and move on with his life. I hope you can forgive me too.'

I wait for a minute and turn around to see Alexis push off from the tree and start walking toward me. She's wearing a long flowing pale pink dress with a cream scarf tied around her neck. Her hair is twisted back and held together with a clip. As she closes the gap between us, a gust of wind sweeps her dress and scarf to the side, taking what breath I have along with it. She is just beyond beautiful.

'Are you ready?' she asks, taking both my hands and holding them in front of us.

I think about the simple question she just asked but interpret it in a different way. *Yes, I am ready.*

I'm ready to live the rest of my life with the woman I love.

PART 2

Thief of my heart

CHAPTER

14

Since becoming a father I have felt many wonderful things: awe, pride, satisfaction; the ability to take on the entire world and those who are in it. Unfortunately, the wonderful joys of fatherhood seem to go hand in hand with the not so wonderful joys, such as confusion, panic and complete exhaustion. All at the hands of one tiny little human being.

Today, my baby boy turns one. Yes, one! As in 365 days old, those days being the best in my life. It feels as if it were only yesterday that I heard his cry, touched his face, looked into his eyes and held him, all for the first time. I just can't believe how quickly this past year has flown by.

Since that miraculous day, I have experienced so much more of what life has to offer. I've experienced hearing the words 'Dad Dad' spoken in such rapid succession that no matter how many times Brayden said it, it still took me several seconds to register that he was, in fact, referring to me as his dad for the first time. I've experienced severe sleep deprivation, sex deprivation and a scarcity of pure silence. I also now know what it feels like to freak the fuck out, and I mean *really* freak out.

When Brayden was ten months old, he somehow managed to get a pea stuck up his nose while he was eating his dinner. And do you think for the life of me that I was able to get it out ... not a chance in hell.

I remember trying to dislodge it with my fingernail, which was inevitably a failure due to his nostril being too bloody small and my finger resembling one that belonged to a giant. So there I was, completely stressed out, panicked and with my phone in my hand about to dial triple-O, when in walked Alexis, calm and composed.

'What's wrong?' she'd asked, obviously sensing from the petrified look on my face that something was clearly out of the ordinary.

Not wanting to waste any more precious time, I explained. 'Bray has a pea stuck up his nose. I'm calling an ambulance.'

She rolled her eyes, took one look at Brayden and, I shit you not, smiled at him. I had started to voice my concern that perhaps it was not the time for smiling, when she gently blocked his other nostril and blew in his mouth, sending the pea flying out onto the benchtop. Alexis then scooped it up, placed it in my hand and picked up Brayden, walking off with him jiggling on her hip and saying, 'silly dadda.' Let's just say I stood there for god knows how long, looking incredulously at the pea that was now in my hand.

Another freak out moment was only the other day when I was cooking dinner. Brayden was playing by my feet banging on the pots and pans I had given him, together with a wooden spoon. One minute he was there and the next he wasn't. I swear the kid has a hidden turbo button which allows him to crawl at high speed when you turn your head for the smallest of seconds. Needless to say, I found him moments later in the walk-in pantry playing with the potatoes.

Despite the fact Brayden stops my heart from beating several times a day, and I'm sure he is the reason for a few new grey hairs on my head, I wouldn't trade becoming a father for anything.

A life I once thought condemned by the wrong decision is now a life I will do anything to protect.

* * *

With Brayden sitting comfortably on my hip, I stand in the middle of his bedroom, pointing out different stars and planets in the painted mural on his ceiling and walls. 'What's that?' I ask over-enthusiastically, which just happens to be the universal speak-to-your-child tone of voice.

He smiles and replies with 'star' while simultaneously clapping his hands because he knows already that he's correct.

'Good boy,' I praise him, holding out my fist for him to bump. He playfully obliges, but misses my hand entirely, inevitably punching me in the chest. 'And what's that?' I ask again, pointing to the moon.

'Star,' he repeats, again clapping himself cheerily. Everything that is painted on the walls around us, to Brayden, is a star.

Not wanting my son to start his astronomy education with the wrong information, I correct him as per usual. 'No, Bray. That's the moooooon,' I say, practically mooing like a friggin' cow.

He giggles at my stupidity and watches my lips intently as I sound the word. His concentration level amazes me, together with just how much information he absorbs at such a young age. Brayden — just like his older siblings — is shaping up to be another little human sponge.

'Bryce, where's Brayden? He'd better be with you,' Alexis calls out from downstairs. 'And he'd better be dressed. Everyone will be here soon.'

Turning toward the door, the direction from which Alexis' bellowing came, I get a playful idea. 'Can you hear Mummy? Should we hide from her? Yeah. Come on, little man, let's play hide-and-seek.'

I look around the room for a hiding place to initiate some secret Daddy business. Then, walking quickly toward the curtains, I position us behind them, not doing a very good job of completely disguising our whereabouts.

'Bryce!' Alexis calls out again, this time sounding more agitated.

'Mummy is getting grumpy,' I tell Brayden.

'Mum mum mum,' he chants in response while poking me in the cheek. Brayden — just like his mother — loves my stubble. Charli ... not so much.

Chuckling like a childish idiot, I kiss him on the head. 'Sh, you'll give us away.'

'Bryce, where are yo—' Alexis says with exasperation, stepping into the room and cutting her words short. I'm guessing her reason being due to spotting our not very inconspicuous hiding spot.

Brayden, hearing his mother's voice, blurts out her name. 'Mum.'

I shake my head, silently laughing to myself. *What the fuck are you doing behind this curtain, you fool?*

Using her mummy-baby voice, Alexis responds. 'What was that? Did I just hear BB?'

Bloody BB, I hate that name.

'BB,' Brayden repeats, forcing a giggle from Alexis.

'I did hear BB! Where is he? Is he under his cot? Nooo. Is he in his toy box? Nooo.'

Hearing her voice get closer and closer with each word that she says, I, along with Brayden, now find myself getting excited in anticipation of her discovering us. *Seriously, how old am I?*

'Where could he be? I know,' she taunts, the curtain now the only thing separating us from her. 'Is he behind the curtain?' Alexis asks, as she gently pokes Brayden in the leg.

He squeals with excitement before she wrenches the curtain aside, revealing our secret Daddy business.

'There you are!' she exclaims.

The look on each of their faces is priceless, their eyes glimmering at each other with elation, their beaming smiles stabbing my heart with a knife forged from love.

'Were you hiding from Mummy? Come here, cheeky boy.' She puts her arms out and, instantly, Brayden lunges toward them. 'Your daddy is naughty,' she says while giving me a sexy grin.

Naughty is one description that fits my current state; another is turned-on and hard as a fucking rock.

Alexis turns away, and I watch with greedy eyes as she sets Brayden down on the floor with his toy cars. The tight-fitting navy dress she has chosen to wear today hugs her body in the right places, sculpting her arse with perfect precision as she bends over.

Swallowing dryly while blood flows from the head on my shoulders to the head on my dick, I adjust my now swelling cock in my pants and map out in my head how I am going to relieve the aching throb underneath my hand.

Visuals of the many ways I can bury myself in between her legs start to filter into my head.

'Okay, sweetheart, you play vroom-vroom while Mummy gets your clothes out,' Alexis says before making her way into Brayden's closet.

Not wanting to waste this perfect opportunity to corner and seduce her, I immediately close and lock Brayden's bedroom door, then follow her into the walk-in wardrobe. As I step into the doorway, I find her stretching on her tiptoes, trying desperately to reach a box on a higher shelf. My initial instinct is to rake the length of her sexy body with my eyes, finding it almost impossible to look past her legs. When Alexis wears stockings, I know that at the tops of her thighs are thick bands of lace that I want nothing more than to remove with my teeth.

I'm now fully aware of my extensive erection and step right up to her side, purposely pushing it into her hip as I slowly reach the box for her. The moment she registers my wanting hard-on, her eyes widen, and the corners of her mouth lift into a seductive smile.

Alexis' smile is hypnotic ... magnetic even, drawing me into a trance-like state. Unable to look away from her captivating and now heavy-lidded gaze, I reach blindly beside us and place the box down on the tallboy.

'We don't have time,' she whispers unconvincingly as I get right up into her personal space, slowly stepping her backward until she is pressed up against the wall.

'We always have time,' I verify, closing the gap between our lips.

The warm wet taste of her tongue as she slides it against mine sets my body alight, waking up every nerve ending I possess. And, with my patience to have her now at a bare minimum, I reach down and lift her right leg, gripping her thigh and holding it to my hip. My other hand finds her jaw and then trails down her throat until I stop it at the hollow of her neck.

'Mm,' I groan while pressing my cock against her, teasing her with my *solid* promise and making her eyelids flutter.

The top of her cleavage provokes my hand's further descent, my fingers now enjoying their journey across the dips and mounds of her breasts, breasts that for the past three months I have had the pleasure of having my way with. Apparently, Alexis decided to stop feeding Brayden due to something called mass-eye-tits ... mass-tits ... massive tits. *Fuck! I don't know what it was called, but it had something to do with her tits.* Either way, she stopped feeding him and I'm not going to lie — thank fuck that she did. My mouth was starting to get nipple-withdrawal.

Licking my lips to moisten them, I wrench down her dress and bra cup, freeing her breast and watching with delight as it bounces beautifully before settling into my hand. The feel of her soft. plump flesh within my fingers triggers my desperation to tease her hardened nipple with my thumb before bending down and taking it into my mouth.

Alexis' reaction to having her breasts teased, licked and sucked, is one of sheer fucking enjoyment to watch. Her chest always rises with her desperate intake of oxygen, all the while pushing her flesh further into my hand and mouth — I love it.

Relishing her perked, hardened nipple underneath my tongue, I tease and tantalise it, flicking the stiff peak with intensity before sucking and stretching it with my mouth.

'Oh, god!' she moans while clenching my hair and tugging it with ardour.

That moan, that go damn fucking moan.

Growling like the beast that she brings out in me, I reach down, pull her underwear aside and caress her moist skin with my fingertips. 'Alexis, just so you know ...' I breathe heavily into her ear. 'You were made to be touched with my fingers, licked with my tongue and fucked with my cock. Honey, you were made for *ME.*'

Her head drops back with a light thump against the wall, exposing her delectable neck. 'Yes,' she murmurs, her tone sexually intoxicating.

I growl once again before undoing my trousers and releasing my cock, positioning it at her entrance before ploughing the fuck into her. I'm needy, eager and desperate for the feel of her, wanting nothing more than to have that privilege without another second wasted.

Digging my fingertips into the skin of her thigh, and bracing my hand on the wall behind her head, I begin to pound into her.

'Fuck, Bryce,' she breathes out while lifting her head back up.

My eyes lock onto her hungry stare, a stare of raw unconcealed passion that blankets my soul and renders me slave to her every whim, need and desire.

'Vroom, bang!' Brayden playfully shouts, snapping me right the fuck out of pussyland and placing me directly into daddyland. I freeze solid, my cock stunned into immobility.

'Don't you dare stop,' Alexis hisses.

'But Brayden sounds like he's —'

'Bryce Edward Clark! *You* came in here, *you* stalked me like a friggin' hungry lion, *you* and your dirty mouth had me all but coming onto your hand, and now *you* want to stop? Well, screw *you*! Either *you* start that cock of yours back up again and make me sink my teeth into your shoulder, or get the fuck out while *I* finish myself off.'

What. The. Fuck?

I'm speechless, impressed, and completely turned-on by her demanding fiery attitude. 'You want my cock to start up again?' I tease with an eyebrow raised. My cock twitches, prompting her face to light up with her sexy, gorgeous smile.

'Yes,' she demands and rocks her hips back and forth, sliding me in and out of her.

Once again, I feel that sensational build-up of pressure as I brace myself and drag my cock out of her, only to drive it back in, again and again until she is doing what she promised — biting my shoulder and muffling her cries of pleasure.

* * *

'Whose freakin' idea was this?' Tash exclaims as she steps into the apartment. 'I know it's a first birthday party and all, but seriously ... you have gone absolutely overkill with the damn balloons.'

I shrug my shoulders at her, as if to say I had absolutely no part in it when truth be told, I knew all along we were practically filling the joint with helium-inflated latex orbs.

Alexis had decided this was the perfect payback for Tash's antics a few weeks back, when Tash had deliberately staged a fake security alert while Alexis took Brayden out shopping. Apparently Tash thought it would be hilarious to pretend Alexis was European royalty, following her around the shopping precinct like a highly trained bodyguard, except she kept speaking a language that did not exist. Needless to say, Alexis ended up cutting her shopping trip short and has been patiently awaiting her moment of retribution.

'Overkill, Taaaash?' Alexis drawls. 'Surely these few balloons are not going to hurt you,' she adds, while picking one up.

'Alexis, whatever you are contemplating, don't!' Tash warns, pointing her finger with a resolute stab. 'I mean it, missy, you come any closer with that balloon and I will lose my shit and haunt you in the afterlife.'

Alexis smiles a devilishly sweet retort and gestures toward the lounge area. 'I don't know what you are talking about. Please, come in and enjoy your afternoon,' she says as she gently serves the balloon in the air and whacks it with her hand tennis-style.

Tash flinches, glares at her, and hesitantly walks past, now in search of Brayden who is playing with his cousin Alexander on the rug.

I wrap my arm around Alexis' shoulder. 'You enjoyed that, didn't you?'

She tries to restrain her laugh. 'You have no idea. And there's plenty more where that came from.'

'Remind me never to cross you.'

'Don't cross me. Or you'll end up in the throes of passion with Krusty the Clown.'

'You're evil at times, you know that?'

'Sucks to be you and have a phobia.'

'Well, everyone is scared of something, even you.'

Alexis bites the inside of her cheek momentarily, then lets go and answers flippantly. 'Nope, not me.'

Leaning in, I whisper into her ear, 'I don't believe you, my love. So guess who is about to dust off his creepy research skills.'

She turns to face me and brushes her lips with mine. 'Dust away, Mr Clark. I know one thing for sure, though ... you don't scare me.'

Before I met Alexis, I was never one to have many gatherings in my home. Sure, I'd invite the boys over for dinner and jam sessions. And Lucy and Nic were always welcome, no matter what time of the day or night. But that was about it. My home was my private space, my sanctuary and kept out of the public eye.

Standing here today, beer in hand, and watching our friends and family enjoy each other's company, I couldn't be more comfortably happy. The seclusion I'd once given myself was now gone, never to return. I'd finally found my purpose in life ... *my* purpose, not a charitable cause, or a brotherly responsibility. My purpose was Alexis and the family we have created. They were now my reason for existence.

'Bryce,' Nate's voice sounds from beside me. 'Mum said it's time for a speech and to cut the cake.'

'Not a problem, buddy. Where's your sister?'

'Playing Twister. Ha ... that rhymes! My sister is playing Twister.'

I can't help laughing at his wit. For a nine year old, the kid is quick. *Shit! Did I just rhyme, too?*

'Can you go tell Charli it's time for cake? I just need to have a quick word with your Uncle Jake.'

Before I even have a second to process what I just said, Nate bursts into laughter. 'Cake and Jake,' he cackles uncontrollably. 'Good one!' *Ah, bloody hell!*

I playfully turn him around and lightly shove him in the direction of Charlotte. 'Go, you crazy kid!'

Shaking my new-found Dr Seuss skills out of my head, I find Jake by the pool with Graeme. 'Got a minute?' I ask him. 'Actually, you both could probably help me.'

'I don't want her back,' Graeme announces. 'She's yours, you wanted her. You can't give her back.'

'You're a funny man, Graeme. But I wouldn't give Alexis back for the world,' I honestly say.

'Good. As much as I love her, I'm too old for her drama-filled life.'

I give him a reassuring squeeze on the shoulder. 'Rest assured, I'm keeping her.'

'I always thought you were a crazy fucker,' Jake pipes in as he takes a swig of his beer. 'From that moment Lex and Jen told me you were flying around the farm in your helicopter, I thought you were cracked.'

I laugh at Jake's stab and give him a *very* firm, manly slap on the back, causing him to choke on some of his beer. 'Thanks, mate. So, I need to know what Alexis is afraid of. She tells me nothing, but that's just bullshit.'

'Spiders,' they both say simultaneously.

Jake then chuckles. 'Big, fat, furry, spiders ... huntsman and wolf spiders, to be exact.'

'You'd think she would be used to them after growing up on a farm,' Graeme adds, while shaking his head in mild disappointment.

'But I guarantee, if one just happened to be in close proximity now, she'd scream the place down.'

'Spiders ... really?' I ponder. 'I thought she just didn't like them.'

Jake slaps my back in return and steps away. 'She doesn't, she bloody *hates* them.'

I smile to myself and tip my beer to my lips, while eye-fucking Alexis with a scheming smirk.

'Whatever it is you are planning on doing, Bryce, don't!' Graeme warns, interrupting my train of thought. 'I'm serious, I don't want her back. And that look you have on your face tells me that could quite possibly be an option.'

* * *

Gently tapping a spoon on the side of my glass, I indicate to the room that we want quiet to make an announcement.

'Star!' Brayden squeals and claps himself while pointing to his big, yellow, smiley-faced, star birthday cake. He leans forward in order to grab it.

'No, not yet, sweetheart. In a minute,' Alexis reassures him while securing him tightly to her hip.

'Just quickly, before Brayden loses patience and attempts to plough headfirst into his cake, we want to say thanks for coming and celebrating this little man's first birthday with us —' I am about to continue when I hear Charli behind me, making a racket. Turning around, I spot her dragging her karaoke machine into position.

'Charlotte, what are you doing?' Alexis whispers.

'I want to sing Brayden a song.'

I subdue a smile with pursed lips and make eye contact with Alexis. She too hides her grin. 'Oh ... okay.' She turns back around and addresses the room. 'Um ... apparently Charli has a little something she wants to share.'

'I want to sing "Happy Birthday" to Brayden,' Charli announces just a bit too loudly into the microphone, sending a high-pitched tone throughout the room. 'He is the best brother ever!' she continues while squinting her eyes and poking her tongue out at Nate.

Alexis slaps her hand to her forehead.

Brayden lunges for the cake again.

Nate smacks a balloon into Charlotte's head.

Tash screeches and dodges its rebound.

Charlotte growls.

And ... I just laugh.

* * *

After Charli performs her entertaining version of 'Happy Birthday', Alexis and I decide to inform everyone of our decision to get married in six months.

'Oh, and one last *minor* detail,' I express playfully, receiving an elbow to the ribs from Alexis. 'We have finally set a date for the wedding! Mark out February fourth on your calendars.'

'About time!' Tash calls out from her position at the bifold doors, the furthest spot from the balloons.

'There's still time to change your mind, Bryce,' Jake calls out, Johanna snorting in response.

Rick and Claire step up to us, Claire smiling meekly while Rick embraces Alexis. Months ago, I would have wanted to punch the fucker for being this close to her.

'Congratulations! Sorry, but we really need to head off. RJ has his soccer semi-final later today,' Rick explains before they make an early departure.

Approximately one month ago, Rick informed Alexis that he and Claire were expecting a child. Alexis — not surprisingly — took the news really well, being genuinely happy for the two of them. Charlotte had refused — and still refuses to this day — to accept that her next sibling would be anything other than a girl. And Nate just carried on as if an extra baby coming into his life was nothing new. Seeing all three of them react with pleasant attitudes, I decided there and then to let go of my grudge and anger toward Rick. If Alexis was happy, then so was I.

Re-entering the lounge area after seeing Claire and Rick out, we are both smothered by Maryann with congratulatory hugs. 'Wonderful. I can't wait. We need to sit down and start planning —'

'Mum, back off. You know what happened last time you interfered with wedding plans,' Jen cautions.

'Yeah, well ... your sister isn't as mean as you. She wouldn't make me wear a stupid t-shirt to her hen's night, would you, Alexis darling?' Maryann says with gag-worthy sweetness.

Alexis rolls her eyes at her mother's attempt at buttering her up. 'Actually, I'm not having a hen's night.'

'Like fun you aren't,' Carly interjects. 'Trust me, you are having one whether you are in attendance or not.'

'Carly, we've decided to just have a get-together here,' I add, taking Brayden from Alexis. 'Set up the band ... that sort of thing.'

'Not gonna happen, mate,' Derek implies as he raises his beer. 'Consider yourself havin' a buck's night.'

Alexis turns to face me, drops her head on her my shoulder and closes her eyes.

''Ake up, Mum,' Brayden shouts, Wiggles style.

Alexis grumbles with a laugh. 'Mummy isn't sleeping like Jeff.'

''Ake up, Mum,' he hollers, again.

We all laugh.

CHAPTER
15

Five months down the track, and it is decided that yes, we are having a hen's night and a buck's night. It is also decided — not by us, mind you — that Carly and Derek are in charge of the entire event.

The plan is to start off together at Opals as one big group, where Live Trepidation will dedicate their entire set to Alexis and play all of her favourite songs. Then we are to go our separate ways, and what will follow is unknown to the both of us. That minor detail I did not like. I didn't like it at all.

* * *

'I can't believe we agreed to this,' Alexis mumbles from our walk-in wardrobe.

I'm standing in the bathroom, latching the buckle on my denim jeans and fastening the last button on my short-sleeved, light grey shirt. 'We didn't really have a choice, honey. Did you want to argue with Carly *and* Derek?'

'No,' she groans. 'Hey! Maybe we could just stay at Opals together? Refuse to leave?' she suggests, a spark of renewed hope sounding in her voice.

'Yeah, don't think that is going to work.'

I finish off with a little gel in my hair and step out into our bedroom to put on my shoes. Sitting on the edge of the bed and bending over, I slide my foot into the black loafer. Before I can reach for the other shoe, I notice two black high heels only centimetres from my feet.

'Can you zip me up, please?' Alexis asks.

I travel the length of her legs until I'm looking up at her with my mouth and eyes wide open. She is wearing an extremely short black lace dress, which reveals quite a lot of her silky smooth skin, more skin than I'm willing to share the sight of with any other man. And even though she looks as sexy as hell, I'll be damned if she is going to look that good so that some loser can discreetly blow a load in his pants.

'What is that?' I ask on a choke.

'What's what?' she asks, quickly glancing toward the roof where she thinks I am looking, her expression indicating she expects to see some type of critter.

'What you're wearing.'

Alexis looks back down and smooths out her dress. 'Um ... I think it's Dolce and Gabbana. I can check if you wan—'

'I don't fucking care who designed it.'

Her face contorts. 'You don't like it?'

Placing my hands on her legs, I pull her toward me. 'Honey, you look sensational, too fucking sensational. It's just ...' I lean back on the bed and run my hand through my hair. *Fuck, she looks irresistible.* 'I'm not going to be with you all night. You can't wear that without me.'

Climbing over my lap and straddling me on the bed, a sly grin creeps across her face. 'Are you telling me what I can and can't wear?'

'Yes, you seriously can't wear that. Remember that time you called me Jackie Chan?'

She screws up her face, then smiles. 'Yeah.'

'Well, I'll be performing Jackie Chan's all night if you wear that.'

Alexis laughs and leans forward, her golden blonde locks cascading around her face as she looks down at me. Even her lips are turning me on — red as a friggin' fire truck.

'Bryce, I'm a big girl. I can take care of myself. And anyhow, we have the apartment to ourselves tonight. Don't you want to wait till we get home so that you can take this dress off and see just exactly what I'm wearing underneath?'

I glance down at her breasts, spying the tiniest hint of red lace covering her chest. *Bloody hell!*

'Fuck the night out. Let's stay here and you can show me now.'

I reach for her tits, but she jumps off and puts her hand up. 'No. We are going. Now, can you please zip me up?'

Alexis turns around, baring her back to me and giving me another sneak peek of her lingerie. The sight of her red corset prompts my dick to stand at attention, poised and motionless, saluting her military-style. Having no choice but to close my eyes in order to try and gather my not so turned-on composure, I lower my eyelids and click my neck from side to side.

After a second of thinking about Dame Edna Everage — because let's face it, she looks like a clown — I reopen them to find Alexis still standing in front of me, her head now turned back in my direction and smiling from ear to fucking ear.

Completely depleted of all willpower and restraint, I grab a hold of her and drag her to the bed, pinning her down underneath me. 'Honey, if you are going to wear that, then first I need to fuck you. I need you wearing me along with it.'

* * *

Alexis and I walk into Opals nearly three-quarters of an hour late, spotting our friends and family scattered around the dance floor. Will, Matt, Derek and Luce are up on stage, preparing for our gig.

'Sorry we are late,' Alexis apologises, blushing profusely.

Carly's eyes widen as they journey up and down Alexis' body. 'No need to explain why. That,' she points to her outfit, 'speaks for itself.'

'What? There's nothing wrong with my dress,' Alexis whines while Tash hands her a drink and a condom-decorated veil. 'Oh, for the love of god ... I am not wearing that! I'm not in my twenties and getting married for the first time. FOR. GET. IT.'

'Told you she wouldn't wear it,' Tash says to Carly, handing her the veil.

'She'll wear it ... give it time ... and alcohol.'

I shake my head, kiss Alexis, and hoist myself up on the stage.

'Nice of you to show, arsehole,' Derek throws my way as I pick up my guitar and begin to tune it.

'I was busy,' I answer, pulling a pick out of my jeans pocket.

'Hmm, yeah ... I can see why,' Matt murmurs, glancing toward Alexis.

'Shut up, dick. I already have to worry about every other sleaze in this joint eye-fucking my fiancée. I don't want to have to worry about you, too.'

'She looks hot!' Lucy says with her back to me.

I turn to my sister. 'Not you, too,' I grimace.

'No. I didn't mean it like that ... although, she does look hot!'

Will laughs as he taps out a light beat.

'Let's just get started, yeah?' I grumble as I glance toward Alexis, taking in the smouldering beauty that she is. I can't say that I really blame them for fucking around with me, she does look exceptionally incredible tonight. And as I watch her greet her family and friends, it painfully dawns on me that my night is not going to be as laidback as hers. Not in the bloody slightest!

We open the show with 'Birth' by 30STM, just like we had at our previous gig. The song is a crowd-pleaser and, quite frankly, a great intro to get everyone — including us — primed for the rest of our gig.

Three songs into our set we decide to play one of our own: 'Chaos'. This particular song seems to sum up my current situation, since during the second bridge I have no choice but to be witness to a group of guys eyeing Alexis, Carly and Jen.

Highly fucking irritated, I watch as the group of douche bags spend a minute planning their approach, the shady thoughts in their minds quite obviously radiating from their over-zealous faces.

Cringing like fuck when they slowly make their way toward the girls, I notice Tash and Steve intercept the group's attempted pick-up, Steve spinning Jen into a dance and Tash wrapping herself around Alexis in a bear hug, pretending to give her a friendly cuddle. I inwardly sigh with relief at the fact I no longer have to jump off the stage and threaten to jam my guitar down any of the guys' throats. Being that Opals is my nightclub, I really don't want to cause a scene.

Tash gives the four guys a vicious snarl, then looks toward me and winks, and I can't help smirking with the knowledge of our agreement that she will be Alexis' bodyguard. Now, it's not as if I formulated this understanding behind Alexis' back. In fact — if I remember rightly — Tash and I discussed our intentions directly in front of her years back when we watched the kids swim at school. So, technically, it is not my, nor Tash's, fault that she did not take us seriously.

After finishing the song and realising I'm going to need more protective reinforcements, I give Dale — my head of security — a quick call.

'Everything all right, mate?' he answers.

'Yeah. Listen, Dale, before you finish and make your way down here, can you send Joey. I need him on Alexis-duty tonight.'

I imagine Dale running his hands over his face in frustration at my request.

'She's not gonna be happy when she catches on, Bryce, and you know she will.'

'Do me a favour. Turn on Opal's lower dance floor camera. You can't miss her. Then tell me I'm going overboard.'

I wait for him to do what I've just directed him to do, anticipating that he is now on my wavelength.

'Right! Yep, I get ya. Joey will be there as soon as possible.'

'Good. Now turn the camera off, you dirty perve.'

He laughs. 'It's off. I know better than to mess with you.'

'So you should. I'll see you shortly.'

'No worries.'

I hang up the phone and turn back to face the crowd, even more pissed off to see the numbers practically doubling. What shits me further is that the male to female ratio is not in my favour. I don't fucking need any more dick-heavy men in Alexis' proximity.

'Bryce, you ready now?' Derek asks, looking annoyed.

I hold up my finger. 'Just give me a minute.'

Before we begin our next song, I quickly call Lisa who is on door-entry this evening.

'Opals Nightclub, Lisa speaking.'

'Lisa, it's Mr Clark.'

'Oh, yes, sir. How can I help you?'

'Tell whoever is manning the door that the ratio is off. Limit the men for the next hour, then get them to do another assessment.'

'Sorry, sir. I will tell Tony now.'

'Good. Thank you, Lisa.'

I hang up the phone once again and find Alexis watching me, concern on her face. Wanting to ease her mind, I make my way to the edge of the stage and squat down.

'What's wrong, honey?'

'You look agitated. Is everything all right?'

'Yes, everything is fine. I just had to arrange a few things.'

'Okay, but this is your buck's night, too. I want you to enjoy yourself.'

'I will,' I reassure her, lightly tapping her nose with my finger. 'But first I want to watch your reaction to the next song.'

She smiles that earth-shattering smile I love so much. 'Ooh, what is it?'

Waggling my eyebrows at her, I stand up. She runs her tongue along the top row of her teeth while her eyes travel the length of my jeans. It has me wanting to abandon the night and take her back to our apartment.

'Alexis,' I growl in warning, her look indicating her inner salacious thoughts.

'What? I'm waiting,' she shouts in response, now smiling innocently.

I'll give her waiting.

Before nodding toward Lucy to begin the song, I notice Joey enter the room. I acknowledge him with a swift lift of my chin as he proceeds to stand not too far from Alexis' position. Just having him here now puts my mind at ease a little.

Taking another step back, I wink at Luce, and just like the time we played in Shepparton she and Derek are the only ones illuminated by light as she begins to play the piano in 'November Rain' by Guns N' Roses.

Alexis — standing at the very front of the stage — blows a kiss in my direction, cementing the fact that I was right when choosing to re-enact this performance for her. I knew she'd love it.

Just like that time, when I performed this song to Alexis with the sole message that I would wait as long as it took for her to realise that we were perfect for each other, I once again serenade her during the guitar solos, even showing off and kissing her passionately while still playing like the freak that I am.

I'm normally not one to show off or flaunt my talents and wealth like an unappreciative flog and wanker. But playing the guitar is something I'm good at, *really* good at. It's also something that made my father extremely proud of me, and he told me to always go hard at it. And it was because of Dad that I had learned to play in the first place. He had given me lessons from the ripe old age of four, he too being a brilliant musician. Music ran in our family. My grandmother had been a violinist and apparently her aunty had been an opera singer.

When I was ten years old and Lucy six, we used to sit around the lounge room and play our instruments. Mum loved the piano and could voice a fairly good tune, in fact, and we all had a natural love for music, a passion for producing a melodic sound. Those particular memories stood out for me the most, being some of the happiest times in my life.

I, too, want those times for my family. To teach Brayden, Nate and Charli — if they want — to play an instrument. I'd love nothing more than to sit back and listen to them harmonise with each other while Alexis sings. It's one of my family traditions that I hope to uphold.

Finishing off the song and standing on top of the piano as a tribute to Slash, I wink at my woman. The twinkle in her eyes is all I needed to know that the complete over-the-top act I just displayed was worth it. My sole reason now for playing the guitar on stage ... purely for her. Alexis' reaction is all that matters to me.

'Okay, ladies and gents. We have one final song to play for this evening then we are off to celebrate our leading guitarist's final night out as a bachelor. Yes, ladies, I'm sorry to inform you, but my man, Bryce, in just a few short weeks will be marrying this beautiful lady in front of him,' Derek says boldly, gesturing toward Alexis.

She raises her hands and I nearly have a fit. The dress she is wearing is strapless and should not be worn by someone who raises their hands, especially someone like Alexis. Not knowing what else to do, I jump down off the stage and wrap my arms around her, covering her nearly-exposed breasts.

She happily welcomes my embrace and drapes her hands around my neck. 'Hi.'

'Hi,' I say back, before taking her mouth with my own.

'Oh, all right you two, hurry up,' Derek complains as the crowd wolf-whistles.

I separate my mouth from hers and whisper into her ear. 'As much as I love to see your tits, my love, please keep your hands below shoulder level. No one else needs to see them.'

Kissing her cheek quickly while she gives me a puzzled look, I pull away and climb back on stage. As I turn around, I notice an expression of anger on her face and her arms are now folded across her chest. Before I can jump back down and ask her what's wrong, Lucy and Will begin playing the intro to 'You're the Voice' by John Farnham and I have no choice but to stand there and wonder what the fuck is wrong with her. *I just saved her from flashing the crowd. Surely that's a good thing.*

By the time Derek starts singing the pre-chorus, her frown has disappeared and she is enjoying the song with her friends. In fact, now that I'm no longer focussed on her change of character, I become aware that the entire club is fully engrossed in our performance.

It really shouldn't surprise me. This is, after all, a great song; an iconic song. And it dawns on me, as I take in the patrons swaying and singing along, that I should've bloody ignored Derek and gone with a live bagpipe player. It would've been perfect. *Fucking Derek!*

Winding down the song and playing the coda till the end, I smile and sigh with relief that our set is finally over. As much as I adore playing the guitar — especially for Alexis — I want nothing more than to spend some time wrapped around her gorgeous body. Not only for the sheer fucking delight and feel of her in my arms, but also to shield her from the many sets of perverted eyes I have spotted around the room.

'Thanks guys,' I say to the band. 'She loved it.'

'Glad my percussion talents have assisted in you getting your dick wet tonight,' Will offers as he pats me on the back. 'Now, let's hope they do the same for me.'

He jumps off the stage and heads toward Carly's friend.

'Has Will got a thing goin' on with Carly's friend?' I ask.

'Her name is Libby,' Derek answers. 'And yeah, kind of ... he hopes to, anyway.'

I inwardly smile to myself, enjoying the fact that Will, too, seems to have taken a liking to someone who doesn't resemble an eighteen-year-old.

'So where are we headed next?' I ask with not much enthusiasm.

'You'll see. Come on, pack up your axe. We're goin'.'

* * *

After putting my guitar away, I make my way down from the stage and head toward Alexis. Her back is to me, and her arms are propped on top of a bar table. She is bent over just a little, and I can't help but stare at her legs, especially the one which is gently rubbing up and down the back of her calf muscle.

As I begin to stalk my prey, I am approached by a couple of women.

'You were so good up there,' one of them says with a suspect smile. 'How long have you been playing?'

'Yeah,' the other agrees, 'you should play professionally or something.'

Never being one who enjoyed being hit on, especially by women who have absolutely no idea of what is going on outside of their own little pick-me bubble, I politely give them the brush-off, thanking them for their empty compliments and continuing on my way until I am pressed up against Alexis.

'I want you,' I whisper into her ear.

'Really?' she whispers back. 'Are you sure you just don't want any-one else to want me?' Her icy response is somewhat sulky.

Confused as to what she is implying — because yes, I sure as hell 'don't want anyone else to want her' — I ask her what's wrong. 'Want to tell me why you sound pissed off?'

She tries to shrug out of my arms, which are still firmly wrapped around her waist I tighten my grip, she isn't going anywhere.

'The only reason you kissed me before in front of everyone was because you didn't want people accidentally seeing a little bit of my skin. And just for your information, I'm wearing Hollywood fashion tape so my "tits" will remain within my dress.'

Not allowing her to dwell on her ridiculousness any further, I spin her around and get right up into her beautiful face. 'Let's get one thing straight. I kiss you because I want to fucking kiss you, because I like it and because you taste good. So don't think for one second that I have an ulterior motive,' I growl on a whisper, as I lean in and get just that bit closer to tasting the lips that required this explanation in the first place. 'And as for your tits, yes, I want them to remain in that dress of yours. They are for my eyes only, honey ... unless ... you have a problem with that?'

Her expression softens and her body become less rigid within my arms. I feel that her resolve is melting away. Leaning in, I remove that final torturous centimetre between us and press my lips to hers, kissing her with as much passion as I'm capable of and holding her head to mine while dipping her in my arms.

When Alexis is secured to me, wrapped around me, completely encompassing everything I possess and breathe, I feel nothing but total satisfaction. She absolutely fulfils me.

'Will you two just get a room,' someone complains, that someone sounding a bit like Lil. 'You have many rooms. Hotels full of rooms, in fact. Go and use one of those for god's sake.'

'Shut up, Lil. Leave them alone. They are getting married soon. Plus watching them is hot!'

Alexis giggles against my mouth at Jade's argument with Lil then locks eyes with me and smiles. 'They are right,' she says a little louder. 'We should get a room. Actually, we should get one now.' She pulls away from me and straightens her dress before threading her fingers through mine. 'Okay, ladies, thanks for everything. We are calling it a night.'

'Oh no, you're not,' Carly interjects with a determination that is not to be argued with. She storms over to Alexis and prises her hand from mine.

Now, if I really wanted to, I could foil her attempts. The thing is, I have a little something up my sleeve, and his name is Joey, so allowing Alexis to go with her friends is no longer an issue. I know he will protect her and report to me as often as I want him to.

'Fine! Fine! I'm coming,' she groans before turning back and giving me one last kiss. 'Be good.'

I shoot her a half-grin as she's tugged away. 'I'm always good.'

'Where are you taking me?' Alexis complains to Carly and Jen as they link their arms through hers.

'Upstairs. We have a surprise for you,' Jen giggles.

I turn to Derek while watching them skip off. 'What surprise?'

'Want a drink?' he asks, ignoring my question and heading toward the bar.

As I wait for him to come back, I can't help but feel uneasy about Alexis' 'surprise'. I hate not fucking knowing what is going on.

A well-built — and if I'm completely honest — good-looking bloke in a cop's uniform, holding a duffle bag, walks past. His shady appearance is distracting and only adds to my already unsettled frame of mind. Derek returns and sets my beer down on the bar table, and we both follow the cop with our eyes as he disappears from the club.

Confusion settles in as I wonder why a police officer has just strolled through my nightclub, a police officer who looks far too pretty to be a cop. Hearing my phone ring from within my pocket, I pull it out and answer it, not even bothering to look who it is, my bewildered state of mind controlling my actions.

'Sir, Alexis has just entered a suite with her friends. Do you want me to wait outside?' Joey asks.

Agitated and not really paying attention, I tell him he can leave, and then disconnect the call. Moments later, the fog covering my mind seems to lift and I begin to comprehend why I suddenly feel slightly ill.

'Derek, what fucking surprise have they got for Alexis?' I ask again, hoping to god that cop wasn't what I thought he was.

The fucker shrugs his shoulders, but clearly knows what the hell is going to happen upstairs.

'That had better not have been some cockhead, wannabe dancer pretending to be a cop, who wants nothing more than to handcuff my fiancée and place her hands all over his spray-tanned, oily body,' I furiously spit out.

Feeling utterly murderous at the thought of another man forcing her to touch him and touching her in return, I begin to follow in the direction the girls headed.

'No, you don't,' Derek says while restraining me.

'Derek, fuck off! Let me go.'

'Dude, it's just for one night. And anyway, Miss Nude Australia awaits you in villa four,' he says as he releases one hand and waves a room key in my face.

'You're an idiot, a deadset idiot. If you think for one second I am going to choose some stripper over rescuing Alexis from some slimy creep, you are dumber than dog shit. Let me go, now!'

'What's goin' on?' Will asks as he steps up to the both of us, assessing Derek's armlock hold.

'Pansy here wants to ditch Nude Australia and act all caveman in front of Alexis.'

'Speak fucking English,' Will complains.

'Carly has arranged a stripper for Alexis. I've arranged one for Bryce. Bryce doesn't want to go. The dickhead doesn't want Alexis to go either. I am currently stopping him from ruining everything. Wanna help me out?'

I apply a compression poke to Derek's L11 pressure point, right in the crook of his elbow joint. This is my warning. If he doesn't let me go in the next second, I will do some serious damage.

'Argh! Fuck, Bryce. Will, a little help, please.'

Will steps in and restrains my hands.

'You arseholes! That dancing pretty-boy cop is about to rub his cock all over our women. How you can be all right with that is beyond me.'

'What pretty-boy cop?' Will queries, stepping back and looking confused. 'You mean the one who walked past just before. That big, dark, handsome police officer is a stripper?'

Derek tilts his head to the side in an assessment of Will. 'Are you gay, man? I don't care if you are, each to their own.'

'No, I'm not gay. I'm actually this close,' he says, holding his thumb and pointer finger in Derek's face, 'this bloody close to having Libby touch *my* cock. And I'll be damned if that dancing cop bloke gets his touched before mine. Let him go, Derek.'

'You're weak. Both of you are fucking weak,' Derek spits out as he lets me go.

'What room are they in?' I ask, picking up my pace and heading for the exit.

'Don't know,' Derek calls back with a shit-eating grin.

I stop, turn fully around and start for him. 'Tell me what room they are in or you'll have no teeth left. And I can tell you, a lead singer without teeth will sound pretty fucking hilarious.'

He studies my face for a second. 'You're joking.'

'Am I? Let me ask you something. You've seen how Carly reacts to men, men with big muscles in particular. Imagine how she is going to react to bodybuilder stripper jerk. You sure you're all right with that, all right with her dragging her hands across his chest, clenching his biceps, his arse and feeling his sweaty junk?'

'She won't touch his junk,' he affirms with not much conviction.

'You sure? Perhaps she likes police officers more than firemen.'

I watch him lose the battle of cockiness. 'Shit! Motherfucking shit!'

'Which room?' I ask for the last time.

'Presidential suite two,' he surrenders.

Not wasting a second longer, I sprint for the elevator, Derek and Will not far behind me.

'If I walk in and see that naked fucker at full mast, thrusting it in Alexis' face, I will kill you,' I say, glaring at Derek as I swipe my card through the security lock on the presidential suite's door.

Will laughs. 'You're a fool, man,' he says sympathetically as he pats Derek on the back. 'I can't believe you thought you'd get away with this.'

'I'm glad you find this funny, Will. You just wait until you find a woman who you can't get out of your head. A woman you will go to the ends of the earth to be with and protect. A woman who becomes your sole reason for breathing. You just wait, mate. Your day will come, and when it does, I will laugh right back at you,' I say as I open the door.

'You're a poetic fucker, aren't you?' Derek teases.

I'm at the point of performing my own chokehold on my best friend, just to knock him out and shut him the hell up, when the Justin Timberlake's 'SexyBack' sounds from within the suite.

'Fuck!' I growl, turning to my idiot best friend. Before taking off in the direction of the music and squealing women, I shove Derek so hard that his back hits the wall.

He laughs at me and starts singing along with JT.

With my heart thumping in my chest over what horrid sight I think I'm about to see, I reluctantly turn the corner. Firstly, I lay my eyes on the massive oily bastard who is straddling Alexis' lap as if he is some fucking rodeo star. She is sitting on a single chair in the middle of the room with her friends standing around in a circle, clapping, dancing and raising their champagne-filled glasses in the air. It really is quite ridiculous and bloody nauseating.

My vision goes back to Alexis who — thank god — has her eyes closed and her hands covering her face, clearly not wanting the dickhead treating her like a horse. My heartbeat calms a little, and all I want to do now is rescue her from her apparent distress.

'Hey! Get out!' Carly yells, pointing in my direction. 'No grooms allowed ... unless,' she wiggles playfully, 'you want to start removing your clothes.'

'You ...' I point to her. 'You and I are going to have some words later. 'And you,' I point to the hairless Chippendale wannabe, 'back the fuck off.'

He steps aside with a knowing expression, as though this is not the first time an irate partner has stormed into the room. Alexis sits frozen, a terrified expression on her face, as I stop right beside her chair and tower over her.

She starts to speak, seemingly to defend herself. 'I didn't know —'

Cutting off her unnecessary apology, I reach forward and take hold of her hand, pulling her up to my chest and pressing my lips to hers in a forceful show of ownership. My intention is to make a clear point that she is mine.

Keeping the kiss brutally short, I pull away. 'Want to go home?'

She smiles and nods.

Not wanting to stay any longer and listen to JT sing about being someone's slave, I bend down, throw her over my shoulder — making sure I cover her arse with her dress — and walk us out of the room.

* * *

When we get back to the apartment, I take the elevator all the way to the second floor, not uttering a word until we are beside the bed.

Before I place her down, I feel her fingers playing with the waistband of my jeans from behind my back.

'Are you mad?' she asks, almost timidly.

'Yep,' I honestly reply, closing my eyes while trying to calm my raging fury together with my raging hard-on which is a result of her teasing touch.

She dips her finger into my jeans, along the crevice of my arse. 'Are you angry with me?'

'No, not with you,' I sigh. 'With our ex-best friends.'

Straightening her back, she encourages me to slide her down my front. 'Good,' she replies with a promising grin, continuing to slide all the way down to her knees. Then, unlatching my belt buckle, she doesn't hesitate in taking me in her hands. 'Because the only man I want dancing around me is you. The only man I want, period, is you.'

Smirking down at her, I caress her stunning face. 'I'm all yours, honey.'

CHAPTER
16

My breath catches when I spot her walk out onto the balcony. I can't see her in detail as I am too far away, but her body, adorned in an ivory gown, is unmistakable. I know they say seeing the bride before the wedding is bad luck, but technically, I can't see her entirely. She is several hundred metres away in the distance.

Hoping that she has her phone with her, I pull out my mobile and send her a text:

29 minutes and 13 seconds — Bryce

I'll admit it. I'm desperate and unable to help myself needing some form of contact. Spending last night without her was agony. So much so, I was highly fucking tempted to sneak into our apartment and surprise her in the middle of the night. I'm sure she wouldn't have minded. Maryann, however, would have. My prospective mother-in-law would no doubt have physically removed me from the premises — or at least tried.

Watching and waiting for Alexis to answer my message, I notice someone, who looks to be Lucy, join her on the balcony. She hands her what I assume is her phone, which makes me smile boldly. Damn,

I adore my sister. She has been the perfect accomplice in my quest for ultimate attainment.

Lucy heads back inside, so I take the opportunity to send another text:

28 minutes, 19 seconds and counting until you make me the happiest man alive — Bryce

I wait, knowing that she is now reading it, and the fact I am watching her without her knowledge leaves me feeling somewhat cocky and powerful at the same time.

My phone beeps, indicating her response:

27 minutes and 21 seconds until I become Mrs Alexis Clark — Alexis

As I read her reply, the smile that covers my face is enormous. Mrs Alexis Clark. It sounds perfect.

I can't wait. — Bryce

Neither can I — Alexis

Smiling like an impish fool, I figure I'll play with her a little longer, loving to wind her up and watch her unleash her inner warrior. The fight she puts up when returning my challenges always ignites a fiery passion within me.

Well then hurry up — Bryce

I love you, you know — Alexis

I do — Bryce

Aren't you supposed to say that in 25 minutes and 33 seconds — Alexis

I laugh out loud. She never fails to amaze me with her wit and responses.

'What are you laughing at, dick?' Derek says from behind as he steps up beside me.

'None of your business,' I reply as I send another message, this one sure to get her excited.

That's it! I'm coming up there to get you — Bryce

'Is that Alexis? Up there on your balcony?'

I look up to my penthouse, still smiling, captivated by her angelic form. 'Sure is.'

'You're un-fucking-believable. You're not supposed to see her before the ceremony.'

'I can't really see her, not closely enough anyway.'

'Sure, keep tellin' yourself that.'

My phone beeps once more:

Okay, okay. I'm on my way ♥ *— Alexis*

'Are you texting her?' Derek asks, incredulously.

A sly grin replaces my smile as I continue to type. 'Yep,' I answer with nonchalance.

You better be ♥ *— Bryce*

'Does she know you are watching her?'

'Of course not.'

'You're a dog, Bryce,' he says as he turns to face me with his back against the railing, trying to block my view.

I raise an eyebrow at the cocky fucker I call my best friend. 'I'm not a dog. I just like to know what she's doing. Get out of the way.' I move him aside and smile once again. 'And anyway, you can't stand there and tell me you aren't well and truly under Carly's thumb.'

'I'm under no one's thumb.'

'Bullshit! Carly owns you.'

'Carly's not like that.'

'It doesn't matter if she's like that or not. You're thumbed ... whipped ... you belong to her. You might as well man the fuck up and admit it.'

'Never, that will never happen.'

'Brayden, come here! Uncle Snakey needs to put your shoes on,' Jake bellows from inside the suite.

I hear Brayden squeal then crack the shits. 'No shoes!'

'Uncle Snakey?' Derek mouths, amusement on his face.

I smile and nod. 'Yep, but don't ask.'

Derek pushes off the railing and heads back inside. 'Come on, man. Let's get you married.'

Taking one last look up at Alexis, who is now hugging her father, I lift my phone and snap a photo. My creepy research is still very much operational.

* * *

Impatiently waiting at the altar for Alexis, my palms are sweaty and my body tense. I seriously need to rein my shit in, having no doubt that I must look like a nervous wreck. It wouldn't surprise me if I've cracked my neck and clenched my fists more times than a pro boxer would before a fight.

Taking a deep breath, I calm my nerves and watch with amusement as Nate follows Brayden around, making sure he doesn't untie any more of the ivory-ribboned bows decorating the large bunches of roses. Seriously, the amount of destruction my son can get up to in the blink of an eye still confounds me.

'Nervous?' Jessica enquires as she steps up to my side. *Nervous? Yeah, if my damp friggin' hands are anything to go by, I'm very bloody nervous.*

'No, not at all,' I lie, leaning forward and giving her a quick kiss on the cheek.

'Hmm,' she responds with a knowing smile. 'Listen, dear. I just want to let you know that your parents and Lauchie ... even Gareth, are all here in spirit. They are proud of you. We all are.'

I manage a small smile and give her a hug. 'Thank you.'

'You're welcome.' She pulls away, gives my arm a quick reassuring squeeze and then finds her seat.

As I contemplate what she just said, Maryann approaches. Her demeanour is both excited and anxious. 'She's just outside,' she explains.

Feeling my pulse pick up a beat, I look toward the door, noticing Alexis' bridesmaids lining up ready to walk down the aisle. 'Bray, Nate, come here,' I call to the boys. Nate grabs Brayden's hand and they make their way over. 'Okay, Mum is just outside those doors. Nate, come stand next to me just like we practised.' He does as he's told. 'Now, little man, see your special pillow,' I say to Brayden as I bend down to his eye level. 'I want you to hold it tightly and go with Nanny, okay?' I hold out my fist for him to bump.

He rears his hand back and then slams it into mine. 'Bang!' he says and then laughs, our fist-bumps now being a playful game to him.

Maryann takes his hand and leads him along the aisle and, just as she reaches the door, I catch a glimpse of Alexis. The sight of her, as per usual, steals what oxygen I have left in my lungs. *Fuck!*

The first thing my overwhelmed mind deciphers is that I'm marrying her today. *I'm marrying her today. I'm* really *marrying her today.*

Completely stunned, and spellbound by her presence, I can't help but start to mentally count my blessings. You see, I've lost a lot in my life, suffering heartache and accepting the fact that I was destined — and deserved — to be alone in love. Don't get me wrong ... yes, I've managed to build a hugely successful business and brand, and I never take my fortune for granted. It's just that ever since Alexis came into my life, I've learned how to truly aspire. I've learned to love, and to live life as it should be lived. And it is for this reason that I will be forever grateful.

Sucking in a deep breath, I properly absorb for the first time since walking into this room that today is my wedding day. Today — after a few years of sharing my life with the woman of my dreams — is the day she becomes my wife. This day is the fucking icing on the cake — the pièce de résistance. This day cements what I have known all along: that Alexis is mine and that she always will be.

Maryann passes Brayden to Alexis and my heart skips a beat as it usually does when I see them together. Watching Alexis and our son interact with one another does things to me that I never thought possible. For one, I can't take my eyes off them, and secondly, I can't help smiling like the fuckin' Joker.

Brayden points in my direction and both he and Alexis hit me with two earth-shattering smiles, smiles that — like hundreds of times before — pierce through me like a bolt of lightning. According to everyone in our life, Brayden looks like me and I must admit, I tend to agree. *The force is strong in my family.* The thing is, he may be a mini-me, but the beam that plasters his eighteen-month-old face is one hundred percent his mother's.

Alexis places Brayden on his stubby little legs. He grabs hold of Maryann's hand and begins to walk toward me. It's in this moment that I finally understand why Alexis wanted to wait two years to get married. She'd pleaded and convinced me the wait would be worthwhile. 'Charli will be at my side and Nate at yours,' she'd said. 'Brayden will then walk down the aisle holding the rings on a cute little pillow ... it will make the day perfect. Please can we wait. I'm not going anywhere, remember?'

I knew that she wasn't going anywhere, that wasn't the point. The point was we were together and had a child of our own; therefore I wanted to be able to call her my wife. So giving in to her pleas had almost killed me, especially after what we had both been through. Waiting was the absolute last fucking thing I had wanted, instead wanting to marry her as soon as I possibly could. After all, I had waited my whole life for her.

Without admitting it to her though, she was right. Watching Brayden as he walks down the aisle toward me is definitely well worth the wait. It's perfect ... the kids are perfect ... Alexis is perfect.

Brayden stops and smiles, obviously pleased with his 'special job'. I bend down and hold my fist out to him, preparing for another right-hook. He indulges me and laughs, then sits down with Maryann.

As the music kicks in, I quickly stand back up and watch Alexis slowly make her way toward me. I'd been picturing and dreaming about this very moment for years, and now it's finally happening. In my dreams, Alexis was angelic ... beautiful ... exquisite. But in reality, watching as she smiles at our family and friends with each step that she takes, she is just pure perfection — fucking breathtaking.

The instrumental musical piece that is playing as she walks down the aisle is one that Lucy, the boys and I composed especially for this moment. We'd spent months on it, making it flawless. I sneak a look over at Derek and watch as he performs an air guitar action, prompting Carly to laugh at him. *Friggin' show pony.*

Shaking my head in amusement, I roll my eyes with a smile. He is definitely whipped whether he admits it or not.

Alexis stops and has a few moments with Graeme. Part of me envies her having her parents here; I briefly wish mine were here, too. Mum would no doubt be crying happy tears and Dad would be patting her arm. Lauchie and Gareth would be standing right by my side, and the day really would be complete. But, as incredibly perfect as that sounds, it is not how it was meant to be. Fate had other plans, plans I would never understand.

Graeme gives Alexis a quick kiss on the cheek before she turns, faces me, and steps up to the altar. *Fuck me, she is gorgeous.*

'Hi,' she mouths, her lips moving seductively yet with a hint of shyness. *Shiiiit! I want at those lips.*

'Can I kiss her now?' I ask, desperately.

The room erupts into an amused chuckle. *I'm glad you all find it funny. I sure as hell don't.* Frustrated at my lack of control, I clench my fist, then open it again.

'I'm sorry, Mr Clark, not quite yet,' announces the celebrant.

Now, if he wasn't the very man who was going to legally bind me to Alexis for the rest of our lives, I would physically remove him from the room for stopping me from kissing her. He should consider himself lucky.

Fighting to refrain from glaring at him, I move my stare back to the love of my life, finding Alexis staring at me, her beauty-filled blue eyes looking deep into mine. 'I love you,' I mouth, having to do or say something to show her how I feel. Apparently, kissing her in this moment is not allowed.

'I love you, too,' she replies quietly as her gaze drops to assess my suit. The way she takes me in with her eyes nearly snaps my dick to attention — nearly. This is my wedding day after all; I do have some degree of control.

Alexis hands her bouquet of roses to her sister, Jen, then turns back to face me, holding her hands out for me to take hold. *Shit! My palms are still sweaty.*

Wiping them on my trousers as quickly and inconspicuously as I am capable of, I take both her hands in mine. She strokes her thumb across my knuckles and, again, my dick nearly snaps to attention. *Bloody hell!* Alexis will always have the ability to charge me with her touch.

Screw this! I raise her hand to my mouth and kiss her wrist, the smell of her perfume intoxicating me. The fight within me to cease my lips further progression up her arm is excruciating. She smiles lovingly at me and, like a magnet, leans in closer. I want to take her in my arms and merge us into one, but the celebrant clears his throat and begins the ceremony.

After exchanging rings and confirming that I never owned my heart to begin with, my heart having always belonged to Alexis, I am now at the absolute end of my tether. I need to kiss her. I need to taste her. I need to feel her in my arms.

With desperation now plaguing my mind, body and soul, I mentally give the celebrant a nice big 'fuck you' and take her in my arms before he has a chance to finish pronouncing us husband and wife. I kiss her like I've never kissed her before. I finally kiss my wife.

CHAPTER

17

Our reception celebrations are a small affair, which we decided to have in one of the function rooms at City Towers. Alexis wanted our entire wedding celebration to be at *our* hotel complex.

As much as I pride myself on our establishment, if Alexis had said that our first night as husband and wife was also going to be in the hotel, I would have probably gagged her. I drew the line at that. Little does she know, we are flying directly to Paris after the wedding reception and I have a few secrets up my sleeve that I can't wait to surprise her with.

* * *

'Excuse me, ladies and gentleman,' Derek announces through the microphone. 'Can I ask the groom to bring his bride to the dance floor for their first dance as husband and wife?'

Alexis has her head on my shoulder while we sit at our table having a quiet moment to ourselves. As she lifts it up and hits me with, yet again, another dazzling smile, I notice something change in her expression and she gets a look I have seen many times before.

'I hope you are wearing that red G-string, husband,' she drawls.

My eyes widen at her suggestion, and I laugh loudly as I pull her to her feet, leading her to the dance floor. 'It was a one-off, wife. I happily destroyed that uncomfortable piece of arse-floss.'

Placing her hands around my neck, she stands up on her tiptoes to kiss my lips. 'You once told me that nothing was absolute.'

'Some things are,' I say with complete confidence as I return her kiss and wrap my arms around her waist.

A familiar sound filters into my ears when the music begins and I recognise almost instantly, as Derek starts to sing, that he is singing the song I wrote for Alexis, 'Thief of My Heart.'

Pressing her head against my shoulder, she squeezes me tightly. 'Loving you is absolute.'

'It better be,' I say with a smirk.

Alexis pulls away and wipes a tear which has begun to slide down her happy face. 'Bryce, I just want you to know that deciding to go back to work three years ago was one of the best decisions I have ever made.' Another tear leaves her eye, heading on a journey south.

'I can't argue with you there,' I agree, wiping it away.

'Giving you permission to kiss me was another.'

'I married a smart woman.'

She scoffs and drops her head for a second, then looks back into my eyes. 'Spending that week with you and allowing myself to believe that what we had was real, well … that was another.'

I hug her tightly, thankful that she took that very big leap of faith. Because when I look back on it now, that decision must've have been extremely difficult for her.

Derek picks up the pace, singing the lyrics to the bridge of the song. I too, mouth them to Alexis.

Let go and feel it.
Just let go and feel it.
You and I, we are it.
Please let go.

The timing of those lyrics couldn't be more perfect, emphasising what we had just been talking about. Alexis smiles and sings the chorus back to me.

You're all that I want and nothing else.
I've fallen hard and will never get up.

I swear that if I die in this very moment, I will die a happy man. Not that dying is an option at this particular point in time. We have a marriage to consummate, and I have some pretty good ideas about how I plan on doing that.

As visions of our honeymoon start to dance across my mind, I feel that all too familiar movement in my pants. Alexis feels it, too.

'Your feet are not the only thing dancing right now, are they?'

I laugh and press her harder to my front. 'No, they are not.'

She stretches up, her face now level with my own, prompting me to lift her off the ground. I don't hesitate, gripping her tighter and raising her up, her feet now dangling centimetres from the floor. She kisses me hard and, during that kiss, it's as though we are the only two people in the room. We move across the floor to the music, her feet dangling, her arms wrapped around my neck, my lips and tongue still connected to hers — I'm the happiest I have ever been.

Hearing the song subside and Derek's voice no longer singing, we both open our eyes and come back to the moment.

'Mrs Clark?' I ask, completely transfixed by her radiant aura.

'Yes?' she answers with a giggle.

'Nothing, I just wanted to say your name.'

Alexis blushes. *I fucking love it when she does that.*

'Did you just blush, Mrs Clark?'

Her blush and smile disappear. 'No, I don't blush.'

'Oh, yes, you do.' I chuckle at her obvious denial.

'I do not,' she states tersely, in her stubborn tone.

'Do you want me to prove you wrong, right here, right now?'

She blushes. *I rest my case.*

Derek interrupts our moment and asks if anyone else would like to join us on the dance floor. He then hands over the microphone to the lead singer of a band that we often play gigs with, and then makes his way toward Carly.

Before I know it, we are joined by our family and friends, even Arthur and Geraldine. Arthur gives me a fatherly slap on the back and kisses Alexis on the cheek with congratulations.

Once again, swaying with Alexis still happily content in my arms, I feel a tap on my shoulder.

'Do you mind if I cut in?' Rick asks, indicating that he wishes to dance with Alexis.

I give him a nod. 'Sure, I need to find that sister of mine anyway.' I lift Alexis' chin with my finger and press a quick kiss to her lips before leaving her to dance with her ex-husband.

* * *

Moments later, I find Lucy sitting with Nic and Alexander, Al driving his toy cars on top of the table. I pick up a car and perform a high speed manoeuvre then crash it into the one Al is holding. He laughs and yells 'Boom'.

'Luce, come and dance with me,' I request, gesturing toward the dance floor.

'Where's your wife? Your wife!' she squeals. 'How does that feel?' She stands up and gives me a quick hug.

I lean in closer. 'Fucking perfect. And she's over there, dancing with Rick.'

Lucy looks over my shoulder. 'Oh. Well, come on then, let's go and keep an eye on them.'

'I don't need to keep an eye on my wife,' I reassure her, knowing deep down that I will *always* keep an eye on my wife.

'Fine, don't. I'll keep my eye on her.'

And I know damn well that she will.

Shaking my head at my devoted sister as we start to sway to 'With or Without You' by U2, I tell her that she can finally stop looking out for me. 'You can stop with the creepy research now.'

'Never,' she cackles like an evil witch.

Knowing this request is falling on deaf ears, I change the tone of the conversation and squeeze her tight. 'Thank you.'

'For what?' she asks with incredulity as she tilts her head up.

'For always being there for me.'

'Bryce, it's the other way around,' she scoffs.

I pull her back to my body and spin us both around. 'That's what you think.'

'Okay, you don't have to convince me twice,' she answers nonchalantly but in a teasing tone. *Cheeky shit.*

I smile into Lucy's hair and, just as we are about to settle in, the music changes and I hear Alexis groan.

'You did this on purpose, Rick!' she exclaims with frustration.

I'm just about to head over there and see what fuck is going on when Rick laughs.

'I don't know what you're talking about,' he fires back, feigning surprise. Then, with a grin on his face he pulls Alexis to him and they both begin to jive to 'Jailhouse Rock'.

My tension alleviates.

'It's like riding a bike,' Rick teases.

'Have you ever tried ridin' a freakin' bike with a wedding dress and heels on?'

I laugh.

'She's got an answer for everything, hasn't she?' Lucy mutters with a smile while shaking her head.

'She sure has.'

'I'm so happy for the two of you. Mum and Dad would've loved her.'

'Yeah, I know.'

'Especially Mum.'

I pull Lucy in for another tight hug, when I notice Brayden spot the wedding cake. 'Shit! Got to go.'

I take off and catch him just before Jake does.

'Jesus, he's quick,' Jake complains, slightly breathy.

'Of course he is. He's going to play football for the Cats, aren't you, Bray?' I declare proudly, picking him up and placing him on my hip.

Brayden looks from the cake then to me and makes a 'meow' noise.

I laugh.

Screwing up his face, Jake smiles like the cheeky fuck that he is. 'Not if Lex has anything to do with it. According to her, he was born a Bomber like his siblings.'

'She won't have anything to do with it. Brayden *will* support the Cats.'

Jake belly laughs, 'Bryce, you are fucked,' he says, right before slapping me on the back and walking off. *Fucking smartarse!*

I like my brother-in law, but he is a cocky son of a bitch at the best of times.

* * *

It doesn't seem too long before Alexis and I are cutting our cake. My lips are deliberately pressed to hers, so that she cannot see what I have coming. 'Remember when you told me how much you loved cake and cream?' I whisper, still keeping her attention fixated on me.

'Yeah,' she blushes.

'Is this just as good?'

I quickly move my hand to her face and mush a bit of cake into her mouth, cream smearing on her nose and chin.

The room fills with laughter and shocked gasps, together with Tash's unmistakable bellow. ''Bout time someone gagged you, Lex.'

Alexis stumbles back in surprise, her eyes wide open, her mouth filled with cake and cream. 'You didn't just do that,' she mumbles as she closes her eyes and swallows her mouthful.

Laughing and somewhat surprised that I actually went through with it, I reply. 'Yeah ... I did.'

Her eyes flick open again, a renewed sense of retribution covering her face. *Crap! I'm going to fucking regret this.* She raises an eyebrow and forcefully ploughs her hand into the top of the cake, grabbing a fistful before taking a step closer to me. I know what she is going to do — obviously, I deserve it — and she looks so damn sexy, I'm willing to let her.

Standing my ground and waiting for the cake to make contact with my face, I refuse to remove my stare from hers. She stops directly in front of me, now only mere centimetres away, her eyes searing me with lust. Then, like the tempting seductress that she is, she lifts her hand and licks the cake off her fingers ... slowly.

'Mm,' she moans quietly. 'This cake and cream is the *best* I've ever had.'

I watch her sensually devour her cream-covered digits with her tongue. *Fuck! Why are we in a room full of fucking people right now?*

'Mrs Clark,' I warn, my voice now gravelly from the lack of moisture that Alexis so easily strips me of.

'Yes?' she mumbles, swallowing her cake and smiling at me victoriously.

'I fucking love you,' I whisper aggressively, grabbing her neck and pressing her cake-smeared mouth to mine, the taste of her mixed with vanilla sponge and cream.

The room breaks into applause, Tash's wolf-whistle dominating the sounds that follow. Nate also voices his opinion that our cake-mushed kiss is 'gross'.

I couldn't care less though, wanting nothing more than to taste my wife, and considering I am not currently in a position to taste other parts of her body, I am more than happy to continue tasting her mouth.

* * *

As the evening progresses, Alexis switches between mingling with our guests and occupying the dance floor. I, on the other hand, switch between the mingling and watching her.

Alexis, Nate, Charli, and Brayden are all dancing in a circle, encouraging Brayden to bring his moves, moves he got from me. I especially like to take responsibility for the little hip and slide action he is currently performing. I let out a laugh and take a swig of my beer.

'Little tacker dances like his uncle,' Jake says proudly, snapping me out of my loving gaze.

I raise my eyebrow at him. 'You dance?'

'I put Patrick Swayze to shame.'

Coughing then choking on my beer, I call his bluff. 'Bullshit! You look like you have two left feet.'

'Don't bait me, Clark. I wouldn't want to show you up on your big day.'

This time I laugh loudly. 'Not going to happen, Jakey Snakey,' I taunt him, Jakey Snakey being Alexis' pet name for her brother, the same pet name Brayden now uses for his uncle. And a pet name I know Jake hates.

He slams his beer down on the nearest table. 'I fucking warned you.' He smiles, then takes off toward the band. I watch with curiosity as he says something to Simon, the lead singer.

Seconds later, the unmistakable sound of the drums in 'Need You Tonight' by INXS sound throughout the room. Alexis and Jen's heads both prick up like meerkats, then they spot Jake walk toward the centre of the dance floor. The smile that spreads across my wife's face indicates she knows what is about to happen.

Jen wolf-whistles and shouts, 'Lexi, get over here.'

Squealing, Alexis meets my eyes and gives Brayden a gentle push on the bum, steering him toward me. And, without further encouragement, he launches himself in my direction at full speed. *I swear to god, one and a half year olds do not know how to walk. Run ... yes; walk ... no.*

I gather him up and throw him into the air before catching him again, the sound leaving his mouth as he soars above my head, the best fucking sound in the world — I could listen to my son giggle 24/7.

'What are Mummy, Aunty Jen and Uncle Snakey up to?' I ask as I walk closer to the dance floor which is now circled by our family and friends.

'Sssssss snake,' Brayden hisses.

I laugh. 'Yes, snakes go hiss.'

He screws his face up all serious-like. 'Woof, woof. Grrr.'

'Are you a cat?' I enquire.

Brayden bursts into laughter and playfully slaps me on the forehead. 'Sill-ee dadda. Bayden a dog.'

'Oh ... of course you are.' I fake stupidity as I kiss him on the cheek.

Lifting my head to look over everyone else's, I spot Alexis and Jen performing simultaneous dance moves as Jake dances his way around the inside of the circle. I have to admit, he isn't bad, sliding when the lyrics suggest, then moving quite raw when the lyrics suggest that.

Johanna — Jake's girlfriend of two years — snorts and giggles as he drags her out into the centre of the circle. Then, lifting his eyebrow up at me in a watch-this-you-motherfucker kind of way, he swings Johanna's arms around his neck and starts dirty dancing with her, Patrick Swayze-style. I shake my head then salute him. *Cocky prick!*

* * *

After the speeches are said, the bouquet tossed and caught by Carly, and Alexis' electric blue garter is removed by my teeth, I can quite happily admit that I've had enough. I now want nothing more than to have Alexis all to myself. I want to spend the next eighteen hours — the approximate time it takes to fly to Paris — buried deep inside her, underneath her, on top of her and wrapped around her.

I can't wait. She is going to flip when she finds out where we are going but, as per usual, she will not find out until we are there. Part of the fun is going to be teasing and taunting her and, if I'm lucky, she will put up a fight. A fight I look forward to winning.

Now eagerly wanting to wrap up our celebrations and jet off to France, I search the room for my bride, finding her sitting with her girlfriends. I head in her direction.

Tash and Jade's expressions as I approach the table have me a little confused. Tash has a shit-eating grin, and Jade appears to be contemplating whether or not to jump off a cliff. But it's Carly's not so subtle indication to Alexis, using a slash-of-the-throat gesture, that she should cease her words, has me concerned the most.

'I hope he doesn't want to divorce me when —' Alexis says, stopping mid-sentence as I come to a halt right behind her. 'Shit! He's right behind me, isn't he?' she stutters.

'Why would I divorce you?' I whisper into her ear as I wrap my arms around her. 'I've only just married you.'

She stiffens in my arms, making my unease heighten.

'I ... I ... I did something yesterday, and I'm not sure if you'll like it or not. You may file for divorce.'

'What did you do?' I ask, not really caring what she did. There's no way in hell I'd want a divorce. I've waited three years to make her my wife.

'I can't tell you. It will have to wait until later.'

I spin her around to face me. 'I will never divorce you, so give me your worst.'

'It's really not that bad. Well, I don't think it is. You might, though. And if you do ... well ...' She starts to stutter nervously again, so I lean in and kiss her, cutting off her babbling words.

'Shh,' I whisper against her lips as I break our kiss. 'We can talk about it later, but for now I want to take my wife on a plane and have her scream her husband's name over and over.'

'Mm, anything you say, you incredibly sexy husband.'

Opening her eyes as if she has just awoken from a trance, she pulls away from me, her mouth wide, her expression embarrassed. I can't help but chuckle.

'Shit! I just said that out loud, didn't I?'

'Yes, you did,' I explain. 'Come on. Let's say our goodbyes.'

Pulling her to my side where she fits perfectly snug under my arm, she rests her head against my shoulder as we walk.

'I'm going to miss the kids. I hope Brayden will be okay staying with Mum and Dad.'

'He'll be fine,' I reassure her, squeezing a little tighter, when truth be told, I have the same uncertainties.

We both take a seat at our table, and Alexis puts her arms out for Brayden, who is sitting on Graeme's lap. 'Give Mummy a big cuddle, BB,' she mumbles into his neck as they bear hug each other.

I automatically clench both my fists, that being my natural reaction to the annoying nickname. But, unfortunately, due to underestimating her ability to pull one over on me, as it stands at this point in time that bloody nickname is not going anywhere.

'You be a good boy for Nanny and Poppa, and Mummy and Daddy will see you in a couple of weeks, okay?'

'He'll be fine, darling. Poppa has some "farmy stuff" we can do to keep us busy, don't we, Bray?' Graeme explains, using his code for farm slavery.

'I am not cleaning out the chicken coop again. That was disgusting!' Charli complains.

'I'll mow the lawns,' Nate pipes in, knowing that particular job comes with driving the ride-on mower.

Graeme laughs. 'See, they'll be fine. Go and enjoy yourselves.'

We hug all three kids and say goodbye before walking through a guard of honour.

* * *

'Are you going to tell me where are we going yet?' Alexis asks, unlatching her seatbelt as Paul — the plane's captain — has just informed us we can do so.

Following suit, I remove my belt and stand up. 'No. You'll find out when we get there.'

'Fine, I won't tell you my surprise then,' she pouts with a smile.

I offer her my hand and pull her up to stand flush with my chest.

'Thank you,' she says, like a stubborn child, and then turns her back to me. I follow closely behind as she walks toward the bedroom, and even though she is clearly shitty due to my refusal to disclose our location, her leading me to our bed is evidence she still wants to make love. I smirk at her cuteness and then place my hand at the top of her arse, firmly guiding her.

She instantly pulls away and winces, sidestepping from me and displaying an expression of discomfort.

'What's wrong, honey?' I ask while reaching for her hand.

'Nothing,' she responds with a fake smile, now stepping backward toward the room.

'Alexis, why did you just flinch when I touched you?'

'Bryce, where are we going?' she answers my question with a question, frustration in her tone.

Her defiance sends a surge of adrenaline coursing through my body and, together with my increasing need to make love as husband and wife, has me stalking her predatorily while displaying a hungry expression.

Noticing my lascivious prowl, she backs herself into the room, inevitably jailing herself. 'Bryce,' she says with less conviction, 'tell me where we are going.'

I shake my head from side to side, slam the bedroom door behind me, then remove the space between us.

Now holding her body against the wall with my own, I pose my question again, deliberately breaking it down for her. 'Why,' I whisper into her ear, 'did,' I say, breathing into her neck, 'you,' I growl, as I lick the top of her cleavage, 'flinch?' I ask as I spin her around and splay her hands against the wall.

Her fingers claw into the panels as I press my erection against her arse. 'Where are we going?' she probes again, still persistently holding her own.

Her fight has me hard as a fucking rock. 'Fine, have it your way,' I advise, as I slowly unzip the back of her dress.

Alexis changed out of her wedding gown right before we left for the airport, her attire now a red mid-length strapless number.

I finish undoing the zipper and begin to peel the dress from her body when she stops me. 'Bryce, wait!' Sucking in a breath, she turns her head to the side and closes her eyes as she breathes out. 'I love you.'

By this point, I have a pretty good idea of what she has done and, to tell you the truth, I'm fucking excited to see exactly what she chose.

'Honey,' I say as I remove her dress completely, letting it fall to the ground, 'I love you, too.'

Taking a step backward, I spot the freshly inked area at the base of her back. It looks a little raw. I drop to my knees, now face level with her tattoo and take in the scripted name and picture.

'Brylexis,' I read aloud, as I trace the letters without touching the mark.

Under our name is a picture of a star.

'Do you like it?' she asks, clearly hesitant.

'Yes,' I hiss. *Do I fucking like it? I more than fucking like it. It's one of the sexiest things she has ever worn.*

She breathes out as her body relaxes. 'Oh, thank god!'

Gripping her arse cheeks with both my hands, I lean forward and trail my tongue around the area, prompting her to tense up again and suck in another breath.

'I love it,' I growl.

Alexis widens her stance just a little, and that slight opening of her legs — an invitation to deepen my exploration — sets a fire within me. I can't help myself and I grip her G-string, tearing it apart before nipping and biting at her soft rear.

'Oh, god, Bryce,' she moans.

'Turn around,' I demand, my tone not one to be argued with.

Slowly, she does as she is told, and even though I love her tenacity at times, her submission is also just as pleasing.

Now staring at her naked flesh before me, I wet my lips in preparation for her taste, fervently anticipating our union.

'Foot,' I request, keeping my eyes on her moist pussy.

She obliges and lifts her heeled foot, placing it on my knee. While I remove her shoe, I trail my tongue up and down her leg, tantalising every nerve ending I possibly can.

'Other one,' I demand, repeating the same action.

With her shoes discarded, I lean forward and lash her clit with my tongue then trail it up her abdomen and in between her breasts until I'm at her mouth. I bend down, slide my arm behind her thighs, and lift her into my arms.

'Where are we going, Mr Clark?'

'To the bed, Mrs Clark.'

Almost instantly, I feel my bottom lip between her teeth as she holds it, stretching it slightly and taking it with her as she pulls away from my face. Her eyes display a mischievous retribution as she lets go, the feeling mildly uncomfortable, yet erotic.

'That's not what I meant, and you know it,' she says with a slightly annoyed tone.

'I know nothing of which you speak.'

'I hate you.'

'You love me.'

'No, I don't. Not right now.'

Laying her down on the bed, I climb over the top of her and look deep into her crystal-clear blue eyes that reveal her innermost feelings. When I pay attention to them, they never lie.

'Not right now?' I question, leaning forward to tenderly kiss her lips.

Pulling away from her perfectly fucking kissable lips, I wait for her answer.

'No,' she answers, her response obviously artificial.

I swipe her peaked nipple with my tongue before sucking on it, deliciously. 'How about now?' I prompt.

'Uh-uh,' she answers on an intake of air.

'Hmm. No?' I mumble as I switch breasts, only to tweak with my fingertips the wet, hard nipple I just abandoned.

Trailing my tongue further down her stomach, I dip it into her belly-button then comfortably position myself between her legs. I smile victoriously as I take in the sight before me, seeing just how turned-on she is — the proof is in the pussy.

Her entrance glistens with arousal, moistened, the view parching my mouth. I swallow heavily and drag my finger along her clit, making circles. 'How 'bout now?'

Her back bows, affording me a stunning view of her chest, but she still refuses to give in.

Having had enough of this game, I go in for the kill, hungrily devouring between her legs. I lash at her clit with my tongue while sliding two fingers into her pussy, moving them in a 'come hither' motion.

'Oh, Bryce,' she moans, her sultry sound eliciting a reverberating groan from within me.

'Do you love me now?' I growl, still pressing my lips to her wet clit.

'Yes ... yes, I always love you, every second of the day,' she admits, her voice rising along with her impending climax.

Satisfied pleasure rushes through me hearing her say those words. They never get old; I never tire of hearing her say them. Now, feeling overly fucking thrilled with her surrender, I suck her clit into my mouth, knowing this will tip her over the edge. I then wait for her body to relax as she comes back down to earth.

Sitting up on my knees, my cock is hard and heavy with desire, desire I want nothing more than to release into my wife. 'Come here,' I say, taking her hand and lifting her to her knees.

She looks down at my erection and a pleased appreciation washes over her face. It's the best fucking expression imaginable. Nothing tops the look she gives me when she admires my cock.

Scooting forward on her knees, she takes me in her hand, squeezing my base and dragging her hand to the tip. Her milking action is rewarded when a bead forms on my crown. 'Taste it,' I suggest, knowing that she wants to.

She smiles and sticks out her tongue, then leans forward and slides it along my sensitive head. I jerk with pleasure. She pumps once more in hopes of another bead and is rewarded when yet again one appears.

'Fuck, honey. Come here.' I pull her close and lift her up, impaling her on my shaft, both of us moaning in succession. I seize her arse with my hands and lift her up and down, thrusting with passionate dedication over and over.

She cries out with exertion as she reaches another climax, the sheer carnality of her scream a fucking pleasure to watch. The way her head falls back under the weight of physical pleasure and mental emotion rewards me for my efforts. I release one hand from her hip and clasp the back of her head, bringing it back to mine. Then, delving my tongue deep into her mouth, I expel my own orgasm.

We both collapse on the bed, thoroughly sated and fucked, and that wonderfully gratifying feeling of attainment washes through me. After seconds of catching our breath, I tug her to my side where she comfortably rests her head on my chest.

Gently, I kiss her on the head. 'So, how does it feel to be Mrs Clark?'

'Perfect,' she replies then hugs me tight.

* * *

Hours later, we are departing the plane and stepping onto the tarmac at Charles de Gaulle Airport. It's fucking freezing, the icy chill in the air piercing my skin like a thousand tiny needles.

'Paris?' she asks, spinning to face me and seeming unfazed by the near zero degree temperature.

The sheer excitement that is radiating from her fills me with so much joy. 'The one and only,' I reply, intertwining my fingers with hers, wanting to keep us both warm.

'Oh my god! Can we go see the Eiffel Tower, now?'

Personally, I want nothing more than to cuddle up to her naked body, the flames of an open fire dancing before our eyes. Except seeing her exhilaration — that resembles a kid at Disneyland — I'm now more inclined to freeze my arse off just to continue witnessing her expression.

'If you want, but it's bloody cold,' I shiver, cursing myself for not having our coats accessible.

'Screw the cold. Paris blanketed in snow is so romantic. It is the only place in the world I would be happy to freeze to death.'

Shaking my head, I lead her toward the waiting limousine, hellbent on not allowing any freezing of her body to occur. 'We can go, see and do whatever you want. Our honeymoon is your oyster.'

She stops once again and I refrain from rolling my eyes, when I see her smile widen beyond normal proportions.

'Anywhere?'

'Yes, honey, anywhere but here. Come on, let's go see *La Tour Eiffel*,' I entice, my French rolling from my tongue.

'*Oui, s'il vous plaît, Monsieur* Clark,' she responds, her French spoken just as perfectly.

I groan at the sound of her words which are like verbal sex to my ears. 'Limousine. Now!'

* * *

Reaching Champ de Mars without burying myself inside Alexis was an impossibility. Her French words as I bucked my hips and she rode me were fucking sensational. '*Oh dieu, oh dieu*,' she'd chanted at my request. Followed by '*Oui, oui*', and finishing off with '*baiser*'.

Needless to say, it was the best forty-five minute drive I have ever experienced.

Standing at the base of the monumental structure that is the Eiffel Tower, I watch with joy as Alexis arches her head back to get maximum perspective. Her obvious excitement feeds my delight, and I can't help but take a moment to absorb what my life now encompasses. The exquisite creature before me, my wife, is the woman who breathed life back in to me, giving me purpose to my existence and the desire to enjoy the life I have. She tempts me, satisfies me, fulfils me in every possible way. She is my greatest achievement.

Reaching into my coat pocket, I pull out a rose I had our chauffeur obtain for me, then take a hold of Alexis' hand, tugging her to my chest. Her eyes sparkle when I place the flower on her forehead and drag it down the bridge of her nose, her sight never leaving mine, not even for a second. Once I have trailed the rose across her lips, I lean forward and replace it with my mouth, sealing us with a passionate kiss. She is mine, and she always will be.

I have attained my ultimate perfection.

EPILOGUE

'Mum! Dad! Come on,' Brayden calls from the lounge room. 'Whatever it is you are both doing up there, stop. We're waiting for you.'

Nate, Charlotte, and Brayden all roll their eyes with a knowing smile, their mother and father's frequent disappearances a common occurrence in their household.

'Listen to this riff I've been practising,' Brayden says to his nineteen-year-old brother before diving right in to some guitar chords.

Nate looks up from tuning his axe, impressed with Brayden's ability to compose so simply, this natural talent obviously passed down from his father. 'Not bad, little bro.'

'I like it, Bray. Are you going to show Mum and Dad?' Charlotte asks before returning to warming up her vocal chords by humming her scales.

'Not yet, it's not finished.'

All three of them continue to prepare their instruments as Bryce and Alexis watch adoringly from the upper level. Bryce, having just listened to Brayden's roughly composed riff, couldn't be more proud of his eight-year-old son. In fact, he couldn't be more proud of all his kids. He never saw Nate and Charlotte as his stepchildren, having always loved them as a father should.

'He's so much like you,' Alexis says to her husband of seven years while dropping her head to his shoulder. Every time she is faced with her youngest child, she is reminded that he is the epitome of his dad. This is both a good and bad thing where she is concerned.

'Yeah ... well ... he has to get his talent from someone,' Bryce playfully boasts, knowing Alexis will fight back. He adores it when his wife puts up a fight; he always has and he always will. Baiting her is one trick he has perfected over the years when wanting to be buried inside her, his taunts always resulting with them both passionately making love.

'Oh, so I am talentless, am I?' she says as she turns to face him. 'What I just did to your cock was something taught in everyday school, then?'

'Fuck! I should hope not,' Bryce laughs.

'I can guarantee, Mr Clark, that what my mouth is capable of is more than just a talent.'

Bryce pulls his wife to his chest and nudges her nose with his own. 'I know, my love. It's a gift.'

'Mum! Dad! Hurry up!' Brayden bellows.

'We're coming,' Bryce retorts.

Laughing, Alexis pulls away to join her children downstairs.

'Where are you going?' Bryce asks, securing his wife's back to his chest. 'I said we're coming and I didn't mean it in an adjectival sense.'

Alexis' body ignites, a natural reaction to her husband's dirty and promising words. 'We've come twice already. A third time is a bit greedy, don't you think?'

'I'm a voracious man.'

'I know, but your voracity will have to wait. We have three eager youngsters down there who want to jam with their parents.'

A battle of choices creates a dilemma within Bryce's mind, because he has to choose between his two favourite pastimes; making love to his wife, and jamming with his family. Knowing deep down that his commonsense will prevail over his lasciviousness, he lightly nibbles Alexis' ear and then lets her go. 'I know. Come on then.'

Bryce seats himself at the piano, now feeling comfortable playing after so long. He had refused to touch the keys following his mother's death, feeling the attempt to be too painful. But when he'd asked Alexis what she wanted for their one year wedding anniversary, she had said just one thing. 'Play the piano for me. It's time, my love.' Ever since that night, he has found a renewed love for the instrument and no longer feels the heart-wrenching pain he once did.

Pressing the keys to begin the song, he looks at Charlotte sitting beside him. On perfect cue, she begins to sing the lyrics to 'Fix You' by Coldplay.

When Alexis hears the first song that she sang to her husband many years ago, she nearly chokes on the emotion she holds so deeply for this man who she risked everything to be with. A man she was inevitably drawn to and could not be without, a man who is and always will be her soul mate. Standing behind him, she leans into his back and drapes her hands down his chest, resting her chin on his head as she joins in and sings with her daughter.

* * *

The moment Alexis presses herself against Bryce's back and her beautiful voice fills his ears, he knows he has picked the perfect song. His wife and stepdaughter sound like angels, the perfect accompaniment to the piano notes filtering the air. But it isn't until the chorus when both Nate and Brayden join in with their guitars, that Bryce truly appreciates his life. He honestly feels that he is the luckiest man alive, and for someone who never believed in luck, this sentiment in itself is a true testament to how far he has come.

His life, his wife, and his family, are his ultimate attainment.

COMING SOON

Attraction

(Book 4 in The Temptation Series)

Carly enjoys her carefree life. She enjoys making her own decisions and not having to answer to anyone. She enjoys the notion of a romantic fling. Her motto is that if you have no expectations and remain unattached, disappointment is less likely to occur.

Carly's life plan is set for a shake-up when she is introduced to Derek at her best friend's birthday. Their instant attraction has them both questioning their outlook on life, on relationships ... on love.

Will Derek and Carly surrender their stance on avoiding commitment, or will they continue to live life free and enjoy the perks of attraction?

ACKNOWLEDGEMENTS

Where do I start? I know. I'll start by thanking the most amazing person I am privileged to share my life with: my wonderful husband. I could not have spent the last ten months of my life writing three novels without you. The way you have adapted to our changing lifestyle has floored me. You floor me. I love you so very much, and I thank you for everything that you are and everything that you do.

My ratbags; my two little adorable loves of my life. You make me smile daily. You make me laugh daily. You make me inwardly curse daily. You make me clean up after you daily. You make my daily worthwhile. Mummy loves you both ♥

I can honestly say I am blessed with two of the most wonderful parents known to man — and woman. Yes, I am that lucky. Mum and Dad, thank you for all that you do. Thank you for loving me. And thank you for being you.

As always, my close friends provide a platform of escapism. You know who you are. Your support, enthusiasm and optimism help to give me the courage to put my heart to paper. Thank you so much.

My beta readers — Sarah and Heather. Sarah, you seriously crack me up. Your comments and advice during the beta reading process are

not only extremely helpful but incredibly hilarious. One of the thrills
I get when writing 'The End' is not only the satisfaction of finally finishing my book, but the knowledge that your feedback is not too far
away. Sarah (Flib) I'm keeping you! Heather, you are a gem. A gram-
mar and spelling goddess. Thank you so much ♥

My fans and followers on Facebook and Goodreads — without
your encouragement and love for everything Brylexis, this series would
not have gone anywhere. I can't possibly thank you all enough for
enthusiastically spreading the word like you have. I love you all ♥ ♥

And lastly, but certainly not least, Annabel, Stephanie, Belinda,
Sue, and everyone at Harlequin Australia who have worked tirelessly
during the revision of these books. I couldn't be happier with the
result. Thank you for making my dream come true and ensuring The
Temptation Series sits proudly on a store shelf.

talk about it

Let's talk about *Fulfilment*.

Join the conversation:

 on facebook.com/harlequinaustralia

 on Twitter @harlequinaus & @KellyGolly

#TemptationSeries

Golland's website: www.kmgolland.com

If there's something you really want to tell
K.M. Golland, or have a question you want answered,
then let's talk about it.